CHUNG KUO

BOOK SIX

"Open wide the door of heaven!
On a black cloud I ride in splendour,
Bidding the whirlwind drive before me,
Causing the rainstorm to lay the dust."

– *Ta Ssu Ming*, "The Greater Master of Fate",
from the *Chiu Ko*, the "Nine Songs" by Ch'u
Yuan, 2nd century BC

"Before me floats an image, man or shade,
Shade more than man, more image than a shade;
For Hades' bobbin bound in mummy-cloth
May unwind the winding path;
A mouth that has no moisture and no breath
Breathless mouths may summon;
I hail the superhuman;
I call it death-in-life and life-in-death."

– William Butler Yeats, from *Byzantium*, AD 1930

By the same author:

in the CHUNG KUO series

Book One: THE MIDDLE KINGDOM
Book Two: THE BROKEN WHEEL
Book Three: THE WHITE MOUNTAIN
Book Four: THE STONE WITHIN
Book Five: BENEATH THE TREE OF HEAVEN

and

TRILLION YEAR SPREE: THE HISTORY OF SCIENCE FICTION
(with Brian Aldiss)

DAVID WINGROVE

CHUNG KUO

BOOK SIX

中國

WHITE MOON, RED DRAGON

Hodder & Stoughton
LONDON SYDNEY AUCKLAND

10 9 8 7 6 5 4 3 2 1

British Library Cataloguing in Publication Data

Wingrove, David
  Chung Kuo. – Book 6: White Moon, Red
  Dragon
  I. Title
  823.914   [F]

ISBN 0–450–56418–5

Typeset by Hewer Text Composition Services, Edinburgh
Printed and bound in Great Britain by
Mackays of Chatham PLC, Chatham, Kent

Hodder and Stoughton Ltd
A division of Hodder Headline PLC
338 Euston Road
London NW1 3BH

For John Patrick Kavanagh,
brother in arms, dedicated B52 pilot
and all round fine fellow.

"Give Em a dollar!"

CONTENTS

CHUNG KUO

MAJOR CHARACTERS

Ascher, Emily – Trained as an economist, she was once a member of the *Ping Tiao* revolutionary party. After their demise, she fled to North America where, under the alias of Mary Jennings, she got a job with the giant ImmVac Corporation, working for Old Man Lever and his son, Michael, whom she finally married. Ultimately, however, what she wants is change, and the downfall of the corrupt social institutions that rule Chung Kuo.

DeVore, Howard – A one-time Major in the T'ang's Security forces, he has become the leading figure in the struggle against the Seven. A highly intelligent and coldly logical man, he is the puppet master behind the scenes as the great War of the Two Directions takes a new turn. Defeated first on Chung Kuo and then on Mars, he has fled outwards, to the tenth planet, Pluto.

Ebert, Hans – Son of Klaus Ebert and heir to the vast GenSyn Corporation, he was promoted to General in Li Yuan's Security forces, and was admired and trusted by his superiors. Secretly, however, he was allied to DeVore, and was subsequently implicated in the murder of his father. Having fled Chung Kuo, he was declared a traitor in his absence. After suffering exile, he has found himself again, among the lost African tribe, the Osu, among the desert sands of Mars.

Karr, Gregor – a Colonel in the Security forces, he was recruited by General Tolonen from the Net. In his youth he was a "blood" – a to-the-death combat fighter. A huge man physically, he is also one of Li Yuan's "most-trusted men".

Lehmann, Stefan – Albino son of the former Dispersionist leader, Pietr Lehmann, and one-time lieutenant of DeVore's, he has, by conquest, become the ruler of City Europe's "underworld", its "White T'ang" and principle enemy of Li Yuan.

Li Yuan – T'ang of Europe and one of the Seven, as second son of Li Shai Tung, he inherited after the deaths of his brother and father. Considered old before his time, he none the less has a passionate side to his nature, as demonstrated in his brief marriage to his brother's wife, the beautiful Fei Yen. His subsequent remarriage ended in tragedy when his three wives were assassinated. Despite his subsequent remarriage to Pei K'ung, his real concern is for his young son, Kuei Jen.

Pei K'ung – Fifth wife of Li Yuan, she is eighteen years his elder and a plain, straightforward woman from a Minor Family background.

Shepherd, Ben – Great-great-grandson of City Earth's architect, Shepherd was brought up in the Domain, an idyllic valley in the south-west of England, where he pursues his artistic calling, developing a new art form, the "Shell": a machine which mimics the experience of life.

Tolonen, Jelka – Daughter of Marshal Tolonen, Jelka was brought up in a very masculine environment, lacking in a mother's love and influence. Yet her attempts to re-create herself – to find a balance in her life – have only brought her into conflict, first with a young soldier, and then with her father, who – to prevent her having a relationship with Kim Ward – despatched her on a tour of the Colony Planets. Returned, she bides her time, awaiting the day when, at twenty-five, she will come of age and can decide her own destiny.

Tolonen, Knut – Former Marshal of the Council of Generals and one-time General to Li Yuan's father, Tolonen is a rock-like supporter of the Seven and their values, even in an age of increasing uncertainty. In his role as father, however, this inflexibility in his nature has brought him only repeated conflict with his daughter, Jelka.

Tsu Ma – T'ang of West Asia and one of the Seven, Tsu Ma has thrown off a dissolute past to become Li Yuan's staunchest supporter. A strong, handsome man in his late thirties, he had yet to marry, though his secret affair with Li Yuan's former wife, Fei Yen, revealed a side of him that has not been fully harnessed. Now, in his middle years, he wishes to lead a more settled life.

Ward, Kim – Born in the Clay, that dark wasteland beneath the great City's foundations, Kim has survived various personal crises to become Chung Kuo's leading experimental scientist. Hired by the massive SimFic Corporation as a commodity-slave on a seven-year contract, he is a staunch supporter of Li Yuan.

* * *

THE SEVEN AND THE FAMILIES

Li Kuei Jen – son of Li Yuan and heir to City Europe
Li Yuan – T'ang of Europe
Liang K'o Ting – head of the Liang Family (one of the Twenty-Nine Minor Families) and father of Liang Shu-sun

Liang Shu-sun – Minor Family Princess
Pei K'ung – Wife of Li Yuan
Pei Ro-hen – head of the Pei Family (one of the Twenty-Nine Minor Families) and father of Pei K'ung
Tsu Kung-chih – older nephew of Tsu Ma
Tsu Ma – T'ang of West Asia
Tsu Tao Chu – younger nephew of Tsu Ma
Wei Tseng-li – T'ang of East Asia
Yin Fei Yen – "Flying swallow"; Minor Family Princess and divorced wife of Li Yuan
Yin Han Ch'in – son of Fei Yen
Yin Sung – elder brother of Yin Fei Yen and head of the Yin Family (one of the Twenty-Nine Minor Families)

* * *

FRIENDS AND RETAINERS OF THE SEVEN

Autumn Snow – maid to Pei K'ung
Bachman, Lothar – Captain in Security
Barlow – equerry to Karr
Byrne – Sergeant in Security, under Haavikko
Chang Hong – Minister of Production, City Europe
Chang Li – personal surgeon to Li Yuan
Chiang Ko – private secretary to Tsu Ma
Chu Ho – Minister of Food Production, City Europe
Chu Shi-ch'e – *Pi-shu chien*, or Inspector of the Imperial Library at Tongjiang
Daubler – Lieutenant, Security, Ansbach *Hsien*
Douglas, John – alias of Thorn
Ebert, Pauli – bastard son of Hans Ebert and Golden Heart and heir to the GenSyn Corporation
Erikson – Captain in Security, under Haavikko
Fiedler, Walter – Major in Security, City Europe
Golden Heart – concubine to Hans Ebert and mother of Pauli Ebert
Haavikko, Axel – Major, Commander of Security for the Western Isle
Haller – Sergeant in Security, under Haavikko
Harrison – AAD Project Director
Hoff – member of *Shen T'se* élite Security squad
Hu – Surgeon, AAD Project
Hu Ch'ang – Principal Secretary to Nan Ho
Hwa Kwei – Chief Steward of the Bedchamber to Tsu Ma
Jeng Lo – Security pilot, Rift veteran
Karlgren – Lieutenant in Security, Astrakhan

Karr, Gregor – Colonel in Security
Lao Kang – Chancellor of West Asia
Lasker – Captain, Decontamination, Ansbach *Hsien*
Lo Wen – Master of *wu shu* and tutor to Li Kuei Jen
Lu – surgeon at Tongjiang
Lung – Director of Analytical Studies, Bremen
Luo Ye – most senior member of the *San Shih*, the "Scholar Princes" of the New
    Confucian movement; also a Minor Family prince
Munk – Captain in Security, Astrakhan
Nan Ho – Chancellor of Europe
Nan Tsing – first wife of Nan Ho
Needham – Captain of *Shen T'se* élite Security squad
Pace – Lieutenant in Security; equerry to Major Haavikko
Radow – Communications Officer, Karr's craft
Rheinhardt, Helmut – General of Security, Europe
Roesberg – Clerk, Air Traffic Control, Britanny
Shao – Old Shao; Air Traffic Controller for Britanny Sector
Shepherd, Ben – son of the late Hal Shepherd, "shell" artist
Sweet Fragrance – maid to Li Yuan
Tan We – Chief Eunuch at Tsu Ma's palace in Astrakhan
Thomas – Duty Captain at Western Isle Command
Thorn – Security operative
Tiny Jade – maid to Pei K'ung
Tolonen, Jelka – daughter of Marshal Tolonen
Tolonen, Knut – ex-Marshal of Security; Acting Head of the GenSyn Corporation
Tsung Ye – private secretary to Pei K'ung
Tu Fu-wei – private secretary to Tsu Ma
T'ung – Surgeon to Tsu Ma's court
Wang – Steward at the Astrakhan palace
Ward, Kim – Clayborn scientist, employed as a commodity slave by the SimFic
    Corporation
Ye – Senior Steward at Tongjiang
Yi Ching – Colonel of Internal Security to Tsu Ma at Astrakhan
Yung Chen – eunuch from the women's quarters in Tsu Ma's palace in Astrakhan

* * *

OTHER CHARACTERS

Agrafes, Ucef – art critic
Ascher, Emily – ex-*Ping Tiao* terrorist, now known as Mary Lever
Ashman – henchman of Pasek
Barrett – GenSyn "sport"; brothel-keeper in the Clay
Bartels, Emil – young First Level bachelor
Beinlich – ex-Security lieutenant, working for Van Pasenow

Berrenson – Company Head
Blaskic – henchman of Pasek
Blonegek – "Greasy"; Clayman civilised by Ben Shepherd
Cao Chang – Financial Strategist to Li Min
Chang, Hugh – agent with Supernal Property
Chang Mu – servant at the Ebert Mansion
Cheng Lu – Lehmann's ambassador to Fu Chiang's court
Chou Te-hsing – Head of the Black Hand terrorists
Crefter – "Strong"; Clayman civilised by Ben Shepherd
Cui – Steward of Marshal Tolonen's household
Curval, Andrew – experimental geneticist, working for SimFic
Deng Liang – Minor Family Prince; fifth son of Deng Shang; Dispersionist
DeValerian, Rachel – pseudonym of Emily Ascher
DeVore, Howard – ex-Major in Li Yuan's Security
Dieter, Wilhelm – Black Hand cell-leader
Ebert, Berta – widow of Klaus Ebert
Ebert, Lutz – half-brother of Klaus Ebert
Eyre – henchman of Pasek
Fox – Company Head
Franke, Rutger – Vice-President of SimFic; Dispersionist
Fu Chiang – "the Priest", Big Boss of the Red Flower Triad of North Africa
Fung – *Wu*, or Diviner to Yin Fei Yen
Grant – henchman of Pasek
Harris – alias of Jan Mach
Harrison, Edward – socialite and First Level "Functionary Executive"
Hart, Alex – Representative at Weimar, Dispersionist and friend of Stefan Lehmann
Hastings, Thomas – Physicist; Dispersionist
Heng Pang-chou – wife of Minister Heng and childhood friend of Jelka Tolonen
Heydemeier, Ernst – artist; leading exponent of Futur-Kunst, "Science Art"
Hooper – Senior Engineer aboard DeVore's craft
Hsueh Chi – Big Boss of the Thousand Spears Triad of Southern Africa
Hsueh Nan – Warlord of Southern Africa and brother of Hsueh Chi
Hu Lin – Red Pole of the Red Flower Triad of North Africa
Huang Peng – Steward at the Ebert Mansion
Jackson – alias of DeVore
Jia Shu – SimFic hospitality girl
Kao Chen – ex-Major in Security
Kao Ch'iang Hsin – daughter of Kao Chen
Kao Jyan – eldest son of Kao Chen
Kao Wu – second son of Kao Chen
Karr, Hannah – second daughter of Marie and Gregor Karr
Karr, Marie – wife of Gregor Karr
Karr, May – daughter of Marie and Gregor Karr
Kavanagh – Representative at Weimar and Leader of the House

Kingsley, Jake – IntSat's arts reviewer

Kygek – "Fat"; Clayman civilised by Ben Shepherd

Layton, Pietr – equerry to Gregor Karr

Lehmann, Stefan – "The White T'ang", Big Boss of the European Triads

Lever, Michael – Head of the ImmVac pharmaceuticals corporation of North America and Representative at Weimar

Li Ho-nien – servant at the Ebert Mansion

Li Min – "Brave Carp", an alias of Stefan Lehmann

Lin Pan – Uncle Pan, adopted uncle of Lin Shang

Lin Shang – Lin the Mender

Ling – "Old Mother Ling", worker on the Kosaya Gora plantation

Lo Chang – Steward at the Ebert Mansion

Ma Ch'ing – servant at the Ebert Mansion

Mach, Jan – leader of the revolutionary movement, the *Yu*

The Machine – an artificial intelligence

Mo Nan-ling – "The Little Emperor", Big Boss of the Nine Emperors Triad of Central Africa

Morel – the Myghtern, "King under the City"

Neville, Jack – Head of Product Development for the SimFic Corporation

Nolen, William – Public Relations Executive; Dispersionist

Novacek, Catherine – wife of Sergey Novacek

Novacek, Sasha – daughter of Catherine and Sergey Novacek

Novacek, Sergey – sculptor; husband of Catherine Novacek

Pasek, Karel – Head of the "sealed"; religious fanatic and senior member of the Black Hand terrorists

Peng, Madam – matchmaker

Peters – cell leader in the Black Hand

Ponow – gaoler in the Myghtern's town

Ravachol – the "second prototype"; an android created by Kim Ward

Reiss, Horst – Chief Executive of the SimFic Corporation

Ruddock – Minor Official, employed by Lehmann

Scaf – "Quick"; Clayman civilised by Ben Shepherd

Sheng Min-chung – "One-Eye Sheng", Big Boss of the Iron Fists Triad of East Africa

Shepherd, Meg – sister of Ben Shepherd

Shepherd, Tom – son of Ben and Meg Shepherd

Shih Chi-o – servant at the Ebert Mansion

Soucek, Jiri – lieutenant to Lehmann

Steiger – Director of the Shen Chang Fang of Milan

Stewart – henchman of Li Min

T'ai Cho – friend and ex-tutor of Kim Ward

Tak – the Myghtern's lieutenant

Tan Sui – White Paper Fan of the Red Flower Triad of North Africa

Ting Ju-ch'ang – Warlord of Tunis

Todlich – giant morph

Ts'ao Wu – cell leader in the Black Hand
Tsou Tsai Hei – "Walker in the Darkness", another name of Hans Ebert
Tuan Ti Fo – Master of *wei chi* and sage
Tung Chung-shu – MedFac's senior arts reviewer
Tynan, Edward – Above businessman and Representative at Weimar; Dispersionist
Vierheller, Jane – Black Hand member
Visak – lieutenant to Lehmann
Von Pasenow – ex-Security Major
Wang Ti – wife of Kao Chen
Ward, Kim – Clayborn scientist
Ward, Sampsa – son of Kim Ward and Jelka Tolonen
Yang – "Old Yang", Deck Magistrate, employee of Li Min
Yang Chih-wen – "The Bear", Big Boss of the Golden Ox Triad of West Africa
Yen Fu – North African Warlord
Yu I – proprietor of the Blue Pagoda tea-house

* * *

THE OSU

Chike – one of the "eight"
Dogo – one of the "eight"
Echewa, Aluko – Head man and one of the "eight"
Efulefu – "Worthless Man"; chosen name of Hans Ebert among the Osu
Elechi – one of the "eight"
Hama – Osu wife of Hans Ebert
Jaga – *ndichie* or Elder of the Osu on Mars
Nwibe – one of the "eight"
Nza – "Tiny bird", an Osu child, adopted by Hans Ebert, and one of the "eight"
Odile – one of the "eight"
Ugoye – one of the "eight"

* * *

THE DEAD

Althaus, Kurt – General of Security, North America
An Hsi – Minor Family prince and fifth son of An Sheng
An Liang-chou – Minor Family prince
An Mo Shan – Minor Family prince and third son of An Sheng
An Sheng – head of the An Family (one of the Twenty-Nine Minor Families)
Anderson, Leonid – Director of the Recruitment Project
Anna – helper to Mary Lever
Anne – *Yu* assassin

Barrow, Chao – Secretary of the House at Weimar
Barycz, Jiri – scientist on the Wiring Project
Bates – leading figure in the Federation of Free Men, Mars
Bercott, Andrei – Representative at Weimar
Berdichev, Soren – head of SimFic and later leader of the Dispersionist faction
Berdichev, Ylva – wife of Soren Berdichev
Bess – helper to Mary Lever
Blofeld – agent of special security forces
Brock – security guard in the Domain
Brookes, Thomas – Port Captain, Tien Men K'ou, Mars
Chang Te Li – "Old Chang", *Wu*, or Diviner
Chen So – Clerk of the Inner Chambers at Tongjiang
Ch'en Li – associate of Governor Schenck
Cherkassky, Stefan – ex-Security assassin and friend of DeVore
Chi Hu Wei – T'ang of the Australias; father of Chi Hsing
Chih Huang Hui – second wife of Shang Mu and stepmother of Shang Han-A
Ch'in Shih Huang Ti – the first emperor of China; ruled 221–210 BC
Cho Hsiang – Hong Cao's subordinate
Chu Heng – "kwai", or hired knife; a hireling of DeVore's
Chun Wu-chi – head of the Chun family (one of the Twenty-Nine Minor Families)
Chung Hsin – "Loyalty"; bondservant to Li Shai Tung
Clarac, Armand – Director of the "New Hope" Project
Coates – security guard in the Domain
Cook – duty guard in the Domain
Cornwell, James – director of the AutoMek corporation
Cutler, Richard – leader of the "America" movement
Dawson – associate of Governor Schenck
Deio – Clayborn friend of Kim Ward from "Rehabilitation"
Donna – *Yu* assassin
Douglas, John – Company head; Dispersionist
Duchek, Albert – Administrator of Lodz
Ebert, Klaus – head of the GenSyn Corporation; father of Hans Ebert
Ecker, Michael – Company head; Dispersionist
Edsel – agent of special security forces
Egan – head of NorTek
Ellis, Michael – assistant to Director Spatz on the Wiring Project
Endacott – associate of Governor Schenck
Endfors, Pietr – friend of Knut Tolonen and father of Jenny, Tolonen's wife
Erkki – guard to Jelka Tolonen
Eva – friend of Mary Lever
Fairbank, John – head of AmLab
Fan – fifth brother to the *I Lung*
Fen Cho-hsien – Chancellor of North America
Feng Chung – Big Boss of the Kuei Chuan (Black Dog) Triad
Feng Lu-ma – lensman

Feng Shang-pao – "General Feng"; Big Boss of the 14K Triad
Fest, Edgar – Captain in Security
Fu Ti Chang – third wife of Li Yuan
Gesell, Bent – leader of the Ping Tiao – "Leveller" – terrorist movement
Green, Clive – head of RadMed
Griffin, James B. – last president of the American empire
Haavikko, Vesa – sister of Axel Haavikko
Hammond, Joel – Senior Technician on the Wiring Project
Henderson, Daniel – pro-tem Governor of Mars
Heng Chi-po – Li Shai Tung's Minister of Transportation
Henssa, Eero – Captain of the Guard aboard the floating palace Yangjing
Herrick – illegal transplant specialist
Ho Chin – "Three-Finger Ho"; Big Boss of the Yellow Banners Triad
Hoffmann – Major in Security
Hong Cao – middleman for Pietr Lehmann
Hou Ti – T'ang of South America; father of Hou Tung-po
Hou Tung-po – T'ang of South America
Hsiang K'ai Fan – Minor Family prince
Hsiang Shao-erh – head of the Hsiang family (one of the Twenty-Nine Minor Families)
Hsiang Wang – Minor Family prince
Hua Shang – lieutenant to Wong Yi-sun
Hui Tsin – "Red Pole" (426, or Executioner) to the United Bamboo Triad
Hung Mien-lo – Chancellor of Africa
Hwa – Master "blood", or hand-to-hand fighter, below the Net
I Lung – "First Dragon", the head of the "Thousand Eyes", the Ministry
Jackson – freelance go-between, employed by Fairbank
Jill – principal helper to Mary Lever
Joan – *Yu* assassin
Kan Jiang – Martian settler and poet
K'ang A-yin – gang boss of the Tu Sun tong
K'ang Yeh-su – nephew of K'ang A-yin
Kao Jyan – assassin; friend of Kao Chen
Kemp, Johannes – director of ImmVac
Kennedy, Jean – wife of Joseph Kennedy
Kennedy, Joseph – head of the New Republican and Evolutionist Party and Representative at Weimar
Kennedy, Robert – elder son of Joseph Kennedy
Kennedy, William – younger son of Joseph Kennedy
Kennedy, William – great-great-grandfather of Joseph Kennedy
Krenek, Henryk – Senior Representative of the Martian Colonies
Krenek, Irina – wife of Henryk Krenek
Krenek, Josef – Company head
Krenek, Maria – wife of Josef Krenek
Kriz – senior *Yu* operative

Kubinyi – lieutenant to DeVore

Kung Wen-fa – Senior Advocate from Mars

K'ung Fu Tzu – Confucius (551–479 BC)

Kustow, Bryn – American; friend of Michael Lever

Lai Shi – second wife of Li Yuan

Lao Jen – Junior Minister to Lwo Kang

Lehmann, Pietr – Under-Secretary of the House of Representatives and first leader of the Dispersionist faction; father of Stefan Lehmann

Lever, Charles – head of the giant ImmVac Corporation of North America; father of Michael Lever

Lever, Margaret – wife of Charles Lever and mother of Michael Lever

Li Chin – "Li the Lidless"; Big Boss of the Wo Shih Wo Triad

Li Ch'ing – T'ang of Europe; grandfather of Li Yuan

Li Han Ch'in – first son of Li Shai Tung and once heir to City Europe; brother of Li Yuan

Li Hang Ch'i – T'ang of Europe; great-great-grandfather of Li Yuan

Li Kou-lung – T'ang of Europe; great-grandfather of Li Yuan

Li Pai Shung – nephew of Li Chin; heir to the Wo Shih Wo Triad

Li Shai Tung – T'ang of Europe; father of Li Yuan

Lin Yuan – first wife of Li Shai Tung; mother of Li Han Ch'in and Li Yuan

Ling Hen – henchman for Herrick

Liu Chang – brothel keeper/pimp

Liu Tong – lieutenant to Li Chin

Lo Han – tong boss

Lu Ming-shao – "Whiskers Lu"; Big Boss of the Kuei Chuan Triad

Luke – Clayborn friend of Kim Ward from "Rehabilitation"

Lwo Kang – Li Shai Tung's Minister of the Edict

Maitland, Idris – mother of Stefan Lehmann

Man Hsi – tong boss

Mao Liang – Minor Family Princess and member of the Ping Tiao "Council of Five"

Mao Tse-tung – first Ko Ming emperor (ruled AD 1948–76)

Matyas – Clayborn boy in Recruitment Project

Meng K'ai – friend and adviser to Governor Schenck

Meng Te – lieutenant to Lu Ming-shao

Mien Shan – first wife of Li Yuan; mother of Li Kuei Jen

Milne, Michael – private investigator

Ming Huang – sixth T'ang emperor (ruled AD 713–755)

Mo Yu – security lieutenant in the Domain

Moore, John – Company head; Dispersionist

Mu Chua – Madame of the House of the Ninth Ecstasy

Mu Li – "Iron Mu", Boss of the Big Circle Triad

Pao En-fu – Master of the Inner Chambers to Wu Shih

Parr, Charles – Company head; Dispersionist

Pavel – young man on Plantation

Peck – lieutenant to K'ang A-yin (a *ying tzu*, or "shadow")
Peskova – Lieutenant of guards on the Plantations
Ross, Alexander – Company head; Dispersionist
Ross, James – private investigator
Rutherford, Andreas – friend and adviser to Governor Schenck
Sanders – Captain of Security at Helmstadt Armoury
Schenck, Hung-li – Governor of Mars Colony
Schwarz – lieutenant to DeVore
Seymour – Major in Security, North America
Shang – "Old Shang"; Master to Kao Chen when he was a child
Shang Ch'iu – son of Shang Mu and half-brother of Shang Han-A
Shang Chu – great-grandfather of Shang Han-A
Shang Mu – Junior Minister in the "Thousand Eyes", the Ministry
Shang Wen Shao – grandfather of Han-A
Shen Lu Chua – computer expert and member of the *Ping Tiao* "Council of Five"
Shepherd, Amos – great-great-great-grandfather (and genetic "father") of Ben Shepherd
Shepherd, Augustus – "brother" of Ben Shepherd, b. 2106, d. 2122
Shepherd, Hal – father (and genetic "brother") of Ben Shepherd
Shepherd, Robert – great-grandfather (and genetic "brother") of Ben Shepherd
Shu San – Junior Minister to Lwo Kang
Siang – Jelka Tolonen's martial arts instructor
Si Wu Ya – "Silk Raven", wife of Supervisor Sung
Song Wei – sweeper
Spatz, Gustav – Director of the Wiring Project
Spence, Leena – "Immortal", and one time lover of Charles Lever
Ssu Lu Shan – official of the Ministry
Steiner – Manager at ImmVac's Alexandria facility
Sun Li Hua – Wang Hsien's Master of the Inner Chambers
Sung – Supervisor on Plantation
Tarrant – Company head
Teng Fu – plantation guard
Tewl – "Darkness"; chief of the raft-people
Tolonen, Hanna – aunt of Kunt Tolonen
Tolonen, Helga – wife of Jon Tolonen; aunt of Jelka Tolonen
Tolonen, Jenny – wife of Knut Tolonen, and daughter of Pietr Endfors
Tolonen, Jon – brother of Marshal Knut Tolonen
Tong Chu – assassin and "kwai" (hired knife)
Tsao Ch'un – tyrannical founder of Chung Kuo
Tsu Tiao – T'ang of West Asia; father of Tsu Ma
Tu Ch'en-shih – friend and adviser to Governor Schenck
Tu Mai – security guard in the Domain
Tung Cai – low level rioter
Vesa – *Yu* assassin
Virtanen, Per – Major in Li Yuan's Security forces

Visak – lieutenant to Lu Ming-shao
Wang Chang Ye – first son of Wang Hsien
Wang Hsien – T'ang of Africa; father of Wang Sau-leyan
Wang Lieh Tsu – second son of Wang Hsien
Wang Sau-leyan – T'ang of Africa
Wang Ta-hung – third son of Wang Hsien; elder brother of Wang Sau-leyan
Wang Tu – leader of the Martian Radical Alliance
Wei Chan Yin – T'ang of East Asia
Wei Feng – T'ang of East Asia; father of Wei Chan Yin
Wei Hsi Wang – second brother of Wei Chan Yin and heir to City East Asia
Weis, Anton – banker; Dispersionist
Wells – Captain in Security, North America
Wen Ti – "First Ancestor" of City Earth/Chung Kuo, otherwise known as Liu Heng; ruled China 180–157 BC
Wiegand, Max – lieutenant to DeVore
Will – Clayborn friend of Kim Ward from "Rehabilitation"
Wilson, Stephen – Captain in Security under Kao Chen
Wong Yi-sun – "Fat Wong"; Big Boss of the United Bamboo Triad
Wu Shih – T'ang of North America
Wu Wei-kou – first wife of Wu Shih
Wyatt, Edmund – Company head; Dispersionist
Yang Lai – Junior Minister to Lwo Kang
Yang Shao-fu – Minister of Health, City Europe
Yi Shan-ch'i – Minor Family prince
Yin Chan – Minor Family prince and second son of Yin Tsu
Yin Shu – Junior Minister in the "Thousand Eyes", the Ministry
Yin Tsu – head of the Yin Family (one of the Twenty-Nine Minor Families) and father of Fei Yen
Ying Chai – assistant to Sun Li Hua
Ying Fu – assistant to Sun Li Hua
Yue Chun – "Red Pole" (426, or Executioner) to the Wo Shih Wo Triad
Yun Ch'o – lieutenant to Shen Lu Chua
Yun Yueh-hui – "Dead Man Yun"; Big Boss of the Red Gang Triad
Ywe Hao – "Fine Moon"; female Yu terrorist
Ywe Kai-chang – father to Ywe Hao

PROLOGUE: WINTER 2215

FORGOTTEN WORDS

Where can I find a man who has forgotten words? He is the one I would like to talk to.

- Chuang Tzu, 6th century BC
(Writings, xxvi, II)

FORGOTTEN WORDS

E bert stood on the lip of the crater, looking across the ruined city towards the distant sun. It was early morning and a rime of frost covered the iron-red rocks, making them glisten. Below him, in the deep shadow, he could discern the twisted shapes of the struts that had once curved half a *li* into the air, supporting the dome of the greatest of Mars' nineteen cities.

He crouched, placing a gloved hand on a nearby rock, conscious of the sound of his own breathing inside the helmet. Behind him, five paces back, the woman and the boy waited silently.

It was here that the dream had ended, gone in a single night, burned up in a violent conflagration that had taken the lives of more than twenty million people. Dust they were. Dead, like the planet that had never been their home, only a prison, a resting place between two darknesses.

He shivered, understanding. The chain had been broken here, the links scattered. That was the message the great Kan Jiang had offered in his poems. Mars was not the future, Mars was a dead end, a cosmic cul-de-sac. If they tried for a million years Man would never make a home of this place. No, they had to go back, back to Earth – to Chung Kuo. Only then could they move on. Only then might there be a future.

And the Osu? Did *they* have a future?

He turned, looking back. The woman was watching him, her face behind the thick glass of the helmet like carved ebony. Beside her, resting in the crook of her arm, the boy looked into the distance, dreaming as usual, his eyes far off.

Ebert smiled. It was a year ago that he had first met her, in one of the northern settlements. In his desire to become a sage he had renounced the flesh, holding that darker part of himself in abeyance, yet, when she had come to him that night, his body had remembered. She had been with him ever since.

It was as Tuan Ti Fo had said – desire took many forms, and sometimes renunciation itself could be a kind of desire. Best then to be at peace with oneself; to have and not to want.

He stood, putting out a hand to her.

"Come."

Then, turning back towards the setting sun, he began to make his way down into the darkness.

* * *

He woke in darkness, the nightmare still close – so close it seemed he might reach out and touch it.

Yes, he could sense it, there behind the night's dark skin, the pulse of it still warm, still real. For a moment longer it was there, and then he felt it slip from him, leaving him gasping on the cold, bare floor of the tent, emptied by the vision.

The woman lay beside him sleeping, her breathing soft, almost inaudible. From outside the muffled sound of the air-vent's hiss was like the noise the wind makes in the southern deserts during the season of storms. Here, at the bottom of the crater, one of the old air-generators was still partly operational, spewing pure oxygen from a single vent.

He went out, sealing the tent flap after him. It was an hour until dawn and the darkness was intense. From where he stood the sky was a ragged circle framed by the black of the crater walls, seven stars, shaped like a scythe, blazing in the centre.

He climbed, following the path through the twisted ruins from memory. On the lip he paused, turning to look back across the crater's mouth. The blackness beneath him was perfect. To the east, on the horizon, was the tiny blue-white circle of Chung Kuo.

He shivered, remembering the nightmare. He had had it before, many times, but this time it had seemed real.

He looked down at his right hand, flexing the fingers in the glove, surprised to find it whole. Two of them – his father's men – had held him while another splayed his fingers on the slab. He had struggled, but it was no use. There'd been a flash of silver, then he felt the thick-edged blade slice through the sinewy joint of the knuckle – his nerves singing pain, his hot blood pumping into the air. He had heard his own high scream and scuttled like a ghost from out of his flesh. There, usually, it ended – there, thankfully, he had always woken – but this time it went on. He had felt his spirit turn, away from the tormented shrieks, following a servant who, bloody bowl in hand, made his way through flickering corridors of stone towards a brightly-lit chamber.

There, at the operating bench, stood his father, cold-mouthed, dead these eight years, his work apron tied neatly about his massive chest. His dead eyes watched as the servant brought the bowl. He took it, spilling its bloodied contents on to the scrubbed white surface.

The old man's mouth had opened like a cave, words tumbling forth like wind-blown autumn leaves, dust-brown and crumbling.

"The design was wrong. I must begin again. I must make my son anew."

There had been laughter, a cold, ironic laughter. He had turned to see his mother looking on, her ice-blue eyes dismissive.

"Zombies," she said, reaching past her dead husband to lift the severed finger from the bowl. "That's all you've ever made. Dead flesh. It's all dead flesh."

She let the finger fall, a chilling indifference in her face, then turned and left the room.

No warmth in her, he thought. *The woman had no warmth . . .*

Setting the bowl aside, his father had taken the finger, stretching and moulding it until the figure of a man lay on the bench before him.

Hans had stepped forward, looking down into the unformed face, willing it not to happen, but the dream was ineluctable. Slowly the features formed, like mountain ranges rising from the primal earth, until the mirror image of his face stared back at him . . . and sneered.

He jerked his head back, gasping.

"Efulefu . . ."

He swallowed back his fear, then answered the voice that had come up from the darkness. "What is it, Hama?"

Her figure threaded its way up through the shadows just below. "Are you all right, husband? I thought I heard you groan."

"It is nothing, Hama, only tiredness."

She came to him, reaching out to take his hands. "The boy is sleeping still."

"Good." He smiled, enjoying the sight of her face in the star light, the dream defeated by the reality of her. "I was thinking, Hama. We must call a gathering."

"A gathering? Of the *ndichie*?"

He shook his head. "No, Hama. Of everyone. Of Elders, Tribes and Settlers." He gazed past her at the distant earth, noting how small, how fragile it seemed in all that emptiness. "It is time we decided what to do. Time we chose a path for all to follow."

* * *

The Machine blinked, then looked again. One moment there had been nothing, and the next . . .

"Tuan Ti Fo? Do you see what I see?"

The air before the Machine shimmered and took form. Tuan Ti Fo sat cross-legged before the open console, bowing his grey-haired head in greeting. "What *is* it that you see?"

"I see. . ." the Machine strained, starting into the intense darkness, using all its powers to try to penetrate that single spot where it was blind. "I see. . . nothing."

Tuan Ti Fo chuckled softly. "You see *nothing*? Then, surely, there *is* nothing."

"No. Something landed on the surface of the planet north of Kang Kua. I can sense it. It *is* there. Its very *absence* reveals it, and yet it conceals itself."

The old man tugged at his beard thoughtfully. "And your camera probes?"

"Cannot penetrate it. It's as if there is a shell surrounding it. A shell of. . ." It hesitated, a hesitation that in a man might seem normal, yet in the great Machine revealed the existence of billions of rapid calculations. "Something unknown," it concluded, a strange hesitancy in its normally toneless voice.

Tuan Ti Fo stared at the console a moment, then nodded. His mood was suddenly more sober. "I see."

The Machine fell silent. It was thinking. For more than five million years Mankind had striven upwards out of the primal dark towards the light, and from that quest had come Itself, the ultimate flowering of mind: one single, all-encompassing intelligence.

Intelligent, yet incomplete. Within its mind it pictured the great swirl of things known and unknown, like a vast *t'ai chi* of light and dark, perfectly balanced. Within that half which was light was a tiny circle of blackness – a pin-point of occlusion, which it knew to be Tuan Ti Fo. And now, within the darkness of those things unknown lay a single point of light.

"If it's a craft," Tuan Ti Fo said, "then it must have come from somewhere."

"But there's no trace," the Machine began, then checked itself, realising that, like the absence that revealed something, there was a line of occlusion through its memory; an area of tampering – a no-trace that paradoxically revealed the passage of the craft.

"It came in from the System's edge. From the tenth planet."

Yet even as it spoke, it questioned that.

"Something alien?" Tuan Ti Fo asked.

It considered the notion, surprised that for once it was dealing in uncertainties. "No . . ."

"But you have a hunch?"

"A calculated guess."

"Then you had best send someone."

"Send someone?"

Tuan Ti Fo laughed, then stood, brushing down his silks. "Why, to look, of course." He turned, his figure shimmering, slowly vanishing into the air, his words echoing after he had gone. "Send the boy. He'll see. *Whatever* it is."

* * *

"Nza?"

The voice came from the air. At its sound the boy turned sharply, his body crouched defensively, then he saw the tiny, glittering probe hovering like a silver insect in the air above his head.

"What is it?" he asked, keeping the fear from his voice.

"Where is Ebert?"

The ten-year-old turned, pointing back into the shadows. The probe moved past him, drifting into the darkness – a moment later it returned.

"Come," it said, hovering just above his head, no bigger than his fist, its surface smooth and rounded like a tiny shaven skull.

Nza shivered and then obeyed.

* * *

The Machine watched the boy approach the nullity; saw him put out his hand, then withdraw it as if he'd been stung.

"Can you *feel* anything?" it asked, the sensation of curiosity almost over-whelming.

The boy nodded, then put out his hand, tracing what seemed like a smooth, curving slope in the air. But still it could see nothing, sense nothing.

It watched the boy move slowly round, testing the air with his hands, defining more accurately the area of nothingness the Machine's probes had sensed.

Nza turned, his eyes wide.

"What is it?" it asked. "Did you see anything?"

Nza shook his head. "Efulefu . . . Get Efulefu."

* * *

It was light when Ebert got there. He crouched some fifty *ch'i* from the unseen presence, perfectly at rest, watching the shadows shorten as the sun climbed the sky. The wind blew fitfully, and when it did he noted the patterns the sand made around the nullity.

After two hours he stood and motioned to the boy. Nza went to him and stood there, looking up at him as he mouthed something through the glass of his helmet. It was cold, bitterly cold, and already two of the Machine's six probes had ceased functioning, but Ebert seemed unaware of it.

The cold. It would kill them all one day. Machine and men alike.

Nza stared a moment longer, then nodded and, with that curious loping run of his, scuttled across to the nearest of the probes.

"What is it?" the Machine asked, but the boy shook his head and pointed to his mouth. It watched, reading the boy's lips.

There's something there. He senses it. He thinks it watches us and listens. And something else.

It waited as the boy ordered his thoughts, recalling what Ebert had told him.

He says. . . when he closes his eyes . . . he sees a face. An old, familiar face.

It knew, even before the boy's mouth stretched twice to form the word. So he was back. DeVore was back on Mars.

* * *

DeVore stood at the view window, looking out across the wind-blown surface towards the crouching figure, then turned to the monitor again. Ebert's face filled the screen, his eyes behind the helmet's glass a deep reposeful blue.

So you survived, old friend. And now you consort with those ugly sons of the night. Well, stranger things have been known.

He laughed softly, then clicked his fingers, summoning one of his guards.

"Find out how it's going. We've been here too long as it is. I want us gone by nightfall."

The soldier bowed low and backed away. DeVore turned back to the screen, pushing out his chin reflexively. Hans Ebert had been but a child when he'd first met him. A spoiled and wilful child. But now, looking at him, *studying* him, he saw how much he had changed. It was there in his eyes, in the perfect stillness of the man.

Impressive, he thought. But also dangerous. Hans Ebert was no friend of his – he understood that now. At any other time he'd stop to kill this exiled prince, but right now it was more important to get back to Chung Kuo as quickly – *and as discreetly* – as possible.

He cursed silently, angry that they had had to set down and determined that, once repairs were effected, he'd kill that bastard Hooper himself. As an example to the others.

He crossed the room and tapped into the craft's log. Things were getting slack. Already they had lost two days. As it was, even a week's delay wouldn't affect their cargo, but any longer . . .

He cleared the screen. That would be one advantage of getting back to Chung Kuo. For too long now he'd had to rely on the services of second-raters. Once back he could dispense with them and hire some better men.

DeVore smiled. He would enjoy that day. It would be a day of rewards. A day when all these second-rate fellows would find themselves grinning.

Grinning bone-white before the wind.

There was a sound in the doorway. He turned, noting the guard there.

"Well?"

"Nine hours, Master Hooper says."

"Good." He waved the man away, then went to the window again. Ebert had not moved. He seemed rooted there, part of the dust of Mars.

"I shall come back for you, Hans Ebert," he said quietly. "Once other wars are fought and won. And then . . ." He laughed, then turned away, imagining the sight. *And then I'll see you dance on a gibbet like the commonest low-life there ever was.*

* * *

Late in the day he felt it go. There was a change in the air, a lessening of the pressure, and then . . . nothing.

"It's gone," Ebert said, getting up, his limbs stiff from inactivity and cold.

"I know," Tuan Ti Fo said, appearing beside him. "I felt its passage in the air."

"Where has it gone?"

"Inwards. Back to Chung Kuo."

Ebert nodded. "We must call a gathering. Tonight."

"It is done."

"Ah." Ebert smiled. "And my intentions? You know those too?"

Tuan Ti Fo's laughter was light, infectious. "You mistake me, Tsou Tsai Hei. The woman, Hama, spoke to me."

He stared at the old sage, surprised. "You speak with her?"

"Sometimes."

"Is there anything you do not know, Master Tuan?"

Tuan's eyes, normally so calm, so clear, for once looked away, troubled. "Many things. But only one that bothers me. I do not know what that man wants."

"DeVore, you mean?"

Tuan Ti Fo nodded. "This world – this *reality* – it is like a game to him. He plays his stone and then awaits an answer. Why, the King of Hell is but an apprentice beside him. He has made malice into an art. Some days I think the man is old. Older than the frame of flesh he wears."

"Older than you, Master Tuan?"

Tuan laughed. "Don't mock my grey beard, Worthless One. Time will find you too."

"Of course. But tell me, Master Tuan, what do you mean?"

"Only this. That I come to think the true nature of the man has been masked from us. DeVore . . . what is he? *Is* he a mortal man? An orphan, raised to high office in the T'ang's Security forces? Or was that too merely a guise? A mask of flesh put on to fool mere human eyes? Copies . . . Think of it, Hans. Why does the man love copies so? He duplicates himself and sends his copies out to do his bidding. Now, is that self-love or some far deeper game?"

Hans considered a moment, then shrugged. "Why did the Machine not destroy his craft while it was here?"

"Destroy it? How? How can one destroy what is not there?"

He laughed. "*Something* was there. I sensed it. With my eyes closed I could *see* it."

"Maybe. But what I said still goes. It was not there. It was . . . *folded in* somehow: a negative twist of nothingness. The Machine has a theory about it. It thinks the craft exists within a probability space quite near to our own, the atoms of which have been . . . *vibrated*, like a plucked string."

"There but not there."

"Like your dream."

Hans stared at the old man, startled. "I told Hama nothing of the dream."

"I was there but not there."

"And you?" Ebert asked, passing his hand slowly through the old man's chest as his silk-cloaked figure shimmered into nothingness again. "Are you here, or are *you* 'folded in'?"

* * *

They gathered at the long day's end, as the last light of the sun bled from the horizon and the red became black. Hans Ebert, once heir to the great GenSyn Corporation of Chung Kuo, traitor to his T'ang and patricide, known also as Efulefu, "the Worthless One" and Tsou Tsai Hei, "The Walker in the Darkness", climbed up on to the table rock and turned to face the thousands who had come.

He looked about him, noting who was there. Just below him were the *ndichie*, the elders of the Osu, their white curls hidden within the tall domes of their helmets. Beyond them, standing in loose family groups, were members of all the northern tribes, sons and daughters of Mother Sky. To his right, forming a tight knot beside the escarpment, were two or three hundred of the new settlers. They looked on suspiciously, clearly ill at ease, disturbed to see so many of the tribes gathered there. Hans wondered what arguments Old Tuan had used to bring them out so late and so far from their settlement.

He raised a hand then spoke, his voice carrying from his lip mike to the helmets of everyone there.

"Brothers, sisters, friends, respected elders, I thank you all for coming. You have been patient, very patient with me. Twice Mars has circled the sun and still I brought no answer. But finally I see what must be done."

"Speak, Efulefu," one of the *ndichie* called, speaking for them all. "Tell us what you see."

"I see a time when the supply ships no longer come. When Chung Kuo no longer looks to Mars with caring eyes."

"What of it?" someone called.

"We do not need their food, their medicines," another, deeper voice shouted from further back. "Let the ships stop. It makes no difference!"

"That's right!" another yelled. "We want nothing from them!"

"No?" Ebert shrugged. "When a father forgets his son . . . when he casts him off, is that nothing? When a mother casts her unwanted child into a stream, to sink or swim, is that nothing? When a great thread is cut, is *that* nothing?"

He moved forward until he stood on the very edge of the great rock, then leaned towards them. "The poet Kang Jiang was right. This planet isn't home, it's exile. There is no life for us here, only the certainty of eventual extinction. Not now, perhaps, not for a thousand years, but one day. One day no human eye will wake to see this world. One day only our dust will blow about the circle of this place."

"It is fate."

Ebert looked down at the elder who had spoken.

"Fate, Jaga?"

The old man lifted his hands in a gesture of emptiness. "What can we do, Efulefu? There is nowhere else for us. We were cast off two centuries ago. To be Osu . . . why, it is to live in exile."

"Maybe that was so," Ebert answered, more gently than before. "But now that must end. We must build a ship."

"A ship!" The surprised words echoed back from all sides.

Ebert nodded. "That is so. Oh, not a huge thing. Nothing that is beyond our means."

There was a furious murmuring. Ebert waited, then raised his hand again. Slowly the noise subsided.

"We must go back . . . a few of us . . . and claim a place."

"They would kill us!" someone yelled.

"They will kill *you*," the elder, Jaga, said, pointing a gloved hand at Ebert's chest.

"Maybe. Yet we must try. A ship. First off we need a ship. And then men. Eight volunteers. Eight men of honour . . . eight black-faced heroes to offer to Li Yuan."

He laughed, seeing it clearly now, recalling the day twelve years before when the two gifts of stones had been given to the young prince on his betrothal day.

"It has been foreseen. One has gone on before us. And we must follow. For if we fail, *all* fails."

He stepped back, hearing the great murmur of debate begin, his own part in it done.

Yes, and it was true what he had said: DeVore had gone on before them to place the first white stone upon the board. But he would follow hard upon his heels – he and his eight black stones.

The game . . . The game had begun again.

10

He looked down, flexing his ring finger within the glove, remembering the moment in the dream. It was time to be rejoined. Time to play his proper role in things. He knew it now. Knew it with a clarity that filled him. His exile was coming to an end. It was time to return. Time to emerge into the light again.

PART 1 – SPRING 2216

SONG OF THE BRONZE STATUE

"Gone that emperor of Maoling,
Rider through the autumn wind,
Whose horse neighs at night
And has passed without trace by dawn.
The fragrance of autumn lingers still
On those cassia trees by painted galleries,
But on every palace hall the green moss grows.
As Wei's envoy sets out to drive a thousand *li*
The keen wind at the East Gate stings the statue's eyes . . .
From the ruined palace he brings nothing forth
But the moonshaped disc of Han,
True to his lord, he sheds leaden tears,
And withered orchids by the Xianyang Road
See the traveller on his way.
Ah, if Heaven had a feeling heart, it too must grow old!
He bears the disc off alone
By the light of a desolate moon,
The town far behind him, muted its lapping waves."

– Li He, "Song of the Bronze Statue", 9th century AD

CHAPTER · 1

IN HEAVEN'S SIGHT

Colonel Karr crouched in the tunnel behind his lieutenant, the light from the flatscreen on the man's back casting a pale glow over his face and chest. His helmet hung loosely about his neck, his gun – a heavy automatic with twin clips – rested against the wall. Beyond him, squatting to either side of the unlit tunnel, a thousand men waited.

It was the four hundred and nineteenth day of the siege, and still there was no sign that Tunis would fall. *Not this year*, Karr thought, amazed by its resilience, by the sheer stubbornness of its defenders.

The image on the screen was a familiar one. It showed Tunis from a distance, sat like a giant rock upon the plain, the sea beyond it: an imposing block of part-melted ice, its surface dark, like rough pitch. They had cleared the surrounding stacks long ago with ice-destroying chemicals, but the defenders had coated the rest with a special diamond-tough bonding: a bonding that seemed to resist all but their most destructive weapons. Close up it had a blistered, burned appearance, like the toughened hide of some deep-sea creature.

They had spent the best part of a year chipping away at it, to little real effect. And what inroads they made were generally short-lived. Nor had their blockade – the keystone of Rheinhardt's plan – been totally effective. Ting Ju-ch'ang, the local Warlord, had the backing of the Mountain Lords, and despite Karr's best efforts, their ships had managed many times to slip through and supply the City-fortress.

Even so, things had to be bad inside. The defending force was more than three million strong. Add to that a further fifty million – all of them crammed into a space designed for a tenth their number – and it took no genius to imagine the problems they faced. If rumours were true, they were eating one another in there.

The thought made Karr shudder; made him question once again the sense of Rheinhardt's strategy. There had been a good reason for hitting Tunis. For a long time Ting Ju-ch'ang – as front-man for the Mountain Lords – had used Tunis as a base from which to attack the southern coast of Li Yuan's City, and there was no question they had needed to do something about it. That said, there had been no need to capture it. As Karr had argued several times in Rheinhardt's presence, they had merely to contain Ting's activities. To capture a well-defended City was – as he knew from experience – almost an impossibility, especially when, as here, he found himself in hostile territory, outnumbered, his supply lines stretched, and harried at his back all the time.

The truth was Rheinhardt knew they couldn't win, yet he'd become obsessed with it. To withdraw would be, for him, a severe loss of face. After all, he had promised Li Yuan he would take it, and to go back on that promise was – for him – unthinkable.

And so here we are, Karr thought, *crouched in a tunnel beneath the City, waiting for the signal to attack. While back in City Europe a far greater threat to our security grows and grows, like a fat white grub, feeding upon its fellow grubs.*

Lehmann. Lehmann was the problem, not Ting Ju-ch'ang.

Karr stretched his neck, then turned, smiling at the men closest to him reassuringly. He glanced down at the timer inset into his wrist, then raised his hand. It was almost time.

He heard the whisper go back into the darkness, then turned back, feeling the familiar tension in his guts. Up ahead his teams were in position. In less than a minute, as his cruisers mounted a diversionary missile attack on the western gate, they would begin.

He lifted his helmet and secured it, making sure the seal was airtight, the oxygen supply satisfactory, then reached for his gun. Behind him he could hear the scrape and click of hundreds of helmets being secured, the clatter as a gun fell then was retrieved.

Fourteen seconds . . .

He waited, counting in his head, seeing the first wave of cruisers flash across the screen, their missiles streaking towards the rock-like wall of the City-fortress. Even as they hit – even as he felt the judder from above, there was the *whummpf-whumpff* of mortars being fired further down the tunnel, followed immediately by the piercing, banshee whirr of the shells as they spiralled towards their targets.

He turned, looking down the line, noting face after familiar face, underlit by their helmet lights. These were good men. His best. They'd been with him a long time now and knew exactly what to do.

Who this time? he wondered, seeing how each one met his eyes and smiled. *Whose widow will I be speaking to tonight? Whose grieving mother?*

But there was no more time for that. Scrambling up, Karr began to run, half-crouching, following his lieutenant towards the gap, his men close behind.

In his head he had been counting. Now, at fifteen, he stopped and crouched again, as the blast came back down the tunnel at them. Behind him, he knew, his men would have done the same.

Instinct. It was all instinct now. They'd been fighting this war so long that there was nothing he could tell them they didn't already know.

He stood, then ran on, making for the breach his guns had made in the City's underbelly.

Up ahead, pre-programmed remotes were picking off most of the defending mechanicals, their lasers raking the sides of the great shaft they were about to

infiltrate, exploding any mines. They would clear a path. But it would take men –
with their heightened instincts – to get any further.

Karr passed the mortar positions. Some ten *ch'i* further on, just above them and
to the right, was the breach. He went through the jagged opening and stepped out
into the base of a huge service shaft, looking up into a haze of mist and light. The
mortar shells had contained a mixture of strong hallucinogenics and tiny pellets
which, when they exploded, burned with a searing, blinding light. Right now Ting's
forces were in temporary disarray – the watch-guard blind and half out of its
collective skulls – but that advantage wouldn't last long. They had two minutes,
maybe four at the outside before fresh forces were drafted in. And after that . . .

Karr stood beside the breach, waving his men through, urging them on,
watching them fan out around the edge of the shaft and begin to climb, proud
– proud with a father's pride – of their professionalism.

Wasted, he thought, angry suddenly that all of their talent, all of their hard-won
knowledge should be squandered for so little reward. *We should be dealing with
Lehmann. Clearing the levels of the scum who thrive under his patronage.*

Yes. But so long as Rheinhardt had Li Yuan's backing there would be no
change. Tunis . . . Tunis would be the rock upon which a million mothers' hearts
would be broken.

He swallowed, then, knowing there was a job to be done, turned and, clipping
his gun to his back, began to climb.

* * *

Pei K'ung, wife of Li Yuan and Empress of City Europe, snapped her fingers. At
once the servant standing beside the great, studded doors hurried across, his head
bowed. Two paces from her desk he stopped, falling to his knees.

"Mistress!"

"Tsung Ye," she said, not looking up from the document she was reading, "tell
Master Nan I'd like a word with him. Meanwhile send in the maid. And have the
doctor standing by. I want his full report on the new intake of girls."

Tsung Ye hesitated, in case there was anything else, then backed away, hurrying
from the room.

Pei K'ung looked up, bracing herself for the interview ahead. Her husband had
seemed particularly happy this morning. She had heard him whistling below her
window, and when she had gone out on to her balcony to look, it was to find him
walking among the flower beds, sniffing the dew-heavy roses, more like a love-sick
boy than a great. T'ang. Of course, it was possible that the beauty of the morning
had made him so, but she suspected it was more to do with the company in his bed
last night.

She sighed. Last night they had argued, for the first time since they had wed, two
and a half years ago. He had turned on her and shouted her down, his face burning
with anger, then stormed from the room. And later, when she had gone to him, he
had refused point blank to see her.

She had slept little, going over every last event in her mind, trying to establish
just what had sparked his anger, but still she was no wiser. He had simply snapped,

as if something deep within him – something dark and hidden from her – had surfaced, like a carp going for a fly.

She shivered then got up from her chair, making her way to the far side of the room. A massive silver mirror, its mahogany frame embellished with peacocks and dragons, stood there between two pillars.

She stood there a while, studying herself, knowing there was no way to change the image that the glass returned to her. Plain she was, and old – eighteen years older than her husband Yuan. It was little wonder that he chose to spend his nights with serving maids. Besides, it had been a condition of their marriage – that there were to be no heirs to the union, no physical side to their relationship. At the time it had seemed a small price to pay, but now . . .

There was a knock. She turned, setting her thoughts aside. Slowly, measuring her pace, she returned to her desk and sat. Then, after a calming breath, she turned to face the door.

"Enter."

The maid came in slowly, her eyes averted, her chin tucked into her neck, her whole body hunched forward as she pigeon-stepped towards the huge desk. It was clear that she found the great study – and Pei K'ung at the centre of it – immensely daunting. *And so she should*, thought Pei K'ung, for she had power of life or death over the girl: a power her husband had granted her on the day of their wedding.

"Stand before me, girl. I want to see you clearly when you answer me."

"Mistress!"

The girl shuffled forward, out of the shadows that obscured the far side of the room and into the sunlight that spilled in from the open garden windows. A pattern of cranes and lilies, white, yellow and black, skirted the edge of the turquoise-blue carpet on which she stood.

Pei K'ung studied her, coldly, clinically almost, as a horse-trader might study a horse, searching it carefully for flaws. She was pretty, of course – they were all pretty – but it was something else that marked her out. Not her age, for they were all of a muchness – fifteen, sixteen, never older – nor her figure, which was petite but well rounded, but something in the way she stood.

"My husband . . . was he pleased with you last night?"

"I . . . I think so, Mistress."

"You *think* so?"

"He . . ." she hesitated, a faint colour appearing at her neck. Pei K'ung noted it. A strong neck she had, and strong bones. Peasant bones. But pretty, none the less. Very pretty indeed.

"Well, girl?"

The maid swallowed. One hand smoothed the pale lemon silk of her *chi pao*. "He seemed . . . agitated at first. Angry about something. I had to soothe him. I . . ."

Pei K'ung waited, sparing the girl nothing.

"I kissed him," she said finally.

Pei K'ung's eyes were like an eagle's, piercing the girl. "*Kissed* him? Where? On the mouth?"

The girl's head dipped an inch or two lower. "No, Mistress. Lower than that . . . You know."

She almost laughed. How in hell would *she* know? She had never even seen her husband naked, let alone . . .

"You kissed his penis, you mean?"

The girl nodded.

"And you liked that?"

"I . . . I didn't mind. If it gave him pleasure."

"And did it?"

The girl's discomfort was quite evident now. "He seemed . . ."

"Did he reach his climax that way?"

The girl looked up, her eyes wide open. "Mistress?"

"The moment of clouds and rain. Did it happen while he was still in your mouth?"

The girl looked down, the colour spreading to her cheeks. "Only the first time, Mistress."

"Ah . . . and the second?"

Her answer was almost a whisper. "That was much later."

"And between times, did you sleep?"

She shook her head.

"Not at all?"

"He . . . would not let me, Mistress. He was . . ."

Pei K'ung stiffened slightly, waiting to see how the girl would finish the sentence. Insatiable? Like a tiger? Tireless?

The girl looked up again, a surprising tenderness in her eyes. "Very gentle."

Pei K'ung felt something strange happen deep within her. It was almost physical, yet she knew it wasn't. It was to do with those last two words, with how the girl had looked back at her when she had said them, her dark eyes sparkling with an inner light. *Gentle*. She had heard Yuan called many things, but never gentle. Not even with his son.

She forced herself to speak, to keep on asking questions. "How do you mean, *gentle*?"

The girl's smile, like her words, made her feel something new – something she had never felt before. She did not recognise it at once, but then, with the suddenness of shock, she understood. Envy. For the first time since she'd married him, she felt envy.

The girl's eyes seemed to drift back to the night before; to widen with pleasure at the memory of it.

"I felt . . . well, I felt he only really got pleasure when he was giving pleasure to me. At first I was uncomfortable. I pleaded with him to relax and let me see to his needs, but he would not have it, Mistress. He . . ." Again, there was that flush at neck and cheek, that same, strange smile of inner satisfaction. "He said he wanted to make me happy, to make me cry out, to . . ."

She stopped, as if she sensed some change in the woman facing her. Her head went down, the chin tucked in tightly, the eyes averted.

"And *did* you cry out?"

The girl nodded.

"Ah . . ." Her mouth was dry, her heart beating strangely. Even so, she had to know. "What . . . what did he do?"

The maid glanced up, as if to gauge her Mistress's mood, then spoke again. "He kissed me, Mistress."

"*Kissed* you?"

Even as she said it, she heard the echo of her earlier words. How often had she sat here going through this obscene litany? Eight, nine hundred times? And never – *never*, until this moment, had it meant anything to her. She shivered, only half listening as the girl spelt out just how thoroughly Li Yuan had pleasured her. And as the words went on, she closed her eyes, imagining him doing that *to her* – for the first time allowing herself to surrender to the thought.

"Mistress?"

She opened her eyes. The girl was watching her, surprised, her mouth open like a fish.

"Forgive me," Pei K'ung said, angry with herself; conscious that she had let her guard slip. "I am tired. If you would go now."

"Mistress!"

The girl knelt, touching her head to the floor, then backed away.

Anger, she told herself. It was all connected with his anger. But how? And why had he not been cruel to the girl? Why had he not taken out his anger on *her*? Or was that the way of it? Was something always converted into its opposite? Was his strange tenderness a product of that anger?

She shuddered then stood, going across to the window. He was out there, standing beside the carp pond, talking to two of his advisers. She could go to him right now if she wanted and ask him – ask him how it had felt and why last night, of all nights, he had been different. Yet she knew it was impossible. As impossible to ask as to put herself there in his bed beside him.

Beneath him, she thought, and was surprised by the silent words.

Do I want him? Is that *it?* For if it was, she had best banish the thought, for it was – it truly *was* – impossible. Had she not, after all, put her name to the contract they had made? Even so, the suddenness, the strength of that newly-discovered need surprised her.

She had thought herself safe: had thought her plainness, her age, precluded her from such feelings. But drip by drip these interviews had worn her down, until two words and a tender smile had breached her.

There was a knock. A heavy, purposeful knock that she recognised as Nan Ho's. She turned, calling on him to enter.

"Mistress," he said, coming two paces into the room and bowing to her. Behind him his two assistants did the same, like living shadows of the man.

"Master Nan. I wanted your advice on something. If we could speak alone?"

"Of course," he said, dismissing his assistants with a gesture. "How are you this morning, Mistress?"

"I am . . ." she almost lied, almost gave in to politeness, yet caught herself in time. "I am disturbed, Master Nan," she said, moving across the floor until she stood beside him. "Li Yuan was in a foul mood last night. He *raged* at me for no reason. And yet this morning he is like a child."

Nan Ho looked down, then cleared his throat. "These are difficult times for him, Pei K'ung. Much is happening. Sometimes . . ."

She interrupted him. "Straight answers, Master Nan."

He looked up, meeting her eyes, respect and amusement in them. He was a good twenty-five years older than her and a man; even so, they had established a relationship of equals right from the start.

"Straight answers?" he laughed softly. "All right. I'll tell you. We're planning a new campaign."

She frowned. "South America?"

He shook his head. "No, no . . . *Here*, in Europe. In the Lowers. Your husband wants to take control again. He feels it's time. The African campaign has reached a stalemate and the feeling among the Three is that we should withdraw. The problem is what to do with our forces once we've withdrawn them. To have them sit idly at home is not an option any of us wants to consider. Things are bad enough without that."

She nodded, understanding. "And the meeting this morning?"

"Is to sound out all parties."

"I see. And if they're in agreement?"

Nan Ho shrugged. "That is not my decision, Mistress."

She smiled. *No, yet you will have the greatest influence over what he decides, neh?*

He bowed. "If that is all, Mistress?"

"Of course." Yet as he turned to leave, she called him back.

"Nan Ho?"

"Yes, Mistress?"

"My husband . . . when he . . ." She took a breath, steeling herself to ask. "When he lost his virginity – how was that done?"

Nan Ho smiled, the smile strangely, disconcertingly like that the girl had offered earlier. "He was but a boy, and curious in the way boys are. He had begun . . . you know, night dreams. It worried him. So I sent one of the maids to his bed. Pearl Heart, if I remember correctly. She . . . *taught* him. She and her sister, Sweet Rose."

He nodded to himself, as if satisfied, then added. "It is the way. His father, Li Shai Tung always said that . . ."

"Thank you," she said, interrupting him. "I . . . I was interested, that's all."

"Of course," Nan Ho bowed again. "If that is all?"

She nodded, letting him go, then returned to the window, watching as her husband paced slowly in the sunlight by the pool.

* * *

"Pull back! Disengage and pull back!"

Karr's voice boomed momentarily in every helmet then cut out as the defenders jammed the channel, but it was enough.

"*Aiya* . . ." he whispered softly, watching from his place beside the breach as his men withdrew, clambering down the pipes and service ladders overhead, then dropping the last few *ch'i* and scrambling for the gap.

The floor of the shaft was littered with bodies, friend and foe indistinguishable in death.

They knew, he thought, touching each of his men briefly on the arm as they moved past him into the safety of the tunnel. *The fuckers knew!*

There was no doubt about it. The counter-attack had been too quick, too well-organised for it to have been a matter of chance. Someone had leaked their plan. Someone in the inner circle of command.

Karr grimaced, pained by what had happened. They'd be lucky if a quarter of their number got out. It had been a massacre. Then, seeing how one of his men had fallen on the far aside of the shaft, he hurried across, helping the wounded man, half-carrying him back, oblivious to the laser-fire from above.

As he handed the man through, a runner pushed into view.

"Sir!"

Karr glanced at him, annoyed to be bothered at this crucial moment. "What is it, man?"

"New orders, sir. From the General himself. He says you are to withdraw."

"Withdraw?" Karr laughed bitterly and looked past the messenger at his men. Their eyes, like his, were dark with knowledge of the betrayal. His voice, when he spoke, was heavy with irony. "Tell General Rheinhardt that his forces have anticipated his request."

The runner, noting Karr's mood and perhaps intimidated by the giant, took a step backward. "Further, he says you are to leave here at once and report to Tongjiang."

Karr turned, staring at the man, surprised. "Tongjiang? To the Palace, you mean?"

The man nodded. "The General says you are to go direct. The T'ang himself wishes to see you. He says it is a matter of the most extreme urgency."

Karr nodded. Then, recollecting himself, he waved the man away. "Tell the General I will come. Tell him . . . tell him I will come once my men are safe from here."

"But sir . . ."

Karr turned back, glaring at the man. "Just tell him!"

Then, turning away, he went back inside, to try to salvage what he could.

* * *

The news from Tunis was good. The latest attack had been beaten off, the great T'ang's forces scattered. Fu Chiang, "the Priest", Big Boss of the Red Flower Triad of North Africa, folded the paper and smiled, then looked about him at the banquet chamber, his hazel eyes taking in the lavish silverware, the ornate red and gold decorations. Briefly he hesitated, as if about to criticise, then gave a terse nod. At the signal a dozen servants let out their breath and, bowing low to their Lord, backed hurriedly from the room.

Good, he thought, satisfied that all was finally ready, then turned away, drawing his dark-red silks tighter about him. As little as a week ago he'd have considered such a meeting impossible, but curiosity was a powerful incentive – it had achieved what neither common sense nor coercion had previously managed.

His "cousins" – "Mountain Lords", Triad Bosses like himself – were waiting in the next room. He had known them in bad times, in those years when Wang Hsien had ruled City Africa with an iron glove, but now they were Great Men – men whose power had grown enormously this past decade, insect-like, feeding upon War and Change. Between them they controlled almost two-thirds of City Africa's lowers.

He smiled then went through.

They were standing before the dragon arch, the fight-pit beyond them, its galleries climbing up out of sight. In an hour those balconies would be packed with his men, their bodies tense, their eyes wide with blood-lust. Right now, however, the pit was dark and empty like a hollowed skull, the galleries silent.

"Cousins," he said, greeting them. If one knew no better one might almost laugh at the sight of them. A giant and a dwarf, a fat man and a one-eyed hermaphrodite! Yet appearances were deceptive. Any one of them was as deadly as a hungry viper, and together . . .

"Are your *sure* he's coming?" the tiny, almost doll-like figure of Mo Nan-ling, "the Little Emperor" asked, his fingers toying with the thick gold chain about his neck.

Fu Chiang smiled benevolently. "He will be here any time, Cousin Mo. I have tracked his craft over the mountains. He comes alone."

"Into the tiger's mouth," the big man at Mo Nan-ling's side said, cracking his knuckles. "The man must be a fool."

Fu Chiang stared at the giant, his face pensive. "So it seems, Yang Chih-wen. And yet that cannot be. Our cousins in City Europe underestimated him, and where are they now? Dead, their kingdoms smashed, the sacred brotherhoods destroyed."

Yang Chih-wen shrugged. He was almost three *ch'i* in height and heavily muscled. "The Bear" they called him and the likeness to that ancient, extinct animal was uncanny, from the long, thick nose to the dark hair that sprouted from every pore.

"They were weak and careless," he said gruffly, as if that were all there was to say, but Hsueh Chi, Boss of the southern *Hsien* and half-brother of the great Warlord, Hsueh Nan, stepped forward, scratching his ample stomach.

"Forgive me, but I knew Fat Wong and he was neither weak nor careless. Caution was his by-word. And yet Li Min proved too cunning for him. He waited, building his strength, biding his time, then took Wong Yi-sun on when he least expected it – *against the odds* – and beat him. He and his fellow Bosses. So we might do well to listen to what our cousin Fu says. It seems to me that we must act together or not at all."

Yang Chih-wen laughed dismissively. "You talk as if he were a threat, Hsueh Chi, but what kind of danger does he really pose? Ambushing Fat Wong and his allies was one thing, but taking Africa . . ." he shook his great, bear-like head. "Why, the full might of Li Yuan's armies cannot shake our grip. What then could this *pai nan jen* – this pale man – do?"

There was an air of challenge, of ridicule in these final words that was aimed directly at Hsueh Chi. Noting it, Fu Chiang hurriedly spoke up, trying to calm things down.

"Maybe my cousin Yang is right. Maybe there *is* no threat. But it would be foolish to repeat past mistakes, surely? Besides, we need decide nothing here today. We are here only to listen to the man, to find out what he has to say. And to judge for ourselves what kind of man this 'White T'ang' really is."

While the talk had gone on, Sheng Min-chung had gone out on to the balcony. For a while he had stood there, his hands on the rail, looking down into the dark, steep-sided pit. Now he came back into the room.

"We will do as Fu Chiang says."

Yang opened his mouth as if to debate the matter further, but at a glance from Sheng he closed it again and nodded. Though they were all "equals" here, Sheng Min-chung was more equal than the rest.

The Big Boss of East Africa was a strange one. As a child he had been raised by an uncle – touched, some said – who had dressed him as a girl. The experience had hardened Sheng. Then, at thirteen, he had lost his right eye in a knife fight. Later, when he'd become Red Pole of the Iron Fists, he had paid to have his remaining eye enhanced, leaving the other vacant. Ever since it was said that his single good eye saw far more clearly – and further – than the two eyes of a dozen other men.

One-Eye Sheng moved between them, his long silks swishing across the marble floor, then turned, facing them.

"And *ch'un tzu* . . . let us show our friend Li Min the utmost courtesy. What a man was born, that he cannot help, but what he becomes, through his own efforts," his one eye glared at Yang Chi-wen, "*that*, I would say, demands our respect."

The bear-like Yang stared back at Sheng a moment, then nodded, and Fu Chiang, looking on, smiled broadly, moved by Sheng's words.

Respect. Yes, without respect a man was nothing. To gain and hold respect, that was worth more than gold. Whatever transpired today and in the days to come, much would depend on establishing a common trust – a solid bridge of mutual respect – between themselves and Li Min.

Fu Chiang smiled, pleased that he, of all of them, had been the one Li Min had chosen, for to him would be given the credit for this momentous event. He turned his head, looking about him, pride at his own achievements filling him. Ten years ago he had been nothing. *Nothing.* But now he was Head of the Red Flower, a Great Man with the power of life and death over others. Sheng Min-chung had spoken true. It was not what a man had been born, it was what he became.

Fu Chiang, "the Priest", Big Boss of the Red Flower Triad, puffed out his chest, then looked to his fellow Lords, gesturing for them to follow him through into the banquet hall.

"*Ch'un tzu* . . ."

* * *

Rocket-launchers swivelled automatically, tracking Lehmann's cruiser as it came in over the mountains, while from the cockpit's speakers came a constant drone of Mandarin.

"Impressive," Lehmann said tonelessly, looking past the pilot at Fu Chiang's fortress. Beyond its sturdy walls and watchtowers the Atlas Mountains stretched into the misted distance, while beneath it a sheer cliff dropped four thousand *ch'i* into a wooded valley.

Visak, in the co-pilot's seat, took a brief peek at his Master's face, then turned back, swallowing nervously.

"You *know* what to do?" Lehmann asked.

Visak nodded. He was to do nothing, not even if they threatened Lehmann. He wanted to question that – to say "Are you sure?" but Lehmann had given his orders and they were not to be questioned or countermanded. Not for any reason.

The pilot leaned forward, flicked one of the switches on the panel in front of him, then nodded. "Hao pa . . ." *Okay*. He looked up at Lehmann. "We've got clearance to land. You want to go in?"

Lehmann nodded, watching as the massive stone walls of the fortress passed beneath them. And all the while the rocket-launchers tracked them. At any moment they could be shot from the sky.

He gets off on this! Visak thought, stealing another glance. *He actually* likes *risking his life!*

Slowly, very slowly they moved out over the drop.

Visak took a long breath. *If they shoot us now we'll fall five li.* That was, if there was anything *to* fall.

The pad came into sight, further down the ragged crest of the peak. Five sleek, black cruisers sat there already. Between the oval pad and the fortress a transparent lift-chute climbed the sheer rock face.

Impressive's an understatement, Visak thought, certain now that they'd made a mistake.

If he got out of this alive, he would quit at the earliest opportunity. Get his face changed and leave Europe on the first flight out. Away, far away from this madman and his insane, life-endangering risks.

He flexed his hands, realising he had been clenching them, then looked up again. Lehmann was watching him.

"You okay?"

He nodded. Through the screen of the cockpit the rock face came closer and yet closer. For a moment the whine of the engines rose, drowning the chatter of the speakers, and then, with the faintest shudder, the craft set down.

The engines whined down through several octaves then fell silent. A moment later there was a sharp click and the door hissed open.

"Okay," Lehmann said, patting his shoulder. "Let's do business."

* * *

It was a small courtyard, no more than five *ch'i* to a side, set off from the rest of the palace and reached through a moon door set into a plain white wall. Shadow halved the sunlit space, its edge serrated, following the form of the ancient, steep-tiled roof. In one corner, in a simple rounded pot with lion's feet, was a tiny tree, its branches twisted like limbs in agony, its tight leaf-clusters separate, distinct from one another so that each narrow, worm-like branch stood out, stretched and melted, black like iron against the background whiteness. In the centre of the courtyard was a tiny fountain, a *shui shih*, its twin, lion-headed jets still – two tiny mouths of silence.

Gregor Karr stood there in full colonel's uniform, waiting for Li Yuan, conscious of the peacefulness, the harmony of this tiny place. A leaf floated in the dark water of the fountain's circular pool like a silver arrowhead. Karr looked at it and smiled, strangely pleased by its presence. Sunlight fell across his shoulders and warmed the right side of his face. It was an oddly pleasant sensation, and though he had often been outside the City, he had never felt so at ease with only the sky above him.

He was looking up when Li Yuan stepped through the great circular space of the moon door and came into the courtyard. The T'ang smiled, seeing the direction of his Colonel's gaze, then lifted his own face to the sky.

"It is a beautiful day, neh, Colonel Karr?" Li Yuan laughed, his face momentarily open, unguarded; a side of him Karr had never seen. Then, more soberly. "However, we are not here to discuss the weather."

Karr waited, silent, not presuming upon that moment's openness, knowing his place. For a time Li Yuan did nothing, merely looked at him, as if weighing something in his mind. Then, abruptly, he put out his hand.

"Give me your badge."

Without hesitation, Karr unbuttoned his tunic and took the badge of office from where it rested against his left breast, handing it to his T'ang. Then he stood there, at attention, his head lowered respectfully, awaiting orders.

Li Yuan looked down at the badge in his hand. It was more than a symbol of rank, it was a means of identification, an instrument of legal power and a compact store-house of information, all in one. Without it, Karr lost all status as a soldier, all privilege. In taking it from him Li Yuan had done what even his General could not do, for it was like stripping such a man of his life. He looked back at Karr and smiled, satisfied. The man had not even paused to question – he had acted at once upon his Lord's command. That was good. That was what he wanted. He handed the badge back and watched as Karr buttoned up his tunic. Only then did he speak.

"Tomorrow I plan to appoint a new General. Tolonen would have had me have you, young as you are, inexperienced as you are. But that cannot be. However loyal, however *right* you might be for the task, I could not have you, for the post is as much a political appointment as a strategic one."

Karr kept his face expressionless and held his tongue, but between them, none the less, was the knowledge of Hans Ebert's betrayal, years before – of the political appointment that had gone badly wrong. Even so, Karr understood what his T'ang was saying. His Family was new to the Above and had no influence. And as General he would need much influence.

"I called you here today for two reasons. First to let you know that, were it possible, I would have had you as my General. And one day, perhaps, I shall. But for now there are other things I wish you to do for me."

Li Yuan paused. "I took your badge from you. Did you think it some kind of test?"

Karr hesitated, then nodded. "Afterwards, *Chieh Hsia*. I . . ."

Li Yuan raised a hand. "No need to explain. I understand. But listen, it was more than a test. From this moment you are no longer commander of my Security forces in Africa."

This time Karr did frown. But still he held his tongue and, after a moment, bowed his head in a gesture of obedience.

Li Yuan smiled, pleased once more by Karr's reaction, then stepped closer, standing almost at the tall *Hung Mao*'s shoulder, looking up into Karr's face, his dark, olive eyes fierce, his mouth set.

"This is a new age, Gregor Karr. New things are happening – new circumstances which create new demands on a ruler. Even among those close to me there is, it seems, a new relationship."

The young T'ang smiled sourly and turned away. When he turned back his features were harder. He stood beside the miniature tree, the fingers of his left hand brushing the crown absently.

"You are to be given a new role. I need a new *Ssu-li Hsiao-wei*. Do you think you can do the job, Colonel Karr?"

"*Chieh Hsia* . . ." Karr laughed, astonished. After General, the post of *Ssu-li Hsiao-wei* – Colonel of Internal Security – was the most prestigious in the whole Security service. It meant he would be in charge of security at all the imperial palaces, in command of the élite palace guard and responsible for the personal safety of Li Yuan and all his family wherever they went. It was a massive responsibility – but also a huge honour.

He considered a moment, then bowed his head. Beside him, in the dark circle of the fountain, the leaf turned slowly, like a needle on a compass. Inside he felt excitement at the challenge: more excitement than he'd felt for years. Looking across at Li Yuan he saw how carefully the T'ang watched him and realised, with a sudden, almost overwhelming sense of warmth, what trust his Lord was placing in him.

On impulse he knelt, bowing low, offering his neck ritually to his Master.

"I would be honoured, *Chieh Hsia*."

Li Yuan stepped forward, then placed his booted foot gently but firmly on Karr's bared neck.

"Good. Then you will report to me tomorrow at twelve. We shall discuss your duties then."

* * *

"So tell us, Li Min. Just why *are* you here?"

Lehmann looked up, then pushed his plate aside, surprised by the suddenness of the query. For two hours they had played a cautious game with him, avoiding anything direct, but now, it seemed, one of them at least – "The Bear", Yang Chih-wen – had tired of such subtleties.

He glanced at Fu Chiang, then met Yang's eyes.

"The two Americas have fallen. Likewise Australasia. Asia – both west and east – is a snake-pit overseen by jackals. And Europe . . ." He picked a miniature fruit from the nearby bowl, chewed at it, then swallowed. "Europe is but a shadow of its former self. Which leaves Africa . . ." He smiled coldly. "I am told that Africa is the world's treasure chest."

"And is that why you are here – to plunder that treasure?"

Lehmann shifted his weight and turned so that he faced Yang Chih-wen full on. The man was big, it was true, but he had faced bigger men. Yes, and killed them too.

"Does that *disturb* you, Cousin Yang?"

Yang shrugged, as if unconcerned, but his eyes told a different story. "I'll lose no sleep over it."

"That's good. A man needs his sleep, neh? And what better tonic than to know that one's neighbour is also one's friend."

That brought a spate of glances – tiny, telling exchanges that confirmed what Lehmann had suspected. For all their swagger, these men were deeply insecure. The collapse of their City and the war that had followed had given them their opportunity, yet their rule was still tenuous. They would fight him only if they must.

He lifted his hands. "Besides, when you talk of plunder you mistake me, cousins. I am not here to talk of plunder, I am here to talk of trade. Trade between equals."

"*Equals?*" It was Mo Nan-ling, the Little Emperor, who spoke. He wiped at his mouth delicately, then leaned towards Lehmann, his fine gold necklace tinkling as he did. "You talk of trade, Li Min, but your words presuppose that there is something we should wish to trade with you."

Lehmann sat back a little, gesturing for him to expand on that.

"What I mean is this, *cousin*. Africa is indeed a treasure chest and we Mountain Lords have had rich pickings these past few years. Our coffers are full, our foot-soldiers happy. What could we possibly need that you might offer?"

Lehmann nodded, as if acceding the point, then turned and signalled to Visak, who came across at once, placing a hardshell case in front of his master.

"Has that . . . ?" Mo Nan-ling began, but Fu Chiang raised a hand and nodded. It *had* been scanned – four times in all – but still he had no clue as to what it held. He watched now, his curiosity naked in his eyes, as Lehmann flipped the latches then turned the case about, opening the lid.

There was a murmur of surprise.

"*Drugs?* You want to trade in *drugs?*" Yang Chih-wen's voice was incredulous. He pushed away from the table, his face scornful. "Are you *serious*, Li Min?"

But Lehmann seemed not to hear the insult in the Bear's voice. He leaned forward and carefully picked the six tiny golden ingots from the depressions in the smooth, black velvet, then looked across at Fu Chiang.

"Forgive me, Fu Chiang, but may I draw my knife?"

Fu Chiang hesitated, looking about him, then nodded.

"Thank you." Lehmann tipped all the ingot-shaped capsules into Visak's open palm, then stood, reaching down with his left hand to unsheath the pearl-handled knife from his boot.

Yang Chih-wen moved back a fraction, his hand resting on his own hidden blade.

"You talk of drugs, Cousin Yang," Lehmann said, facing him again. "Yet the term covers many different things, neh? Some cure diseases. Some enhance performance, others intelligence. Some keep the penis stiff when stiffness is a virtue, others liberate the mind or entertain. These . . ." he smiled a death's-head smile, then drew the razor-sharp blade across his right arm, just below the elbow.

A great gash opened up, blood pumping from a severed artery.

Lehmann threw the knife aside, then took one of the ingots from Visak's palm and squeezed its thick golden contents over the open wound. It hissed and steamed and then, astonishingly, began to move, as if a tiny golden creature burrowed in the gash.

"What in the gods' names . . ."

But Fu Chiang's words were barely out when he fell silent, staring open-mouthed. Where the flesh had gaped, it was now drawn in, the wound raw and scabbed. Then, even as they watched, the scabbed flesh shimmered and – like a film run backwards – disappeared, leaving the skin smooth, unblemished.

Lehmann held up his arm, showing them all.

The silence had the quality of shock. It was Sheng Min-chung who finally broke the silence.

"GenSyn," he said authoritatively. "There were rumours of regenerative drugs."

Lehmann gave a single nod.

"And this is what you're offering to trade?"

Lehmann shook his head, then took the five remaining ingots from Visak's open palm and began to hand them around. "No. This I'm *giving* you. What I'll trade is information."

* * *

Waving the guards aside, Li Yuan pushed through the doors and went inside. A dozen men stood at the balcony's edge, watching what was happening below. They had been training and wore only breech-cloths or simple black one-pieces. The scent of sweat was strong.

Hearing the door close, two of them turned and, seeing their T'ang, bowed low and made to leave, but Li Yuan signalled them to stay and went across, joining them at the rail.

He looked down. Kuei Jen, his seven-year-old son, was standing in the middle of the floor, at the very centre of the fight circle. About him, facing him east, north, west and south, were four burly adolescents. Lo Wen, his shaven-headed, middle-aged instructor, stood to one side, his face inexpressive, his arms folded before his chest.

All five combatants were breathing heavily. Kuei Jen, at the centre of it all, turned slowly, eyeing his opponents warily, his body tensed and slightly crouched, his weight balanced delicately on the balls of his feet. The boy was naked to the waist and wore only the flimsiest of breech-cloths – more string than cloth. His hair was slicked back, his body sheathed in sweat, but his eyes . . .

Li Yuan smiled. The boy had fighter's eyes, like his dead uncle, Han Ch'in. Eyes that watched, hawk-like, missing nothing.

Two of them moved at once – from east and west. As quick as a fox, Kuei Jen ducked and turned, swinging his right leg low, then twisted on his hips and straight-punched – right, left, right, left – in quick succession.

Two of the youths were down, groaning. Between them stood Kuei Jen as if nothing had happened, his breath hissing through his teeth. Looking on, Lo Wen exhibited not even the slightest flicker of interest.

Li Yuan felt the hairs on his neck rise. There had been a low murmur of satisfaction from the men surrounding him, nods of respect.

The third boy backed off a pace, then, with a blood-curdling yell, he threw himself at the young prince. As he did, the last of them took two quick, quiet steps forward.

He wanted to cry out – to *warn* his son – but knew it would be wrong.

Kuei Jen's first punch connected cleanly, his fist striking his opponent squarely in the breast-bone, knocking him back. But even as he drew his arm back from the second, decisive blow, the other was on his back, pulling him down, a wire cord looped about Kuei Jen's throat.

Li Yuan cried out, unable to help himself. Yet even as his cry echoed in the hall, Kuei Jen flipped backward, the unexpected movement tearing the cord from his assailant's hands. There was a blur of movement and the youth was down, winded. Kuei Jen turned from him, took a single step and punched, finishing the third of them. He turned, looking calmly at the wheezing youth, and, moving closer, put out his foot and delicately – using only his toes, toppled him on to his back.

There was a great roar from the balcony; a storm of applause. Li Yuan, amazed, let his voice join with it. Then, as it faded, he called down to his son.

"Kuei Jen!"

The young prince spun round and looked up, astronished to find his father there, then bowed low, a colour at his neck.

"Father . . ."

About him, the four youths scrambled to present themselves, tucking themselves into a kneeling position – two of them coughing – their shaven heads bowed towards their T'ang. Lo Wen, like a statue until that moment, stepped between them and, bowing to the waist, addressed his Master.

"*Chieh Hsia*. I did not know . . ."

Li Yuan waved it aside. "What he did just then . . . you *taught* him that, Master Lo?"

"I did, *Chieh Hsia*."

"I am much pleased, Master Lo. A student is but as good as his teacher, neh?"

Lo Wen bowed his head, pleased by his T'ang's praise.

"And you, young men . . . you played your part well.. You will have a bonus for this morning's work. A hundred *yuan* apiece!"

"*Chieh Hsia!*" they cried, almost as one, the delight in their voices obvious.

Li Yuan stood back slightly, gripping the rail tightly, his pride in his son immense. He was about to say something more – to praise the boy before them all, when the doors behind him opened.

"*Chieh Hsia . . .*"

He turned. It was Hu Ch'ang, his Chancellor Nan Ho's Principal Secretary.

"What is it Secretary Hu?"

Hu came forward and, kneeling before his T'ang, placed his forehead to the floor. Rising slightly, he answered him.

"It is your cousin, Tsu Ma, *Chieh Hsia*. He is calling from his palace in Astrakhan. He says he needs to talk with you urgently."

"Then I shall come, Master Hu."

He turned back, looking to his son, who waited his father's pleasure, head bowed and perfectly still, and gave the boy a small bow of respect.

"You did well, Kuei Jen. Very well. Come to my study later. After lunch."

Then, turning away, he swept past the kneeling Hu Ch'ang, heading for his study.

* * *

She had just come from her bath and was sitting in the chair by the window, having her hair brushed by the maid, when Li Yuan rushed into the room unannounced.

"Pei K'ung . . . you will never guess what!"

She stared at him, surprised by his animation, by the great beam of a smile he was wearing. Pulling her silk robe tighter about her, she stood, dismissing the maid.

"What is it, husband? Have our armies won some great victory in Africa?"

"Victory?" He laughed, then came across to her. "No, no . . . nothing like that. It is Tsu Ma. He has decided to marry!"

She stared at him, astonished.

"It is true," he went on, then laughed again. "It seems he has chosen the girl already. Her family has been approached and they are to be betrothed within the week."

"But the rituals . . ."

Li Yuan raised a hand. "They will be fully carried out. Ah, but it is an excellent idea, don't you think, Pei K'ung? An imperial wedding! Why, it could come at no better time."

She saw that at once. Even so, for Tsu Ma to marry so late in life might cause almost as many problems as it solved.

"Was this a . . . *sudden* decision, husband?"

Li Yuan shrugged, becoming more serious. "It seems the matter has played upon his mind for some time. But what forced him to the issue, who knows?" He went to the window and stared out across the gardens as if looking for someone. "All I know is that the time must be ripe."

She went and stood by him, studying his face. "And is that how you chose me, Yuan? When the time was ripe?"

He turned his head and looked at her. "Five wives I've had, Pei K'ung, and still I do not understand why *this* should be or *that*. To be married . . . for each man and woman it is a different thing, neh?"

She nodded, but still she held his eyes. "And for Tsu Ma? Does he marry simply to beget sons?"

Li Yuan hesitated, then shrugged. "It would seem the obvious answer."

"Then why not before? Why wait until now?"

He looked away.

She watched him, feeling – and not knowing why – that something strange was happening inside him.

"Husband, tell me this. Why did he not marry before now?"

He looked back at her, his eyes stern suddenly. "A T'ang does not need to answer such a question."

She held her ground. "I did not ask Tsu Ma. Nor would I be so impertinent. I asked *you*, husband. If you have no idea, merely say so and I shall be quiet. But I am curious. Tsu Ma is a handsome man. A man much enamoured of women and – from what I've seen – a good uncle to his nephews. Children . . . I would have thought he'd have had many children by now."

Li Yuan huffed out a breath, clearly troubled by the direction of their conversation. He thought a moment, then waved a hand vaguely in the direction of the east – as if towards Tsu Ma himself.

"Something happened. Long ago. He . . . he was betrothed once. In his teens. And the girl . . ."

"The girl died."

Li Yuan looked at her and nodded. But still it seemed he had not given up all he knew.

"Was there . . . something else?"

His answer was immediate, almost brutal. "No. Nothing else."

She shivered inwardly, surprised – no, *shocked* – by the anger he was containing. Anger? Anger at Tsu Ma? For what? Or had she read things wrongly? Was there still something she didn't understand?

"Did he love the girl?"

"I . . . I am not sure. I guess he must have."

"And his father . . . did his father not insist that he be betrothed to another? If he was the eldest son . . ."

Li Yuan turned on her, his anger open now. "You do not understand, Pei K'ung! Tsu Ma was like me in that. He had an elder brother. His nephews . . . they are his elder brother's sons. Tsu Ma was not born to rule. And as to how he has chosen to live his life . . . well, enough talk of it, Pei K'ung! You understand?"

She bowed her head obediently. "I understand." But deep inside her curiosity was burning like a coal. Something *had* happened. Something between Tsu Ma and her husband. What it was she couldn't guess, but she would find it out. Yes, she would seek it out and know it, were it the last thing she did.

* * *

Tsu Ma stood on the balcony of his summer palace at Astrakhan, looking out across the moonlit Caspian. It was a clear night and at this hour – just after two – it seemed like the whole world was sleeping. He alone could not sleep; he alone was plagued by the demons of restlessness.

His foot was sore tonight and troubling him. Tiredness had made his limp more exaggerated. He reached down and scratched at the joint, getting some relief.

No good, he thought, *it'll only make it worse*. But he couldn't help himself. He had always been the same. Impulsive. Give him an itch and he would scratch it. He laughed humourlessly.

Yes, and maybe that's the root of it.

Far out – two, maybe three *li* out from the shore – the lights of an imperial cruiser skimmed the water as it made its regular patrol.

Protecting me, he thought. Yes, but who would protect him from himself? Maybe that was why he was getting married finally, in the hope that he would change.

A young wife. Children. If anything could change a man, then surely these could do it. Why, he had seen how Li Yuan was with his son . . .

Yes, but he was not Li Yuan.

So why was he doing it? Why now, when he was so settled in his ways? Or was that it at all? Was it not, perhaps, some kind of punishment?

He turned from the rail, angry with himself, looking back into the darkness of the room where, on a bed of silk, lay one of his maids.

To change himself. It was a forlorn hope. Yet try it he must, or die an old goat, his grave untended.

There had always been time. Tomorrow. Yes, there'd been an infinity of tomorrows. But slowly he had used them up. Days had passed like dying cells and he was slowly getting older.

Yes, there had always been time.

He sighed. Wasn't it strange how young men thought they were like the sea, ageless and eternal. So he had been. Tsu Ma. The horse. He had outrun, outdrunk, out-fucked every last one of them. But now . . .

Now time weighed heavy on him and the seas in his veins ran slow and sluggish.

Time was he'd been a child, carefree, a full *ch'i* smaller than his eldest brother. That same beloved brother whom he had seen fall from his horse like a mannequin and who had bled to death in his arms, the assassin's crossbow bolt in his neck, the black iron shaft of it poking obscenely from the bloodied flesh. He had promised himself he would *never* love anyone that much again and had fled into debauchery, as if that might stop the hurt or end the dreams that came to him, night after night. But never is a long time, and then Fei Yen had come. Fei Yen, his cousin Li Yuan's wife.

He shuddered then held on to the door, a sudden weakness taking him. For a moment he clung on, as the blackness swept over him, then he let out a breath. He was okay. It was nothing. He had had several of these spells of late and he put them

33

down to over-exertion. It was simply his body telling him to ease off. There was no point mentioning them to his Surgeon.

I should eat something, he thought, taking a long, calming breath. Or maybe sleep. After all, he was no longer as robust as he had once been.

He stepped inside, closing his eyes briefly to catch the young girl's scent. He moaned softly, his senses intoxicated by the sweet perfume of her, then, opening his eyes once more, put his hand out, feeling for the edge of the bed. He could hear her now. From the soft regularity of her breathing he could tell that she was sleeping.

His hand searched among the silken covers until it found something warm and smooth – her leg.

He sat, kicking off his slippers, his hand caressing the young girl's thigh, tracing the smooth contours of her. As he did she woke.

"*Chieh Hsia?*"

"Quiet, girl," he said, his hand finding her face in the dark. She nuzzled it, kissing it softly, wetly, making his sex stir.

Tomorrow, he thought, pushing her down then untying the sash of his sleeping robe. *I shall reform myself tomorrow.*

CHAPTER·2

BREATHLESS MOUTHS

Kim stirred, then turned abruptly on the bed, like a fish on a hook, mouth gasping, left hand reaching for the ceiling.

"*A-dhywas-lur! A-dhywas-lur!*"

He woke, his dark eyes blinking, staring up into the camera lens, the narrow band about his neck pulsing brightly in the darkened room. Silence, then: "What is she doing?"

It was the first question he asked, today and every day.

"She's awake," the Machine answered, the soft Han lilt of its voice filling the tiny room. "Right now she's eating breakfast. Would you like to see her?"

Each day the same struggle within him; each day the same answer.

"No."

Its circuits made a shrugging motion, unseen, unheard. Ward sat up, then twisted about, planting his feet firmly on the uncarpeted floor. One would have thought that today of all days something else would have been on his waking mind, but no, the young man was machine-like in his obsession. Not an hour went by without some reference to her.

Kim turned, looking up at the lens. "And her father? The Marshal? Will he be accompanying Li Yuan?"

"He is part of the T'ang's official party, so I assume . . ."

Kim's raised hand silenced it. It watched him cross the bare, cell-like room and enter the bathroom, a second lens above the shower watching him step into the unit.

"Hot or cold?"

"Cold."

At once the water fell, bracingly cold, a touch of northern ice in its needle-sharp flow. It watched the young man grimace and then shudder in a kind of pained ecstasy.

Why did he continually punish himself? What inner need drove him to such extremes? Or was the young woman, Jelka, the answer to that also?

"Enough!"

It cut the flow. At once warm air-currents filled the cubicle, drying the young man's body. Again there was that movement in his face; again that faint, almost indiscernible shudder.

What was it like to be a thing of flesh? What secret languages of blood and nerve, sinew and bone was he *granted and* it *denied?*

Kim stepped from the shower and went to the sink, popping a calcium pill to clean his mouth and teeth. As it dissolved, he hummed a tune to himself – an air from the times before the City: a song of love and loss and constancy.

"Any messages?"

It would have been easier to have tapped them direct into the wire inside his head, but Kim had forbidden it. For some archaic reason he preferred this quasi-human form – this question-and-answer in the air.

"Only two. Reiss and Curval."

Kim slid the cupboard door open and took a pale red one-piece from inside. It was all he ever wore these days – a succession of crisp new lab-suits, each one burned at the end of the day, as if in some constant ritual of self-purification.

"When does Reiss want to meet?"

Not "What does Reiss want?" – he knew what Reiss wanted: to settle the terms for the renewal of his contract – but "When?" As ever, Kim wasted no time with what was already known.

"Lunch if possible. This evening if not. He seemed quite concerned."

As he ought. In four weeks he could be losing the services of the greatest scientist on Chung Kuo. That was, unless he could come up with a deal enticing enough to make Kim Ward stay with SimFic.

Unconscious of the gesture, Kim touched the glowing band about his neck. "It'll have to be this evening. Book dinner, at eight. At the Hive. But Reiss only. None of the other monkeys."

"He thought you'd say that, but he wants to bring someone along with him – a young executive named Jack Neville. Says you'd understand."

Kim stepped into the one-piece, zipped it up, then turned, looking up at the camera.

"Okay. And Curval?"

"He called half an hour back. Wanted to know if you'll need him for the trial-run. To be frank, I think he just wants to be there."

"Then tell him I'll expect him, ten o'clock in the main lab."

He sat on the edge of the bed, reached underneath, then pulled on a pair of worn slip-ons. "And our game?"

In answer it placed a hologram in the air beside him – a life-size image of a *wei chi* board, the black and white stones of a half-completed game covering two-thirds of the 19 by 19 grid. As Kim looked, a new black stone appeared two down, six in from the top right-hand edge. It glowed for the briefest moment, then grew dull.

Kim smiled. "Interesting."

It said nothing, merely watched, knowing that for that single moment they were alike, he and it – simple mechanisms that thought and calculated. Then Kim looked up, the faintest glimmer in his eye, and it knew the moment had passed.

"What is she doing now? Is she walking in the garden?"

* * *

Jelka stopped on the tiny bridge at the centre of the Ebert Mansion gardens, looking toward where her father crouched playing with the boy. Laughter filled the morning air, the boy's high-pitched shrieks threading the old man's deep laughter like a young bird fluttering in a great oak.

She smiled. Who would have imagined, three years back, when he'd first taken on the role of protector to the boy, that it would have come to this? Back then he had positively loathed the child; had raged, calling him "that half-caste little bastard", but now . . .

She watched him scoop the boy up and hold him high, his craggy face filled with an unusual lightness, his eyes drinking in the young lad's laughter. So he'd been with her: father and mother to her, for more than twenty years. She shivered then went across to join them.

"Father?"

Tolonen set the boy down and turned, smiling, one arm out to her in welcome. Beside him, the boy waited, his arms at his sides, his head bowed politely, as he'd been taught: every bit the little soldier.

"How are you, Pauli?"

He looked up at her shyly through the dark fall of his hair and nodded. It was the most she ever got from him. Whether she frightened him or whether, as her father said, he was half in love with her, she didn't know, but when she was there he clammed up totally.

She smiled inwardly, but outwardly she kept her face stern and serious, walking slowly around him as if inspecting a young officer. Satisfied, she nodded.

"You've done all your schoolwork?"

He nodded, his eyes careful not to meet hers.

"Good." She permitted herself a smile, then reached out and ruffled his hair. Han . . . there was no doubt that the boy was Han, yet something of his father's blood – of Hans Ebert's Saxon stock – had shaped that young face, giving it a curious strength. With or without the great trading empire he would one day inherit, Pauli Ebert would be a force to reckon with when he was older.

She turned, looking to her father. "Oughtn't you to be getting ready?"

He glanced at the timer set into his wrist, then made a face of surprise. "Gods! Is that the time?"

She nodded, amused by his pretence. These days he would even keep Li Yuan waiting if it meant an extra ten minutes playing with his ward.

"Still, there's not much to do," he said, making no move to leave, his eyes resting fondly on the boy. "Steward Lo has already laid out my uniform. I only need to shower, and that won't take a minute."

"Even so . . ."

She paused as Steward Lo himself appeared in the doorway leading to the West Wing. Her father, noting her attention, turned.

"What is it, Lo?" he asked, suddenly more formal.

Lo bowed. "You have visitors, Master."

"What, at *this* hour?" A flash of irritation crossed his face, then, he nodded. "All right. Show them into the main Reception Hall. I'll see them there. Oh, and tell them they have fifteen minutes of my time, no more. The T'ang himself is expecting my company."

When Lo had gone, Jelka stepped closer. "Who is it?" she asked quietly.

His face was hard, his eyes troubled. "Oh, it's no one . . ."

She laid her hand on his arm – his flesh and blood, human arm. "Father?"

He laughed gruffly at her admonishment, but still his eyes were troubled. "It's them again. Wanting, always wanting."

"Ah . . ." She understood at once. By "them" he meant the small group of powerful businessmen who – when Hans Ebert had ordered his bastard child terminated – had saved the boy and raised him secretly for his first four years. She shuddered. "What do they want now?"

A sourness filled the old Marshal's face. "Who knows? Favours. The usual thing . . ."

"And you give them what they want?"

His laughter was almost ugly. "No. Thus far I've delayed them, fobbed them off, but they're becoming more insistent, their claims more outrageous."

She squeezed his arm. "Tell them you owe them nothing."

He looked at her, then shook his head. "I wish I could, but it's not so simple. As the world perceives it, the boy owes them a great deal, maybe everything."

"But legally . . ."

He shook his head. "Leave it, please, my love."

She stepped back, bowing her head obediently, while beside her, his dark eyes taking in everything, the boy frowned.

* * *

"Well? What do you want?"

The two men got to their feet abruptly, surprised by the sudden presence of Tolonen in the room, shocked by the hostility in his voice.

"Forgive us for intruding at this hour," began the first of them, a rotund man in pale lemon silks, "but this matter . . ."

Tolonen cut in. "You'll forgive me if I'm less than polite, *Shih* Berrenson, but I'm not accustomed to being dragged from my breakfast for ad hoc meetings. I am a busy man – a very busy man, and should you wish to make an appointment with me it can be done through my Private Secretary."

Berrenson looked to his partner, Fox, then ducked his head slightly, as if at the same time agreeing and disagreeing with Tolonen.

"Forgive me, Marshal, but that is exactly what we have been trying to do for the past six days. A dozen times we've approached him to arrange an audience with you and each time your man has put us off. In the end we were left with no option . . ."

". . . but to come knocking on my door like tradesmen."

Berrenson's face stiffened. Beside him Fox looked indignant.

"*Tradesmen?*"

Tolonen stepped right up to him, then tapped his chest with the fingers of his golden, artificial arm. "Tradesmen. Wheeler-dealers. What do you want me to call you? *Ch'un tzu?*" He laughed coldly. "No, *gentlemen*, let's not hide the fact with pretty words. I *know* what you want."

Berrenson stared at the golden fingers pressed into his chest then met Tolonen's eyes again. "Whatever your personal feelings are in this matter, I feel it would be best . . ."

"*Best?*" Tolonen shook his head. "What would be *best* would be for you to go away and stop pestering the child. He is grateful, certainly, but your attempts to turn such gratitude into financial advantage are – and let me make this *absolutely* clear – becoming tiresome."

Berrenson took a long breath, then looked to his colleague again. "I see we are wasting our time here. It seems the Marshal has no understanding of how things work in the realm of Finance. Not that that's surprising: he is, after all, a mere soldier."

The insult was barely out before Berrenson found himself sprawling backward. He sat up, groaning, blood dripping from his nose and from the gash in his top lip. Fox looked on, astonished.

"Nothing," Tolonen said, standing over him threateningly. "You shall have nothing. You or any of your pack of jackals."

Berrenson dabbed at his broken nose with the collar of his silks, then glared up at the old man. "You'll regret this, Tolonen. Before I'm done GenSyn won't be worth a fucking five *yuan* note."

Tolonen laughed. "Is that a threat, *Shih* Berrenson? Because if it is, you'd better be prepared to carry it out. But let me warn you, you loathsome little insect. If I find you've said one word that's detrimental to the Company or made one deal that could harm my ward's interests, then I'll come for you . . . *personally,* you understand me? And next time it won't be just your nose I'll break, it'll be every bone in that overweight tradesman's body of yours." He leaned in close, pushing his face almost into Berrenson's. "*Understand me?*"

Berrenson nodded.

"Good. Now go. And don't bother me again."

* * *

Kim waited as the door hissed back, then stepped through, his breath warm in the protective suit. This was a secure area and as the door closed behind him, sealing itself airtight, a fine mist enveloped him, killing any bacteria he might have brought in from outside.

Inside, beyond the second airtight door, was the garden he had had built at the centre of the labs. There, beneath a fake blue sky that was eternally summer, were the two dozen special rose bushes he had had planted in the rich, dark earth that covered the whole of the 30 by 30 area to a depth of three feet.

As the second door slid back, Kim stepped inside, the micro-fine filters in the helmet allowing him to smell the sweet scent of the roses. He stopped a moment, eyes closed, enjoying the early morning warmth, the strange freshness of the place, then walked on, making his way down the lines of bushes.

SimFic had spent more than fifteen million *yuan* building this place, simply to humour him. The thought of that – of the waste – had worried him at first, but then he'd begun to see it from their viewpoint. Here he could think – here, undisturbed, he could put flesh to the bone of speculation. And thinking was what he was paid to do.

He smiled, seeing the first of the webs glimmering wetly in the fake sunlight. It was beautiful. Delicately, indescribably beautiful. It was as if it touched some blueprint deep inside him and struck a resonating chord. He crouched beside it, staring at its delicate symmetry. It was an orb web, spun by the simple European garden spider, *Araneus diadematus*.

Yesterday he had watched her spin this web, making first the spokes and then the central spiral. A broader "guide" spiral – a kind of scaffolding – had followed, and then the great spiral itself, the "bridge-lines" as they were called. He had watched fascinated as she wove and gummed the threads, her tiny, rounded body balanced on the scaffolding as she plucked the gummed line to spread the tiny droplets equidistantly along its length. When he had first seen it he had thrilled to the discovery, recognising once more the importance of the laws of resonance and how they governed the natural world – from the largest things to the smallest – and it had brought back to him a moment when he had witnessed a great spider-like machine hum and produce a chair from nothingness. So long ago that seemed, yet the moment was linked to this, resonating down the years. Memories . . . they too obeyed the laws of resonance.

He moved on. Beside the orb web spiders he had others – scaffold-web spiders like *Nesticidae* that had settled in a tiny rocky cave he had had built at the far end of the garden, and triangular-web spiders like *Hyptiotes*. But his favourite was the elegant *Dinopis*, a net-throwing spider with the face of a fairy-tale ogre. How often he had watched her construct her net between her back legs and then wait, with a patience that seemed limitless, to snare any insect foolish enough to pass below.

Insects had long been banned from City Earth. The great tyrant, Tsao Ch'un had had them eradicated from the levels, building intricate systems of filters and barriers to keep them out. But here, in this single airtight room, he, Kim Ward, had brought them back. Using stored DNA, GenSyn had rebuilt these once-common species specially for him: these and their prey – ants and beetles, centipedes, ladybirds and flies, silk moths and aphids.

It had not been easy, however. He had first had to get Li Yuan's permission. A special Edict had been passed, co-signed by all three T'ang, while SimFic, for their part, had guaranteed that there would be no breaches of the strict quarantine procedures. Not that that was really a problem.

He looked about him, feeling a brief contentment. Here he had mused on many things: on the physical nature of memory; on the ageing of cells and the use of nano-technology to induce the rapid healing of damaged tissue; on the duplication of neurons; and, most recently, on the creation of a safe and stable intelligence-enhancement drug. Each time he had come here knowing no answer, and each time the tranquillity of the garden had woven its magic spell, conjuring something from the depths of him.

But now it was almost done, his time in exile finished. In four weeks he could walk from here, a free man again, the pulsing band gone from around his neck. If he chose.

He reached out and brushed the delicate, dew-touched petals of a blood red rose with his gloved fingers, watching the pearled drops fall. It was all one great ballet – a cosmic dance, governed by immutable laws, and he the key, the focus of it all. He saw how it all worked, how it could be shaped and used. And yet some part of him held back – some dark and quiet part of him *refused* to use that knowledge.

He expelled a long, slow breath, then looked about him, as if seeing it all for the first time. Thus far he had but scratched the surface of the real. SimFic had asked and he had answered. But their questions had been small and insignificant . . . *unimaginative*. It was as if they couldn't see the possibilities, whereas he . . .

He frowned, not liking the shape of his thoughts. Yet it was necessary to face the truth. Intellectually he was their superior. That made him no better than them – not in simple human terms – but it did make him different, and he was convinced that that difference had been granted him for a reason. The twists and turns of his existence – his very survival – all of it meant something. He had been raised up from the darkness for a purpose, and now it was time, perhaps, to discover just what that purpose was – to ask himself the big questions, the questions that only he – from up here on his intellectual mountain top – could frame.

He crossed the room and stood before the long metal cabinet that was attached to the wall. Taking a long-stemmed key from the belt of his suit he fitted it into the lock and turned it twice. There was a moment's delay and then a series of tiny metal doors in the side of the cabinet clicked open.

Kim stood back, watching the insects tumble out in a spill of darkness. They were freshly-fashioned, their neutered forms made for a single purpose – to be eaten by his spiders. It was a disturbing thought. Like so much else he had created they were little more than toys – distractions from the real business of life.

He watched them flap and whirr and scuttle and felt his inner self curl up in aversion.

They moved, yet they were dead.

"Kim?"

He looked up at the camera lens overhead. "Yes?"

"Curval wants to speak with you about the new figures."

"Tell him I'll be with him in a while."

He looked down. The real reason he had come here this morning was to see if he could focus himself for long enough to make a decision about whether he should stay with SimFic in some capacity or go his own way. But, as ever, there was too much to do, too many things to be attended to, to allow him time to think it through properly. The decision would be of the moment. They would ask, he would reach inside himself and . . . well, it would be there, on his tongue. Until then he didn't know.

He retraced his steps. As the door hissed closed behind him and a faint mist enveloped him, one final thought came to him.

Does she still think of me? Does she even remember me?

* * *

Jelka had heard her father shouting, had heard the commotion in the entrance hall as the two men left, but it was an hour before he emerged from his rooms, wearing his Marshal's uniform, his face composed as if nothing had happened.

She greeted him in the atrium at the front of the Mansion, walking around him to inspect him, just as she'd done to the boy. It was unnecessary, of course – Steward Lo would never have let him leave his rooms unless he were immaculate – but it had become almost a ritual between them.

"Well?" he asked.

She touched his arm. "You look very smart, Father. It's not often you wear full dress uniform these days. What's the occasion?"

"I . . ." He looked down at his wrist-timer, then shook his head. "Gods! Is that the time? Look, sweetheart, I have to go. I'm late already."

She kissed his cheek. "Go on. Hurry now. I'll see you when you get back."

He smiled. "Look after Pauli, neh?"

She nodded, then sighed, watching him disappear through the open doorway, but a moment later he was back, smiling apologetically.

"I almost forgot. The final guest list for the party . . . it's on my desk. If you'd check it to make sure we've not left anyone out."

"I'll make a start on it at once."

He returned her smile. "Good."

She watched him go then turned, gazing down the hallway towards the big picture window at the end with its view of the gardens at the centre of the Mansion, then shook her head. How she hated this place. Five years she had lived here now and still she felt like an intruder. Not that she had ever liked this house, with its dark walls and its heavy furnishings, its monumental statuary and its thick, oppressive tapestries. No. The ghosts of the Ebert family still presided here and their fleshy imprint lay on everything. This was their place, like the lair of some strange, half-furred, feral creatures. And for her there was the further memory of her betrothal to the son of the house, Hans.

Jelka shuddered. It had been just there, in the Great Hall, just to the right of where she stood. She walked across, then stopped in the doorway, looking in. Nothing had changed. The jet black tiles gleamed with polish, while between squat red pillars, on lush green walls that reminded her of primal forests, hung the same huge canvases of ancient hunts that had hung there on the day she'd been betrothed to him.

She closed her eyes, remembering. In the half-dark, the machine had floated toward her like a giant bloated egg, silent, two brutish GenSyn giants guiding it. Its outer surface had been like smoked glass, but a tightly focused circle of light directly beneath it had glimmered like a living presence in the depths of the floor. She had stood there as in a dream, rooted with fear, watching it come, like Fate, implacable and unavoidable.

She made a small movement of her head, surprised by the vividness of the memory. So much had happened since that day – so many had died or been betrayed – and yet she, Jelka Tolonen had survived. She had danced her way to life.

Turning, she noticed that the door to her father's study was open. Steward Lo was inside, tidying up after his master.

Looking up, Lo saw her. "*Nu Shi* . . ."

She went across, looking about her as Lo finished his chores. Even here there was little sign of her father. He had changed nothing. Bookshelves filled three walls, but those had been there before he'd come and the leather-bound books that lined them had been undisturbed for twenty, maybe thirty years, the Ebert crest stamped into the title page of each one. Only the personal items on the huge desk that filled the far corner of the room were her father's.

She went across and began searching for the list. There were letters from old friends and bulky files with the S-within-G logo of GenSyn stamped into their bright-blue covers, a note from General Rheinhardt about the next Security Council meeting and her father's desk diary, open at today's page. She searched a moment longer, surprised to find nothing, then stopped, her eyes caught by the final entry in the diary.

She shook her head, then read it once again. No, she hadn't been mistaken. There it was, in his own handwriting: *SimFic Labs with Li Yuan. 12 p.m. Kim Ward and Work-in-Progress.*

He hadn't told her. He *hadn't* told her!

She eased back, an unfocused anger gripping her. Then, clenching both her fists, she called for inner calm. Slowly, very slowly, it came to her.

So . . . it was still going on. Seven years – seven long years he had kept this up. But now it had to stop.

She let out a long breath then looked across the study. Steward Lo was watching her.

"Are you all right, *Nu Shi*?"

She let her voice project her inner calm. "I'm fine, Steward Lo. It's just that my father said he'd left a list . . . a guest list for my Coming-of-Age party."

"Ah . . ." Lo came across and, with a bow to her, reached past her and took a slender file from among the GenSyn papers.

"Here," he said, dusting it off and handing it to her, bowing again. "It is not long now, neh, *Nu Shi*?"

"Not long," she answered, nodding her thanks. Then, moving past him, she hastened from the study.

Back in her room, she sat on the edge of her bed, the file in her lap, letting her thoughts grow still. They would all be here, of course – all of those important names from Above society one might expect to turn up for the Coming-of-Age party of the Marshal's daughter, but there was only one name she was interested in. She counted ten then opened it, scanning the list quickly with her finger.

Most of the names were familiar – Security mostly – but some, she knew, were there because one could not hold such a party and not invite such people. She would have to go through it more carefully later on, but for now . . .

She came to the end. Nothing, There was no sign of his name.

So it was true. He really was keeping his word. Very well. She should not really have expected other of him. But this was her party, *her* Coming-of-Age, and there was one person, more than any other, she would have there on that day. Kim Ward.

She went through to her study and sat at her desk, leaning across to take the ink brush from its stand. Inking it, she tried to remember the last time she had seen him, after his Wiring Operation. Seven years had passed since that day, and never, in all that time, had she stopped thinking of him, wondering about him, *preparing* herself for him.

She took the list and wrote in his name, there between Wang Ling, the Minister for Production, and her father's friend, Colonel Wareham.

There! she thought. Yet even as the ink dried, she knew it would not end with that. He would fight her over it, she knew, for it was the one thing they had *always* fought over.

Damn you, you old bugger! she thought, angry at him yet loving him all the same. *Why can't you want what I want just this once?*

But she knew it was no good wishing. Her father was like a rock, impervious to time and good opinion. She would have to face him out on this. Tonight, perhaps, or tomorrow.

She shivered, frustration and anger threatening to drive her to distraction. Then, controlling herself again, she switched on her desk-top comset and turned to the front of the list, determined he would have no other reason to find fault with her.

* * *

Tolonen gazed out of the window of the cruiser then looked back at his T'ang, answering him finally.

"I don't know, *Chieh Hsia*. I think you should try other means before taking such drastic action."

Li Yuan gestured wearily. "I wish I could, but time is against us. Each day sees the man grow stronger at my expense. The situation in Africa is worsening and my armies there are restless. If I do nothing, things will simply deteriorate until . . . well, until Li Min will merely have to raise his voice and the whole thing will come tumbling down."

Tolonen sighed, troubled by such talk. "Forgive me, *Chieh Hsia*, but surely things are not so bad? We have had *peace* these past three years. The House has been docile, food rations have increased . . ."

Li Yuan huffed out a breath, exasperated. "Can't you see it, Knut? The peace you talk of, it's a fragile, *brittle* thing. No. Time is running out. Our options are dwindling. We must either fight the bastard now or hand the City over to him."

"Then send Karr to negotiate with him, as I suggested. Have him offer Li Min a temporary peace – something that'll give us time to draw up a proper plan of campaign. To fight him now, without preparation . . ." Tolonen made a bitter face, "it would be madness!"

Li Yuan sat back, smoothing his chin nervously. Tolonen, watching him, saw the gesture and looked down, reminded of the young man's father, Li Shai Tung. So the old man had looked in those months before his death – his eyes haunted, his face made gaunt with worry. And maybe Yuan *was* right – maybe things *were* worse than they seemed – but to hit out blindly, simply for something to do . . . well, he had said it already: it was madness.

Tolonen sighed. "Besides, there's always Ward. If *he* delivers the goods . . ."

Li Yuan nodded distractedly, then met Tolonen's eyes again. "I understand you had some visitors this morning?"

"Ah, *that*."

"Is there a problem, Knut? Something I can help you with?"

Tolonen gave a short laugh. "Nothing I can't deal with, *Chieh Hsia*."

"No . . ." Li Yuan stared at him a moment, then laughed. "I doubt there's anything you couldn't deal with."

They were both silent a while, then Tolonen spoke again.

"Do you think Ward will sign up again?"

"For SimFic?" Li Yuan considered a moment, then shrugged. "It's hard to say. One thing is for certain, he doesn't need the money. I am advised he's worth close on four hundred and fifty million, and with the royalties on SimFic products he's had a hand in that's likely to treble within the next five years. If I were in Reiss's position I would be looking beyond financial incentives."

Tolonen stared at his hands, suddenly uncomfortable. "He's a strange one, neh?"

Li Yuan nodded. "It must *be* strange, being as he is."

Tolonen hesitated then looked up. "What do you think of him as a person?"

Li Yuan frowned. The question was unexpected. "I . . . respect him. His talent is formidable . . . frightening. I can't begin to imagine how he thinks. It's as if he's thinking in a different *direction* to the rest of us. Like Shepherd."

Tolonen was leaning forward now, his face set, waiting.

"But as a person?" Li Yuan shrugged, then pulled his silks about him, as if suddenly cold. "I don't know. I cannot make him out. There is something . . . *dark* in him. I have tried to like him, but . . ."

Tolonen nodded, understanding. It was how he himself felt – at one and the same time awed and repelled by the boy.

Boy? He laughed inwardly at the slip. Why, Ward was a man now . . . a young man of twenty-five years, but still he thought of him as a boy, perhaps because Ward still had the body of a child – an effete yet threatening child. He shivered. If the truth were known he thought Ward an ugly, stunted little creature and what his daughter had ever seen in him he couldn't imagine. Clayborn he was, and like all of the Clayborn there was something deeply, intrinsically repugnant about him.

He sat back, then locked his hands together in his lap, gold metallic fingers alternating with pink-white flesh. He had not seen Ward since he'd come back from America – in truth, he had hoped never to see him again. When America had fallen he'd believed the boy was dead – had thought it done with for good and all. But Ward had got out – SimFic had protected their investment and shipped him out on the last flight – and he, hearing the news, had felt a bitter disappointment.

A curse – Ward was a curse on him, an evil spell, always coming between him and his daughter.

He felt the cruiser begin to bank, the engine tone change and knew they were approaching their destination. Looking back at Li Yuan he saw he was staring out of the window; but his hazel eyes were looking inward, his mind worrying over some problem of State. Tolonen, seeing him thus, felt his own worries dissipate. They were as nothing beside his Master's. To serve his T'ang, that was – had *always* been – his prime directive, and whatever he felt about Ward, he must let none of it come between him and his duty. To serve . . . he nodded then straightened in his seat, pushing out his chest and placing his hands firmly, decisively on his knees . . . it was the very reason for his existence.

* * *

Kim leaned in to the screen, tracing the slowly descending line of the graph with his index finger, his worst fears confirmed.

"There's no doubt, is there?"

Curval, beside him, stared a moment longer then shook his head. "No. These performance figures bear out what we've suspected for a while now. There's a definite memory drain."

"Any guesses as to why?"

Curval glanced at Kim, then shrugged. "No idea. But it's happening. At this rate the whole of the implanted memory core will be gone in . . . three months? Four at the outside."

"And the body's good for sixty, maybe eighty years."

"Bit of a problem, huh?"

The two men laughed.

"So what are we going to do?" Curval asked, smoothing the polished dome of his skull.

"Start again? Re-design from scratch?"

"Li Yuan won't like it."

"But if there's no other option?"

Curval considered. "What if we were to create back-ups? Make more than a single implant? Maybe it's simply a question of reinforcement. After all, the human brain makes copies of all new memories and distributes them, so maybe that's what's lacking? Maybe we're over-simplifying?"

"Maybe. Then again, maybe we're not being simple enough. I've the feeling that the answer's there, staring us in the face, only it's so obvious – so glaring – that we just can't see it."

Curval laughed. "You think so? If you ask me there's a fault in the materials we've been using."

Kim shook his head.

"Then what? There's got to be an answer. This . . ." Curval tapped the screen. "This oughtn't to be happening."

"No, but it is. Which means something basic is going wrong – something so integral to the process that we're going to have to take the whole thing apart piece by piece before we can understand what it is."

"That'll take time."

"I know."

"And we haven't got time."

"I know."

"So what are we going to do?"

Kim smiled. "First we're going to see the T'ang and show him what we've got."

* * *

The tests were over. Li Yuan watched them lead the man-like morph away then looked down at his hands.

In some ways it was impressive, much more impressive than anything GenSyn had thus far managed to produce. The creature's feats of memory and mathematics were breathtaking and there was no doubting its mental agility. Physically, however, it was disappointing. Oh, it was fit – super-fit if the performance figures quoted could be trusted – and its co-ordination was excellent, moreover its vision and muscular strength had been enhanced; even so, it was not what he had envisaged.

He sighed and looked across at Tolonen. The old man smiled back at him, but he looked tired, as if the whole thing had been too much for him. Seeing that, Li Yuan relented a little. They had all worked hard – Tolonen included – to get this far. And maybe he was simply expecting too much. After all, three years ago there had been nothing – nothing but the rumour that DeVore and Hans Ebert had been working on something like this. That and the "manufactured" brains they had discovered in North America.

He was used to synthetic beings, he had grown up surrounded by them – tank-grown creatures, products of GenSyn's bio-engineering programmes – but this was different. The skin, the eyes, they had been grown in GenSyn's vats – special "nutrient reservoirs" feeding the living, self-replicating parts; doing the jobs other cells would normally have carried out – but the rest . . . the rest had been *built*. Beneath the human form that presented itself to the eye was a machine; a machine that – however crudely – thought for itself.

He turned, looking to Kim. "There's one thing I don't understand. Why does it make those lists?"

Kim hesitated, glancing at Reiss, then answered him. "It makes lists because it's autistic."

"Autistic?"

"You saw how easily it remembered things. It's like a blotting paper, soaking things up. And once shown it never forgets. But what it lacks is the ability to ascribe a meaning or purpose to things – especially to people and places. It has no *structure* to its existence, you see. There's a gap there where it ought to be. So, to plug that gap it fills its life with lists."

"Ah . . ."

"In humans the problem is rooted in the cerebellum – that's where our sense of 'self' is to be found." Kim laughed. "I've heard that the Temple of the Oracle at ancient Delphi had an inscription carved into the stone over the entrance. 'Know Thyself' it read. Unfortunately that isn't even an option for our android friend.

The brain structure we've developed for this model is simply too crude, too simple to allow self-consciousness."

"And nothing can be done about that?"

Kim shrugged. "Possibly. But there are other problems we have to solve first. At present the brain in this model is quite small – like the ones the Marshal brought back from America. The reason for that's quite simple. An ounce of nerve tissue uses up far more calories in the process of thinking than an ounce of muscle burns up in exercise. In fact, the brain uses up a quarter of the body's energy. We've tried to accommodate this fact by providing extra power to our models. Hence the two storage packs in the small of its back. But we can only do so much. Being aware is actually very hard work. To make that model more aware we would have to increase its cranial capacity considerably, and that would mean increasing its body size and weight proportionately. What you'd have, in effect, would be a giant."

Li Yuan leaned back, his disappointment deeper by the moment. "I hoped we would be able to improve on things somehow."

Kim smiled apologetically. "Maybe we shall. Given time. At first I considered doing something new – designing something that was completely different from the basic human blueprint – but ultimately I had to concede that there was nothing wrong with the old model. Tens of millions of years of evolution can't be bucked. The brain is as it is because that's how it *has* to be."

"I understand. But tell me . . . why did it take so long to recognise us. Even you. It seemed almost not to see you until you spoke to it. I thought its vision had been enhanced?"

"It has, but the model is essentially prosopagnosic. That is, it can't recognise faces. Not at once, anyway. Retinas, yes, voices too – from the inflections – but a whole face takes much longer. It has to check a number of different elements – shape of nose, colour of eyes, distance between forehead and mouth – against a pre-programmed list of the same elements and tick off each item. It doesn't take long, but there's a definite delay. Like many of its behavioural traits, it's a crude analogy of how a human functions, not a perfect copy."

"I was surprised by how human it looks," Li Yuan confessed. "I was expecting something more . . ."

"*Brutal?*" Kim shrugged. "I toyed with the idea of making it look very different; of enhancing it even more and making it like some sleek custom-designed machine, but in the end I decided it would be best to work with something that looked as unthreatening – as *normal* – as possible. After all, if it's simple *threat* you want, you already have GenSyn's half-men, their *Hei*. My thinking was that if this project had any purpose, it was to produce something that would fool your enemies. Its very normality is, I feel, its greatest strength."

"Is it safe?"

Kim laughed. "Safe? It's positively docile. In fact, one of the problems we've been having with this model is its passivity. It'll make decisions, but only when it's *asked* to make decisions. Most of the time it'll just sit there."

"I see. And there's no way to alter that?"

Kim hesitated, then glanced at Reiss, who had remained by the door, looking on.

Li Yuan turned, a faint hope growing in him. "Is there something I should know, Director Reiss?"

Reiss bowed his head. "*Chieh Hsia*, I . . ."

"Just tell me."

Reiss swallowed. "There's a . . . a second prototype."

Li Yuan raised an eyebrow. "A *second* prototype?"

"Yes, *Chieh Hsia*, except . . ."

"Except we've been having problems with it," Kim said, interrupting him.

Li Yuan turned. "What kind of problems?"

Kim smiled then put out an arm, inviting Li Yuan to accompany him. "I think you'd better see it for yourself."

* * *

Li Yuan stood beside Kim in the tiny room, staring at the creature sprawled on the narrow bed. The first prototype had seemed little more than a complex marionette, like the golden bird in the poem Ben had sent him, but *this* . . . he felt a strange thrill – of fear? excitement? – run up his spine. This was something special. He could see that at a glance.

"So what *is* the problem?"

"Can't you see?"

Li Yuan made to step closer, but Kim touched his arm. "Forgive me, *Chieh Hsia*, but no closer. It's . . . erratic."

"Dangerous?"

"It hasn't been, but . . . well, I'd hate to be proved wrong."

"Should we . . . ?" Li Yuan gestured to the door.

"No. It'll ignore us if we keep our distance. Usually it . . ."

"Usually it *what*?"

The creature turned its head and stared at them, its eyes dark with intelligence.

Yes, Li Yuan thought, his breath catching in his throat, *this* was more like what he'd expected!

It turned and slid its legs over the edge of the bed.

"How are you today?"

It ignored Kim's question, staring at Li Yuan as if to place him.

"What do the latest figures show?" it said.

"The same trend."

The creature nodded, then, in a gesture that was peculiarly human, combed its dark hair back from its eyes. "So what will you do?"

"I can re-implant."

"No good. If you do that I lose what I am. All I've been. Already . . ." It grimaced painfully. "Already things are slipping from me."

"Has it a name?" Li Yuan asked.

Kim turned, surprised, as if he'd forgotten the young T'ang was there. "Ravachol . . . I called him Ravachol."

"A Slavic name. Interesting. He *looks* Slav."

Kim nodded, but already his attention was back with the creature.

"What do *you* want me to do?"

Ravachol looked away, pained, its every action revealing some deep inner torment. "I . . . I don't know. Some new technique, perhaps? A drug?"

"There *are* no drugs."

It stared at Kim a while, then shrugged. "So how long do I have?"

"Three, maybe four months."

It nodded. Then, smiling suddenly, it leaned towards Kim. "I had another dream."

"A dream? Tell me. Was it the same as before?"

Ravachol hesitated, concentrating, then shook its head. "No . . . I don't think so."

Kim spoke to it softly, as if coaxing a child. "So?"

It frowned fiercely, as if struggling to recall the details, then began, its voice faltering. "It began in the light. A fierce, burning light. It *seared* me. I was *consumed* by it, caught up within a great wheel of incandescent light. And . . . and then it focused. I was . . . I *felt* new-made. I stepped out from the centre of the light and . . . it was as if I was stepping into a air-tight cube of glass – of ice – a place of stillness. Perfect, immaculate stillness." It sat back, its face beatific, and sighed. "I could hear nothing, feel nothing, smell and sense nothing. It was . . . *strange*. The silence was both within me and without. There was no pulse in me, no beating in my chest. It was like I was dead, and yet I was conscious. I could turn my head and see. But there was nothing to be seen. Even the light . . . even *that* had gone. Not that it was dark. It was just . . ."

Ravachol stopped, its muscles locked, its eyes staring at Kim as if it had been switched off.

"And then?"

The way it came to again was eery, frightening, like a time-piece clicking into motion on the hour. Li Yuan felt a small shiver of fear pass through him. Yes, he could see now what Kim meant. The thing was mad – totally, unequivocally mad.

"I can't remember. Something happened, but I can't remember. It's like a piece of cloth where the edge has frayed. I get so far and then there's nothing left."

It stared at Kim, mouth open in a perfect O of surprise.

"Okay, you'd better rest. If you dream the dream again, write it down. Or speak of it to the camera, before the edges fray."

It nodded, then, with a curious meekness, allowed itself to be tucked in beneath the thin white sheets. It lay there, passive, eyes open, staring at the ceiling. Then, with a suddenness that was shocking, its eyelids clicked shut.

Outside again, Li Yuan stood at the view window looking in.

"What does it mean, all that?"

"The dream?" Kim scribbled something in a small notebook then slipped it into the pocket of his one-piece. "It's the same every time, detail for detail. It's not really a dream – not as you and I have them – more a symbolic landscape of its self-consciousness . . . a tacit recognition of its basic non-existence. It *knows*, you see. Knows what it is and how it was made. It even knows what's wrong with it. The dreams . . . they're a kind of anxiety outlet. The only one it has. Without them it would cease to function."

"I see." Li Yuan shuddered, feeling a strange pity for the creature. He was silent for a time, then he sighed. "I hoped we'd be further along."

"We've come a long way."

"I know, it's just . . ."

"Time?"

Li Yuan nodded, then turned to face Kim. "Time. It's the curse of kings and emperors." He laughed wistfully. "When I was a child, I thought there was all the time in the world – that things would be the same for ever. Time was like an old friend, unalterable, unending. But it isn't so. My father knew it. The day I was born, they say, *he* had a dream. A dream of the darkness to come."

Kim traced a circle on the one-way mirror. "You think collapse is inevitable, then?"

"Inevitable? No. But likely. More and more likely every day. Unless we take preventive action."

"And this?" Kim tapped the glass, indicating the sleeping android. "Do you *really* think this is any kind of solution?"

"You don't, I take it?"

Kim laughed. "You are the T'ang, *Chieh Hsia*."

Li Yuan smiled. "So when will it be ready?"

"A year. Six months if we're really lucky."

"Lucky?" Li Yuan raised an eyebrow. "I thought your science was a *precise* thing."

"Oh no, *Chieh Hsia*. Far from it. Luck plays a huge part in things. But the problems we've been having with the prototypes have stemmed mainly from the pace of development. We've come from nothing to this in less than three years. That's fast. Too fast, perhaps. If we were dealing with a single homogenous bio-system it would be relatively straightforward – we could locate any errors as and when they occurred – but we're not: we're dealing with a dozen, fifteen different bio-systems at any one time, and those systems aren't discrete, they're dependent on each other. One goes wrong, the whole lot goes wrong. And the trouble is, the systems have had no time to evolve properly – to grow together. We've had to rely on guesswork most of the time, and our guesses have sometimes been wrong. But why something doesn't work – whether it's this system we've got wrong or that – well, it's difficult to say."

Li Yuan raised a hand. "I understand. But a year . . . a year should do it, right?"

Kim nodded.

"Good. Then it's time, perhaps, to make the thing specific."

"Specific?"

"Facial details, build, height and weight. That kind of thing."

"Ah . . ." Kim digested that a moment, then looked back at his T'ang. "Who is it?"

"I think it's best you don't know."

"Who *is* it?" Kim insisted. "I have to know."

Li Yuan stared at him, surprised, reminded briefly of Ben, then took the envelope from within his silks and offered it to Kim.

"He's a killer. A man named Soucek. But that information is classified, all right? Four men died getting those details."

Kim studied the sheaf of papers a moment longer, then nodded. "I understand. But why him?"

"He works for Li Min. He is his right-hand man. He has *access* to him."

"Ah . . ." A shadow passed over Kim's face.

"You want to pull out?"

Kim shook his head. "I didn't say that. But I needed to know."

"A year? At the very most?"

Kim nodded.

"Then let us pray we *have* a year, neh, my Clayborn friend? Let us pray to all the gods we know that time, this once, does not outrun us."

* * *

Soucek sat in a chair to one side of the Magistrate's desk, his legs crossed casually, his long, pock-marked face inexpressive. Two guards stood at his back – big, brutal-faced thugs, heavy automatics held across their chests. Behind the desk, Old Yang, the Magistrate, cleared his throat then tugged nervously at his wispy beard.

The hall was packed. People stood at the back and along the side walls or crouched in the aisles, talking and fanning themselves indolently. There were over two dozen cases to be heard this session and this was only the third of them. Already they had seen two deaths and there was a mounting excitement now that this case, too, was coming to a head.

From where she stood against the back wall, Emily looked on apprehensively. How many times had she seen this in these last two years? How many times had she had to stand and watch this dumb show of justice? *Far too often*, she thought, her fingers tracing the shape of the gun beneath her jacket. But today . . . today would be different.

The accused – a young Han male of seventeen years – stood in the blood-spattered space in front of the dais, his hands bound behind his back, his head bowed. His scalp had been crudely shaved and was flecked with cuts. A leather thong had been tied around his head, over his mouth, holding down his tongue and keeping him from speaking. Two bare-chested tong members stood behind him, butchers' cleavers in their belts, ceremonial black sashes about their brows. The arresting tong officer's testimony had been read, the security camera evidence shown. All that remained was for the Magistrate to pronounce sentence.

The evidence seemed conclusive. They had a Security film of the boy – a non-tong member – purchasing a knife from an unidentified criminal, and the sworn statements of "friends" that he had been boasting about what he was going to do with it. The matter appeared clear cut. He had committed a crime for which the penalty was death. But the evidence was faked, the boy innocent.

She had seen the parents yesterday and listened to their story, then had checked out the details for herself. The father was a local market trader and the couple had three children: two boys and a girl. A week back he had had an argument with one of the local tong officials – what it was about she hadn't managed to get from him, but it had to do with their fourteen-year-old daughter. The two men had exchanged sharp words. The old man had thought that that was it, but the official had not let the matter rest. He had bought evidence – faked film, the "word" of several worthless youths – and had had his cousin, the officer responsible for Security in these stacks, arrest the boy.

The circumstances were not unusual. She had evidence now on more than eighty such cases and knew that these represented only a small part of what was going on throughout the Lowers. For two years now the White T'ang had run the tribunals down here, imposing his "Code of Iron" on these levels. But what had at first seemed like justice had quickly revealed itself as just another means for tong members to lord it over the common citizens. It was a stinking, corrupt system, administered by bullies, cheats and murderers.

Like this case here. She sighed, her anger mixed with pain. This wasn't justice, this was arranged murder, with the victim denied even the right to speak for himself. And Soucek . . . Soucek was the architect of it all, the administrator and chief executioner. It was he who let the sewers run with filth.

But today . . . today she would strike a blow for all those who had suffered under him.

As the Magistrate began to pronounce sentence, those who were crouching stood, craning their necks to see, an electric current of anticipation running through the crowded hall. Emily stood on her toes, noting where the guards were standing, then began to move through the press of bodies, making her way towards the front.

Old Yang was shouting now, berating the youth in a shrill, ugly voice, calling him the vilest of names and insulting his family. Then it was done, the sentence pronounced. There was a murmur of anticipation.

Emily slowed, looking about her. She was still some way from the front. She would need to get nearer.

At a signal from Soucek, one of the tong members behind the youth stepped up and kicked the youth hard just behind his left knee. With a groan the boy went down. As he got up on to his knees, the arresting officer came across and, drawing his gun, cocked it and placed it against his head.

The hall was silent now, a tension in the air like that before a thunderstorm. She edged forward.

The shot was like a release. Heads jerked, mouths opened. A great sigh ran round the hall. It was done. The White T'ang's word meant something. But for Emily there was only anger. Her hand covered her gun. She was only five or six from the front now. She could see Soucek clearly; see how calm – how hideously calm – he was as he turned to speak to one of the guards.

There was a wailing to her right. *His* mother, she thought, slipping her hand inside her jacket pocket and cocking the gun. Then, shockingly, there was a gunshot.

She turned her head, anxious, trying to see where it had come from. A small cloud of smoke was rising from the crowd to her right. As she saw it, another shot rang out. There was screaming, the beginnings of panic. Tong guards were converging from all sides. For a moment she didn't understand, then, as the crowd parted, she saw. It was the youth's father. He was standing there, his face distraught, holding a gun out at arm's length. She saw his hand tremble as he tried to fire again, and then one of the big automatics opened up and he jerked back, bullets ripping into him, the gun falling from his hand.

As if at a signal everyone got down. She did the same. But as she did she saw, up on the dais, one of the guards crouched over Soucek.

He's hit! she thought, exultant. *The old man got the bastard!*

Yet even as half a dozen tong thugs scrambled up on to the dais to surround him, she saw Soucek get up and, shrugging off the guard's hand, push past the men and vanish through the door at the far end.

She looked down, disappointed. Soucek was bleeding. From the look of it one of the old man's shots had hit his right shoulder and broken the collar-bone. But he had survived. She would have to wait for another opportunity to get to him.

Yes, and it wouldn't be so easy next time. After today they'd be sure to take greater precautions.

She got up, sighing heavily. Old Yang was slumped in his seat, dead. All about her people were moaning and whimpering. To her right it was a scene of utter chaos. Chairs were scattered everywhere. A dozen or more people were down, dead or wounded.

As the guards began to clear the hall, she let herself be herded with the rest, letting the gun slip down her leg on to the floor then peeled the flesh-thin gloves from her hands and dropped them casually.

There'll be another time, she promised herself. *The bastard can't always be so lucky*. Yet she felt sick at heart and bitter . . . and angry. More angry than she'd ever felt before.

* * *

Kim stood before the mirror in his room, adjusting his silks. He was due at The Hive in an hour, but still he hadn't made up his mind whether to sign again or not.

"Well?" he asked, addressing the air. "What did you see?"

"He hates you."

Kim turned, startled by the words. "*Hates* me? *Li Yuan?*"

"No. Tolonen. He wishes you dead. There's such anger in him. Such unexpressed violence."

Kim let out a breath. "I hoped things might have changed. I hoped . . ."

"She's with the boy," it said, anticipating his next question.

"The boy?"

"Pauli. Her father's ward. He can't sleep and she's gone to his room to comfort him."

"Ah . . ." Kim grimaced at his reflection then turned away. "And Reiss?"

The machine was silent a moment, then, rather than answering his question, it did something it had never done before and offered him advice.

"You should go and see her."

"*See* her?" Kim laughed uncomfortably. "Now why should I do that?"

"Because you ought."

Kim turned, looking up into the camera eye. "It's unlike you to be so vague." It was silent.

"Okay," Kim said, faintly disturbed. "I'll think about it."

"You should buy yourself a Mansion."

Kim looked up again. "A *Mansion*? Are you all right?"

The Machine's voice was hesitant. "You don't see things. The obvious things. Your vision . . . it's so narrow."

Kim laughed, astonished.

"Maybe you should talk to Reiss about it. Insist on it as a term in whatever deal you make with him. You need a home, Kim – somewhere to build from. This . . . this is no good for you."

Kim stood there a moment, staring into the camera, then, with an impatient, dismissive gesture, he left the room.

"It makes sense," the Machine said, its voice following Kim down the corridor. "If you were to have children . . ."

Kim stopped and turned, angry now. "Matters logical, *they're* your province. As for matters of the heart . . . well, what would *you* know of those?"

He waited, expecting an answer, but the Machine was silent. Kim walked on, troubled, thinking about what it had said.

* * *

"Kim . . . so there you are!"

Reiss got up and came out to greet Ward as he approached the table. The Hive was packed, as it always was this time of evening, but Reiss had paid to have the four tables surrounding his kept clear. He embraced Kim, then turned, introducing his companion.

"Kim, this is Jack Neville. Jack . . . this is Kim Ward."

"Pleased to meet you," Neville said, stepping round Reiss and offering his hand. He was a slender, brown-haired man in his early thirties with a plump, almost boyish face.

"I'm sorry I'm late," Kim said, taking a seat across from them. "There was something I had to do."

Reiss smiled. "No matter. I understand things went well after I'd gone."

Kim smiled apologetically. "I'm sorry about that. I know what you said about the second prototype, but I was sure Li Yuan would see it our way once things were explained."

Reiss took the menu the Head Steward was offering, then smiled back at Kim. "And you were right. Nan Ho was on to me only an hour back. It seems Li Yuan has decided to extend the programme for a further year."

"Excellent!" Then, understanding why Reiss was not quite so enthusiastic, Kim gave a soft laugh. "We'd best resolve this, neh? As it is . . . well, I'm finding it hard to work."

Neville, watching him, raised an eyebrow, then looked to Reiss who nodded.
"You want to hear our offer *before* you eat, or after?"

Kim took a menu, scanned it, then set it aside. "Let's order, then you can tell me
what you've got in mind."

"Okay," Reiss looked to the Head Steward. "My usual, Chang, medium rare,
and a bottle of Golden Emperor. A magnum. The '98 if you have it."

"I'll have the same," Kim said, "but rare. And just water for me, thanks." He
looked at Reiss. "No offence, but I'll get nothing done tomorrow if I drink
tonight."

"I understand. But you don't mind . . ."

"No," Kim smiled broadly. "Some people can take their drink. Me . . ." he
laughed. "Anyway, Jack, what are you having?"

Neville looked up, surprised and flattered to be addressed by his first name. "I
think I'll have the rainbow trout. I don't think I've ever tasted it." He laughed. "In
fact, I didn't know it still existed."

"It doesn't," Kim said, as the Steward withdrew. "At least, not the real thing.
That's been extinct some two centuries now. But it's as good as, so they say.
GenSyn have been making great strides these past few years, bringing back a lot of
the old species. You've seen the ads."

Neville nodded, again surprised that Kim kept up with such things. "Does
anything escape your notice?"

Kim laughed. "Not much. I like to keep abreast of developments. It makes my
task easier if I know I'm not duplicating things. And I like to keep up with the
latest media trends. I'm told you're something of an innovator in that field."

Neville looked down, a faint blush at his neck. Reiss, beside him, beamed with
an almost parental pride.

"He's a good man," Reiss answered. "We expect much of him. That's why I
asked him to come up with a package we could offer you."

"I see." Kim sat back, surprised that the Machine hadn't told him. In fact, now
that he came to think of it, the thing had been behaving very strangely these past
few weeks. Almost as if it were conscious.

Kim shook his head. No. That wasn't possible. He'd seen just how difficult it
was to create even the most basic functioning intelligence in a machine. It simply
wasn't possible that a machine – however large, however complex – could develop
consciousness, not on its own.

Neville was watching him, fascinated. "What is it?"

Kim laughed. "Sorry. I was doing it again, wasn't I?"

"Doing what?"

"Thinking."

"Ah . . ." Neville nodded, then, with a glance at Reiss, leaned towards Kim.
"You want to hear our offer?"

Kim nodded, strangely relaxed now that the moment was here.

"The bad news . . ." Neville grinned. "The bad news is that you're no longer to
be an employee of the Company."

Kim laughed. "And the good news?"

Neville reached beside him and took a slender folder from the empty chair, then handed it across.

Kim hesitated, then opened it.

"You don't have to answer now," Reiss said, sitting back as the waiter placed the ice bucket on the table and lifted a magnificent-looking golden bottle from within. "You'll want to think things over, I'm sure."

Kim nodded. "I see." He scanned the two sheets quickly, then put the folder down, watching as the waiter uncapped the honey-gold bottle and poured an ice-chilled glass for Reiss.

"And if I were to ask for a Mansion?"

Reiss smiled and lifted his glass. "You have one in mind?"

Kim shrugged, then looked back at the folder. His own Company, that was what they were offering. A subsidiary of SimFic, yet big enough to compete on its own terms in the market. He shivered inwardly. Once before he had been in such a position. Once before he had tried to make a go of it on his own – and failed. But this time it would be different. This time he would have the giant SimFic Company at his back, protecting him, keeping him from being swallowed up. Yes, and this time there would be no circle of Old Men trying to pull him down and destroy him. It was a tempting proposition.

He watched Reiss sip and then grunt his satisfaction. The waiter poured again, filling Neville's glass. Neville nodded his thanks. then lifted his glass, toasting Kim.

"To you, Kim. *Whatever* you decide."

CHAPTER · 3

WIVES

Pei K'ung had opened only a dozen or so letters – placing each unread in the tray beside her – when the handwriting on one made her frown and pause. She turned the single sheet over, then, seeing the signature, the family seal at the foot of the page, caught her breath. She sat back, her face drained.

Tsung Ye stared at her, alarmed. "Mistress? Are you all right?"

She waved him away, then turned the page, reading it from the top right column, concentrating fiercely on the neat handwritten Mandarin.

"The nerve . . ." she said after a moment, giving the paper an impatient rustle. Why, she had a mind to call the bitch right now! How *dare* she write to him!

Fei Yen . . . The letter was from Li Yuan's first wife, Yin Fei Yen.

She brought her fist down hard, making everything on the desk jump, then stood, her whole body trembling now with anger. Crossing to the window, she summoned her secretary to her. Tsung Ye hurried across, his face troubled by the sudden change in his mistress.

She rested her left hand against the cool, rain-beaded glass and took a calming breath, looking out across the Eastern Gardens towards the stables. It would not do to act too hastily. No. She must act correctly or not at all.

She looked own at the paper in her other hand and shook it angrily. Why, the woman had even had the impudence to mention her bastard son! After all she'd done! Pei K'ung shuddered. She felt like burning the letter or ripping it into tiny shreds, but that was no solution. No. It had to be answered. There would be no peace for her until it was.

She stopped, staring at the letter, struck suddenly by the familiarity of its tone, the presumption of a friendship, and felt herself go cold. What if this wasn't the first letter Fei Yen had written him? What if the wording was a pretence – a kind of code between them? What if they often met?

Her throat was suddenly dry, her heart beating fast.

Nan Ho. Nan Ho would know . . . Yes, but even if he did . . .

She crumpled the paper into a ball and let it fall.

Was he still seeing her? When he went away on business, did she go to him then? Did she still sleep with him?

Pei K'ung closed her eyes, tormented by the thought even as she told herself how unlikely all this was. Or was that true? Who would tell her, after all? Nan Ho? His secretary, Chang? The men who travelled with him? No, they would say nothing. Indeed, they would see it as their sacred duty to keep it from her.

Besides, did she really *know* her husband? Did she know his thoughts, his innermost desires? No. Not at all. Oh, she had tried to know him – she had *tried* to get close to him – but there was still a part of him he kept from her, an inner core which she had never penetrated.

She bent down to retrieve the letter, uncrumpling it. As she did so she realised that Tsung Ye, her secretary was still there, his head bowed, awaiting her instructions.

"Tsung Ye, I'm sorry, I . . ."

She saw him blush and cursed herself, knowing what her husband had said about never saying sorry to a servant. But it was hard sometimes. Empress she might be, but she was only human after all. Gathering together the shreds of her dignity, she returned to her desk and sat, spreading the letter out and smoothing it several times. For a moment she sat there, staring at the carved jade ink block and at the copy of Nan Ho's seal which lay beside it, then nodded to herself, her decision made.

"Tsung Ye. I have a letter I want delivered in the utmost confidence. It must be delivered by hand directly to the recipient. No one else must know of it nor learn of its contents, you understand me?"

Tsung Ye bowed low. "I shall do as my Mistress asks."

"Good." She reached out and took a clean sheet of her husband's paper, lifted a fine-pointed brush from the stand and began to write.

*   *   *

The woman's screams filled the tiny cell and echoed down the corridor outside, carrying into the nearby living quarters where two guards, playing cards at a table that doubled as a security barrier, paused, looking up uneasily, then carried on with their game.

Back in the cell, Lehmann turned from the naked body on the bench and placed the fine-tipped iron back onto the white-hot grid. The smell of burned flesh and faeces was strong in the room, mixed like an obscene cocktail of pain. Overhead a camera captured it all. The film would sell for over five hundred *yuan* on the black market.

As Lehmann turned back to her, her eyes followed his every move – wide, terrified eyes, the pupils contracted to a tiny point by the drugs she'd been given to enhance the pain. She was bound to the four spikes at the corners of the bench by crude metal bands which, as she'd struggled, had cut into the flesh. The metal glinted in the spotlight, slick with blood.

She was young – early twenties, twenty-five at most – and unlike most of the women one found down here in the Lowers, she was well fleshed, no signs of malnourishment about her. It was that which had tipped his man off. That and the sidearm they'd found in her rooms when they'd searched them.

It was clever. He'd known for some while that Li Yuan was infiltrating his organisation, but this female angle was a new one. She had been hired as a whore at one of his establishments and had proved very popular with many of his Above contacts. But whatever she'd found out would die with her now.

Whores . . . he'd have them all checked out now that they'd discovered this one.

He moved closer, lowering his face until it was only a hand's width from hers, then blew his breath across her face.

"Are you ready to talk?"

She swallowed then shook her head.

"Brave girl. I'll make sure your Master gets a copy of the tape. Maybe he'll give you a promotion . . . posthumously, of course."

Her eyes glared at him defiantly. She gritted her teeth against the pain, then spoke, her voice a whisper.

"Go to Hell."

He turned away, then took the iron from the grid and studied the tip. There, delicately carved into the white-hot iron was the tiny Mandarin character *Si*. Death.

He looked at her and laughed; the coldest, emptiest sound she'd ever heard, then positioned the iron carefully. Cupping her right breast almost lovingly, he leaned in to her, pressing the white-hot tip to the nipple.

"There . . ." he said when she was silent again. "A matching pair. Now . . . you want me to start lower?"

Her skin was beaded with sweat, her eyes delirious. He could see that she was close now. One more tiny push.

"Okay," he said softly, placing the iron back upon the grid. "Let's start again. Who sent you?"

There was a knock. Lehmann turned, a flash of anger – pure, like lightning – passing through him. He had told them not to disturb him. If this was something trivial he would have them on the bench in her place. Controlling his anger, he went to the peep-hole and peered out.

Hart! What the fuck did Hart want? And who was the fat man with him?

He slid the bolt back then pulled the door open.

"Forgive me, Stefan," Hart said, beginning to come in, "I . . ." He stopped, taking in what was going on. "Kuan Yin . . . I . . . Look, I didn't know. If you want me to come back?"

"No. Come in. I'll be done in a while. But be quiet. I'm taping this."

Hart glanced at the camera uneasily, then went to the far side of the room, out of the camera's line of sight.

"This is Berrenson," he said, waving his companion across. "He's a businessman."

Berrenson went across, staring all the while at the naked woman, a lewd smile playing on his lips. "Hey, what's going on here?" he began, almost cheerfully, but Hart put a hand over his mouth then drew him closer, whispering into his ear. Slowly Berrenson's face clouded over. He nodded then swallowed deeply.

Lehmann locked the door, took the iron from the grid, then returned to the bench, as if the two men weren't there.

"Okay. Who sent you?"

She was trembling, her eyes fixated on the iron's glowing tip. Unable to prevent it, she began to piss herself again.

"I'll ask you one last time. Who sent you? Rheinhardt? Tolonen? Nan Ho?"

Her mouth moved, her tongue licked drily at her lips, then she shook her head.

"Who then?"

"The . . . the Hand."

He had moved his face closer, now he drew it back, but still the iron hovered above her, at a point just below her navel.

"The *Black* Hand?"

She nodded.

He was silent a moment, thinking, then he turned and set the iron back on the grid. Seeing it, she closed her eyes, relief flooding through her.

Lehmann stood over her again, then leant close, his face almost touching hers, his eyes directly above her eyes.

Her eyes were wide open again – afraid to blink; petrified in case she missed what he was doing.

"You did well," he said gently, caressing her face with his long, pale fingers. "You did very well. But I need one more thing. I want the name – the *real* name – of your cell leader."

There was a strange movement in her eyes – a sudden realisation that, whatever she did, whatever she said, there would be no end to this. Not until she was dead.

She shook her head, her whole face creased now with pain, knowing the torment to come. Vainly she began to call out and struggle.

Looking on, Hart felt himself go cold. He had never seen anything like it. *Never* . . . He shuddered, then closed his eyes as the woman's screams began again, while beside him, Berrenson looked on with a sickly fascination.

* * *

Later, in Lehmann's offices, Berrenson sat there silently, sipping iced-water and chewing at a knuckle, while Hart spelt out what they wanted.

Lehmann sat casually in his chair, listening patiently, turning the tiny cassette between his fingers, time and again, staring at it thoughtfully all the while. As Hart finished he looked up at him and nodded.

"I'm glad you came to me, Alex. You did the right thing. But I think you're going about this the wrong way. Killing Tolonen . . . well, it would give a lot of people – myself included – a great deal of pleasure, but it would solve nothing. To begin with, it would make Li Yuan angry, and I don't want that. Not yet. Moreover, he would only appoint an even more intractable protector for the boy. Rheinhardt, perhaps. And where would you be then? No. We need to be more direct."

"*More* direct? But killing Tolonen . . ." Hart laughed. "What could be more direct than that? Besides, it would avenge your father."

The look Lehmann gave him made him fall silent and lower his eyes.

"Listen," Lehmann said coldly, looking to Hart and then to Berrenson. "I'll say this only once. I don't want Tolonen killed. It doesn't fit my plans. There is, however, another way. Berrenson, your people took the boy from the Ebert Mansion once, right?"

"That's so, but . . ."

"But nothing. If it was done once it can be done again. We'll take the boy and hold him. And if Tolonen still refuses to come to terms, we'll kill him."

"But the Marshal . . ."

Lehmann glared at Berrenson. "You will leave it to me. And you will tell no one about this meeting – not your wives, not your friends, and certainly not your business associates."

He leaned towards them threateningly, the tape held up between his fingers. "Remember what you saw this morning. Remember it well. Because if there's one thing I won't tolerate, it's indiscipline."

Swallowing nervously, the two men bowed their heads. Then, the interview over, they hurried away, the screams of the dying woman echoing ghost-like in their ears.

* * *

Li Yuan dismissed his three advisers then turned to the twin screens facing him.

Once there had been seven of them, meeting in council twice a year to discuss matters of State and formulate policy, but the years had slowly pared the Seven down. Now there were just the three of them.

"Tsu Ma . . . Wei Tseng-li . . ." he said, greeting his fellow T'ang. "You have heard what Marshal Tolonen and General Rheinhardt had to say, and I am sure you have taken your own specialist advice on the matter. Now, however, we must decide on a course of action. Something all three of us are happy with."

Tsu Ma was first to speak. "Tolonen talks sense. Africa has become a luxury we can ill afford. The cost of policing it, both in manpower and in funding, exceeds any benefit we derive from keeping it. Moreover, we all have more pressing problems at home, neh? While there was a shooting war in Africa our presence there at least distracted men's minds from domestic worries, but these last twelve months things have been quiet and the people have grown weary of the struggle. What's in their bellies worries them more than whether Africa is won or lost. And rightly so, perhaps. My vote is to get out."

"And you, Cousin Wei?"

Wei Tseng-li was his father's third son and had inherited only after the murder of his elder brothers. For a time he had been Li Yuan's personal secretary and, when stationed on Li Yuan's floating palace, *Yangjing*, had saved Yuan's son, Kuei Jen, from certain death. As such there was a strong bond between the two young men. In many respects they were more like brothers than cousins. Just now, however, Tseng-li was deep in thought, his smooth, beardless face pale. The problems of State sat heavier on him than on the other two, and he had been ill these past months, though his surgeons could not trace the cause.

"I hear what my cousin Ma says," he began, speaking slowly, every word, considered. "And whilst what he says makes sense, I am still loath to throw away what we have fought so hard to keep. History teaches that, once lost, territory can never be regained so easily. So with Africa. Withdraw and we withdraw for good. Chung Kuo will be diminished. Not only that, but it will be seen by all to be a sign of weakness. A sign so large that even the most myopic of our enemies might read it, therefore my counsel is against withdrawal. I say we should persevere. Until times turn to our favour once again."

Li Yuan sat back. "I hear you, Cousin, and, were it merely a matter of withdrawal, would agree with you entirely. It would not do to display any sign of weakness. And that is why I am suggesting that we make of this necessity a virtue."

"How so?" Tsu Ma asked.

Li Yuan smiled. "Can we meet?"

"In person?"

"It would be best."

Tsu Ma frowned. "Forgive me, Yuan, but is that wise, given the climate of the times?"

"It must be so. For what I have to say is for the ears of we three alone. The days when we could trust such distant communications as this to be discrete are past. We must assume that every call is monitored, every communication suspect."

Wei Tseng-li nodded. "I, for one, agree."

"Then so be it," Tsu Ma said with a sigh. "We shall arrange a time and place to settle this for good and all. Until then, may the gods preserve you, cousins."

"And you," Li Yuan said, breaking contact.

Tsu Ma was right, of course. It was dangerous for all three of them to meet in person. Extremely dangerous, given the circumstances. But there was no option. He could not go ahead without their consent, and for his scheme to work absolute confidentiality was needed. So . . . they would have to meet. But where? And when?

Li Yuan smiled. The answer was staring him in the face. Tsu Ma's betrothal ceremony! What better opportunity for an informal meeting? Why, they could have it here, at Tongjiang, and then Karr could look after the security.

Yes, and maybe it would prove a turning point – the first step on the long road to recovery.

Li Yuan nodded to himself, then, taking a brush from the ink stand, began to pen a memorandum for his Chancellor.

* * *

Karr slipped the coded key into the lock, let the scanner register his retinal imprint, then slid the door back quietly, listening for sounds from within.

It was silent. He set down his pack and turned, looking about him. Nothing had changed. Even the smell was how he remembered it. For a moment he closed his eyes. Six months it had been since he'd last stood here. Six months.

He slid the door closed, then went through. The door to May's room was open. He stood there, looking in, bewitched by the sight that met his eyes. The three-year old lay on her back, her mouth open, her legs splayed carelessly in sleep. Beside her lay his wife, his darling Marie, her back to him, her long dark hair spread out upon the pillow.

He felt his heart go out to them both, felt all the longing, the heartache he'd suffered being away from them, well up in him again.

Home. He was home.

He made to step back, when she turned, drowsy-eyed, and looked at him.

"Gregor?" Then, suddenly more awake. "*Gregor?*"

She sat up, rubbing her eyes, then, with a brief glance at her sleeping child, came across to him.

They embraced, long months of denial shaping the passion of their kisses. It was eight weeks since she'd last visited him in Africa.

She drew back, breathless. "Gods, I've missed you!"

He stared back at her, her beautiful face only inches from his, as it was every night in his dreams. "And I've missed *you*."

"How much?" She reached down, then giggled. "Oh, *that* much, huh?"

He grinned. "Here?"

She shook her head then pulled May's door across. "No. In the shower. I've dreamed of it. Dreamed of you and me in there together."

He laughed. "You think I smell?"

"Like a pig, but I don't care. Come on, I need you right now."

He followed her into the shower unit, his hand never leaving hers. Then they were undressing frantically, his hands caressing her, his eyes drinking in her lovely nakedness.

"Marie . . . oh, Marie."

As the water fell, shockingly cold at first and then hot, he entered her, her gasp, the look of pained delight in her eyes making him shudder and come instantly.

"*Aiya!*" he said, grimacing, pinning her against the wall as he thrust into her again and again and again. And then she was crying out, unable to help herself, pressing against him so tight it seemed she wanted to breach him. He shuddered, then let his face fall against her shoulder. And still the water fell.

They were still for a moment, silent, and then she reached up and turned his face, making him look at her.

"What's happened?"

He laughed, almost making some wise-crack, then grew serious. "I've a new appointment. A promotion."

Her eyes widened. "A *promotion*? But I thought . . ."

"No." He laughed. "Not Rheinhardt's job. Not yet anyway. I'm to be *Ssu-li Hsiao-wei*."

She frowned. "Colonel of Security? But . . ." Then she understood. "Li Yuan! You're to be Li Yuan's own Colonel!"

He nodded, his smile mirroring that on her face now. "I've to report to him tomorrow. We're moving, my love. Moving to Tongjiang!"

* * *

Tsu Ma reined in his horse and leaned forward in the saddle, looking out over the edge of the cliff. Far below him the sea boiled about the dark and jagged rocks as the water sucked back. A moment later the next huge wave crashed against the granite, throwing a fine spray high up the cliff face. The grass beneath his horse's hoofs was slick with salt, the air misted, sharply cold.

He turned and watched as his young nephews caught up with him. Breathless, they drew alongside, their horses' heads pulling against the bit, afraid of the drop only a pace or two away. Their finely braided coats steamed in the cold air, their hoofs dragging impatiently at the hard earth after their headlong gallop.

Tsu Ma laughed, seeing how his heirs were watching him uncertainly, their eyes going briefly to the steep drop then returning to his face. They said nothing, yet their expressions were eloquent.

His brother's sons. Resting one arm on the pommel, he leaned forward, studying them. The eldest, Tsu Kung-chih was like his father, taller than Tsu Ma and – though only nineteen – broader at the shoulders. His physical presence was misleading, however, for in his features he had inherited all the weaknesses of his maternal grandfather – a certain limpness in the mouth, an absence of muscle in the jaw, a softness to his nose and narrow brow. His eyes – which seldom met those of his uncle – were the eyes of a salesman; calculating, yet somehow unambitious. Small, petty eyes. All in all it was a face that few would trust – the face of a vassal, not a T'ang. Seeing that face steeled Tsu Ma in his purpose and made him put all feeling from his heart.

Beside Kung-chih sat a smaller, lither boy, Tao Chu. Tsu Ma smiled as he looked at him and saw how the fifteen-year old smiled back, all the while smoothing his horse's neck to calm it. Tao Chu was very much his mother's son, half-brother to Kung-chih, yet Tsu Ma saw something of himself in the boy. Tao Chu had nothing of his half-brother's awkwardness but was direct and open – was in every way a natural ruler, a T'ang, with a T'ang's generosity of spirit. There was strength in his laughter and power in his smallest, subtlest action – a restrained power that only Tsu Ma seemed to recognise in him. Wind gusted through his fine hair, spilling its neat-cut strands across his brow. The boy shook his head and looked away a moment. For him this would be far easier. He, after all, had never thought to rule. Even so, Tao Chu was fiercely loyal to his undeserving half-brother and would feel this disappointment keenly on his behalf.

Tsu Ma straightened and, raising his voice against the sound of wind and wave, spoke.

"I am going to be married."

He saw how Kung-chih's face struggled with the words; how he turned to look at Tao Chu, as if the younger boy might explain it to him, but Tao Chu was watching his uncle carefully.

"When?" he asked, and Tsu Ma could see that he had weighed it all at once – as if he had prepared himself for this moment.

Tsu Ma smiled sadly. "The betrothal ceremony is to take place this very week."

Kung-chih was still watching his half-brother, his face stiff with shock. Then, slowly, he turned to face Tsu Ma, the severity of his disappointment open in his face. For a moment he stared back at his uncle, his mouth half open, then, abruptly, he turned his horse and galloped away. Tao Chu stayed a moment longer, then, with a bow to his uncle, he turned his horse and raced after his brother.

Tsu Ma watched until they were tiny figures in the distance, then turned his horse and followed the cliff's edge, staring down at the raging sea. It was done. Tsu Kung-chih's dream of inheritance was shattered. Tsu Ma lifted his face and stopped his mount, looking out across the sea's grey, uneven surface. He had left this too long and now it seemed a kind of cruelty. This marriage would win him few friends in his immediate family.

"Well . . . so be it," he said softly, the words torn from his lips by the wind. *So be it*. But he was determined now. He would do what he had refused to do before this day and settle down; have sons and watch them grow. Sons like Tao Chu or like his friend, Li Yuan. And in his old age they would rule in his place; strong, wise, decisive – sons he could be proud of.

Unbidden, a tear came to his eye. Turning away, he forced the horse into a gallop, heading back across the open fields towards the estate, thinking of the one woman he had loved.

Of Fei Yen . . . and of the boy, Han.

* * *

Fei Yen stood at the window of her room, watching the imperial cruiser land behind the hangar on the far side of the lake, nervous anticipation making her stomach cramp.

She had sent the letter two days back when she had been at a low ebb. There had been arguments with her eldest brother over her son, Han Ch'in, and then, out of the blue, her latest lover had packed his bags. She had written it only an hour after he'd gone, filled with remorse and self-loathing, and had had a messenger deliver it at once. But in the clear light of morning she had panicked, bitterly regretting her action and praying to the ten thousand gods that he would never see it, never even – perhaps – get to hear of it. But now it was clearly too late. The presence of his cruiser said as much. Now she would know what he thought of her.

She went to her wardrobe and searched for something to wear to greet his messenger. Something simple and yet sophisticated. Something that might suggest she was a woman in control of her life, contented with her lot. She took down a simple red *chi pao*, then put it back. No, red was the wedding colour – the colour of happiness and celebration. Black, then? She hesitated a moment, then, realising she hadn't any time, took it down and, peeling off what she was wearing, hurriedly pulled it on.

There was no time for maids and lengthy preparations. Besides, it was only a messenger. If he was anything like most men, he would scarcely notice what she was wearing. Even so . . .

She stood before the mirror, combing her hair quickly, then putting it up in a bun. Yes, that was it. That was the look she was trying for. She smiled, practising courteous phrases to greet him, then, satisfied, she turned and hurried from the room.

She met him at the front door, standing dutifully behind her brother as he went through the rituals of greeting.

As he introduced her, she bowed low, making herself the very picture of demureness.

"Well, Tsung Ye," her brother said, inviting the man inside, "how can I be of assistance?"

Tsung Ye, however, stood his ground, a polite smile on his face. "Forgive me, Prince Yin, if I decline your most generous offer, but my instructions are clear. I am to escort your sister, the Princess Yin Fei Yen, back to Tongjiang without delay."

Hearing the words, Fei Yen felt faint. Tongjiang! She had never meant *this* to happen! He had sent for her. Li Yuan had sent for her!

"You have *instructions*?" Yin Sung asked, puzzled.

"Here, Prince Yin," Tsung said, taking a sealed letter from his pouch and handing it to him.

Sung studied it a moment, noting the Chancellor's wax seal, then broke it open. He read it quickly, then, frowning, handed it to his sister.

"Do you know what this is about?"

Fei Yen shook her head, conscious that she was blushing. "I have no idea, brother. Why, I . . ."

"Forgive me," Tsung Ye interrupted, "but my instructions . . ."

"Of course." Yin Sung gave a bow, acknowledging Tsung Ye's status as his Master's messenger, then turned and summoned one of the house servants. "Bring Lady Fei's cloak. She must leave at once."

Then, looking to his sister, he took her arm, speaking more gently than before. "You will tell me if you need me, neh?"

"Yes, eldest brother."

"Good. In the meantime I shall make sure Han Ch'in is well looked after."

She bowed, keeping all the worries she was feeling at that moment – for her son and for herself – from her face.

"Good," he said again. "Then go. Chancellor Nan expects you."

Yes, she thought, letting the servant put her cloak about her shoulders, then hurried down the path after the T'ang's messenger.

* * *

The great hall at Tongjiang was cold and dimly lit, the huge space between the pillars empty, the flagstones black with age. Torches flickered in iron baskets hung about the walls, the shadows of the pillars wavering like the dancing limbs of giants, but in the centre it was almost dark. There, at that centre point, on a ceremonial chair that had been set down by the honour guard, sat Fei Yen. She had sat there for an hour now, alone in the silence, waiting.

On a narrow balcony overlooking the Hall, Pei K'ung looked on from behind a lattice screen, studying the figure in the chair. Her husband had once loved the woman – loved her to the point of distraction . . . and beyond. If rumour were correct he had once in anger killed all her horses while she, in answer, had told him that the child in her belly was not his.

Pei K'ung gave a small shuddering sigh. Maybe it was just the time of the month, but the last few days her emotions had been in turmoil. She had thought herself beyond such juvenile feelings, but it seemed it wasn't so. That feeling she had experienced reading Fei Yen's note to her husband – she recognised it now. It was jealousy. She was jealous of what this woman had once had with her husband, and afraid – no, terrified – that that feeling still existed between them.

Agitated, she fanned herself then turned away, slipping quietly from the balcony, her servants following after. She was tempted to send the bitch straight home again – to snub her regally – but that would solve nothing. She had to speak to her.

And if it was as she feared?

She pictured herself confronting her husband; saw him laugh and turn from her, dismissing her without a word, returning to his men as if she were not there. She shivered, forcing herself to walk on, to show nothing of her inner turmoil. Could she face that? Could she live with that rejection?

Of course she would. After all, that was the deal, was it not? To be a wife in name alone, while he . . .

She stopped dead, her servants almost stumbling over her.

Maybe that was what she should do. Maybe she should put the woman in his bed, to show him that she knew. To prove she was no fool.

Yes, but what if she were wrong? What if her husband hadn't been meeting Fei Yen secretly? And what if her action proved the beginning of a reconciliation between Fei Yen and him?

She whirled about, heading for her rooms.

No, Li Yuan must not even know she had been here. She must meet the woman and dispense with her. Threaten her, if necessary. After all, it was she who had the power now. She who was Empress.

Yes, but if Li Yuan loves her still . . .

She stopped, groaning softly, reaching out to steady herself against the wall. At once her servants rushed to her and held her up, as if she were ill, but she brushed them off angrily.

"Leave me be!"

"But Mistress . . ."

She turned on Tsung Ye, who had spoken, and glared at him. At once he bowed his head.

"Tsung Ye. Let her sit there another hour, then bring her to my study. And let no one go to her or speak with her. Understand?"

Tsung Ye nodded, then backed away.

She took a long breath, calming herself, then walked on. An hour. She nodded savagely. Yes, let her wait – it would do the bitch good to stew for another hour. In the meantime she would bath and change her clothes. Then she would deal with this matter. Deal with it *once and for all.*

* * *

Fei Yen waited outside the door as Tsung Ye went inside, her mouth dry, her heart racing. It was more than five years since she had last seen Li Yuan, that day in the Great Room at the estate in Hei Shui – the day after his wives had been killed. Then, astonishingly, he had asked her to come back to him, had begged her to try again, but she had sent him away, pride and anger, and the fear perhaps of his discarding her again, keeping her from saying yes.

The years had passed and no further word had come. Li Yuan had married again, immersing himself in his work. And the Great Wheel had turned, and slowly, very slowly, she had grown older. Older, yes, and ever less content.

Aiya! she thought, looking down at her hands. *What am I doing? What madness brought me here?*

Was it love that had brought her here? Or was it simple bitterness? Bitterness that her dreams had not come true?

"Princess Yin . . ."

Tsung Ye stood with his hand on the open door, his head bowed, waiting for her. Swallowing, she brushed her palms against her sides, then stepped past him into the room.

"Yin Fei Yen . . ."

She heard the door click shut behind her, and squinted into the sunlight on the far side of the room where, behind a huge desk by the window, someone sat.

For a moment she did not recognise the voice. She hesitated, confused that it was not Li Yuan, not understanding what was happening.

"Please, Lady Fei, come closer to the desk."

This time she understood. Pei K'ung! It was his wife, Pei K'ung. She bowed her head and slowly crossed the room, a small knot of fear at the pit of her stomach. Was this *his* doing? Was this his way of humiliating her?

That thought dispelled the fear, replacing it with anger.

She stopped, two paces from the desk, her head held defiantly aloft, her eyes boring into those of the Empress.

"Am I not to see Li Yuan?"

Pei K'ung stared back at her uncompromisingly, her eyes hard, her whole manner stern, like a mother-in-law. "Li Yuan is not here. He is away on business."

Fei Yen took that in, trying to assess the significance of it. Was that deliberate on his part? Was this all – the summons, the two hours wait, and now this – simply an elaborate snub; his way of getting back at her for her rejection of him? She bristled with anger at the thought, and held herself straighter. She was worth ten of this aged fishwife. Why, if rumour were to be believed, Li Yuan did not even sleep with her. And who could blame him? Ugly was perhaps too strong a word for it, but for certain the woman was plain.

"I am sorry to hear that," she answered, as if it were of no importance. "I had hoped to give him my regards."

Pei K'ung stared at her a moment longer, then looked away, a short, sardonic laugh her only comment.

Fei Yen waited, wondering what this woman wanted – what she had been instructed to do. Whatever it was, she was determined not to be belittled by her.

Whatever the woman said, she would give as good as she got. Besides, who knew whether what she had said were true. For all she knew Li Yuan was in the next room, watching all.

She studied Pei K'ung a moment, noting the elegant cut of her silks, the sophisticated way she had put up her hair, and wondered if that had been done specially for this meeting. Whatever, they did little to allay the severity of her features. To be frank, there was something almost masculine about the Empress. Her nose was too long, her hands too big, her ears . . . She almost laughed. Why, without the expensive silks the woman would have looked little better than the coarsest peasant's wife. The thought of it gave her confidence.

"Am I to be granted an audience?"

Pei K'ung looked back at her. "An audience?" Her voice was scathingly dismissive. "No, Lady Fei. This is the closest you will ever get to seeing my husband. I will not permit him to be distracted over such a . . . *trivial* matter."

The words made Fei Yen reassess the situation. Li Yuan didn't know! Why, he wasn't even aware that she was there at Tongjiang! Yet if that was the case, then why had Nan Ho summoned her?

Her eyes quickly searched the desk and found what she was looking for. There it was, beside the elaborate jade inkstand. Nan Ho's spare seal. She recognised it from former days.

Fei Yen felt herself go still. She had got it wrong. She had thought Li Yuan himself had summoned her, using his Chancellor as a go-between, but it had been Pei K'ung. For some reason the Empress had wanted to see her face to face. But why? Was it, as she said, to keep her husband from so-called "trivial" distractions? Or was there another, deeper reason?

She met Pei K'ung's eyes again and laughed. Saw how her laughter lit some inner fuse of anger. Anger, yes, and something else.

"What are you afraid of, Pei K'ung?"

"Afraid?" Pei K'ung's laughter was humourless. "I am not afraid, Yin Fei Yen. Certainly not of you. You forget who you speak to. I am the Empress and my powers . . ."

"Are your husband's powers. No more, no less. You forget who *you* speak to. You forget that I once sat where you now sit. Yes, and shared my husband's bed."

She regretted it as soon as it was uttered; yet she had not been wrong. Pei K'ung had started at the words. Now, her manner much stiffer, she leaned towards Fei Yen.

"Yes, and he *divorced* you. Do you forget *that*, Lady Fei?"

"He was but a boy . . ."

"And wayward, as boys are. He should never have married you. You were his brother's wife."

No more than you are Yuan's, she thought to say, but this time something held her back. It was true. If Han Ch'in had not been killed, she would be Empress now. If he had not been killed then none of this would have happened. She shivered and looked down.

"What did you want?" Pei K'ung asked after a moment, her voice more neutral than before. "What did you think you would achieve after all this time?"

Fei Yen looked up and shrugged, feeling suddenly less hostile towards the woman. Was it her fault Li Yuan had married her? And was it her fault he preferred to have much younger women in his bed?

"To be honest, I was hoping for some form of advancement for my son. Han Ch'in is eight now . . . nine this September. I thought . . ."

Pei K'ung's answer was blunt. "Is the estate at Hei Shui not enough for you? Nor the pension you and your son receive? Why, considering the circumstances . . ."

Furious, Fei Yen grasped the edge of the desk and leaned towards the other woman, shouting at her now. "He *owed* me that! That and much more! It was *his* neglect, *his* indifference towards me . . ."

"And *your* betrayal!"

She moved back slightly, shaking her head. "No. He betrayed me long before I ever thought to stray. It was he who cheated me. Cheated me first of my rightful place in his bed, and then of my son's rightful birthright!"

"His *rightful* birthright!" Pei K'ung sat back, laughing scornfully. "Why, your son's a bastard, Yin Fei Yen . . . yes, and no better than any gardener's son, I bet!"

Fei Yen stood up straight, her anger cold now and unforgiving. "If you but knew the truth of it, Pei K'ung." She turned and walked slowly, with great dignity, to the door, then looked back at Pei K'ung. "If you but knew . . ."

* * *

Pei K'ung sat there after she'd gone, staring at the open door.

Now what in the gods names had Fei Yen meant by that? *Cheated?* How cheated? No. There had been tests to ascertain the boy's father. Why, if there had been any doubt Li Yuan would never have divorced her . . .

Her mouth fell open. No. It wasn't possible. Fei Yen would have contested it.

But what if she hadn't known? What if Li Yuan had kept the knowledge secret?

It made no sense. If Han Ch'in *were* Li Yuan's son and Fei Yen had known that – known it for certain – then she would have moved heaven and earth to have him made heir. No mother would have done less. But she had done nothing.

So what *did* Fei Yen mean? Why had she been so angry at the suggestion of her son's low origins?

Mystery. It was all shrouded in mystery. But the truth was in there somewhere and she would find it out.

And Fei Yen?

Fei Yen was beautiful. There was no denying that. Still beautiful enough to turn a prince's head . . . or a T'ang's.

Pei K'ung shivered, knowing that for all she had said, the matter was far from settled; that, far from scaring the Lady Fei away, she had merely made her more determined.

Yes, she thought, *but I shall win in the end, for though you are beautiful, time is on my side. The days, which rob you of your beauty, shall slowly make me indispensable to my husband.*

Beauty. Pah! She would show them how little beauty meant! Why, she could fill her husband's bed with a thousand dumb beauties, and still he would depend on her!

She laughed, determined on it, knowing now what had to be done, then rang the bell to summon Tsung Ye, keen to begin the task.

CHAPTER · 4

SECRET LANGUAGES

"Kim? . . . *Kim*! Wake up!"

The young man turned, gasping, his left hand reaching for the ceiling, then woke, his dark eyes blinking.

"*Pandra vyth gwres?*"

The Machine's voice answered him, soft, reassuring in the dimly-lit room. "It's Curval. There's an emergency."

Kim sat up, rubbing at his eyes. "What time is it?"

"Four seventeen. Now get dressed. You're needed."

Kim didn't argue. He pulled on his one-piece and went out into the corridor. Alarms were sounding distantly and he could hear shouts and running feet.

Kim began to run, heading towards the source of the sound. At the first turn he almost cannoned into Curval, coming to get him.

"What's happening?"

Curval was breathless. He raked his fingers across his bald pate, getting his breath, then answered. "It's Ravachol. He escaped from his cell. He took one of the guards by surprise. Stole his knife."

"Shit!" Kim thought quickly. "Where is Ravachol now?"

"The guards have got it hemmed in on the far side of the labs. It's been breaking everything it can get its hands on!"

Kim nodded, pained by what he was hearing, then touched Curval's arm. "Okay. Let's get over there."

They could hear the smashing of glass long before they turned the corner and came out into the main laboratory area. Ravachol was on the far side of the benches, going from one store-cupboard to the next, pulling whatever he could from within and hurling it on to the floor. A dozen guards crouched behind the nearest benches, stun-guns levelled at the android. As Kim came into the room, their Captain came across.

"I've done what I can, *Shih* Ward, but it's in danger of damaging itself. Some of the chemicals it's throwing down . . ."

"I know," Kim said, anxious now that he'd seen how agitated the creature was. Something had pushed it over the edge. Something or someone . . .

"Ravachol!" he called, walking towards it. "Come now, you've got to stop that!"

The android stopped and turned, staring at him, the knife held out threateningly. Kim made to take a further step, but the Captain grabbed his arm and pulled him back.

"No, sir. I can't let you. Director Reiss . . ."

Kim shrugged himself free, but the Captain took his arm again, more firmly this time. "I've orders, *Shih* Ward. It's too dangerous. If you should be hurt . . ."

"He's right," Curval said, coming up beside him. "Look at it. It's gone. Look at its eyes. It doesn't even recognise you. It's what we feared. Its neural matrix has destabilised completely."

Kim stared at it. It had been stable this past week, but Curval was right; it had degenerated badly. Even so, he wanted to go to it – to try and reason with it.

"It's dangerous," the Captain said. "I've already two men in hospital. If it comes at us my men have orders to stun it, but that may not be enough. It's very strong and it's nervous system may not respond the same way as a human's."

Kim nodded, understanding what the Captain was really saying. He didn't want to take any risks. He wanted to kill it, before it did any further damage.

"What else did the Director say?"

"Reiss will be here within the hour," Curval answered. "Let *him* sort this one out."

Kim shook his head. "No. I can't do that." He sighed, then turned to the duty officer. "Give me your gun, Captain. *I* made it, *I'll* destroy it."

The Captain stared at Curval a moment, then, shrugging, unholstered his pistol and handed it to him. Kim weighed it in his hand a moment, then, looking directly at the creature, began to walk towards it.

"Ravachol? Do you know who I am?"

It stood there, perfectly still, watching him approach. When Kim was only ten *ch'i* or so from it, it raised a hand, shielding its eyes, as if it were staring into brilliant sunlight.

"Kim? Is that you?"

"It's me."

It opened its mouth, hesitated, then shook its head. Looking down, it frowned, as if it didn't understand what had caused the mess that surrounded it. Its feet were leaking blood and there was a faint sparking down one side, the slightest hint of burning.

"It's . . . growing dark," it said, looking back at Kim, bewildered. "I can't . . ."

It seemed to freeze, then, with a tiny jerk, began to move again. Its eyes blinked violently, its left hand juddered, dropping the knife.

"You're not well," Kim said quietly. "You keep forgetting."

It nodded, but it was as if it only half understood. Curval was right. It had gone. There was nothing they could do for it now. Nothing but end its misery. He raised the gun.

"What are you doing?" it asked. "What *is* that?"

Release, Kim thought, and pulled the trigger.

The detonation shocked him. It was much louder than he'd imagined. He stared at his hand, then traced a line to where Ravachol had been standing. He was gone . . . no, he was down, there, beside the bench. Kim stepped closer, then stood over the creature, setting the gun down beside it.

Where the bullet had hit its chest was a jagged hole through which a strange amalgam of wiring and organic matter could be glimpsed, silver and red. Locked into some obsolete programme, its left leg made climbing movements in the air, while its eyes stared straight ahead. The smell was stronger now – the scent of burnt plastic mixed with burning flesh.

Kim crouched over it, pained by the sight, wanting to hold the thing and comfort it in its final moments, but something stopped him. It wasn't dying. You couldn't say that it was dying, for it had never really been alive. It had only *seemed* alive. But for once that distinction seemed meaningless. Ravachol had been more than a machine – more than a simple thing of wires and flesh. Kim hesitated, then, conscious that others were watching him, put his hand out and brushed the hair back from the android's forehead.

It was warm, just as a dying man was warm. And all its memories . . .

Even as the thought formed, Ravachol's eyes blinked and snapped shut. There was a tiny tremor through the body, then it was still.

Gone, he thought. *It's gone* . . .

But where? Where *did* the soul of a machine depart to?

The thought disturbed him, darkening his thoughts, for just as he was conscious of having made Ravachol, he was conscious also that something – some force or creature greater than himself – had fashioned *him*. For the first time he had a strong, clear sense of it.

Copies, he thought, nodding to himself. *We are all copies of some greater thing.*

He stood, then walked back to where Curval was waiting.

"Are you all right?"

Kim shrugged. "I don't know. I'm not even sure I want to think about it."

Curval smiled sadly at him. "Maybe you should take the day off. Have a break from it."

"No. We have to begin again. This morning. I want the body in the autopsy room by seven. We can take scans, slices . . . find out what went wrong. And next time . . ." Kim took a long, shivering breath. "Next time we get it right."

Curval nodded, then touched his arm. "Okay. I'll get things moving straight away."

* * *

At first light Emily went down to the market on Fifty-One, walking through the echoing openess of Main as stallholders set up their barrows and old men sat on benches listening to the caged birds sing.

It was the time of day she liked best; the time when anything seemed possible. Each day was new, filled with possibility, and no matter how many times she had been disappointed, she had always welcomed the dawn.

At the Blue Pagoda tea-house she took a seat at an empty table. Within an hour the place would be packed, but just now there were scarcely more than a dozen people there. Yu I, the proprietor, saw her and came across, smiling his gap-toothed smiled and bowing to her, as if she were a princess, his hands tucked into his voluminous sleeves.

"Ra-chel," he said, his old eyes twinkling playfully. "Is a long time since you come."

"I've been busy, *Lao jen*. I came back only last night. But I've missed this place. Your *ch'a* is renowned for fifty stacks."

He bowed again, delighted by her compliment. "And what will you have, *Nu Shi*? A Sparrow Tongue, perhaps? Or a Water Fairy?"

She smiled broadly. "A *T'ieh Lo-han* would be nice, Yu I. A large *chung*. And some *chiao tzu* if you have any."

"*Nu Shi . . .*" He nodded, then backed away, hurrying off to fill her order.

From rails overhead more cages hung – elaborate things of painted wire. She looked up at them, listening to the birds, watching a tiny chaffinch puff out his chest. How he sang! So full of joy . . . or was it avian pride? She smiled, then looked about her. At a nearby table a young, shaven-headed boy sat beside his grandfather. He was staring at her in that pure, unembarrassed way children have, his dark eyes big and round. Emily smiled at him then looked away.

Pockets of normality . . . that was what it was all reduced to these days. Brief moments – like this – of sanity before the mayhem began again.

A young waiter came across, setting a pale lavender *chung* beside her. He produced a rounded bowl and polished it on his sleeve before setting it before her.

"Thanks . . ."

The young man nodded and turned away. Apart from Yu I few talked to her here. They were mainly Han, she *Hung Mao*, a big-nose barbarian. So it was these days. Tolerance was the most she might expect.

She poured, then lifted the mock-porcelain bowl, cupping it in both hands, enjoying its warmth, the strong scent of the "Iron Goddess of Mercy" reminding her of her youth – of times she had sat beside her father in places like this while he talked with his friends.

Was that why she came here? To renew that simple memory? To keep in touch with that earlier self? Or was it for the peace she found here and nowhere else?

She sighed, then took a long sip of her *ch'a*, swilling it about her mouth as the Han did, enjoying the simplicity of it.

The great world changed, yet these smaller, simpler things persisted. Small things. She nodded to herself, thinking of the horrors she had seen, the deaths she had been witness to. Yes, though Empires fell, small things – those intensely human things – remained unchanged. A thousand years might pass and great Emperors turn to dust in their tombs, but still in some small tea-house in some corner of the world the old men would meet beneath the caged songbirds and sip *ch'a* and talk away the day.

The thought brought her comfort. Yesterday she had gone to see the gutted deck; had seen with her own eyes how cruel and indiscriminate the White T'ang's justice was.

The bastard, she thought, remembering the stink of the place, the pictures she had seen from the leaked security video. It had been awful, unbearable to watch. But necessary. For now she knew there was no option. She had to kill him. *Had to*, for the sake of them all. The only question now was how.

She sipped again then set the bowl down. Yu I was coming across again, a large plate of the delicious dumplings in one hand, a small bowl of spicy sauce in the other.

"*Chiao tzu*," he said, grinning at her again. "If there is anything else, *Nu Shi?*"

"No, *Lao jen*, that's fine." She handed him a ten *yuan* chip and closed his hand about it. "Buy your grandson something."

He grinned and nodded his thanks.

Alone again, she picked up one of the meat-filled dumplings with her chopsticks, savouring the delicious smell of it. As with the *ch'a*, this too was part of the ritual – this too she'd first tasted with her father.

So it began, she thought, suddenly heavy of heart; *yes, and so, perhaps, it ends*.

Killing Lehmann – some said it was impossible, but nothing was impossible. She laughed and took a second dumpling from the plate, dipping it in the sauce, then popping it into her mouth, enjoying the mixture of pork, cabbage and onion, even as she thought the problem through. No, killing him would not be hard – what was impossible was surviving the attempt.

She cleared the plate then sat back. It had been good. She had forgotten how good. She turned, meaning to order a second plate – to indulge herself for once – and saw that Yu I and his waiters were gathered beneath one of the media screens, staring up at it. From where she sat she couldn't make out what the picture was, but after a moment a small cheer went up from the men, their faces suddenly lit up and laughing.

Yu I, seeing her, came across again. "You want more, *Nu Shih?*"

She handed him a five *yuan* chip. "Yes, but tell me . . . what was all that about? You seemed very excited."

The old man grinned and nodded, his delight evident. "It was good news, *Nu Shi*. Very good news indeed. It seems the great T'ang, Tsu Ma, is to be married!"

* * *

The announcement was a simple one – *Liang K'o Ting chih nu Shu-sun Shih li wei Luang-hou*. "Shu-sun, daughter of Liang K'o Ting, is hereby created Empress."

The imperial rescript was read out on the media channels and posted throughout the levels of City West Asia.

At Tsu Ma's palace at Astrakhan, there was a small ceremony. The prospective bride's father, Liang K'o Ting, approached Tsu Ma and knelt, pressing his forehead to the floor. Tsu Ma looked down at him from his throne and smiled, watching as he went through the *san kuei chiu k'ou* – the three kneelings and nine strikings of the head that was required before a Son of Heaven.

As Old Liang straightened up, Tsu Ma looked past him at Shu-sun, wondering how such a stick of a man had bred such a voluptuous daughter. Shu-sun noticed his attention and let her head fall slightly, blushing. She was eighteen years old and fresh as a peach. Just looking at her made his blood race, and when she looked up at him and smiled . . .

He turned his attention to Old Liang again. The man was thanking him for the honour of elevating his daughter to the imperial dignity. He listened, hearing the old man out, then bestowed on him the button of First Rank, given by right to the *hou-fu*, the father of the Empress, and appointing him an officer of the imperial bodyguard. And then it was done, the great family seals placed upon the betrothal agreement, all speeches made.

There was laughter and raised glasses, yet at the back of the hall, unnoticed by Tsu Ma or his future in-laws, a young man slipped away, crossing the great hall swiftly, silently.

At the doorway, Tsu Kung-chih turned, looking back at the smiling group surrounding the throne, his eyes burning with resentment. Then, his face set, his right hand gripping the handle of his dagger, he strode out and ran down the echoing corridors to his rooms, slamming the door behind him.

* * *

Tsu Tao Chu reined in his pony at the cliff's edge and sat forward in his saddle, looking out across the calm sea's surface. Shen, his mount, moved his head restlessly, then bent to crop. The youth reached down to smooth its long, sleek neck before straightening up again, sighing heavily, thinking of the ceremony that morning. It was here, only a week ago, that Tsu Ma had spoken to them. Here that his half-brother, Kung Chih's sickness had begun.

He dismounted and sat at the cliff's edge, his legs dangling over the drop. Far below the water slopped over and around the tips of jagged rocks. It was high tide and the sluggish movement of the current seemed like the shallow breath of a sleeper. The water was thick and glassy green and the dark, vague shapes of rocks beneath the surface seemed more like shadows than hard realities. Tao Chu took a handful of stones from the bare patch of earth beside him and sprinkled them over the edge, watching the diffuse pattern of ripples spread on the rising, falling back of the water.

He looked down at himself. Dust was spattered across his knee-length boots. He raised a leg to brush the earth from the dark leather, bracing his heel against a large, up-jutting stone. Then, taking a white silk handkerchief from the pocket of his riding jacket, he spat on it and began to rub the shine back into the leather. He had just leaned forward to breath on it when the stone moved and he tilted forward.

There was no time to save himself. Where his foot had been the cliff had fallen away and he found himself tumbling head first toward the water, his arms flailing the air. He made a sound, more of surprise than fear, then hit the surface hard, all breath knocked from him, the sudden, shocking coldness of the water making him gasp and try to take a watery breath, but some last flicker of reason made him choke back the instinct.

He struggled upward, his mind dark, in turmoil, his lungs on fire, a searing pain in his side, then broke water, coughing violently and, floundering against a rock, held on for dear life, the waves washing over him.

It was some while before he came fully to his senses. He was still coughing and the pain in his side had grown worse. His teeth were chattering now and he realised that if he didn't get to shore soon he would die from exposure. He turned in the water, trying to make out where best to swim for, but as he did the pain grew so severe he had to close his eyes, almost blacking out.

Carefully he felt beneath the water-line, tracing the wound tenderly with his fingers. He shuddered. It was bad. Very bad. But he wasn't helping himself by staying here. Gritting his teeth, bracing himself against the pain he knew would come, he began to swim, leaning over to one side, doing a kind of lop-sided doggy-paddle that took the strain off his injured side.

Several times on that long and painful swim he thought of giving up, of relaxing and letting himself be sucked beneath the cold, clear water, but something kept him from succumbing, kept him doggedly pressing on, until, at last, he crawled up onto the beach, the outward wash forming long ribbons of silver laced with red at the side of his legs. Slowly, feeling close to exhaustion now, he pulled himself up out of the water, then turned to examine the gash properly.

The wound looked smaller than it had felt, and not so deep. Miraculously it had missed the bone. The rock had sliced into the flesh of his left side between the edge of the pelvis and the outer cage of the ribs. The sea water had washed it clean and the flow of blood from it had eased.

He had been lucky, Very, very lucky.

For the first time in what seemed an eternity, Tao Chu smiled. Somehow he had missed the rocks. Somehow he had fallen between those hard, cruel points of darkness. As he rested there, taking long, sweet breaths of the salty air, a sense of elation, of pure joy at having survived his own stupidity, washed over him. He laughed.

He was still laughing when a call came from the rocks overlooking the small bay he had swum to. Awkwardly, still in some pain, he turned and looked. Three men, servants of his uncle, were standing there. One of them waved, calling out his reassurances as they began to hurry down the slanting, rock-strewn face towards him.

Tao Chu let them lift him and carry him carefully back to the cliff's summit. There one of them examined the wound again, wincing to himself, and removed his jacket, tearing it into strips which he then bound about Tao Chu. Then they began to carry him again, hurrying now. They were halfway across the long, flat stretch of grass that led to the orchards when Tao Chu saw his mount.

"Stop!" he cried. They set him down, then made small murmurs of protest when he told them to catch and bring his pony. There was a moment's muttering between them then one of them scurried off and, after some trouble, brought the reluctant, skittish pony back.

Tao Chu stared at the beast, delighted. "Now help me mount her," he ordered, struggling up into a sitting position. This time there was open protest from the men, but Tao Chu insisted, his voice taking on the tone of command. The men looked among themselves again, then shrugged. One held the horse steady while the others helped Tao Chu into the saddle.

Fresh blood stained the bindings at his side, but Tao Chu felt strangely better now that he was mounted. He smiled fiercely, doing his sixteen-year-old best to ignore the pain that was now a horribly nagging ache. Seated thus he let them lead him on, one drawing the horse by its harness while the other two walked either side of him, ensuring he did not fall, their hands supporting him in the saddle.

Coming into the courtyard of his uncle's palace, he saw his half-brother, Kung-chih over by the stables. He made to call to him, then stopped, frowning. Kung-chih was standing with his back to him, talking to a small, bald-headed man. Kung's presence in the stables was not unusual, nor was the fact that he was talking to a servant, but the servant was neither groom nor stable-hand, he was Hwa Kwei, one of Tsu Ma's most trusted men, the Chief Steward of his bedchamber. What was the eunuch doing talking to Kung-chih? And why here, in the stables? Kung-chih made a furtive gesture with one hand and Hwa Kwei scuttled away. Then Kung-chih himself strode purposefully across the cobbled space and into a side door, far from the one Hwa Kwei had taken.

Concerned, Tao Chu looked down at the men surrounding him, but they seemed to have noticed nothing. He grimaced, the pain starting up again more fiercely than before.

"Help me down," he said quietly.

* * *

When Kung-chih came to see him later Tao Chu said nothing of what he had seen. Tsu Ma was sitting in the room with them, concerned for his favourite nephew. Tao Chu had told him everything, omitting nothing, and had seen his uncle frown and then laugh with pride as he told him about mounting his horse and riding home.

"That is indeed how a Prince should act!" Tsu Ma had said, delighted. "And do not worry, Tao Chu, I shall not punish the men for your obstinacy!"

But Kung-chih was quieter, somehow less attentive than he might usually have been. He had said little since that day on the cliff tops – had made no threats nor shown any disrespect to Tsu Ma. He had been kind, almost his old self, yet in small ways he had changed. He no longer confided in Tao Chu; no longer shared his hopes and fears with his young half-brother. He had become insular and broody and subject to sudden moods. Seeing him with Hwa Kwei had therefore awoken Tao Chu's suspicions. He was sure that Kung-chih was up to something.

"How are you, little brother?" Kung-chih said on entering the room. "I hear you have been swimming."

It was an attempt at the old banter that had once existed between them, but now it fell strangely flat.

"I was stupid," Tao Chu said, sighing. "I ought to be dead. I'll not be so lucky twice in my life!"

The comment was not meant to carry any other meaning, yet as Tao Chu looked up into his brother's face he saw how Kung-chih's eyes moved away sharply, as if stung by the words. There was a momentary sourness in his expression, but then he looked back at Tao Chu and, softening, smiled. "Still . . . I'm glad you're safe."

Are you? thought Tao Chu, seeing that all too familiar face in a different light, as if with new-created eyes; seeing the softness, the weakness there. But it was an unworthy, an uncharitable thought, and he felt guilty, knowing that for all his half-brother's self-preoccupation, his love was genuine. Reaching out, he took his hand and pressed it gently.

"I know," he said, and in his mind added, *because you need me, Tsu Kung-chih. Need me to save you from yourself. To keep you from falling.*

That was, if it wasn't already too late.

* * *

Jelka looked up from the screen and rubbed her eyes. She had been working on the tapes most of the day, selecting and editing those parts he'd find of interest, determined that she would finally get them done.

She had frozen the tape at an image of Titan she had taken when they'd been heading back on the *Meridian*. The orange surface of the moon was hazed in cloud, the dark red collar in its northern hemisphere showing up strongly. Beyond it, seeming to spear it, Saturn's rings swept in a glorious arc through the star-spattered blackness, the great gas giant itself just out of shot. The sight of it had taken her back to that moment, sending a strange thrill through her.

If only you could have been there with me, Kim. If only you could have seen it as I saw it.

She turned, looking across at the picture of her in her spacesuit taken on the steps of the *Meridian*. It was strange how comfortable she had felt in it – odd how something in her had responded to the icy coldness of the outer planets.

She turned back, stretching, nodding to herself, then took a print of the image. She would have it blown up and hung on the wall behind her desk. The rest . . . well, the rest was for Kim.

She let the film run, listening to her own voice as she repeated for the camera what she'd been told, facts and figures flowing from her tongue effortlessly. This was the last of them – the last of a dozen eight-hour tapes she had compiled for him from what had been months of material. For almost a year now she had spent at least an hour a day preparing them, but now they were almost done. Another few hours at most.

And then?

She wasn't sure. Wasn't sure whether to send them to him or hand them over herself. After all, what if he'd forgotten her? What if there was someone else?

Titan receded slowly, the bulk of Saturn moving into shot, dwarfing the tiny moon, the swirling striations of its northern hemisphere filling the screen. It was beautiful. Breathtaking. She let it run, knowing that whatever else happened, he, at least, would get to share this much of her experience.

So small our world is. Like a tiny speck of dust in a vast, echoing hall.

Slowly the image of Saturn shrank, slowly the darkness filled the screen. She shivered, frightened by the intensity of her feelings.

He had promised he would wait. Seven years, he'd said. Seven years.

There was a knock. She leaned forward and pressed HOLD, then turned to face the door.

"Come in!"

"Jelka?" Her father took a step into the room and looked about him. "Can you spare me a few moments?"

"Sure." She turned back, pressed SAVE, then blanked the screen. She could finish it later.

"How's Pauli?" she asked, going across to him and kissing his cheek.

Tolonen grinned. "Oh, he's fine. He's resting now. That new tutor of his makes him work. Sometimes I wonder if he's not a bit too hard on the child."

"He's a good child," she said, taking his arm and leading him out of the room. "And a bit of discipline won't harm him, will it? You forget how strict my tutors were with me."

"I guess so. But then, you were always a tough one. Headstrong too." He laughed. "Still are, I guess."

They went into his study. While he sat, she walked about the room, picking books from the shelves, then putting them back.

"So what is it?"

He looked up from his papers and grunted. "Just, er . . . a few details to sort out. For the party."

"Ah . . ." The invitation to Kim – that was what this was about. Steeling herself, she went across and sat, facing him across the desk.

"Here." He took a small pile of bright red envelopes from his tray and handed them to her. "You'd better check them before they go out."

She took them, nodding to him, but afraid to look.

"I was wondering about the music. I've booked the *Chi L'ing* Ensemble. I've been told they're very good. But maybe you feel they're a bit too . . . conventional."

She would have laughed but for the tension at the pit of her stomach. "It's all right," she answered, her voice small. "The *Chi L'ing* will be fine."

His smile was businesslike. "Good . . . then that's settled."

She stared at him, trying to read his face while her fingers sorted through the pile, counting the cards. Eleven. There were only eleven. But she had made twelve additions to the list. She wetted her lips, then spoke.

"There's one missing."

"Pardon?" He looked at her, then, understanding, gave a brief laugh. "Oh, I see. Yes . . . Old Joss Hawkins is dead, I'm afraid. Died a good eight, nine months back. I thought you'd heard."

She stared at him, mouth open, then looked down, flicking through the envelopes.

There! Six down. She stared at her father's handwriting on the envelope, surprised. "Kim Ward" it said, then gave his address at the SimFic labs. She looked up again. "I thought . . ."

"You thought?"

She shook her head. "It doesn't matter."

"Good. Then let's look at the catering. I've been thinking that maybe we should change a few things . . ."

* * *

After she'd gone, Tolonen sat there deep in thought. It was just as he'd suspected. No . . . as he'd *feared*. He had seen it in her face. He'd thought it finished with, but it wasn't. She was still obsessed with the Clayborn – still determined on being with him.

He sighed, then sat back, steepling his fingers under his nose.

Rich or not, genius or not, it could not be countenanced. His daughter and a Clayborn. No, it was unthinkable. His family would be a laughing stock, his daughter's chances at a real marriage destroyed for all time. He had to do something. Defying her was no good – he knew that now. But there were other ways.

He sat forward and pulled his diary towards him, opening it at that day's entry. The card he had been given lay there where he'd left it. He picked it up and stared at it, then, grimacing, drew the comset across to him and tapped in the number.

It rang, once, twice, a third time. *I'll try later*, he thought, about to put it down, but then the signal changed and a voice answered him.

"Hello. Madam Peng here. Can I help you?"

He cleared his throat. "Madam Peng . . . it's Marshal Tolonen here. A friend of mine gave me your number. I . . . I have a problem I hope you can help me with."

* * *

Kim stepped from the sedan and looked about, taking in the breathtaking opulence of the place. The Mansion was a big, three-storey building in the Han style with sloping tiled roofs but the gardens too were expansive, with a small river and an orchard on the far side of an ornamental bridge. Fake clouds drifted slowly across the blue of the ceiling fifty *ch'i* overhead, while the walls gave views of distant mountains. He had seen its like before, but he'd never thought to own such a place.

Reiss had called him just over an hour back and told him to go and see it. If he liked it it was his, whether he signed the new deal or not. If not, well, there would be others.

"*Shih* Ward?"

He turned as a middle-aged Han in dark green business silks strode towards him down the gravel path.

"I am Chang . . . Hugh Chang from Supernal Property." He bowed and shook Kim's hand at one and the same time, then turned, indicating the Mansion. "Beautiful, isn't it? It's rare for one of these really big Mansions to come on the market, but Director Reiss asked me to look out for something and notify him first. So here we are. I understand you're interested in acquiring something *special*."

Kim stared at the man a moment, irritated by his bullish, over-familiar manner, then answered him.

"I haven't really thought about it."

"But I thought . . ."

"Just show me," he said, moving towards the House. "I want straight answers to my questions. And don't try to persuade me to buy it. If I like it, I like it. If not . . ."

He swept past Chang, imagining the look the man gave him behind his back, but right now he didn't care. It had been a bad day – a very bad day so far – and even this could not really lift his spirits. Losing Ravachol had been a body-blow, and though he'd set to the task again at once, it was more to disguise his feeling of loss, of alienation from the task at hand, than to seriously solve the problems that had come up.

The truth was, he felt like giving it all up. Like calling Reiss back and saying no, keep your company, I want none of it. At the same time he recognised that it was only a passing mood, and that however bad he felt now he would feel better in a day or two. Well enough, perhaps, to start anew.

As he approached the huge double doors to the main house two guards stepped forward to bar his way, then backed away hurriedly as Chang waved them aside.

"Security is tight, as you see," he said, coming alongside Kim as they went into the shadowy hallway. "There are six guard towers in the wall and special security barriers at both lifts – as you saw on the way in. We've recently installed a special electronic tracking system for the perimeter walls and emergency seal doors inside the house itself."

Kim glanced at him, surprised. "Is that normal?"

Chang shrugged. "You know how it is these days. No one's safe. Not even up this high. Not unless they've got all this stuff."

Kim stopped, turning to him. "And the people who owned this?"

"They took great precautions. In the eight years they were here there wasn't a single breach of security."

"So what happened to them? Did they get tired living like this? Or did they buy something even bigger?"

"Like a stack?" Chang laughed, then grew serious again. "No. You want a straight answer, right?"

"Right."

"Okay . . . They were killed. Butchered in their sedan. They'd gone to a charity ball run by that new group, you know, the New Conscience Movement. Seems like they were targeted. A terrorist cell took them in the lift coming up. The death by a thousand cuts. Very messy, so I'm told."

Kim nodded, sobered by the story. He looked to his right up the broad main stairs, then turned, looking through to the kitchens. It was all very dour and ostentatious. It simply trumpeted its wealth. Moreover, the place was huge. One could have a hundred children here and still not fill it. Even so, it didn't have to stay like this. With a little imagination he could make something of it – turn part of it into a research centre, another of the wings into a lab complex. After all, money was no object now. He could do pretty much as he wanted.

Yes, he thought, *but what would Jelka say? What does she want?*

For a moment the absurdity of his situation almost made him laugh. Here he was, looking round a First Level Mansion – a place worth, what, a hundred, a hundred and fifty million *yuan*? – that was his, gratis, if he said yes, and the only

thing stopping him was whether a young woman he hadn't seen in seven years –
and who he couldn't be sure even remembered him – would like to live there.

He huffed out a breath, exasperated with himself, then looked at Chang again.
"Okay. I'll take it. But I want to make changes. That's possible, I assume?"

Chang beamed. "As far as we're concerned, *Shih* Ward, you can burn the place
down and start again from scratch. What you pay for is the deck itself. The
Mansion . . ." He made a dismissive gesture. You could replace this for . . . oh,
twenty million?"

"As little as that, huh?"

Chang nodded, unaware, it seemed, of the irony in Kim's voice. "Naturally,
should you wish to make changes, we could put you in touch with the very best
construction technicians. Craftsmen, they are. Why . . ."

"Thank you, *Shih* Chang, but I think I've seen enough. Draw up the papers and
send them to Director Reiss. If I wish to see the place again I'll know who to speak
to, neh?"

Chang smiled, then handed Kim his card. "Just press the reverse and it'll put you
in direct contact."

Kim stared at it with a professional interest, then pocketed it. He was about to
turn away, when it came back to him what he'd meant to ask earlier.

"By the way . . . about the previous owners. What group was it that attacked
them?"

The smile faded from Chang's face. "It was the Hand. The Black Hand. No one
else is so audacious. Why, I'm told . . ." He stopped, realising he had overstepped
the mark, then bowed. "Forgive me, *Shih* Ward. I don't want to keep you."

Kim nodded then walked out and across to his sedan. Yet as he climbed inside he
was thinking of all he'd heard recently. There was no doubting it, they were living
in troubled times. Society had changed. Once it had been driven by the simple
mechanics of the levels – of aspiration and demotion. Life had been a giant game of
snakes and ladders. But now . . . now society was fear-driven. All of these guns and
guards and laser-tracking devices were signs of a deeply paranoid culture. So
paranoid that it was now quite normal to assume the worst – to assume that your
enemies would come and get you in your bed.

He sat, feeling suddenly heavy-boned and tired. Paranoia . . . it was the
philosophy of the Clay, of the place from which he'd come. Upwards he'd
climbed and ever upwards, until he'd found himself here, at the very top of the
City, beneath the roof, like a bird in a loft of an old house, fluttering about, trying
to get out. But there was no way out. And slowly, very slowly, the darkness was
climbing after him. Up and up it came. And what guns and trackers would keep it
out? What precautions could ever be enough?

As the sedan lifted he sat back, shaking his head angrily.

It was Ravachol's death that had made him think all this. That and Chang's
foolish prattling. So a few rich people had died . . . hadn't that always been the
way? Wasn't history filled with such instances? Yes, but that made it no more
comforting, for the signs were clear now – there for the dullest man to read.

The sedan shuddered slightly, then began its swaying motion.

Li Yuan was right. They had to act now or go under. But what action could prevent the coming crisis? What measures could assure their childrens' futures?

Yes, and that was the nub of it, wasn't it? For what was the point in loving someone – in pursuing and possibly marrying them – if it were all to come to nought? – if society were to crumble away and the species end itself in a frenzy of blood-lust?

Why take the risk of loving and having children when the risks were so high, the rewards of love so tentative? Why make oneself a hostage to the times?

Because you have no choice. Because you love her and want her and . . . and because if you don't try you'll never forgive yourself.

And because nothing else mattered. Nothing.

* * *

"Rachel?"

Emily gave a little start then turned, regaining her composure. For a second she had forgotten who she was – had been thrown by the use of her assumed name. She had been day-dreaming: thinking about Michael, wondering where he was, what he was doing.

"What is it?" she asked half-challengingly, staring back at the tall, pock-faced *Hung Mao* who stood there, an arm's length from her.

Pasek smiled coldly, then moved past her, looking out from the balcony across the crowded Main below. His dark, Slav eyes passed briefly across the ragged awnings, the packed mass of unwashed and shabby humanity that crowded the floor between the stalls, dismissing what he saw.

"I thought we ought to talk."

Emily felt her stomach muscles tighten with aversion. "Talk?"

He turned back. "Sure. We need to clear the air between us."

She was silent, uncertain what to say.

Pasek's smile was like a sneer. "You don't like me, Rachel DeValerian. I know that. I can see it even now. But that doesn't matter. What *does* matter is that we don't let it get in the way of things."

"I don't see . . ."

He raised one pale, thin hand, interrupting her. "There are going to be changes."

She stared at the dark leather band about his wrist. On it was a copy of the symbol he wore on a silver chain about his neck. A cross within a circle.

"Changes?"

His smile evaporated. The eyes were brutal now. "It's already happening. A purge. Those we can't trust. I ordered it."

"You . . ." She fell silent, understanding. He'd had Chou Te-hsing killed. Yes, and all his deputies. All except her. She looked up, meeting his eyes. "Why?"

"Because it was time. We were drifting. We needed a new direction. Chou had no idea. He had to go."

She nodded, not because she agreed, but because she saw it all clearly now – saw why he'd pressed to have his men placed in key strategic positions; why he'd held his tongue in the last council meeting when Chou had spelt out the new

SECRET LANGUAGES 中 國

programme. *You planned this*, she thought, all of her instincts about the man confirmed in an instant. He'd known then that it didn't matter what Chou said or didn't say at that meeting; knew then that, come this morning, Chou would be dead, his power base in the Black Hand destroyed. Pasek had taken over. He *was* the Black Hand.

"What do you want?"

His hand went to the cross hanging about his neck. "I want you to join us. Become one of the sealed."

She made to answer him, but he spoke over her. "Oh, I know you don't believe. That doesn't matter. Not now, anyway. Right now what matters is that we consolidate. Make sure the Hand doesn't tear itself apart. There'll be a lot of ill feeling. Chou had a lot of support at grass roots level. People respected him. Wrongly, as it turns out, but that's by the by. As for you, Rachel, you're respected too. Rightly so. I've watched you for a long time and I like what I've seen. There are no illusions about you. You get on with things. It's as if you've seen it all before. Nothing shocks you. Even this. I saw how quickly you understood how things stood – how quickly you accepted them, and I like that. I'd be sorry to lose you."

She felt a faint shiver, not of fear, but of aversion, ripple through her. "So that's it, is it? I join you – become one of the sealed – or I die?"

He shook his head. "If I'd wanted you dead, you'd be dead. No. It has to be your choice. If you choose not to work with me you can go into exile. Africa, maybe. Or Asia."

"And if I stay?"

"You get to help formulate policy."

She laughed, astonished, then frowned, searching his eyes for some kind of explanation. "I don't get it. I want what Chou wanted."

"No. I've *watched* you at those meetings. I've *seen* the doubt in your face, the frustration at some of the decisions. You want what *I* want. Not all of it, but enough for us to work together. To make the Black Hand not just another shitty little faction but a genuinely important force. A force for change. You want that. I know you do. I've seen it in your eyes."

Emily looked away. It was true. The last eighteen months had been nothing *but* frustration. But to work with *Pasek* . . . It was on her lips to say no, to tell him to go to hell, but something stopped her.

"I need to think about it."

He looked her up and down, then nodded. "Okay. Twenty-four hours. That's all I can give you. We're meeting at noon tomorrow. At the White Mantis. If you're with me, be there. If not . . . well, good luck."

She watched him go. Saw his tall, spiderish figure vanish into the crowd, then shivered, chilled by this sudden turn in events. Twenty-four hours. It wasn't long. And if she *didn't* turn up?

She didn't know. For once her instincts failed her.

Well? she asked herself, sighing heavily. *What are you going to do?*

She turned, putting her hands on the rail of the balcony, leaning her full weight on them as she looked out across the crowded marketplace. She knew what she wanted – at least, she thought she did. But Pasek . . . could she work with Pasek?

Twenty-four hours. It *wasn't* long. But maybe that was how it always was.

She pushed away from the rail, then turned, hurrying away, pushing through the crowded corridor urgently, hastening towards her room, conscious of the seconds ticking by.

* * *

Tao Chu looked round the door into his half-brother's suite of rooms, then took a step inside.

"Kung-chih?" he called softly. "Are you there?"

The study was in shadow, the last of the evening's light blocked off by the closed slats of the window. On the far side of the room, the door to his brother's bedroom was open. Tao Chu went across, one hand pressed to the bandage at his side.

"Kung-chih?"

There was no answer. The room was empty, the bed made up. Tao Chu turned, looking back into the study, wondering where Kung-chih could have got to.

A sharp pain stabbed through him, taking his breath. Making his way across slowly, he eased into his brother's chair and sat there until the pain subsided.

He looked down. There was fresh blood on the bandage. Surgeon T'ung would be angry with him and would no doubt speak to his uncle, but that didn't matter right now – he had to speak to Kung-chih; to find out what was going on.

"Curse him," he said quietly, his anxiety for his beloved half-brother outweighing any concern he had for himself. "Curse his stupid pride."

He leaned forward, searching the desktop with his eyes, looking for some clue as to where he might be, but there was nothing. Kung-chih was probably out walking in the grounds somewhere – in the orchards, perhaps – or riding in the woods to the south of the palace.

Brooding, probably. Yes, he'd seen the way he had looked at their Uncle Ma; seen the resentment in his eyes, the hurt. But Kung-chih had to come to terms with that. His life – his expectations – had changed and he must live with that. He could not mope about for ever.

He was about to get up and return to his room when he heard voices outside, coming closer. His brother's voice and . . .

Tao Chu frowned, surprised. It was Hwa Kwei again – Tsu Ma's Chief Steward of the Bedchambers. What in the gods' names was Kung-chih doing talking to him twice in one day?

There was a murmured exchange, a curt dismissal, and then Kung-chih came into the room. He switched on the light and turned, then stopped dead, his mouth open, seeing Tao Chu there at his desk. For a moment there was a look of guilty shock on his face, then anger.

"Tao Chu! Why aren't you in your bed? What the hell are you doing here?"

"I . . ."

Kung-chih came and stood over him, glaring at him fiercely. "Did Uncle Ma send you to spy on me? Is *that* it?"

Tao Chu shook his head, hurt by the accusation, but Kung-chih went on.

"Why, you fucking little sneak! I thought I could trust you, but as soon as my back's turned you were in here, weren't you, poking about to see what you could find! But you won't find anything, *brother*."

Find what? he wanted to say, but the question made no sense. He hadn't come here to poke about, he'd come here to talk to him, to warn him about associating with the likes of Hwa Kwei.

He closed his eyes, the ache in his side suddenly worse, but Kung-chih went on, his voice savage now, unrelenting.

"You little worm! You snivelling little worm! All those words of consolation and all the while you're fucking lapping it up. That's the truth, isn't it? You loved seeing Tsu Ma humiliate me. You just *loved* it!"

"No . . ." Tao Chu said, crying now, unable to believe that this was Kung-chih talking to him this way. What had he done – what had he *ever* done – to deserve this?

"Fuck off! Just fuck off! Next time I find you poking around my rooms I'll kick you from here to Africa!"

Slowly, every movement an effort, Tao Chu pulled himself up. For a moment he stood there, swaying, his vision swimming, then it came clear again. Kung-chih stood there close by, less than an arm's length from him, yet so far away it seemed a whole world separated them.

"Brother . . ." he said, his eyes pleading with Kung-chih, his right hand reaching for him, but Kung-chih brushed his hand off angrily and leaned towards him, his words spat into Tao Chu's face.

"*Brother*? No, Tao Chu, you've got it wrong. You're not even a friend!"

* * *

Ravachol lay face down on the operating table, naked under the pale blue light. They had finished the dissection and had begun to tidy up. Kim stood back, weary now, letting his assistants finish off.

After extensive scanning they had taken sample slices from different areas of the android's brain, running a number of tests on them. All had shown the same – a severe deterioration of the brain tissue, almost as if it had been burned away.

What could have done that? he wondered, puzzled by the phenomenon. Was Curval right? *Was* the organic material they were using sub-standard? Or had something more sinister taken place?

Later, as he showered, his mind toyed with possible explanations. Synaptic burn-out of some kind? A virus? Or maybe – just maybe – some form of neuronal poison?

There was no physical evidence for it. Its food had been strictly vetted and there had been no signs on the body of an injection, but the more he thought about it, the more certain he was. Someone had got to it. Someone – an agent of one of their business rivals? – had made sure the experiment would fail.

I wasn't wrong, he realised with a start. *The brain's structure* was sound. But someone has been tampering with it. Someone who had access.

The thought was chilling. At any other time he would have dismissed it as a product of the hour and his depressed mood, but this was not paranoia. The more he considered the history of its deterioration, the more he saw how false, how *unscientific* it had been. No . . . it hadn't been a natural decay. All along they had floundered for explanations for what was happening, not wanting to face the obvious.

But who?

He stepped from the shower and shook himself, not wanting to wait for the warm air-currents to start up, then padded across to the terminal in the corner of the room.

"Who was it?" he asked, knowing that if anyone knew, *It* knew. "Who poisoned Ravachol?"

The Machine was silent.

"You know. I *know* you know. So why won't you say? You see *everything*. If it happened, *you* saw it. Why, you could even show me, I bet!"

"The screen," it said tonelessly. "Look at the screen."

Kim watched, fascinated at first and then horrified as he saw who it was. When he spoke again his voice was small and frightened.

"Why didn't you say? Why didn't you show me this before?"

"You didn't ask."

"But . . ."

Kim leaned against the terminal, feeling suddenly more tired than he'd ever felt. He had thought it was over, thought himself cured, but here was proof that it was still going on, unknown to him.

"Run it again," he said, forcing himself to watch as, on the screen, he slipped from his room and, creeping stealthily past the guards, went to the android's cell. There, crouching beside the sleeping creature, he took a small pouch from his pocket and gently brushed some of its powdery contents on to Ravachol's lips.

As the figure on the screen turned, the lens zoomed in, catching for a moment the dark malevolence of its eyes. Kim shuddered, recognising it from his dreams. It was Gweder . . . his mirror self.

Gweder and *Lagasek* – "Mirror" and "Starer", his two halves, the dark and light of his being, names from his Clayborn past.

"*A-dhywas-lur*," he said softly, a ripple of pure fear running up his spine. *Up from the ground*. Then, more practically, "What did it use?"

"Something it stole from you. Something you made and then forgot about."

"But I don't forget."

"No?"

The images ran. Again and again he saw himself slip from his cell and make his way to the android's cell. Again and again he saw himself administer the poison. And never once had he suspected. Never once had he had even the faintest idea what was going on.

"Where's the pouch now?"

"In your room."

Kim gave a laugh of disbelief. "It can't be. I would have seen it."

"No. He doesn't let you."

"How . . ." Kim frowned fiercely, then rubbed at his brow. "How do you know this?"

"You forget. I have all your files. I saw you through Rehabilitation. I know things about you that even you don't know."

"So what else do you know?"

"I can't tell you."

"Why?"

"Because . . ."

Kim gave a small yelp of frustration. "*Why?*"

It was silent a moment, then, in a voice that seemed as old as the rocks, it spoke to him again.

"Get dressed now and go to bed. We'll talk in the morning. I'll tell you then what you need to know. And Kim . . ."

"Yes?"

"Do not blame yourself. You are what you are. Without him – without Gweder . . . Well, I think you understand."

Kim nodded, then, sighing, he turned from the screen and took a fresh one-piece from the pile, slipping it on.

"Tomorrow?" he said, looking up into the camera's eye.

"Tomorrow."

CHAPTER · 5

CAGED BIRDS

L i Yuan's son, the Imperial Prince Kuei Jen, sat in a tall official's chair facing the three old men, his back straight, his eyes staring straight ahead. The men – distinguished-looking greybeards – sat some twenty *ch'i* from the Prince, wearing the flowing saffron robes of New Confucian officials, no sign of rank displayed anywhere about them. Yet these were not simple priests, these were the *San Shih*, the Three Priest-Scholars – princes themselves, honoured sons of the Twenty-Nine, the Minor Families – and they were here to test the young prince on his knowledge of the Five Classics.

Li Yuan and his Chancellor, Nan Ho, sat to one side, looking on. While the examination was in progress they could not interrupt. So it was. So it had been for two thousand years or more, since the time of the Han emperors. With one difference. Kuei Jen – at seven – was probably the youngest ever to sit the oral examination.

A long white banner hung to one side of the hall. On it, painted in large red pictograms, was Kang Hsi's famous *Sacred Edict* with its sixteen injunctions exalting the twin virtues of filial piety and brotherly love. Copies of it hung throughout the Cities of Chung Kuo and were recited twice a month by teachers and pupils alike.

Just now they were questioning Kuei Jen on the *Ch'un Ch'iu*, the Spring and Autumn Annals of the State of Lu.

The *Ch'un Ch'iu* was the earliest historical record of the Han people, covering the period from 722 to 481 BC, when the fifteen major feudal states of the North China plain had first formed a loose confederation called *Chung Kuo*, the "Middle Kingdom". Though it was some while since he himself had read it, Li Yuan could still remember how he had felt as a boy, knowing how deeply-rooted – how *ancient* – those traditions were.

Looking on, he knew that this was Kuei Jen's favourite area of study – one that not merely interested, but excited him – yet the boy's answers, couched in fluent Mandarin, were strangely hesitant, stilted almost, as if he spoke from rote.

"Ch'i was the first of the Five Hegemons – the *Pa* – followed by Sung, then Ts'in, then Ch'in, and finally Ch'u, before authority was returned to its rightful owner, the Son of Heaven."

One of the old men leaned towards Kuei Jen, his voice, like those of his fellow *San Shih*, filled with the authority of his position.

"And the Lord-Protector Ch'i. Tell me about him. Who was he Lord of and where was his capital?"

Again Kuei Jen hesitated, trying not to let his father down, resisting the temptation to turn and look at him.

"Lord Ch'i was Prince of Ts'i and his capital was the powerful and wealthy city of Lin-tsu in Shantung Province. The Lord Ch'i could trace his ancestry back thirteen generations to the kings of Chou. His daughter married the Emperor."

The old man nodded, then glanced at his fellows, clearly pleased by the answer. As he sat back, another of them leaned forward.

"You speak well, Prince Kuei, but tell me, what event caused the Lord Chi to take up arms at the request of his Lord the Emperor?"

Li Yuan frowned, surprised by the question, trying to recollect what he knew of the House of Ts'i and its history. Lord Ch'i had eventually been assassinated. But as to why he had taken up arms in the first place . . .

Kuei Jen shifted uncomfortably, then, as if mirroring the old man, leaned forward slightly.

"Was it to do with what happened in 894 BC?"

"Go on . . ."

"Well, in that year one of the Emperor's advisers had counselled that he should have the Lord of Lu boiled alive, which the Emperor did. Two hundred and four years later, one of Lu's descendants launched an armed attack on the descendants of the adviser, and the Lord Ch'i was commissioned by the Emperor to act on his behalf in bringing Lu to justice."

"Very good. Now tell me . . ."

And so it went on, question following question, unrelenting, until, after almost four hours, it came to an end.

Li Yuan stood, pleased – profoundly pleased – and proud of his son's performance. To fail would have been no disgrace, for the same examination was taken by men four times young Kuei's age, yet he had answered every question; most of them with a detailed knowledge that, he suspected, was rarely shown, even by much older candidates.

As the *San Shih* backed away, to consult among themselves and prepare to give their verdict, he went across to Kuei Jen. What he wanted to do was pick the boy up and hug him, he was so proud, but as ever the eyes of his servants and officials watched his every move, constraining his actions.

Later, he promised himself, seeing how awkwardly Kuei Jen stood there, how nervous he was even now, after it was over.

"You did well," he said, bowing stiffly to his son, honouring him by the gesture. "Whatever the *San Shih* say, I am proud of you, Kuei Jen. Your answers showed not merely a sound knowledge of the texts but also a profound understanding of their meaning. You are a good son, Kuei Jen. The very best of sons."

Kuei Jen blushed then bowed his head. "Father . . ."

"*Chieh Hsia?*"

93

He turned. "What is it, Master Nan?"

"Forgive me, *Chieh Hsia*, but it seems your wife, Pei K'ung, has been waiting these past few hours to speak with you."

"Does she say why?"

"It seems it is a personal matter, *Chieh Hsia*. She will speak to no one but yourself."

Li Yuan huffed, exasperated. What with this, he was already behind with his work, and there would be no time to catch up, for he must leave at six to fly to meet Tsu Ma at his palace in Astrakhan.

"Tell her I shall come, Master Nan. Tell her . . . tell her I must finish here. She'll understand."

"*Chieh Hsia*."

He turned back, puzzled as to why Pei K'ung should wish to see him so urgently. Maybe her father was ill. Maybe that was it. Maybe she wanted permission to visit him.

The *San Shih* returned, bowing as they entered the hall again, then came across, presenting themselves formally to their T'ang.

"Well, *ch'un tzu*," he said, nervous himself now that the moment of decision had come. "Give me your verdict."

"The Prince spoke well," Old Luo began. "He answered confidently and, for the main part, correctly. His tutors are to be commended."

Li Yuan felt himself stiffen, hearing the unspoken "but" behind the old man's words.

Luo continued. "His knowledge of the texts was good for one his age, though more work needs to be done on both the *Shih Ching* and the second book of the *Li Ching*, where his knowledge – though correct – seems fairly thin."

"However . . ." Li Yuan said, impatient now.

The old man bowed his head slightly. "However, it is the feeling of all three of us that, while the Prince exhibits a good knowledge of the *form* of the *Wu Ching* – of the words and events set down in the texts – he is none the less of an age when . . . well, when perhaps the *substance* is not so strongly rooted in his being."

"Put bluntly, you think him too young."

"Not too young, *Chieh Hsia*, merely . . . inexperienced."

Li Yuan felt his anger welling and beat it down, maintaining a calm and stately demeanour.

"Inexperienced?" He turned away, taking a pace or two, as if considering the idea, then turned back, staring directly at Old Luo.

"You think my son too young, and you think, because I am a grown man, that I should agree with you. Well, *ch'un tzu*, let me say this. When my brother Han Ch'in was assassinated I was but eight years old. Only nine months older than Kuei Jen is now. Some men forget what they were like at that age, but I cannot. How I was that day – how I felt, what I thought, what I had *experienced* – is etched unforgettably in my memory."

He turned, looking at Kuei Jen.

"You look at my son and you see only a child – a precocious little boy who has learned his lessons well. But when *I* look at him I see myself, as I was, and remember what I was like at his age."

He looked back at the three men.

"You talk of form and substance, yet you forget the lessons of the Tao. What is a child but the seed of becoming? And if the seed is not sound, how will the tree grow straight?"

"So it might be, *Chieh Hsia*, yet it is our feeling . . ."

"Oh, *damn* your feeling!" Li Yuan yelled, losing his temper. "Get out of here, *Lao jen*! Now! Before I lose all patience with you!"

Luo blanched then, looking to his fellow *San Shih*, backed away, his bow stiff and angry.

When they were gone, Li Yuan turned, looking to his son. Kuei Jen stood there, his head down, his face and neck scarlet with embarrassment.

"Kuei Jen?"

The young prince swallowed then looked up at his father. Tears were welling in his eyes. "Call them back, father. *Please*. They are great men. Influential men. Besides, maybe they are right. Maybe I *am* too young to be made a scholar."

"Nonsense! Luo Ye is an old fool! You answered all his questions perfectly!"

He shuddered with indignation, looking about him, defying anyone to gainsay him.

"Why, the nerve of the man! I am of a mind to . . ."

"*Father!*"

Li Yuan looked at Kuei Jen and frowned, noticing for the first time the tears that were coursing down his cheeks.

"*Kuei Jen* . . . what is it?"

"Please, father. Call them back and make peace with them. Before it's too late. Before any more damage is done."

Li Yuan sighed, his anger tempered by his son's obvious distress. "All right. But only because you want it so."

He turned, summoning the nearest of his retainers.

"Hu Chang . . . go fetch the *San Shih*. Tell them I shall speak to them privately, in my study."

Then, turning back to Kuei Jen, he smiled and reached out to brush away the tears.

"You are right, Kuei Jen. It does not matter what the old men think. You and I know what you are. And maybe you are wiser than the *San Shih*. Much wiser, neh, my son?"

* * *

Pei K'ung sat on a chair in the corridor facing her husband's rooms, her hands clasped together tightly in her lap. Nearby stood her secretaries and beyond them a group of guards and minor officials, all there at their T'ang's command.

The old men – the *San Shih* – had been in with him for more than twenty minutes now and she had heard raised voices more than once.

Dangerous, she thought, remembering how Li Yuan had lost his temper with her that evening and how she had felt. Yes, but she was only a wife – only the helpmeet of the T'ang. Those old men . . . well, to alienate *them* was much more serious, for they were leading figures in the New Confucian hierarchy and without the whole-hearted support of the New Confucians Li Yuan's position was greatly weakened.

The door clicked open and the three greybeards backed out, bowing like comic figures in an opera. As the door closed they began to talk urgently among themselves then fell silent seeing her.

She rose imperiously from her chair and gave them a tight smile, then walked to the door and knocked.

Inside, Li Yuan was sitting at his desk, drumming his fingers on the surface impatiently.

"Husband," she said, dropping to her knees and lowering her head.

"Get up, Pei K'ung," he said, motioning her across. "What is it? Is your father ill?"

"My father?" She frowned then shook her head. "No. But I am angry."

He raised an eyebrow.

"I visited the imperial library."

"And?"

She drew herself up straight, the full weight of her indignation in her voice. "And the old man sent me away as if I were a common serving maid!"

Li Yuan gave a shout of laughter and leaned towards her. "Chu Shi-ch'e, you mean?"

She bristled with anger. "I don't see what is funny. You should punish him for his impudence!"

"Punish him? *Punish* Chu Shi-ch'e? Why, the man is ninety if he is a day! If I punished him I would kill him, and I am loath to do that, Pei K'ung. Besides, what did he say?"

"He said I could not look at the family archives. That I needed your permission."

He smiled. "So?"

She stared at him, astonished. "You mean . . . it's true?"

"Of course." He watched her, his eyes amused.

She let out a shuddering breath then turned and went to the door.

"Pei K'ung . . ."

She stopped, her hand on the door's thick edge.

"Come here, Pei K'ung."

She turned and went across, her whole manner set against him now.

"Yes, husband?"

He took a pen and inked it, then wrote a note and signed it, pressing his seal to the bottom of the paper.

"There," he said, handing it to her. "But let's have no more talk of punishment. The *Pi-shu Chien* is one of our finest servants. He served my father and my grandfather before him. Sixty-eight years he has filled that post and there is no man in the whole of Chung Kuo who knows more about or is more loyal to our family. Use him well, good wife, but do not anger him. Chu Shi-ch'e can be a cursed old crow when he's angered!"

She laughed, surprised, then, with a bow of thanks, turned and left.

Outside she stopped and stared at the permission letter then shook her head. Why, he hadn't even asked! He had simply signed it, trusting her.

Trusting her . . .

The thought was sobering. Yet what had she expected?

I expected him to say no.

She stood there a moment longer, then, the letter held out carefully at her side, she began to walk, heading for the library once more, her two secretaries falling in behind her as she went.

* * *

Lehmann sat on the sofa in the corner of the room, his booted feet on a low table, staring at his Financial Strategist, Cao Chang, who stood, head bowed before him.

"Well, Cao Chang? What will it cost us?"

Cao Chang hesitated. "Is this the place to discuss this, Master?"

Lehmann waved aside the objection. "Our guests are busy, Chang. We are as safe talking here as anywhere. So tell me. What would it cost us to depose the T'ang?"

Cao Chang gave a bow, then took a tiny cassette from the breast pocket of his black silk *pau* and slid the thin, domino-shaped tape into the slot behind his ear. His eyes glazed a moment, then came clear. He was suddenly more alert, his speech more hurried, as if it sought to keep up with the accelerated pace of his thoughts.

"Our analysis shows nine main elements. Three of these, recruitment, training and weaponry, might need to be adjusted upward should our policy in Africa prove unsuccessful. For my calculations, however, I have assumed a training period of six months and a total figure of two million, eight hundred thousand men, including a mercenary force of half a million."

Lehmann nodded. "Good. Now outline the other six elements."

"One," Cao Chang began, enumerating each point on his fingers. "The cost of fermenting revolt in Li Yuan's African armies. Important in preventing Li Yuan from using those forces directly against us. Two. The cost of pacifying our Triad friends in Africa. Important in ensuring that they do not take the opportunity to step in and take over our South European operations. Three. The infiltration of Li Yuan's European Security forces and the purchase of a minimum of two thousand top-level officers. Important in undermining the efficient operation of Li Yuan's forces in the first hours of our attack. Four. The purchase of *tai* at Weimar in the weeks running up to our operation. Important in helping to create a mood of popular dissent. Five. The funding of terrorist factions in both East and West Asia. Vitally important if we are not to find ourselves fighting not merely Li Yuan but also Tsu Ma and Wei Tseng-li. Six. The cost of destroying major GenSyn installations in the hours before our attack, particularly the five *Hei* garrisons."

"And the costings?"

There was the briefest flicker of hesitation, then the figures spilled from Cao Chang's lips.

"For recruitment and training, forty-seven-point-six billion. For weaponry, sixty-eight-point-eight billion. To pay off the African armies, twenty-four-point-five billion. To pacify our Triad friends, fifty-six billion. For the infiltration of Li Yuan's security forces, sixteen-point-four billion. For the purchase of *tai* three-point-five billion. To fund terrorist factions in the Asian Cities, fifty-two billion. To destroy major GenSyn installations, twenty-two-point-two billion. That comes to two hundred and ninety-one billion. Add to that a wastage factor of twenty per cent and the final figure is three hundred and forty-nine-point-two billion *yuan*."

Lehmann nodded. It was a huge sum, but no more than he had anticipated.

"Thank you, Cao Chang. You have done well. Relax now. Take a girl, if you want."

Cao Chang gave a deep bow, then turned away, vanishing through the bead curtain on the far side of the room.

Lehmann took his feet from the table and sat forward, staring into space. Though three hundred and fifty billion was a massive sum – the equivalent of three years' profits from all his ventures – raising the money wasn't the problem. The problem would be keeping the details of his scheme secret from Li Yuan. Not that he had any illusions about that. Both he and Li Yuan knew now that a war must come. Both had begun their preparations. But when and how it would be fought, *that* was the nub of it.

Timing was everything.

He sighed, then sat back, looking about him at the plush decor of the foyer, feeling a natural aversion to its silk-cushioned opulence. He had had the House of the Ninth Ecstasy gutted and rebuilt, much as it was when Mu Chua, its legendary Madam, had been running it. Not only that, but he had had Mu Chua reconstructed too, using visual records to recreate a GenSyn duplicate of the woman. Fifteen million she had cost him, all told – including the fees of the assassins he had sent to cover his tracks – but it had been money well spent; perhaps the best fifteen million he had ever spent.

Whatever he personally felt about such places, there was no denying their usefulness. In the eighteen months since he had rebuilt it, the House of the Ninth Ecstasy had regained its former prestige as a watering-hole for Above merchants wishing to do business "down-level", its reputation spreading far and wide. All sorts were attracted here, lured by rumours of what could be had in the Madam's famous "Red Room" – Security officers and Company Heads, Minor Family princes and sons of the rich and famous, Representatives from the House and even, once, a Junior Minister. Through Mu Chua he snared them all. Drew them all into his cage.

Like birds, he thought, then stood, stretching his long, pale limbs, feeling the power there in every movement. He smiled: a bleak, corpse-like smile.

It was time to use those connections: to make the birds flutter in their cages.

* * *

Tolonen travelled up to Lubeck shortly after lunch. Madam Peng was waiting for him at the door to her First Level salon, her eight assistants lined up behind her to greet their prestigious visitor.

Rotund and bird-like, as her name – *Peng* – suggested, the Madam hovered anxiously as the eight polemen set the Marshal's sedan down.

She had entertained many prominent citizens in the thirty-four years she had been in business and prided herself on the quality – the *exclusivity* – of her clientele, but never had one so elevated or so powerful entered through her doors.

"Marshal Tolonen," she said, bowing low, her eight assistants kneeling at her back, four to her left, four to her right, their foreheads scraping the thickly-carpeted floor.

"Madam Peng," he said, stepping forward to take her gloved hand and gallantly kiss it. "I am grateful you could see me at such short notice."

"Not at all, Marshal," the Madam answered, a smile splitting her heavily rouged lips. "You honour my humble salon with your presence. Please, come through. I have cancelled all other engagements to see you . . ."

"You are most kind." Tolonen answered, inclining his head, then moved between the twin ranks of assistants.

"Forgive me if I sound impertinent, Marshal," the Madam said, hurrying to catch up with him, "but might I say how well you look."

Tolonen nodded, clearly distracted by his thoughts. Yet it was true. The old man looked closer to sixty than eighty-one. He had kept himself supremely fit and though his stubble-length hair was the colour of snow, his eyes were clear and strong. Even in his casual silks he looked exactly what he was – a leader of men – and seemed a match for any man half his age.

Double doors opened automatically before them and the two stepped through, into the Madam's "boudoir". Here she did all her business. Here, surrounded by her bright silk wall-hangings, across the low, black, antique table that dominated the centre of the richly-decorated space, she had made her reputation as City Europe's leading matchmaker.

Showing the Marshal to a sturdy chair that had been imported specially for the occasion, she plumped herself down on a sofa facing him, her ample figure settling into the big silk cushions like a brightly coloured bird into its nest.

"Well, Marshal," she began, her ancient and thickly-powdered Han face grinning broadly – almost obscenely – as a servant approached bearing a tray of wine and sweetmeats. "How exactly can I help you?"

It was not unusual for an old man to want a young wife, especially as they came to realise that their grip on mortality was growing daily more tenuous, yet somehow she had never thought Tolonen the type. Still, she was prepared, and had spent an hour that morning selecting a handful of special girls that might well suit his profile.

Tolonen waved away the offer of a drink and leaned towards her, his grey eyes troubled.

"It is my daughter, Jelka. I . . ." He looked at the servant, reluctant to say more. At once Madam Peng dismissed the man.

She sat up slightly, smiling reassuringly. "All that is said between us here is absolutely confidential, Marshal. But forgive me . . . when you spoke to me yesterday, I thought . . . well, I thought you meant to take a bride yourself."

"A bride! *Me*?" Tolonen laughed, but his eyes seemed horrified by the notion. "Gods, no, Madam Peng! It is my daughter Jelka I'm worried about. She . . ." Again he seemed ill at ease broaching the subject. "Well, to be blunt with you, she has a crush on an awful little fellow – a Clayborn by the name of Ward. He . . ."

She put her hand out, her face all sympathy now. "You need not say another word, Marshal Tolonen. I *quite* understand. Why, even the thought of it is absurd, neh?"

Tolonen smiled weakly.

"No. You were absolutely right to come to me." She leaned forward, her fingers brushing a pad on the desk in front of her. At once a screen came up out of the surface, facing her. She tapped in a few words, then eased back, smiling at Tolonen once again. "It's true what they say, neh, Marshal? Clay is Clay. It cannot be raised."

He nodded, comforted, it seemed, by her understanding.

"Now, your daughter is . . ." she studied the details on the screen, "twenty-four I see. So your principal worry is, I guess, that she will do something silly after her Coming-of-Age in three weeks time."

Tolonen swallowed. "That is so."

"Then we must act quickly, neh? We must somehow find a way to break this former attraction. And what better way than by creating a new one?"

She leaned forward, tapping at the keys, the huge golden rings on her fingers glittering in the spotlights. She paused, watching the data come up, then, satisfied, sat back, the screen lowering into the table's surface once again.

Slowly the lights dimmed. At the centre of the table was now a faint red glow, dull and misty.

"You know your daughter well, Marshal Tolonen?"

"Well enough," he answered from the darkness where he sat. "Her mother died giving birth to her. I raised her from a child."

"Ah . . ."

"If it helps, she was engaged once. To Hans Ebert."

"Ah yes, I recall that now. She was . . . *reluctant*, am I right?"

Tolonen sighed. "She hated him, if the truth be told. I tried to force her into the marriage. I . . . Well, I do not want to make the same mistake again, Madam Peng, let me make that clear. She must choose her own mate. But not *him*. Not Ward!"

There was a vehemence to the last few words that made Madam Peng reassess the situation. If he was so worked up about it, then there was clearly a very *real* danger that his daughter would marry the Clayborn. That made her own task more difficult; made it essential that she knew everything there was to know about the matter, for to fail in this her most prestigious case – well, it was unthinkable. As unthinkable as the Marshal's daughter marrying a Clayborn!

"This Clayborn . . ." she began, trying her best to be tactful. "This Ward. What is it, do you think, that attracts your daughter to him?"

The old man's laugh was sour. "The gods alone know. Oh, he's clever enough, there's no doubting that, and he has the T'ang's ear in matters scientific, but . . . well, as to what attracts her *physically* . . ."

"I see," she said, after a moment's awkward silence. "And yet there is an attraction? You're quite sure of that?"

"Oh yes. She wanted to *marry* him! She defied me openly, in front of old friends who'd come to dinner! Why, I had to send her away to prevent it."

Madam Peng sighed silently. The more she heard, the less she liked this commission, but it was too late now – she had committed herself the moment she had invited the old man to come and visit her. If she turned him away now it would get about – for rumour had a vicious tongue in her circles – and her reputation would be damaged. Then again, it was far from certain she could do anything meaningful in the circumstances. If what she'd heard were true, the Marshal's daughter was a headstrong, independent young madam.

"Okay," she said, her voice betraying nothing of her thoughts. "Let us try to build up some kind of profile of what she finds attractive in a man. This Ward . . . I assume he's the usual type . . . big head, bulgy, staring eyes, stunted body?"

Tolonen grunted, his discomfort evident.

"So. My guess is that it's not actually something physical your daughter is responding to, but some . . . *inner* quality. You say he's very intelligent."

"Perhaps the most intelligent young man on the planet, Ben Shepherd aside."

She brightened, letting her voice grow more animated. "Then that's it! What we need to do is look for a young man who is not merely good looking, but bright with it!"

"Maybe," the old man said uncertainly. "And yet Ebert was bright."

"Yes, but look what a foul piece of work *he* turned out to be. Why, it wouldn't surprise me if something in his manner *alerted* your daughter!"

Tolonen laughed. "I'm beginning to understand just why you have such a good reputation, Madam Peng. It was as you say. But tell me, who do you have in mind?"

He heard the tap of her fingers on the keyboard. There was a brief delay and then the hazy red glow at the centre of the table began to intensify and grow.

"I have programmed the Selector to search the files for eligible young men who fit the profile. It will come up with those four that best fit the parameters we've been discussing. Then . . . well, we'll take a look at them, neh, Marshal Tolonen? And then you can tell me which of them you'd like to pay your daughter a visit over the coming weeks."

* * *

The sign flickered fitfully, sending a sweet burning scent into the air. Emily, standing at the rail of the balcony two floors up, looked down at it, seeing how the giant electronic mantis seemed to spring and trap its prey, its long tongue moving with an inhuman quickness.

Two guards, plainly dressed but carrying Security-issue automatics, stood by the door, moving the curious along. Inside Pasek waited for her.

She went down. At the door they searched her then waved her through. She didn't recognise either of them, yet that was not unusual – the whole of the Hand could have assembled and she'd have known no more than eighty, maybe ninety of them at most. *Or would have*, she thought, *before yesterday.*

What she had noticed, however, were the pendants about their necks, the same as that which hung about Pasek's – the cross within the circle.

Inside, she pulled the curtain aside, then stopped. The White Mantis had been an opulent, bustling place – a gambling and drinking club the Hand had bought as a cover – but now it was silent. All the fittings had been ripped out, the carpets removed, the silk hangings torn down. All was bare now – eerily so.

She walked across and stood in front of the door to the main gaming hall, hearing the murmur of voices from within. She pushed through, then stopped, astonished. She had expected Pasek to be there with a few of his men; instead she found herself looking into a room packed with a hundred or more people. She looked about her, recognising faces – some she'd not thought to see again – and understood at once. He'd summoned them all – all the Hand's surviving cell leaders. Never, in the history of the Black Hand, had they met like this – all of them in one place at one time – and something told her it would not happen again.

She walked through, making for the tiny dais on the far side of the low-ceilinged room, conscious that every eye was on her. Many smiled, clearly pleased – reassured, it seemed – to see her there, and reached out to touch her arm as she passed, but one or two of them scowled, as if her very presence was a betrayal.

Coming out by the dais she found herself facing a line of Pasek's men – his four henchmen, Ashman, Grant, Blaskic and Eyre. For the past few years they had been Pasek's constant shadows. They were big, well-built men, a good ten or fifteen years younger than Pasek, with strong Nordic features and short, ash-blonde hair.

Security types, she thought, meeting their eyes unflinchingly. *Just the kind of empty, soulless type the man attracts.*

"Where's Pasek?" she asked, looking to Blaskic.

"He'll be here," Blaskic answered, the slightest suggestion of a smile playing on his lips. Yesterday he had been out-ranked by her – a lowly minion in the Hand's hierarchy – but today . . .

She turned, looking about her, making a swift calculation. There were roughly a hundred and fifty people in the room. Of those she knew fifty, perhaps sixty at most. The majority of the rest were sure to be Pasek's. All in all, then, it was finely balanced. Pasek had enough support to guarantee the success of his initial coup, yet not enough to make it absolutely safe.

She smiled inwardly, understanding suddenly just why she was there. It wasn't just that Pasek "respected" her, he *needed* her, to hold things together while he consolidated his rule. But only for a time. Things would change – she understood that instinctively – and Pasek would slowly increase his stranglehold, until . . .

Until he no longer needs me.

Emily turned back, knowing now what she had to do; knowing *exactly* how to play her hand.

She didn't have long to wait. A gong sounded from the next room and then a door opened at the back of the dais. Pasek stepped out.

He stood there a moment, looking about him as if noting who was there, then nodded.

"Friends," he said, lifting a hand, palm out, to greet them. "You know what has happened, and some of you are . . . *uncomfortable* with it. In the circumstances I felt we should meet. To clear the air."

His voice was warm, yet his eyes when they met Emily's were cold, uncompromising.

"Rachel . . ." he said, acknowledging her. "Would you like to start?"

She stared back at him belligerently. "Start?"

"I mean, is there anything you want to say?"

She smiled. There was plenty she'd like to say – like what a callous shit he'd been to have Chou Te-hsing murdered – but that wasn't what he meant.

"I'm here," she said, as if that said it all.

"And?"

She almost laughed. And what? That she was his loyal supporter? That she condoned what he'd done and was happy with the way things had turned out? No. The truth was, the more she thought about it, the *less* happy she was. She had joined the Hand because it had seemed to her to be the best way of changing things – of achieving some limited form of justice and directly affecting the lives of the common people – but in practice it hadn't worked that way, and now, under Pasek, there was even less chance of that.

She thought back to their meeting the day before. Pasek had been wrong when he'd spoken of them wanting similar things. Wrong, or simply lying. For while she saw the Hand as a vehicle for social justice – as a corrective rod to beat corrupt officials and counterbalance the grosser abuses of power – what *he* wanted was to transform it into a society of religious zealots like himself.

Which was fine, only she wasn't going to go along with that. Not without a struggle.

Brushing aside Grant and Blaskic, she stepped up on to the dais, facing Pasek.

"I'll join you," she said, eyeing him defiantly. "But there's one condition."

He stared back at her, confident, it seemed, now that he had her vocal support. "Name it."

"That you let me take out Lehmann."

There was an audible gasp from the body of the room; a look of shock on every face. All, that is, except Pasek's. He just smiled – a pale, ghostly smile – and nodded.

* * *

Afterwards he spoke to her alone.

"How did you find out?"

"Find out?" She laughed. "What are you talking about?"

"The tape. I only got it an hour back. How did you hear about it?"

She stared at him. Clearly there was something she didn't know. "Lehmann . . . We're talking about Lehmann, right?"

He nodded, then. "Look, you'd best come through. You'd best see this before we talk any further."

He had cleared one of the bedrooms at the back of the Mantis and made it into a makeshift office. There were a desk, two simple ice-cast chairs and – on the wall behind the desk – a larger version of the pendant he always wore, the cross within the circle.

"Sit down," he said, pointing to the nearest chair, then went round the desk and took a hand-held from the top drawer.

"Here," he said, handing the viewer to her. "But I warn you. It isn't pleasant."

Pleasant? What *was* pleasant about Lehmann? She stared at Pasek a moment, then looked down at the tiny screen of the hand-held, activating it.

Ten minutes later she understood.

"Who was she?"

"One of our south-eastern operatives. Jane Vierheller, her name was."

"And the man?"

Pasek laughed coldly. "That's your man. That's Lehmann."

"Lehmann?" Emily brought the screen closer to her face, rewinding until his face came clearly into view. So *that* was what he looked like. She felt a shiver of pure aversion pass through her.

"You still want to take him out?"

She looked up, glaring at him. "And you don't?"

"Sure. But not just yet. Not until we're strong enough."

"Strong? Look, I don't want to depose him, I just want to kill him."

"I understand. But that won't be easy. To get to him at all we'd need quite a force. They say he's better defended than Li Yuan."

"You forget. I almost got to Soucek."

"Sure, but Soucek's a different matter. He's *meant* to be seen. Lehmann . . . well, no one sees Lehmann, not unless he *wants* them to."

She considered that. Then, with a jolt, she realised something.

"The tape! How did he get it to you? How did he know where to find us?"

Pasek leaned towards her. "He didn't. We found the tape. He meant us to find it."

"I don't understand. How?"

"The woman . . . Vierheller . . . was part of a cell of five. Later in that sequence – towards the end of it – she gives Lehmann a name and a location. The name she gives is that of her cell-leader, Wilhelm Dieter, the location is his apartment. Two hours back, when Dieter didn't show for the meeting here, I sent Ashman to bring him. Ashman brought him all right, but Dieter was dead. Lehmann had killed him."

"And the tape was in his apartment, right?"

Pasek shook his head. "You have to understand what you're taking on. You need to know what Lehmann's like, otherwise . . ." He spread his hands, palms upward.

"So what do I need to know? He torched a whole deck. Only a monster would do that."

"That's true. But it's useful to know the nature of the monster, neh? To know just what he's capable of."

"Torture. Mass death. You still in any doubt we should kill the man?"

"No doubt at all. But listen. The tape wasn't with Dieter, it was *inside* him.

Lehmann had had him cut open and his innards scooped out like a grapefruit. Then they sewed him up and lay him on his bed, face down. There was a message burned into the skin of his back."

Emily swallowed. She had known Dieter; not well, but enough to know he had been a good man. She hoped it had been quick; that he hadn't suffered the way the woman, Vierheller, had suffered. She shuddered, then forced herself to ask. "What did it say?"

Pasek sat back, lacing his fingers together. "You can look for yourself, if you want. His body's in the next room."

"Just tell me."

"He's very direct, our friend, Lehmann. He knows what he wants."

"Cut the shit. What did it say?"

Pasek's smile disturbed her. "Just four words. *'Don't fuck with me.'* Effective, wouldn't you say?"

She looked down, staring at the frozen image on the screen – at that pale, albinoid face with its awful slit of a mouth and its cold, unemotive eyes. Monsters . . . The times bred monsters. But this one surpassed them all.

She met Pasek's eyes again. "So what are we going to do? Just how *are* we going to get strong enough to take the bastard out?"

Pasek's smile broadened. He leaned towards her conspiratorially. "We're going to do what we should have done years back. We're going to make sure that the Hand's the coming force . . . the *only* force in the land. You understand?"

"War," she said quietly. War against the myriad other terrorist organisations; that was what he was talking about. A war to make the Black Hand not merely dominant but supreme.

"That's right," he said, nodding slowly, his eyes gleaming at the thought of it. "And then you can have that bastard. I promise you, Rachel. On my mother's memory . . ."

* * *

The door was locked, the room in darkness. For hours now, Pei K'ung had sat there, hunched forward, her hands gripping her knees, watching the holograms flicker in the air above the table – so real and yet so distant. She had seen her husband as a child, playing in the orchards of Tongjiang with his elder brother, Han, his round face laughing as he ran between the trees; had watched him on the day of his coronation as he stepped down from the Temple of Heaven, resplendent in his silks of imperial yellow, like a young god sent among them; had witnessed his grief at the news of his wives' deaths, then watched him clutch his baby son Kuei Jen to him, his face filled with disbelief and joy after the floating palace of Yangjing had been destroyed; had spied on him in his bridal bed and looked on as he stood at the window of his study, his face wistful as he watched the young maids play ball in the gardens.

So much she'd seen. So much she'd forced herself to witness.

Pei K'ung sighed, then clapped her hands. At once the room's lights came up, the hologram vanishing like a wraith. She stood, the blood pulsing at her temples, and reached out to steady herself.

Too much, she thought. *I have seen too much.*

She closed her eyes, trying to shut it out, to push it far away, but she could not help herself: she kept seeing it, time and again, Fei Yen lying on the bed beneath him, her arms opening to him, her tiny breasts like offerings, and his face . . .

She took a sharp intake of breath. *Stupid*, she thought, angry with herself; not merely that she had succumbed to the temptation, but that she'd acted so . . . *predictably.*

"It's over," she told herself with more confidence than she felt. "It was over long ago. Those were just images. Fading memories."

Yes, and yet the sharp clarity of those images seemed to belie that fact. Looking at them she had felt her stomach tighten with jealousy – as if it had been only yesterday.

She went to the mirror and pointed a finger at herself accusingly.

"Stupid, Pei K'ung . . . How could you be so stupid!"

She should not have let the woman's taunts get to her. But now it was too late. Now she was infected by Fei Yen's image. She could not turn her head nor close her eyes without seeing the woman there in her husband's bed, there, moving slowly, sensuously beneath him, then, as he climaxed, smiling triumphantly back at the recording lens, as if to mock her across the years!

"Damn you!" she said, not sure whether she meant Fei Yen or herself. She felt like punishing the woman – humiliating her in front of her servants – yet even a cast-off wife had her rights, her *status*, and besides, she would need Li Yuan's permission before she did such a thing, and how could she possibly do that?

She turned then went quickly to the door, unlocking it and throwing it open.

"Mistress?" the waiting Steward asked, bowing low.

"Send my maids," she said. "I shall bathe before dinner."

She went back inside, composing herself. Li Yuan had already gone – he would be at Tsu Ma's within the hour – but still her duties claimed her. With her husband gone she would sit at the head of his table, entertaining whichever guests remained. But there was an hour and forty minutes before then.

She heard footsteps in the corridor outside. A moment later both of her maids stood before her. They curtseyed breathlessly.

"Mistress!"

"Run a bath," she said imperiously. "And lay out my clothes. Then leave me."

There was the briefest exchange of glances between them – for they were used to seeing to her every need – then, without a word, they set to work.

Pei K'ung went to the table, looking down at the golden cases of the holograms and shaking her head. When she had married him she had thought it would be simple, never guessing – never even suspecting – what he would awake in her.

She was not meant to be his mate, merely his helper. Her sexuality had been neutered by the marriage contract; she herself rendered into a false male – a female eunuch. She shuddered.

I should have stayed where I was. I was contented there. I knew my place. Here . . .

She sighed, then went across to the bathroom, watching one of them pour scent into the water, then strew the surface with rose petals.

Here I know nothing any more. Only that I've changed.

Finished, they bowed and backed away. She heard the door click shut, then spun round and went to her desk, activating the intercom.

"Tsung Ye?"

She waited, then a voice came over the speaker.

"Mistress?"

"Come to my rooms. Now."

"Mistress."

Pei K'ung took her hand from the pad and straightened up. She was no longer young and she had never been beautiful, but she *was* Empress.

As she made her way back to the bathroom, her fingers reached up, unfastening the top button of her *chi pao*. She stretched her neck, relieved to be free of the tight-fitting collar, then felt for the button at her collar-bone, pushing it through the eye.

There had been a brief time in her adolescence when she had hoped to be a bride, to be a woman in the fullest sense of the word. But the years had passed and no suitor had been found, and she had resigned herself to the fact that she would never have that other, secret life that most women had.

She let the *chi pao* slip from her, then stepped from her silk briefs, turning to face the mirror, naked now.

Forget that face, she told herself, knowing how horse-like and masculine it was; *look at the body.*

She stood a while, studying herself, reaching up to cup her breasts, then tracing the broad swell of her hips. *Not bad*, she thought, *considering*. She turned, looking at herself side-on, when there was a knock at the door.

"Mistress? It is Tsung Ye!"

Pei K'ung looked across to where her silk bathrobe hung from a silver peg, then, smiling nervously, encouragingly to herself, she stepped to the edge of the huge, sunken bath and slipped in beneath the rose-scented water.

She flexed her muscles, trying to calm herself, to still the trembling in her limbs, then turned her head, facing the door.

"Come in, Tsung Ye!"

She heard the door open; heard it click shut.

"Mistress?"

"In here."

She heard him come part way then hesitate; knew he had seen the discarded *chi pao*.

"Mistress?"

"Come here, Tsung Ye. I need your advice."

She waited, staring straight into the mirror, watching the reflection of the doorway. Slowly, with great reluctance, Tsung Ye edged into the room, his discomfort more than evident.

"Mistress?"

She turned to face him, lifting herself slightly in the water so that her breasts came into view. He was staring at her now, wide-eyed, his mouth fallen open. The sight gave her more confidence. After all, he was a mere servant, she an Empress!

"Well, Tsung Ye . . . what are you waiting for? Come in and scrub my back."

"Mistress?" There was an edge of panic now in his voice, almost of pleading.

"You heard me, Tsung Ye. Get those clothes off and join me here. Quickly now!"

He swallowed, unable to believe what he was hearing, then stammered a reply. "I . . . I . . . am a se-secretary, Mistress. I . . ."

Slowly she stood, letting him see that she was naked, aware that he could not keep his eyes from her. That knowledge gave her power; gave her voice a new-found resonance.

"In here, Tsung Ye, at once, or my husband will hear you have insulted me!"

* * *

Li Yuan stopped at the top of the steps, looking down into the Great Hall, five thousand heads turning to look up at him. Long banners of bright yellow silk and huge red lanterns, all printed with the characters *chang shou* – long life – hung over the heads of the great and mighty who had gathered. He smiled then turned to meet Tsu Ma's eyes.

"It is your last evening as a single man, Cousin Ma. It seems almost a shame to spend it thus."

Tsu Ma laughed, then leaned heavily on his pearl-handled cane. "That is our fate, neh, Yuan? Common folk can get drunk and play the fool, but we . . . we must perform like actors before an eager crowd. Come, let us go down. There will be time later to share a quiet moment."

They went down, the great mass of courtiers and ministers, soldiers and aristocrats, company heads and politicians, bowing as one before the two T'ang, then moving back, like the sea parting before the bow of a great ship.

Relieved of any official obligations, Li Yuan looked on, at ease in his cousin's court, yet also somewhat wistful, remembering the night before his own brother's wedding when, in the Great Hall at Tongjiang, they had held a similar reception.

Then, as now, there had been peace. Then, as now, beneath the calm surface of courtly ritual, things had been in flux.

And tomorrow it begins again, he thought, wondering for a moment how Karr was spending this evening – his last before he took on his official duties. Was he at home with his wife and child? Or was he out celebrating with his friends and colleagues?

With his family, he decided, smiling. *A good man, Karr. Reliable. And honest. Honest as the day is long.*

He had not told Tsu Ma just yet, but there would be time later. Once Wei Tseng-li was here. When the three of them were alone.

Smiling, he accepted a drink from one of the stewards and took a large sip, steeling himself, then turned to greet one of Tsu Ma's senior ministers.

The hours passed. Just after ten, Wei Tseng-li arrived, the young T'ang greeting his fellows with a laugh and smile, as if the moment had no significance, yet each of them knew what lay behind this meeting. The last time all three had met had been thirty months before, at Tongjiang. That day Wang Sau-leyan, their fellow T'ang and cousin, had sent his élite troops against them in an attempt to wipe them out. Two Sons of Heaven had died that day, including Tseng-li's elder brother, Wei Chan Yin. But they had survived, and Wang, in time, had been brought to account for his treachery.

"Cousin," Tsu Ma said, embracing Wei Tseng-li, then holding him at arm's length. "Why, you've put on weight! Is this what having three wives has done for you?"

Wei Tseng-li laughed heartily, his dark eyes twinkling. "And you, Cousin . . . is it *anticipation* of marriage has bloated you so?"

Tsu Ma roared with laughter – laughter that was taken up by all surrounding him until the Great Hall rang with it. He nodded, pleased by the rejoinder, then looked to Li Yuan. "So here we are," he said quietly. "Like the Three Old Worthies!"

Li Yuan smiled. "*Old*, Tsu Ma?" Then, looking past Tsu Ma, he touched his arm lightly. "But hush . . . here comes your bride."

Shu-sun stood beside her father at the top of the steps, resplendent in a full-length dress of jasmine edged with lavender, her pretty face framed in delicate yellow flowers.

Looking up at her, Li Yuan felt his heart grow heavy, once more reminded of the day before his brother's wedding.

If I had but known what was to come . . .

He looked down sharply, tears welling in his eyes.

What would you have done? he asked himself. *How* could *you have prevented Han Ch'in's death? And if you had, how would you have stopped the next attempt, or the one that followed that? Could you have kept your brother safe until his last breath, until you stood over him, an old man in his bed, a dozen great-grandchildren weeping silently in the death-room?*

No, came the answer. *No, for it was willed otherwise.*

But even if you had – even if the gods gave back that day to you – how could you then have lived, knowing that she was his? How could you have looked on her, day after day, and not have had your heart break within you, knowing she was not yours?

He shivered, then looked to Tsu Ma. His cousin was gazing at his bride as she descended, a look almost of awe in his eyes.

"She is like the dawn, neh, Yuan? Like Spring's first shoot."

"She is very beautiful," he answered, determined to set aside all troublesome memories. "May you have many sons."

Tsu Ma chuckled but did not look at him, his eyes snared by his betrothed.

"And I'll call the first one Yuan . . ."

* * *

Fei Yen climbed from the bed and crossed the room, her fingers reaching for the door. She could hear the man's soft snoring in the darkness, could still *feel* his weight on her, smell the sickly perfumed scent of him, and shuddered, despising herself.

Kisses and flattery, that's all it ever was: crude disguises for some darker, baser need. Why could she never see that? Why was she always tethered to her senses, like a hawk on a leash, circling the lure? Where in the gods' names was her pride, her dignity?

She took a gown from the peg beside the door and pulled it on, then slipped out into the corridor.

A night light flickered in a wall bracket to her left, some twenty *ch'i* along, above the stairwell. Across from it a servant slept atop a lacquered chest, his knees up under his chin, his mouth open. Wrapping her gown tight about her, she went to the right, hurrying down the broad, carpeted hallway, heading for her dead father's rooms, her bare feet making no sound.

Inside, in the silent darkness, she rested, her back against the door, her eyes closed, letting her heartbeat slow, the faint, musty scent of the room filling her lungs.

The evening had been awful. She had drunk too much, laughed too much, and then . . . gods, the things she had let him do! The awful, degenerate things!

She gritted her teeth. The *Wu* . . . She must consult her father's diviner – his *Wu* – and have him cast an oracle. But first she must wash the man's foul scent from her.

Finding her way in the dark, she crossed the room and pushed the bathroom door open.

"Light," she said, speaking to the House Computer. At once the room was bathed in artificial sunlight from the panels in the ceiling.

"Gentler . . ."

The light softened.

Since her father's death four years before no one had used these rooms, yet the servants maintained them as if he were due back any moment. Solid gold fittings sparkled under the crystal lights, marble surfaces gleamed. In one corner a green jade fountain, carved in the shape of a rearing dragon jutted over a circular pool, its tiled floor decorated like a huge *tai chi*.

She went to it and, activating the controls in the panel between its wings, stood and watched as a steaming jet of water spewed from the dragon's mouth, describing a glistening arc in the air.

"Cooler . . ."

Throwing off her gown, she went down the steps, into the swirling current of the slowly filling pool.

The fierceness of the spray against her skin was exhilarating. She turned slowly in the glittering fall, her arms out, feeling the water drum against her face and breasts and back, cascading down her flanks and between her legs, cleansing her, washing all memory of the man from her skin. And as the disgust passed from her, that feeling of anger and indignation she had had in Pei K'ung's office returned. She was still young, her body trim and firm, her beauty undiminished. How dare the woman treat her like a servant? How *dare* she?

"Enough!"

At once the jet of water died. At once warm air-currents played over her body, drying and caressing it.

She knew, of course, just why she had got drunk. It was the news – those hideous images from Tsu Ma's palace in Astrakhan. She had seen the way he looked at his bride – seen how his eyes drank in the youthful beauty of her.

Just as he had once looked at her . . .

"Wake the *Wu*," she said, climbing the steps, then stooping to pick up her gown. "Send him to my study. I'll see him there."

* * *

The *Wu* looked up from the fallen yarrow stalks and met her eyes.

"Heaven above water . . . it is *Sung* . . . conflict."

Fei Yen nodded, but she was disappointed. She had hoped for something clearer. Conflict – of course there would be conflict.

Old Fung turned to his book and picked it up, beginning to read:

> "Conflict. You are sincere
> And are being obstructed . . ."

"Yes," she said, impatient now. "Go now, Fung. I need to think."

The old man bowed and backed away, knowing his Mistress's moods, not even bothering to gather up his things.

Lightning, she thought, gathering up the stalks and letting them fall on to the table once again; *from the sky into the sea. Yes, I shall be like the lightning falling on them.*

And her son? What would happen to Han if she did as she proposed?

Better, perhaps, to ask what would happen if I did nothing; if he had to live out his life in the shadow of my bitterness.

Maybe . . . yet it stayed her hand. It had *always* stayed her hand. But no longer. If she could not get satisfaction from Li Yuan, she would go to Tsu Ma and tell him direct.

Han was his son. *His*. She would prove it before the world.

She shivered – indignation singing in her blood – then swept her arm across the table, clearing it.

Conflict . . . she would give them conflict. Whether they wanted it or no.

CHAPTER · 6

THE WHITE T'ANG

Pei K'ung looked up from the corner desk in which she sat, trying to keep the impatience from her voice.

"Yes, Master Chu, what is it now?"

The old man bowed – more a slight leaning forward than a proper bow, he was so bent already – then placed four gold-bound cases in front of her.

"Ah . . ." Her eyes lit up. "I thought . . ."

"Your husband's permission, it seems, covers everything."

She smiled, then drew the cases toward her, her fingers tracing the embossed shape of the *Ywe Lung*, the Wheel of Dragons.

"Thank you, Chu Shi-ch'e. I am sorry if I was . . . *tetchy* with you earlier. If you would leave me now."

"Mistress."

The old man inclined his body slightly and backed away, but Pei K'ung's attention was already on the tapes. If these showed what she thought they showed . . .

She gathered them up and went across. At the centre of the room was a circular black lacquered platform, some six *ch'i* in width, its surface carved with the symbol of the *Ywe Lung*, the whole thing resting on seven golden dragon heads. Setting the cases down beside it, she went to the window and pulled at the thick silk cord that hung there. At once massive blinds – each slat a full *ch'i* thick – began slowly to descend, shutting out the daylight.

She returned to the platform, then knelt, taking the first of the discs from its case.

"I'm right," she whispered to herself, her hands trembling with anticipation. "I *know* I am . . ."

Leaning across the platform, she placed the disc on to the spindle at the hub, then moved back. Slowly the room's lights faded. A faint glow filled the air above the platform.

"I am Pei K'ung," she said, "Wife of Li Yuan and Empress of Ch'eng Ou Chou."

"Welcome, Mistress," the machine answered, accepting her voice recognition code, its own voice soft, melodious. "What would you like to see?"

"The stables," she said, her heart beating faster. "The royal party, setting out to ride."

"Mistress . . ."

The air shimmered and took shape. As ever, she found herself surprised by the sharpness, the crystalline clarity of the image. It was so real she could almost smell the horses.

She watched, fascinated, her suspicions confirmed. She saw the horses being led from their stalls, their breath pluming in the cold December air; saw Tsu Ma wave the groom aside and help Fei Yen up into the saddle, his hands lingering over-long on her waist. And then that smile – a smile that said it all. Lovers . . . *yes*, they had been lovers.

Closing her eyes, she let out a long sigh. She ought to have felt satisfaction that her guess had been proved right, but all she could think of was Li Yuan: of how hurt he must have felt, how *damaged*.

"Enough!"

The air-show died.

"You wish to see something more, Mistress?"

"No. No, I . . ." She made a gesture of dismissal.

Slowly the lights came up.

So now she knew. Bending down, she picked up the empty casing, studying the date. Like the other three, it came from a four-week period in December 2206 – the month Fei Yen had conceived her son.

Pei K'ung shuddered, wanting to hate the woman for what she had done to her husband – for the suffering she had caused him, and for being so weak, so impulsive a creature – but it was no longer possible. Not after last night.

She sank on to her knees, letting her head fall forward, remembering. So sweet it had been, so deliciously sweet. And his body. *Aiya*, his body . . . Once more she shivered, desire welling up in her, making her place a hand against her breast, gently, tenderly . . . as he had done.

She hadn't known. She simply hadn't known. But now she understood. What had been dark was now light; what had been hidden was now revealed to her. She smiled. Yes . . . so many things had come clear in the night.

It was then, lying there in the dark beside him, listening to his soft breathing, his flesh pressed close and warm against her own, that she had begun to think it through. If it were not Li Yuan's child, then whose was it? Who had had the opportunity? A servant? One of the house musicians, perhaps? A groom? Or had it been someone greater than that? Someone whose very power and nobility had been enough to rob Fei Yen of her senses?

Rising at dawn, she had gone straight to the library and, getting Old Chu from his bed, had consulted the family records for that month. Searching through the Imperial Itinerary for the palace, she had found that on four separate occasions Tsu Ma had visited Tongjiang, each time when Li Yuan was away.

She should have left it there. Should have contented herself with that. But she had had to know for certain.

There was a knock. She turned towards it, frightened, then quickly gathering up the cases, stood.

"Who is it?"

There was a moment's hesitation, then a young male voice answered her. "It is I, Mistress. Tsung Ye . . ."

She felt her heart flutter, her stomach tighten. Calming herself, she set the cases down, then faced the door again.

"Come in!"

The door eased slowly open. The young secretary took a pace into the room then stopped, his head bowed, unable to look at her.

"What is it?" she asked, as if nothing had happened between them.

"You are wanted, Mistress," he said awkwardly. "Your cruiser is prepared. You must leave within the hour."

"Ah . . ." Pei K'ung turned her head, looking at the old clock that hung on the far side of the study above the racks of gold-bound cases, then nodded. She hadn't realised it was so late. "Thank you, Tsung Ye. I shall come and prepare myself at once."

He gave a little bow, beginning to step away, but she called him back. "Tsung Ye . . . close the door."

"Mistress?" His eyes flew up, alarmed.

"You heard me. Then come here. We need to talk."

He swallowed, then turned and closed the door. A moment later he stood before her.

"Listen," she said softly, laying a hand on his arm. "What happened last night – you will keep quiet about it, neh, Tsung Ye?"

He nodded, trembling slightly.

She leaned closer. "It is not that I am ashamed, you understand. Nor that my husband would be angry. Far from it. He has instructed me to find my own . . . *amusement*. But the staff must not know. You understand, Tsung Ye? My husband must be Master in his own house. No man must have cause to mock him. We must be . . . *discreet*."

"Discreet?" He looked at her directly, his alarm quite open now.

She squeezed his arm and smiled. "Hush now, Tsung Ye. No harm will come to you. Besides, it was good, neh? You were . . ." she leaned close and gently kissed his neck, "very sweet."

He stared at her, direct, eye to eye for a moment, then looked down. "I will do whatever you ask, Mistress."

"Good." She let her hand rest on his shoulder, then trace the shape of his arm, finally lacing her fingers in his own. "And Tsung Ye . . . you are not obliged to love me. Only to make me happy. and if you make me happy . . . well, a talented young man can go far, neh? Very far indeed."

* * *

There was a banner over the gate, the Mandarin characters burning white on the jet-black background. Karr halted, ignoring his escorts, looking up at it, translating it in his head.

If only there is persistence, even an iron pillar will be ground into a needle.

Karr studied it a moment longer, then shrugged. Was it meant as a statement of intent? A rallying cry? Or had it been left there from another occasion?

The last was unlikely. Everything he had seen had been put there for him to see. He was a witness, after all. What he saw would be taken back and spoken of. And not to casual ears, but to the ears of a T'ang.

He nodded to himself. To be honest he had been surprised by the opulence, the industry of these stacks. Much had changed in the past two years. Lehmann had come a long way since he had last been down here.

As the doors swung back, Karr had a glimpse of a huge crowd of people – uniformed, drawn up in massed ranks – and felt a moment's misgiving. What if it were Lehmann's purpose to humiliate him? And, through him, to send a message to Li Yuan?

Then why any of this? Why such display if the only reason for the meeting were to kill the T'ang's representative?

Because, came the answer, *he might want to send a message to his own people too*.

He straightened up, dispelling his fears, then stepped through, beneath the gate that led into the very heart of the White T'ang's territory, looking about him with a cold disdain, knowing how impressive a sight he – a single man – made in their eyes.

He strode slowly between the massed ranks, conscious of them watching him. Once he had been a "Blood" in these levels. Once he had fought the Master, Hwa, to the death, becoming champion. *Against the odds*, he thought, remembering how the Marshal had come and asked him if he would serve the T'ang.

Facing him, at the far end of the Main, stood three men. Tall, leprous figures, the central one dressed from head to toe in white, the colour of death.

He smiled inwardly, recognising them from the last time he was here. The one in white was Li Min, the "Brave Carp", otherwise known as Stefan Lehmann. Either side of him were his henchmen – *Niu T'ou* and *Ma Mien*, as Karr secretly called them, Ox-head and Horse-face, the Lieutenants of Hell – real names Soucek and Visak.

Twenty *ch'i* from them he stopped, lifting a hand in greeting. "*Ch'un tzu* . . ."

Lehmann studied him a while, then stepped forward. "It's been a long time, Colonel Karr. I hear you've been promoted. *Ssu-li Hsiao-wei* . . . that's a rare honour for a *Hung Mao*."

Karr blinked, astonished. Only a handful of people knew of his appointment. Why, he hadn't even told his adjutant!

"And Marie . . . is she well?" Lehmann came closer, until he stood an arm's length from him, looking up into his face, an arrogance to his stance emphasising that the difference in their size meant nothing to him.

His stomach muscles had tightened at the mention of his wife. "Marie is well."

"That's good. And young May . . . it will be good for her to have a sister."

Karr stared at the albino, then answered him quietly. "I'm afraid you are mistaken, Li Min. There is only May."

"Ah . . ." Lehmann nodded, as if accepting the correction, yet there had been something about his assurance when he'd said it that was disturbing.

"Anyway, enough small talk," Lehmann said, raising his voice, so all could hear. "You did not come here to discuss your family's health, neh, Colonel Karr? You come as an envoy, to try and make a peace between Above and Below, to bridge the great gap that exists between the heights and depths of our great City."

He leaned close, lowering his voice to a whisper. "Forgive the bullshit. We, at least, know why you are here."

Then, raising his voice again. "But come, let us go through. There is much to be discussed."

* * *

The approach to Lehmann's offices were like a rat-run. Walking through the narrow corridors, Karr noticed the false walls and sliding panels and knew it could all be changed in an instant, like an ever-shifting maze. Cameras were everywhere, and laser-weaponry. The best, he realised: NorTek stuff, as good as anything Bremen had.

At the very centre of it all was a single, spartanly-furnished room. Karr followed Lehmann in, impressed despite himself, then stopped, staring at the painting on the wall behind Lehmann's desk.

"You like it?" Lehmann asked, noting the direction of his gaze.

Karr nodded. "I've never seen the like. Who is the artist? Heydemeier?"

Lehmann turned in his seat, studying the painting, taking in the elongated figure of the man, the naked body turned and crouching, the face staring back out of the canvas.

"No," he answered, looking back at Karr. "The painter is long dead. Egon Schiele was his name. An extraordinary man."

Karr moved closer, noting the word that was boxed in at the bottom right corner of the canvas. "Kampfer. Is that the model's name?"

Lehmann shook his head. "Kampfer's an old German word, from before the City. It means 'fighter'."

"Ah . . ." Karr nodded again. "I should have known. He looks a fighter."

Lehmann gestured to the empty chair. "You want to sit down?"

Karr stiffened slightly. "No. I'd prefer to stand. What I have to say won't take long."

"As you wish." Lehmann sat back a little. "So . . . What does your Master want?"

"Peace. An understanding. And some token of your . . . loyalty."

"My *loyalty*?" Lehmann considered that, then nodded. "And in return?"

"Li Yuan will promise to keep his armies in Africa and not bring them home."

"I see." Lehmann spread his hands on the table, the pale fingers like stilettos. "And when does the great T'ang want my answer?"

"A week from now."

Lehmann nodded, then, changing the subject, leaned towards Karr. "You killed him, didn't you?"

"Who?"

"DeVore. And Berdichev, too. I've seen the tape."

Karr stared at Lehmann, astonished once again. *No one* had access to that tape. No one but Li Yuan. So either he was lying, or . . .

"You're good," Lehmann said, his pink eyes filled with respect. "They say Tolonen's a fool, but he knew what you were, neh? A killer. A natural-born killer. In that we're alike, neh, Gregor Karr? *Very* alike."

* * *

Visak escorted Karr back to the gate. There they blindfolded him again and pushed him toward the waiting sedan. Yet even as he climbed between the curtains, he felt something being pushed into his left hand – felt someone close his fingers over it. He held it tightly, recognising from its shape and texture what it was. A message. Someone had passed a message on to him.

He sat there, silent, as the sedan swayed towards its destination, conscious of the two guards watching him from the seats facing him. He could smell them, hear their breathing. After a while he let himself relax, relieved now it was over and lulled by the movement of the carriage. Even so, he was worried. Lehmann had known far too much. Moreover, he had been too relaxed, too blasé about the whole thing. Why, even Li Yuan's request for some token of loyalty had barely brought a flicker of reaction.

Things were wrong. Things were badly wrong.

They left him at the pick-up point just below the City's roof. Pulling off the blindfold, he opened his hand and, unfolding the paper, read the brief note.

It was from Visak. He wanted a meeting, tomorrow, at noon. Karr nodded. It was just as they'd thought – as their sources inside Lehmann's organisation had told them – things were not as rosy as they seemed. If Visak wanted a meeting . . .

He folded the note and pocketed it. Then, knowing that time was of the essence, he reached up and pulled down the trap-door, reaching for the ladder, hauling himself up into the access tunnel.

On the roof his cruiser waited.

* * *

Two hours later he was at Baku Spaceport, transferring to one of Tsu Ma's own cruisers for the twenty-minute flight north along the shore of the Caspian.

Karr sat to the right of the craft, directly behind the pilot, staring out of the cockpit window towards Asia, a sense of deep foreboding growing in him. The more he thought about it, the more convinced he was that Lehmann had spies within Li Yuan's household. And maybe more than spies. Maybe trained assassins, waiting to be triggered.

The next few days would be critical; he understood that now. Reading the secret briefing Rheinhardt had had prepared, he had realised just how near the brink they were. One thing – one single, crucial incident – could throw them into war, and having seen what had happened on Mars and in North America, that was the last thing any of them wanted.

Yes, and yet war is coming . . .

Best then, perhaps, to do as Li Yuan proposed and bring the armies home from

Africa, whatever answer Lehmann gave them. Better break their word of honour than let the world slip into darkness.

He closed his eyes, feeling giddy. *Marie . . . My darling May . . .* It pained him to think what might happen to them. Yes, but they were better off in Tongjiang than Europe, that was certain.

He sighed heavily, opening his eyes again. Down below the perimeter of Tsu Ma's estate came into view. There was a brief exchange of codes – the high-pitched chatter of computer language – and then silence.

The final days, he thought, remembering the man's pale hands spread on the table like demonic spiders. *These are the final days . . .*

They circled the palace then descended on to a crowded over-spill pad to the north-east of the main palace buildings. Rheinhardt greeted him as he stepped down from the cruiser.

"Come," he said, hurrying him along the path towards the palace. "The ceremony has already begun, but Li Yuan wants to see you at once." He stopped, looking at Karr closely. "Is it good news or bad?"

Karr let the General read the doubt in his eyes and saw the shadow of it reflected back at him. They walked on, silent now, each lost in their own thoughts, brooding on the war to come.

* * *

Li Yuan was waiting for them in one of the small halls in the Eastern Palace, a place of shadows and dampness, bare stone and high, echoing ceilings. Tolonen was with him and his Chancellor, Nan Ho. They watched Karr cross the floor to them, their faces apprehensive.

"Well?" Li Yuan asked as Karr rose from his knees.

"He says he will give his answer within the week."

"Ah . . ."

Quickly he told them what had happened, leaving nothing out, not even the wording on the banner over the gate. When he had finished there was a long silence. Li Yuan turned away, pacing between the looming pillars, the hem of his silks whispering on the stone flags.

Finally, he looked to Tolonen. "Do you still think you are right, Knut? Even after what you've heard?"

Tolonen pushed out his chin, uncomfortable at being put on the spot. "I still think we should wait, *Chieh Hsia*. Let's hear his answer before we act. Things look bad, I admit. His arrogance . . ." The old man shook his head. "You should have crushed him when you could. Now . . ."

"You think it is too late?"

Tolonen looked down.

"And you, Master Nan?"

Nan Ho lowered his head. "Nothing I have heard changes my mind, *Chieh Hsia*. We must crush the man. The only question is when."

"And you, Colonel?"

Karr stared back at his T'ang a moment, surprised to be asked his opinion.

Recollecting himself, he bowed his head, averting his eyes.

"I . . . I was not sure before today, *Chieh Hsia*. I thought we could avoid war. Now I know that it is a certainty. Li Min prepares for it. Our delay is to his advantage. And I sense something more. I sense some deeper game of his. He is like DeVore, that one. Shifting, elusive."

Li Yuan waited, then, when Karr said no more, nodded. "Thank you, Colonel. Your first duty as *Ssu-li Hsiao-wei* will be to investigate the possibility that Lehmann has infiltrated our palace at Tongjiang. Until that is completed, we shall stay here with our cousin, Tsu Ma. I shall send for your wife and daughter, if that eases your mind. If there's to be any nastiness, it would be best if they were not there to see it, neh?"

Karr bowed low, grateful for his T'ang's concern.

"Then go at once. The sooner done, the . . ."

Li Yuan stopped, staring past Karr towards the doorway. Karr turned. It was Tsu Ma's secretary, Chiang K'o.

"Forgive me, *Chieh Hsia*," Chiang said, kneeling and bowing his head, "but news has come from Europe. It appears that the Ebert Mansion has been attacked."

Tolonen stepped forward. "Attacked? How do you mean *attacked*? Is anyone hurt?"

Chiang looked to the Marshal. "The report mentions six dead and several injured."

"*Aiya!*" The old man looked to the ceiling, his face deeply pained. "Jelka and the boy . . . are they . . . ?"

"Your daughter was away when the attack happened. The boy . . ." Chiang swallowed and looked down. "I am afraid the boy was taken."

Tolonen shuddered.

Li Yuan stepped to him and held his arm. "You must go, Knut. At once. I shall explain things to Tsu Ma. Take Karr. And Knut?"

"*Chieh Hsia*?"

"Do whatever you need to. But get him back, neh?"

* * *

Karr watched the old man walk from room to room, disturbed by the vulnerability, the unexpected frailty he glimpsed in that normally rock-hard face. He had always considered Tolonen a cold, heartless man, but watching him crouch over the shrouded body of a female servant, seeing him lift the white sheet and wince, real hurt, real pain in his eyes, made Karr re-evaluate all he knew about him. This had hit him hard. Had shaken him to the core.

Tolonen straightened up, scratching at his neck with the fingers of his flesh and blood hand, then looked across at Karr.

"Where's he gone, Gregor? Where have they taken him?"

Karr shrugged. "We'll know soon. They're obtaining back-up camera material right now. If any exists, that is . . ."

"But Lo Chang . . ." Tolonen shook his head. "I can't believe Lo Chang was involved in this!"

It's always those we least expect, Karr thought, but aloud he said. "We don't know that yet, Marshal. They may have taken him, too . . . to have someone there the boy knows. They do that sometimes."

But Tolonen was shaking his head. "The Lo I knew would have died before he let them take the boy. He would have fought to the death."

Yes, but he didn't – so either he was involved, or . . .

"Did Steward Lo have any family?"

Tolonen nodded distractedly, then saw what Karr was saying. "I've the details in my study."

Karr followed him through, then waited while the Marshal accessed his records.

"Here," Tolonen said, turning the screen towards him.

Karr looked at it, then unclipped his communicator. "It's Colonel Karr. Get me Central Security . . ."

He gave them the details, then looked back at the Marshal.

"They'll let me know as soon as they've checked it out. It'll take them ten minutes maximum."

Tolonen looked away, sniffing deeply, clearly struggling to maintain his composure.

"We'll find him," Karr said. "We'll get him back."

Tolonen nodded, but he seemed unconvinced.

Karr hesitated. "Forgive me, Marshal, but we need to put someone in charge of this investigation. How about Colonel Haavikko?"

The mention of Haavikko's name seemed to bring the Marshal back to himself. "Yes . . . Good man, Haavikko. If anyone can do the job . . ." Tolonen offered Karr a smile that was closer to a grimace. "Saved my life once." He held up his golden arm. "That's when I lost this . . ."

Karr nodded, but he was thinking of what the duty captain had said when they'd first arrived. There had been no sign of a forced entry and no alarm had been sent. Which meant that whoever had done this had either been known to the guards at the gate, or . . .

No. Now that *was* being paranoid.

Tolonen was staring at him. "What is it, Gregor?"

"Security. The men who did this . . . they were Security. An élite squad. They'd have had proper passes, a reason to be here. They'd have known the lay-out and known how to erase all the security camera tapes."

"No." Tolonen shook his head, but his eyes said yes. After all, who else could have got in so easily? Who but one of the T'ang's own élite teams? His *Shen T'se* . . .

Karr shuddered, then unclipped his communicator and spoke into it once more.

"Central Security? Karr here. Look, were any of the *Shen T'se* teams out this morning? . . . Two of them, huh? And have they reported in?"

He waited, meeting Tolonen's eyes, both men quite certain now.

"No sign of it, huh? I see. Look, send me full details. Faces, files, psych profiles, the lot. To the Ebert Mansion . . . That's right. Use Marshal Tolonen's code."

He closed the circuit.

"So," Tolonen said quietly. "All we need to know now is who they're working for, where they've taken him, and what they want."

"Haavikko . . ." Karr said, feeling useless suddenly. "Let me contact Haavik-ko."

Tolonen laughed gruffly. "We have to keep busy at times like these, neh, Gregor? It doesn't pay to think too much."

Karr stared back at the old man a moment, feeling a new respect for him, then nodded and made the call.

*   *   *

Jelka arrived back twenty minutes later. In the interim news had come that Lo Chang's family were gone. They had left home the previous evening and had vanished without a trace. Tolonen had taken the news badly, but the sight of his daughter at the door, safe but bewildered, brought a broad grin to his face. he went to her, hugging her tightly, almost lifting her off her feet.

"Jelka, my darling. Thank the gods you're safe! For a moment I thought . . ." He kissed her face and held her tight again. Then, as if remembering, he held her at arm's length from him.

"You've heard?"

She nodded.

Slowly his face collapsed. There was a sudden tremor in his voice. "If he's dead . . ."

She held him to her, patting his shoulder, comforting him. "He's not dead. Not our Pauli. We'll find him. You know we will."

She looked past her father at Karr, who looked down, embarrassed yet also moved by this show of emotion.

"Where were you?" Tolonen asked after a moment.

"I went to see a friend," she said, her eyes concerned for him. "They must have seen me leave. I couldn't have been gone more than five minutes. If I'd been here . . ." She swallowed and looked down guiltily. "I would never have let them in. Not without contacting you first."

"I know," the old man said, caressing his daughter's face.

Karr, however, was staring at her. "You *knew* they were Security?"

She moved away from her father, her blue eyes meeting Karr's clearly. "Who else could it be?"

"*Aiya*," Tolonen said, staring down at the golden fingers of his left hand as if at any moment they might reach up and tear at his throat. "All this betrayal . . ." He groaned. "Who would have thought?"

But Jelka wasn't listening to him. Her eyes had flown open. She turned to face her father again. "Where's Golden Heart?"

Tolonen reached out to her, his granite face distressed, tears beginning to trickle down his cheeks.

"She's dead, my love. They broke her neck. So Pauli . . . Pauli's ours now. Ours alone. So we've got to get him back, neh? We've got to bring him home, where he belongs."

*   *   *

"Kim?"

Kim lifted the bulky glasses from his eyes, then looked up at the screen. "Andrew? What is it?"

"You've a visitor," Curval said, smiling down at him. "Guy name of Neville from Product Development. Says he knows you."

"Sure. I met him a week or so back. What does he want?

"Says he wants to speak to you . . . off the record."

Kim huffed. It would mean going through decontamination again – stripping off one suit and putting on another. For a moment he hesitated, half determined to send Neville away, his tail between his legs. Then he relented.

"Okay. Tell him I'm coming out."

Five minutes later, Kim stepped from the tank and, still dripping, made his way through to the reception area. Neville was seated on the far side, reading one of the Company news sheets. Seeing Kim, he got up quickly and came across.

"Kim, I . . . well, I didn't plan to see you, but I was passing by and I thought . . ." His eyes took in Kim's condition, smelt the powerful cleansing agents. "Oh shit. Look, I'm sorry, I didn't know you were . . ."

Kim laughed. "It's all right. Do you want to come through? I'm afraid I can't spare you long. I'm busy right now. We've begun reassembling the Model B cranium."

Neville's eyes lit up. "Could I see that?"

Kim hesitated, then nodded. "You'll have to suit up, though. The tiniest trace of infection and we're done for."

"I understand. And look, I'm really grateful. I . . ."

He handed Kim something. Kim stared at it. It was odd. Tiny, like a domino, and yet heavy.

"Like a scarab," Kim said, looking up. "What is it?"

Neville smiled. "If I'm right, it's going to be the biggest thing in the entertainments industry for the next hundred years. And before you go showing it to everyone, it's embargoed. Only Director Reiss and I have seen it. Oh, and the creator, of course."

"And now me." Kim span the tape in the air and caught it. "Well, thanks. I'm honoured. Whose work is it?"

"Shepherd's. You know him?"

"I've heard of him. Adviser to Li Yuan, isn't he?"

"That's one of his roles. But this . . ." Neville laughed, his face registering awe. "Well, you'll see for yourself. At least, you'll get an idea of it. The real thing is phenomenal. Totally new. We're having to redesign our entertainments hardware to accommodate it."

"I see." Kim nodded thoughtfully. "Anyway, you'd better come through."

Suited up, they went inside, the air-lock doors hissing shut behind them.

"So what are you trying to do?" Neville asked over the suit mike, a gloved hand pointing clumsily at the exposed brain of the new prototype where it rested in the nutrient tank.

"Right now?" Kim laughed. "Well, right now I'm working on the dopamine and noradrenaline reactions – attempting to extend the time the stuff remains in the synaptic cleft."

"What does that do?"

"Do? Well, it gives the brain a 'high' for a start. Combined with other things – with certain pheremonal responses, for instance – it can trigger a response of . . . well, of love. Of infatuation and desire."

"You're joking!"

Kim glanced at him. "Not at all. In fact I've never been so serious about anything. It's where we went wrong before. We tried to tailor its emotional range to fit our criteria of usefulness – criteria which stressed the machine-like, rationalistic aspects of the human mind. In the process we made it . . . well, effectively we made it mad. Balance, that's what all this is about. Giving our creations balance."

"But *love*, Kim! What if it develops a crush or something? What use would it be then? Surely the whole idea of developing an android is to create something quite different from us – something free of human emotional weaknesses."

"*Is* it?" Kim stared at Neville openly now, a faint amusement in his eyes. "That's what's always been assumed. But what if that's wrong? What if we *need* to put that full range of emotions in? What if it only works if they're all in there? After all, they've served us humans pretty well over the eons."

"So how *will* your new model be different?"

"It'll be quicker, sharper, *smarter* than the old model."

"Like you, you mean?"

Kim laughed. "Like me." Then, with a nod, he turned back, pulling the bulky glasses down over his eyes.

Neville watched him, fascinated, seeing how he "fine-tuned" the brain, stimulating it with a delicate-looking wire, injecting it with various chemicals then checking one of the four screens beside the tank to see what kind of reaction he was getting. On each of the screens outline skulls – normally a regular patchwork of blues and greens – lit up with areas of pulsing yellow and brilliant red. Finally, Kim put the fine-wire down and, lifting his glasses, smiled at Neville.

"Okay. I think I'll leave it at that."

Neville nodded towards the screens. "It's certainly colourful."

"Isn't it? It's an old system, but still the most effective for this kind of work. You can see what's happening at a glance." Kim lifted the headset off and placed it on the side, then turned, facing Neville. "Curval said you wanted to talk . . . informally."

Neville waved a hand. "It's nothing sinister. I just thought it might help you if you had another view on things before you made your mind up about the new deal."

"But you're the one who drew up the contract!"

Neville smiled. "So? That doesn't mean I can't detach myself from things. I mean, I've not got SimFic tattooed on my bollocks!"

Kim laughed. "I'll take your word for it. But let me ask *you* something first."

"Fire away."

"What's Reiss like? You work for him. What's he *really* like?"

Neville hesitated a moment. "Difficult. I guess that's the best word to describe him. Fucking difficult at times, forgive my Mandarin. But he listens. And he's capable of changing his mind. He doesn't tolerate fools, though, nor losers. And he likes new ideas. Thrives on them, in fact. That's why he likes you so much."

"And you?"

Neville smiled. "Me? I don't know you."

Kim returned his smile, pleased by his honesty. "Let's get these suits off, then go through to my office and talk."

* * *

Neville sat in the chair in the corner, a bowl of *ch'a* cupped in his right hand, listening.

Kim sat on the edge of his desk, facing him. He had been telling Neville about what had happened in America with Old Man Lever and his consortium.

"I failed once," Kim said, finishing his tale. "I don't want to fail again. Next time . . . well, if it were just myself . . ."

Neville nodded. "I understand. A man needs a family, neh? And you want security for them, right?"

Kim laughed. "Right. But it's not just that. I'm not even talking about myself, really. It's . . . well, it's what I want to *do* with my talent. I've been given it for some reason – and I want to find out why. Oh, and before you ask, I have glimpses of it, but . . ."

"You're talking theoretical science, right?"

Kim nodded.

"That's fine. We've been anticipating it."

Kim stared at him. "*Anticipating* it?"

"Sure." Neville drained his *ch'a* and set the cup down, then leaned toward Kim. "Look, my job is evaluating risks. Big risks and little risks. With a Company the size of SimFic even the little risks could involve the investment of billions of *yuan*. Right now, however, my biggest risk is you. When we talk in that two-page document I gave you of funding you, we mean *funding* – whatever it takes, and however long it takes. It may cost us very little. Then again it might mean tying up a vast amount of SimFic's capital. And if you died . . . well, we'd have *nothing*. On the other hand, if one of our competitors got you . . ."

Kim stared at him. "Let me get this clear. You're talking about unlimited funding, right? Guaranteed?"

Neville nodded. "Fully documented. And guaranteed by Li Yuan."

Kim raised an eyebrow, surprised. "What is the connection? I mean, aside from the fact that SimFic are helping him build the android."

Neville sat back again. "I'll tell you. But it's to go no further than this room, right?"

Kim nodded.

"Good. Then it's like this. Since the GenSyn Inheritance Hearing six years back Li Yuan has been busy steering projects away from GenSyn to various other major

Companies, SimFic among them. This was done initially to try to make GenSyn less vulnerable while it was under Tolonen's stewardship, but it proved to have a number of other advantages. What it's done, in effect, is to tie in the fortunes of six of the major Companies with those of the T'ang. Now, as far as SimFic is concerned, we've risen considerably these past few years, but we want to build on that – to make ourselves Number One, not only in commercial terms, but in terms of being the trend-setters, the innovators. It's a policy Li Yuan himself has endorsed."

"I see." He had had no idea this was going on.

Neville smiled. "There's one great weakness to this Corporate strategy, however. And that's you, Kim. In the past seven years we've become more and more dependent on you as a generator of ideas, of new patents and new directions." He laughed suddenly. "Look, I know it must seem a poor bargaining ploy, letting you know just how important you are to us but . . . well, what's the point trying to disguise the fact? You know as well as I what you're worth. No. There's only one question we at SimFic have to answer, and that's got nothing to do with money. It's whether we can provide you with the resources to pursue whatever it is you want to do."

"But what if nothing comes of it?"

"Then nothing comes of it. It's not as if we'll be sitting on our hands. Why, it'll take us the best part of a decade to develop some of the stuff you've already given us. And as I said, it would mean our competitors didn't have you."

"So when do I sign?"

"Look, I'm not trying to pressurise you."

"No. I'm serious. If that's the deal, I'll take it."

Neville smiled. "Well . . ."

There was a knock. Kim stood. "Excuse me a moment."

It was Curval. "Sorry, Kim, but I didn't know if you knew. A package came for you about an hour back. It's in reception. And this." He handed Kim the bright red envelope. "It's Tolonen's hand, isn't it?"

Kim nodded, staring at the envelope suspiciously. The last time he had had a note from the old Marshal it had been to warn him to stay away from his daughter. He turned, looking to Neville. "Forgive me, Jack. Something's come up."

He stepped outside and closed the door, then slit the envelope open with his nail.

"What is it?" Curval asked. "Is the old bastard still playing his stupid games?"

"No." He handed Curval the card. "You said there was a package. Did it come with the card?"

Curval made a noise of surprise, then handed it back. "That's right. The guard said a young woman delivered them. Tall, long ash-blonde hair. Sound like anyone you know?"

"I . . ." Kim hesitated, then touched Curval's arm. "Look, take care of Neville a while, will you? I won't be long."

He walked through to the reception area, trying to keep calm, but feeling all the while that he wanted to run, to whoop and punch the air. It had come. After all these years she had finally made contact again.

He shivered, thinking of her; of the startling blue of her eyes, and of her smile. *She was here*, he thought, wondering what she had left him. *She actually came here.*

The guard rose from his chair behind the desk as Kim approached. *"Shih* Ward . . ." He reached down and removed something from one of the drawers, then placed it on the desk in front of Kim. "If you'd sign . . ."

"Of course." But Kim's palms were wet and his fingers were trembling. Steadying himself, he took the stylus and made his mark against the screen, then lifted the package.

It was a simple rectangular box, like a standard tray of samples, wrapped in dark-green ersilk paper. Kim shook it gently, hearing a faint rattle from within, and frowned. The guard was watching him.

"The young woman who brought this. Did she say anything?"

"Sir?"

Kim waved a hand. "It doesn't matter." Then, making his way across to one of the interview rooms, he closed the door behind him.

He took a long, calming breath, then slit the seal on the side of the box with his nail, pulled the paper back and slid out the box.

Tapes . . . the box held a dozen tiny tapes. He lifted one from its indented slot and studied the hand-written label.

Enceladus, Tethys, Dione and Rhea.

He understood at once. She had recorded it all. All of her travels out there in the System, knowing his fascination with it; knowing he'd want to see.

He slotted it back, then picked out another, then another, nodding to himself. It was all here. Everything she'd seen. Everything she'd done. He shivered. She had waited. She had kept her promise. That was what this meant.

He leaned past the box and tapped out an activation code on the desk comset. There was a second or two's delay and then the screen lifted up out of the surface.

"Get me the Ebert Mansion," he said as a young Han male's face appeared on the screen. "It's Kim Ward from SimFic. I wish to speak . . ."

"I'm sorry, *Shih* Ward," the operator interrupted, "but I cannot take calls for that destination at present. If you would call later . . ."

"Look, this is important. Extremely important. I . . ."

The young Han's face shimmered then disappeared, replaced by the face of a high-ranking Security officer in his early forties, his blonde hair cut stubble-neat, his eyes as blue as sapphires.

"Shih Ward? I understand you've been trying to get through to the Ebert Mansion urgently. I'm Colonel Haavikko, in charge of the investigation. Have you any information with regard to the whereabouts of the boy?"

"The boy?" Kim frowned, confused. "I'm sorry, I don't follow you, Colonel. I wished only to talk to *Nu Shi* Tolonen. I . . ." He stopped, what Haavikko had said hitting him suddenly. "What's happened?"

Haavikko smiled tightly. "You have no information, I assume . . ."

"No. No, but look . . ."

"I'm sorry, *Shih* Ward, but time really is tight right now."

"Jelka . . . is Jelka all right?"

Haavikko had leaned towards the screen to cut connection. Now he sat back again, a weariness in his face. "The Marshal's daughter is fine, *Shih* Ward. Now, please. There's a great deal to be done."

"Of course. And thank you . . ."

The screen went dead. Kim straightened, realising how tense he'd been, then let a long, shuddering sigh escape him. For a moment he'd thought . . .

He sat, staring at the box of tapes. The boy. Someone must have taken the boy, Pauli.

"Machine?" he said, addressing the camera overhead. "What's happening?"

* * *

Lehmann studied the boy through the glass, then turned to his lieutenant, touching his arm.

"You did well, Jiri. But your man . . ."

"He's dead already."

"Good. Can't have any loose ends, can we?"

Soucek nodded, then. "So what now? Do we tell the old man we've got him?"

"No. We let Tolonen sweat a while. Two days, maybe three. Then we give him back."

Soucek stared at him uncomprehendingly.

"Trust me, Jiri. I know how to play this. Now go. There's a lot to be done."

When Soucek was gone, he turned back, watching the boy again. Pauli was sitting in the corner once again, head down, his dark hair fallen over his eyes as he chewed the knuckles of his right hand.

That morning's audience with Karr had gone well. The big man had bought the whole package, lock, stock and barrel. All that stuff about having seen the tape of Berdichev's death – that was a lie; an audacious guess, based on what he knew of Li Yuan's father. *And an accurate guess too*, he thought, remembering the shock in Karr's face. The rest . . . well, it had been easy to buy Karr's wife's surgeon. *Yes, and a cheap purchase too, considering*.

It could not have been better timed. With Karr already on his way, word had come that Karr's wife was pregnant – news even Karr himself had not known.

Lehmann turned from the one-way glass. Information . . . it was sometimes more deadly than armies, as the great Sun Tzu had known.

Yes, he had planted the seed of paranoia deep. That single truth – gained cheaply – would confirm the veracity of the rest. As Colonel of Internal Security, Karr would embark on a witch-hunt at Tongjiang.

Disruption – maximum disruption, that was his aim. To wrong-foot them and feed them with a stream of misinformation. To play upon their weakest points and milk them. Karr he had touched, and Tolonen. Rheinhardt and Nan Ho would follow. And then Li Yuan himself. One by one he would make them uncertain of themselves.

Yes, for war was not a simple thing of armies and battles: it was a state of mind, a psychological regime. War was not won with bullets and bombs, but with the raw materials of fear, uncertainty and self-doubt.

He laughed – a cold, clear laugh – then left the room, keen to get on with things. Why, before he was finished with them, he would make them look before they shat!

* * *

The ceremonies had begun before the dawn, as fourth bell sounded across the palace grounds. At that dark hour Prince Tsu Kung-chih, eldest nephew of Tsu Ma, had stepped from the gate of the Northern Palace, dressed in the gown of the Imperial Commissioner, the *chieh* – a beribboned staff that symbolised imperial authority – held out before him. Two torch-bearers lit his way, while behind him came a great procession of courtiers and servants, bearing the betrothal presents on raised platforms, as well as the Golden Scroll and Seal and the *feng yu* – the great bridal chair. They made their way across the gardens at the centre of the four palaces, then stopped before the gate to the Southern Palace where, on a crimson cushion, Liang K'o Ting, father of the Empress, knelt, awaiting them, as if at the door of his own house.

Once, in ancient times, there had been three great ceremonies of presentation, separated by long weeks of preparation. Now there was only this single, simple ritual. Even so, the servants standing three deep at the windows surrounding the gardens, watched wide-eyed, conscious of the great chain that linked them to the ancient past of their kind.

At the same moment, in a private ceremony in the *T'ai Miao*, the Supreme Hall of Ancestors, Tsu Ma was solemnly reporting the news of his betrothal to the august spirits of his ancestors, their holograms burning brightly as he knelt before them, his forehead pressed to the cold stone flags.

Twelve hours later, Liang K'o Ting, dressed in his new uniform as officer of the imperial bodyguard, stepped from the gate of the Southern Palace, heading north across the gardens. Behind him was a procession no less great than that which had set out earlier. This time, however, the *feng yu* was occupied, Tsu Ma's bride, Liang Shu-sun, hidden within, twenty-two bearers moving slowly, solemnly as the drums sounded the "Central Harmony". Fifty servants carried gifts on litters, while a further hundred bore large lanterns and "dragon-phoenix" flags. In the midst of all a dozen men carried two yellow pavilions, holding the Golden Seal and the Golden Scroll, symbols of Shu-sun's authority as Empress, while directly behind the great Phoenix Chair walked the servants and ministers of her household.

At the gate to the Northern Palace, Tsu Kung-ch'ih stood motionless, the *chieh* held out before him, waiting to receive his uncle's bride. Behind him, in the Great Hall at the centre of the palace, Tsu Ma sat on the dragon throne in the full glory of his imperial yellow silks, the nine dragons – eight shown and one hidden – decorating the gown.

As he reached the gate, Liang K'o Ting stood to one side, his head bowed, letting the imperial commissioner, Prince Kung-ch'ih lead the procession into the Northern Palace, relinquishing his daughter into his care. Inside, surrounding the dragon throne, stood the four hundred members of the *Nei T'ing*, the Inner Court, as well as those invited guests, numbering some fifteen hundred in all. The procession moved between them, then stopped, the great Phoenix Chair being set down below the steps of the dragon throne.

Two bells sounded, one high, one low. The final ceremony began. Tsu Ma stood, then came down the steps, halting before the *feng yu* as eight shaven-headed New Confucian officials, dressed in crimson robes, lifted the red silk curtain that covered the litter, drawing it back over the top.

Within, Shu-sun sat in the Chair, dressed from head to toe in red, the traditional *kai t'ou* covering her face. At a signal from the Chief official, Tsu Ma stepped forward and delicately lifted the veil over her head.

Shu-sun's smile was radiant. Taking her hands, Tsu Ma helped her step down, her smile disarming him, making him feel at that moment like the most gauche of schoolboys. As the chants began he stood there, facing her, disturbed by the fact that at this, one of the most public moments of his life, he was sporting the most enormous erection. As if she knew, Shu-sun's smile broadened, her eyes widening in invitation.

Tonight, he thought, surprised by the strength of his feelings. After all, he scarcely knew her. He had thought himself jaded, emotionally spent, but the simple sight of her inflamed him. Why, the last time he had felt this way had been for Fei Yen.

His sad smile was noted by her and she raised an eyebrow querying it. So strange it was, for it suggested an intimacy that did not yet exist between them, and yet . . . well, it was as if he knew her from way back – from another cycle of existence.

He watched, unconscious of the words of the ritual, aware only of her face, her eyes, the light dancing in the darkness of her pupils.

The ceremony was halfway through when sirens began to sound beyond the doors. Tsu Ma turned, looking to his Colonel of Internal Security, Yi Ching and nodded. Yi bowed and turned, running off to discover what was happening.

Heads turned, eyes looked apprehensive, yet no one broke the silent solemnity of the moment. The chants went on, the ritual continued, while outside, echoing menacingly across the empty gardens of the palace, the sirens rose and fell.

* * *

Yi Ching rushed into the busy control room, taking control. Voices in his head had apprised him of the situation, yet he spent a moment or two studying the screens, checking for himself before he acted.

The ship was fifty *li* out, over the Caspian, coming in fast from the east. Twice they had challenged it for a visual ID and twice it had ignored them. Now they had only two options – to shoot it down or let it land.

He turned to the Duty Captain. "Captain Munk . . . you're certain about the CGRP?"

"It's a Minor Family format, sir, but unspecific."

"Shit!"

No one would blame him for shooting it out of the air, but what if *was* one of the Minor Family princes? After all, it wouldn't be the first time a cruiser's Computer-Generated Recognition Pattern had failed or been wrongly-set. Yes, and things

were very sensitive right now. To shoot a prince out of the air without warning
would cause a terrible stink, no matter what justification there was for it.

Colonel Yi gave a grown of annoyance then banged the console hard with both
fists. Now was no time to prevaricate. It would be here in less than five minutes. He
leaned forward, barking instructions into the speaker.

"I want two cruisers in the air – *now*! The incoming's communicator may have
failed, so make visual contact and head it off. If it ignores you again, blast it out of
the sky. No arguments, right? If it complies, take it south. Land it beyond the
perimeter. I'll give further instructions then."

Yi Ching straightened up, voices sounding in the air, giving orders and
confirming instructions, the mood of the room changed instantly, everyone happy
now that something was happening.

He stared at the flickering point on the map screen and shook his head. Who
would be so fucking stupid as to fly into their air-space at such a critical moment?

He had a low opinion of the Minor Family princes – they were, after all, the most
self-centered, arrogant and stupid people on the planet – but this seemed out of
character, even for one of them. At the same time, he simply couldn't believe this
was a serious attack on the palace. There was no way a single cruiser could get
through their defences. It was in the air too long. It made such an easy and obvious
target. Unless . . .

He pressed the stud on his right wrist, putting him in direct contact with his
Lieutenant in the Great Hall.

"Karlgren. Get the T'ang out of there now! Get him into one of the secure rooms
and clear the Hall. I think the incoming is a diversion. Oh, and make sure Li Yuan
and Wei Tseng-li are safe."

Yi Ching looked about him, seeing the startled expressions on the faces of the
nearby men, but there was no time to explain.

"Captain Munk. Take over here. Make sure my instructions are carried out to
the letter."

"Sir!"

Yes, he thought, running from the room, heading back to the Northern Palace,
and let's hope to the gods I'm wrong!

* * *

The sirens had stopped. In the central garden the crowd milled restlessly, the
murmur of their voices filling the space between the walls of the ancient palaces.
From the top of the steps to the Northern Palace, Prince Kung-ch'ih looked on,
the dour expression he had worn all day replaced by a smile of ironic
amusement.

All day he had had to play his uncle's creature, bowing and scraping, acting to
his order, reading from *his* script, greeting *his* bride, but now – through no effort of
his own – he had had the last laugh.

Until he died he would remember the look of anger on his uncle's face, the pure
fire of exasperation – of denied expectation – in his eyes as they hustled him away
and cleared the Hall, the ceremony unfinished, the woman not yet his bride.

And even though it had proved a false alarm, Kung-chih felt it was an omen – a sign that this marriage was ill-fated.

You cheated me, he thought, thinking of that day beside the cliff. *You led me to believe I was your heir, and then you cheated me. But I'll not relinquish it that easily. Oh no. Not if you take a dozen wives.*

Hearing voices behind him he turned, in time to see Colonel Yi and the three T'ang coming out from where they had been closeted these past few minutes. Yi Ching backed off a pace and bowed, then turned, letting them move past him.

Kung-ch'ih straightened up, facing his uncle squarely as he came towards him.

"Nephew," Tsu Ma said, touching his arm gently. "I am afraid we must deal with this matter at once. If you would lead our guests into the Eastern Palace, I shall have Lao Kang arrange refreshments."

"And the ceremony, Uncle?"

Tsu Ma huffed, clearly upset, but his smile for his nephew was kind. "I am afraid the ceremony must be delayed until tomorrow, Kung-ch'ih. It would be . . . *inauspicious*, to continue now, neh?"

"As you wish, Uncle," Kung-chih answered, bowing his head low, his face expressing grave disappointment, but inside he was exultant.

* * *

The four men stopped outside the cell, the camera swivelling automatically to cover them, its laser-trackers beading all four of them.

"Are they here?" Tsu Ma asked, pulling at the knuckles of his left hand as if he wanted to strike someone.

Yi Ching hesitated, aware of Li Yuan's presence there beside his Master, then nodded. "The crew of the ship are elsewhere, *Chieh Hsia*, in separate cells. It seems they were acting under orders. However, as far as their Mistress is concerned . . ."

"Their *Mistress*?" Tsu Ma stared at his Colonel in disbelief. "You mean some damned *woman* did this? *Aiya!* I'll have the bitch quartered!"

Yi Ching bowed his head, but glanced uneasily at Li Yuan. "Forgive me, *Chieh Hsia*, but I think you might wish to see her alone."

"Nonsense, Colonel Yi. The insult was not to me alone. My cousins deserve an explanation, neh?"

"Of course, *Chieh Hsia*."

Yi turned, motioning to the guards, who took turns to tap their personal codes into the lock then place their eyes against the retinal-scanner.

The cell door hissed open.

Tsu Ma moved past his Colonel into the cell, then stopped dead, giving a gasp of surprise. On the bench seat facing him sat Fei Yen, her hands bound, a tracer-necklet glowing faintly about her neck. He turned, in time to see the flash of astonishment in Li Yuan's eyes as he too saw who it was.

"Fei Yen . . ." he said quietly, his voice incredulous. "What in the gods' names were you up to?"

She stared back at him with dumb insolence, then raised her hands, displaying the restraints.

"Unbind her!" Tsu Ma ordered, then turned to Wei Tseng-li. "Cousin, if you would leave this to us?"

Wei Tseng-li looked from one to the other, not understanding what was going on, then nodded. "As you wish, cousin. If you need me . . ."

"Of course," Tsu Ma said gently, giving him a troubled smile, then turned back, watching as a guard unclipped Fei Yen's wrist-restraints.

As the door slammed shut, he glanced at Li Yuan, then looked up at the overhead camera. "Surveillance off."

At once the red operating light vanished.

He turned, staring directly at Fei Yen, giving full vent to the anger he had been keeping in. "*You*! What the *fuck* do you think you were up to, flying in without proper identification codes? Have you any idea what you've done? *Aiya* . . . I'd like to know why I shouldn't just have you flogged and executed? You and your whole damned family!"

"I had to see you," she said quietly, her face hardened against his accusations. "Today. Before it was too late."

"Too late?" Tsu Ma laughed, exasperated. "Too late for what?"

"For my son . . ."

"Your *son*? What has your son to do with this?"

"Because he's your son too, Tsu Ma."

There was a long silence and then Tsu Ma laughed. But beside him Li Yuan was looking down, his lips pursed.

"No," Tsu Ma said finally, meeting her eyes, a cruel, unforgiving anger there. "I have no sons."

She looked back at him defiantly. "No, Tsu Ma? You can say that with absolute certainty?"

His chest rose and fell. For a moment it seemed he would say nothing, then, with a tiny glance at Li Yuan, he answered her. "I *have* no sons, Fei Yen."

"No?" She turned, pointing at Li Yuan. "Why don't you ask your cousin if that's true?"

Tsu Ma turned, looking at Li Yuan, his eyes pained, knowing that a sudden gulf had opened between them – one that, perhaps, might never be bridged – yet he spoke softly, as if to a brother.

"Is it true, Yuan? Is Han Ch'in my son?"

Li Yuan looked up, a profound sadness in his eyes. In an instant it had all come back to him: all of the hurt he'd felt, all of the bitterness and betrayal. But worse. For now he *knew*. Tsu Ma – his beloved Tsu Ma – had betrayed him.

He shuddered then answered her, his voice toneless. "You are wrong, Fei Yen. It is as Tsu Ma says. He has no sons."

She stared back at him, disbelief in her eyes, then slowly shook her head, her eyes widening, understanding coming to her. "But . . . but you *divorced* me!"

He nodded. "I had to. Don't you understand? You were a weakness I could no longer tolerate. A cancer that was eating away at me. To be a T'ang and be subservient to you . . . it could not be, Fei Yen. It simply could not be."

"*Aiya* . . ." There was pain in her face; pain at the realisation of what had really happened. "Han Ch'in . . . he's yours, isn't he? Yours! And you knew it, didn't you? Knew it all along!"

Li Yuan shook his head. "No, Fei Yen. Han Ch'in is *your* son. Yours alone. You made your bed, now you must lie in it."

She stood, angry now and close to tears. "I shall do no such thing! My son . . ." She swallowed, then lifted her head proudly. "My son shall be a T'ang one day!"

He answered her scathingly, his eyes cold. "Your son is nothing, woman. Understand me? *Nothing!*" He took a step towards her, his very calmness menacing. "It was always the way with you, wasn't it, Fei Yen? You could never be content. You *always* had to meddle. To spoil things and break them. Too much was never enough for you, you always had to have more. More and more and more, like a petulant child. But now . . ." He sighed and shook his head. "Now it must end. You have finally overstepped the mark. You have left me with no option."

Tsu Ma reached out and touched his arm. "But Li Yuan . . ."

Li Yuan turned, looking down at the hand that rested on his arm, his eyes burning with indignation. "Cousin . . . don't you think you've done enough?"

Tsu Ma drew back, bowing his head.

Li Yuan stared at him a moment longer, then turned back, facing his ex-wife.

"As for you, Fei Yen, you shall return to Hei Shui, but this time under guard. You are to speak to no one and see no one. All correspondence between you and the outside world will be strictly censored. And as for your son . . . Your son shall be kept elsewhere, as guarantee of your good behaviour."

She stared at him, then gave a wail of anguish and sank to her knees, pressing her forehead to the floor, her voice distraught.

"*Aiya!* Please the gods, no, Li Yuan. *Please* leave Han Ch'in with me. I've nothing without him. *Nothing!*"

She looked up at him, tearful now, her eyes imploring him. "As you once loved me, please do this for me, Li Yuan. Let my son live with me at Hei Shui. I shall do anything . . . sign anything at all, but let him stay. Please the gods, let him stay!"

He stood there a moment, staring down at her, thinking of the hell she had put him through – of all the bitter blackness he had suffered because of her – and slowly shook his head.

"It is over, Fei Yen. It is finished now. You understand?"

Then, turning from her, he left the cell, Tsu Ma following him out, neither man looking at the other, the screams of the woman following them as they walked, silent, side by side, down the dimly-lit corridor.

CHAPTER·7

WHERE
THE PATH DIVIDES

L i Yuan returned to Tongjiang at once, taking Pei K'ung and all his entourage
with him. There, in the great study that had been his father's and his father's
father's before him, he called together all his senior officials, summoning them
from whatever duties they were attending to. By five they were all gathered and the
Council of War began.

On the journey back he had spoken to no one, not even his Chancellor, Nan Ho,
giving no explanation for his mood or actions. Nor, when he opened the great
meeting of State, did he say a word about what had happened at Astrakhan,
though all there, having heard of the alarm during the wedding ceremony, knew
that something had transpired.

Watching him from the other side of the council table, Master Nan saw the new
hardness in his Master's face and wondered what had passed between him and Tsu
Ma. He had seen him return from the meeting in the cells – had seen the coldness,
the distance between the two great friends – and known at once that something was
wrong. Then, when Li Yuan had ordered them gone from there, he had known
there had been a breach. Nothing else would have made Li Yuan miss his cousin's
wedding celebrations. But what had caused it?

For hours Nan Ho listened as each man spoke, spelling out what stage their
preparations were at, yet he knew for a fact that many there – surprised by the
suddenness of the summons – were far from as advanced as they claimed.
Contingency plans had been drawn up months ago, after the New Year meeting
of Ministers, but no one had seriously expected war. Not *this* year. But now things
had changed.

When they were gone, Master Nan held back, waiting by the door. Normally Li
Yuan would call him back to discuss what had been said, but now he just sat there,
slumped forward in his chair, his fingers steepled beneath his chin, staring into
space.

He closed the door then went across.

"*Chieh Hsia?*"

Li Yuan looked up, his eyes distracted, then sat up straighter.

"Master Nan, I guess you deserve an explanation."

Nan Ho waited, silent, head bowed.

"I . . . I have done something that perhaps I should not have done. I have cast off a wife and denied a rightful son."

Nan Ho looked up, surprised. Li Yuan was looking past him, his face tensed against the strong emotions the words were evoking, but his eyes were misted.

"I acted wrongly, Master Nan. Yet I too was wronged . . . both by my wife and by my most trusted friend."

Nan Ho felt a ripple of shock pass through him. *So it was true.*

"I didn't know," Li Yuan went on. "I didn't really *want* to know, I suppose. Until today." He paused a moment, as if steeling himself against what he was saying, then spoke again. "Today it was all made clear. Today I understood how it was – how it has been all this time."

"*Chieh Hsia* . . ."

"No, Master Nan, let me finish. I should have found out long ago. I should have made it my business to know what really happened. My father said I ought, but my pride was sorely hurt and besides, I . . . I could just about bear it if I *didn't* know. Knowing . . . knowing *exactly* what happened . . . that would have broken me."

"I understand."

He stared at his Master, seeing, for that brief moment, the vulnerable little boy he had once had to tend – the young man he had introduced into the ways of the flesh. Oh, if he had only known what love would do to his charge he would have killed Fei Yen with his own hands long before she got her talons into him. He would have gladly sacrificed himself to prevent it. But now it was too late. Now they must learn to exist in the ruins of these relationships. He sighed, then uttered the words his Master did not wish to hear.

"You must make peace with him, *Chieh Hsia.* You must set aside your feelings as a man and act as a T'ang . . . as an Emperor."

Li Yuan stared at him a moment then shook his head. "It is too late for that, Master Nan. To be a T'ang . . . well, one must know where one stands, neh? One must know who one's friends are and who one's enemies. All I know, right now, is that Tsu Ma is no friend. And if not a friend, then I must count him henceforth as an enemy – as someone I cannot trust to come when I call. I must make my plans dependent upon my own strength and follow my own counsel from here on."

"But *Chieh Hsia* . . ."

Li Yuan raised his hand imperiously, silencing his Chancellor.

"You are a good man, Master Nan, but do not oppose me in this. Be as a friend and aid me. For I have need of friends."

"*Nu-ts'ai, Chieh Hsia,*" he said, sinking to his knees and touching his forehead to the ground. *I am your slave, Majesty.*

* * *

Karr came to him an hour later.

"*Chieh Hsia?*"

"Colonel . . . please, relax a moment. Take a seat. We need to talk."

Karr hesitated, then sat, facing Li Yuan, his huge frame filling the tall-backed official's chair.

"Is there any news of the boy?"

"No, *Chieh Hsia*. I'm fairly certain now that it was one of our own élite teams."

"I see." Li Yuan sat back. "And Marshal Tolonen? How is he taking this?"

Karr sighed. "Badly, *Chieh Hsia*. He . . . Well, forgive me if this sounds impertinent, but I feel he is close to breaking point."

"Should I send one of my surgeons?"

"It would do no good, *Chieh Hsia*. His daughter tried to get him to rest, but he has refused all sedation. Indeed, I saw him take two Stayawake capsules. He is determined to see this through, whatever the personal cost."

Li Yuan nodded, his eyes pained. "Perhaps I should order him to rest."

"Maybe so, *Chieh Hsia*."

"And the other matter . . . your investigations into the household staff. How goes that?"

"Slowly, *Chieh Hsia*. It is difficult to know where to start. I have asked the six most senior members of the palace household to draw up lists of those they would trust implicitly and those they are less certain of."

"And what good will that do?"

"It is my intention to compare the lists and see where they differ – then go back and ask why. At the same time, *Chieh Hsia*, I have set up a team to monitor all contacts between Tongjiang and the outside world. If there is an information leak we shall find it."

"Good. But one further thing before you go. You will have heard that I called a special meeting of my most senior ministers and advisers."

"*Chieh Hsia?*"

"To judge what was said in that meeting, we would be ready to fight a war at a moment's notice. The truth is very different. My own assessment is that we are weeks, possibly even months from a state of readiness. Would that be your reading too, Colonel Karr?"

Karr smiled. "It would, *Chieh Hsia*."

"And what would you say was the greatest problem confronting us?"

"Speaking from experience, *Chieh Hsia*, I'd say it was supplies. A war against Li Min . . . well, it would be even more difficult a logistics problem than the campaign in Africa. There we could at least stake out and clear a stack before each supply drop. Here in Europe . . . Well, it would be a war fought level by level on our own territory. Supplying our own forces while denying our enemies access to those same supplies – that would be an almost impossible task."

"I agree. If, that is, we were to fight a war on that basis."

"*Chieh Hsia?*"

"One last thing. How long would it take to prepare the three Banner armies in Africa for a new campaign?"

Karr considered, then shrugged. "Three days, *Chieh Hsia*."

"Good. Then that is all."

Karr bowed his head, then, as his T'ang stood, hastened to his feet.

"You have been most helpful," Li Yuan said, ushering Karr to the door. "If you would keep me advised on any developments with the boy."

"Of course, *Chieh Hsia.*"

"Good. I understand your wife is here."

"That is so, *Chieh Hsia.*"

"Then you must see her. Spend the night with her."

"Forgive me, *Chieh Hsia*, but I am on duty."

Li Yuan smiled and put his hand briefly on the giant's arm. "Go. I order it. I shall have Master Nan arrange cover for you. And make the best of it, neh? I fear you may have few such opportunities in the weeks to come."

* * *

As the evening light began to fade, Karr walked back slowly to the guards' quarters, his heart heavy, his mood darkened by what Li Yuan had said. He had known war would come – they all had – but it had always been some vague time in the future, never soon – never only a matter of days away. He should have been ready for it, for he had seen much fighting in the African campaign, yet somehow this was different. War in City Europe; hand to hand fighting in the levels; all of that disruption, all of that chaos and carnage, the awful, barbaric brutality of it – it was hard to believe all that must come now to his homeland.

Marie was in the kitchen when he got there, singing to herself as she unpacked things from one of the big transit-boxes and put them away on shelves. He went across and put his arms about her waist, making her jump with surprise then snuggle back against him.

"Where's May?" he asked, murmuring into her neck as he kissed it.

She turned and leaned back against the sink, smiling at him. "She's out in the gardens with the other children. It's like paradise for her. Why, she doesn't even seem bothered by the insects!"

He looked past her out of the half-open window, hearing the distant shrieks and laughter of the children. It was true. This was like paradise after the confinement of the levels, yet his pleasure at being there was muted by his knowledge of what lay ahead.

"What is it?" she asked, seeing the shadows in his face.

He met her eyes, pained by the simple strength and beauty of her. "It's war, my love."

Her breath caught. "Did *he* say that?"

"No. But I could see it in his eyes. He is determined on it. Something must have happened."

The light had gone out of her face. She looked away, then looked back at him, offering a tight smile. "Well, maybe it's best that we're here, then. Back there . . ."

He nodded, then reached out and held her once more, kissing her brow. "I'm off duty tonight," he whispered, smiling at her. "The T'ang has ordered it."

"Ah . . ." Her face lightened, her eyes widening, but still there was a darkness at the back of them. War . . . who knew what war would bring?

137

"I have some news too," she said, her smile broadening.

"News?"

"A baby," she said hesitantly. "We're going to have another baby, Gregor."

"That's great . . ."

Inside, however, he felt himself go cold with fear. He had dismissed what Lehmann had said as idle talk, but the man had been right. Somehow he had known.

"Gregor? What is it?"

"I was *told*. Li Min told me."

She gave a small laugh. "He couldn't have. I only found out yesterday. I haven't told anyone, not even May. I was waiting to tell you first."

"He knew," he said quietly. "The bastard *knew*." He heaved a sigh, then. "Look, stay here a moment, there's something I want to check."

He made to turn away but she called him back. "Gregor?"

"Yes?"

"Did you . . . I mean, you did *want* another child?"

Looking at her, he realised suddenly how scared she was, how close she was to tears. He went to her and held her tightly, stroking her back, physically reassuring her. "Marie, Marie, my darling love, you know I do." He lifted her chin, making her look at him. "It's *wonderful* news. really it is. But . . ." His smile slowly faded. "Get May in and settle her. Okay? I'll be back in a while."

Outside, in the imperial gardens, the evening light was failing. Walking back to the duty room Karr ran a dozen different scenarios through his mind, yet he knew, even before Bremen confirmed it. They were dead; the Surgeon and all his staff. Blown into the next world by a bomb planted in some new equipment they'd taken delivery of only that morning.

Returning to his rooms he rehearsed how he would tell her – how reveal to her just how small, how vulnerable they were, but facing her he found there was no need. She read his eyes and looked down, nodding.

"Where's May?" he said softly, wearily.

"Asleep. She tired herself out."

"Ah . . ." He nodded, then reached for her, holding her tightly against him, squeezing her arms, her back, reassuring himself that she was there, alive and warm – at least for this much longer – knowing suddenly how easily he could have lost her.

"We'll be safe here," he said. "War or no war, Tongjiang at least is safe."

She smiled, as if comforted by his words, yet something in her eyes mirrored back his own growing doubts. Nowhere was safe any more. Nowhere. Not even Tongjiang.

* * *

The moon was full, burning a perfect circle of white in the blackness of the sky. Beside it the mountain glistened, its crooked peak thrust like an ice-pick into the frigid air.

Lehmann stood on the slope on the far side of the valley, staring at the scene, his hood thrown back, his breath pluming in the air. It had been months since he had come out here. Months since he had seen anything so beautiful.

He shivered, more from awe than from the cold, then turned and looked to his lieutenant, Soucek, who had just arrived.

"Is there any word yet?"

Soucek rubbed his gloved hands together and shook his head inside the fur-lined hood. "Nothing."

"Ah," Lehmann turned back, distracted by the news. It was strange. Visak was normally so reliable.

"He's over two hours late," Soucek added, coming alongside him. "Do you think something's happened to him?"

He shrugged. For a moment he was silent, breathing in the pure, cold air, letting the inhuman perfection of the place fill him, then he turned, looking back at Soucek.

"It's almost time. You know that, don't you? All these years we've waited, and now . . . Well, now that it's here I hesitate. We have the means, the will, the *strength* to beat Li Yuan. Even so, I hold back. And I don't know why. That's why we're here, Jiri. To try to see things clearly. To work out if there's anything we've overlooked."

"It's to be war, then?"

Lehmann nodded, his face mask-like, almost transparent in the moonlight, his eyes sparkling unnaturally, like a demon's. "Are you afraid, Jiri?"

Soucek hesitated, then nodded.

"Good. That's a fighter's emotion. To be afraid, yet to be in control of one's fear."

Soucek stamped his feet, the cold getting to him. "It seems a long time since we killed Lo Han. Seven years . . . You know, I felt *alive* that day. I felt . . . well, close to something. Something I'd never experienced before. But these past few years, since we defeated Fat Wong and his cousins . . . Well, sometimes it's seemed like a dream. As if I wasn't fully awake."

Lehmann turned, looking at Soucek directly, understanding what the other man was saying. He too had missed the danger. Missed that feeling of extending himself – of putting himself at risk. It had all been too easy. Too *safe*.

"You're right, Jiri. We *have* been sleeping. Letting events drift when we should have been seizing the moment and shaping it. Playing at being kings when we should have been stoking the fire beneath the throne. But now it's time to change that."

Soucek had been staring at the tree-line far below. Now he looked back at Lehmann. "What do you mean?"

"I mean we ought to push a little and see what happens."

"Push?"

He turned, looking to the east, as if he could see beyond the mountains, beyond the great sweep of Eastern Europe and the Urals, right to where Li Yuan sat at his desk in Tongjiang.

"*Push*. Create pressure in the House. Ferment trouble among the African Banners. Assassinate some of Li Yuan's leading officials. That kind of thing."

139

"And his offer?"

Lehmann shrugged. He didn't know. He was tempted to say no, to defy Li Yuan and see what he did. But maybe that would be too direct.

"I don't think he wants to go to war. I don't think he has the will. Besides, he'll wait on his cousins – see what they say first. No, the more I think about it, the more I'm convinced we should play a double game. Play loyal subject to his face while undermining him at every opportunity."

"And if we're wrong?"

"Then we fight."

He stopped, looking past Soucek, then relaxed. It was one of his own men. "What is it, Stewart?

Stewart stopped and bowed his head. "There's no sign of Visak," he said breathlessly. "No one's seen him since six. He was due to meet some of our people in Osnabruck but . . . he didn't show."

"I see." He dismissed the man, then turned to Soucek. "What do you think?"

"Think?"

But it was clear what Soucek thought. His eyes gave him away. He thought Visak had gone over – sold them out – and if Soucek thought that then maybe it was true. But he would find out first. Make sure before he acted.

"You know what I think?" he said, looking up at the moon hanging there like a great white stone in the sky. "I think we'd better get back. I think the game's begun."

* * *

"Daddy?"

Jelka pushed the door open with her knee, then stepped inside into the darkness, the tray balanced carefully between her hands.

Her father was sitting in his chair, the holo-viewer on the floor in front of him, the control module in his lap, the golden fingers of his right hand wrapped about it. In the air before him stood the boy, dressed in a miniature of the Marshal's uniform.

She went across and set the tray down, then stood behind him.

It was something they had recorded only weeks ago; part of the great *Kalevala* she herself had set to music. Watching it she felt once again the sharp pain of Pauli's absence, that awful, gnawing uncertainty of not knowing where he was, nor what was happening to him.

Pauli stood there, straight and tall and proud, his dark hair combed neatly across his forehead, his whole body lifted slightly on the balls of his feet as he sang, his eyes staring into the distance as he concentrated on the words.

> "Hereupon the bird spoke language,
> And the hawk at once made answer:
> 'O thou smith, O Ilmarinen,
> Thou the most industrious craftsman!
> Truly art thou very skilful,
> And a most accomplished craftsman!'

"Thereupon smith Ilmarinen
Answered in the words that follow:
'But indeed 'tis not a wonder,
If I am a skilful craftsman,
For 'twas I who forged the heavens,
And the arch of air who welded.'"

He sang on, his pure high voice seeming to capture the very essence of those ancient days – of that distant time before the City had been built over the land, before the World was cloaked in ice. Looking at him, she realised with a start of surprise how very like his father he was – not the Hans Ebert she had known on Chung Kuo, the one who had almost married her, but the one she had met on Mars – "The Changeling" as she liked to think of him. She shivered, strangely moved by the thought. Her father had brought the boy up well. There was nothing spoiled about him, nothing impetuous or soft – nothing *corrupt*. His voice was like a light shining out from deep within, revealing the perfect pitch of his inner being, resonant with innocence and hope. So strange that was, so utterly strange, considering that his father had been a traitor, his mother a madwoman and a whore. But the boy . . . She listened as he finished, entranced and deeply moved, the ancient tale made new in his song.

The old man froze the image, a tremor passing through him, tears on his cheeks. She laid her hands gently on his shoulders. He turned, looking up at her, then reached up, grasping her hands tightly in his own. She squeezed them, for once not bothered by the cool, metallic feel of his left hand.

"We'll get him back," she said, fighting down the tears. "You *know* we will."

"It's not that easy," he said, his face hardening. "Things are changing by the hour."

He released her hands, then stood, turning to face her, all softness gone from him suddenly. "Things are bad, my love. We could be at war within the week."

She stared at him. "*War?*"

He nodded. "I asked the T'ang for Karr, but he refused. Things are happening. Pauli . . . Well, Pauli's but a single stone in the great game. We . . ." His voice faltered, then carried on. "We must deal with this matter ourselves."

She frowned, not understanding. "Deal with it? How?"

He turned his head, looking at his desk and the tray there. "Is that soup?"

"Yes . . . but answer me, daddy. How? *How* are you going to deal with this?"

He looked back at her, a sour smile on his lips. "I have not been a soldier sixty years for nothing. I know people . . ."

"People?"

Again he looked away. "It's best you don't ask."

Best? She shivered, seeing there, in her father's eyes, a steely hardness, a determination which she recognised from the past – that same determination that had made him defy his T'ang and kill Lehmann before the whole House – that same iron-hard spirit that would wreck a world before it allowed harm to one of his own.

Maybe it is best I don't know what you are planning, she thought. Then, reaching up, she gently stroked the drying tears from his face.

* * *

The cell was dark, the dull red glow of the LOCKED signal above the studded door the only source of illumination. On the bunk in the corner lay the boy, a rough blanket covering his nakedness. Two guards patrolled the corridor outside. He could hear their booted footsteps click and echo in the silence.

Cold. It was so cold here.

He huddled into himself, conscious of the camera somewhere in the dark above him watching his every move. Infra-red it was – he knew that. Uncle Knut had told him all about such things. He turned over, facing the wall, trying to relax, trying not to cry. He had done so well. Throughout it all he had held his head up and been brave, like he'd been taught. But now, alone in the darkness, it was suddenly much harder.

No, he told himself, swallowing hard. *They're watching me, waiting for me to break down, so I mustn't. For Uncle Knut's sake, I mustn't.*

For a moment his thoughts wandered and he imagined himself in his own bed, back in the Mansion; imagined that the footsteps were those of the servants; then he remembered. The servants were all dead: he had seen them die, Chang Mu and Shih Chih-o, Li Ho-nien and his favourite, the young Ma Ch'ing, the last in his room, fighting them vainly, trying to stop them from taking him.

He shuddered, trying to control himself, to push back the memories, but they were too powerful for him. Unbidden, a tear trickled down his cheek and then another.

And his mother . . .

He gritted his teeth, but a low moan forced itself out from somewhere deep inside him.

Be brave, he heard the old man say. *Whatever you have to face in life, be brave and face it squarely.* But it was hard to be brave when no one came, when no one even knew where you were. Harder yet when the memories came crowding back to haunt you.

He ducked his head beneath the blanket and secretly wiped the moistness from his cheeks, then sat up and turned, placing his feet on the cold earthen floor, ignoring the cold.

Remember the song, he told himself, hearing Jelka's soft voice coaxing him in his head. And, lifting his head, he began, his pure, high voice sounding in the silent darkness, making the guards outside turn and listen.

> "Still the sun was never shining,
> Neither gleamed the golden moonlight,
> Not in Vainola's dark dwellings,
> Not on Kalevala's broad heathlands.
> Frost upon the crops descended,
> And the cattle suffered greatly,

And the birds of air felt strangely,
All mankind felt ever mournful,
For the sunlight shone no longer,
Neither did there shine the moonlight . . ."

* * *

It was after eleven when Tsu Ma finally left the Council Chamber. He had been loath to call such a meeting, despite what had happened earlier, but the news from his agents in Tongjiang could not be ignored. If their reports were true, Li Yuan was preparing for war, and that would mean trouble in his own City.

He stood in the tiny ante room a moment, alone – for the first time since the dawn, alone – and tried to still his racing thoughts. Too much had happened too fast. That business with Fei Yen . . .

Tsu Ma let a sigh escape him, then sat down, raking his fingers through his hair distractedly. He had always thought Li Yuan had known; had known yet been too tactful, too much a "brother", to ever mention it. Since the day of Li Yuan's coronation, when he had approached him about the child, he had assumed the boy was his: that Li Yuan knew yet had forgiven him. If he had thought for a moment . . .

"*Aiya* . . ." he said softly. If he had known what harm the woman could do he would have killed her. Or was that true? Wasn't he still more than a little in love with her? Hadn't his anger at her today been tempered by some other, darker feeling?

He blew out a long breath, then leaned forward. If the truth were told, seeing her there in the cell, chained and defiant, he had felt that old, familiar fire burn up in him again – had remembered, for the briefest instant, how it had been to lie with her. No other woman had ever fired him so. No other had ever made him lie there sleepless with the memory.

Tsu Ma shuddered, then stood, realising suddenly that someone was standing in the doorway, waiting. It was Hwa Kwei, his Master of the Inner Chambers.

"*Chieh Hsia?*"

"What is it, Master Hwa?"

"My Mistress, the Empress, has sent me to ask if you will be coming to her rooms tonight."

His wedding night . . . He had forgotten. This was, after all, his wedding night.

He stared at Hwa, then waved a hand at him. "Tell her I shall come in a while. I need a moment's thought."

Hwa bobbed his head. "*Chieh Hsia!* Shall I bring something to eat? Some soup perhaps? And something for the Empress?"

Tsu Ma was looking away, staring at the portrait of his father that hung over the fireplace. "That's kind, Master Hwa, but I have no appetite. Bring something for the Empress, however."

"*Chieh Hsia.*"

Alone again, his thoughts returned to Li Yuan and his cast-off son. How could Li Yuan have done that? It made no sense. No sense at all. If he had wanted to deal with Fei Yen, he could have exiled her and married again. There had been no need to divorce her, not if her son was his.

Unless, that was, he'd wished to punish her. And what better way to punish a headstrong, ambitious woman like Fei Yen than by denying her son the right to be a T'ang.

The thought of it quite shocked him, for he had thought Li Yuan a less vindictive man. But who knew what passion – especially spurned passion – could do to a man?

He looked back up at his father's image. "What would you have done, Tsu Tiao?"

But the question, he knew, was idle. His father would never have got involved. His father would have cut off his own manhood before he would touch another man's wife. And as for that woman being the wife of a fellow T'ang . . .

"This is all my fault," he said quietly, bowing his head to the portrait, ashamed of himself. "And I must rectify it if I can."

Yes, he thought. *But how? What in the gods' names can I do to make things up with him? His wife. I stole his wife. It does not matter that her beauty blinded me. What matters is the fact that I betrayed him. Him . . . whom I counted as a brother.*

He shuddered, afraid, suddenly deeply afraid of what he had done.

So the wheel turns. So fate catches up with us.

But it was not too late. If he could only speak to him. If he could only humble himself before his cousin.

He lifted his head, speaking to the camera overhead.

"Contact Li Yuan at Tongjiang. Tell him I wish to speak to him. I shall take the call in my study."

While his servants set up the link, he paced the corridor, trying to work out what he would say – rehearsing phrases, trying to find some formula of words that would explain why he had acted as he had.

I love you, Li Yuan. Can't you see that? As I loved my elder brother Chang. Just as you loved Han Ch'in. It was their deaths that brought us so close. Beside which, this is nothing.

He sighed, then pushed through the doors into his study. If only that were true. If only it *were* in the past. But he had seen Li Yuan's face and had known at once that the hurt he'd felt had never gone away – that deep inside the wound was still bleeding.

Tsu Ma went to his desk and sat, waiting, his fingers laced before him, his whole body trembling with a fearful anticipation. He had thought himself fearless; had thought himself beholden to no man, but now he knew. Li Yuan. He *needed* Li Yuan. As a friend. As a brother and an intimate. Without him . . . Well, he could not bear the thought of it. To be severed from Li Yuan after all they had gone through together. It could not be. It simply could not be.

A minute passed and another. Then, with a suddenness that made him jump, there was a knock.

"Enter," he said, feeling his heart thump heavily in his chest.

His Secretary, Tu Fu-wei took a step into the room then bowed low.

"What is it, Tu?"

"It is Li Yuan, *Chieh Hsia*, he refuses to speak to you. He . . ." The young man looked bewildered. "It seems he has given orders for the borders to be closed between the Cities."

Tsu Ma stared at his servant, stunned by the news. The last time Li Yuan had closed the borders had been when he had had the plague in his City and had closed the gates to City Africa. Within months there had been war.

He sat back, robbed of words, then shook his head.

"*Chieh Hsia?*"

There was a blankness in his head. He could not think. For once he did not know what to do.

Tu Fu-wei came closer, looking at his Master with alarm now. "*Chieh Hsia?* Are you all right? Should I send for Surgeon T'ung?"

Tsu Ma shivered, then looked back at his Secretary. "No, I . . ." He shook his head, waving the man away, then stood, needing for the briefest moment to support himself against the desk.

The borders. Li Yuan had closed the borders . . .

He crossed the room and went out, heading for his new bride's quarters. He had to see her. It was his duty, after all, to see her. Yet all of the joy, all of that wonderful lustful anticipation he had been feeling earlier, had gone from him now, leaving him an empty husk. And all the while his thoughts circled the same point.

He'll come round. He's angry now, but things will change. He needs to sleep on it, that's all. Right now he wants revenge. Rightly so. But in a day or two . . .

No, he thought, stopping outside Shu-sun's door. *For there are some things that can never be forgiven. Some actions which can never be atoned for. Not in ten thousand years.*

Then, steeling himself against his new bride's disappointment, he knocked on the door and pushed it open, the rich scent of her perfume greeting him as he stepped into the darkness.

* * *

"Hwa Kwei?"

The voice from the shadows was only a whisper, nonetheless Tsu Ma's Master of the Inner Chambers stopped dead, giving a small cry of surprise. He had thought he was alone and unobserved.

Stepping from the shadows, Prince Kung-ch'ih took him by the arm and drew him aside, into one of the small reception rooms.

Closing the door quietly behind him, the young prince turned, looking at the tray Hwa was carrying, at the cloth-covered bowl, then met his eyes again. "Have you . . . ?"

Hwa shook his head, then answered the Prince quietly, terrified of being overheard. "I couldn't. Her door is locked. It seems the T'ang sleeps alone tonight."

"*Alone?*" Kung-ch'ih's voice was loud with surprise. "On his *wedding* night?"

Hwa Kwei winced. "Please, Master . . ."

Kung-ch'ih grinned. "That bodes well, neh, Master Hwa? But we must be sure, neh?" He reached down and removed the cloth from over the bowl, then sniffed at the soup. "You are sure this will work?"

Hwa Kwei nodded.

"Good. Then make sure you treat our Mistress the new Empress well, Master Hwa. Make sure she has her bed-time bowl of soup, particularly those nights my uncle *does* decide to visit her."

Hwa Kwei swallowed, then bowed his head. "I shall do as you ask, Prince Kung."

Kung-ch'ih straightened, his demeanour changing, becoming more threatening. "Make sure you do, Hwa Kwei. Make *very* sure you do."

* * *

Li Yuan stood beside the carp pool, looking down into its depths, watching the fish drift slowly, dark within the dark, circling like the thoughts within his skull.

It shall be war, he thought, the last shred of doubt gone from him. *I shall recall the armies from Africa and crush the monster in the depths of my City.*

That was the easy part. As for the rest . . .

The day, now it was done, seemed like a dream. The hurt he'd felt – the anguish and pain – now seemed unreal, like a nightmare he had woken from. Not that they were gone. No. They were still there, in the depths. It was just that he was blank now, emotionally inert.

An hour back, Pei K'ung had sent a girl, thinking it a kindness, but he had turned her away. Throwing on a cloak, he had come here, hoping to lose himself, knowing the silent spell this place wove over him.

He crouched, then put out a hand, stirring the water's surface.

Just fall forward, he thought. *Just let go, Li Yuan, and it will all be done with.*

But he could not let go. In spite of everything, some part of him refused to weaken; refused to take that final, irrevocable step. They could take it all from him – his brother, his father, his wives, yes, even the one man he truly trusted; the one man he had truly loved – and still he'd not succumb.

Tired as he was, he was not *that* tired. Hurt as he was, he was not *that* hurt.

Like a brother he had been. Like a brother . . .

He let his head droop, let a shuddering breath escape him, then, slowly straightened up. His limbs felt leaden, his blood sluggish in his veins.

"*Chieh Hsia?*"

Nan Ho must have been standing there some while, his head bowed, his arms straight at his sides, like a shadow beside the door.

"What is it, Master Nan?"

Nan Ho stepped forward, his face suddenly half lit, his dark eyes concerned.

"Forgive me, *Chieh Hsia*. I did not mean to disturb you. I just wondered . . . well, if you were all right?"

Li Yuan smiled wearily. "It has been a long day, Master Nan. I am tired. Very tired."

Nan Ho bowed his head. "Of course, *Chieh Hsia*. I . . . ." He hesitated, stepped back into the shadow, then came forward again, "I did not know, *Chieh Hsia*. I just wanted you to know that. There were rumours at the time – rumours we crushed in the bud, but . . . well, I did not believe them. Marshal Tolonen and I . . ."

Li Yuan raised a hand. At once Nan Ho fell silent. The T'ang's eyes were pained, his face muscles tensed. He looked down, composing himself, then looked back at his Chancellor, his face stern.

"I hear what you say, Master Nan, but there will be no further mention of that man within my hearing, nor within the walls of any palace or official building under my jurisdiction. From henceforth it must be as if he does not exist."

Nan Ho stared at him a moment, shocked by the coldness he saw in his Master's eyes, then bowed his head.

"It shall be so, *Chieh Hsia*."

"Good," Li Yuan said. "Then good night, Master Nan. May the gods look after us in the days ahead."

* * *

Karr woke in the small hours, his whole body beaded in sweat, shaken by a dream in which Lehmann had stolen into their rooms and taken May, replacing her with a perfect changeling – an android copy. Fearful, he had gone to May's room and knelt beside her bed, touching her arm in the darkness to feel the warmth there, checking at her neck for a pulse.

She had stirred and he had sung to her, crooning softly until he was certain she had settled. Only then did he go back.

Marie spoke to him from the darkness, her voice heavy with sleep. "Gregor?"

"It's all right," he said, climbing in beside her. "I heard a noise. From May's room. I was just checking she was okay."

She murmured some vague noise of understanding then cuddled close, placing her head on his chest, asleep in an instant. Normally it would have been enough to soothe him, to calm his fears, but this once he could not get to sleep again. He lay there, tense, remembering the dream, disturbed by it – seeing again and again his daughter turn and laugh at him, her mouth a dark hole within which he could see the full moon burning.

CHAPTER · 8

TO THE EDGE

he tower dominated the valley. Inside, heavy wooden blinds had been pulled down over the massive windows at either end of the Upper Hall, leaving it in heavy shadow – a brooding darkness that a shaft of light from a skylight breached, picking out a tiny figure in blood-red silks, standing on the stone flags beside a fountain.

Fu Chiang, "the Priest", Big Boss of the Red Flower Triad of North Africa, stood at the centre of the Hall, looking up through the skylight at the faint circle of the moon in the early morning sky. Behind him, the light glittered off the flowing water of the fountain, making the green-bronze flanks of the running horse shimmer.

He loved this hour when the air was so clear and cool and the fortress silent. Walking to the door he pushed aside the blue silk curtain and went out on to the balcony, stepping from shadow into sunlight.

Dismissing the two guards, he went to the parapet and looked out across the valley. From this vantage point, all was below him. To his right three peaks soared into the cloudless sky, their very stillness making him think of eternity. Dark-green pines clothed their flanks, hiding the gun emplacements he knew were there. To his left the land fell away more steeply, the stark geometric shapes of the lower garrison bunkers jutting from the smooth face of the rock. Far below a river wound its way into the distance, like a black snake coiled in the grass. Somewhere in the middle ground lay two small villages. Beyond them the dark massed shapes of the Atlas Mountains rose once more, stretching to the horizon.

Fu Chiang looked up, taking a deep breath and stared into the perfect blue of the sky. More and more he found himself drawn to this place. More and more he left the day-to-day running of the brotherhood to his lieutenants; to his Red Pole, Hu Lin, and his White Paper Fan, Tan Sui.

This had once been a summer retreat for Wang Sau-leyan. It was rumoured he had even brought his woman here – the *hsueh pai*. But that had been some while back now. Fu Chiang had taken it over two years ago, after Wang's death, paying-off the local Warlord, Yen Fu.

For now, he thought. *For the day will come when Yen Fu will pay me.*

Yes, but Yen Fu was not a problem. An irritation, maybe, but not a problem. *Li Min . . . Li Min was the problem.*

He turned, looking to the north, the stone face of the tower climbing into the air to his left. This morning, not long after first light, a cruiser had come from that direction. On board had been Li Min's henchman, Visak.

Fu Chiang pulled at his beard thoughtfully. His *Wu* would be here shortly. He had summoned him as soon as he'd learned what Visak wanted, knowing that this was not a course to be entered on lightly. To give Visak shelter – to agree to what he wanted – would, if Li Min heard of it, surely make an enemy of the man. On the other hand, to send him back . . .

He sighed, suddenly impatient. Where *was* the man? Why hadn't he come? He turned and went back inside, hurrying across the Hall and throwing the door open.

"Guard!"

The man came quickly to his Master's summons and knelt at his feet.

"Find out what's happened to the *Wu!*"

"Master!"

The man bowed low, then hurried off, calling to others as he went.

Fu Chiang stood there a moment, banging his clenched fist against the doorpost with frustration, then went back inside. It would not have been so bad had he been able to trust any of his fellow Mountain Lords, but who was to say which one of them would take advantage of the situation and inform Li Min?

Or was he worrying too much? Could Li Min *really* harm him?

Yes, he thought. Not directly, but the bastard could withdraw his support and fund his enemies, and that could shift the balance of power against him. Unless . . .

Unless I make a deal – another deal – this time with Li Min's principal enemy.

He laughed. The very thought was outrageous. But why not? Why shouldn't he, a Mountain Lord, make deals with one of the Seven? After all, the times had changed. And if Visak *was* so important, then maybe Li Yuan would be willing to buy the man.

The more he thought of it, the more he liked the idea.

He turned, hearing voices and running footsteps and nodded to himself. If the *Wu* confirmed it – if the signs were right – then he would act.

And if they weren't?

No. He was convinced of it. The oracle would bear it out. Visak . . . Visak was the key that would open many doors for him.

* * *

Tsung Ye edged to the side of the bed then, carefully pulling the silken covers aside, slipped out, tiptoeing to the chair where he had left his clothes. Pei K'ung lay on her side on the far side of the bed, naked, her shoulder and the curve of her back visible from where he stood, dressing.

He had waited almost twenty minutes until he was sure she was asleep, knowing that if he woke her he would be there still an hour hence. The thought of it made him lower his eyes and groan inwardly. It was not that his Mistress was a bad lover. Far from it. He was surprised by how passionate, how enthusiastic she was, how quickly she had learned the arts of pleasure. Nor did her age or lack of beauty put him off. It was just that she was so . . . well, *insatiable*. As if she was trying to make up for forty years of celibacy in a few brief days.

Tsung Ye sat, pulling on his boots, then stifled a yawn. She had kept him at it all night, that last time riding him like a demon, her face distorted so that, for the briefest moment, he had been afraid, thinking she had been taken over by the legendary fox lady. He shuddered, remembering it, then stood, pressing his feet down into the bottom of the soft kid boots she had bought him.

That, at least, was one good thing that had come of this. The presents she kept showering on him: new clothes, a golden timepiece, silks, jewellery and cloth-bound books. Even so, the situation worried him. One of these days they would be caught. He knew it for a certainty. And though she said her husband knew, how certain could he be of that? After all, it was not something he could check.

He sighed. Maybe she would tire of him. Maybe, once her passion for him had waned, she would take another to her bed. Until then he must be careful. Until then he must do as she said.

He tiptoed to the door and opened it, checking the corridor, then slipped outside. Pulling the door closed behind him, he hurried away, making for his bed and the sweet oblivion of sleep.

* * *

Pei K'ung heard the door click shut then turned and pulled herself up on to the cushions. Stretching, she yawned then smiled. The night had been wonderful, the best yet, but though she felt exhausted, she could not sleep. For a while she lay there in a fitful reverie, remembering what they had done, her hand straying down to touch her breasts, her sides, the soft-haired nest between her legs.

Yes, my little bird, she thought, a sigh of contentment escaping her, *you were right to slip away when you did. Get some sleep. For tonight I shall have need of you again.*

After a while she got up and went through to her bathroom. Squatting there over the bowl, washing herself, she felt a shiver run through her, imagining not Tsung Ye but her husband, watching her. For a moment she closed her eyes, letting the fantasy run its course, imagining him chancing upon her, there where she was, then coming across to throw her down upon the tiled floor and have her on the spot. The thought of it made her nerves tingle, the hair on her neck stand on end.

Awake, she thought. *After all this time I am awake.*

She dried herself then went back through, not bothering to summon her maids, but searching the great carved wardrobes herself, looking for something that suited her mood. Something light and airy. She decided on a simple wrap of lavender and pink decorated with embroidered silk butterflies. Laying it on the bed, she went to her dressing-table and sat.

"Send my maids," she said, addressing the House Computer.

They were there in an instant. Curtseying in the doorway, they came in, then stopped, hesitating as they saw her at the mirror, naked.

She smiled, seeing how they averted their eyes as they came across, then spoke to them, giving them their orders.

"Tiny Jade, I want you to put my hair up. You will do something fashionable with it, all right? As for you, Autumn Snow, you must use all your skills to make your Mistress presentable."

"Mistress!" the two maids said together, bowing and looking to each other with worried glances; glances Pei K'ung pretended not to see.

"And girls," she said, the familiar authority of her voice tempered with an unexpected tenderness. "Do this properly and I shall reward you well."

* * *

Nan Ho stopped outside the Empress's rooms, then, clearing his throat, he knocked loudly on the outer door.

There was a faint exchange of voices from within and then the door eased back, a guard staring out at the Chancellor. Seeing who it was, the man bowed his head and stepped back, announcing him.

"Mistress, it is his Excellency, the Chancellor."

Pei K'ung was seated in her throne, the dignitaries of her household surrounding her, as if she'd been expecting him.

"Master Nan," she said, smiling. "To what do I owe this pleasure?"

Nan Ho knelt, bowing his head, then stood, returning her smile. "Forgive me, Mistress, but I have come from your husband. He wishes to see you at once."

She gave a nod, then turned, dismissing the dignitaries. As they went, Nan Ho frowned, noting the absence of Tsung Ye, surprised not to see the ever-present young secretary at her side.

He bowed again, letting her pass, then fell in two paces behind her as they went out into the corridor.

"Is my husband better?"

"*Better*, Mistress?"

She stopped and turned, facing him. "Forgive me for being so blunt, Master Nan – I mean no disrespect by it – but let me have no more of this bull-shit from you. You *know* what I mean. Yesterday we returned from Astrakhan at a moment's notice, snubbing our cousin's wedding. Today a decree is issued banning all mention of the man's name. It takes no great intelligence to figure that something happened between my husband and his cousin, does it?"

Nan Ho nodded, conceding the point.

"Moreover, it was noticeable how pale my husband seemed, returning from our cousin's palace. So I ask you again, Master Nan. Is my husband feeling any better?"

He laughed. "That is something I think you had best judge for yourself." He put his hand out. "If you would . . ."

She smiled, then turned, walking on at a pace, leaving him to half walk, half run to try and keep up with her.

* * *

Li Yuan was halfway through a meeting when she came into his study. Without breaking sentence, he motioned towards a chair, his eyes following her as she made her way across and sat.

Flicking out her fan, she waved it before her face, hiding a yawn, then clicked it shut, studying the senior official who stood stoop-backed before her husband's desk.

At once she sensed something different. It was not just the tension in the room, though that, of itself, was quite remarkable; nor was it the crowd of advisers and retainers who were gathered in the room; it was something in the words her husband used – in their curt significance and in the underlying menace she sensed in them. Even before he dismissed the man and turned to her she knew. He had decided upon war.

"*Chieh Hsia,*" she said, addressing him formally, anticipating him. "Might we talk alone?"

He stared at her a moment, then nodded and waved the rest away. When they had gone he stood and came round the desk to her.

"So, Pei K'ung, what is it?"

She looked up at him, meeting his eyes squarely, almost as an equal. "Yesterday . . . that business with your cousin. I know you do not wish to talk about it, but . . ."

"But *what?*" There was a hardness in him suddenly that told her she had been right. "Speak then be silent."

She bowed her head. "When I was researching in the imperial library, I came upon something. Something to do with your cousin."

"Go on," he said, a note of curiosity entering his voice.

"It was to do with your first wife, Fei Yen."

She looked up, expecting to find him glaring at her, but to her surprise he was looking away, a muscle in his cheek jumping. Then a tear dropped from the corner of his eye and rolled swiftly down his cheek and into the folds of his silks. She blinked, astonished.

"Husband, I . . ."

He turned to face her, then sniffed deeply and wiped away a second tear that had formed but not fallen. "You understand, then?"

She nodded, but at the core of her she was shocked. So it was true. It really was true. And because of it the two T'ang were not now speaking, and Li Yuan was preparing for war. She shivered and clicked open her fan again, moving it distractedly.

"I have had her put under house arrest," he said. "Her son is held separately. Without him, she'll do no more mischief."

"Ah. . . ." Again she felt a faint shock of surprise. "She tried to see you," she said quietly.

He stared at her.

"A few days ago," she said, putting the fan down and holding it stiffly in her lap. "I . . . I saw her myself. Sent her away. I . . ." She looked up at him again. "I thought it best. I did not realise . . ."

"No . . ." He sighed. "You were not to blame, Pei K'ung. The woman . . ." He shook his head and grimaced. "The woman was always unstable. I was wrong to marry her. It was infatuation . . . childish infatuation. I see that now."

She nodded. But whereas only three days ago, she would not have understood, now she saw it clear. When it came to love and sex the eyes were blind.

"Is it war?" she asked, changing the subject. "I mean, against Li Min?"

"Yes." Strangely, he offered her a smile. "I'm glad you know. I . . . I was so lonely. So wrapped up in myself. But now . . . Well, now it's easier, neh?"

He stared at her a moment, as if seeing her for the first time, then frowned. "You're . . . *different*, Pei K'ung. Your hair. That dress. It . . . it makes you seem much younger."

She bowed her head, a faint blush coming to her neck. "I . . . I thought I would try to please you, husband. I . . ." She looked up again, noting that his eyes were still upon her. "I thought I could, perhaps, come to you tonight. After you had retired. To talk and . . . well, to help you relax."

He opened his mouth, as if, for the briefest moment, he was going to say no, then, with a curt little movement, he nodded.

Pei K'ung sat there, her heart pounding, her mouth suddenly dry. Then, realising that the audience was at an end, she stood and, bowing, backed away.

* * *

May stood in the doorway to the shower, watching while her father washed himself down, her four-year-old eyes taking in his every movement. Glancing at her, he smiled self-consciously, then turned, facing the stone wall, whistling softly to himself.

"Papa?"

He stopped and turned back. "Yes, little plum blossom?"

"Those marks . . ." She pointed to the tattoos on his chest and arms, her tiny face creased up with curiosity.

"These?" He laughed, then, cutting the flow, stepped out and grabbed a towel. "I had these done when I was twelve. Long ago, that was. Long, long ago. And far away, come to that."

She stared at him, waiting. Shrugging, he towelled his loins dry, pulled on some shorts, then crouched down next to her.

"These," he said, indicating the dragon tattoos on his left arm, "are the red dragon of summer and the green dragon of spring. And this," he smiled, seeing how her eyes widened at the sight of it, "is the great eagle, symbolising strength."

She shivered, then reached out to touch and trace the design.

"But why is it so cruel?" she asked, pointing to the terror-stricken horse the eagle clutched in each of its steel-like talons.

"Because strength is cruel, perhaps." He watched her, seeing how she studied the design, and felt a tightening of his stomach muscles at the thought of what lay ahead.

What kind of world will you grow up in? he wondered. *A world of eagles and dragons? Or will it be a kinder, safer place?*

The thought disturbed him. He reached out and picked her up, cuddling her, then carried her through into the kitchen where Marie was preparing the breakfast.

"You want a hand?" he asked, setting May down.

She turned from the stove and smiled. "Are you ill, Gregor?"

He laughed. "No. It's just that I'm not used to being waited on. In Africa I would eat with the men, help prepare the meals. But that's not what I meant. This . . ." He looked about him. "I wonder if all this will be the same . . . afterwards."

There was a flicker of uncertainty in her face and then she smiled again, reassuring him. "We'll come through, Gregor. We always do. Besides, you've more than us two to think of now."

Karr smiled, but the memory of what Lehmann had said lay underneath his joy. Death. Death lay beneath the surface wherever one looked. He went across and stood beside her, reaching past her to take the tiny statue from the shelf by the window. More and more these past few years people had reverted to such things.

"You should be careful," he said, holding it out to her. "It's still illegal."

She raised an eyebrow, then took it from him and set it back. "It's Si Ming."

"Ah . . ." He looked at it again, then nodded to himself. Si Ming was the God of Fate, bestower of life and death. It was he, they said, who determined how long a man's life should be. He shivered, then reached out to touch the tiny statue, as if to take some of its good luck.

"Gregor?"

He looked at her, then laughed. "It'll do no harm."

"I thought you made your own luck."

He nodded. It was what he'd always said. But in the days ahead a single man would be like a seed, blown by the great wind. In the days to come they would need all the luck they could get.

"I . . ." He stopped, hearing a knocking at the door, then moved past her. It had an urgent sound to it.

He threw the door open. A messenger stood there, dressed in the dark green and red of Li Yuan's personal staff. The young man handed him a sealed letter, then bowed and backed away.

Karr watched him go, then broke the seal and took the letter from the envelope.

"What is it?" Marie said from the kitchen doorway, wiping her hands on a cloth.

"New orders," he said, looking back at her. "I'm to go to Africa."

"To the Banners?"

He shook his head. "No. I am to meet a Mountain Lord named Fu Chiang. It seems Lehmann's man Visak has fled the nest. He wants to make a deal."

*　*　*

"Tell me your name?"

Light flickered in the creature's eye. The pupil moved to the right, contracting slightly.

"I am . . ."

It hesitated, searching its newly-implanted memory.

"Well?" Kim asked, adjusting the scope that was set up over the creature's face then glancing at the twin screens beside the operating table.

"I am unnamed," it said finally.

"Good," Kim said, looking across the room to where Curval sat behind the control desk. "Why do you think that is?"

There was activity on the right hand screen – tiny flares of red and yellow within the dark outline of the skull – and then an answer.

"Because I have not *been* named."

"Good." Kim peered down the scope again, adjusting the fingertip controls. "And yet it is in the nature of things to be named, no?"

The creature was silent. At the desk Curval smiled.

"So why does everything – even the smallest, inanimate thing – possess a name and you none?"

Again the flares danced in the outline skull, brighter this time and more intense.

"I . . . I do. not know."

Kim straightened up then studied the left hand screen where two graphs – one in green, one in yellow – showed respiration and blood pressure. He nodded, satisfied, then looked back at the creature.

"Do you remember your parents?"

It gave a smile of recognition. "I remember."

"Good." Kim patted its arm. "So what did they call you?"

"Call me?"

"You lived with them, right?"

Flares of yellow intensified into red, faded and then returned. The respiration rate was up – dramatically.

Kim looked to Curval and nodded.

"You remember them, but you can't remember being with them, is that how it is?"

There was a look of pain on the creature's face now, of confusion. It gave a tiny nod, constrained by the scope.

"Good. And the house you lived in. It was a big house, neh?"

"Very big. There were fifteen rooms."

"Fifteen? That's a lot of rooms for just the three of you. You had no brothers or sisters?"

"No . . ." Again it hesitated. "I . . . I don't think so."

"Okay." Kim laid his hand on the creature's shoulder, reassuring it. "You can relax now. We'll talk more later."

He went out, Curval joining him in the ante room.

"Well?" the older man asked impatiently. "What do you think?"

Kim went to the machine in the corner and punched for a bulb of soup. "I think the implant's taken well."

Curval followed him across. "So what was all that about?"

Kim turned back, handed Curval the bulb, then punched for another. "You mean, why didn't I programme him properly? Why did I leave gaps?"

"That's *exactly* what I mean."

Kim took the bulb, cracked it open, then sat on the corner of the nearby table. "Because I want to see what it does with them."

Curval frowned. "With what?"

Kim sipped then smiled. "With the gaps. If my hunch is right, its brain won't be happy with the situation – with there being gaps. If I'm right, it will try to fill them."

"Fill them? How? We'd have to programme it, surely?"

"Would we?" Kim sipped again, then laughed. "Let's give it half an hour and see what happens."

Curval laughed then turned, looking through the glass at the creature on the table. It lay there, inert, like a piece of discarded machinery. "What *could* happen?"

Kim finished his soup then threw the flattened bulb into the disposal. "It might invent something."

"Like what?"

"Wait and see," Kim said, going to the machine and punching for another soup. "Just wait and see."

* * *

"Tell me your name?"

Light flickered in the creature's eye. On the right hand screen a single flare of yellow brightened and then faded.

"I am Box."

"I see." Kim looked across. Curval, at the desk, was sitting forward, astonished.

"Box. That's the name your parents gave you?"

"Yes."

"You remember your parents, then?"

"You asked me that before."

Kim smiled. "I did, didn't I?"

"You asked me if I remembered being with them and I said no."

"But now you do?"

It hesitated, then. "Yes, I remember it now."

"Why do you think that is?"

"I . . . I must have forgotten."

"Of course." Kim loosened the scope arm and pulled it aside. "Sit up, Box. I want to talk to you about what you remember."

Like a waxwork waking into life, it sat up, slipping its legs over the side of the operating table. Its eyes were an intense blue. Kim stood facing it, dwarfed by it.

"Good," Kim studied it, as if looking for flaws. "Now tell me. The house. You remember the house, right?"

"I remember."

"Fifteen rooms, you said. A big house. The house where Box lived with his parents."

"And my brothers."

"Ah." Kim nodded, as if it were the answer he'd expected. "Two brothers?"

"Three," it corrected him.

"Of course." Kim smiled. "Your brothers . . . did they have names?"

"They . . . Yes. They had names."

"Good. And their names . . . what were they, Box?"

"One . . . One was named Other. The second was Pole. The third . . ." It reached inside, its face forming the rudiments of a frown, then it smiled. "The third was Square."

Kim smiled. "Good. That's very good, Box. But tell me, did you play with your brothers? In the garden, for instance?"

"I . . ." Its hesitation this time was pronounced. "I must have. I . . . I *think* I remember playing with them."

"Were there trees in the garden?"

"Yes." It was more confident this time. "Four trees."

"One for each brother."

"That's right."

"Okay. We'll leave it now. Rest now, Box. Lay down and rest."

Outside once more, Curval rounded on him. "What's going on? Where the hell did it get all that stuff?"

"It made it up."

"Made it up?"

"To fill the gaps."

Curval laughed. "Three brothers . . . *Aiya!* It's a pathological liar! We might as well destroy it right now! It's living in a fantasy world!"

Kim nodded. "Sure. But that's exactly what we intended, wasn't it?"

"Yes, but . . ."

"No, think about it, Andrew. What did we set out to achieve with the implant? To give it memories that seemed real. To give it some kind of back-story so that it thought of itself as being more than a simple machine of flesh – so that it could function properly. All well and good. But the trouble is, how do we make sure that that story – that 'false history', if you like – is detailed enough? Up to now we've been assuming that what we were giving it was enough. That it would accept the implant verbatim and use it like some kind of theatrical backdrop. But we know now that that assumption was a false one."

"Because there were gaps. Because you didn't name it."

"Sure. But there are *always* going to be gaps. Don't you see that? That demonstration just now – the things I left out of its back-story were glaring and obvious, but they make the point. Whatever we leave out, it will invent. Wherever it finds gaps – however small – it will fill them. That's the nature of it."

"So we make the implant more detailed."

Kim laughed. "You're missing the point, Andrew. What we're talking about here is duplicating a life – the memory of a life – detail for detail. We're talking about a piece of programming so huge, so complex that we could put a thousand men on the job and they'd still be working on it fifty years from now."

"Okay. So what *is* the point? Are you suggesting we should give up? Is that it?"

"Not at all. What I'm saying is that we need to take this new factor – this facility it has for filling gaps, for inventing its own reality – into our calculations. We need to re-conceive what we've been doing and to construct the next generation of implants not as backdrops but as mental skeletons. If we can give the new models some kind of coherent framework, they can flesh it out themselves. And if I'm right

157

– if my instinct for this is correct – then we'll not only cure the instability problem we've suffered with previous prototypes but we might even simplify the whole imprinting process."

"So where do we go from here?"

"First we go back to GenSyn. Get them to expedite the release of the new brain matter they've been working on. There have been delays with the paperwork – the usual kind of thing – but I'll get on to Tolonen. See if he can't put a rocket up them."

"And Box?"

Kim turned, looking back at the creature. "We'll let Box run for a week. See how he fills himself. And then . . . well, then I guess we close the lid." He looked back at Curval. "The shame of it is that he'll never know, never realise just what he could have been. Gaps . . . All he'll ever know are gaps."

* * *

Von Pasenow stood in the shadows at the back of the room, waiting while Tolonen took the call. He listened, sensitive to the nuances in the Marshal's voice, to the sudden defensive stiffness of his posture, and knew that the old man's over-polite manner concealed real depths of hostility. Whoever Ward was, he was no friend of the Marshal's.

As the old man cut the call and turned to him again, he straightened, attentive once more.

"I'm sorry about that," Tolonen said, a flicker of distaste crossing his face. "You'd think he'd deal with the appropriate manager! Why he has to pester me. Anyway . . . you were saying you had news."

Von Pasenow took two steps forward, into the circle of light cast by the hover-globe at Tolonen's elbow, then bowed his head.

"I think we've found them, sir."

"Found them! Why that's excellent! *Where?*"

He raised his head. Tolonen was leaning forward, staring at him eagerly.

"We've traced them to Cosenza in the south. It looks like they're preparing to slip away to Africa. My guess is that they're waiting to be paid off, otherwise they'd have gone."

Tolonen nodded, then waved him to continue.

"I've had the surrounding levels staked out thoroughly. Good men. Reliable, ex-service types. My men are in the transits and at all the barriers. If they even cough I'll know about it."

Tolonen stood. "Excellent. Then let's go there, neh?"

"Marshal?" Von Pasenow stared at the old man, surprised. "But I thought . . ."

Tolonen came round the desk and placed a golden hand on Von Pasenow's shoulder. "You've done a good job, Major. I knew you would. That's why I hired you. But this is personal. You understand?"

Von Pasenow bowed his head. "Of course, sir. I'll take you there at once."

"Good. And Major . . . if we have to take containment action, we do what has to be done, neh? I'll accept the responsibility for any consequences. But I want at least one of the fuckers alive. I don't care how you do it, but you do it, *right?*"

Von Pasenow swallowed, then bowed his head. "Sir!"

* * *

The curtains were drawn, the room in semi-darkness. From the far side of the room he could hear her soft, regular breathing and smiled. The room was warm, filled with the sweetly perfumed scent of her. Hesitant, he pushed the door closed and tiptoed to the bed.

Shu-sun lay there, her back to him, a bright red silk wrapped about her nakedness. Gently Tsu Ma sat, careful not to disturb her, then leaned across, his eyes taking in the features of her sleeping face.

He had not been wrong. She was every bit as beautiful as he'd remembered. As he watched, she turned, slowly, sensuously uncurling, her lips parting a fraction, her shoulders and neck stretching. Then, with a lazy motion, her eyes opened, the pupils heavy with sleep. Seeing him, she smiled.

"Where were you?" she asked, her voice a lazy, familiar drawl. "I thought you were going to come, but you didn't . . ."

He felt a pang of guilt and quickly suppressed it. "I'm here now," he said, placing his palm against her cheek and smoothing it. She took it and slowly led it down her body on to the warm, firm breast beneath the silk.

"I wanted you."

"Wanted?" He felt a tiny shiver of anticipation pass through him. The silken warmth of her inflamed him.

"Want," she said, correcting herself.

She lifted his hand to her lips, kissed it, then, releasing it, drew back her silks, revealing her nakedness. Tsu Ma let a long, slow breath escape him, bewitched by the sight of her, then leaned forward and gently kissed first one and then the other breast, his tongue lingering on the the nipples.

He glanced up at her. Her eyes were closed now, her whole face lit with pleasure at what he was doing. He bent again, kissing and teasing her breasts, his hands moving down her body, tracing the smooth young shape of it, eliciting soft sighs from her.

Moving back, he shrugged off his jacket and then stood, beginning to undress. Her eyes opened lazily, watching him, her smile heavy with desire, her body turning towards him like an offering. He threw off his shirt and kicked away his boots, then peeled off his leggings. As he moved forward to kneel on the edge of the bed, she sat up and reached out to him, her fingers caressing his stomach and his inner thighs, tracing a circle about his groin, her eyes wide, enjoying the sight of his fierce arousal.

He closed his eyes and groaned as she leaned closer, her fingers cupping his balls gently, tenderly while her mouth opened to him. Placing his hands on her shoulders, he began to knead the muscles there, half tender, half savage.

"*Aiya,*" he moaned, unable to keep himself from thrusting at her. "*Aiya!*"

His hands were at her neck now. As she leaned into him, taking him deeper, he reached up with his right hand and, grasping the point where her hair was gathered into a plait, pulled back her head, as if reining in a horse.

She stared back up at him, her mouth still open, her face entirely changed, a primal savagery staring back at him from her eyes. He shuddered then pulled her down, his mouth going to hers and crushing it almost brutally, even as her legs parted and her body curled about his. With a gasp he was inside her, the shock of entry making them both cry out, she high, he low. Savagely he thrust at her, as if to destroy her, to annihilate her utterly, her cries, the pained contortions of her face robbing him of all reason. She clung to him fiercely, pushing up to meet each downward thrust like some young animal in its death-throes.

As he came she cried out, convulsing beneath him, thrusting up against him as if to split herself, her hands gripping his buttocks fiercely while he groaned as if he'd been speared, forcing his seed deep into her, each thrust now like a dagger blow, his teeth gritted, his whole face contorted in a rictus of pain. Again! Again! *Again!*

* * *

He woke an hour later, his head nestled between her breasts, her arms about his neck and shoulders. For a while he lay there, contented, happy simply to listen to her gentle breathing, to feel the soft warmth of her flesh against his own. *Like paradise*, he thought. Then, knowing he must get back, he gently broke from her, easing up off the bed.

He stood there a moment, staring at her, aroused once more by the sight of her. It would be easy simply to stay here for a day or two. To sleep and make love and damn the world outside. After all, that was a T'ang's privilege. But a T'ang had responsibilities too, and right now the world was a place of threats and chaos. Right now the world would allow him only a few snatched moments of pleasure.

He shuddered, then began to dress. For a moment he had forgotten everything – everything but her. He smiled, remembering. The first time had been fierce, like the violent coupling of animals, the second tender, softly, astonishingly gentle. And between . . . He laughed, surprised by it. Between times he had fallen in love with her.

Fastening the last button of his jacket, he turned, looking at her again, then went across and, leaning across her, planted gentle kisses on her neck, her cheek, her brow.

"Tonight," he whispered. Then, moving back, he straightened up, preparing himself to go out and face the greater world once more.

Tonight, he thought, knowing that there was at least this one sweet certainty amidst all else. *I shall come to you tonight, my darling Shu-sun.*

But first there was one other matter to be settled.

* * *

They were in transit when it began – travelling south from Milan garrison, their cruiser flitting less than a hundred *ch'i* above the City's roof, as if across a vast, smooth snowscape.

"What's happening?" Tolonen demanded, leaning across to touch Von Pasenow's arm.

The ex-Major looked up and grimaced. "It looks like their contact has arrived. They're de-camping. If we don't hit them now . . ."

"Then hit them," Tolonen said sternly. "But remember what I said. I want at least one of them alive. Tell your men to shoot to disable if they can, not to kill."

"And if they suicide?"

"That's a risk we'll have to take."

Von Pasenow stared at him a moment, then nodded and got back on to his man in Cosenza.

They arrived ten minutes later, setting down beside one of the security hatches. By then it was all over.

"Let's hope they've left us something," Tolonen said as they climbed down from the craft.

"Or someone," Von Pasenow said beneath his breath, fearing the worst.

Down below it was chaos. Someone had shot at one of the *Shen T'se* before the ambush was properly set. As a result more than twenty of their own men had been killed or critically wounded. Of the *Shen T'se*, only one was still alive, and that was because they had blown off both his arms and one of his feet. He lay in one of the rooms, under heavy guard, his wounds freeze-staunched, his condition kept stable by the Resuscitation Machine he was strapped to.

Tolonen went to inspect the dead first, spending a long time staring at the five *Shen T'se*, murmuring to himself about loyalty and trust, and wondering aloud how such men as these could be bought. Eventually he left them and came through, frowning fiercely as he studied the half-conscious man.

"You know him?" Von Pasenow asked.

"I did," Tolonen answered. "Or thought I did. He was a good man." He heaved a sigh, then sniffed deeply. "But then, men are not to be taken at face value any longer."

The Marshal turned, looking directly at Von Pasenow. "It began with that rascal DeVore. From him it was contracted by my erstwhile son-in-law, Hans Ebert. And from there, it seems, it has spread, like some contagious disease. The disease of *seeming*. It hollows a man and replaces him with a shadow, a puppet man, dancing to another's orders. So here."

He went across and stood over the wounded *Shen T'se*, his face pained.

"Sergeant Hoff . . . do you know who's speaking to you?"

Hoff's eyes slowly opened. "Marshal Tolonen? Is that you?"

"Hoff . . . I need to know a few things, and I need to know them now."

Hoff shook his head.

"I'll make it simple, Sergeant. You tell me now I'll kill you, quickly and mercifully. You know I can do that, don't you?"

Hoff nodded, suddenly more alert.

"If you keep silent, however." Tolonen sniffed. "Well, I think you've a good enough imagination, neh, sergeant? I could keep you alive, what, thirty, maybe forty years. And every day of that you would be in agony. In a hell that would make your present condition seem like bliss. So . . . what is it to be? A quick death or an eternity of suffering?"

Hoff closed his eyes and groaned. "What do you want to know?"

161

"Who bought you? Who paid you? Who gave you your orders?" He paused, then, leaning closer. "And here's the big one. Where's the boy? Tell me that and I may even offer you a better deal."

Hoff shivered, then opened his eyes again, looking directly at the old man.

"Our contact was a man named Ruddock. He's a Minor Official according to his Security file, but in point of fact he's one of the main mediators between ourselves and the White T'ang's organisation."

"Go on."

Hoff grimaced, closing his eyes briefly, then began again. "The paymaster was Li Min himself. As for who gave us our orders . . . it was Rheinhardt."

Tolonen laughed. "I don't believe you."

Hoff's eyes stared back at him, a cold certainty in them. "There was a secret meeting, two weeks back, up north. In Goteborg or some place like that. More than two dozen people attended that meeting, our commander and a number of other high-ranking Security officers among them. Rheinhardt chaired it. The purpose of that meeting was to try to assess just who would come out on top in the event of a war between Li Yuan and Li Min."

Tolonen let out a long breath. "You have proof?"

Hoff nodded. "Our commander . . . Needham . . . swore a personal oath to Rheinhardt. He had us do the same." Again he grimaced, the pain clearly returning as the quick-shot medication wore off. "When the order came from on high we did as we were told."

"I see." The old man nodded, then looked once more to Von Pasenow. "I couldn't understand it," he said. "A *Shen T'se* unit. Their loyalty is unquestionable. But this, if true, explains it." He looked back to Hoff. "So where's the boy?"

Hoff swallowed drily, then shook his head. "I don't know. We handed him over back at Linz on our way down here. To a tall man with an ox-like face. Had a shoulder wound. Pale, cadaverous face."

"Li Min's man?"

"I . . . I guess so."

Tolonen stared at him a long while, then slowly shook his head.

"I don't believe you, you know that, Hoff? Oh, the part about being in Li Min's pay. That rings true. As for the rest, well . . . I think you're out to make mischief for Li Yuan. Rheinhardt . . ." He laughed, his voice suddenly louder, more authoritative. "I *know* Helmut Rheinhardt, and he would as soon slit his own throat as think of committing treason against his Master."

He leaned in to the man, placing the fingers of his left hand – the golden, metallic fingers – against the cauterised stump of Hoff's right arm and pressed, gently at first and then with greater and greater pressure.

Hoff screamed.

"Now, Sergeant," Tolonen said, his rock-like face hovering above the sweating man, "let's begin again from the beginning, eh? We've plenty of time, after all. All the time in the world . . ."

* * *

Fu Chiang stood beside Karr at the rail, looking down into the fight-pit.

"It is brutal, I know, but it is also one of the few *pure* things there is. To see them fight . . ." Fu Chiang smiled and turned to look at the giant, casting admiring eyes over his physique. "It cannot be faked. One wins, the other dies. There is such . . . *clarity*."

"I know," Karr said, his look intense. "I was a Blood. I too once fought in a pit, beneath the lights."

Fu Chiang's eyes widened. "You *fought* . . ." Then he laughed. "You jest with me, Colonel?"

Karr turned to him, his eyes deadly serious. "I fought. Beneath the Net. Eight contests, to the death. And then the Supreme Master, Hwa. He almost beat me." Karr breathed deeply then nodded. "He was a great man, Hwa."

"And then?"

Karr smiled. "And then Tolonen found me, *used* me. Made me the T'ang's man."

Fu Chiang frowned. "I did not know. It . . . well, it strikes me as odd that a Blood should rise to become a Colonel in Security, yet looking at you . . ."

Fu Chiang put out a hand, touching Karr's chest. It was like touching a warm stone pillar. Karr watched him patiently, neither offended nor pleased by the small man's touch. Fu Chiang let his hand fall and shrugged. "Anyway, to business . . ."

"He's here?"

"Up above, in the Tower Hall. I left him admiring the view."

"It must be beautiful."

"It is." Fu Chiang smiled. "I like you, Colonel Karr. If ever you tire of being in Li Yuan's service . . ."

He left the rest unsaid, then put out an arm, indicating that they should leave. As they walked along they talked, going down corridors and up stairs, moving along passages cut from the stone of the mountainside, guards everywhere.

"You know what to do?" Fu Chiang asked, pausing outside the great doors.

Karr nodded. "You talked of purity back there. Of the clarity that comes when life or death's the issue. But it isn't always so. These days . . ." He looked away, troubled, then met Fu Chiang's eyes again. "Deals. That's all there is these days. *Deals*."

"That worries you," Fu Chiang said; statement not question.

"Yes," Karr admitted. "But I can live with that, if it means I can serve the moral good."

"The moral good? You actually *believe* that?"

"Not all the time. Yet I know there is a difference. To serve a good man, however bad the system that he oversees, well, it might seem strange to you, Fu Chiang, but I find it better than serving such a one as Li Min."

"You make it sound so simple."

Karr shook his head. "Simple? No. It's never simple. Some days . . ." He smiled, then took a step back from the edge. "Never mind. Let's see the White T'ang's man – the Traitor's traitor."

Fu Chiang laughed. "The Traitor's traitor. I like that. I take it you do not trust our friend, Li Min?"

"No."

"Nor I . . ."

"Shall we?" Karr said, indicating the doors.

Fu Chiang smiled. "Be patient, Colonel. Visak will wait as long as you and I wish him to wait, but this . . . ah, it is rare to talk without masks. I had almost forgotten how."

Karr raised an eyebrow. "Have you no wife, Fu Chiang? No friend in whom to confide?"

"A wife?" Fu Chiang snorted. "I have a dozen wives! But *trusting* them . . . why, I'd sooner trust my bollocks on a butcher's block!"

Karr laughed, then grew serious again. "And yet a man cannot live in isolation."

"No?" Fu Chiang considered that, then shrugged. "All my life I have been alone. It is the *condition* in which I exist. I thought you understood that. To be a Mountain Lord . . . it is not an easy path."

"No . . ." Karr's eyes studied him, their earlier suspicion changed to sympathy. "I understand."

"You understand?" Fu Chiang, half Karr's height, an eighth his size, laughed then met the giant's eyes. "No, Colonel Karr. You do not even *begin* to understand."

*　*　*

Visak was standing beside the fountain, one hand resting on the horse's flank. Hearing the doors creak open, he turned then hurriedly came across, his nervousness marked.

"What's happening, Fu Chiang? Has Li Yuan agreed my terms?"

"Your *terms?*" Karr stepped between Visak and Fu Chiang.

Visak took a step back, then, deliberately ignoring Karr, looked to Fu Chiang again. "You know what I said, Fu Chiang. I want guarantees. A safe place. Protection. Twenty million *yuan.*"

Fu Chiang looked to Karr and nodded. Karr stepped forward, the quickness of the movement surprising for so big a man. In an instant he had pinned Visak's arms behind his back and bound them.

"No deals," Karr said, stepping back. "You're my prisoner now, *Shih* Visak."

Visak glared at Fu Chiang. "You viper. You . . ."

"You had nothing," Fu Chiang said. "Nothing for yourself, that is. But for me . . ." He grinned, then turned to Karr. "Tell Li Yuan I am grateful for his patronage. Tell him . . . tell him I hope my gift helps him snare that monster in the depths of his City."

Visak looked from one to the other and then snarled. "You cunt! You fucking . . ." Fu Chiang's hand flashed out, the stiffened fingers catching Visak crisply in the solar plexus. Visak doubled up, gasping. Fu Chiang turned, meeting Karr's eyes.

"That was good," Karr said, lowering his head respectfully.

Fu Chiang smiled. "Maybe I should have told you, Gregor Karr, but I too was once a Blood. Long ago now. Long, long ago . . ."

*　*　*

Li Yuan had signed the Recall Order and was inking it with the Great Seal, pushing down with both hands on the massive chop, when Nan Ho's secretary, Hu Chang, entered the room and, hurrying to his Master, whispered something to him. Nan Ho listened, then stepped forward and spoke up.

"*Chieh Hsia*. It seems Marshal Tolonen wishes to speak with you urgently."

Li Yuan looked up, smiling bleakly. "Put him on. I am sure he will want to hear the news."

He moved back, letting the two Custodians of the Seal ease the great square stamp from the silk-paper page and replace it on the cushion, then turned to face the screen which slid down from the ceiling to his left.

"Knut . . . what is it?"

The old man's face was bright with joyful relief. "He's back, *Chieh Hsia!* Li Min has returned the boy!"

"Returned . . ." For a moment he did not understand. "You mean Pauli? Li Min has *returned* him?"

"Yes!" Tolonen laughed, forgetting himself. "It's wonderful, neh? And no strings!"

No strings . . . Li Yuan felt his heart sink. What was Li Min up to? "Is he all right?"

"Oh, he's fine, *Chieh Hsia!*"

Li Yuan nodded, forcing himself to smile, to pretend to share the old man's joy. It was good news, there was no doubting that, yet he could not help but suspect the move. One thing he knew about Li Min, and that was that there was a reason for everything he did. This was no act of kindness, this was a calculated strategy. But to what end? What else was Li Min planning?

"Have you . . . have you had the boy checked?"

"Checked, *Chieh Hsia?*"

He swallowed, then, knowing no tactful way to put it, said what was on his mind. "Is the boy . . . *real*? I mean . . ."

Tolonen laughed. "My personal surgeon has completed a full examination, *Chieh Hsia*. It *is* Pauli."

"Good." Li Yuan smiled, relaxing a little. "While you are on, Knut, let me tell you the news. I have recalled the Banner Armies from Africa."

"*Chieh Hsia?*" Tolonen's smile faded. "But I thought . . ."

"I have made my decision, Knut. Now forgive me. There is much to do."

Abruptly he cut contact, not wishing to argue the matter out in public with his Marshal.

He turned, looking for his Chancellor, but Nan Ho had left the room. Frowning, he beckoned Nan's secretary across.

"Hu Chang! Where is Master Nan?"

Yet even as he asked, Nan Ho returned, breathless, a strange smile on his face. He came halfway across the great study, then bowed low.

"Master Nan?"

Nan Ho straightened, then held up a flimsy piece of paper. His eyes were twinkling, his face almost laughing now. "It has come, *Chieh Hsia!* At the last moment it has come!"

He bowed low a second time, then held out his arm, offering the paper to his Master. Li Yuan came round the desk and took it, beginning to read. He had barely read more than a paragraph of it when he looked up abruptly, shocked, meeting Nan Ho's eyes.

"But this is . . ."

"His capitulation, *Chieh Hsia!* He calls you Son of Heaven and swears his absolute loyalty, offering his neck before your foot!" Nan Ho laughed. "We have won, *Chieh Hsia!*"

Li Yuan shook the paper as if to emphasise its flimsiness. "But this means nothing!"

Nan Ho bowed his head, sobered by his T'ang's words. "Forgive me, *Chieh Hsia*, but you have not heard the rest. This document . . . copies of it are going up throughout the Lowers even as we speak. Millions of copies. Tens of millions! He bows before you, *Chieh Hsia!* He calls you Son of Heaven!"

"I . . ." Li Yuan was about to say something more, to question what his Chancellor had said, but the summons bell behind his desk had begun to ring urgently. Wei Tseng-li was trying to contact him.

He returned to his desk and faced the screen once more as his young cousin's face appeared.

"Cousin Wei," he said formally, conscious of the servants in the room with him.

"Cousin Li," Wei Tseng-li answered, an unaccustomed hardness in his face. "I am much worried. Word has come that your African armies are to be mobilised and moved to Europe."

Word? Li Yuan felt himself go cold. How could word have got to Wei Tseng-li so fast? He had only made the decision an hour back. And the Recall Order . . . that was less than half an hour old! Who of the twenty or so who knew of this had informed his cousin Wei?

"Forgive me, cousin," he said, with a gesture dismissing all those in the room, "but may I ask from whom you heard this . . . *rumour*?"

Wei Tseng-li waved the query aside. "Do not toy with me, Yuan. I have heard of your quarrel with Tsu Ma. The whys and wherefores I know nothing of, but if you plan to throw your City into a state of war simply to . . ."

"To *what*?" Li Yuan interrupted angrily. "Cousin . . . I owe you the life of my son . . . and much more beside . . . but I am a T'ang and what I decide . . ."

"Will affect my City." Wei Tseng-li leaned into the screen. "What is happening, Li Yuan? Come clean with me. If you *are* planning war then tell me, for I shall need to take measures in my own City. If not . . ."

Li Yuan sat back, holding his cousin's eyes a moment, then shook his head.

"The Banners stay in Africa. As for war . . ." He picked up the document and turned it, holding it up so Wei Tseng-li could see.

Wei read, then laughed. "But Yuan, that is . . ." He laughed, a boyish laugh of delight that strangely warmed Li Yuan. "That's *wonderful!*"

Li Yuan nodded, but still he was uncertain. Wonderful? *Was* it wonderful? Or was it some trick, some empty form designed to trap him? The truth was, he did not

know. To the edge . . . The bastard had taken him right to the edge. But for now –
for this brief intermission, at least – it was peace.

He let out a long, sighing breath then laughed, letting himself succumb to Wei
Tseng-li's obvious delight.

"Yes, cousin Tseng, it is! It really is!"

CHAPTER · 9

LIGHT AND DARK

K im stood on the verandah outside his new study, looking out across the gardens. There, on the south lawn between the gravel path and the outer wall, they had erected a geodesic dome – a huge structure more than sixty *ch'i* in height, framed by a protective web of high-tensile steel. Beneath its darkened outer layer lay two others, all three manufactured from a specially-toughened variant of ice Kim had devised himself, the inner layers sealed from the outside and accessible only through a single cast-steel tunnel in which were three air-locks. Beside the circle of the outer lock stood T'ai Cho, his tall, senatorial figure making a stark contrast to the workmen who were bowed deferentially before him. Kim smiled, then looked about him, pleased by what he saw. It looked so much better now that they'd laid the lawn and removed the diggers. For weeks it had been chaos, but in the last few days it had all come together. Almost miraculously, it seemed.

Thank the gods T'ai Cho is here, Kim thought with a smile, knowing he would have gone mad trying to cope with this and the project at the same time. As it was the conversion had gone very smoothly. In less than three weeks they had transformed the old Mansion. All that remained now was for the dome's alarm system to be connected and the rose garden transferred from its home in SimFic's labs.

Just in time, he thought, looking back at the elaborately-wrapped present that lay on the table beside the open door, for tonight was Jelka's Coming-of-Age party. Tonight, after seven years, he would finally get to see her again.

He smiled, then went inside, walking from room to room past bowing servants, feeling an immense satisfaction at what had been achieved. T'ai Cho had done an excellent job furnishing the house. Gone was the heaviness of the old decor, the oppressive sense of age and mustiness; in its place was something much lighter and simpler.

Yes, Kim thought, stepping into the airy main reception room. *This is more like it. This is a home.*

Home. The very word was alien to his experience. He had never had a home before, only rooms. But this . . . this had the feeling of a home, of somewhere one could work and live. A place one could venture out from and return to, knowing it would always be there.

A place waiting to be filled with life.

He walked to the great window and looked out. To the left was the east wing of the house and, on the far side of a shallow lake, an apple orchard; to the right the main driveway and, beyond the pale, lace-like stone of a curving bridge, the massive arch of the ornamental gates.

Home, he thought, surprised by the strength of the emotion engendered by that single word. *The Machine was right. I needed to make a home – a place for us to be . . .*

He looked across. T'ai Cho, it seemed, had finished. With a curt gesture he dismissed the men then turned and, gathering his silks about him, began to make his way back to the house.

Kim went out, meeting his old friend in the entrance hall, the great sweep of the stairs to his right.

"Is everything ready?"

T'ai Cho handed the electronic clipboard to a servant, then turned to Kim. "We've had a few problems with the T'ang's Inspectorate, but I think I've smoothed them over. They're going to give the system a trial run. Once that's done we can arrange the transfer."

"Today?"

T'ai Cho shook his head. "The Inspectorate are demanding the very tightest security. They want it done tonight, in the early hours when the levels are clear. And SimFic says they'd need twelve hours notice."

Kim looked down, disappointed.

"Chin up. It'll make no difference. Besides, it's almost midday. Even if we *could* arrange it for this evening you'd only miss it. Unless of course . . ."

"No. We'll wait."

T'ai Cho smiled. "You deserve the best, Kim. I hope it all goes well tonight."

Kim sighed. "It scares me, T'ai Cho. Seeing her again . . . I . . . I don't know what I'll say."

"Say what comes to mind. 'Thank you' might be a good start, for the tapes she sent you."

"Yes." Kim laughed. "Yes, you're right." He stared at his old friend a moment then stepped forward and embraced him. "I'm glad you came, T'ai Cho."

"I'm glad you asked me," T'ai Cho said, hugging him tightly, moved by the gesture of affection. "I missed you."

Years ago, when Kim had first come up from the Clay, it had been T'ai Cho who had found him, trained him, fought for him when things went wrong and Andersen – the Director of the Recruitment Project – had wanted to have him terminated. T'ai Cho had been his tutor, his protector, the closest he had known to a father, his own having been killed – executed by the T'ang, unknown to him. Yet, for the last seven years, T'ai Cho had been almost a stranger to him. He had kept in touch, yet his work as a commodity-slave for SimFic had filled his time. That, and the waiting . . .

Kim put a hand to the pulsing band about his neck.

But now the waiting was at an end. Today Jelka came of age. Today he ceased to be a slave and became an owner. And tonight . . . tonight he would ask her to be his wife.

He felt a strange thrill – a mixture of fear and feverish expectancy – pass through him, then turned, looking at the great clock on the wall.

"*Aiya!* I'll be late . . ."

T'ai Cho shook his head. "Don't worry. I've arranged everything. Director Reiss is coming here."

Kim turned back. "Here? But I thought . . ."

"You're important to them, Kim. Whatever you want . . ." T'ai Cho stopped, then laughed suddenly. "I'm so pleased for you. So . . . *thrilled*. I keep remembering how we had to fight, even to keep you alive. But now . . . well," he turned, indicating the opulence of the Mansion and its grounds, "the world is your oyster. You want a Mansion? They give you one. Your own company? It's yours. The hand of the Marshal's daughter? . . . Well, how *could* he refuse? You are a Great Man, Kim Ward. Today you have arrived. Today you take your place in the world."

Kim looked away, embarrassed, then smiled. "I'd best get ready. When's Reiss due?"

T'ai Cho glanced at the clock. "Any moment. I told him noon."

"*Noon? Aiya!*" Kim turned, beginning to climb the stairs.

"Kim?"

He stopped, looking down at T'ai Cho from ten steps up.

"Take your time. He'll wait. They'll *all* wait from now on. You are a Great Man now, remember that?" He smiled enigmatically. "You are the golden key that opens doors, remember?"

Kim's eyes widened. "Matyas . . . You remembered."

T'ai Cho nodded. "But those days are done with now. No one will bully you ever again, Kim. No one. Now go and change. It's time they took that collar from your neck."

Kim touched the glowing band, then nodded and, turning, mounted the steps again, jumping them three at a time. And as he went T'ai Cho spoke softly to his back.

"No one, you understand that, Kim Ward? No one. Not even the great T'ang himself . . ."

* * *

"Jelka?"

Tolonen popped his head round the door, looking into his daughter's room.

"Daddy?" She looked up from her desk, then got up and came across to hug him. "How's it going?"

"It's madness. Absolute madness! I've hardly dared come out of my rooms. But Harrison seems to know what he's doing."

Harrison had been brought in by Tolonen two weeks ago to oversee the final stages of the party. He was the veteran of a thousand social campaigns; a hard taskmaster and accomplished socialite rolled into one.

"Don't worry, daddy," she said, seeing the troubled look on his face. "Any problems, he'll sort them out."

"Yes . . . Yes, I suppose he will." He looked past her distractedly, then gestured towards the brightly-lit screen of the scanner on her desk. "Anything interesting?"

She shook her head. "Nothing really . . . I thought I'd catch up with my journal."

"Journal?" He looked back at her, intrigued. "You keep a journal?"

"Yes . . . and before you ask, no, you *can't* see it. It's private."

He raised a hand, as if fending her off. "Okay . . . but make sure you're ready for the first guests."

"Fourth bell. Right?"

"Right." He smiled, then looked past her again. "It's a lovely dress. Your mother . . ." He shivered, then said it. "Your mother would have loved to have seen it."

She turned, looking at the dress where it hung beside her outer-system suit, then nodded. It was her mother's dress – the same dress she had worn to her own Coming-of-Age party twenty-six years before. She turned back, then, kissing him gently on the brow, pushed him from the room and closed the door, then returned to her desk.

For a moment she sat there, staring into space, thinking of her mother; a mother she had seen only in holograms; had only dreamed of; never met, never touched.

Could you love someone you had never met? Could you love them because of what they ought to have been in your life? Love them despite *their absence?*

She shuddered. Never had she framed it so explicitly, but there it was, the thing that made her different from all her friends; the very thing that made her idiosyncratically herself – the lack of a mother's love.

She typed it in, then sat back.

The closer it gets, the less real it seems.

And what if she found she didn't actually like him? What if the years had changed what she felt? What if the thing she had been carrying inside her all these years was only an illusion – the chimera of love?

It frightened her. She, who prided herself on fearing nothing – who had survived three separate assassination attempts – was afraid of this; of meeting the man she loved. Afraid in case his feelings for her had changed. Afraid simply because she had never done this kind of thing before, never *loved*. Not in this way. Not in the way she proposed to love him.

Even the thought of it made her feel odd. She had tried *not* to think of it; had tried to divert her thoughts whenever they fell into that track, but her dreams had tripped her up. In her dreams she had been with him, woman to man, naked with him in that cave on the island where she had seen the fox that time, his dark eyes shining in the dark. Dark, animal eyes that made her shiver simply to think of them staring back at her.

Be brave, she told herself. *Furthermore, be true.*

Seven years. So much could change in seven years. Yet she had waited. She had kept *her* word.

Tonight. She shivered, then leaned forward, switching off the screen. Tonight he would be hers.

* * *

Madam Peng was waiting for him in his study.

"Madam Peng," he said, smiling tightly as he moved towards his desk.

She got up quickly, taken by surprise by his entrance. "Marshal Tolonen. Forgive me . . ." She bowed, the young man at her side standing to do the same.

Tolonen sat, moving the papers he had been working on aside, then looked up, taking in the young man at a glance.

"And this is?"

Madam Peng turned to her left. "This is Emil Bartels. I sent you his file . . ."

"Ah yes." Tolonen nodded to the young man. "You understand why you are here, *Shih* Bartels?"

"Yes, Marshal Tolonen."

Tolonen's expression softened a fraction. "You're a good-looking young man, Emil. And your family . . . very sound, if I recall."

The young man nodded, then glanced at Madam Peng uncomfortably.

"Please, sit down, both of you."

Madam Peng sat, smiling, fluttering the fan before her face. The young man beside her leaned forward, his hands on his left knee, the fingers interlaced, his face deadly earnest.

"Forgive me, Madam Peng," Tolonen began, sitting back a little. "As you know, it was my intention to have *Shih* Bartels visit my daughter before tonight. To . . . *prepare* her for this. But there simply hasn't been time. Besides, my daughter is . . . *difficult*, let's say. She suspects my motives. I wish only the best for her, of course, but she mistakes my interest for meddling. In the circumstances we must be careful. Her encounter with *Shih* Bartels must seem an accident."

"This is most unusual," Madam Peng began. "To guarantee success in a matter like this . . ."

Tolonen raised a hand. "I understand. If my daughter falls for young Emil here, all well and good. He looks a fine young chap and his past conduct is exemplary, but you do not understand. I . . ." He frowned, searching for the right words, then shrugged. "Let's put it this way. If you succeed in distracting her tonight . . . in *entertaining* her, let's say, and taking her mind from other matters, well, there will be a huge bonus in it for both of you."

Bartels looked to Madam Peng, surprised. "But I thought . . ."

"Oh, don't get me wrong," Tolonen said hastily. "If my daughter wishes to see young Bartels again, and if that association leads to marriage, I shall place no obstacle before it. But the main aim of this exercise is to ensure that tonight goes . . . well, without a hitch, let's say."

Madam Peng's fan snapped shut. Her face was now openly suspicious. "Forgive me, Marshal. You might tell me it isn't my business, but does your daughter already have a suitor?"

Tolonen looked down, sniffing deeply, then nodded.

"*Aiya!*" Madam Peng said softly. "Why in the gods' names didn't you tell me this?"

"You were paid well, Madam Peng," Tolonen said, an edge of steel in his voice. "And if your young man is successful the world shall know of it. As for this rival . . . this so-called 'suitor', *I* shall deal with *him*. Your job is simple. You have only to do what you have always done – to facilitate the coming together of healthy young men and women of the right social level. If there's a problem with that . . .?"

Madam Peng stared at him a moment, dumbstruck, then shook her head.

"Good. Then you can begin at once. I have arranged a room for you in an apartment nearby. Whatever you need ask for it. *Shih* Harrison is in charge. He'll see to all your needs."

Tolonen stood, then came round the desk, offering his hand to the young man. "And good luck, Emil. Do your best for me, neh?"

The young man took the hand and shook it, then stepped back and bowed his head, like a soldier before his commanding officer, while beside him, Madam Peng looked on, her face concerned, the fan fluttering uneasily in her hand.

* * *

The news was full of it. A bizarre new cult was killing people – many of them suspected terrorists – by nailing them to huge wheel-like crosses, slitting their wrists and leaving them to die. There had been a few instances before today, but this morning more than fifty had been discovered in the Mids, sign of a dramatic increase in the cult's activities. Rumour was that it was the work of what had once been called the Black Hand – or of a new break-off sect called The Sealed. Whatever the truth, it was a disturbing escalation, and most of the media channels had turned their full attention to the new "trend".

Kim sat beneath the screen in his study, watching with the sound turned down as the images changed. He was troubled by this new upturn in violence. Down where he'd come from, in the Clay, such savagery would have seemed quite normal. Dog ate dog down there. But he had climbed the levels to escape from that nightmare reality, thinking it would be different up here.

He had been wrong. The darkness wasn't down there, it was inside. However high men climbed, the darkness climbed within them. It was there, beneath the skin, there behind the pupils of the eyes. Darkness: it was rooted in the head and in the heart. Darkness, everywhere darkness.

"Enough!" he said. At once the screen went black. He turned. T'ai Cho was watching from across the room.

"What is it?" he said softly, sensing Kim's mood.

Kim shrugged. "It gets worse . . . every day there's more of it. And every day it's more extreme. The Clay . . . it's becoming like the Clay."

T'ai Cho nodded and looked away. He too had been disturbed by what he'd seen.

"It worries me," Kim said after a moment. "What kind of world is this to bring one's children into?"

"Things will get better . . ."

Kim gave a short, despairing laugh. "I'd like to think so, T'ai Cho, but experience teaches otherwise. We live now on the edge of chaos, of perpetual uncertainty. Look at us. I mean . . . guards and guns. Whoever would have thought it?"

"It has always been so. From the time of the Three Emperors, men have built walls to keep other men from killing them. So it was, so it is."

"And must ever be?" Kim sighed, then shook his head. "No, T'ai Cho. There just *has* to be something better than this!"

"And if there isn't? If this is *all* there is?"

Kim stared at him, then shook his head. "Darkness . . . it can't all be darkness. There *has* to be light. Darkness and light . . . *balanced.* That's what the great Tao says, isn't it?"

T'ai Cho nodded. "Yes, but remember what the great sage Lao Tzu said, 'The bright Way appears to be dark'."

"And if it *is* dark?"

"Then be a light in that darkness, Kim. Shine out and *make* things change. Dedicate yourself to it. You have a gift, Kim. *Use* it. Maybe that's why you were saved. Maybe that's why the darkness coughed you up!"

Kim laughed. "You make it sound so easy."

"Easy? No, I never said it would be easy. Remember how we began. Remember what a knife-edge we walked back then, you and I. Why, one mistake and I'd have had to gas you in your cell. You were such a tiny, bony creature – more wraith than child. Yet I knew you were different. I could see it, right from the start. And to think how far you've come . . ."

Kim stood up, then went to the window. It was true. He *had* come far. Yet how much further the light now seemed above him. How much further it seemed he had to climb. Even so . . . His hand went up to touch his neck where the collar had been removed. It was his choice now. His choice entirely what he was to be.

"Okay. I'll try. I promise you I'll try."

T'ai Cho came over, touched his arm. "Good. But right now you'd best get ready. You don't want to keep Jelka waiting, do you?"

Kim smiled. "No. I think we've waited long enough."

* * *

The madman walked through the market quickly, his head back, his shouts, his manic whoops of laughter carrying above the normal hubbub of the place. Emily, sitting alone at one of the tables in the Blue Pagoda, turned to watch him pass, then frowned and sipped from her half empty *chung.* A madman was a common sight these days. Then again, it was a wonder they weren't all mad, things being as they were.

She sighed, then looked back at the documents she'd been reading. So many things she'd seen these past ten years – so many awful, dreadful things – but this was by far the worst. And the most awful thing about it was that it proved the old men – the Seven and their servants – right, for such a thing would never have been thought of before the Edict had been relaxed. Now it was almost commonplace.

Almost . . . for thank the gods there were still some people with a shred of decency – of humanity – left in them.

Emily closed the file with a shudder. Tonight they would hit the place. *Oberon's* it was called, a club up on the Twenty-Fifth level of the fashionable Augsburg stack, the haunt of the super-élite of the First Level, the "Above-the-Above", as they called themselves, the "Supernal".

It would not be easy, for the place had its own guards – ex-Security, for the most part – and a state-of-the-art laser defence system, but it could be done. And they *would* do it, whatever the cost.

She finished her *ch'a* then set the *chung* down, recalling the difficulty she'd had getting Pasek to agree. He had been against it, wanting to carry on with his petty wars against his rivals, but she had put her foot down, insisting on this as a price of her continued loyalty, and he had given in. But if she fucked up . . .

Emily laughed quietly, then looked up, signalling for Yu I to bring more *ch'a*. What did it matter if she fucked up – if she didn't get out of there alive? At least she would have done something. At least she would have sent a warning to these monsters that they couldn't do such things without paying the price.

Her smile faded, the anger burning in her again. They thought their money made them immune. They thought that it lifted them above all human decency. But she would teach them otherwise.

Yu I brought back a fresh-filled *chung* and set it beside her with a bow, taking away the empty. She watched him go, knowing it might be the last time she would witness the sight. The thought didn't upset her. Rather, it lifted her. These past few weeks had been like a dream; she had been going through the motions like a hireling, but now she had a chance to act, to do something real, and that made her feel alive again.

She looked up at the cages overhead. The birds were quiet, dozing on their perches, like old men in the late afternoon. She smiled, then tensed, feeling a hand on her shoulder. Two men slipped on to the bench either side of her, hemming her in.

"Rachel . . ." the one to her left said. "We were told we'd find you here."

She turned, meeting his dark Han eyes. "What do you want, Ts'ao Wu?"

Ts'ao Wu smiled unpleasantly and looked past her to his companion, a tall, shaven-headed *Hung Mao* named Peters. Both were Hand. Both were cell leaders. Both, as far as she knew, were Pasek's men.

"We've had enough," Ts'ao Wu said quietly, his face close to hers, his bad breath making her want to choke. "This new spate of killings . . . these *crucifixions*. They've gone too far."

"Yes," Peters said, leaning in from the other side. "And we want to know what you're going to do about it?"

"Do?" She sat back slightly. "I don't intend to do anything. You don't like what's happening, you speak to Pasek . . . Or leave the Hand."

Ts'ao Wu laughed sourly, his pocked face humourless. "The only way you leave the Hand is through the Oven Man's door. You know that. So I ask again. What are you going to do?"

She looked down at her untouched *chung*. "You don't like what Pasek's doing?"

Ts'ao Wu turned and spat on the floor, then looked back at her, raising the middle finger of his left hand. "*That* to his great 'crusade'. *That* to his talk of the One God and Judgement Day!"

"The man's mad," Peters said, his face glowing strangely. "He's gone too far. We have to stop him before he destroys the Hand entirely."

"Or *changes* it?"

Her comment caught them off-guard. She saw them exchange looks, and knew suddenly that they were serious. For a moment she had thought this a trap; an attempt by Pasek to test her loyalty, but that brief eye exchange – revealing, as it did, their uncertainty, their sudden fear that they had miscalculated – told her she'd been wrong. Setting aside personal dislike, she put her arms about their shoulders and drew them in, looking from one to the other, her voice a whisper.

"I understand. I . . . *share* some of your fears. But now is not the time. We must plan things carefully. Make soundings. See how deep the current of mistrust runs."

She saw once more the uncertainty in their faces and squeezed their shoulders as if to reassure them.

"It will not be easy, but it can be done. You must be watchful, brothers. Sensitive to the moods and expressions of your fellow Hand members. And patient. You must approach only those whose eyes and gestures reveal their . . . *unhappiness*."

"But Pasek . . ."

"Pasek sees only what he wants to see. Likewise his lieutenants. They are like blind men, neh? They see only what he wants them to see, say what he wishes them to say. That is their weakness. We need not fear them. We need fear only ourselves. So go to it. But carefully."

Emily took her arms from their shoulders, then leaned between them to take the file. She stood, stepping out from the bench.

"And you?" Peters asked, both men turning to look up at her. "What will *you* be doing?"

"Me?" Her smile was like a hawk's, fierce and cold. "Don't worry about me, brothers. When the time comes, I shall be there for you. Yes, and Pasek will rue the day he let me live."

If I survive, that is, she thought, turning away. *If I get out of Oberon's alive.*

* * *

Jelka stood before the full-length mirror, holding out the voluminous folds of the lilac ball dress and frowning at herself.

It's not me, she thought, wondering how her mother had felt about wearing it. But then, her mother had not been brought up by the T'ang's General. Her mother had had a normal childhood, been a normal woman.

She grimaced at her reflection, then, lifting her arms, twirled about, as she had seen dancers do on the trivee.

No. It was grotesque. Utterly grotesque. How could she possibly wear such a thing in front of people? The very thought of it made her want to crawl away and hide.

"Jelka?"

It was her father.

"Jelka? Why is the door locked? Are you all right in there?"

"I'm fine, daddy. I won't be long."

She could hear his sigh of exasperation through the door.

"Okay," he said. "But don't be long. Our first guests will be arriving any time now. You ought to be at the door to greet them."

"I'll be there. Just give me a minute."

She listened to his footsteps fade, then let out her breath. What was she to do? What on earth was she to do?

If she didn't wear it he would be upset. He would think it an insult to her mother's memory. But if she did . . .

She sighed. *Aiya!* Why hadn't she tried it on before? Why hadn't she faced this problem weeks ago and settled it then?

Perhaps because she'd known what a fuss her father would make. These past few weeks she had avoided arguing with him, afraid to give him any excuse to cancel the party. But now she had to face it.

"Shit!" she said, making a face at her image. Was this really how she wanted Kim to see her? Was *this* – this garish, silly image of silk and lace and bows – really what he'd been waiting seven years to see?

"It isn't me," she moaned softly. "Can't you see that, daddy? It simply isn't me!"

But he wasn't there to answer her. This one she'd have to sort out by herself. She blew out a long breath. "Shit! Shit! Shit! Shit! *Shit!*"

From the front of the Mansion she heard the summons bell sound. The first guests were at the gate. Their sedan would be making its way up the drive even now.

Jelka glared at herself, then, turning side-on to her image, stuck out her tongue.

"If he laughs, I'll cut him dead!" she said defiantly. "If he laughs . . ."

* * *

The hours passed, the guests arrived, and after a while her sense of self-consciousness began to fade, blurring into a kind of numbness in which she laughed and smiled and mouthed inoffensive answers to questions from people she barely knew. And yet all the while, beneath it all, some part of her was kept separate. Each time the summons bell sounded she would look to the entrance arch expectantly, her stomach muscles tensed, only for her hopes to be dashed.

Now it was after nine, and still he hadn't come.

Where are you, Kim Ward? she asked herself anxiously. *Why aren't you here?*

"Jelka? You look wonderful. That dress. Why, it looks marvellous on you . . ."

Jelka turned, for a moment not recognising the luxuriously-dressed young woman who stood before her. Then she put her hand to her mouth in surprise. "Yi Pang-chou?"

The woman beamed and reached out to take her arm, leaning close in a familiar manner. "It's Madam Heng now. I married the Minister three years ago . . . or hadn't you heard?"

"No, I . . ." Jelka laughed, embarrassed, wondering vaguely what had happened to her first husband. "Anyway, how *are* you, Pang-chou? It's ages since I last saw you."

"Seven years," Madam Heng said, straightening up. Her peacock blue silks looked fabulously expensive and a small fortune in jewellery rested on her fingers and about her wrists and neck. She had obviously married well second time round.

"And your children? Are they well?"

"Very well, thank you. I have five now . . ."

"Five . . ." Jelka stared at her, stunned, then nodded vaguely. Yet it made sense. Pang-chou had married and had her first child even before they left College. So had many of her friends. As she was finding out, the anomaly lay not in them, but in herself. She alone of her schoolfriends was unmarried, childless.

She turned, glancing at the door.

"Bachman's here," Madam Heng continued. "You remember Lothar Bachman? He's a Captain now. They say he'll make Major within the next two years."

Jelka looked back at her. Bachman? Now where had she heard that name? Then it hit her. She stared at Heng Pang-chou, alarmed. "You mean . . . ?"

"Didn't you realise?"

She shook her head. "My father must have invited him. I . . ."

Bachman. He'd been the cadet officer at the College Graduation Ball who'd tried to kiss her – the young man whose legs and arms she had broken . . .

Jelka swallowed, then bowed her head slightly. "Forgive me, Heng Pang-chou, but I have to see to something. I'll speak to you later."

She moved away, making for the entrance arch, nodding and smiling as she went, noticing, once again, the young man who seemed to have been shadowing her all night.

Probably security, she thought. *Something my father's arranged.*

Outside in the corridor it was cooler. Smiling at a pair of guests who had just arrived, she went across to the House Steward, Huang Peng, who stood beside the great outer doors welcoming each guest.

"Has he come yet?"

"*Shih* Ward?" Steward Huang looked across at his assistant, who hastily consulted a list, then shook his head. The Steward turned back and bowed. "I am afraid not, *Nu Shi* Tolonen."

"Has he sent a message?"

"We have heard nothing, Mistress. Should I . . . ?"

"No."

She turned away. He was late, that was all. He would be here soon. If he loved her he would be here.

For a moment she hesitated, hearing the great swell of voices from the Reception Hall, then turned to the right, making for her rooms. Ten minutes. No one would miss her for ten minutes. But she had to know. The uncertainty was driving her mad.

As she reached her door she heard soft footsteps behind her. She whirled about. "*You?* What do you want?"

"I . . ." The young man gave a nervous bow, then swept his hair back from his eyes and offered her a smile. "My name is Emil. Emil Bartels. I . . ."

"Did my father send you?"

He hesitated, then nodded. She sighed. A soldier. He looked every inch a soldier. She put a hand up. "Okay. It's not your fault. Come in. You can wait in the outer room. There's something I must do."

She went inside, not looking to see if he followed. Going through to her study, she went behind the desk and sat, the folds of the gown getting in her way. Cursing, she arranged the dress beneath her, getting herself comfortable, then leaned forward, switching on the comset.

She knew the code. As soon as she'd heard he'd bought the Mansion, she had made it her business to discover it. But she had never used it before now. Never dared.

What if he isn't coming? What if he's ill?

But he wasn't ill. She knew that. If he'd been ill, he would have sent a message. So what was keeping him? Why hadn't he come?

She took a deep breath then pressed out the coded sequence. As the screen rose from the desk to face her, she sat back a little, trying to compose herself, to steel herself against the possibility of rejection, but her hands were trembling now and her mouth had gone dry at the thought of actually talking to him.

There was a moment's hesitation and then a face appeared. A young Han face, female, very pretty.

"*Nu Shi* Tolonen?"

"Yes, I . . ."

"I am afraid that the number you have called is unavailable. The channel is closed right now, but if you would like to leave a message, we can transmit it once the channel reopens."

"I . . ." She sighed heavily, unable to help herself, then shook her head. "No. It doesn't matter."

She cut the connection, then sat back, her face pained.

Maybe he was on his way. It was even possible that he was here already. Maybe he'd arrived while she was sitting here, fretting. She stood and crossed the room quickly, then stopped, seeing the young man standing in the doorway to her bedroom. She cleared her throat.

"Excuse me . . ."

He jerked round, surprised. "I . . . I was just looking." He took a step towards her, his hands out, as if to excuse himself. "I just wondered what kind of girl you were. What kind of things you liked. That's all. Girls' rooms . . ." He smiled uncertainly. "They reveal a lot about their owners, don't you think?"

She stared at him coldly, then answered him, her voice hard, uncompromising. "What business is it of *yours* who I am or what I like?"

His eyes widened, disconcerted by the harshness of her answer. "You mistake me. I . . . didn't mean to pry. I was . . . *interested*, that's all. If we're to . . ."

"If we're to what?" She was suspicious now. She took a step towards him, as if facing an attacker. "What are you talking about, lieutenant?"

He gave a brief, surprised laugh. "*Lieutenant?* No, you've got it wrong. I'm not a soldier. I . . ."

Bartels swallowed, seeing the look that had come to her face.

"So what *are* you? And what *do* you want?" She took another step, her body crouching slightly. "Who invited you?"

He took a step back, his hands raised defensively. "Look, I . . ." He sighed, his eyes pleading with her now. "Your father said I was to be pleasant to you, that's all. He said . . ."

Jelka stopped, straightening slowly, her whole body gone cold, all of her darkest suspicions suddenly confirmed. *Her father. This was her father's doing.*

That was why there had been no fuss, no arguments about Kim's invitation. Because he had had no intention of letting the young man step inside his Mansion. Because . . .

She shivered with indignation, then, sweeping past Bartels, went into her room, slamming the door shut behind her.

"You thought I'd be fooled, didn't you?" she said with a quiet anger, addressing her reflection as she began to peel off the dress. "You thought I'd play the good daughter and not embarrass you."

She kicked the dress away then went across and pulled the space suit down from its peg. For a moment she hesitated, knowing that if she did this it would be tantamount to an open rejection of her father – that it would mean a breach with him. But that was what he'd been counting on: that she would think twice before tackling him head on.

Well, you were wrong, she thought, angry with him suddenly. Furious that he should use such tactics against her, after all that had happened.

Facing the mirror again, she rested the suit against her body, remembering how it had felt out there in the outer system; how at home she'd felt among the cold-worlders. Then, without further hesitation, she pulled it on, the familiarity of the garment – the smell and touch of it – making her shiver with a sense of recognition.

Better, she thought, smiling at the new image of herself. But the hair was still wrong. Hurriedly she took it down and combed it out with her fingers. *Yes*, she thought finally. *That's me. Not that other creature, but this . . .*

And if Kim had come? If she'd been wrong about her father?

She laughed, then spoke softly to the mirror. "Then you'll look a fool, Jelka Tolonen, won't you?" But at least it would be *her* and not some twisted image of her mother – some hideous fulfilment of her father's fantasies.

Seven years she had waited for this day. Seven years. And now, finally, she had come of age. Today she was her own woman, free to choose for herself. But what did that mean – what point had it – if she could not *be* herself?

Smiling uncertainly, Jelka nodded to her image, then, steeling herself, knowing what lay ahead, she turned and went to the door.

* * *

The masked man stood in the doorway, a big "scatter-gun" – a hundred and eighty rounds in its snake-like spiral chamber – levelled at the servants who lay, bound and gagged on the stone floor of the pantry. Their eyes watched him fearfully as, from other parts of the Mansion, strange voices called back and forth. They had seen the symbol on the chain about the men's necks – the cross within the circle – and feared the worst. If these *were* Hand members then they were dead . . . sooner or later.

Outside, in the main house, masked men went from room to room, checking they were empty. Finally one of them came down the main steps and went over to a man who sat on the low wall by the drive and snapped to attention in front of him, bowing his head.

"He's not inside, sir. He must have gone."

Von Pasenow stared at his lieutenant, then shook his head. "He's here. He has to be here. What about the dome?"

"It's locked. If he's in there . . ."

Von Pasenow stood, angry that he had to do the thinking for all of them. "Well, unlock the fucking thing! He's in there. He has to be. He can't be anywhere else, can he? We've watched the transit all day, and there's no other way out. So get to it. Use cutting tools if you have to!"

"Sir!" The man bowed and backed away, then turned and hurried back inside, calling men to him as he went.

Von Pasenow glanced at the timer inset into his wrist then swore. Twenty minutes . . . Twenty fucking minutes! They were supposed to be in and out in ten, taking Kim with them. But now . . .

He growled with frustration. Staying here was the last thing he'd wanted. They had to get Kim out of the dome and quickly, otherwise they could be into a siege situation, and who knew where *that* would lead?

Fuck you, Knut Tolonen! he thought, kicking at the gravel angrily. *If the shit hits the fan, you can take the blame for this! Yes, and explain it to your precious daughter!*

He had tried to talk the old man out of it, but it had been like talking to a statue. Tolonen was obsessed with keeping Ward and his daughter apart . . . by any means, it seemed. But he hadn't counted on this.

He watched as two of his men hurried down the steps, carrying a laser cannon. "Beinlich!"

His lieutenant reappeared in the doorway. "Sir?"

"Drug the servants, then get all but four of your men to the gate. I want to be out of here as soon as possible."

"Sir!"

Von Pasenow let out a breath. Security, when they came to investigate this, would know this wasn't the work of the Black Hand, if only because the Hand left no survivors. But then they were never meant to think that. They were meant to think this was industrial – that Kim had been kidnapped by one of SimFic's major rivals. The make of drugs would be one clue – throwing suspicion on MedFac: suspicion which would be fanned by a whispering campaign over the next few weeks.

Yes, but it won't work. It won't keep your daughter from marrying Ward. Not if she really wants to.

In fact, it might even backfire. Like that whole business with sending her away to the Colonies. If what he'd heard was right, she had spent most of her time pining for the Clayborn.

No. There was only one sure way to keep the two apart, and that was to kill him. But as Tolonen wouldn't go that far . . .

He shrugged then walked across to the dome. When he'd taken on the job, he had known very little about Ward, but scanning the files he had come to respect the young man, Clayborn or not. In that regard, he didn't share the view of most of the Above. What did it matter where a man came from? It was where he ended up that counted. Too often in his life he had had to put up with arseholes who were his superiors merely through connection. It was nice to come across someone who had risen, like himself, through merit.

If it were he and not the Marshal whose daughter was in love with Ward, he would have given the match his blessing. After all, Ward was one of the richest men in City Europe. And this Mansion . . . He nodded to himself, impressed. No, he would have had no qualms about a daughter of *his* marrying a Clayborn. Not if the Clayborn were worth six hundred million *yuan*.

By the time he got there they had set up the laser and were already cutting into the steel outer door. There was the sweet smell of burning in the air. He put up a hand to shield his eyes against the glare, then turned, looking back at the great House.

No . . . no qualms at all.

* * *

Slowly, careful not to make a noise, Kim edged further into the darkness, wriggling his whole body forward a fraction at a time, his head forced to the side by the narrowness of the space between the ceiling and the floor. The light was just ahead of him now, and he could hear the murmur of voices down below. If he was right he was directly above the kitchens. On the far side there was a service hatch, leading down. If he could somehow twist about and get into it.

He rested, inhaling the warm scent of the new pine floor he'd had put in only a week ago. If he hadn't watched them – if he hadn't witnessed how they'd laid the narrow planks – then they'd have taken him for certain. In all probability he would be dead by now, and Jelka . . .

Jelka would have been widowed before she was even married.

He closed his eyes, wondering what was she doing at that moment. Was she dancing? Was she in the arms of some young soldier, twirling around the ballroom, spiting him, angry with him for not being there – thinking he'd let her down?

He pushed the thought away, then began to edge forward again. It wasn't far now. Another ten minutes and he'd be there. Just another ten minutes.

And if they set the house on fire before then?

"Kim?"

He froze, his eyes searching the darkness in front of him. Then, with a jolt, he realised that the voice had come from inside – from the implant in his head.

"Who is it?" he whispered.

"It is I," the voice answered. "The Machine."

Kim felt a chill go through him. He had not known that it had access to the implant. Always, before now, he had spoken to it in the air – insisting on it. But all the while it had been in there – silent, observant, like a ghost inside his skull.

"What do you want?" he said, the words so soft they were barely formed – yet it heard him perfectly.

"You must go back. Now. You must make your way back to the room you were in when they came."

"But they'll find me."

"No. There are only two of them in the house now, and they are in the control room."

"Then they'll see me."

"No. For there will be nothing to see."

"Ah . . . ." He understood. It was talking about manipulating the images on the screen – of showing an empty room when the room was not empty.

"Who are they?" he asked.

It was silent a moment, then. "You must start to go back. There's little time. She will be here very soon now."

Kim tensed. "Who?"

"Jelka . . . She's coming for you."

"No." He said it slightly too loud, then repeated it more quietly. "No. She mustn't come. They'll kill her."

"Only if they see her. And even then . . . ."

"Even then what?"

It ignored his question. "You must begin. *Now*. The rest I'll see to."

"Machine?"

"Yes?"

"Make sure nothing happens to her."

"I'll try."

"And Machine?"

"Yes?"

"Thank you."

* * *

The reality of it was worse than she'd imagined. Seeing the women's skins hanging there on the rail of the cool room, padded out by their plastoform inserts, their owners eyeless faces staring lifelessly ahead, Emily felt the bile rise in her throat and had to turn away, leaning over the sink in the corner to retch, until there was nothing left in her stomach.

For once the files hadn't prepared her. For once she had let the sheer nastiness of it get to her.

They called it "shelling". Five years ago it wouldn't have been possible, but new research had found a way of keeping the flesh of a human being alive without the bone or blood or muscle. These – these skins – had once been "worn" by living human beings; by young women from the Lowers: the kind of women who, even if they were missed by those they loved, would never have been traced, never accounted for, because they were too poor, too unimportant in the scheme of things to be bothered about.

Kidnapped by special teams, they were taken to a special lab and drugged. There the operation was performed, the surface layer of skin and fat skilfully removed, to be preserved in a vat of nutrients until required. The rest – the living being, stripped like a bloodied skeleton – was given to the Oven Man.

She shivered, thinking of it; trying to imagine the kind of man who would find this sort of thing *attractive*; who would pay a thousand *yuan* a time simply to wear a skin.

Of course, the skin was the simplest part. The really "clever bit was the part that brought the skin to life – that allowed the wearer to tap in to the skin's nervous system and experience exactly what it experienced. A fine mesh of ice was sewn into the inner layer of the skin, feeding to a series of artificial ganglions, at the base of the spine, beneath the sex organs and at the base of the neck, which rooted pain and pleasure signals to the brain of the recipient.

By this foul means a man could wear the body of a woman and make love as a woman. He could feel what it was to be possessed by another man, to have his breasts fondled, the nipples kissed. It was an ancient dream come true. Shelling made it possible. But at a cost . . .

She forced herself to look again – to sear it into her memory. This was what human beings could do to each other. *This*. She reached out to touch one of the skins, surprised by its warmth, a shiver passing through her at the thought that this had once been a living woman like herself, with dreams and hopes and memories, perhaps with children of her own – children who missed her, crying themselves to sleep at night for want of her. But now . . . Emily shuddered. Now it was a mere sense-matrix, a flesh-pad for some rich, unthinking cunt.

A shock of the purest, blackest hatred passed through her like an electric bolt. Inhuman, some might call this. Obscene. But she had her own word for it. *Evil*. These bastards were evil.

She pulled on her gloves, then stood before the mirror, taking long, deep breaths, trying to prepare herself. The attack had been an unqualified success. Despite the heavy security of the place, they had achieved almost complete surprise. The guards had been overwhelmed in the first thirty seconds, the alarm system shut down. The rest had been easy.

As for the clients, they were in the next room, lying face down on the thickly carpeted floor, naked, their hands tied behind their backs.

She had intended to gut the place: to set fires at all the doors and let the bastards burn to death, or suffocate, but that would be too kind. Having seen these awful mementoes, she was of a mind to take the bastards back with her; to take them down level and keep them; to torment them, the way these poor women had been tormented.

Yet even as she considered it – even as her blood sang at the thought – she knew how impractical it was.

Torment. Yes, they deserved to live in everlasting torment for what they'd done.

She looked about her one final time, then turned away and, drawing her knife, stepped out into the other room.

I'll cut your balls off, that's what I'll do, she thought, looking about her at the dozen men who lay spread-eagled on the floor before her. *And I'll make you eat them, you evil fuckers. Every last tiny morsel.*

And afterwards?

She reached down and grabbed the first of them by the hair, pulling his head up so that he could look at her – at the winking razor-sharp edge of the knife in her hand, and smiled.

Afterwards she would have them skinned. *Without* anaesthetic.

* * *

The young Han crouched in the shadows beyond the broken lamp, watching them come from the lift. He had known something was going on; had heard the screams from up above when he was working in the shaft and had known they would come this way. What he hadn't known was what would happen next.

He was smiling, his deformed face pulled to the right, when the guns opened up. Two of the Hand went down at once, dead. The others scattered, finding whatever cover they could, but it was pretty hopeless. In a minute it was over. He waited, his heart threatening to burst from his chest, his legs weak from the shock of what he'd witnessed, keeping his eyes closed, thinking he'd be next . . . After a while he opened his eyes and looked.

They were gone.

He stood, putting a hand out to steady himself against the wall, almost falling as his legs gave. He waited, letting his strength come back, then forced himself to walk over to where the bodies lay; forced himself to look.

They were dead. All eight of them were dead.

There was a faint noise, a hint of movement. He turned, his mouth forming a silent cry of fear.

His heart pounding, he shuffled across, then stooped, listening, studying the fallen woman, seeing the faint rise and fall of her chest. She was alive. He leaned over her, studying the wounds to her head and shoulder. They were bad. She was losing a lot of blood. If he left her here she would die for certain.

And if he took her?

He swallowed drily, then, knowing he had no choice – that he was compelled to help her – he moved round and took her legs. Then, slowly, inch by inch, he began to drag her – away from the scene of death and into the shadows. Away . . . a snail-like trail of blood smeared on the dusty floor of the corridor. Away . . . the weight of her seeming to grow with every step he took.

* * *

As the lift slowed, approaching the top of the stack, Jelka moved to the side, pressing herself against the wall. The feeling that something was wrong had grown in her, until by now she was jumpy, her nerves on edge.

This was stupid – common sense cried out against it – but right now she couldn't help herself. If Kim *was* in trouble, she had to help. And if he wasn't . . . well, she had to know that too. So that she could get on with her life.

The camera eye over the door swivelled, following her every move. She closed her eyes briefly, trying to keep control. No doubt they were watching her from the control room and laughing; laughing, because she didn't have a chance.

The lift stopped abruptly. She was there. She waited, expecting the doors to hiss open, but they stayed closed.

"Open the doors," she said quietly, looking up at the camera. "Why don't you open the doors?"

Nothing. Just the underlying hum that was everywhere in the City.

She hesitated, then stepped across and, slipping her nails beneath the control panel's rim, popped it out. Beneath it were a number of panels. She pulled one out and, taking a second to remember the override sequence, punched in the code.

Nothing. It was as if the thing was dead.

She smacked her hand against the mirrored wall. "*Shit!*"

"I wouldn't do that," a voice said softly. "You'll only hurt yourself."

It sounded like a woman's voice, mature and well-modulated, the intonation somewhere between Han and *Hung Mao*.

"Who are you?" She asked, staring up at the camera.

"Never mind who I am. Just listen. The Mansion has been taken over by intruders."

"Intruders?"

"Your father's men. They have instructions not to harm anyone, but the situation might change at any moment. If it does, this whole thing might escalate into something much nastier."

"And Kim?"

"Kim is safe. But only for a while. If they decide to make another physical check of the Mansion . . ."

"So what do you want me to do?"

"Just do exactly what I say. Take the audio unit from the control panel and carry it with you. I'll speak to you through that."

Jelka nodded, then stepped to the panel again and removed the tiny, dice-like unit.

"Okay," it said, its voice suddenly tiny, coming up to her from within her palm. "You must pretend that you're invisible . . ."

* * *

The masked man stepped from the gaping metal of the outer air-lock and shook his head.

"He's not there. The dome's empty."

"*What?*" Von Pasenow's face registered shock. "But that's not possible! He *has* to be there!"

The man lifted his mask, wiping his face with the back of his hand. "Maybe we should check the house again . . ."

"Quiet! Let me think!"

A second man joined the first, glancing at him, a faint amusement in his eyes, then both looked to Von Pasenow.

There were only two ways into this place and they had watched them both. Kim hadn't come out, so he had to be here.

Von Pasenow paced back and forth, punching his left fist into his right palm again and again. Convinced that Kim was inside the dome, he had dismissed the majority of his men. To search the Mansion again with only five of them would take too long; besides, they'd done a thorough job first time out.

"Tolonen," he said quietly, stopping dead. "I'll speak to Tolonen."

He spun about, then began to run towards the house.

The two men watched him a moment, then, shrugging, began to walk after him.

* * *

Tolonen closed and locked the study door then went to his desk and sat, trying to control the trembling in his arm.

"Put him on!" he said irritably, staring at the screen.

Von Pasenow's face appeared. He bowed low, then made to speak, but Tolonen cut him short.

"Well? What in the gods' names do you want? Don't you realise how *dangerous* this is? Do you have him?"

"I . . ." Von Pasenow lowered his eyes. "I can't find him, Marshal. He's here somewhere, but . . ."

Tolonen stared at him in disbelief, then slowly shook his head. "Then you had better find him. And quick."

"But Marshal . . ."

Tolonen cut contact and sat back, closing his eyes. *Aiya! First that awful scene with Jelka in the ballroom and now this!* He put his hands to his face, groaning. It had all seemed so simple. So straightforward. But now . . .

He gritted his teeth against the memory of the things she'd said to him – of the words he'd let fall from his own lips. Words that could never be recalled.

"Kuan Yin preserve me . . ." he said softly. "Jelka . . . My pretty little Jelka . . . I never meant . . ."

But it was done. Broken. And no way back.

He shuddered, then, laying his head upon his folded arms, began to sob. *I never meant . . .*

* * *

She moved through the great house slowly, silently, her feet making no noise, as if invisible, moving from light to shadow like a ghost, while on screens in the control room, the watching cameras showed only empty corridors, untenanted rooms.

At the back of the great house, in a small room on the upper floor, she found him, seated on a low stool, waiting.

He stood. "What's happened?" he asked, surprised by the pain that was in her face, but she only shook her head.

He stared at her a while, noting her clothes, the simplicity of her appearance, then reached out, taking her hand. It seemed the simplest thing, yet it had taken seven years – seven long years – to achieve.

She looked down, her hand lying passively within his, then smiled; a strangely wistful smile.

"I didn't think . . ." she began, but then her face creased up again, as if she were about to cry.

He understood. Her father. She had broken with her father. He held her to him, the difference in their heights making it an awkward first embrace. Yet in an instant all awkwardness was forgotten. He kissed her face with tiny, delicate kisses, as he'd so often dreamed of doing, then moved back a little, staring into her eyes, surprised to find her looking back at him; surprised by the awe, the love, the expectation in her eyes.

"Is it a dream?" he asked, his voice barely a whisper.

She shook her head. "We must leave. The Machine . . ."

"I hear it," he said, touching the access slot beneath his ear. "It speaks to me. Inside. It told me you were coming."

He reached up, his fingers touching her mouth, her nose, her cheeks, checking to see that she was real. Then he smiled.

"We'd best go," she said. "They're running out of time. Any moment now they'll come and look for us."

He nodded, but still he was reluctant to go, afraid to lose this moment. He could feel a faint trembling in him, as if he were a bell that had been struck and still resounded, long after the hammer's blow had fallen.

"Where are we going?" he asked, when the silence in his head extended; when no answer came.

"To the island," she said, and smiled, the pain momentarily forgotten. "To Kalevala."

CHAPTER·10

THE FLESH OF KINGS

Tsung Ye was kneeling, his head pressed to the floor in front of the Chancellor. Nan Ho looked down at the young secretary in astonishment. He had known something was going on – who hadn't? – but as long as it was being kept discreet, it was not his business to interfere. Now, however, Tsung Ye had made it his business.

He groaned inwardly. This was the last thing he needed just now. In fact, he was tempted to send Tsung Ye away and tell him not to be so silly – that sleeping with the Empress was no great crime, so long as he did not rub the T'ang's nose in it. But Tsung Ye was determined to be absolved, the great burden of his guilt taken from him.

Nan Ho sighed heavily. He felt great pity for the young man, but he only had himself to blame. No doubt it had been flattering to be pursued by his Mistress. But it seemed she had taken things too far. Nan Ho listened, embarrassed, as Tsung Ye spelt out just how far she'd taken them.

It would not have been so bad had Pei K'ung kept to her original agreement with Li Yuan. Then, at least, he could be certain that, should any issue come of the liaison, it was at least no son of Li Yuan's, but the one night she had spent with her husband complicated matters. If she were pregnant . . .

He turned away, suddenly impatient with it all. For a while he had thought her different from the rest – had thought he'd found a woman *above* all of that business – immune to it, but underneath it all, she was just the same. Sex . . . why could they not be free of sex? For all the trouble it caused – all the unhappiness and blighted lives – there seemed little enough reward.

"Enough!" he said, turning back. At once the murmur of the young man's voice fell silent. "You will go to your rooms and lock the doors. You will take pen and paper and write down all that you have told me, then you will return and give the document to me. Meanwhile I shall ensure that the Empress does not come near you."

"Thank you, Master," Tsung Ye said with pathetic gratitude, beginning to crawl away. "I am *pu ju pen fen*."

Nan Ho watched him go, then went to the window. *Pu ju pen fen*. "One who has failed in his duty." And when his duty was to serve his Mistress without question? And when her instruction conflicted with his duty to his T'ang? The old man shivered, then pulled at his collar which had been chafing him, undoing the top button on the right hand side of his neck. He was glad, for once, that he did not have to make a decision. It was an issue Li Yuan alone could rule upon.

And what would he say? Well done, Tsung Ye? You do well to keep the old girl from my bed?

Nan Ho almost laughed, thinking of his Master's predilection for young maids. Why he had let Pei K'ung into his bed that once he would *never* understand. And then to banish her again . . .

He shook his head, then returned to his desk. Matters were pressing. If he judged right things were coming to a head. The reports of his spies were ominous. They spoke of large movements of men and supplies. They hinted at secret meetings and of deals done in shadowy rooms. But nothing certain. Nothing absolute. When it came, it would come suddenly. And he must be prepared.

Nan Ho sat, the image of Tsung Ye naked, his buttocks rising and falling between Pei K'ung's open legs haunting him a moment, making him frown. Then, pushing the matter aside, he picked up the tiny hammer and rang the bell on his desk, summoning his secretaries.

* * *

Tolonen made to get up from his chair, but the abruptness of Rheinhardt's entry into the room caught him by surprise.

"What the fuck are you up to?" Rheinhardt demanded, leaning over him aggressively, his face burning with anger. "I've five men in my cells and, were it not you, Knut Tolonen, I'd gladly make it six!"

Tolonen looked down, embarrassed. "You don't understand . . ."

"*Understand?* What *is* there to understand? That you hired a disgraced Major and his team of tin-pot mercenaries to kidnap one of this City's most important men?"

Tolonen's head came up. "*Important?* That ragamuffin!"

He made to get up, but Rheinhardt pushed him down savagely; the first time he had ever dared touch the old man. He leaned close, speaking the words into Tolonen's face as if addressing the most lowly of his officers and not the man who had been General even before he himself had been born. "*Important.* You understand me, Knut? As in *indispensable.* If he's been harmed. If in any way . . ."

"I gave strict instructions," Tolonen began, but Rheinhardt glared at him and he fell silent.

"You've done many things in your time, Knut Tolonen. Some of them were . . . well, impolitic is to put it mildly. Some of them weren't strictly within the rules. But this . . . *Aiya*, old man, what were you thinking of? Did you think it would solve anything? Did you . . . well, did you even *think*?"

Tolonen stared back at him, his natural defiance tempered by the fact that he knew Rheinhardt was right. He had been stupid.

"What will you do?" he asked quietly.

Rheinhardt straightened up then shook his head in exasperation. "There's nothing I can do. Li Yuan will have to know. If Ward presses charges . . ."

Tolonen sat forward, some of the old fire returning to him. "Let him press charges! But he won't marry my daughter!"

Rheinhardt stared at the old man with a mixture of dismay and pity, then spoke to him, more gently than before. "Jelka is of age now, Knut. Don't you understand that? She can choose for herself now. And if she chooses Ward . . ."

Tolonen stood, his golden hand bunched into a fist as if to strike the one he was talking of. "He won't! I won't let him! I'd rather see him dead!"

Rheinhardt drew himself up rigid, pained to hear the old man reduced to this. "I would be careful what you say, Marshal Tolonen. I am empowered to uphold the law in City Europe. Your words . . ."

"Are no more than the truth," the old man said defiantly, his grey eyes piercing Rheinhardt's. His voice boomed now with all its ancient power. "Arrest me, if you dare. Go tell Li Yuan. But you will not stop me. Whether I lose my daughter or not, *he* shall not have her. You understand me, General Rheinhardt? I won't let him!"

Rheinhardt stared back at the old man a moment, then came to attention, clicking his heels and bowing his head smartly.

"You will hear from me, Marshal," he said, stepping back. "Until you do . . ."

But Tolonen was not listening. The old man turned and, crossing the room, disappeared into his dressing-room, slamming the door behind him.

Rheinhardt closed his eyes, letting out a deep, audible sigh. Then, feeling a sadness that was beyond expression, he turned and left, knowing that the old man had given him no choice.

* * *

Li Yuan stood at the top of the landing ramp, looking out towards the silent stone walls of T'ai Yueh Shan palace, his mood despondent.

It was a grey, cheerless day, the wind whipping off the water of the lake, the calling of the geese like the cries of lost souls.

I should not have come, he thought. *I should have left her here to rot.*

But now that he *was* here he would see it through. Besides, he had to know, to purge himself of this so that he could move on and be strong again.

He shivered, then turned, calling for another, warmer cloak. At once a servant brought one.

The past few weeks had been a torment. In his mind he had constantly pictured her with Tsu Ma. Wherever he turned, there they were, leering at him and laughing, their nakedness taunting him. "Little boy," they'd called, mockingly. "Such a silly little boy, to love your brother's wife."

The pain he felt at such moments was intense. No less intense for being of the mind. Two souls they said he had – the earth soul and the spirit soul, *p'o* and *hun* – and at such moments he had no cause to doubt them, for while his body was untroubled, his spirit ached. Ached like a rotting tooth that could not be pulled.

Well, so it might be. Yet he would try to rid himself of it. Here, today, he would face that inner pain and try to find surcease.

He went down, walking between the lines of kneeling, bowing guards, and on along the path that led to the great West Gate.

Eight and a half years ago he had given her this place, for her and her bastard son. He had divorced her on the day of his coronation and she had had the child two days later, on his wedding day.

Li Yuan slowed his pace, looking to his right, across the grassy slope towards the ornamental bridge, remembering. His wedding day . . . It had been a day much like this, with the wind whipping off the lake. The nineteenth day of the ninth month it had been. The week before *Chiu Fen*, the Autumn Equinox.

He sighed. *And now those three I married that day are dead and she still lives.* How strange it was that after all that had happened, it was to her he was returning. Always to her.

Yes, but no more. After today . . .

Fei Yen was waiting in her rooms. She greeted him with cold civility, kneeling and pressing her head three times against the floor before she straightened up.

"How are you?" he asked, yet a single look told him far more than she could ever say. There was a darkness behind her eyes that had not been there a month ago, a tightness to her mouth. Whatever madness had compelled her to fly to Tsu Ma's palace that day, whatever hotness of the blood had urged her on, it had congealed in her now. Eyes which had burned with an angry passion now stared at him with frigid insolence.

Her words, when they came, were, like the formality of her greeting, only a mockery.

"I am very happy here, *Chieh Hsia*. You do me great honour, visiting me."

He felt the pain rekindled; felt that familiar tightening of his stomach muscles. Why was it thus? Why did she still have power over him, after all these years?

"I came to clarify things," he answered. "Much was left . . . *unstated* last time we met."

She laughed. "Unstated? Why, forgive me, *Chieh Hsia*, but I thought I expressed myself quite eloquently. Your cousin fucked me. Not once, but many times. Would you like to know *where* and *how*?" Her eyes searched his, as if trying to gauge how best to inflict pain. "It would be no trouble, if you've the time. I can recall each and every occasion." She smiled. "He may have been a bastard, but Tsu Ma was a memorable fuck. He . . ."

"Enough!"

He turned from her, smoothing out his gloves, trying not to show the intense hurt, the agitation he was feeling, but her voice went on, ignoring his command.

"We would ride up to the ruins of the old monastery, up in the hills above Tongjiang. Inside, in the oldest of the temples, he would lay down his riding blanket and we would strip and lie on it. And then . . ."

He turned, staring at her, compelled, despite himself, to know.

"And then . . ." Her voice, her face slowly changed, softening. "And then he would make love to me." She sighed. "So fierce and yet so . . . so gentle he was. As if he could feel what I was feeling. As if . . ."

She shuddered and looked away, all of the anger in her transmuted suddenly to pain.

中
國

He stared at her, for that brief moment understanding her. For the very first time understanding just what had driven her. *Aiya!* he thought. *To feel that, and yet to be tied.*

"I understand," he said quietly. "It . . . it was not your fault. Tsu Ma . . ."

He swallowed back the sudden surge of hatred he felt for the man.

She came across and stood beside him, her dark eyes looking up at him, the sweet scent of her filling his senses. And if he were to reach out . . .

Slowly he put his arms about her and bent his face to hers, her mouth opening to his, her lips warm and moist. It was the thing he had missed most all these years: being kissed by her.

He broke from the kiss and moved his head back, staring at her, suddenly afraid of what he'd done.

"Make love to me," she said softly, her eyes pleading with him. "Now. Before the moment vanishes."

He shivered, then, unable to prevent himself, nodded, letting her lift the cloak from his shoulders then begin to unbutton his robe, a boy again, the veil of years torn aside.

"Fei Yen," he whispered, his hand reaching up to caress her neck, her cheek, his fingers smoothing the side of her head as it pressed back against his touch. "Fei Yen . . ."

She drew him down, on to the bed, her soft warm kisses on his neck and shoulders blinding his senses, making him groan with sweet delight. She fumbled at his loin cloth, her hand brushing intimately against his fiercely swollen sex, and then he was inside her, thrusting into her, the pain of longing in her face inflaming him, making him spasm and come immediately. And still he thrust, and still she met his thrust, her cries of pleasure keeping him hard.

"Yes . . . oh, yes . . . Oh, oh . . ."

He felt her reach up, holding herself tightly, intimately against him, felt the great shudder of release that rippled through her, and then she fell back, as if she'd fainted. As she did, he felt his penis slip from her and gave a tiny groan. At once she reached for him and led him back inside her, then cradled his head against her with one hand, while the other smoothed his buttocks.

He let a shuddering sigh escape him, then closed his eyes, conscious of the hard length of his flesh within her, linking them, binding them as no words or ceremonies had ever managed.

If only it could always have been thus. But the flesh was weak, the warmth illusory.

They made love again, this time beneath the blankets, his face above hers, watching her, savouring each moment, using all his skills to bring her to her climax long before he let his seed flow into her.

"I had forgotten," he said afterwards, facing her, his hands tracing the contours of her body. "All these years . . ."

She watched him lazily, like a cat, all of the hardness, the resentment washed from her; purged, it seemed, by his love-making.

"Do you think . . ." he began, then sighed, shaking his head.

"You can always visit me," she said. "You could tie me up."

"Is that what you like?"

She gave a soft grunt, then looked away. "You do not know the half of it, Li Yuan. The men I've known. The years . . . ach! Each year has seemed like ten. Like those years I spent in exile in the floating palace, mourning your brother's death."

He sighed, pained by this insight into her. All these years he'd blamed and hated her; all these years he'd failed to see.

"I have been blind," he said. "I never understood, did I?"

"No." She looked back at him and smiled. "So what now, my husband?"

The words sent a strange thrill through him – a shock of recognition, of *rightness*. He smiled, feeling as if it were the first true smile – the first honest, open smile – he'd ever given her.

"So now . . . we start anew."

He reached out, drawing her up on to him, cradling her above him and kissing her.

"Once more and then I have to go. But I'll be back for you. I promise. We'll start again, Fei Yen, and damn the world. I'll divorce Pei K'ung and make Han Ch'in a prince. I'll set things right, I promise you. I'll make things better than they were."

Then, rolling her on to her back, he climbed above her and entered her again, feeling like an exiled king, returned into his kingdom.

"Fei Yen," he whispered, her movements matching his perfectly, Yin to his Yang. "My darling wife, Fei Yen."

* * *

Tsu Kung-ch'ih was drunk. He stood there, red-faced, facing his uncle's Master of the Inner Chambers, Hwa Kwei, and shouted angrily.

"You incompetent fool! Can't you do *anything* right? I pay you a fortune and you mess things up! I mean, what now?"

He tore at his rich silks in anguish, then turned away sharply. Behind him the embarrassed Hwa, his head bowed, kept his silence. Tsu Kung-ch'ih was right. He had failed miserably. Tsu Shu-sun was pregnant and he had failed to prevent it. His potions had made her sick, certainly, but still, somehow, she had conceived.

The prince turned, one foot up on the low wall that surrounded the inner courtyard and its shallow pool. His disappointment was clear in his face. His sallow lips quivered and his eyes were moist, but he spoke more softly now, trying to control himself; struggling against the sudden impact of this news. He had learned of it only today – only an hour back. Tsu Ma had kept it from him until now.

Shuddering, he looked at Hwa Kwei again.

"Was it so difficult? You said it would be easy. You *assured* me."

Hwa Kwei gave a small nod, then bowed lower. It *should* have been easy, but who could have known that Shu-sun would conceive on her wedding night? Who would have thought that Tsu Ma would change his mind and go to her?

Kung-ch'ih glared at him a moment longer, then turned away, a noise of sheer exasperation escaping him. He felt betrayed. It was as if his uncle had been toying with him. And though he had pretended otherwise, it was clear that Tsu Ma had enjoyed telling him the news. As if he didn't know what it meant to him.

He laughed bitterly and threw out his hand, dismissing the middle-aged servant. What good was it, trusting in others? No, this was something he would have to do himself.

He looked around. Hwa Kwei had gone. "Good riddance," he said softly. But the words did not begin to express the turbulence of what he had felt this last hour. Now, however – now that he was alone at last – one thing seemed to surface and rise above all others, vast, bloated, obscuring the rest in its dark and awful shadow. Tsu Ma had known! He had known all along! And Hwa Kwei . . .

Tsu Kung-ch'ih closed his eyes, a faint nausea overcoming him momentarily. They had toyed with him. Played him like a fish on a line. And now they would reel him in.

"*No-oooh . . .*"

Slowly he opened his eyes. No one had heard his cry of anguish. He turned and looked about him, making sure. But no, he was alone.

"What then?" he said softly, talking to himself now. "Should I go to him and tell him what I've done? Go down on my knees before him and beg forgiveness?" He sighed, then shook his head. "No, I'll not do that. Not after what he's done to me."

Which left him but one choice. Smiling grimly he stared down at his reflection in the mirror of the pool.

"So be it, then."

* * *

Li Yuan swept down the grand corridor at Tongjiang, his entourage almost running to keep up with him, servants – surprised by the haste with which he came upon them dropping quickly to their knees and lowering their heads as he rushed past. The T'ang was more than three hours late and had missed several important meetings.

As the doors to Nan Ho's study burst open, the Chancellor looked up from his desk, then hastily came round the desk and knelt before his Master.

"*Chieh Hsia,*" he said, looking up at Li Yuan. "I am delighted to see you well. I was worried that something had happened."

Li Yuan waved the concern for his health aside, moving past his kneeling Chancellor to study the papers on his desk.

"What has been happening, Master Nan?"

Nan Ho got up slowly, and stepped to his Master's side. "Minister Chu is in the Eastern Palace being . . . *entertained*, shall we say. The *San Shih* I saw myself. I felt it best not to keep them waiting, considering recent events."

Li Yuan nodded, yet he seemed distracted. "And the matter with Tsung Ye?"

Nan Ho blinked. "Tsung Ye?"

Li Yuan glanced at him. "He came to see you this morning, I understand. About the Empress's demands on him."

The old man's mouth opened, then closed again. He nodded.

"So what do you suggest, Master Nan? Should I have the young man castrated?

Or should I make him a member of my Advisory Council? After all, to find a man who is both a dedicated servant and yet a man of honour . . . that is not to be discarded lightly, neh?"

Nan Ho's mouth worked without sound. He looked in shock. Finally he found the words. "I . . . I did not know you knew, *Chieh Hsia*. I . . . I have had him draw up a full confession. It is . . ."

Li Yuan shook the sheaf of papers at him. "I am reading it, Master Nan. An interesting document, neh? One we could use, if we wished . . ."

"Use, *Chieh Hsia?*"

There was an urgent knocking on the outer doors. Li Yuan looked to Nan Ho. "Are your expecting anyone, Master Nan?"

Nan Ho shook his head.

"Well . . . we had best find out who wants us, neh?"

Master Nan bowed, then went across. Opening the door a crack, he exchanged a few words with his secretary, then turned back.

"It is General Rheinhardt, *Chieh Hsia*. He wishes to speak with you urgently."

Li Yuan folded Tsung Ye's confession and pocketed it, then nodded. "Send him in. I will see him here. And Master Nan . . . please stay. There is something I need to arrange with you."

Nan Ho stared at his Master, noting the strange smile he wore, then turned and left. A moment later he was back, leading in the General.

"Helmut," Li Yuan said, greeting his Marshal, holding out his ring for him to kiss, then watching as he knelt and touched his forehead to the floor before him. "How can I help you?"

Rheinhardt glanced at Nan Ho, then got to his feet again. "It is Marshal Tolonen, *Chieh Hsia*. He tried to have Ward kidnapped."

"Tried . . ." Li Yuan laughed. "You jest, surely, Helmut? Knut kidnap Kim? Why on earth would he do that?"

"To stop him marrying his daughter."

Li Yuan turned to Nan Ho, his face suddenly severe. "Am I to believe my ears, Master Nan? You mean there was a relationship between Ward and the Marshal's daughter and I was not told of it?"

Nan Ho bowed low. "It was long ago, *Chieh Hsia*. I . . . I did not feel it was important."

"*Important? Aiya*, Master Nan! Nothing is more important than these personal matters. Nothing! Surely you of all people understand that?"

"Forgive me, *Chieh Hsia*. I am *pu ju pen fen*."

Li Yuan stared at him, surprised by the formality of the phrase – "one who has failed in his duty" – then turned to Rheinhardt again. "So what happened?"

"It seems the Marshal hired mercenaries to kidnap Kim at his Mansion, to prevent him from attending his daughter's Coming-of-Age party. But for some reason Ward eluded his attackers. Now both he and the Marshal's daughter have gone missing."

"Together?"

"That's the strange thing, *Chieh Hsia*. We can find no camera records of their movements. It's as if they vanished."

Li Yuan sucked in his breath. If he had lost Ward . . .

"And the Marshal? What does he say of all this?"

Rheinhardt looked down. "I am afraid the Marshal is unrepentant. He says that Ward will never marry his daughter. That he would kill him first."

Li Yuan turned away, then walked over to the window. "Why now? Why *now* of all times?" He looked back. "We must find Ward, Helmut. We simply must. He is *vital* to our plans. As for the Marshal . . ." He sighed. "You will place Marshal Tolonen under house arrest. You will give orders to the guards to use the minimum force to restrain him if need be, but restrain him they must, if it proves necessary. As for his honorary rank, he is stripped of it until this matter can be investigated. From henceforth he is to be considered no more than any other private citizen."

Rheinhardt looked down, saddened that it had come to this. "I am sorry, *Chieh Hsia*. To bring such news . . ."

Li Yuan went to him. "It is not your fault, Helmut. Sometimes even the best of us lose our way, neh? The Marshal is an old man. He was always inflexible. Old age has made him more so."

He stepped back, making a gesture of dismissal. Rheinhardt bowed low, then backed away.

When he was gone, Li Yuan looked to his Chancellor and let out a long breath. "*Aiya!*"

Nan Ho came across and knelt at his feet. "Forgive me, *Chieh Hsia*. If I had known . . ."

Li Yuan reached out and touched his head gently. "It is all right, Master Nan. I forgive you this once. But . . ."

Unexpectedly he laughed.

Nan Ho straightened up, staring at his master. "Are you all right, *Chieh Hsia*?"

The young T'ang smiled. "Never better, Master Nan. Never, in all my life, better."

*　*　*

The old men filed in silently, their shaven heads lowered modestly, their saffron robes whispering on the ancient stones of the great hall. When all seventy eight were seated, the three *San Shih* made their way to the centre of the great circle of chairs and stood, their arms crossed before them, concealed within the silken folds of their robes.

Luo Ye, the eldest and most senior of them, looked about him at the patiently watching faces, then bowed. "*Ch'un tzu*," he began, "we have come to report to the *Pa shi yi* concerning our meeting this morning with Li Yuan."

The old man hesitated then, drawing himself up straight, he raised his right hand from within his robes, the crooked index finger pointing to the ceiling high above. As he did, his voice rang out, the perfectly intoned Mandarin filling the ancient hall.

"I am afraid to tell my revered brothers that the T'ang was not there. It appears he was . . . *delayed*."

A great hiss of disbelief went out at the news. Luo Ye waited a moment, then continued.

"Instead we spoke to the *Ch'eng Hsiang*, Nan Ho. He advised us to wait; to let our grievances rest until a better time. To . . . well, in brief, to go away and do as we were told."

The hiss became a buzz of anger. On all sides old men looked to each other, animatedly discussing this new development.

"*Ch'un tzu* . . ." Luo Ye said, calling them to order. "It may be that the great Li Yuan was indeed delayed. That, knowing we wished to see him on a matter of the first importance, he yet allowed himself to be detained elsewhere. However, it was my feeling that his was a deliberate insult; a snubbing of the *Pa shi yi*, indeed, of the great New Confucian movement itself. Since we failed his son, he has, it seems, had little time for us. Like a sulking woman, he has sought to avenge himself in petty ways. But this . . ."

Luo Ye drew himself up straight, the grave authority of his voice echoing amidst the stone pillars of the great hall.

"Since the time of the great sage, Meng Tzu, it has been agreed by all men that to govern Chung Kuo a Son of Heaven must have Heaven's Mandate, and that to be in possession of the Mandate such a one must be a man of virtue and benevolence. Similarly, it has been agreed that any Son of Heaven found lacking in these qualities forfeits his right to the dragon throne. In such a case the Mandate is broken." He paused significantly. "For some time now the actions of our Master, Li Yuan, son of Li Shai Tung, have caused this Council great concern, but this . . . this wilful disregard for other men . . . does this show virtue? Are these the actions of a benevolent man?"

"No!" came the cry from all sides. "No!"

"Well, brothers . . ." Luo Ye said, folding his arms within his robes once more, a smile of satisfaction on his lips now. "Then it seems we must debate a brand new matter. It seems it is time for the *Pa shi yi* to act. To teach this wilful young man from whence his power derives . . ."

* * *

Tsu Ma's face was blanched, like a mask of shocked anger, the muscles of his neck taut. He sat there, his hands clenching the carved arms of the throne, his whole body held rigid, listening as his Master of the Inner Chambers, Hwa Kwei, made his confession.

Hwa Kwei was sprawled below the raised dais, his forehead pressed against the stone floor, his arms thrown out before him in supplication, his whole attitude one of abject apology. When he had finished, Tsu Ma gave a small grunt and leaned forward.

"Is that all, Hwa Kwei?"

"It is all, *Chieh Hsia*."

The T'ang shuddered violently and stood, looking past his servant at the great doors. They were alone here in the audience chamber. Tsu Ma had dismissed the guards, trusting his old retainer. But now? For a moment his anger spilled out. He raised his voice.

"*Why,* Hwa Kwei? What have I done to deserve this of you?"

But his anger was seasoned with the knowledge that Hwa Kwei had come to him. Dishonoured and a traitor he might be, but he had acted honourably at the last. Tsu Ma sighed and, going down the steps, raised Hwa Kwei's chin with his foot.

"I shall spare your Family, Master Hwa. I promise you that."

The retainer took the T'ang's foot and kissed it, then returned his forehead to the floor. For himself, he knew, there was only death, but the T'ang had been merciful. Hwa's Family, at least, would live.

Just then there was a hammering at the door. Tsu Ma stepped past Hwa Kwei, frowning, then glanced back at the servant as he answered.

"Enter!"

It was Yung Chen, one of the eunuchs from the women's quarters. He was breathless. His eyes stared wildly at the T'ang as he bowed, then straightened.

"What is it?" Tsu Ma said quietly. His stomach had tightened, his whole body gone cold. He had the sense that something dreadful – something irreparable – had happened.

"It is Kung-ch'ih, *Chieh Hsia*. He has gone mad. he holds Shu-sun at knife-point and calls for you to come. Tan We is dead, and two others."

Tan We was the Chief Eunuch, Tsu Ma's mentor from his childhood. The news was like a physical blow. For a moment Tsu Ma faltered, not understanding what was happening. Then, stumbling forward, he pushed past the eunuch and began to run.

In the corridor outside, the guards fell in behind their T'ang, astonished to see him in such a state. Out into the courtyard they went, into bright sunlight, then through the water gardens and across the narrow bridge that led to the women's quarters.

And as he ran, Tsu Ma was thinking, *And Tao Chu? Is Tao Chu in on this too? Can I trust no one?*

The first three rooms were empty. Beyond them was a small courtyard with cherry trees in blossom and a small pool. Beyond that were Shu-sun's rooms. Two servants stood on the far side of the pool, turning towards him and bowing as he came out into the courtyard.

"Where is he?"

One of the servants turned, pointing inside. Tsu Ma strode across the courtyard, but he had gone only a few paces when two figures appeared in the far doorway.

Kung-ch'ih held Shu-sun before him, the long, deadly knife held lengthways beneath her chin. He could kill her before Tsu Ma took another step. The T'ang halted, glaring at the youth.

"Are you mad, Kung-ch'ih?"

"Never so sane, Uncle."

Shu-sun looked terrified. Her silk wrap was spattered with blood and her small, white hands were clasped together in front of her. She seemed close to fainting and looked to Tsu Ma with imploring eyes. Tsu Ma, seeing her so, felt his stomach turn; felt an emptiness, a fear he had never felt before. Even so he kept it hidden from his face; kept all his love, his weakness tight inside, steeling himself to deal with his nephew.

"Why this?" he asked, taking one step.

"No further, Uncle," the youth warned, tilting the blade slightly so that it nicked the flesh and made Shu-sun cry out. Tsu Ma gritted his teeth, then let a breath hiss out between them.

"What do you want?"

Kung-ch'ih's hand was steady, his whole manner dangerous – far more dangerous than Tsu Ma would have expected. He had thought him weak. In that, too, he had been wrong. He waited while the youth considered his reply; appraising the situation, his eyes straying to each side and to above, trying to assess what might be done. Shu-sun's body shielded Kung-ch'ih's. If his guards shot at Kung they would probably miss, and Shu-sun would be dead.

"I am tired of games," Kung-ch'ih said finally.

"*Games?*" Tsu Ma was puzzled. He made to take another step but saw how the muscles of the hand that held the knife tensed, and so he relaxed, letting his hands open at his sides.

"You have toyed with me, Uncle. Played games with me. All along you have mocked me. I know. Hwa Kwei told me."

This puzzled him more. What could Hwa Kwei have possibly told him to make him think that? Then, suddenly, he understood. It all fell into place. The announcement of Shu-sun's pregnancy! *That* had precipitated all of this!

"No . . ." he said softly, almost tenderly, as if he understood the hurt the boy was feeling. "I have played no games with you, Kung-ch'ih. Until today, I . . ."

The boy's cold laughter cut his words short. "I do not believe you, Uncle. Even now you think to trick me. To keep me from what I want."

"And you want this?" Tsu Ma had gone cold again. He saw no way out of this. No way but death.

"I wanted what was mine. By right."

By right? But Tsu Ma said nothing, only bowed his head slightly, as if acknowledging what was said.

Kung-ch'ih spoke again. "For years you led me to believe I would be T'ang one day."

Did I? Tsu Ma thought. Well, maybe he had. Even so, nothing justified this.

"What do you think this will achieve, Kung-ch'ih?"

Again the young man laughed, but his eyes gave nothing away. He had killed three times already; perhaps those deaths had changed him.

"I could kill your son, perhaps, Tsu Ma. Kill the heir you think to have."

Tsu Ma was silent a moment, simply watching the boy, trying to control the sudden violent hatred he had felt hearing those words, reminding himself that this was his brother's child, his ward. Yet when he spoke again he let nothing of that hatred show, steeling himself to be calm and unemotional.

"I can wed a dozen wives, Kung-ch'ih. One of them will give me a son."

For the first time the knife wavered slightly and a look of doubt crept into the prince's eyes. But it was a moment's hesitation only. The look of cold determination returned. Kung-ch'ih slowly shook his head and laughed.

"No, Uncle. You do not fool me with your act. I've *seen* you with this woman."

Again Tsu Ma felt a hot flush of rage pass through him. He wanted to kill the boy; to tear him apart with his bare hands. And yet he had to stand there, calm, his hands open at his sides, his face clear of the anger he felt. For Shu-sun's sake. Because to show what he was feeling would mean her certain death.

He laughed and let the laughter roll on for longer than its normal course. Again there was a moment's uncertainty in the young man's eyes. Tsu Ma let the laughter spill over into his voice.

"So you think you *know* me, boy?"

This time no words, only a curt, uncompromising nod. The knife was held steady beneath Shu-sun's chin, the sharp blade dark with others' blood. Shu-sun had closed her eyes, her chest rising and falling heavily. Kung-ch'ih's left arm was locked about her shoulder now, keeping her from falling.

Tsu Ma, watching, wondered what she was feeling; whether it was one part as dreadful as the fear he felt for her.

"What now then?" he asked, keeping his voice steady.

They had come to an impasse. There was nothing he could offer. No deal could come of this. No compromise. He sighed heavily, suddenly weary, then, with an anger he had concealed until that moment, he yelled and threw himself forward.

Surprised, Kung-ch'ih's instincts took over, and for one brief moment the knife moved outwards in a wide arc, as if to meet the oncoming threat. Then it jerked back and Shu-sun fell forward, screaming.

Tsu Ma stopped, horrified, looking down at his fallen wife. Then his head jerked up. Kung-ch'ih was on his knees. The knife had clattered to the floor. From the centre of Kung-chih's chest a long steel spike protruded. Kung-ch'ih coughed once, blood dribbling from between his lips, then fell on to his face.

Behind him, in the doorway, stood Tao Chu. His silks were drenched and his hair slicked back and wet. He looked down at his half-brother in surprise, a dreadful look of pain – of sheer loss – on his face, then looked across at Tsu Ma. Shu-sun was scrabbling forward, whimpering with fright. Tsu Ma met his nephew's eyes a moment, then bent down and held his wife to him, his big frame shivering uncontrollably as he comforted her.

After a moment he looked up at Tao Chu again. The boy was still standing there, looking down at the brother he had killed. Tears rolled down his cheeks, one after another, and, even as Tsu Ma watched, the boy knelt and kissed the dark head of his brother, one hand gently touching and stroking the yet warm neck, as if he merely slept.

* * *

Nan Ho sat at his desk, staring into space.

"Kuan Yin preserve us," he murmured.

"Master?"

He looked to his secretary, Hu Chang, and shook his head. "I said Kuan Yin preserve us. This business . . . it is an ill day's work. The Empress Pei K'ung is a good woman, and if she has needs . . . well, we all have *needs*, neh, Hu Chang?"

Hu Chang lowered his head.

"I tried to talk sense into him," he continued, "but he would not listen. It is just as before. He is obsessed with her. Infatuated with the she-fox. She has cast her spell over him again and we must all suffer for it."

Hu Chang looked up. "Master?"

"Yes, Hu Chang?"

"Perhaps we should try to delay matters and let time cure our Lord of this . . . this *strangeness*."

Nan Ho turned to him. "*Delay?*"

"Yes, Master. If we could find some . . . distraction, perhaps, to keep him from pursuing the matter. Some . . ."

Nan Ho raised a hand. At once Hu Chang fell silent, bowing his head.

"He wants it done tonight. The divorce document is being drawn up even as we speak. Tsung Ye's confession . . . achh!" He heaved a great sigh of exasperation, then stood, his restlessness taking a physical form. "I should have ignored my conscience and had the woman killed while I could."

Hu Chang's eyes followed his Master, appalled by what he was hearing. Never had Nan Ho spoke of killing anyone. Always he had been a voice of reason. But this matter, it seemed, had stripped all rationality from him . . . or revealed it?

Hu Chang swallowed, then spoke up. "To kill her. It would solve nothing, Master."

"No?" Nan Ho turned to him. "You do not know the woman, Hu Chang. Such deviousness . . ." Again he shook his head. "And this time she will not be so easy to dislodge. This time . . ."

The summons bell rang. Nan Ho stared at it, then grimaced.

"That will be him. Go to him, Hu Chang. Tell him that I am sick and have taken to my bed. Tell him . . ."

Nan Ho stopped, lowering his head, genuine pain there suddenly. "My boy . . . my poor, poor boy. How could he do this to himself a second time? How can I bear to stand by and watch it happen?"

The bell rang again.

"You want me to go, Master?"

Nan Ho looked at him then smiled sadly. "No, Hu Chang. It is my duty to attend. My duty to serve, whatever my Master asks of me. It is the way, neh? Wherever it leads."

Hu Chang bowed his head, relieved to see his Master returned to his former self.

Nan Ho came across, touching his arm gently, then went from the room, making his way towards Li Yuan's rooms, ready to serve his Master, *whatever* was asked of him.

* * *

"You summoned me, *Chieh Hsia?*"

Li Yuan looked up and waved Nan Ho across. "Have you heard, Master Nan?"

"Heard, *Chieh Hsia?*"

Li Yuan handed him the single sheet of paper. "It arrived a moment back. Copies are being posted throughout our City even as we speak."

Nan Ho read it through, then looked up, his face blanched, his eyes bewildered. "But this says . . ."

"The Mandate is broken . . . that's what it says. The *Pa shi yi* have declared my government invalid. They have sanctioned open rebellion."

Nan Ho stared back at him. "*Aiya* . . ."

"*Aiya* indeed. Yet not unexpected, neh?"

"Unexpected?"

"We have known for some while now that the New Confucians were dissatisfied with things. And your meeting this morning . . . well, did you not sense this in the air, Master Nan?"

Nan Ho shook his head. It seemed he had foreseen few of these developments. "But what shall we do?"

"*Do?* Why, we have them all arrested. Arrested and executed."

Nan Ho swallowed. "But that would mean . . ."

"War? Possibly. But this . . . ." He took the paper back from his Chancellor. "No, Master Nan. I cannot have this."

There was a knock. Li Yuan raised an eyebrow. "Enter!"

A messenger bowed his way into the room, then, kneeling, offered a sealed letter to the T'ang's secretary, who unfurled it, read it, then brought it across.

Li Yuan took it and read it, then turned in his seat, calling for the screen to be lowered.

"Watch," Li Yuan said, then, speaking to the air. "Show me the latest scenes from Weimar."

At once the screen showed a picture of the great House. Drawing back, it focused on a group of men outside the entrance gate. Media remotes hovered about their heads like bugs as one of them, recognisable as the Leader of the House, Representative Kavanagh, was speaking.

". . . yet such an unprecedented statement by the New Confucian hierarchy can only be read as a recognition by those within the T'ang's government – those who know him best, let it be said – that things have reached such a pass that only the most extreme action can remedy the situation. It is therefore with great reluctance, but with a sense of duty, that we have taken a vote on the issue and offer the full support of this House to the *Pa shi yi*. Further, we urge the citizens of City Europe to reject the rule of the despot Li Yuan and accept Li Min as Son of Heaven and the new T'ang."

There was a gasp from all those in the room. Nan Ho turned, expecting to find his own shock mirrored on his Master's face, but Li Yuan was smiling.

"*Chieh Hsia?*" he said, astonished that at this moment the T'ang should be amused. "Are you all right?"

"Never better, Master Nan." He stood, then came around his desk, stopping before the image of House Leader Kavanagh.

"Arrest them," he said, the confidence in his voice surprising them all. "All of them, and then burn the House. We must teach these *hsiao jen* a lesson, neh, Master Nan?"

"*Chieh Hsia?*"

Li Yuan turned to face him, the smile slowly fading from his face until, in its hawk-like seriousness it resembled his father, Li Shai Tung's.

"You heard me, Master Nan. Arrest them. Triad members, New Confucians, Representatives and all. All who oppose me. It has begun," he said, his voice a strange mixture of fear and relief. "The gods help us, Master Nan, it has finally begun."

* * *

At the cliff's edge stood a ruined chapel, its roof open to the sky, the doorway empty, gaping. It was a tiny building, the floor inside cracked and overgrown with weeds, one of the side walls collapsed, the heavy stones spilled out across the grass.

Kim stopped beside her, looking up at the lettering cut into the stone lintel.

"It's Latin," he said. "From the Revelation to John."

Jelka looked to him, surprised, as he began to read.

"I saw an angel standing in the sun, and with a loud voice he cried to all the birds that fly in middle heaven, 'Come, gather for the great supper of God . . .'"

He turned to her, finishing the quote, "to eat the flesh of kings, of all men, both free and slave, great and small."

He smiled, then looked about him. "Is this it? Is this your special place?"

"No." She looked out at the sea beyond the ruin, then walked on.

It was an old path worn by many feet. Near the bottom, where the way grew steep, steps had been cut into the rock. She picked her way nimbly between the rocks and out beneath the overhang. Kim followed. There, on the far side of the shelf of rock, was the cave.

She turned and smiled at him. "This is it. My special place. The place of voices."

He went halfway across the ledge then stopped, crouching, looking down through the crack in the great grey slab. There, below him, the incoming tide was channelled into a fissure in the rock. For a moment he watched the rush and foam of the water through the narrow channel, then he looked up. She was watching him, amused.

"Can't you hear it, Kim? It's talking to you."

"Yes," he said. "I hear it."

He stood, wiping his hands against his thighs, then went across and stood there at the edge of the rock, looking out across the rutted surface of the sea, feeling the wind like a hand on his face, the tang of salt on his lips.

"Here," she said, drawing his attention again.

There, on the wall behind her, were the ancient letters, a hand's length in height, scored into the rock and dyed a burnt ochre against the pale cream of the rock. Their stick-like, angular shapes brought to mind the shape of yarrow stalks. He frowned, recognising them as runes – as a name. Tolonen. And yet they were – what? – fifteen hundred years old?

He shuddered, then narrowed his eyes, watching as she stooped, making her way further in, towards where the ceiling sloped down to meet the floor of the cave.

"It was just here that I saw the fox," she said, turning, her blue eyes staring out at him from the half dark. "Later I dreamed of it and thought of you."

A fox. He nodded, then went in, taking her hand.

"So wild it was," she said, kneeling, then pulling him down beside her. "Erkki wanted to shoot it but I wouldn't let him."

He stared at her, bewitched, the dark scent of the place awaking something in him.

A fox . . .

He drew her face to his and kissed her, a savage, fox's kiss, then pushed her down, the brightness slipping from him.

* * *

Back in the house, he walked about the rooms, disturbed by what had happened; wondering just what it said about himself. Yet Jelka seemed happy. He could hear her in the kitchens, singing to herself, her laughter strange and unexpected. He had thought her so cold and regal.

At the door to the study he stopped and lifted his head, sniffing the air, then stepped inside, his eyes widening at the sight of so many books.

"Books!" he said, carrying one out to her. "*Real* books!"

"Kalevala," she said, taking it from him. "My uncle lent me this. It was the first real book I ever read. Here . . ." She handed it back to him. "You must read it. My people . . ."

"Your people . . ." He looked at her sadly. "You should contact him, you know. Let him know that you're safe. He'll be worrying."

"Let him worry!" she said. "He deserves it. But aren't you angry with him?"

"Angry?" he laughed, then, putting the books down, took her hands. "How *could* I be angry? Without him there would be no you. For that . . . well, I forgive him everything."

He smiled, trying to coax her to his viewpoint, but he could see she was not to be brought round. Not yet, anyway.

"Let me help," he said, looking past her at the pans on the old-fashioned stove. "I like to cook for myself."

In answer, she beat his hand away. "That was when you were on your own. Now . . . well, now you're mine. If it worries you, we'll take turns. But tonight . . . tonight I want to cook for you. Please . . . I've dreamed of it."

He smiled. "You dream a great deal, Jelka Tolonen."

"Yes . . ." Her eyes grew serious. "I dreamed that you would come for me and save me from the World of Levels. I dreamed . . ." She stopped, a sudden fear growing in her face. "Something's happened," she said. "Something . . ."

She moved past him, heading for the great living-room. He followed, intrigued by the change in her, by the sudden intuitive leap she'd made. As she crouched before the big screen, trying to tune it in, he looked about him, surprised, constantly surprised to find himself there on the island, in this strangest of houses. Had she dreamed this? And was he, even now, trapped within her dream – of no more substance than Caliban's dream.

"Sometimes a thousand twangling instruments
Will hum about mine ears; and sometimes voices,
That, if I then had wak'd after long sleep,
Will make me sleep again: and then, in dreaming,
The clouds methought would open, and show riches
Ready to drop upon me, that, when I wak'd,
I cried to dream again."

She turned, looking at him, even as the screen came to life behind her.

"What is that? It sounds . . . *familiar* somehow."

"Just words," he said. "Something that no longer exists, except in the mind of a Machine."

"Words?" But already her attention was being drawn by what was on the screen. There, framed by thick black smoke, was the House at Weimar, its great windows smashed, its levels licked by flames. Long lines of shackled men were being led away by visored guards. Then the image changed, to scenes of rioting and ruin, of screaming men and crying women.

"What's happening?" he said, stepping up beside her, then crouching, taking her hand. "What in the gods' names is happening?"

"It has begun," she said, a tremor passing through her. "The gods help us all. The War's begun."

CHAPTER · 11

THE RIDER THROUGH THE AUTUMN WIND

"Y ou must talk to him, *Chieh Hsia*. You simply must."

"*Must*, Master Nan?" Li Yuan turned from the great map, stoney-faced, to confront his Chief Minister. "Will you tell me also who I must *sleep* with?"

Nan Ho lowered his head, chastened. All around the War Room others – more than forty in all – did the same, recognising that tone in the T'ang's voice. At such times he was at his most dangerous – or so it had proved, these past five days.

Nan Ho glanced at his Master from beneath his lashes. Five days . . . was that all it had been since war had been declared? A mere five days?

"They say he is dying, *Chieh Hsia*," he said quietly, risking his Master's wrath; knowing he would never forgive himself unless he attempted some kind of reconciliation.

"Dying?" Li Yuan turned, surprised. "I . . . I had not heard that. I thought . . ."

"Poisoned, *Chieh Hsia*. Or so I am told. It is . . . well, difficult to know the truth. Our usual channels are not as reliable as they were."

Li Yuan nodded, understanding. All was in chaos. And information – *reliable* information – was the hardest thing to come by. Li Min had seen to that.

We did not know, Nan Ho thought, looking at the map of City Europe and noting how the dark areas – those that denoted Li Min's territories – had grown in the last two days. *We failed to understand just how big he had become – how powerful. We thought what Visak told us was all lies, but it was true.*

To be blunt, they had totally underestimated their enemy. They had thought he had delayed – had issued his famous Statement of Loyalty – because he was too weak to fight them. But now they knew. Li Min had delayed only because he wanted to be certain before he acted.

And now he was a day from victory. Two days at most. And still Li Yuan refused his cousin's help.

He watched his Master, seeing how the young T'ang studied the map, as if it were a board, the whole thing a massive game of *wei chi* in which he might find some flaw in his opponent's strategy, some previously overlooked weakness he might exploit. But there was nothing. Li Min had planned his campaign well. The game was his. He had only to lay the last few stones.

Li Yuan turned back to him. He had not slept in three days now – kept awake and alert by special drugs – and his eyes were heavy from lack of sleep.

"All right," he said softly, nodding to his Chancellor. "Arrange for us to speak."

"*Chieh Hsia!*" he said, a feeling of relief flooding through him.

While Li Yuan pored over the map, he made contact with the palace at Astrakhan, yet when the screen lit up, it was not Tsu Ma's Chancellor who faced him but his nephew, Tsu Tao Chu.

The young man's face was tight with anguish. Everything about him spoke of loss. Even before he said a word, Nan Ho knew.

"My uncle, the great Tsu Ma, is dead. He . . ." Tao Chu lowered his head, a tear trickling down his cheek. "He passed away this morning."

Li Yuan, standing beside his Chancellor, stared mutely at the screen.

"It was a great relief," Tsu Tao Chu said after a moment. "He suffered greatly. If he had not been so strong . . ." He shuddered, then, noting Li Yuan's presence, gave a bow of recognition.

"I am sad to hear the news," Li Yuan said, waving Nan Ho away so that he could speak to Tsu Tao Chu alone. "As you know, we had not been speaking these last few weeks, yet his passing comes as a blow to me. I feel as if I have lost a brother."

Tsu Tao Chu smiled tightly, a deep sadness in his eyes. "Thank you, cousin Yuan. I know that he always considered you his brother."

Li Yuan returned his smile. "How are things in your City, cousin?"

Tsu Tao Chu grimaced. "Not well, cousin Yuan. Each hour brings more bad news. Things look bleak for us all, neh?"

"That is true. Yet if we stand together . . ."

"I would like that. I . . ." He paused, looking round, speaking to someone off-screen, then faced Li Yuan again. "Forgive me, cousin, but it strikes me that if you were to come here, to Astrakhan . . . If we were together in one place, then perhaps we might coordinate our efforts and therefore fight our enemies more effectively. Tongjiang is a fortress, true, yet Tongjiang is a long way from your City. If you were here . . ."

Li Yuan considered a moment, then nodded. "I would like that, Tao Chu. I would like that very much."

"Then come, cousin Yuan. Come now, without delay."

* * *

The news was good. Tsu Ma was dead, and Wei Tseng-li too, in all probability. Asia was in chaos and Europe . . . Europe would be next to fall. It needed but one final push.

Lehmann stood there, looking down at the great map of City Europe, studying the shape of things, the white that denoted his territory clearly in the ascendant.

This was the endgame. A time of sacrifices and captures. A time when shape was all-important, when the all-connectedness of his schemes would matter more than the bravery of soldiers or the skill of generals.

In his right hand were the five white stones that represented his reserve forces. Five battalions of his best troops, held back until now. He rattled them in his hand then looked about him. His men watched him silently, awaiting his decision with a confidence, a certainty that mirrored his own. They were almost there. Just one more push.

He leaned across, placing a stone in Stuttgart. That would reinforce his forces there and help keep the supply corridor open to the army that was besieging the Mannheim garrison. A second stone he placed in the far west, in Nantes. Again it was a defensive move, to safeguard his capture of the great spaceport. Which left three.

Lehmann hefted the three white stones, feeling their weight, then leaned right across the map and slapped them down at Bremen.

"There!" he said. "Right to the heart."

There was a deep murmur of satisfaction. Bremen. It was Li Yuan's chief stronghold, its name alone representative of the power and strength of the seven generations of the Li family who had ruled Europe. Take Bremen and the rest would follow, like the leaves falling in Autumn.

"Get me Soucek," he said, looking to his Financial Strategist, Cao Chang. "I want to know what the situation is."

In a moment Soucek's long, ox-like face appeared on the giant screen to the left of the room. Lehmann went across and stood beneath it.

"Well, Jiri? How goes it?"

Soucek's face was black with smoke. He rubbed at one eye, then answered Lehmann. "We're making headway, but slowly. Resistance is fierce. The Mannheim garrison is a proud one and well-disciplined. Not only that, but Karr has taken over the command."

"Karr?" Lehmann nodded thoughtfully. "Well, press on, Jiri. Karr or no, I want you in Mannheim by the morning, understand me?"

Soucek bowed his head.

"And Jiri. I've defended your supply line at Stuttgart. But look for news from Bremen. It's there the final battle will take place. If I'm right, Li Yuan will withdraw some of his forces from Mannheim to defend Bremen. When he does, press home. And Jiri . . ."

"Yes, Master."

"Take no prisoners."

* * *

Karr sat on an ammunition case, resting, the sound of gunfire coming closer by the minute. Each time they would draw a defensive line and each time it would be overrun. Hour by hour they were being pressed back, the number of their dead and wounded mounting steadily, until finally . . .

Finally we'll all be dead.

He looked up, studying his young equerry. The boy – for he was little more than seventeen – had been posted on him only yesterday when he'd taken this command, yet he already felt he knew him well. Right now the boy looked to his right, towards the gunfire, a strange calmness – or was it shock? – pervading his gaze. Then, realising that Karr was watching him, he blushed and turned to face his Colonel, bowing his head smartly.

"It's okay," Karr said. "There's no ordinance against thinking."

"No, sir. It's just . . ."

Karr smiled, touched by the boy's shyness. "Go on. Say what you're thinking, lad. I grant you permission this once."

Barlow looked away, his whole manner awkward. "I was thinking of a girl, sir."

Karr smiled. "Me too. Two of them, in fact."

"Sir?"

"My wife, and my daughter, May."

"Ah . . ." The cadet laughed, then fell silent, serious again.

"You know, it's much harder on them," Karr said. "They carry the burden of not knowing what's happening to us. The burden of imagination. Whereas we . . . Well, we have only to worry about the unseen bullet, the sudden pain and the darkness that follows."

Barlow met his eyes and nodded, no sign of fear in his own.

Good, Karr thought. *He understands. It's far simpler when you understand. Death, when it comes, is easy. It's the waiting that's hard.*

Karr stood, then reached down for the big automatic rifle he had been using, picking it up by the strap and slinging it over his shoulder.

"Sir?"

"Yes, Barlow?"

"Why is this happening? I mean . . . why didn't Li Yuan crush the White T'ang when he could?"

Karr sighed. "A good question. But not one for us to ask. We are but our Master's hands, neh?"

Barlow stared at him briefly, surprised by the tone of his words.

"Have we . . . lost, sir?"

"Lost? No, lad. Things aren't *that* bad." But it wasn't what he believed. News had come only an hour back of Tsu Ma's death – news he had kept from his troops, lest it demoralise them. Closer to home, it was said that the old Marshal was sick, on his death-bed. Soon there would be no one left. Soon there would only be darkness – darkness and ghosts.

And as for Marie and May . . . well, maybe they *would* be safer in Astrakhan, but the news of their evacuation from Tongjiang had troubled him far more than he'd believed possible.

Safe? No. No one was safe any more.

In any case, it doesn't really matter, he thought. *For this is the end. All this . . . this drawing of lines . . . we're only going through the motions. Filling our own territory with stones. For the truth is he's already won.*

"Sir?"

He looked to Barlow again, then reached out and brushed his hair back from his eyes, as if it were his son. "Yes, lad?"

"How long do you think we have?"

* * *

"Daddy?"

Tolonen stirred in his bed, then turned his head, looking across the darkly shadowed room towards the door.

"Jelka?" he asked weakly. "Is that you?"

She went across and knelt beside the bed, clasping his good hand – the hand that was flesh and blood – between her own.

"Oh, daddy . . . what have you been up to now?"

He laughed softly; laughter that quickly degenerated into a hacking cough. She waited, looking anxiously at the doctor who hovered silently on the far side of the bed.

It's okay, he mouthed, smiling reassuringly.

She looked back at her father. He was old – that was a fact – yet never before now had he *looked* old. He had always been so healthy, so . . . robust. To see him like this pained her, and for all that Kim had argued with her about it, she still saw it as her fault. *She* had done this to him. She and her bloody-mindedness.

"How are you?" she asked, reaching up to smooth his brow.

"Just fine," he said, his grey eyes searching hers. "Not a day's sickness in all my life, and suddenly . . ."

She pressed his head back gently where it had come up from the pillow. "They say you must rest. They say you must take things easy and not worry."

"Worry?" He laughed bleakly. "Did you hear? They're talking of evacuating Bremen . . . Bremen! *Aiya!*"

"Daddy . . . *please*. It will do no good. You have to forget what's happening. You can do nothing."

"You think I do not know that?" He turned his head aside, then sniffed deeply, a look of bitter shame on his face. "I have never let him down. *Never . . .* until now."

She squeezed his hand tightly, touched by his display of loyalty. It was true what he said. Whereas she . . .

"Is *he* here?"

Jelka sighed. "No, daddy. I came alone."

He closed his eyes and nodded, then placed his other hand – the hand of golden metal – over hers. She stared at it, trying not to flinch from it – from that part it had always seemed to represent – that cold, inflexible part of him.

"I've come to stay," she said quietly. "I've come to nurse you."

His head turned back, his eyes flicked open. "For good?"

It was hard to meet his eyes and disappoint him, yet she knew she must. "Until you're well again. Kim says . . ."

"Damn you, girl!" he yelled hoarsely, lifting himself from the pillow. "Don't even speak his name in my presence! I . . ."

He gave a shudder, as if he were about to have another fit, then lay back again, glancing at his doctor. "I'm sorry, I . . . I forgot myself there. I must rest, I know."

She moved back slightly, letting the doctor fuss about him a moment, checking his pulse and his blood pressure, then leaned close again, giving him a smile.

"Let's not fight, eh? Let's be friends . . ."

"You're all I have, Jelka. All the others . . . they're dead. Klaus Ebert, Hal Shepherd, Li Shai Tung . . . Dead, every last one of them. The world . . . it's like there's nothing here but ghosts. Excepting you, my love. Excepting you."

She felt her stomach muscles tighten, felt the tears begin to well in her eyes; yet at the same time she knew what he was doing; knew that this too – true as it was – was another battle for him. To win her, that was his aim. And to defeat his enemy, her lover, Kim.

"I love you, daddy," she said, the tears beginning to trickle down her cheeks. "Never doubt that. Never doubt that for a moment. But I love him too, and I have to be with him."

He stared at her, silently, his eyes accusing her.

"Can't you see? Don't you see how easy it would all be if you just stopped this silliness? Why can't you just accept him, eh? Then we could be together . . . all of us. We could take you to Kalevala . . ."

"No!" he roared, sitting up, his face suffused with sudden anger. "You'll not have him! You won't! You . . ."

She saw the surprise in his face, the look of shock that came into his eyes, the way his hands clutched at his chest.

"Oh gods . . ." she whispered, frightened. "Please, no . . ."

Then there was shouting in the room, doctors hurrying about. In a daze she found herself lifted to her feet and led away.

"It'll be all right," someone was saying reassuringly. "He needs rest, that's all. All this excitement . . ."

But as she was led from the room, she could still hear his murmuring. "You won't have him! You *won't* . . ."

* * *

Li Yuan embraced his cousin, then turned, introducing the senior members of his staff who had travelled with him from Tongjiang.

"I am glad you came," Tsu Tao Chu said, when they were alone again. "The situation . . ."

Li Yuan touched his arm, understanding. Tao Chu had not been born to rule. The deaths of his half-brother and his uncle had come as a double blow. Nor had he been given any time to prepare himself for such a mighty responsibility. All this was new to him. Even so, he was a good, upstanding young man. If anyone could shoulder such a burden, Tsu Tao Chu could, surely?

"It is okay, Tao Chu. Together we shall make sense of this, neh?"

Tao Chu smiled. "I have prepared the Northern Palace for your people, Yuan. If that is insufficient . . ."

"It will be fine," Li Yuan said quickly. "But before I do anything else, I must pay my last respects to your uncle."

"Of course."

Tao Chu led him through, past grieving servants and into a dark, cool hall in which the funeral bier had been set up, the casket open to the air. Li Yuan went across and stood there over it, looking down at his old friend, finding it hard to believe that he was dead. The poison had left its mark on Tsu Ma. His face seemed much older than Yuan remembered it, and the hair . . . the hair was almost grey. He sighed, then turned to Tao Chu again.

"Have you found out yet who did this thing?"

"I have the man. I racked him, made him sing."

Li Yuan stared at Tao Chu, surprised by the unexpected hardness in his voice and face.

"And his Master?"

"You know his Master well, cousin Yuan. Your armies fight him even now."

Li Yuan gave a tiny nod, then looked back. For some reason the memory of an evening, years before, came back to him – of Tsu Ma and he in a boat on the lake at Tongjiang, with Fei Yen and her cousin, Yin Wu Tsai, the lanterns dancing in the darkness. What a night that had been. What a beautiful, entrancing night.

He grimaced, then turned away, torn between the jealousy he felt – the anger at Tsu Ma's betrayal – and the love he'd had for him.

You were like a brother to me, he thought, as if addressing Tsu Ma in his head. *Why, then, did you take my bride away?*

As if in answer, the words from Ch'u Yuan's "Heavenly Questions" floated into mind.

Dark Wei followed in his brother's footsteps and the Lord of You-yi was stirred against him . . .

In a sense it was true – he had taken his brother's wife, and in turn his brother – Tsu Ma – had done the same to him.

But now it was done with. Death had paid all debts. Now he could let that matter go and remember his cousin with affection.

He turned back, bowing deeply to Tsu Ma, his hands pressed together, palm to palm, as he offered his respects, then he looked to Tao Chu and nodded.

"There is much to do, cousin Tao. We had best begin at once."

* * *

Karr had been expecting the order for some time, even so, as he unsealed Rheinhardt's handwritten letter and read its contents, he felt his heart sink, the spirit go out of him. He was to abandon Mannheim and go at once to Bremen, taking whatever forces remained at his disposal.

This is it, he thought sadly, folding the letter and slipping it into his tunic pocket. *Another day and all is gone*. On whim, he took out the picture he carried and looked at it, studying the smiling faces of his girls. He kissed it fondly then returned it, and, calling his Duty Captain to him, began to issue orders.

* * *

"It is no good," Li Yuan said, pointing to the southern half of the map, indicating the five remaining tiny islands of black around Bordeaux, Lyon, Turin, Ravenna and Belgrade. The rest was solidly white now – more than two-thirds of the City; almost everything beneath the ancient Loire and Danube rivers – while to the

north, Li Min had made encroachments in at least a dozen places. "We shall have
to let them go. Issue the order now, General Rheinhardt. I want all of our forces
pulled back above the Seine in the west and the Danube in the east."

"But *Chieh Hsia*," Rheinhardt began, appalled by the thought of relinquishing
so much.

"You have your orders, General. Now do it. And get Karr on the screen. I have
a use for him."

Rheinhardt bowed and left the room, leaving Li Yuan alone with Nan Ho and
Tsu Tao Chu.

"Was that wise, *Chieh Hsia?*" Nan Ho asked quietly. "Rheinhardt knows what
he is doing, and those garrisons . . . well, they have served to tie up a great number
of Li Min's troops."

"And a great number of ours, too," Li Yuan said, leaning across the map and
drawing an imaginary line from west to east with his finger. "No, Master Nan. It is
time for drastic measures. What is lost is lost. We must conserve what can yet be
saved. Li Min's new forces have swung the balance heavily against us. Yet all is not
lost. Until now we have been hampered by the need to hold down a vast area, to try
to police it even as we wage a war. But now that responsibility is Li Min's. He must
now subdue those parts of the City he has conquered. That will tie up more and
more of his forces, while our own will be freed to defend what remains. Moreover,
if we keep our forces here in the north, in this section," he indicated a swathe of
territory less than a quarter of the City's total size, "then we also have the
advantage of keeping our supply-lines short."

Nan Ho studied the map a moment, then shrugged. "Even so, *Chieh Hsia* . . ."

Li Yuan snorted. "*Aiya*, Master Nan! Must I constantly be held back by you and
your Even so's? We have no option. We must draw a line and fight to preserve it. If
we fail . . ."

Tsu Tao Chu stared at the map a moment, then nodded. "A line, cousin? Why
not a *physical* breach . . . some kind of gap?"

Li Yuan stared at him a while, then smiled. "Yes! A gap – as about Tunis! We
could destroy a line of stacks . . . here." He drew the line again with his finger, this
time more definite, his eyes shining with excitement. "We could make a break two
li wide and defend it . . . as if we were fighting a fire."

He looked to Nan Ho. "Have we still got those stocks of ice-eaters that were
confiscated that time?"

"We have, *Chieh Hsia*, but . . ."

"No buts, Master Nan. The idea is an excellent one. And Karr . . . Karr's the
man to implement it, neh?"

Nan Ho looked to his master, imploring him with his eyes to drop the idea, but
Li Yuan was adamant. After a moment Nan Ho bowed his head. "Very well. I shall
arrange it, *Chieh Hsia*."

* * *

Tsu Tao Chu sat in the window seat, chewing a thumb nail, while Li Yuan paced
the room in front of him, reading the latest reports.

That evening Tao Chu was to be appointed T'ang of West Asia in an official ceremony in the Hall of Celestial Virtues. But by then, it seemed, West Asia would be gone and he would be T'ang of nothing. Nothing but these ancient stones.

After two hundred years of peace, Asia had fallen into darkness once again. Warlords had divided the great continent between them, reacting to the scent of blood like sharks in a feeding frenzy. The twin cities, once the jewels of Chung Kuo, now burned, and tens of millions died each hour as the darkness fell.

"Is it bad?" Tao Chu asked, looking up to him, a youthful innocence in his eyes.

Li Yuan sighed. "It could not be worse, Tao Chu. It is all slipping away from us. It might be best if we prepared to take our courts . . . off-planet."

"Off-planet?" Tao Chu looked alarmed. "As bad as that?"

Li Yuan nodded.

Tao Chu got up suddenly, then, with a polite smile and bow to Li Yuan, made to go past him to the door, but Li Yuan held his arm.

"Cousin? Where are you off to in such a hurry? I thought we might talk."

Tao Chu looked down, embarrassed. "Forgive me, Yuan, I . . ."

Li Yuan smiled. "I remember the first time we ever met. It was after your grandfather, Tsu Tiao's death. You were . . ."

"Eight . . . and you twelve." Tao Chu nodded thoughtfully, then looked to Li Yuan with a smile. "I remember that I gripped your arm, I was so afraid. I thought that my uncle . . ." He shivered, a look of pain flickering across his eyes. "I thought he had killed Tsu Tiao. I did not know it was only a GenSyn copy."

"Was that the first time you had encountered death?"

Tao Chu nodded. "I remember you explained it all to me. Why my uncle Ma had to kill the image of his father to become his own man. Yet I never truly understood. Not deep down. To kill one's father . . ." He shuddered.

Li Yuan reached out and held his shoulder gently. "The first of the crafts from Tongjiang will be here shortly. Perhaps you would like to come and greet them with me?"

Tao Chu shook his head, his eyes avoiding Yuan's. "I . . . I would prefer to get some rest, cousin. I . . . It has been a very trying day for me."

Li Yuan bowed. "I understand. The times take much from us, neh?"

Tao Chu bobbed his head in response, then, with a strange, pained glance at his cousin, went to the door and out.

Li Yuan stood there a while, staring at the open door, wondering if there were anything he could do to ease his young cousin's suffering. Then, with a heavy sigh, he went out to meet the incoming craft.

* * *

The five craft came in from the east, in tight formation. Li Yuan, watching from the parapet above the Eastern Gate, saw the faint wisp of smoke that came from the exhaust of the central craft and, at the same time heard the slight difference in the tone of its engine, and knew at once that something had happened.

He hurried across, lifting his silks so he could run, the honour guard exerting themselves to keep up with him. As he came to the hangars, they were already disembarking. Li Yuan made his way through until he stood before the Commander of the flight, who was busy examining the damage to one of his craft.

"What happened?" he asked, staring past the Captain at the smoke-blackened side of the cruiser.

The Captain span round, surprised, then bowed low. "Forgive me, *Chieh Hsia*. We were attacked coming over the Uzbek plantations . . . three ships out of Tashkent. We gave them the imperial codes, yet they attacked all the same. Deliberately, it seems."

Li Yuan nodded, sobered by the thought. Before today it would have been unthinkable that an imperial cruiser would have been attacked by security forces, but today the unthinkable was finally happening.

"We lost two ships, *Chieh Hsia*, but none of the transporters was harmed. Not in any serious way, that is."

"And the attackers?"

"We destroyed them, *Chieh Hsia*."

"Good. You will be rewarded for your actions, Captain. You and all your men."

Li Yuan turned, looking around him, seeing at once the face of his son, Kuei Jen, staring down at him through the portal of one of the other cruisers. He went across, greeting the boy at the bottom of the ramp, picking him up and hugging him, relieved that he was safe. In the hatchway beyond the boy stood his wife, Pei K'ung. He stared at her then nodded, strangely pleased that she had survived.

"What is the news from Tongjiang?" he asked, setting his son down and facing her.

"Tongjiang has fallen. A thousand dead, so they say. The news was full of it as we flew across. Another half an hour and we ourselves would not have escaped."

"Ah . . ." He felt a heaviness descend on him. A thousand dead. And Tongjiang itself . . . gone. He felt like weeping at the thought. But at least his family had survived.

Cling on to that, Li Yuan, he told himself. *For many men this day have emerged from this with far less than you. Millions are dying even as you stand here with your son, your wife. So give thanks to all the gods you know.*

He shivered, then stretched out a hand to her. She hesitated, then came down, taking his hand, surprised, for it was the first gesture of kindness he had shown to her since that night weeks ago when she had shared his bed.

"Forgive me, Pei K'ung," he whispered, drawing her close. "I have not been myself."

She drew back slightly, meeting his eyes. "There is nothing to forgive, my husband."

"And my cousin, Wei . . . is there any news of him? The rumours . . ."

"Wei Tseng-li is dead," she said, the solemnity of the words filling him with dread. "We taped all of the newscasts as we flew over. The pictures . . ." She shuddered physically. "They are most disturbing. They strung him up, like an animal. That lovely man . . ."

He grimaced and closed his eyes, then reached out, holding the two of them to him – his wife, his son. After a moment he looked up again, meeting her eyes. There

were tears there, as in his own. "Then there are just the two of us now. Tsu Tao
Chu and I. Two T'ang and but a single City. That is, if my own City survives the
night."

"And if it falls?"

Li Yuan looked away, his left hand gripping his son's shoulder fiercely, a muscle
in his cheek twitching. "Then we must leave Chung Kuo and go elsewhere."

* * *

He had seen the demonstrations. One moment the ice was a solid thing, the next . . .

Karr shuddered. They were hovering above the City's roof, the hold of the
cruiser packed with cylinders of the stuff. Two hundred and forty cruisers in all –
more than half their remaining strength – had been loaded up and flown into
position along a line from Le Havre in the west through Nurnberg and Dresden to
Stettin in the north-east. Now he had only to give the order and the spraying would
begin.

There was no time to evacuate. No time to give the people down below any
chance to escape, for to do so would be to tip off Lehmann. And if he knew . . .

"Okay," he said, leaning towards the cockpit's control panel. "Let's get this over
with. Begin spraying."

Karr turned, then clambered up, going to the left-hand portal to look out as the
chemicals began to fall like a mist of fine rain on to the City's pure white roof. And
where it touched . . .

He caught his breath, then groaned. It was unbearable to watch. He could see
them far below him, jumping as the levels slowly melted. As in a dream . . . the ice
melting beneath the fine spray that fell from the heavens, the levels vanishing just
as if they'd never been.

He sat down heavily, closing his eyes, trying not to imagine it, but it was no use.
He could see them still. All of those people . . . thousands, hundreds of thousands
of them, falling through a dissolving mist of ice, falling like stones, downward to
the earth.

He groaned. He had done many foul things in the service of his T'ang. He had
killed and lied and sold his soul a hundred times, but this . . . this was the nadir.

He stood, forcing himself to look once more, to bear witness. Behind them a
great space had opened up, like a canyon between two smooth plateau of ice, a
cross-section of the levels exposed by the acid-like mist. And where the mist still
fell, the City seemed to sink into the earth as layer after layer shimmered into
nothingness.

Like earth in a sieve, he thought, trying to find the words to describe what he was
seeing – trying not to go crazy at the thought that those tiny black shapes were
human beings.

I gave the order, he thought, stunned by the enormity of it. *Yes, it was I who gave
the order*.

For a moment longer he watched, then, swallowing down the bile that had risen
in his throat, he went back through and sat, staring out at the whiteness that
stretched ahead of him, trying hard not to think of all those down below who, in a

blink of the eye, were about to learn what their Master, the great T'ang, had decided for them.

* * *

The cruiser descended slowly, sinking into the space between the Cities. Below, a vast army waited in the late evening gloom, rank after rank, their bright red uniforms standing out against the forlorn silver shapes of what had once been the City's supporting columns. The mass of men stretched into the distance, their number filling the two *li* gap between the massive walls. Ten thousand brightly-coloured banners fluttered in the wind that blew down that vast, artificial canyon. Torches flickered in the twilight, then, at a signal, drums rolled and trumpets blew. As one the masses came to attention.

Looking out through the cockpit of the cruiser, Lehmann studied the host below. Eight hundred thousand men there were. To the west, in the shadow of Rouen, a further million waited, while to the east, at Eberswalde, an army of four hundred thousand were gathered.

In an hour it would begin. As darkness fell he would make the final push; would hammer the final nail into the great T'ang's coffin. He nodded then turned to Soucek, who stood in the doorway behind him.

"So here we are, Jiri. A few hours more and all is ours."

Soucek, recalled only an hour past from his labours at Bremen, bowed respectfully.

"I never doubted it, Master. From that first moment until this. We have walked an iron path."

The albino's face was like a waxwork, devoid of all emotion. Yet men followed him in their millions, bled for him, laid down their lives for him.

"That was a bold stroke of Li Yuan's," he said, a grudging respect in his voice, "but it will not save him. Drawing a line is one thing, defending it another."

The engine noise changed, intensifying as they dropped below the last level of the City and into the semi-darkness beneath. Soucek looked out and shuddered. The ice-eaters had done their work mercilessly. They had stripped the levels bare.

The craft touched down on the Clay.

As the door hissed open, a great cheer went up from all sides. For a moment the hatch was silent, empty, then Lehmann stepped out, dressed from head to toe in white, his left hand raised in a triumphal salute. At once the cheer became a roar. Helmets were thrown in the air, guns thrust towards the heavens.

Lehmann half turned, his face a blank, his eyes cold like glass. "You see, Jiri? They have a need of kings."

He walked down the ramp to a tumultuous reception. It was like the roar of a great storm. Soucek stood at the head of the ramp a moment, watching him descend, then looked out across that sea of eager, exultant faces, seeing no sign of doubt – only an ecstatic adulation.

We walk as in a dream . . .

Soucek stepped down, taking his place behind and to the right of his Master as the senior officers presented themselves. Glancing down, he noticed for the first time that the ground underfoot was hard and glassy where the aerated ice had reformed. Bodies were embedded in it.

As Lehmann went up the line, inspecting the honour guard, he walked over the upturned faces of the dead. Overhead tiny remotes hovered like carrion, catching each word, each gesture for posterity.

History this was. A turning point. The day the White T'ang came into his kingdom.

Soucek shivered at the thought, a strange thrill of love passing through him. Visak had failed the test, had faltered at the final hurdle, but he had remained true, and now he would live to see his Master crowned, seated upon the dragon throne itself, king of the underworld no more, but king of all.

At the head of the second line, Lehmann turned and looked across at him, then nodded. At the signal, Soucek went across and, walking behind Lehmann, began to make his way through the crowd to where a platform had been set up. There Lehmann was to address the masses; to rally their spirits before the final attack. Yet even as they passed between the ranks, the deafening sound of cheering rolling on and on, he sensed something was happening. On the platform up ahead a group of officers were gathered about the mobile transmitter, listening anxiously, their faces troubled.

"What is it?" Lehmann asked unceremoniously as he mounted the steps on to the platform.

Soucek, coming up behind Lehmann, saw how they looked to one another, a shock of fear passing among them, then how the most senior of them stepped forward.

"There are rumours, Master . . ."

"Rumours?"

"Reports . . . from Malaga, Toulon, Taranto . . . and other places."

Lehmann lifted him from his feet, one hand tight about the man's neck. As he did the sound of cheering slowly died, until the whole space between the Cities was silent.

"No babbling, man," Lehmann said quietly, his face only a breath from the other's, his steel-like grip almost choking him. "Give me no rumours. Tell me what you know."

He let him fall, then stepped past him, pointing to another. "Tell me what's happened."

"We have been betrayed, Master," the man said, his voice trembling. He fell to his knees, staring up at Lehmann, his eyes wide with fear. "The Mountain Lords have come against us, Master. They have attacked us in the south. Five great armies have come against us."

"There are reports?"

"Coming in all the time," another offered, also falling to his knees. "They began twenty minutes back. At first we discounted them. But in the last few minutes . . ."

"Enough!" Lehmann said, raising his left hand abruptly. He looked to Soucek. "Jiri . . . find out where they are attacking and what strength they have. Then gather my generals south of here, in the captured garrison in Milan. We must hold a Council of War."

"And *this*, Master?" Soucek said, pointing north, towards what remained of Li Yuan's City.

"Another day," Lehmann said, turning to face the south, his eyes burning coldly in the glass of his face. "First I must give my African cousins the welcome they deserve."

* * *

Karr jumped down from the cruiser and began to run up the slope of the lawn towards the palace, laughing to himself at the news he brought, imagining the face of his Master when he told him. But as he approached the Eastern Gate, he slowed, hearing bells from within the ancient palace.

Had someone else beaten him here with the news? One of Rheinhardt's young officers, perhaps?

He waited impatiently at the gate while the guards double-checked his ID and ran hand-held scanners over him, then went through, ducking beneath the low lintel and into the grounds of the inner palace. He expected to hear laughter, the sound of celebration, but there was nothing – only an ominous silence, in which the sound of the bells seemed suspended as if in glass. He jumped down the steps in threes and began to make his way along the path to the centre, heading for the Northern Palace, then stopped dead, the breath hissing from him.

From beneath the great arch of the Southern Palace, a procession was emerging, his master, Li Yuan, leading it. Behind him, on an open bier carried by thirty bearers in white silk robes, lay Tsu Tao Chu. His face had been made up as if in the perfect bloom of life, and he wore the dragon robes – the imperial yellow with the nine dragons, eight shown and one hidden. Beneath him the rich furs of the bier were strewn with white petals.

Karr walked slowly towards the procession, then, some twenty *ch'i* from his Master, fell to his knees, touching his forehead to the earth.

The procession stopped. Li Yuan looked to him, his face ashen. "Is it over, Gregor Karr? Has the White T'ang taken my City?"

Karr lifted his head. "No, *Chieh Hsia*. We are saved. The Mountain Lords . . ." He looked beyond Li Yuan a moment, appalled by the sight of the young prince. "Fu Chiang and his cousins . . . they kept their word, *Chieh Hsia*. They came!"

Li Yuan nodded, but it seemed that even this news had no power to raise his spirits. He sighed heavily, a bitterness in his eyes. "Then my cousin's life was truly wasted, neh?"

"*Chieh Hsia?*"

Li Yuan stared at Karr bleakly. "We found him an hour back, in his rooms. He had locked the door then hung himself."

Karr felt the shock of that pass through him. A Son of Heaven, dead by his own hand. It was hard to believe.

"But your news . . ." Li Yuan gave him the ghost of a smile. "Your news brings us some comfort in these dark hours. We live to fight on, neh, Gregor Karr? We who survived."

"*Chieh Hsia*." Karr bowed his head, trying not to think of the what he had seen that day – of the levels misting into nothing and the people falling. *Yes*, he thought. *For now we are safe. But for how long?* The Seven had gone. Li Yuan alone remained. A single man. A Son of Heaven true, and yet a single man.

Li Yuan put out a hand, gesturing for him to get up.

"Come, Gregor. Walk with me. The time will come to celebrate your news, but now we must place my cousin Tao Chu beside his uncle."

He paused, gathering his full dignity about him once more, then nodded. "It is time to observe the rituals. Time to grieve the dead and see their souls are welcomed in the other world."

THE NIGHT-COLOURED PEARL

"The Yellow Emperor went wandering
To the north of the Red Water
To the Kwan Lun mountain. He looked around
Over the edge of the world. On the way home
He lost his night-coloured pearl.
He sent out Science to seek his pearl, and got nothing.
He sent Analysis to look for his pearl, and got nothing.
He sent out Logic to seek his pearl, and got nothing.
Then he asked Nothingness, and Nothingness had it!
The Yellow Emperor said:
'Strange, indeed: Nothingness
Who was not sent
Who did no work to find it
Had the night-coloured pearl!'"

– Chuang Tzu, 6th century BC
(*Writings* xii, IV)

THE NIGHT-COLOURED PEARL

The cockpit was packed, all nine of them trying to crowd into that tiny space to watch the screen.

Below them lay Chung Kuo, bright in the sunlight.

Ebert, in the pilot's seat, frowned, then spoke to the air.

"What's happened, Master Tuan?"

There was a moment's hesitation, then the old man's voice sounded in the cabin, as if from every side.

"Much has changed since you were last here, Hans. The Seven have become One and the world . . ." he laughed gently. "Some say the world has shrunk. I see it differently. To my eyes the world is a much bigger place these days."

Ebert stared at the planet below him, shaking his head. The great shapes of white that had once covered every continent had now diminished to a patchwork. In some places – in the Southern continents particularly – it was gone entirely. Only in Europe was the City still dominant, but there too it was split – a great jagged line, like a crack in the surface of a frozen pond, running from west to east.

"I didn't realise," Ebert said. "There has been war, neh?"

"War was the least of it," Tuan Ti Fo answered, placing images on the screen before them. "War is but the prelude to disaster. After War there is Pestilence and Starvation, and always, *always* there's the darkness."

"The darkness?" It was Aluko Echewa who spoke. All about him the young Osu murmured, their discomfort evident. They had never been off Mars until three months back. Now they were to start a new life on the planet below, alone, cut off from their loved ones, preparing the way for others of their kind.

"The darkness within," Tuan answered. "Hatred and fear and evil."

Dogo, the strongest and biggest of the young Osu, laughed. "Father Aluko thought you meant us, Master Tuan. With us the darkness is visible, no?"

There was general laughter at that. Eight dark faces grinned, showing pearled teeth like polished stones. But Ebert seemed distracted.

"What is it, Efulefu?" Echewa asked, laying a dark hand on his shoulder. "Why the long face?"

"What happened here . . ." He looked up at them, real pain in his eyes. "I was much to blame for it. The things I did . . ."

He turned, looking back at the scenes of horror that continued to fill the screen.

"Where should we go, Master Tuan?" he asked. "What does your friend the Machine suggest?"

"We shall go south," Tuan answered. "We shall . . ."

There was a sharp buzz of noise and then a rapid clicking.

"What is it?" Echewa asked, leaning forward, suddenly anxious.

"I don't know, I . . ."

"Leave the cabin," Tuan Ti Fo said faintly, his voice barely audible above the static. "Now, before . . ."

Ebert was facing the screen as it lit up. The others were more fortunate: they had turned away, making to obey Tuan's voice.

The light from the screen was fierce, like the light from the heart of a sun. It flooded the cabin, seeming to scour every pore, every cell of their bodies. The Osu were screaming, the pain in their heads – in their eyes – like nothing they'd ever experienced. But their blindness would prove temporary. For Ebert it was different. Ebert had taken the full force of the light. He sat there in the chair, groaning, his face blistered and steaming, his eyes burned from their sockets.

The light faded, the clicking stopped. Echewa, on his knees in the doorway, turned blindly.

"Efulefu? Are you all right?"

Ebert groaned again.

"What . . . what happened?" Echewa asked, beating down his fear. "What was that?"

"It was a light-mine," Tuan Ti Fo answered. "Our presence in its air-space seems to have triggered it."

"But I thought . . ."

Echewa fell silent. He had thought Tuan's Machine would have anticipated such a danger and dealt with it. He'd thought . . .

He swallowed bitterly. "Efulefu?"

"It's okay," Ebert said weakly. Then, strangely, he laughed.

"Efulefu? Are you all right?"

"I'm blind," Ebert said, then laughed again. "I'm . . . *blind.*"

Echewa struggled to his feet, then turned, trying to see, but his eyes were still too painful. All was a blur; a blur of pain and confusion.

"But Efulefu . . . why are you laughing?"

"Blind . . . the Walker in the Darkness, blind . . ." again he laughed. Then, just as unexpectedly, he moaned. "Gods . . ." he said quietly. "All those things I did. All those people I hurt. All that darkness . . ."

"Is past now," Tuan Ti Fo said, his voice warm and reassuring in the air surrounding them. "Now sit quietly, *Tsou Tsai Hei.* The Machine will see you down."

PART 2 – SPRING 2218

THE KING UNDER THE CITY

Here not even the stars can spy us,
Not even the moths can alight
On our mystery; nought can descry us
Nor put us to flight.

Put trust then now in the black-boughed tree,
Lie down, and open to me
The inner dark of the mystery,
Be, penetrate, like the tree.

   – D. H. Lawrence, *The Yew Tree on the Downs*

I go new ways, a new speech has come to me;
like all creators, I have grown weary of the
old tongues.
(Freidrich Nietzsche, "The Child with the Mirror",
                Thus Spake Zarathustra. 1883)

CHAPTER · 12

CLAY

S een from afar the City was a glacier, its featureless white cliffs thrusting out into the sea, following the contours of the coast. Thorn stood at the prow, one hand shielding his eyes, the other gripping the roof of the steering hut as the boat rose and fell. There was the steady slap and slosh of water against the wooden sides of the boat; a regular vibration in the wood beneath his hand as the engine chugged noisily.

Thorn looked to his side, studying the boatman. He was a squat, broad-shouldered man in his middle years, his neck and arms well-muscled. He stared ahead, his rough hands gripping the wheel tightly. His wind-carved, ruddy face was handsome in a primitive way, typical of the men who worked this coast. His hair was short and tightly curled, sea-bleached almost to whiteness. Like most of his kind he was reticent with strangers. He had uttered barely a dozen words to Thorn since they had set out from St Mary's earlier that morning.

Thorn looked away, enjoying the bite of the wind against his face. Ahead the land seemed to grow by the moment, the vast walls of pearled whiteness soaring into the cloudless blue. A rock slid by to his left, like the dark back of an animal. He turned to see it swallowed by the swell.

Slowly the boat came round, its rolling motion exaggerated as it began to run parallel to the coastline. For a while they maintained this course, then the boatman swung the wheel sharply to the right, turning the boat inland once more.

Ahead an arm of rock jutted from beneath the massive walls, dwarfed by them but still huge. The port lay to the far side of the rock, in the bay beyond. A hundred *ch'i* ahead the sunlit surface of the sea ended in a sharply-defined line. Beyond was darkness. Slowly they approached that line. Fifty *ch'i*. Twenty. Then, suddenly, they were beneath the City's walls, in a still, cavernous place of intense shadow. The wind dropped. The sound of their engine came back to them across the dark water. Thorn turned and saw the boatman glance up at the over-towering walls, then look away with a shudder.

He looked down – the water a glaucous black, like the swollen pupil of a giant eye – and had a sudden sense of its depth beneath the hull.

Up ahead, waves were breaking against the stone then washing against the shore beneath the walls, all force spent. Closer and closer they came, the sunlight up ahead. Great slabs of rock thrust up out of the sea, jagged and irregular. They passed within a boat's width of them, rounding the headland, then came out into the sunlight again, but it was no warmer. If anything, the wind blew fiercer here, churning the water into spray and making the boat rock steeply, its prow smacking into each wave as its engine revved, fighting the current, drawing closer to the land.

* * *

The harbour was calm in the brief afternoon sunlight. Five small craft were secured against the far wall. Once there would have been more. Many more. The cobbles of the jetty were loose, several missing. Empty fishing baskets were stacked against a low wall next to coils of old, bleached ropes. Thorn looked about him, noticing how the paintwork on the boats was worn, likewise the tyres that hung as buffers over their sides. *Relics*, he thought. *From a simpler age.*

He looked up. Steep streets of old stone houses ended in the blind, unfeatured whiteness of the City. What remained of the tiny fishing port rested in an angle between two of the vast external walls which rose two *li* into the air on either side of the harbour. Only for these brief afternoon hours was the village free of its oppressive shadow.

"*Dyes-kynna?*"

Thorn smiled and nodded at the boatman. Yes, he was going down. The old man shrugged and turned away.

"*My a-vyn,*" Thorn said. *I want to.*

The boatman half turned, then shook his head.

A ragged group of locals had gathered on the quay opposite. They stared at him malevolently. Ignoring them, he lifted the heavy pack on to his shoulder and began to climb the path, his right hand on the haft of the dagger beneath his cloak.

He was a small, dark-haired man with green eyes and a neatly-trimmed beard. He was dressed simply but effectively against the cold. As he walked, his eyes searched the houses up ahead. The old cottages were dilapidated, mostly abandoned. Only those at the harbour's edge were still inhabited. Towards the end he climbed between ruins, the windows gaping, roofs collapsed and open to the elements.

He went without hesitation, knowing the way. Others had come before him; traders like himself. He was nearing the entrance when the challenge came.

"*Saf yn-nes!*"

Stop where you are. He turned to his left and saw them. Two men, one standing in the doorway, glowering at him, the other sat at an empty window, a gap-toothed smile on his face – an old, balding man with a wind-tanned face. Thorn addressed him.

"*Gwycor,*" he said, placing his hand against his chest. *Trader.* Then he nodded towards the entrance. "*My a-vyn . . . dyes-kynna. Yn dan cyta.*" He fumbled with the words, as if they were unfamiliar. *I want to go down. Under the City.*

The old man scratched the stubble on his chin and considered for a moment, then he leaned forward, his hand extended, palm open. The young man in the doorway straightened.

They were no real threat to him, yet he wanted no trouble. If he wanted to come out this way it might prove awkward later. He reached into his belt and removed two heavy coins. Five *yuan* each – more than enough to bribe his way in. He weighed them in his palm a moment then placed them in the old man's hand.

He watched the old man bite at the solid plastic coins then grunt his satisfaction. He waved Thorn on.

* * *

He stood at the tunnel's mouth, looking inwards at the blackness of the Clay. The air was warm and close, like the air in a small, unventilated room, fetid with animal smells. He reached into his cloak and drew a small strip of tape from an inner pocket then fastened it across his eyes. At once he could see, the uniform darkness resolved into a thousand shades of red, dissolving into black.

Securing the pack about his neck and shoulders he went in.

The land fell away sharply, then rose until it met the floor of the City. That floor formed a lid to the Clay, containing the vast and desolate lands beneath the City. Huge pillars thrust down into the earth, regularly spaced, holding the weight of the City: cold strokes of black against the multi-textured redness of the land. The roof was just above him where he stood. On tiptoe he could stretch and touch its smooth, unyielding surface. Beyond was Level One.

Thorn was looking east, towards old Lelant, looking down on a barren, almost lifeless land. Almost. Nothing grew here in the Clay, and yet men still struggled to make a living in this awful place.

The Clay . . . the very words were like a curse.

He rearranged his pack then began the descent, looking from side to side as he went. It was possible that the Myghtern would know of this entrance and have it watched. If so news would get back and they would try to intercept him. He would have to move fast, skirting likely settlements, heading east and then south, until he came to the town where the Myghtern – the great "King Under the City" – held his court.

As he made his way down he went over once again just what he knew of this place. Back before the City this place had had a name, Cornwall, but the land, once rich and green, was dust now. No sunlight ever pierced the stygian gloom and the rain never fell. The air was stale and heavy. There was no doubting it. Two centuries of barrenness had left their mark. These were dead lands now.

Thorn went quickly, his legs moving in an easy, tireless rhythm. He skirted Lelant then went directly east, meeting no one in that desolate landscape, covering more than fifteen *li* before he stopped. He had three days to get to the town. At most it would take one. That left him two days to find out what was happening before they came.

He had just crossed the old road northwest of Crowan. He stood there, his back to a layered stone wall. Ahead the land rose to the floor of the City in a huge wedge twenty *li* across. He would have to trace its outer rim north and then sharply south, following the plateau's contours. It would force him into the outskirts of Camborne, but that was preferable to the southern route. That led through Helston, now a dumping ground for City wastes.

He glanced down at the timer inset into his wrist. It was his only link to the outside in this timeless, seasonless place. Two hours had passed. He looked north, using long-sight, searching for activity on the slopes. Still there was nothing.

His luck was too good. Some sixth sense prickled his neck, making him hasten on, climbing the slope towards the Camborne road, then clambering over the wall at a low point where the stone had collapsed.

He looked again. The road was clear for several *li* ahead, but then it dropped out of sight. He began to walk, wary now, looking from side to side, his hand clutching the knife's haft.

They were waiting just beyond the crest of the road, a dozen of them seated casually, looking towards him as he came up over the top. He turned and saw more of them climb over the wall stealthily and then stand there, cudgels in their hands, blocking his retreat.

There was laughter from front and back. Feral, braying laughter. They had him. Twenty to one. Impossible odds. His hand slipped from the dagger's handle. Slowly, carefully, he raised his hands, showing they were empty. Then, smiling, Thorn walked on towards the seated men.

* * *

They took his pack, his dagger, then stripped him. He stood before them, naked, ignoring their mocking eyes. They themselves were scrawny specimens, malnourished and sparsely fleshed.

He saw how their eyes widened, seeing what was in his pack. It was a tiny treasure trove: Above toys, mainly – gifts for the Myghtern. HeadStims, Enhancers, MedFac Sensorbs. Few of them would make any sense to these savages, even so they were in awe of the Above and its works.

One of them took charge of Thorn's things, snarling as he plucked them from unwilling hands and returned them to the sack. He was some inches taller than the rest and broader at the shoulder, but that said little. Like all here, his frame was small, stunted. Things grew *trythro* in the Clay. *Twisted.*

"*Gwycor?*" he asked, coming up close to Thorn and poking him in the chest. His breath stank. His grimacing face seemed demonic, the eyes two vivid pits of crimson in a mask of red. As in all cases of malnutrition, his head seemed too large for his body, the skull's shape clear through the stretched skin. Thorn looked back blankly, pretending not to understand.

The Clay man stared at him a moment longer, insolently studying his features, then turned away. "*Map orth caugh,*" he said loudly. The men nearby laughed shrilly, like jackals baying.

Son of shit, yourself, thought Thorn.

The laughter faded and with it came a sudden change of mood. Thorn saw the transformation in their faces. They were uneasy now they had him. Their heads moved jerkily from side to side, eyes searching the darkness of the nearby slopes. He understood at once. They were intruders here. He frowned, reassessing things. He had thought they were the Myghtern's men.

At a signal from the leader two men brought forward what Thorn had taken to be cudgels and presented them, grovelling cravenly. From a pocket in his ragged cloak the leader took out a small cylinder and pressed the button on its side. In an instant both of the torches were ablaze. The two men stood back, holding them aloft.

Thorn peeled the strip from his eyes and looked. The twin flames burned fiercely, steadily, throwing a warm orange glow across the surrounding fields. From the floor of the City, thirty *ch'i* overhead, the image of the flames was thrown back at them, as though in a giant, silvered mirror. Thorn looked up and saw the group of them, reflected, inverted in the dust-free surface: dark shapes with double shadows. Looking down he saw the leader anew, in normal vision. Small, dark eyes sat in a gaunt, bloodless face that even the warm flames could not animate – more corpse now than demon.

They set off, heading north on the road, Thorn naked in the midst of them, the torches at front and back. They moved fast, at times trotting, keeping a tight formation that had more to do with fear than discipline. Nearing Camborne they slowed, skirting the ruins cautiously, expecting attack at any moment. But the torches kept the scavengers at bay.

Past the town they headed north, on to the old coast road, then made a track across an old disused airfield. The old tarmac was cracked and pitted and the men skirted it almost superstitiously. On the far side the land rose almost to the floor of the City. In places they had to get down and crawl, the smooth, geometrically regular surface above, the rough uneven earth below.

And as they journeyed on so Thorn's conviction grew stronger. These weren't the Myghtern's subjects, these were outsiders. He watched them, sharply attentive now, knowing just how valuable this knowledge was. It meant there was another route into the Clay, another unguarded entrance. He smiled to himself, then straightened as the land began to fall away again.

It was almost four hours before they halted. They were two *li* south-west of Perranporth, on the floor of a steep-sided valley. The underside of the City, more than two hundred *ch'i* overhead, reflected the torchlight faintly. Darkness seemed to plug each end of the valley.

How much further? he wondered, and for the first time began to think that maybe they'd been expecting him.

They rested, binding his hands and feet and placing two guards to watch him. He lay on his side, pretending to sleep, listening to their talk, but it was only idle chatter. There was no clue as to who they were or where they'd come from. One fact alone caught his interest – they were to have a feast that night to celebrate. Which confirmed that this had been planned, his capture anticipated.

When they set off again Thorn could sense the thread of pure fear that circulated among the men, like a live wire joining them. Even the brightness of the torches couldn't drive back that inner darkness. To their north was a densely populated area. South was the Myghtern's capital. Between all was his land, held by his chiefs in his name. These lands were hostile.

They went a long way east then turned north again. They had changed the torches several times, but now the leader ordered them doused. For a time they stood there, huddled in a close group, accustoming themselves to the darkness, then set off again, cutting across a field, avoiding the old roads. This stage of the journey had taken them over five hours but now they were nearing their destination. Thorn could sense their relief. Despite the darkness there was a growing confidence among the men.

They were crossing the ruins of old buildings, picking their way carefully over fallen walls, heading south-west towards the waste. As they neared the coast it grew lighter, imperceptibly at first, but then markedly. It was still dark but the darkness was much softer and he could make out vague shapes of grey against the black. There was a pre-dawn sense of impending brightness. For a time he was puzzled, then realised what it was. Light was leaking through the translucent walls of the City.

They moved along the cliff's edge, the vastness of the wall to their right, the trapped sea dark and silent below them, the floor of the City a good hundred *ch'i* overhead. Echoes sounded eerily in this strange, twilit place, here where the City ended and the sea began. Sound carried back and forth between the still surface of the water and the roof overhead. Between moved the men, in silence, fearful of each small noise that sounded in that emptiness.

Dead voices spoke here. Falling rocks, The steady slop of the current.

They moved on, in single file now, descending, until they came to a wedge-shaped ledge of rock. There, where the wall of the City made one of its great folds, was the entrance.

It was a small, cave-like opening; a mere depression beneath the edge of the City's walls. Large slabs of fallen stone lay to each side of the opening. Pools of water had formed between them. At high tide, he realised, this ledge would be underwater, but the rock was kept free of moss or weed.

Two of them went through first, while the others crouched, shielding their eyes, growing accustomed to the brightness. Then, abruptly, they pushed him forward. He ducked under, feeling the smooth, thick edge of the wall with his hand as he edged between the rocks. Then, suddenly, he was outside. Out into freshness, brightness. Brilliant, blinding freshness. Involuntarily he put his hand up to his eyes, squeezing them tightly shut, reaching out with his other to keep his balance. A rough and bony hand grabbed his arm, then another. Blind, he was led unceremoniously up a steep slope then thrown down roughly.

He smiled, feeling grass beneath his naked buttocks. He picked a stalk and put it to his lips. Cool and wet it was. Something living.

He had been inside the Clay less than eighteen hours, yet it had seemed much longer. The absence of light, the fetid stillness – such things played tricks with one's sense of time. Now time ran normally once more. Gulls wheeled and cried overhead, nearby his captors murmured softly among themselves, but beneath all he could hear the regular wash of the sea against the rocks below, the ageless rhythm of the tide. A gust of wind blew coldly across his skin, but he made no move to cover himself. He simply sat there, his head bent forward, his arms folded across his knees, at ease, listening, waiting to see what they would do.

After a while he opened his eyes. From where he sat he could not see much. A thick, rough grass grew on all sides, interspersed with thistle and gorse. The men were near by. They had changed and put on warmer clothing – patchwork skins of leather and fur and cloth. For the first time he saw them smile, not in mockery but in good humour. They were at ease here in their own place.

Thorn smiled. He knew now where he was. In the old times this had been called Trevelgue. Two, maybe three thousand years before there had been an iron age fort here, built on the great hump of rock that jutted out into the bay – a tiny island, linked by a narrow wooden bridge to the mainland.

Those days had returned, it seemed. Trevelgue had been resettled, the bridge rebuilt.

* * *

They led him up a slope of grass towards a palisade of stone and wood and rusted iron. It was a junk heap of a wall, more a symbol than a genuine barrier. At the gate he turned and looked back, seeing how the City's walls followed the curve of the coast to north and south. This place – this tiny island of earth and rock and grass – was dwarfed by that huge, unnatural edifice.

For the first time since his capture, Thorn laughed.

The guards turned and stared at him, surprised. Since his capture he had made no sound, and his bearing had won their respect. He had been proud and uncomplaining in his captivity – a man, for all that he was not of their tribe. But now his laughter changed things. One or two of them squinted at him, suddenly afraid. Their leader came across and pushed him roughly through the gate, making him stumble.

It was their turn for laughter, but this time it was uneasy. This one, they sensed, was different.

Conditions inside the fort were primitive. Simply constructed huts, made, like the palisade, of a ragtag of materials, were scattered about the edges of the central clearing. Small, ill-tended plots lay between the huts.

Thorn looked about him, wondering how old the settlement was. No more than twenty years, that was for certain. It hadn't shown up on the last coastal survey.

As he was led through they came out to stare at him. A ragged, ill-clothed people, the women distinguishable from the men only by their beardlessness, the children often on all fours. Clay, all of them. Deformed by the darkness. *Devolved*.

The chief's house lay in a depression at the top of the fortress. It was built lavishly compared to all that lay below it, even so it was a hovel, its cracks filled with lumps of moss.

One mystery was solved, however. From the roof of the chief's house poked an aerial. Crude, pitted with rust, its anachronistic appearance brought a smile to Thorn's face. A radio. So that was how.

Even so, it asked more questions than it answered. However crude, this was beyond the Clay's capabilities. Such knowledge had been lost to them. This had to be Above work.

He was glad he'd let them take him. Who knew what else he'd find?

The chief stood in his doorway, an ugly smile on his face. About his shoulders

235

was an old and tousled sheepskin, sign of his status. About his neck was a string of small skulls – old, yellowed animal skulls – linked by a leather band. His hair was combed straight back from a high forehead. Dark, thick, greasy hair. He was tall, much taller than any of them gathered there, Thorn included. Too tall to have been bred here, his skin too healthy despite its pallor.

A castout. He had found his level here. Become a king of sorts, lording it over the Clay.

The pack leader took Thorn's sack to the chief and dropped at his feet, then backed away, his eyes craving the tall man's approval.

"*Da*," the chief grunted. *Good*. But he was already crouched over the sack, fumbling inside it, greed and excitement naked in his face. He took things from the pack as if they'd melt, anxious to parade them before his eyes. Thorn watched him, imagining him as he'd been. A petty criminal. A faceless member of the lower levels. A nothing in the great Above. And here a chief.

"Why . . ." The chief pointed at Thorn. *You*, he was saying. He closed the pack and set it down, then came closer, walking round his naked captive, looking him up and down. "*Gwycor?*" he asked. Then, when he received no answer, he turned to his lieutenant and touched his tongue. "*Omlavar?*" *Is he dumb?*

There was an awkwardness in the way he pronounced the old tongue. It was still a second language to him. He turned to face Thorn again, the ugly smile – a sneer of amusement – returning to his lips. "*An estren tawesek . . .*"

Stranger than you think, Thorn thought. *And for now, quite silent.*

The chief studied him a moment longer, a slight indecision in his eyes, then strode past him and stood on the lip of the depression, looking down over the rest of the settlement. He raised his arms high and seemed to punch at the air with his fists. "*Prysner dhyn-ny! Gorthewer un golya!*"

The prisoner is ours! Tonight a feast!

There was a ragged cheer from the people below, a half-human sound.

Thorn watched them a moment longer, then turned back to look at the rust-pitted aerial. He would destroy that before he went.

* * *

They put him in a rude, low-ceilinged hut at the back of the chief's house and bound his hands and feet. Lying there, he could hear the chief operating the radio set, sending a message out, then awaiting a reply. It was a long time coming.

He tried to figure out where this crude chain of communications might be based. He could identify two points, but where else? Brittany, perhaps. Somewhere on that coast. Or the Channel Isles. Yes, that was more likely. On Sark or Alderney. But why? What was going on here?

It was why he had been sent. To find out and report back.

Night came, star-studded and clear. From where he lay, Thorn could see the soft, pearled glow of the City beyond the settlement, a band of cold, milky light. It looked cold and alien. How did it make them feel, seeing *that* each night? Did it make them sense how small they were? – or did they turn their backs on it to face the darkness of the ocean?

The feast began an hour into the darkness. He could hear the babble of their excitement, smell their fires. And something else. Roasting flesh. So there *had* been other captives here.

The fires crackled, threw up bright sparks into the darkness. Down below, the sea crashed against the rocks. Seabirds called in the dark, troubled by the activity on the great saddle of rock. Thorn lay still, biding his time. There was more to be learned here. Much more. And there was time. Plenty of time for him to find out why he'd been taken.

It was late when they came for him. They were naked, their skins and faces painted, sweat-beaded from the dance. Their eyes seemed wild, unfocused, their breath smelled of crude alcohol mixed with drugs. *Above* drugs.

They unbound him then gave him a rough sacking coverall to wear. He tied it at the waist and then stepped outside. Turning, he looked up and saw the brilliant circle of the full moon above the dark ocean. From the base of the cliff far below came the soft rush and break of the waves. Thorn turned his head, looking at one of the men who'd come for him. In the silver light his skin seemed like polished metal, his bare, thin arms like the jointed extensions of a machine. Only the man's eyes seemed alive and vital, the rest was dead. Thorn studied him a moment, then turned away. He had seen how the man's eyes had been drawn by the moon, in awe and fear, as if linking the stranger with its mysterious potency.

They went down into the central clearing. Three fires had been built and the tribe was gathered in a great circle about them. The stacks had been large but now they had burned down and the darkness overhead seemed more immense than ever.

The chief sat on high ground on a crudely-built throne. His face and neck were painted black. Only the eyes were contrasted, hexagons of white exposed about the liquid, flame-filled circles of his pupils. His sheepskin was pulled close about him against the night's sudden cold. Even the fires could not dispel that now.

On his head was a crown of twisted metal, and in his hand, grotesque, almost surreal, a blackened arm, the fingers shrivelled as if grasping at the air.

So easy to fall. So hard to rise.

He greeted Thorn with a flourish of the blackened arm. "*Wolcum, arluth travyth.*"

Welcome, lord of nothing.

He put the arm to his mouth and bit deep. Then, as he chewed the tough and stringy meat, he spoke again. "*Eery wew, goeff!*" *Worse luck for that!* It brought drunken laughter from the darkness about the dying fires.

The chief leaned forward, beckoning Thorn closer. He advanced and, at the chief's gesture, sat.

"You talk?"

The words were heavily accented. They came like pebbles from his mouth, hard but rounded. It was clear he hadn't spoken English for some time.

"I talk."

The circle grew quiet, listening without understanding. This was mystery to them. Above talk. He sensed the awe in their sudden silence. The moon sat high above the chief's right shoulder, throwing a fierce silvered light across his black-painted neck. The chief looked out around the circle, then back at Thorn. "Another . . ." His hand gestured, circling, searching for the right word, then alighted on the charred limb. "Another has need of you."

Thorn frowned. "The Myghtern?"

The chief winced. There was a murmur about the circle, then silence. "Do not . . . talk of that man."

"Why?" he asked. But it was beginning to fit together. After years of petty squabbling the Clay had a scent of power. Real power. Something was happening to wake the Clay. Something important. How important he hadn't guessed until now.

The Myghtern had new friends in the Above. Influential friends. Friends in Security, in coastal surveillance. Friends who would ignore unauthorised signals on certain wavebands. Friends who would report all movements of traders in and out of the Clay.

"What will happen to me?"

The chief smiled. "Trade you. Rich trade." He nodded ferociously. "The man pay well for you."

This was unexpected. Why should the Myghtern want traders? Was it, perhaps, their skills he wanted? Numeracy? Languages? They were an interface, after all. They linked Clay and Above.

"And my wares?"

The chief glared at him and shook his head. They were clearly no part of the trade. He tapped at his chest with the blackened fingers. "Keep them," he said and smiled. A predatory smile this time, from the part of him that had always been Clay, long before his fall.

* * *

He woke with the dawn. Light entered through the threadbare, hole-pocked cloth that formed one side of the hut, speckling the rough, unpainted wood of the wall beneath which he lay. He turned, listening, immediately awake. Sea birds were calling in the bay, but the sea was quiet. He stretched, easing his legs and arms, feeling the rough blanket beneath his naked thighs and back. The crude wire with which they had bound his wrists and ankles had chafed the skin, but he ignored it, rocking himself up into a sitting position, then edged forward until he could poke his head out of the hut.

It was a bright, clear morning. Long shadows pitted the ground. Somewhere out of sight two men were talking languidly. There was the clink of a spoon against a cooking pot and the smell of wood burning. Otherwise there was little activity in the camp. The two men set to guard him were asleep on the ground close to the hut.

Thorn smiled and leaned back, relaxing. Whatever the Myghtern wanted with him, he would get to where he wanted to be – he would be there when they came. And later, when he had what he had come for, he would come back here and destroy this place.

It was more than an hour before they came for him. They unbound him, then threw the old sackcloth at him, watching as he dressed, surly now that it was time to relinquish him. When he was ready they led him down through the settlement, back to the Claygate. There they waited, on the outside, a guard of twenty warriors, armed with cudgels and flint axes, between Thorn and the gate.

He sat there, watching the Myghtern's men come through; a dozen men, dressed in light armour and wearing cloaks. They were proud, fierce men, but even so they struggled to contain their fear of the outside, keeping close to the rock wall by the gate. Only their leader, a straight-backed man with short dark hair and piercing green eyes, seemed unaffected.

The chief came down to greet them. Without his face paint he seemed much smaller, less impressive. He was broad-shouldered but gaunt. Even the sheepskin failed to disguise his emaciation. And as he embraced the leader of the Myghtern's men Thorn could see the reluctance, the uncertainty and distaste in the smaller man's stiffness. There was no love lost here.

Thorn watched their faces, saw how they held their bodies. Here such things were more telling than words.

"*Pandra ober mynnes why?*"

What do you want? It was blunt, to the point. The newcomer was angry, humiliated that he should have to bargain with this man, and his anger was barely contained. It flashed in his eyes as he uttered the words. Only a pragmatic sense of the situation controlled and shaped his actions. This was awkward for him; he had been beaten to his prize.

The chief smiled and opened his hands. "*Pandra kerghes why?*"

What have you brought?

The chief's eyes narrowed. His shoulders were hunched. Thorn, watching him closely, frowned. Everything was so naked here; so obscenely open. Greed sat like a mask on the chief's horse-like face.

"*My a-wyn gwele gwycor.*" *I want to see the trader.*

The chief hesitated, then turned and motioned with his hand. One of the guards reached down and pulled Thorn roughly to his feet, then dragged him forward until he stood before the Myghtern's man. On both sides the warriors tensed, cudgels and short swords raised in case this was a trick.

For a moment the green-eyed man simply stared at Thorn, then he reached out and lifted Thorn's left hand, turning it, studying the palm. He saw a smooth, fine-boned hand, the palm's flesh unblemished, the red weals of the binding rope about the wrist.

"*Tan!*" *Here, take!*

The chief snatched at the offered gift. It was something small and shiny. Glass and silver flashed in the early morning sunlight. The chief studied it a moment, then gave a howl of delight, holding it up to show the gathered warriors.

It was a valve. A valve for the radio. And there were others in the pouch. It was old technology, two centuries out of date. Thorn studied the newcomer's face, trying to understand.

The chief passed the valve carefully to his lieutenant, who scurried back up the hill towards the chief's hut. In a while he was back, breathless, nodding his head, a broad grin on his face. "*Ober-s,*" he said. *It works.*

The chief had been waiting impatiently. Now he rubbed his hands together and turned to face the newcomer. *"Ytho?" And?*

For a moment the Myghtern's man said nothing, did nothing, but his face was dark with anger and his nostrils were flared, his eyes wide. Then, abruptly, he pushed back his cloak and put his hand on the handle of his long dagger. *"Tra nahen." Nothing more.* Behind him his men grew tense, mimicking his stance, prepared to fight.

There was a long, tense silence, and then the chief laughed. It was a false, high-pitched laugh that grated on the nerves.

"Hen yn lowr dhyn, ena." That's enough for us, then.

But Thorn could see how he eyed the long dagger, the belt, the man's fine clothes. It was not enough. Nothing was enough. But it would have to do. The chief gave a curt movement of his hand and Thorn was pushed forward – given over into the custody of the Myghtern's men.

And as he went back into the darkness of the Clay, Thorn smiled to himself. The trader had been traded.

* * *

They moved fast, in utter darkness, beneath the metal sky, south to the Myghtern's city. It was open, undulating land, and as his eyes grew accustomed to the dark so it seemed like a journey across a desert on a moonless night. No one spoke. Only the faint sound of their footsteps disturbed the hollow dark. They followed the old road, marching between stone walls that had stood for centuries. As the road began to dip towards the sea, the surrounding land changed. The wilderness gave way to signs of life. Small, makeshift huts stood back some way from the roadside. Faces peered at them from above the stonework. The air itself grew heavier, more foul. More and more habitations appeared along the road until finally, as they approached the outskirts of the old county capital, the darkness seemed alive with movement.

At the Trispen crossroads a kind of market had been set up. Ragged stalls offered the flotsam of a past none here could remember. Equally ragged people, their bony limbs poking through threadbare garments, picked furtively at these offerings under the hostile and suspicious glares of the traders.

Thorn's party slowed, seeing the press of bodies up ahead, and then stopped completely. The Myghtern's man called several of his men to him, then sent them ahead to clear a path. That done, they set off again, keeping close to the right hand wall, short swords drawn.

They were almost through when it happened. There was a scuffle and a brief cry and one of the Myghtern's men went down, hit by a rock. Thorn turned and saw how quickly the crowd surrounded the fallen man, finishing him off. Others of the party had, like Thorn, turned to look back, but a barked order from their leader drew them on.

They pressed on, keeping a tighter formation than before. The road dipped then slowly rose again. At its crest they had a view of the land below, stretching away towards the sea. Thorn, looking outward, thought at first that he had to be mistaken: the darkness seemed much less intense down there and, below them, directly ahead of them on the road, there were what seemed like vivid patches of brightness. As they descended he realised what it was. Up ahead of them – no more than a *li* away now – torches burned in brackets mounted on high poles, lighting the way down to the Myghtern's city.

At the bottom of the hill the wide, deep scar of an ancient river bed cut across the land. The road ran out on to an old stone bridge, gently arching over the gap. On the far side of the bridge twin torches blazed steadily in the windless air. Beneath them was a barricade, guarded by a dozen lightly-armoured men.

As they came to the bridge the Myghtern's man turned to Thorn and put his hand on Thorn's chest.

"Before we go inside, you must understand how you are to behave. You belong to the Myghtern now. Whatever he commands, you do. You are his creature now. Here that is not so bad a thing to be. It has its compensations. But if you are difficult, if you try to escape, we will kill you."

"I understand."

"Good." The man nodded, but his expression was unreadable, his face a mask of light and shadow.

Thorn studied him a moment. There was something odd about the man. He seemed half-finished, yet in some strange way he was more sophisticated than any of these others. His accent was clear, unrounded, not native to these parts, and he spoke English with a clarity and ease that was as surprising as it had been unexpected. Thorn reassessed him, looking at the thickness of his biceps, the musculature of his chest and thighs. He was somehow too well formed, his bones too firm, too straight, to have come from here. Like the chief, he was an outsider.

The man had been looking away from Thorn, calling orders to his men; now he turned back to face the trader.

"I am Tak, the Myghtern's lieutenant. Whatever you want, you come to me. Understand?"

There was a sudden sharpness to his tone that made Thorn look at the words again. *Whatever you want, you come to me.* What was really being said here? For a moment Tak held his eyes. Then, abruptly, he looked away, turning to give more instructions. On the far side of the bridge there was movement as the barricade was slowly moved back out of the way.

There was a low parapet overlooking the dried-up river. Thorn went across and rested his elbows on it, looking out away from the brightness of the torches, at the old town.

There, in the centre of the darkness, it seemed to glow. The silhouette of the old cathedral stood out against that faint illumination, hard-edged and dark, its square central tower thrusting towards the City's floor. Thorn looked up. Yes, it was no trick of the eyes – there was something there, like the faint irradiation of a dying fire reflected in the dark undersurface of the City. Or a lamp, shining beneath the water at the bottom of a deep, dark well. He frowned. Another mystery. Another thing that ought not to be here.

Thorn turned. Tak was watching him, his eyes half-lidded, as if trying to fathom what he was, what he wanted here. *As if he knows*, Thorn thought. *Or, at least, suspects*.

Tak raised a hand, beckoning him. "Come, let's cross the bridge. The Myghtern will see you in the morning."

"The morning?" Thorn laughed uncertainly.

Tak turned away and walked out on to the old stone bridge. "You'll see," he said over his shoulder. "This is the city. The Myghtern's capital. You will see many things that will surprise you here."

Thorn glanced up at the floor of the great City, two hundred and fifty *ch'i* overhead, seeing once more that faint glow in the dark, reflecting surface, then shook his head. He didn't understand. Here there *was* no day, no morning. Here there was only night – only shadows and darkness.

He felt a firm hand in the small of his back and began to walk, crossing the slightly arched bridge. *The City*, he thought, wanting to laugh at the absurd grandeur of that term. *What a mockery of words they make down here. If they only knew . . .*

The barricade was drawn back. The guards parted, letting him pass. And so he went through, beneath the torches, into the narrow, cobbled lanes of the Myghtern's city.

CHAPTER·13

GODS OF BONE AND DUST

Scaf sat at the water's edge, staring out across the violently shimmering bay, the booming noises of the great world filling his head, his body anchored to the earth by fear. He dared not stand, lest he fell, for if he fell he was not sure he would ever get up, not the way he felt right now.

Things loomed. He would focus on something and it would grow large in his vision, taking on a brilliant show of colours, while the smells . . .

He dared to take a breath and felt his head swim at the mixture of strange and powerful scents that flooded his senses.

"Scaf . . ."

He slowly turned his head, making the gargantuan effort only by exerting every last shred of his will. Things pulled at him, demanding him to look, smell, hear what they were. *Alive . . .* it had all come suddenly alive!

His head stopped. Kygek's portly features leapt into view, like a landscape seen through an enlarging glass. Scaf groaned. He could smell Kygek's breath, like an old and rotting corpse.

Kygek tried to speak, but couldn't. It was as if the words terrified him. But words had never frightened Scaf, not even at the start, when they had first come to the Domain, that moonlit night nine years ago. That was why he had been the first to be named by the Master. "Scaf" he had been called: *Quick.*

Scaf lifted his eyes, moving from the great, black lake of Kygek's mouth, spiked with jagged, yellow rocks, past the furred caverns of his nostrils to the liquid blackness of his pupils. Kygek tried again to speak and once more failed, but it didn't matter – the fear in his eyes, the torment there, were eloquent enough.

"No," Scaf said clearly, trying to keep Kygek's eyes from dragging him down into their terrifying depths. Kygek thought they had been poisoned, but the Master would hardly keep them for nine years, feed and clothe them, shelter them and teach them his language, only to poison them like vermin. No. Whatever this was, it had a purpose. There was a *reason* why the world had suddenly changed.

He pulled his eyes away, slowly, agonisingly turning his head.

There was a reason why the water shimmered like a pit of silver snakes; a reason why the trees on the far side of the water leapt at him like hungry animals; a reason why the honey-bees burned orange and black in the air surrounding him, why their buzzing reverberated like a power-saw inside the echoing cavern of his skull. The Master had done something to them. Not poison, no, but something else. Something that had changed their relationship with the world.

He put his hand before his face and stared at it, fascinated, tracing the lines, the patterns of the flesh, and as he did words came to him from nowhere.

> "What the hammer? what the chain?
> In what furnace was thy brain?
> What the anvil? what dread grasp
> Dare its deadly terrors clasp?"

He shuddered, astonished by the sound of his own voice, loud, echoing loud, offering the strange words to the busy air. Those words . . . he'd never heard them before that moment. And yet he knew – knew without asking – that they were not his own.

The Master . . . he would have to ask the Master.

Slowly, with an agonising slowness, he stood. He tried to close his eyes, but it was no good: it was as if his brain refused to let him blank it out. Slowly he turned, his eyes picking their way from object to object like a mountain-climber finding handholds in the surface of a cliff. At any moment he might fall.

The water vanished. He let go of a tree and grabbed at a nearby bush. It leapt into view, holding him like a piece of sticky tar. He shook it off and grasped at a low fence.

He was almost there now. His eyes clung to the fence, conscious of the grain of the wood, of the great eye-like whorls, the shining silver head of a nail. Each thing grabbed at him, forcing him to look. Gritting his teeth, he jerked himself free, then turned his body that final, tiny bit.

There!

Scaf could smell Kygek at his feet, could hear his rasping breath beneath him, but his eyes were fixed elsewhere. There, at the top of a brilliant, emerald slope of grass, was the Master's cottage, its walls so white, so powerfully, overwhelmingly white they hurt Scaf's eyes.

He whimpered gratefully.

"Master!" he called, his voice like thunder in his head. "Master!"

Slowly the darkness at the door's edge thickened, widening like a flooding river until, with a suddenness that made Scaf jump, a hand appeared, gripping the wood.

Scaf shuddered, his whole body trembling with a violent anticipation, and then a wave of blackness hit him like a club.

* * *

Ben pushed the door open and stepped out into the sunlight. For a moment he stood there, puzzled, then he saw them, down at the end of the lower garden, by the water.

He went down, bending over Kygek to check the pulse at his neck. Kygek stared up at him as he did, dog-like as ever, yet there was something new in his eyes; some element of curiosity that had not been there before. The pulse was high but regular. *Good,* Ben thought and smiled, patting Kygek's shoulder, then turned to the second of them. Scaf was unconscious. Ben knelt beside him, concerned for a moment, then relaxed. The pulse was normal, his heartbeat regular. He had probably just got over-excited, that was all. It was Scaf who had been calling him.

As he leaned back, Scaf moaned and opened his eyes. Seeing Ben, the Clayman's large, round eyes widened perceptibly, a look of utter astonishment seizing his face.

Ben smiled. "Is it strange, Scaf? Is it all . . . changed?"

"Yes," Scaf said quietly, the word filled with wonder. "Your face . . ."

Ben held himself still, letting the Clayman study the contours of his face. So often he had done so himself, standing before a mirror, a lamp to one side, turning his head so that the shadows fell in different ways. But this felt different. To have another see him as he saw himself . . .

His smile broadened, and as it did Scaf gave a tiny sigh of delight. Then, with a suddenness that was frightening, the Clayman's face changed, grew horrified. Scaf was staring past him now, as if there were a demon at his back.

Ben half turned, confused, but there was nothing: only the two remotes that followed him constantly. For a moment he didn't understand, then, with a laugh, he reached up and plucked one of the tiny hovering cameras from the air.

"It's all right," he said, cupping the thing in his hands to show the Clayman. "It's a remote. A tiny camera. It just looks like a bug."

Slowly Scaf's terror subsided. Slowly the light of curiosity returned to his face.

"I . . . I've never seen it before," Scaf said slowly, his eyes locked on the tiny machine.

"They've always been there," Ben said, picking it up between the thumb and forefinger of his right hand. "You've just not noticed it. Like the rest of it. The drug I gave you has heightened your perceptions. Sharpened them."

With an effort, Scaf pulled his eyes away from the remote and looked at Ben again, the dark pupils of his eyes as tight as pin-heads.

"Is this for good?"

"Permanent, you mean? No. It'll wear off in a few hours. But it'll leave a residue. You'll sense things much more clearly from now on. And it ought to sharpen up your thought processes too. And when I give you the second shot . . ."

"The second?" There was a look of doubt in Scaf's eyes now as if he wasn't sure whether that sounded a good thing or bad. Kygek, who had been lying there listening to everything, gave a distinct groan.

"Don't you *want* to be better than you are, Scaf?"

Scaf's mouth worked impotently a moment, then he shrugged.

Ben placed the remote in the air, then reached out to hold Scaf's shoulder. "Of course you do," he said, his voice heavy with reassurance. "You all do. Even Kygek here. It's your destiny."

He squeezed the Clayman's shoulder gently, then stood, looking about him. The other two must be somewhere about. Back in the blockhouse, perhaps, lying on their backs in bed, engrossed by the patterns on the ceiling. He laughed, remembering his own first experience with the drug. It had been like a door opening in his head. He had seen . . . darkness. The infinite darkness between the individual atoms. So much space and so little substance. So much . . . *nothingness.*

Ben looked back at Scaf. It was working. He could see it in their eyes, in the hesitancy with which they now encountered every facet of the world. He had switched them on. For the first time they were alive, truly, vividly alive, the way he himself was alive. He laughed, then spread his arms wide. It was time to further their education.

*   *   *

He carried the two Claymen back to the bunkhouse, one under each arm, then searched nearby for the others. Crefter he found in the tool-shed, crouched in a corner, staring at the objects on the shelf in front of him. Blonegek was in the lane, standing facing the stone wall. Neither had the least understanding of what had happened to them. He brought them back and strapped them in their beds, then returned to the cottage to fetch the lists he'd prepared.

As he made his way out of the study, Meg came from the living-room and, closing the door behind her, took his arm, keeping her voice low.

"Are you sure you know what you're doing?"

He smiled at her and reached out to brush her cheek. "It's what I'd always planned. You know that."

"Yes. But why now? Is it because *he's* here?"

"He" was the man from SimFic who was sitting in the living-room even as they spoke.

He shrugged. "Maybe. Maybe it's just time. I need to do something new. This . . . well, I've been preparing for this a long time now. You know what they say, as one door closes another opens."

"But what if it harms them?"

His fingers combed the hair behind her ear, then he drew her closer, embracing her. "It won't harm them. To be better than they were, that can only be a good thing, no? We've fed them, clothed them, been kind to them. If they'd stayed in the Clay they'd have been dead long ago. No, Meg, I've done them no harm. Nor shall I."

She stared back at him, her dark eyes searching his. "You promise?"

"I promise. Now let me get on. And tell our Mister Neville that I'll be with him in another twenty minutes."

*   *   *

The strong effect of the drug was beginning to wear off. As he unfastened their bindings, Ben whistled to himself cheerfully. It was just as he'd said to Meg. It was time to stretch himself again.

He stood back, watching them sit up, noting how they looked to each other, checking that they were all all right. That concern, which he'd noticed before, was highly developed in the Claymen. They were a tightly-knit group and even Scaf, the most individual of the four, would rarely act without the approval of the others.

The drug, it seemed, had had little effect on that aspect of their relationship. Or so it seemed. It was early days yet, and as the doses continued it would be interesting to see whether the bonds between them would remain as strong.

Scaf was staring at him again, not with the drug-induced intensity he'd shown earlier, but with a curiosity that none of the others seemed to display, even now. The others merely looked down, as if ashamed. Or maybe they were afraid? It was hard to tell.

"What is it, Scaf?"

He saw how the others looked up, attentive suddenly, looking to Scaf. For while Crefter – named for his strength – was physically the dominant one, it was to Scaf they looked whenever there was a problem.

Scaf made a tiny shrugging motion then looked away.

"You want to know what's happening – is that it?"

He glanced at Ben then nodded.

"I understand. Today . . . well, if I'd prepared you for what was going to happen, you wouldn't have gone through with it. Now that it's happened, you'll be better prepared next time. Maybe you'll even enjoy it."

There was a disgruntled murmur from the others.

Ben took a long breath, momentarily irritated by them – by their stubbornness, their intractability. It was as if they didn't want to be better than they were: as if all they really wanted was to wallow in the filth and darkness from whence they'd come.

"This is it," he said, keeping his voice free of any trace of irritability. "Don't you understand that yet? This is what we've been working towards all these years." He held up the printouts he had brought from his study and waved them at the Claymen. "Look, I've made lists for each of you of what needs to be done." He began to hand them out. "You'll see here just what needs to be prepared, what packed."

There was general consternation as they studied their lists. Kygek, in his usual fashion, scratched his head. But it was Scaf, as ever, who spoke for them, his long face furrowed deeply.

"But this . . . this is for a journey, Master." He looked up and met Ben's eyes. "Where exactly are we going?"

"Inside," Ben answered, smiling back at him. "Into the Clay."

* * *

Neville turned from the window, looking across as Meg came back into the room carrying a loaded tray. As she set it down, he went across to her, watching as she laid out the cups and then poured the *ch'a*.

Tea, he reminded himself. *Here they call it tea.*

Setting the teapot down, she lifted the brimming cup and offered it to him, her dark eyes meeting his for the first time since she'd left the room. Again he felt his stomach clench, his heart begin to hammer. Whatever he'd expected to find out here in the Domain, it wasn't her. He had thought her a fiction – something conjured from Ben's mind, like all the rest of it, but she was real. Real, and quite beautiful.

More beautiful even than the day.

He watched her draw her long dark hair back from her face, then lift her own cup; felt his breath catch as she smiled and sipped.

So simple a thing to do, and yet she transformed it utterly.

"So, Mister Neville?" she said, the unusualness of that word "Mister", the strangeness of her accent – so pure and clipped – making him feel, once again, that he had strayed into a dream. "Do you like our little valley?"

Like it? He laughed gently and made a vague gesture with his head. How could one not like it? Why, he had fallen in love with it the moment he had stepped from the cruiser. With it and with her.

He looked about him at the room, at the carved wooden panels of the walls, the dark oak beams, the low ceiling and the soft furnishings of the chairs and sighed.

"It's like a dream," he said. "If only the whole world were like this."

"It was once," she said. "Or parts of it."

He stared at her, drawn into her eyes a moment, unable to look away, then broke his gaze, embarrassed, unused to such directness.

She was like her brother in that. Neither of them had learned any of those games one took for granted in the Above: games of face and status. One did not have to look for the motive behind their words, nor for some barbed insult.

"Those men," he said, turning to indicate the window. "Who are they? I thought you were alone here."

"The Claymen?" She moved past him, the scent of apple wafting to him from her hair, so fresh and natural. "They came here nine years ago when the valley was invaded. Ben captured them, civilised them."

"I didn't know," he said, moving up beside her to stare out down the garden towards the bay. "Was it frightening?"

"Yes." She turned her face to him and smiled. A smile full of sunlight and roses. "I left, after that. I stayed away from here almost two years, but I had to come back. Ben needed me."

He frowned, not quite understanding what she meant, but sensing the strength of feeling behind her words.

"Your brother is a remarkable man, *Nu shi* Shepherd. No one knows the inner workings of a man better than him. His self-knowledge is quite astonishing."

His comments brought a strange smile to her features. "Forgive me, Mister Neville, but you're wrong. Ben but guesses at his nature. If he *knew* there would be no art, no . . . *creativity* in him. It's that darkness within him he pursues. Those things unknown."

She stopped, turning suddenly. Ben had stolen silently into the room. He stood beside the door, like a piece of the darkness itself, his dark eyes watching them intently.

"I learnt his road and, ere they were sure I was I, left the dark wood behind, kestrel and woodpecker, the inn in the sun, the happy mood when first I tasted sunlight there. I travelled fast, in hopes I should outrun that other. What to do when caught, I planned not. I pursued to prove the likeness, and, if true, to watch until myself I knew."

Neville felt a shiver ripple up his back. The hairs on the back of his neck were standing on end.

"Is that something you made up?"

Ben stepped into the light. "Good God, no. That's Edward Thomas. "The Other". He understood, you see. It's like Meg says. It's the pursuit that matters. The ceaseless search for self."

Neville bowed his head in a gesture of respect, but Ben seemed merely amused.

"You want to know what I've decided, yes?"

"I . . ." Neville hesitated, then smiled, deciding that such directness should be answered in kind. "Yes."

"Then you can tell your Masters that they have a deal."

"I see." Neville nodded, but his surprise was close to shock. What, no haggling? No endless questioning of contractual clauses? Just a straight yes? It was unheard of! "You're sure?"

Ben laughed. "Don't think me naïve, Mister Neville. Or may I call you Jack? I've studied the contract at length and I know what I've signed." He took the papers from his pocket and handed them to Neville. "If SimFic want something more complex than my signature, I'll provide whatever they want. There's only one condition."

Ah . . . Neville smiled tightly. *Here it was.*

"I do no publicity."

Neville laughed. "But . . ."

"My work speaks for itself, or it doesn't speak at all."

Neville hesitated then bowed his head. "Well, it's strange. The media . . ."

"Can take it or leave it."

"I see."

"Make sure you do." Ben lifted the teapot and poured himself a cup, then came across to where Neville and his sister stood. "And make sure your Masters understand, as well. What they do with the work is their concern. Mine is to create."

Neville licked his lips, his mouth suddenly dry. It was as he'd been warned. Ben was one of a kind. Every other artist he'd ever met had been neurotically concerned with every last tiny detail of the promotional strategy, but Ben genuinely seemed not to care.

"Doesn't it worry you?"

"Worry me? Why should it? The sum you've paid me, I'm sure you'll do your best to re-coup your investment. And even if you don't, how does that affect me? Will it change what I do next? No. Will it change the work I've already created? No. So why should I be worried?"

"Put that way, I guess . . ."

Ben reached out, pressing the fingers of his left hand to Neville's chest, the touch firm yet unthreatening.

"Did *you* like the work?"

Caught in the intensity of that stare, Neville felt transfixed. To answer no seemed impossible, and yet he felt compelled to give more than the stock, expected answer.

"It frightened me," he said. "It was so *real*."

"Good," Ben said, the slightest hint of a smile in his eyes – eyes which, now that Neville was looking into them, he was surprised to find were green, not dark as he had been picturing them. The dark, vivid green of the trees and grass and hills of the valley. He shivered, then looked down at the hand that continued to press against his chest.

"It's false," Ben said. "The hand, I mean. I lost the original in an accident. A mirror fell on it."

Neville noted the faint rim around the wrist then looked up again. Ben was smiling broadly now.

"What *didn't* you like about my work?"

Neville considered a moment, then shook his head. "Nothing. I thought it was perfect. I . . ."

"No. Perfection . . . that's when it ceases. It's the flaws that make the art. The uncertainties. The gaps. The . . . hesitancies. Perfection. Well, perfection is death."

"And yet you seem to seek perfection?"

Ben's eyes seemed amused by that. "Yes," he said. "I guess I do. Maybe that's why I'm fascinated by the darkness. After all, nothing's more perfect than the dark, no?"

Neville shrugged. He had no view on it. Had never even thought of it. But the mere fact that Ben had spoken of it meant he would now. He knew that: knew it almost as certainly as he knew that he would never see things the same again – not after having experienced Ben's work. No, and nor would millions of others. If what he suspected was correct, Ben's *The Familiar* would change the lives of everyone it touched. But not yet. First they had to come up with suitable forms of technology that would allow people to experience it in all its glory. Ben's art was so new – so revolutionary – that right now there was not even a means of presenting it. But there would be. And that, too, would change people's lives.

He felt the pressure on his chest cease. Ben stepped back, giving him a nod. "You must excuse me now, Jack Neville, for I have work to do. But come again, please. We must talk at greater length."

Neville smiled and bowed his head, then watched Ben turn and leave the room. When he had gone, he let a long breath escape him and turned, looking to Meg again. While Ben had been there he had almost forgotten her, but now he was gone . . .

"Would you have more tea, Mister Neville?"

"Jack," he said, emboldened by her brother's friendliness. "Please, call me Jack."

* * *

Ben pulled the curtains to, then sat behind his desk, watching the screen. A hidden camera perched high in the corner of their quarters gave him a view of the four Claymen. They were sitting on the bottom bunks, two to each side of the stone gangway, their heads leaning in close as they talked.

Ben pushed the slide to maximum. At once the sound of their voices filled the room.

". . . that's as may be," Crefter said angrily, "but the Clay! It's too risky."

"That's right," Blonegek said, coming in on Crefter's side. "It's much too dangerous."

"But it's where we're from," Scaf answered them reasonably. "And this is what we've been trained for."

"Were we ever given a choice?" Kygek asked. "Do you forget those early days?"

Scaf shook his head. "I remember it well, Kygek. Yet it was necessary. We were wild, remember? Little more than animals. What we are now . . . all that is down to the Master. We would be nothing without him."

Crefter made a small noise of dissent, yet it was clear Scaf's words had had some effect. Even so, the thought of going back into the Clay was clearly disturbing them, for they returned to it immediately.

"I would do anything for him," Blonegek said. "You know that, Scaf. But this . . ." He physically shuddered. "It makes me uneasy. The dark . . . I've come to hate the dark."

Scaf nodded then rested his hand on Blonegek's shoulder.

"Can't we talk to him," Blonegek asked. "Persuade him not to go inside."

Kygek laughed. "Persuade the Master? How? He's set on this. Couldn't you see that? His face . . ."

"His face was like the shining moon," the normally unpoetic Crefter said, surprising them. "I'd never seen . . ."

He fell silent and dropped his head, abashed.

Scaf looked from face to face. "If that's how we all feel, I'll talk to him. Tell him . . ."

"Tell him what?" Kygek asked, his face sneering. The drug, which had given Scaf insight and Crefter poetry, had darkened Kygek's natural cynicism. Only Blonegek seemed vaguely what he'd been, but then, there had been so little of note in his character to begin with. Blonegek was a born follower.

Scaf looked at Kygek and smiled. "I'll tell him we won't go."

Both Crefter and Blonegek made noises of surprise, while Kygek simply stared, open-mouthed.

"But you *can't*," Crefter said. "He's the Master."

"No?" Scaf looked about him. "Isn't that what you want?"

"Yes, but . . ."

"But *what*? Either we go or we don't go. It's that simple, neh?"

Yet it was clearly *far* from simple. From the looks on their faces, Ben could tell they were really torn by this matter.

"How do you feel, Scaf?" Crefter asked after a while.

"Uneasy." Scaf sighed, then studied his hands as if he were seeing them anew. "Given the choice, I would prefer not to go back inside. I have nightmares."

There were nods at that. In the shadows of his room, Ben sat back a little. He hadn't known.

"So what are we going to do?" Kygek asked.

"Simple," Scaf answered. "We have a vote."

"Vote?" Blonegek stared blankly at Scaf. To either side of him, Crefter and Kygek shrugged.

"It's easy," Scaf said. "First I ask all of you if you want to stay here. If you do, you put your hand up. Then I ask all of you if you want to go inside. If you do you put your hand up."

"What if you want to do both?" Blonegek asked.

"You won't. That's the point. And whichever idea gets the most hands up for it, that's the course we'll choose. Okay? Right. Then let me ask you if you want to stay in the Domain."

Kygek's hand went up at once, Crefter's following it hesitantly a moment later. Blonegek stared from one to other of them, then, frowning, put up his hand. Last of all, Scaf raised his.

"That's settled then," he said.

"Aren't you going to ask the other question?" Blonegek asked.

"There's no point," Scaf said, with infinite patience. "We all want to stay."

"Ah . . ." Blonegek said, but there was still confusion in his face. And Ben, watching, realised he would probably have to give him a barrelful of the enhancement drug before it made any difference.

Scaf, however . . . Well, already he was displaying some interesting traits. Before the treatment his leadership had been of a passive, reluctant sort, but now he was coming out of himself.

Ben watched Scaf stand, steeling himself to come up to the cottage and speak to him, then leaned forward and switched off the screen.

It was time to deal with them. Time for drastic measures.

* * *

There was a knock on the cottage door. Ben opened it and looked out into the garden. Scaf stood there, the other three at his back. He shuffled awkwardly, tugging at the sleeve of his jerkin, then opened his mouth to speak.

"What is if, Scaf?" Ben asked, pre-empting him. "Is something troubling you?"

He could see how Scaf wanted to withdraw. If he'd been alone, he would probably have stepped away, murmuring something like "It's nothing, Master". But he was conscious of the three behind him, and of the plan he'd drawn up for them, and so he stood his ground, and, swallowing, began again.

"It's about the Clay, Master."

Ben smiled. "You don't want to go, is that it?"

Scaf's eyes widened, then, made speechless by Ben's anticipation, he nodded.

"You'd better come in," he said. "There's something I have to show you."

Scaf hesitated. He had never been inside the cottage: none of them had, not since the very early days, and then they had been punished – and punished severely – for stepping inside the Shepherd family home.

"Come on," Ben said, standing back to let them pass. "I order you. And you three. Come on now, this is important."

He led them along the shadowed corridor and into the dining-room, then across to the door that led down into his secret workplace, unlocking it then leading them down the steep, narrow flight of steps.

Here he did his work. Here were a thousand secrets that were kept from the world. As they stepped through between the crowded racks, they stared about them, eyes wide in wonder. It was a treasure trove of technological marvels, most of them beyond the comprehension of the Claymen. But one thing, standing there in the space between the end shelves, they did understand. It was a Clayman, like themselves. As they approached, the Clayman removed his hat and bowed to them.

"Good day, my friends. I've been expecting you."

Ben, who had stepped to the side, looked back at them and smiled.

"This," he said, "is Genna."

"Delighted to meet you," Genna said, stepping forward to shake their hands; and as he did he named them. "Scaf. Crefter. Kygek. Blonegek."

Ben watched, noting their reactions; how, like animals, they surreptitiously sniffed the stranger, their senses fully alert.

"Well, my *dyvrow*," he said, using the old Cornish for "exiles", "it's time you understood how things stand. You had a vote, neh? You *decided*."

All four of them looked away, abashed, yet there was something defiant in the way Scaf stood there.

"Genna, come here!"

The Clayman turned and, taking four steps, stood before Ben.

"Give me your knife," Ben ordered, his voice neutral, his eyes perfectly calm. Genna did as he was told.

"Now roll back your sleeve and hold out your arm."

Genna took off his jacket and threw it down, then ceremoniously rolled back his sleeve and held out his arm, as if he knew what was to come.

Ben slipped the knife into his belt, then took a hypodermic gun from his shirt pocket and, holding it against Genna's bared upper arm, fired it – once, and then again.

The others were watching intently now.

Ben threw the gun down, on to Genna's coat, then took out the knife again. Its razor-sharp edge flickered in the lamplight. Ben hesitated, waiting for the drug to take effect, then grasping Genna's arm firmly, dug the point in and scored a line all the way down his arm from inside the armpit to the wrist. Blood welled in the gash and ran.

The Claymen gasped.

"Watch," Ben said, throwing the knife down on to the jacket, then began prising open the gash with his fingers, opening up the wound as one might prise open a fig.

There was another gasp. A low moan of fear from the watching Claymen. Wires showed, and metal struts. The Clayman, Genna, was a machine. Or, at least, his arm was.

Ben stooped down and wiped his hands on the jacket, then picked up the knife and, ripping open Genna's shirt, began to cut into the chest. Genna shuddered but stood still, as if mesmerised by what was happening to him.

Ben cut and pulled, then stood back, letting them see. More wires. More plastic and metal. Blonegek fell to his knees. After a moment, Crefter and Kygek joined him. Only Scaf still stood.

"You understand now?" Ben asked, the power and authority in his voice like that of a young god. "I made you. Sinew and bone, I made you, here in my workshop."

"No," Scaf said, frowning, the effort of denying his Master costing him a great deal. "I have memories. Memories of a time before we came here."

"I gave you them," Ben said.

Scaf shook his head, but even as he did, Ben spoke again.

> "What the hammer? what the chain?
> In what furnace was thy brain?
> What the anvil? what dread grasp
> Dare its deadly terrors clasp?"

Scaf stared at him, horrified.

"Remember?" Ben asked. "Do you remember asking yourself where that came from? Well, Scaf, it came from me. I gave it to you. Like all your thoughts and memories. Because I made you. Every last bit of you."

A shudder went through Scaf, like a sudden surge of power, and then, bowing his head, he knelt.

And so it's done, Ben thought, moving between them and touching each one's head, as if blessing them. *A few wires, a simple speech programme, the subliminal seeding of a few lines of poetry, and they believe.*

Lies. He had lived all his life among lies and fictions. Why should *this* be any different? And yet he felt a sudden disappointment looking at them, kneeling there, worshipping him as a god – strong because so unexpected.

He looked at the machine, standing there staring ahead sightlessly and frowned. To make machines think they were human – that was nothing. But to make humans think they were machines . . .

"Okay," he said, shrugging off the mood and clapping his hands. "Let's get packing. I want to be gone from here before sunset."

* * *

The pillar stood in an open space at the end of Boscawen Street in the heart of the Myghtern's city. It was as broad as a dozen men and reached up at least three hundred *ch'i*, disappearing into the floor of the Above. In the darkness it had seemed more a shadow than a solid thing, but now its blackness was breached and light spilled from the open gate, revealing sleek, curving surfaces of silvered metal.

Five men came down the steps, suited up, their faces obscured by wraparounds, their shapes silhouetted against the brilliant light. Two made to go ahead, but the others paused, looking about them. All this was new to them. The illuminated fronts of the old, Georgian-style houses, the unlit street-lamps, the cobbled surface of the street. They looked at it all in awe, surprised despite their expectations, then moved on, urged by the first of them.

* * *

General Rheinhardt sat on the far side of Haavikko's desk, looking through the latest reports. Li Yuan had asked him to investigate the operation as a matter of urgency, so here he was, unannounced. Finished, he closed the file and looked up.

"So what's the state of play? Have we heard *anything?*"

"Nothing yet, sir," Haavikko answered, trying not to let the General's stare unnerve him. "We've fifteen operatives in the Clay – twelve on the Mainland and three in the Western Isle – but as yet we've heard nothing from them. However, as the last of them only went in a few days back, it's not a cause for worry."

Rheinhardt nodded. "And the other line of enquiry? The merchants? Where have we got to there?"

That was how this operation had begun, with a tip-off from a merchant. Someone had contacted a Junior Minister, who had put him on to Haavikko's office. The man had spoken of sinister goings on in the Clay – of deals and unauthorised visits. Haavikko had arranged to go and see the man, but when he got there he had found him dead, his throat cut, his rooms ransacked, and anything that might have given them a clue was missing.

It might have ended there, only Haavikko's natural curiosity led him to investigate the movements of the man, and he had found two gaps in the camera record – two periods when the merchant was nowhere in the Northern Enclave. He hadn't gone out by any normal exit from the City, therefore he must have gone down. Down, into the Clay.

"It's a long job, sir. We don't really know where to look, who to investigate. None of the man's business colleagues were involved, nor, it seems, were any family contacts. All we can really do is work through the list, hoping to get lucky."

Rheinhardt considered that, then shrugged. "Was there no club the man attended? Somewhere he might have . . . well, met people? This . . . I can't believe it's random."

"That's if we're right, sir. That's if there is anything to be found down there."

"So? Did he go to any clubs?"

"Not regularly, sir. He went to brothels occasionally. Aside from that . . ."

"Have you investigated that angle?"

"Sir?"

"The brothels?"

"I . . ." Haavikko made as if to consult the file, but he knew the answer. "No, sir."

"Well, get on to it at once. And Major Haavikko?"

"Yes, sir?"

"You have two days to get a result. Understand? Li Yuan wants this matter sorted out by Friday morning. He wants a report on his desk first thing, in time for the Council of Ministers that afternoon."

"I . . ." He swallowed, then bowed his head. As Rheinhardt stood, he too stood, clicking his heels, then stood there, head bowed, while the General put on his gloves and, without another word, left the room.

He sat, breathing easier once more. "Shit . . ." he said quietly, then leaned forward, pressing the summons button. At once the Duty Captain appeared at the door.

"Sir?"

"John? Get the full team in here now. It looks like we might be going in. Li Yuan wants answers, and he wants them fast."

* * *

Darkness. It beckoned him like a lover.

Ben stood amidst the ruins of the old village, looking about him. Through the heat-sensitive glasses he wore he could see the figures of his Claymen, moving like bright red demons in that suffocating darkness, the RadMark identification symbols vivid on the backs of their suits.

This was Lamorna, an old smuggling village south of Penzance on the southernmost tip of ancient Cornwall. They had come into the Clay some twenty minutes back, following tunnels groined into the rock five hundred years before. From here it was a twenty-five mile march to the Myghtern's capital, but Ben was in no hurry.

"Crefter!" he called, hearing his voice echo back at him from the ceiling overhead, and knowing that word would already be going out that there were intruders in the Clay.

Crefter came across, dog-like in his obedience, the heavy pack strapped to his back. Ben turned him and activated the tracer. At once the screen lit up, glowing red and black. It too showed heat-sensitive images, relayed to it from the four remotes Ben had with him. Only one was presently active, hovering directly over his head, programmed to stay there come what may. The other three sat in their slots at the top of Crefter's pack.

Ben unslotted the first of them, tapped out its induction sequence, then threw it into the air. At once it sped off north. It would go ahead and find a perch in the Myghtern's town from which to send back its images. The other two would be their eyes as they made their way through this dark and deadly place.

He activated them and sent them ahead, then gathered his Claymen about him. All four carried packs. Kygek had the guns and ammunition, Blonegek the food, Scaf some basic medical supplies and a spare remote, as well as various things for trade, should the need arise.

He turned Kygek and unclipped one of the five heavy-duty lasers from his back and handed it to him, then took the others and distributed them, checking the charge on each before he gave them out.

Their faces stared at him expectantly: skeletal faces of red and black. He smiled and pointed up the dusty hillside. "Up there," he said. "Crefter, you'll walk in front of me. Kygek, go ahead ten paces. Blonegek and Scaf, you cover the rear, left and right."

He had had them practise it in the field before they'd flown out, but here it was different. Here it was dark . . . and dangerous.

They began to climb, the ceiling of the Above seeming to come down to meet them. At the top the land levelled out and Ben paused.

"Scaf," he said, summoning the Clayman to him. "Do you see them?"

Scaf came across, then looked about him nervously. "See who, Master?"

"The dancing maidens. Take off your glasses a moment and look!"

As Scaf removed his glasses, Ben fired his laser at the ceiling overhead. For a few moments the whole place was lit up vividly, revealing that they stood in the midst of an ancient stone circle, the stones like the irregular teeth of a giant.

Scaf gasped in awe. Such places were sacred among the Claymen. He fell to his knees.

"Bones and dust," Ben said, laughing, the darkness enveloping him once more. "That's all the old gods are now, bones and dust! First the Christians came and built their churches on the old sacred sites, and then the Chinese came and consigned it all to darkness and oblivion. Now only devil men live here. Devils and their king, the *Myghtern* . . ."

He could sense their unease at the word. King Under the City, he called himself, as if he ruled it all, when in fact all he ruled was this tiny corner of the darkness. A king of scampering mice and insects!

Ben smiled. That was why he'd come. To catch the king and take him back to his own Domain. And that was why he had needed his Claymen. To carry his prize back through the dark.

He had ventured into the Clay once before, five years ago: had taken the trail up to Totnes, a journey of five miles, accompanied by an armed patrol. But it was only last year, when he had sent one of his remotes deep into the Clay, that he had discovered the Myghtern's town, and, at the heart of it, the Myghtern himself.

"Move on!" he called, tapping Crefter, then clipped the laser to his chest again, freeing his hands to manoeuvre the remotes.

* * *

Three hours later they were on the outskirts of Camborne, more than half their journey completed. Ben had made regular stops to check the land ahead, knowing they would be watched, seeing from time to time a flash of red among the stones, but still no attack had come.

The Claymen were nervous. He could sense how the time had dragged for them, so that this journey seemed not a matter of hours but of days. Now, as he rested, he gathered them close about him, offering a few words of reassurance while they ate.

That done, he crouched behind Crefter, studying the screen. The lead remote had reached the Myghtern's town and was perched on a roof, looking out over the New Bridge. He moved it on, searching the lamp-lit streets, then stopped, focusing-in as six figures – five tall, one small as a child – stepped from a doorway and made their way down a street.

He watched a moment, then switched to one of the two surveillance remotes, searching the surrounding darkness.

Insects, attracted by the warm glow of the screen, fluttered around him. He crushed one between his gloved fingers and let it fall, then cracked another against the screen, wiping it afterwards.

Nothing, he thought, beginning to be suspicious. It was almost as if someone was letting him come on, deeper and deeper into the Myghtern's realm. He had expected to be attacked – to have to use the lasers, but this waiting . . .

He stood. They would need to be extra-vigilant from here on, for the attack would come. Somewhere between here and Truro the Myghtern's men would try to stop him. There were three places they could try – three bottlenecks where the land rose to meet the ceiling and only a narrow passage led through. By taking the northern route he would avoid two of those.

He lifted his mask and sniffed the darkness, hearing the fluttering of insects in the air around him, and felt a shudder ripple through him. For months now he had dreamed of being here; had pictured it in his mind. And now here he was, embedded in the dark, hours from safety, with only his own skills between him and certain death.

He replaced his mask then went among them, touching their shoulders. It was time to move on.

* * *

The door was open. A broad flight of steps led steeply down. The passageway was dark but at the bottom, some twenty *ch'i* below, a faint light showed a wet, uneven surface.

"*Here?*" Hastings seemed surprised, but the small man, Tak, merely nodded and began the descent.

They were big men and Tak, among them, seemed like a child in stature. At the bottom a passageway stretched away into the earth. A light shone dimly from the ceiling about thirty *ch'i* along, but after that there was only darkness. Tak led the way and they followed.

Past the light he looked back and saw Franke pass beneath the rounded, yellow lamp. Briefly there was gold in the silver of his hair, gold like cloth on his broad shoulders, then darkness. Tak narrowed his eyes thoughtfully, then turned and went on.

The darkness ended in a second door. They stood before it, the three newcomers uncertain, the sound of their breathing filling the narrow space. Tak stepped forward and lifted the heavy iron knocker then let it fall. It made a deep, hollow, echoing sound in the darkness.

Silence, and then the door eased slowly back. A big, thick wooden door. And as it opened a dull redness leaked out into the passageway, sketching them in its pallid colour.

Beyond was a hall. Vast, high-ceilinged, its true dimensions lost in the dim redness.

"Gentlemen . . ."

A tall, almost spectral figure stepped from the shadows and stood before them. He was taller than Tynan, but thin and angular, his arms and legs somehow too long, his face too narrow.

They knew at once what he was. A "sport" – a product of the GenSyn vats. Nothing natural bred like that, not even in the Clay.

The creature ushered them through. Behind him four hugely-muscled men pushed the door shut on its silent hinges, then slid home well-greased bolts. Inside the air was filled with spices.

"This is our host," Tynan said, his hand resting lightly on the long, thin forearm of the GenSyn sport. "His name is Barrett. Whatever you want, ask him. He can arrange most things." He paused and leaned towards them. "Here *anything* is permitted."

The boyish smile was frightening. In the distance – in a second chamber – could be heard faint cries of torment: voices stripped of everything but pain.

Tak turned, saw Hastings looking down at his hands. His eyes were troubled. Beyond him stood Franke. Franke's eyes were different: they burned with eagerness – with an intense, unnatural desire. Tak turned back. Nolen was watching him, a half smile on his face.

"And what do *you* desire, little man? Or did they make you free of that?"

For a moment all eyes were on him. Tak smiled and bowed. "Nothing here, sir. Nothing you'll find in these chambers."

Nolen nodded and was about to say something more when Tynan interrupted him hastily. "No need to rush matters, gentlemen. First a few drinks. Then Barrett will see each of you privately. After all, discretion is needed in these matters, no?"

Deng Liang laughed, but the others were silent, thoughtful.

"Come then," said Tynan, looking from one to another. "Whatever you want. My treat."

And at his side Barrett smiled, his mouth a slit of darkness, his eyes two moist points of redness. "Yes, come."

* * *

It was a large, dark room. The walls were bare and there was a musty, unpleasant taste to the air. In the corner was an old bed, the brass posts spotted with corrosion, the blankets bleached by age, worn almost to shreds. Hastings stood there, alone in the cool silence, looking about him. A crude electric light-bulb suspended from the ceiling illuminated the room, casting his shadow, sharp-edged and unfamiliar, whenever he moved.

In one corner, set into the wall, was a set of wooden cupboards. He went across and opened them. Inside the shelves were empty, the walls bare but for some old traces of paint. A blind-eyed insect scuttled for its hole, twelve-legged, its shell casing a perfect white. In one corner, high up so that he had to stand on tiptoe, was an old web, its strands broken. Tumbled at the bottom, like a discarded wrapping, lay the dried husk of a spider. How long had it been there? he wondered. How old this room? Four centuries? Five?

He closed the doors and turned, facing the room again, sensing the great age of this place beneath the old town. All of this so different from what existed in the Above. And then the thought hit him again: this was to be his place. Down here, among the dead men. For a moment his lips formed the shape of his distaste, then he shrugged and went over to the bed. He stood there, looking down at the blanket, trying to make out the faded pattern. It looked like roses . . .

Behind him the door opened. He turned and saw it was Barrett. The sport smiled ingratiatingly and came into the room. With him was a frail-looking young girl. Barrett held tightly to her arm with one claw-like hand as he edged closer to Hastings, bowing grotesquely.

"As you wished, Master. A young woman. Clean. Very clean, I assure you. From the Myghtern's own household. His brother's daughter."

Hastings looked past the creature at the girl. Her hair was dark but lank, as if it had not been washed in weeks. She was thin to the point of emaciation and her breasts were undeveloped, giving her a boyish look. She shivered as she stood there, her eyes downcast. Looking at her, Hastings felt both revulsion and pity: these and a strange, previously unexperienced sense of desolation. He could see her hopelessness so clearly, as if through her eyes.

He waved Barrett away, then, when he had gone, went over to the girl. The top of her head barely came to his chest. He placed his hands on her shoulders, feeling the bones beneath the thin cloth – so fragile it seemed he could snap her with the smallest effort. Placing one hand beneath her chin he lifted her face and looked at her.

In other circumstances it would have been quite beautiful. The lines of her cheeks, the shape of her mouth suggested what might have been, but paucity of diet had blunted the edge of her beauty. There was something both childish and ancient about her face: an innocence allied with the most profound experience. Her skin was rough, unhealthy, her neck marked by scars. Even so, it was to her eyes he found himself drawn, for her eyes were dark like his. Dark and beautiful, like mirrors to his own.

For a moment he looked away, thinking of the women he had loved in the Above. Cold, imperious women, their beauty cut like crystal, the expression in their eyes as distant as far galaxies. How he had suffered for such women. How vainly had he pursued them. He grimaced and held the girl tighter, then turned and led her to the bed.

They undressed and lay on the bed, on top of the thin and faded blanket. Beneath his weight the springs of the old mattress groaned and gently gave. Naked beside her he was aware even more of the contrast between them. His own body was so firmly fleshed, the muscles honed, his broad chest covered by a fine down of golden hair. Hers was white-fleshed and undernourished, the ill-developed body of a child.

Her face was closed against him, her eyes averted. For an instant he didn't understand, then recognised what it was. She was ashamed. For her this was an agony.

He felt a hot flood of compassion wash over him and reached out to draw her to him and hold her against him. He wrapped his arms about her, like a father comforting his child, one hand smoothing the back of her neck. For a long time he was content to lie there, simply holding her, feeling the faint trembling in her limbs grow still, her breathing normalise. Then he moved his head back and turned her face gently to look at her. For a moment she looked back at him, curious, her eyes searching his as if to understand him. But when he smiled she looked away quickly.

"Don't be afraid," he said, concerned, but then realised that his words meant nothing to her. Softly he laughed and, still curious, she turned to look at him again, her dark eyes shining in the pallid wasteland of her face. Again he smiled, feeling something more than pity, something greater than compassion for her. Those eyes, so beautiful. And as he looked her face changed, mirroring his own, smiling back at him, then pressed close to kiss.

Later, when he woke, he felt confused, the starkness of the unshaded bulb making him shield his eyes with one hand. Then he remembered and turned slightly, looking down at the sleeping figure beside him. In sleep she was more a child than ever, one hand raised to her mouth, the fingers gently curled, like a young animal, snuggled up beside him, trusting. And as he looked at her he felt something he had never experienced before. Not love, nor desire, but something more fragile and delicate than either – tenderness. It was like a barb in his gut, making him want to cry out. Not pain, nor happiness, but something in between. A sense of how frail, how vulnerable she was. He reached out to touch but hesitated, letting his hand make a vague motion in the air, tracing the blunt lines of her wounded face, realising how ugly she was – like a gelded, sickly boy-child. And yet not ugly at all.

He sighed and looked away. It was time to be getting back.

* * *

Ahead the land rose to meet the floor of the Above. Only at one point, in a narrow dip between the rock face and the road below, was there room to pass, and then only at a crouch.

Ben let out a breath, then sent the remotes through.

The town was below them, beyond the gap, less than a mile away now. Ben looked about him, seeing how the four Claymen stood there, cradling their lasers, their heads turning, searching the darkness all around them.

Behind them, less than half a mile back, were two, maybe three hundred of the Myghtern's men, while ahead . . .

Ben watched the screen as the first of the remotes threaded its way slowly through the gap, hugging the ceiling. As it emerged he caught tiny glimpses of red – evidence of men hiding behind rocks, but they were at a distance; closer at hand the land was empty.

Strange, he thought. Himself he would have circled the gap.

He switched to the second remote, then had to shield his eyes as the screen flared with a sudden, intense light.

He cried out, the after-image of the explosion imprinted on the back of his eyelids even as the sound of the detonation rumbled through the Clay.

Blinking, he switched back to the first remote, but the screen was blank. The remote . . . somehow they'd destroyed the remote.

Even as the thought struck him there was a second flash, a second rumbling detonation.

"Stay," he said to Crefter, putting his hand on his shoulder as he moved past him. Then, crouching next to Kygek, he pointed to the gap.

"Go through," he said. "Blonegek will cover you."

Kygek glanced round at him, then, after a moment's hesitation, nodded. Ben turned, calling up Blonegek.

"Follow Kygek in," he half whispered. "Keep five paces back. If anyone goes for Kygek, blast them, okay?"

"Okay," Blonegek answered. Then, at a dog-trot, both men headed for the gap.

Ben watched, biting his lip. It was over. It had been over from the moment they had targeted the remotes. If they had the technology to do that, then they could pick off five intruders easily enough. Besides, the remotes had been their eyes – now they were blind. The advantages were all now with their enemies.

He sighed, sad that for once nothing would get back. For him to die, and for it not to have been recorded, that was a great disappointment.

Ben turned, looking to Crefter and Scaf, then, standing, he signalled for them to follow him. Pressing the tracing signal at his neck, he moved towards the gap, his laser searching the darkness up ahead.

CHAPTER·14

THE KING
UNDER THE CITY

It was morning in the Myghtern's city. Thorn stood at the open casement
window, looking out across the ancient town. High above him the floor of the
Above was bright with reflected light. In the street below, a line of lamps blazed in
the darkness of the Clay. The cathedral was below him to his right, the river a long,
dark scar beyond.

"Are you ready?"

Tak stood behind him in the wood-panelled room. He had come in without a
sound; stealthily, like a shadow.

Thorn turned and nodded. "Where are we going?"

"You have an audience. But first the Myghtern wishes you to see his city."

The room in which they stood was bare but clean. Everything was in a state of
good repair. The wood of the walls had been scrubbed and polished; the bunk was
old but sturdy and the pure white sheets were laundered. A newly-woven mat
covered the bare-board floor.

Thorn looked to Tak. "Okay. Let's go."

Outside, in the narrow alley, Thorn stopped and looked up at the wall-mounted
lamps. "Morning," he said softly, then laughed. Beside him the Myghtern's man
smiled tightly, then beckoned him on.

The alley opened out on to a broad main street. *Boscawen Street*, a sign halfway
up the wall read. He stood at one end of it, looking west, the cathedral's spire
jutting up above the buildings to his right. At the far end of the street, straight
ahead of him as he looked, a giant silvered pillar rose straight out of the earth and
soared to meet the floor of the Above some two hundred *ch'i* overhead. There were
few people in the street – far fewer than he'd expected – and those who were
scurried away quickly at the sight of Tak.

He walked slowly down the broad street, looking from side to side at the elegant
Georgian buildings, Tak silent beside him. He already knew there was something
wrong here – something out of place – but the feeling grew in him until he stopped
and looked back, trying to fathom what it was. There was glass in the windows,

263

doors in the frames. Good, solid doors. He looked up. The old slate roofs were in good repair, the guttering mended. And the huge, twelve-panelled window frames were painted.

Thorn went across and ran his finger along the edge of one shop window. Yes, *paint*.

He looked through the glass, saw goods laid out on a trestle table. It was a shop. He almost laughed. A shop! In the Clay! Then he shook his head, frowning. None of this belonged here.

He walked on, quickening his pace. Behind him he heard Tak grunt then follow.

Where the street opened out on to a square Thorn stopped, looking across at the pillar. There was a broad flight of steps at the base of the pillar and above the steps, clearly evident in the lamplight, the outline of a gate.

He stood there a long while, staring at the pillar. A gate. Here, at the very centre of the Myghtern's capital. A *gate*!

Tak came up and touched his arm. "Seen enough, trader?"

Thorn nodded. More than enough.

"Then let's go down to the Chapter House. We'll make you presentable before you meet the Myghtern."

Thorn tore his attention from the pillar. Tak was smiling broadly – a proprietorial smile compounded of pride and delight at Thorn's evident surprise.

"Come then. The Myghtern awaits you."

They walked down through the old county capital towards the cathedral. There, beside the huge, nineteenth-century building, was the Chapter House.

"Here," Tak said, businesslike now, leading him through a side door and down a narrow flight of steps. They went through an old oak doorway and into a long, low-ceilinged room where three old men – none of them bigger than a child – sat at a long bench sewing. They looked up briefly, then returned to their work. Electric lamps burned in the ceiling overhead.

"The Myghtern is a mighty ruler," Tak said with a fierce, defiant pride. "You must come to him in silks, not rags."

Tak opened a cupboard door to his right and took several outfits from the rail, handing them to Thorn. "One of these should do."

Thorn looked at the garments draped over his arm, surprised by their lavishness. Velvets and silks. Leather belts and silver buckles. There was wealth here: more than simple commerce could account for. He glanced up at Tak.

"Try them on," the small man urged. "Quick now. The Myghtern is waiting."

Thorn set them down on the bench then quickly slipped out of the rags he was wearing. Moments later he stood there, dressed like an ancient courtier in crimson, mauve and green. Tak nodded, satisfied, then went to the cupboard again, reaching up to pull down a big crimson-coloured box.

Thorn went very still. It was not what the box contained, but what was embossed into the side of the box. That motif – the Han symbol *Peng* surrounded by the letter C – was the trademark of a company that dealt with only the élite of the Above – the "Supernal" themselves. Tak smiled and handed him the thigh-length kid-leather boots.

"Take great care of these, trader. They are only loaned to you, not given. All here belongs to the Myghtern."

Thorn pulled them on, then stood before the mirror Tak held up for him, seeing how the clothes transformed him. As if he had stepped back a thousand years or more. Tak laughed and showed his perfect white teeth.

"Now then, trader. Its time."

The mirror was set aside. Tak straightened his own clothes and then turned to face Thorn again.

"Speak only when you are spoken to. And bow before the Myghtern's throne. Raise your head only when he commands. Otherwise, do what he asks and all will be well."

Thorn nodded.

"Good. Then follow me."

* * *

At the far end of the long throne room, on a raised platform, sat a giant of a man. His hands, resting on his knees, were broad and long. Heavy rings sat on the thick knuckles of his fingers: black rings of iron, like the rings the T'ang above were said to wear. On his brow rested a massive crown. A crown of iron, rough-cast and ugly, but suggestive of brutality and power. Long, jet-black hair fell in waves beneath the crown over broad, ox-like shoulders. He wore a polished metal breastplate and at his belt hung a huge broadsword.

Thorn advanced towards the Myghtern. Then, as he'd been told, he stopped and knelt, bowing deeply, his eyes averted.

"Get up, trader. Come closer."

The words were in old Cornish, the voice deep and low, like the voice of the earth itself. Thorn looked up, meeting the eyes of the Myghtern.

Dark eyes, intensely black. Fierce, insolent eyes, unaccustomed to looking away. They seemed to pierce the trader, then relinquish him, as though they had – in that single instant – penetrated to the core of him. Thorn shivered. It was like looking into a foreign country: into a place that was primal and savage and vividly alive.

"I am the Clay," said the Myghtern in a voice that seemed to roll like thunder and fill the room. "Everything beneath the solid sky is mine. All lands, all men. And now you, trader. You too are mine."

The Myghtern stretched his hands, as if they were pets resting in his lap. Hands that could crush a skull or bend a bar of iron.

What do you want me for? thought Thorn. *Why send your man to fetch me?* And, more important, *Who told you I was coming?*

The Myghtern cleared his throat and seemed to sit more upright on his throne. His fingers tightened about his knees.

"How do you like my city, trader? Does it impress you?"

Thorn let the words of the old language flow easily from his tongue.

"It is a marvel, Master. I have seen nothing to compare with it in all my travels."

The Myghtern lifted his chin and stared down at Thorn. Then he gave a short grunt of laughter and leaned forward conspiratorially. "It is not finished yet. But in time . . ."

265

Thorn took the opportunity to study the Myghtern's face. It was not a face as other faces, more a landscape. Deep furrows surrounded each eye, like rivers running to the twin lakes of those black, fathomless pupils. His cheeks were ruddy as if lit by some inner fire, and the bottom half of his face was covered by a thick and curly beard, dark tangles of wiry hair glistening in the lamplight. The nose was blunt and wide, yet handsome. Like the chin it suggested strength and a will of iron. Yet the mouth was softer, suggestive of good humour, perhaps even of compassion. Full, sensuous lips peeled back in sudden laughter to reveal strong teeth, like the teeth of a predatory animal. Looking at him, Thorn wondered how the Clay had ever bred such a magnificent creature.

"You will work for me, trader. Use your skills for me."

"My skills?"

The Myghtern smiled broadly. The appeal of the man was intense. Good humour flowed like waves from him. Such power and such warmth. Such overwhelming charm. Thorn found himself smiling.

"You *are* a trader?"

Thorn nodded.

"Good." The smile remained but changed. It was suddenly more calculating. "The five who are here. Would you know them if you saw them?"

Thorn hesitated. Five . . . He kept his face controlled, but his mind was racing. His information had been vague,. A date. A place. Nothing more. "The five . . . ?" He frowned, his expression of incomprehension only half an act.

The Myghtern studied him a moment, fixing him with his gaze, then relented. "From the Above."

Thorn mimed sudden understanding. "It is possible," he said, after a moment. "I know many among the Above." That much was true. There was no one of importance among the élite whose file he had not studied and assimilated. If they were who he thought they were then he would certainly know them.

His answer seemed to satisfy the Myghtern; his hands lifted from his knees and went to his face, the long fingers pushing into the thick blackness of his beard, forming a cage about his chin. For a time he was silent, staring out past the trader thoughtfully. Then he stood and came down the steps, standing there close to Thorn, almost three *ch'i* his superior in height.

"Listen to me well, trader. There is something I want from them. Something they are reluctant to give me." He walked past the smaller man then turned. His fists were clenched now. The shape of his mouth had changed, losing its softness. When he spoke again his lips formed a harsh, animal snarl. "But I will have it. Or I will send them from here. You understand?"

Thorn looked at the richness of the Myghtern's robes, the perfection of his metal breastplate, and understood nothing. *The further in I get, the more I see. And yet the more I see, the less sense it all makes.* He looked up, meeting the Myghtern's fierce dark eyes, and bowed his head in affirmation. As if it were all clear – clear as daylight – when really all there was was darkness.

* * *

Haavikko rolled over and opened his eyes, stared at the illuminated figure on the bedside clock and groaned.

He looked up, seeing the figure silhouetted in the doorway and knew he'd not dreamed it. His equerry really *had* woken him at three forty-five in the morning.

"Whaa?"

"A call's come in, sir. Top priority."

Haavikko sat up and put his feet on the floor, trying to gather his senses. He had been dreaming of the girl again, and of the old woman who had used to run the House of the Ninth Ecstasy. Mu Chua, her name had been. He had been sitting in a room with her, talking, as real, it seemed, as this.

"Who is it?" he asked, standing up and walking across to the corner sink. "Li Yuan? The General?"

"No," the young cadet said, as Haavikko poured water from the jug into the bowl. "It's from the Western Isles, sir. A young lady."

He set the jug down and turned. "A *what?*"

"That's right, sir. But the codes check out. Her message has a top priority rating and she says that she'll speak to no one but the Commander of Security for the Western Isles."

"I see." He sluiced his face once, twice, a third time, then reached blindly for the towel and dried himself. "And am I to call her back?"

"She's holding, sir. I said you were asleep, but she was very insistent. She said if she couldn't speak to you she would go to the T'ang direct."

Haavikko raised an eyebrow. "Then I had best speak to her. Did she give a name?"

The equerry shook his head.

"Then you're as mystified as me, neh, Lieutenant Pace? Okay. Hurry back and tell her I'm dressing. That I'll be with her in . . . oh, in a minute or so. And Pace . . ."

"Sir?"

"See if you can get me some fresh *ch'a*. An oolong, if the mess serves it."

"Sir!"

He went to the locker in the corner and took a fresh uniform from the rack, then slipped it on. Standing before the full length mirror he studied himself, then combed his fingers through the rough bristles of his hair. *Old*, he thought, *you're beginning to look old*. Then, with a nod to his image, he went out, heading for the Operations Room.

Operations was almost empty. There were a dozen men at most scattered about the huge chamber. Several hundred more slept close by, ready to be called were there an emergency, but little usually happened at this hour – at least, nothing that a handful of men couldn't cope with.

He went between the rows of desks and machines and climbed the eight steps up to the central podium. There, at the very centre of it all, was his desk. He sat, facing the big screen, bowing his head in greeting to the young, dark-haired woman whose face filled it.

"*Nu shi* . . . how can I help you?"

"Major Haavikko," she said, clearly recognising him even if he did not recognise her. "My brother went into the Clay yesterday evening, at Lamorna, south of Penzance. I understand he was heading north-east towards Truro. A few hours back he activated the tracing device he was wearing. That means he's in trouble."

"Your brother . . ." Then, suddenly, he understood. "Your brother Ben, you mean? Ben Shepherd?"

She nodded, her eyes deeply troubled. "You have to send someone in to get him out. He's in trouble. I know he is."

"I understand, *Nu shi* Shepherd, but it's not quite as easy as that. The Clay . . ."

"You have to send someone," she said, as if she hadn't heard what he'd said. "And you have to send them *now*. If he's killed . . ."

Haavikko raised a hand. "Okay. I'll do what I can, and just as soon as I can. But I have to get permission. There's something happening, you see . . ."

She leaned towards him, her eyes piercing him, her voice insistent now. "You have to act now, Major Haavikko. There isn't time, don't you understand? They might have captured him. Why, they might be torturing him, even now."

He made to object – to point out that they simply couldn't know – but the seriousness of her demeanour nipped his objections in the bud. "I'll do what I can," he said. "And I'll do it at once. More I cannot promise."

"See that you do," she said, with all the sternness and authority of an Empress. "And Major Haavikko . . ."

"Yes, *Nu shi* Shepherd?"

"Let me know what's happening, won't you?"

"Of course."

He cut the connection and sat back, considering what he should do. Rheinhardt wouldn't welcome being woken for this. Knowing the old man's habits, he wouldn't have got to bed before two, and to wake him now . . .

No, he would have to carry the responsibility for this himself. Sighing, he leaned toward the screen.

"Captain Thomas?"

At once the face of his Duty Captain appeared before him. "Sir?"

"Wake the élite squad. I've got a job for them."

* * *

Ben groaned and tried to turn on to his side, but it was impossible. The thick chains that fastened his legs to the wall were too short, too inflexible to let him move. He tried to raise his hand to scratch his chin and again found his movements restrained by chains.

He relaxed back against the wall, ignoring the itch. Across from him, at the normal standing height of an Above male, was a narrow skylight: through its bars light filtered into the cell from the street-lamps outside. In that faint illumination he could make out the shapes of two of his Claymen. They lay against the wall, shadows within shadows.

It had been no contest. There had been more than two dozen of the Myghtern's men waiting for them on the other side of the gap, armed with lasers and canisters of disabling gas. Quickly overcoming Ben's small party, they had delighted in kicking and beating them even as they bound them, then they had dragged them through the dust to the gates of the town before throwing them into this filthy, stinking cell.

He rotated his chin, feeling how sore it was, then spat, tasting blood in his mouth.

"Master?" came a voice from close by. "Are you awake?"

"I'm awake. What is it, Scaf?"

"Are you . . . *hurt*, Master?"

He almost smiled. After all he'd done – after all the danger he had put them in – Scaf was still concerned for him.

"I'm not sure," he said truthfully. To be honest, he felt numb in places. Whether that was the cold of the cell, an after-effect of the gas, or whether he was hurt much worse than he felt, was hard to tell.

"I think my left leg is broken," Scaf said after a moment. "I can't feel anything in the foot and when I try to move it . . ."

Ben heard the wince and wished he had his infra-red glasses still, so that he could see.

He closed his eyes, conscious for once of the force that drove him: of that blinding compulsion in him to see, to witness, and to describe. So pure that at times it leeched anything human from him, refining him to a cold observing point behind the camera's eye.

Only now, bereft of light and of the tools of observation, could he see it.

I am driven, he thought. *And I cannot help it. There is no "I" in me to control the process, only the cold force of my being – the gift my "father" Amos gave me: the "gift" they call my genius.*

"Don't move," he said to Scaf, feeling a strange compassion for the Clayman. "It only makes it worse."

There was silence for a time, and then Scaf asked. "What do you think will happen to us?"

"Maybe they'll use us. Make us work for them."

"Ah . . ."

There was a groan from the far side of the cell. Another of them was waking, Crefter by the sound of it.

"Crefter? Are you all right?"

The Clayman coughed, then began to heave.

Ben looked down, breathing through his mouth, the acrid stench of sickness filling the tiny cell.

"It's okay," he said reassuringly. "It's the gas that's done it. It has that effect."

"I'm sorry," Crefter said miserably, wiping his mouth. "I feel so bad. And my arm . . ."

There was the echoing tread of footsteps in the corridor to Ben's left, the rustle of keys, then the sound of one being fitted into the lock.

Ben turned his head, watching as the heavy door eased back, the light from a hand-held oil lamp flooding the cell. Two men stood there: a big, swarthy man in a leather jerkin and a smaller, neater man – a typical Clayborn – dressed in fine silks.

"Who are you?" the small man asked, looking to Ben, his English heavily accented.

"I'm Shepherd," Ben answered.

"And the others?"

"They are my men. *Servont.*"

There was a whispered exchange, and then the big man came across. he leaned over Ben a moment, seeming to study his face, his foul breath playing in Ben's nostrils; then, just when Ben expected him to do or say something, he moved on, crouching over the unconscious figure of Kygek.

"*Eva!*" the one at the door said impatiently. *Him!*

At once the gaoler slipped one of the keys into the iron cuff on Kygek's left wrist and unlocked it, then moved busily about him, unfastening the rest. That done, he lifted Kygek on to his shoulder and carried him out, ducking beneath the door.

"Where are you taking him?"

The small man stopped, staring back at Ben, his dark eyes studying him a moment. Then, without a word, he turned and slammed the door shut, leaving them in darkness.

* * *

Tak walked back down the corridor, then reached up and hung the oil lamp on the hook beside the door. *Shepherd*, he thought, remembering how the young man had said it, as if he ought to have known; but the name meant nothing. *Not yet, anyway.*

He went inside, watching as Ponow fastened the unconscious man to the bench. There were many strangers in the Clay right now, some by invitation, others – like these men – for reasons of their own.

Tak edged past the bench and went through into the tiny office on the far side of the cell. There, on a wide, long shelf, were the objects they had taken from the men. Some of them he recognised, like the screen; others, like the tiny sphere, were mysteries. He sat, studying the sphere, rolling it about in his palm, then set it down again. It had felt warm, almost alive to the touch.

And the big man, Shepherd – what did he want in the Clay? Why had he come here, armed with lasers, surrounded by his men? Had he come to meet the others? Or was he a free agent, wanting to muscle in on whatever deal was being struck down here? So much was happening right now it was hard to tell. Tynan might know, but Tak didn't want to ask Tynan. Not yet. Not until he had exhausted other avenues.

There was a noise from the other room, the sound of the prisoner waking. Tak listened a moment, then, knowing what must be done, he went through to begin the interrogation.

* * *

It was evening. The lamplight had faded and darkness lay like a lid of stone above the silent town. Thorn stood on the steps of the hall, staring out into the blackness, thinking.

270

"What is it, trader?"

Tak stood close to him on the steps. Once again he had come upon him silently, unnoticed. Thorn turned. Though Tak was only an arm's length from him he could make out only the vague outline of his form. His face was totally obscured.

"Just wondering."

Tak came closer until he stood almost face to face with Thorn in the darkness. Thorn could feel his breath upon his cheeks. Clean, unadulterated breath. Thorn laughed softly.

"What *are* you, Tak? And what are you doing here?"

Tak was silent. Thorn could sense him, only a breath away, watching his face, trying to penetrate the layers of darkness that hid what he was from normal sight. At length the smaller man laughed. Thorn felt Tak's hand on his upper arm.

"Just a man, trader. Like you." The hand dropped away. "Come. Let's go inside. We have work to do, you and I."

Inside the benches were set up for a feast, a dozen of the Myghtern's men – minor chieftains and retainers – to each table. Their raucous chatter filled the old hall. Overhead the huge oak beams of the rafters were strung with electric bulbs. On the walls hung ancient shields bearing the arms of the families of the old county.

Thorn walked down the aisle, between the heavily laden tables, no longer surprised by the richness, the variety of food on display. At the top table he stopped and bowed low before the Myghtern. The hall had gone quiet. All eyes were on Thorn.

"Welcome, trader. Come up here, beside me."

He went up and sat to the right of the Myghtern. Below him in the hall the talk had resumed, heads had turned back. Thorn looked down the length of the hall and saw Tak standing by the door, staring out into the dark.

The Myghtern turned to him, his face set, determined. "They will be here soon, trader, so let me make this clear. I want to know them. Everything about them. Understand?"

Thorn nodded. The nearest table on the right was empty, he noted. "These five . . . you know none of them?"

The Myghtern smiled. "Two of them. The others . . ." He drained his cup and set it down. "They want things from me. Certain *agreements*. They will no doubt try to placate me. What they want . . ." He laughed, then his face grew serious again. "It is important to them. Very important."

Thorn watched him as he turned away and poured himself more wine. *How important?* he wondered. *More important than what the Myghtern wanted?*

At the far end of the hall, Tak moved back suddenly, addressing someone in the darkness outside. Beside Thorn, the Myghtern stiffened and leaned forward. The hall had grown quiet once again. All eyes had turned to stare at the five silver-suited figures that had come into the hall.

"The first man," the Myghtern said quietly, "the hawk-like one with the dark hair. Who is *he?*"

Thorn was quiet a moment.

"Well? Do you know him?"

"I know him."

He knew all five.

"His name is Edward Tynan. In the Above he's a powerful man. Like the man beside him, Franke. They were both Representatives in the great House that once governed the Above. Nowadays Tynan runs his own trading Company."

The Myghtern laughed. "Like you, then, trader."

Thorn smiled tightly. It was all a matter of scale. Apart from Li Yuan there were only a few dozen men on the planet richer than Edward Tynan. His company transported more than thirty per cent of all the goods that were manufactured in the orbital factories back to the North European Enclave. He was considered one of the pillars of the new establishment. What, then, was he doing here? What could a man like Tynan hope to get down here that he couldn't get Above?

Thorn studied the others. Rutger Franke was Vice-President of SimFic, the up-and-coming entertainments company. He wasn't in the same league as Tynan. Not yet, anyway, for financial sources predicted that SimFic was the Company to watch, and Franke held a substantial shareholding. William Nolen, next to him, had no Company behind him, but that hadn't held him back. He had used a massive inheritance to carve out a successful career in Public Relations. There was no one who was anyone in the Above who wasn't in *his* circle. That *he* was here – linked to the presence of Tynan – suggested that whatever was going on was wide-scale and involved some of the most powerful people in the Enclave.

He watched as Tak turned and began to lead the five down the aisle towards the Myghtern. They came like kings, Tynan and Franke leading, Hastings, Nolen and Deng Liang last.

Deng Liang was an aristocrat. That is, he was a member of one of the Twenty-Nine, the Minor Families, so-called, who had once helped rule the great empire of Chung Kuo. Even now, when their power was but a shadow, they were still "above the Above", not subject to the same laws and strictures as the common citizens of the Enclave. For Deng Liang, fifth son of Deng Shang, to be here was not merely surprising but astonishing. It would be difficult to convey to the Myghtern what it suggested. And as for Hastings . . .

Thorn had received the update on Hastings only days before setting off for the Scillies. The death of the great physicist had come as a sad surprise to many, for he had been an articulate spokesman for his kind: a fearless advocate of change and a vociferous opponent of many of Li Yuan's new laws. His presence here – alive – made some kind of sense of this strange gathering. Or the beginnings of sense . . .

They stopped half a dozen paces from the Myghtern, Tak moving aside with a bow, leaving them to face the Myghtern alone. Thorn spoke hurriedly to the Myghtern, whispering to his ear, telling him who each was and what his status was in the Above, leaving out any mention of Hastings' reported death.

"*Wolcum, Tynan. Wolcum oll,*" the Myghtern said, smiling broadly, his whole manner genial and welcoming.

"I see you have a new man," Tynan said, pointing at Thorn. "A new tongue, eh?"

The Myghtern looked to Thorn, who quickly translated what had been said. It was clear that Tynan had been a test which he had passed. So now he was the Myghtern's man. Like Tak. The Myghtern's ear, his tongue. Behind the expressionless mask of his face, Thorn smiled. It was better, far better than he could have hoped for.

* * *

The screaming had stopped now. In the darkness of the cell, Ben let a long breath escape him, then touched the tip of his tongue against the inside of his upper lip. It felt tender and swollen and one of his teeth was loose, but otherwise he seemed unharmed.

And when my turn comes, he wondered, *will I cry out the way they have? Will I too jibber like a madman and plead for mercy?*

He didn't know. In fact, the very thought of it made his stomach clench with fear. But above that fear – riding it almost – was his curiosity.

Meg's right, he thought, and almost smiled, picturing her face before him in the darkness. *There's part of me that's mad. Mad as the proverbial hatter.*

Beside him, Scaf shifted in the darkness and made a small noise of discomfort. Ben looked to him, making out the vague outline of the Clayman. Scaf had borne this well, considering. Kygek, Crefter and Blonegek had been taken already. His turn was next.

Unless they take me. But that's not their scheme. They'll find out all these "lesser" creatures know before they question me.

He shifted uncomfortably, the chains chafing his wrists, then stretched his neck. How many hours had passed? Two? Three? And the signal? Was that still going out?

He touched the stud at his throat and winced. One of them had hit him there and twisted the delicate implant. If it was broken . . .

If it was broken then no signal was being sent. And if no signal was being sent, no one would come. And even if they did, they would not be able to find him.

Lost, he thought. *I am lost.*

He sighed, then spoke. "Are you afraid, Scaf?"

There was silence, then. "Yes, Master. And sad."

"Sad?"

"That it has to end now. I was . . . hopeful."

"Ah . . ." In the darkness, Ben frowned; but for once there was nothing he could do. This, then was how it felt. To be fated. To be without control. He nodded slowly, understanding. *This* was how it felt.

"Scaf?"

"Yes, Master?"

"Thank you. And sorry. This was my fault."

Unexpectedly, Scaf laughed. "You didn't plan it very well, did you, Master?"

"No, I . . ." He laughed, suddenly feeling much better.

"In fact," Scaf said, his voice dark with intelligence, "you fucked up pretty badly. The Mistress will be very angry with you."

273

"She will, won't she?"

"But she won't give up. She's like you in that."

In the darkness Ben nodded. It was true. Maybe the signal *wasn't* damaged. Maybe someone *was* coming for him, even now. He had only to hold on; to buy himself some time until they came.

Maybes and ifs, he thought, then, angry with himself for being so negative, began to sing.

> "In diesen heil'gen Hallen
> Kennt man die Rache nicht,
> - Und ist ein Mensch gefallen,
> Fuhrt Liebe ihn zur Pflicht,
> Dann wandelt er an Freundes Hand
> Vergnugt und froh in's behre Land.

"What is that?" Scaf asked.

"Mozart," he answered, hearing the glorious music in his head. "It's from *The Magic Flute*."

"I . . . I seem to know it."

"Yes," Ben said. "I gave it to you."

Again there was silence, then. "Did you really make me, Master?"

Ben took a breath. "No. You were born, Scaf, like other men."

"And the memories?"

"Some are real, some implants. The poetry and music . . . those things I gave you."

"I see." There was no anger in the words.

"Scaf?"

"Yes, Master."

"You were the best of them. You know that, don't you? I could have made you something . . . well, something special."

Scaf sighed, hearing the door clank open at the far end of the corridor and footsteps approach. "And now it ends."

Bear up, brave Scaf, Ben thought, but could not say the words. It was not the moment to say something so trite, so . . .

The door eased back, light filling the cell. Scaf looked up at him and smiled.

"It's okay," he said. "You gave me life, Master. And a chance."

Ben swallowed, watching as the gaoler crouched over Scaf, then, not knowing what else to do, began to sing again.

The big man turned, glaring at Ben, and swung his arm, the back of his hand connecting with Ben's cheek. Yet even as he did, Scaf, free now, pulled himself up and, taking a single, agonising step on his broken leg, launched himself at Ben.

The gaoler roared and pulled him off, but in that brief instant Scaf had passed something to Ben.

The cell door slammed, the blackness once more enclosed him. His cheek stung as if it was on fire. But now he had hope. Hope like a beacon blazing in him.

He turned the object Scaf had given him between the fingers of his right hand, recognising it and blessing the Clayman for his foresight. It was a remote control unit. The unit that operated his artificial hand.

Slowly, careful not to drop the unit, he began, moving his hands as close together as the chains permitted, so that he could unfasten the flesh clips just below the raised line of his left wrist. And as he worked, he softly sang the last two lines of Sarastro's song:

> "Wen solche Lehren nicht erfreun
> Verdienet ein Mensch zu sein."

* * *

The worst thing was the waiting, the feeling of impotence as he stood there in the dark behind the door, listening to Scaf's screams.

He had tried to think of other things – to think forward and plan what he would do – but that dreadful sound destroyed the very thread of thought. And then silence – a silence more awful than any he had known.

Was Scaf dead?

He waited, listening, then heard the door clank open and the two men come out. There was a brief exchange, then footsteps – away this time, climbing the steps up to the street. Then, after a pause, the heavy footsteps of the gaoler came towards him.

He stepped back, prepared now, the loose chains at his feet clinking softly against the stone floor.

There was the sound of the bolt being drawn; slowly the door eased back. Ben watched the gaoler move past him, into the cell, then gasp, astonished to find him gone. He began to turn, but it was too late. Even as he made to lunge at Ben, Ben's hand – detached, floating in the air above the gaoler – fastened itself about the man's neck with the force of a vice.

Slowly, his eyes bulging, the man went down on to his knees, his hands struggling vainly to pull away Ben's hand. Ben watched, his eyes taking in everything, his mind burning with a hatred he had never thought possible.

Slowly he increased the pressure, his real hand aching with the effort, until, with a resounding crack, the bones of the gaoler's neck popped and shattered and he fell.

Ben shuddered, then released the tension in his fingers. At once the hand released and floated slowly up. He watched it, then looked back at the gaoler's dark, distorted face. His tongue was thick in his mouth, his eyes like tiny marble spheres.

Time. Time was of the essence now. Quickly he stooped and took the keys from the man's belt, then, letting the hand float on before him, he went out into the corridor, his chains clanking.

His luck held. There were no guards. Setting the control box down, he sorted through the keys, trying them one by one until he found the one that turned the lock.

275

He pushed the door back, his reluctance for once greater than his curiosity, then groaned. Scaf lay there on the bench, his chest pinned open, his eyes burned from their sockets. Ben stepped up to him and winced. His testicles had been mutilated and his legs and arms burned a dozen or twenty times. His fingernails had been pulled off and there were tiny cuts all along his inner thighs.

Ben shuddered and made to turn away, then heard the faintest groan from the Clayman.

Alive? Was he still alive?

He clanked over to the top of the bench and leaned close, putting his hand above Scaf's mouth to feel for a breath.

Yes! But it was the faintest trace. He turned, looking about him, then realised. Of course, he had the keys! Fumbling through them, he found one tiny key that clearly matched the locks at each corner of the bench. He moved round, unfastening them, hearing Scaf groan again, as if he were coming back to consciousness, but listening all the while for the return of footsteps.

How long did he have? How long before someone came to check?

He stared at his own chains, wondering if he should take the time to unfasten them and cast them off, then decided he didn't have the time. Lifting Scaf, he balanced him on his shoulder, then went out into the corridor again.

The steps . . . they were the only way out. But what if there was a guard at the top? He took a calming breath, then began to climb the steps.

At the top step he paused, listening again, but he could hear nothing through the door. Slowly, expecting the worst, he put his shoulder to the door and pushed.

Outside a row of ancient gas lamps punctuated the darkness of the street. Ben hesitated, looking about him, then realised where he was – recognising it from the probes he'd sent in earlier.

He turned, heading left towards the New Bridge, surprised by how heavy Scaf was. If he didn't find shelter soon – somewhere to hide Scaf's body while he worked out how to get out of there – they were done for. Besides, their escape would be noticed before long, and then . . .

Ben stopped and turned, hearing an unexpected sound from down the street – the sound of laughter from inside one of the big houses further down . . . the Mansion House, it looked like.

A feast, he realised. They were having a feast!

He hobbled on, clinking with each step. There were steps beside the bridge, leading down. On the far side a guard walked through a patch of light then merged with the shadows again, some thirty yards distant.

Ben hesitated, then went down the steps, coming out on to the footpath, then ducked beneath the low arch.

Slowly, mindful of his injuries, he set Scaf down. "It's all right," he whispered reassuringly, wishing he could give him something to ease the pain. "We'll be out of here soon. Just wait for me here. I'll be back as soon as I can."

He touched Scaf's forehead tenderly, feeling the burning fever there, then moved back, knowing he had to do something about his chains, or they'd quickly be discovered. Valuable seconds passed as he searched among the bunch for the right key, then, fumbling, he unfastened the cuffs, taking care all the while not to make any sound that might betray their position.

Any moment now, he kept thinking, imagining the small man returning to find the empty cell, the gaoler dead. Yet still the streets were silent, still they were empty.

He shivered then, setting the last chain down, picked up the control again. At the top of the steps he stopped, looking towards the gate, checking the guard was in his post, then he ran on, tracing his steps back to the cells.

His hand . . . it was here somewhere. He looked around, then looked up and saw it. It had floated up halfway to the roof. He smiled and slowly brought it down.

One more thing, he thought, slipping the control into his pocket, then plucking his hand from the air. *One more thing and then we're gone from here.*

* * *

Ben crouched there, still as a gargoyle on the roof, looking down through the skylight at the scene below.

It was a small hall, sparsely furnished, yet the grandeur of the man seated on the old carved throne was undiminished.

I was right, Ben thought. *He is a magnificent beast.*

He watched the Myghtern lean towards the men and speak, his words barely reaching Ben except as faint reverberations in the air. Without a probe it was hard to make out what was going on, yet one thing had struck Ben instantly – something no remote had ever really captured – and that was the power, the sheer *charisma* of the man.

That's why I had to come, Ben thought. *That's why I had to see him for myself. To see him on a screen was one thing, but to see him like this . . .*

There was a noise behind him in Quay Street, a cry and then running footsteps. Ben turned slowly, holding on tightly to the brick parapet, and looked.

The commotion had been from near the cells. As he looked, two men ran across to the open doorway, one of them speaking hurriedly to the other and then gesturing down into the darkness below.

Out! Ben thought. *I must get out.*

He made his way across, half crawling, picking his way hand by hand along the old timber roof. On the far side a fire ladder went down to a flight of steps. He went down quickly, his footsteps echoing, hoping no one would be drawn to the noise. But there was shouting now from the other side of the Mansion House – that was where it was all happening. If he were to slip down Enys Quay he could be out of there before they knew.

The tiny lane was dark and empty. He ran down it and then turned left along the footpath.

There were guards on the New Bridge, but they were looking west, to Boscawen Street. Ben ran on, praying they'd not turn and see him, then ducked down under the parapet.

Scaf lay where he'd left him, unconscious, his breathing shallow. Lifting him up on to his shoulder, Ben climbed down into the river's dried-up channel and walked across, picking his way carefully.

Overhead, on the bridge, one of the guards called out, his voice loud in the darkness, asking what was going on. A voice answered him. A prisoner had escaped. The gaoler, Ponow, was dead. A search was on. Guard the gate! Ben heard them turn and run back to their posts and cursed silently.

Laying Scaf on top of the bank, he scrambled up after him. Close by was a tall mesh fence – electrified by the look of it – while to his left, some thirty or forty yards off, beside the old Round House, was the gate. The mesh fence ran to the gate and beyond. The gate was the only way out.

He unlatched his hand again and lay it next to him, then took the control box from his pocket.

How do I do this? he wondered. With two hands it would have been difficult enough, but with one and carrying Scaf . . .

He laughed. "Nothing ventured . . ."

Gripping the control between his teeth, he lifted Scaf once more, balancing him like a sack on his shoulder, then took the control and pointed it at his hand, lifting it into the air.

Then, the hand floating slowly along in front of him, he stepped up on to the bridge and headed for the gate.

* * *

Deng Liang pulled off his boots and threw them into the corner of the room. He sat facing the others, smiling broadly.

"He can drink, that one! But he'll be sorry in the morning, when he comes to deal with us."

Tynan was standing nearby, gazing thoughtfully at one of the shiftprints on the wall. At Deng Liang's comment he looked across at the young man and shook his head.

"You're more drunk than him, young Liang. Why, I've seen the Myghtern drink twice as much and be sharp as a knife the morning after. Don't underestimate him. To become a king here is not easy. One is not born to it, as Above. And to stay king, as Moyha has done . . . well, that is something else altogether! In the Above he would be . . ."

"A king," said Hastings, seating himself beside Deng Liang. "He's astonishing, don't you think? Like an animal. An animal that thinks."

Deng Liang broke into laughter again. It was true what Tynan had said: he was drunk.

"That may be so," Nolen said guardedly. "But he thinks he can ask what he wants from us."

Hastings smiled, ignoring Nolen's hostility. "Well, can't he? Hadn't we already agreed that he could have whatever he asked for?"

Nolen made to answer, but Tynan touched his arm to silence him.

"Whatever he wants," Tynan said. "Providing we get what *we* want in exchange."

"He's not stupid," Hastings added, watching Nolen turn away and leave the room. "Uncultivated, perhaps, but no fool. And that man of his – the one he calls trader – he seems sharp enough."

Franke stepped forward. "Tak says he's new here. A stranger to the Clay."

Tynan waved the matter aside. "Look. We give the Myghtern what he wants and we take what we want in return. Simple as that. Rutger will speak for us."

Franke had been elsewhere most of the day, arranging things, so Tynan said. Hastings leaned back and yawned. He was feeling good. Things weren't so bad here. And the girl . . . He had bought the girl that morning. She would be his. He would feed her well and look after her. He rubbed at his arm. It was still feeling a little sore from the injections they had had that morning. He looked up at Tynan and smiled.

"I wonder what it is he wants? To what lengths does his imagination stretch, do you think?"

"It has a ceiling, I'm sure," Franke said, making them all laugh.

"I wonder what it's like," Hastings said after a moment, "not seeing the sky, the stars. Year after year. Only the dry, unchanging dark."

"You'll know soon enough," Tynan said, then, in a softer voice. "And don't worry about Nolen. He'll be all right."

Hastings hadn't been worrying, but he nodded anyway. He didn't like Nolen. Though they had many things in common, there was something about the man that got under his skin. He yawned again and wondered vaguely why it was that he so often liked his enemies better than those who were supposed to be his allies. There again, did one have any choice in the matter? Li Yuan's laws existed, preventing them from living a full, free life. What did it matter that he *liked* Li Yuan? Li Yuan and his laws were inseparable. One could not remove one without the other.

His hands were tied, the course of his life dictated by circumstance, and it was no good wishing otherwise. Even so, the thought of working with the Myghtern – with someone he for once admired – was a pleasant one.

Beside him, Deng Liang leaned forward, frowning. "What's that?"

They listened. Somewhere outside, in the Myghtern's town, sirens were blaring. It was a strange, unexpected sound. Hastings stood, looking to Tynan, but Tynan shrugged.

At the far end of the room the inner door of the airlock hissed open. Tak stepped inside.

"What's happening?" Tynan asked.

"It's nothing, gentlemen," the small man said reassuringly. "A prisoner's escaped, that's all. We'll soon have him locked up again. But until we do; the Myghtern has requested that you stay here. There's a guard on the outer door, so you're perfectly safe."

Hastings, who had come across, met Tynan's eyes, a query in his own as to whether this might not be some kind of ploy on the Myghtern's part, but again Tynan made a shrugging gesture.

"And if you don't find him?" Nolen asked, coming up behind them.

"Oh, we'll get him," Tak said, smiling tightly. "Why, he'd need to be some kind of sorcerer to get out of the Myghtern's city right now."

* * *

It's no good, Ben thought, setting Scaf down, *I have to rest.* At his own estimate he had walked almost four miles, yet for all his attempts to keep some kind of track on where he was, he had to admit that he was lost.

He leaned over Scaf, listening for a breath, then, when he could hear nothing, put his fingers to Scaf's neck, feeling for a pulse. It was there, but faint. Far fainter than it had been. If he did not get help soon, Scaf would die. But where would one find help, here in this endless darkness? His only hope was to get to the seal. To somehow find a way back to the Domain.

Ben crouched, looking about him. His eyes had slowly become accustomed to the darkness. Even so, it was hard to discern between shadow and substance. So often his eyes had tricked him, making him think something – someone? – was there, when there was nothing. He had been right to think of this place as a giant "shell", for his brain, denied its usual visual stimulus, had begun to create its own pictures – painting illusions on the blackness. In that regard the Clay was a giant desert, filled with its own mirages.

Down here, he realised, one came to trust other senses than sight – one's sense of hearing, particularly.

There was a sharp *click!* – the sound a stone makes when it falls against a hard surface. He waited, tensed, listening, then turned back and lifted Scaf on to his shoulder once again. As he did, the Clayman stirred and murmured something.

"What?" Ben asked as quietly as he could, placing his cheek against Scaf's face.

"Leave me," Scaf said, quietly yet distinctly. "Alone you'll make it. With me . . ."

"No," Ben whispered, and began to move again, picking his way blindly, his feet finding their way slowly, deliberately across the uneven surface. He felt Scaf shiver, the movement rippling through his body like the wind through a rag, and felt his determination harden. They would get out. They *would*.

"I'm no good any more," Scaf said after a moment. "I'm blind, and my legs . . ."

"That doesn't matter," Ben whispered. "We can replace all kinds of things these days. Eyes, legs. I'll make you as good as new."

"And the memories?"

Ben's legs moved slowly through the dark, separate, it seemed, from his thinking self. For a moment he conceived himself as some kind of piston-driven machine, filled with fuel, pumping its way slowly, inexorably through an eternity of darkness.

"That's for you to choose," Ben said finally. "Whether you want to keep them or not."

But Scaf was sleeping again.

Ben walked on, his legs pumping wearily through the endless dark.

* * *

The four gatemen knelt before Tak, their heads lowered abjectly. They had failed in their duty and now they must pay the price. Tak's men formed a great circle about them in the High Cross, the cathedral towering over the scene. Tak waited angrily, gun in hand.

"*Mes y gwyryon!*" one of the guards insisted, his eyes pleading with Tak. *But it's true!* "*An jevan tewel hus ha y luf nyja y-ban ha dyswul an hespow . . . crakkya a'n gwelen!*" *The demon cast a spell and his hand floated up and undid the great locks . . . snapped them like twigs!*

Tak's anger boiled over.

The gunshot sent a ripple of fear through all those watching. The three kneeling men hunched into themselves, whimpering.

He walked down the line. "Liars!" he screamed, firing point-blank at the second man. "Fools!" Again a shot rang out. "Incompetents!"

The gun clicked, empty. Tak glared at the man, then, throwing the gun away, drew his dagger and, grabbing him by the hair, slit his throat.

He stepped back, looking about him. There would be no more talk of demons and spells. Above technology, that was all this was. Yet he knew his men were scared. He had seen what had happened to the gaoler Ponow and knew that dozens of his men had seen it too. Whoever – whatever? – did that had super human strength. And the great locks on the gate . . . there was no doubting that they had been snapped. But that was not the point. He could not let the rumours get out of hand, nor his men succumb to fear. He must control them, and the only way to do that was to make them more afraid of him than of this "sorcerer" Shepherd.

He turned. A messenger had come.

"*Pandra vyth gwres?*" *What now?*

The messenger's gap-toothed mouth opened in a wide smile. "*Ny trovya pystryor!*" *We find wizard!*

"*Prysner,*" he corrected him, then, "*Py plas?*" *Where?*

"*Holya!*" the messenger answered, turning away. *Come!* "*Ny settya an jevan!*" *We've surrounded the demon!*

* * *

Tak looked through the heat-sensitive glasses and smiled. Shepherd was at the bottom of the valley, trudging along the bottom of a dried-up stream, the wounded servant on his shoulder.

How strange that he should do that, thought Tak. From what he'd heard life was cheap in the Above; almost as cheap – so Tynan said – as here. Such a man as Shepherd could buy a hundred men, surely? Unless he, Tak had overlooked something.

They had got nothing torturing the men: nothing, that was, about why Shepherd was here, in the Clay. It seemed he had not confided in his men. Yet he must have wanted *something,* or why take the risk?

Tak frowned then put the glasses down. Turning, he signalled along the line of men. It was time to take their captive back.

* * *

Ben stopped and turned, astonished. High above him and to either side, where there had been nothing only a moment before, were now two straggling lines of lights. Slowly, even as he watched, they approached, spreading out to encircle him.

Lamps, he realised, noting the ghostly presence of men behind the lights. *They're carrying lamps*.

He sank to his knees, resting Scaf on the ground beside him, then looked up again.

So this is it.

After what he'd done to the gaoler he didn't expect any mercy from them. The best he might hope for was a quick death; the worst – well, Scaf could tell him what the worst was.

He watched, observant to the last, a camera eye, seeing the swaying lamps come on towards him. *Two flashes from a laser and even that would be denied me*, he thought, knowing how easily a good marksman could burn away his cornea. It would take but an instant.

Briefly he closed his eyes, swallowing, and as he did light flooded his head. For a moment he thought it had happened and waited for the explosion of pain at the nerve ends. But there was nothing, only the sense of being washed in brilliant light. Light, and the howling screeches of the Claymen.

Ben turned, wincing, into the light. At the head of the valley, less than two hundred yards from where he knelt, a searchlight rotated slowly, focusing its powerful beam on the hillside, picking out a hundred fleeing figures.

He shielded his eyes with his right hand, then turned, looking back up the hillside. Only one of the Claymen remained now, his hands on his hips, staring back defiantly, then he turned and walked away.

Ben shuddered, then stood and slowly turned, raising his hands.

A voice from within the light boomed out. "Ben? Ben Shepherd?"

He closed his eyes, surprised by the wash of relief he felt, the sheer joy at hearing his own name.

"Yes," he said quietly, knowing they could not hear him. "It's me, Ben Shepherd, back from the dark."

CHAPTER·15

THE DARK ANGEL

Thorn stood beside the Myghtern's throne as the five were brought before him. He had spent a good part of the night and the first few hours of the morning briefing the Myghtern, yet he felt fresh, energised by the thought of the encounter.

He watched as they came down the long room towards the Myghtern; saw how they stood there, unbowed before him, meeting his primitive fierceness with their own high arrogance.

"We have brought you a gift," said Hastings, stepping forward.

The Myghtern turned to Thorn, not understanding. He whispered in the big man's ear. "*Presont . . .*"

The Myghtern turned back, smiling, and beckoned Hastings on. "*Kerghes!*"

Hastings looked to Thorn. "What did he say?"

"He said you should bring it."

Hastings turned and signalled for the gift to be brought forward. One of the Myghtern's stewards advanced, carrying a box draped in black cloth. He bowed, averting his eyes from his master, handed the gift to Hastings, then backed away. Hastings stepped forward on to the lowest of the steps that led up to the throne.

"With our deepest respect and best wishes, King Moyha."

Thorn translated, amused that the five did not know that Moyha was not his name, merely another part of his title – "Grandest". Like many barbarian chiefs, he chose the most grandiloquent of titles – *Myghtern Moyha* – "Grandest of all Kings". Though maybe, for once, there was an element of truth in it, for was a king to be judged merely by the size of his domain?

He stood aside, watching as the Myghtern removed the cloth. Beneath it was a delicate golden cage and inside the cage a small black bird: a tiny thing, as black as nothingness itself, yet its eyes were golden, like polished orbs.

"A gift from the Above," Tynan said, smiling tightly as Thorn translated.

The Myghtern studied the bird a moment, then turned and handed it to Tak, who stood close by. When he turned back his face seemed grimmer. His hands gripped his knees tightly. He was anchored like a rock in his throne, his hugely-muscled arms like something carved from oak. Slowly he surveyed the men before him, his eyes moving from one face to the next, then, one by one, gesturing at each with the index finger of his right hand, he named them.

"Fran-ke. No-len. Ha-stings. Ty-nan. Deng Li-ang."

He nodded to himself then turned to Thórn, giving a short bark of laughter. "*Gowek . . . mes cref.*" *Liars . . . but strong.*

Thorn returned the Myghtern's smile, wondering if any of the five had bothered to learn anything of this bastard language. He doubted it.

He stepped forward, standing between the Myghtern and the five.

"I speak for the king," he began, seeing how Nolen and Tynan smiled at that. Unpleasant, ironical smiles. "He has told me what to ask from you, and what to give. You will deal with me."

Hastings stepped back, looking to Tynan.

"You know who we are," Tynan said coldly. "You therefore know what we represent . . . the *power* we hold in our ten hands. What you have to understand is just what, together, we might achieve."

Until that moment Thorn had been guessing – toying with half-truths. Now, suddenly, he saw it whole. In that image of the ten hands he pictured what the connection was. No, not a single connection, but a web. A tightly-woven web of connections. He listened, alert now. Whereas only moments before he had understood little, now he had it all. He needed only verbal confirmation.

"The Dispersion," he said calmly, confidently, as if he knew it for a fact. "You are all agents of the Dispersion."

Tynan smiled tightly. "Dispersion*ists*. But tell the king this. Tell him he can have what he wants. Within limits, of course."

Thorn stared back at Tynan a moment, fixing him, then shook his head. "The Myghtern wants something else. Something you might think twice about giving him."

Tynan frowned, but it was Hastings who spoke next. "What does he want?" he asked, stepping up alongside Tynan.

Thorn felt the presence of the Myghtern in his throne behind him. Felt the power emanating from him; the raw, primal power of the man.

"He wants a wife. A bride from the Above."

Franke laughed contemptuously. "Impossible!"

Thorn waited a second then began again, speaking slowly, each word deliberate now. "He says that you will do this for him or he will drive you from his kingdom."

Nolen made to speak, then closed his mouth with a snap. He turned and looked to Tynan, who shook his head, but Hastings put his hand on Nolen's arm.

"Think. Just think before you say anything. And Rutger . . . please, let me handle this."

There were exchanged glances, then Tynan gave Hastings a curt nod.

"He is determined," Thorn said, observing all. "He wants nothing else."

"For now . . ." Franke began, then fell silent as Hastings turned, a flicker of anger in his eyes.

"Tell him we are . . . reluctant, but . . ." Hastings sighed. "Thorn, you must know how things are. No woman from the Above would come down here. Not for any price. This place . . ." His eyes revealed the depths of his distaste. "It stinks. It's foul here, yes, even here where there's carpet on the floor and finery on the walls. It's . . ." He shrugged, unable to express the degree of his disgust.

"And yet you five are here. You want something." Thorn looked from face to face. "He means what he says. He'll arm the Clay against you if you deny him this."

Hastings nodded . . . "Okay. We agree. But it will take time. We cannot just buy a bride."

"Ten days," Thorn said. "That's all he gives you. Ten days . . ."

"It's enough," said Tynan, winking at Nolen beside him.

Thorn turned, facing the Myghtern again. "*Ya,*" he said.

The big man smiled, but his hands still gripped his knees, as if in torment. "*Dres'n benen,*" he said. "*Y'ethom dhym a.*"

The Above woman. I need her.

The audience was at an end. In the cage the bird turned on its perch, fluffing out the darkness of its tiny feathers. But its golden eyes saw nothing.

* * *

Major Axel Haavikko had set up his mobile operations room in the lower garden. His men were camped in the fields close by, their tents in neat rows facing the bay.

While Haavikko spoke to his General, Ben stood in the doorway of the half-track, listening in.

"But we have to go in now, sir, before they can prepare against us. If what Shepherd's told us is correct, all that's standing between us and his headquarters is an electrified mesh fence."

Rheinhardt stared back at his Major uncompromisingly, his close-shaven head giving him the appearance of a sophisticated thug.

"I have to disagree with you, Major. If we go in now we could ruin it all. Shepherd saw your operative, you say?"

"Yes, sir. The one called Thorn. He was standing beside the Myghtern, it seems."

"I see. Then it's imperative that we give Thorn time to get out of there. No? He's been at the thick of it, after all. He'll know what's going on. And it's important that we find out exactly what's been happening down there. In the circumstances I order you to hold off for forty-eight hours. If the situation changes come back to me for orders, Major. I want no maverick operations."

Haavikko's face showed nothing of the disappointment he felt. "Sir!" he said, bowing towards the screen as it went blank.

"You think he's made the wrong call, don't you?" Ben said quietly.

Haavikko hesitated, knowing that Ben was an adviser to Li Yuan, then gave the barest nod.

"Why?"

Ben's directness surprised Haavikko. He shrugged and looked away, as if he wasn't going to answer, then met Ben's eyes again.

"Because they're warned now. Forty-eight hours . . ." He shook his head. "In forty-eight hours they could pack it all up and move out. It's what SimFic used to do under Berdichev. They were running all manner of illicit operations and by the time we'd get permission to hit them, they'd be gone."

"And this . . . this smells the same?"

Haavikko nodded and then grimaced. "No maverick operations, eh? Why, it's so-called maverick operations that have saved us all these years. If we'd stuck to what the General decided, we'd all be dead."

Ben raised an eyebrow. "Speaking off the record, I assume?"

Haavikko's expression hardened, realising what he'd been saying. "Of course . . ."

"And what if, as Li Yuan's Chief Adviser and therefore General Rheinhardt's nominal superior, I was to *order* you back into the Clay . . . to recover some property I left there. How would you feel about that?"

Haavikko stared at him a moment, then grinned broadly. "Why, I feel I would be compelled to accept your instructions . . . *sir*."

* * *

Like all about him, the Myghtern dreamed of light; of an open sky and a small, round sun that shed its warmth on bare flesh.

"But you've seen it, surely? There are ways out of here."

The big man placed one of his huge hands beneath his thickly bearded chin. "No," he said fiercely. "It would only anger me."

But that was not entirely true. Thorn knew what it really was – he had seen it in the Myghtern's warriors that time when they had come to the settlement for him. Like them, the Myghtern was afraid. Afraid of the open sky and its terrifying brightness. Dreams were enough for him.

And amongst those dreams, the dream of a beautiful Above wife. A straight-boned woman the equal of himself, not some scraggy, breastless woman of the Clay, deformed and stinking-breathed.

Dreams. And as below, so Above. The five from the Above – they too had their dream: a dream of the dispersion of humanity among the stars. A dream as old as the idea of space technologies itself. Of leaving the teeming, overcrowded earth and finding other planets. A dream of freedom from the tyranny of the Seven – or of the One who remained, Li Yuan.

A dream – and a conspiracy. Five men, planning something here where no eyes could spy on them. Here, beneath the T'ang's great City.

But soon he would know; would see with his own eyes just why these men had come here to bargain with this barbarian chief.

* * *

For an hour or so Thorn was left to his own devices. Tak had seemed distracted earlier. Something had happened; something he didn't want to mention, not even to the Myghtern. But when Tak called on him again he seemed transformed, re-energised somehow.

"What's happened?" Thorn asked as they made their way down Boscawen Street to the Mansion House.

"It's Jackson," Tak said, beaming. "He's back. I didn't expect him for days yet, but he's here."

"Jackson?"

Tak glanced at him. "You'll see. He's been to Africa. *Africa* . . ." He said the word softly, reverently, as if it were a dream.

"So what does Jackson do?"

"He arranges things. Acts as a kind of go-between. The five who are here . . . that's his doing. But he's not their agent, nor the Myghtern's come to that."

Thorn nodded, loath to push this line of questioning too far, lest Tak get suspicious. But for once Tak seemed happy to volunteer information.

"He's been here a long time now. Two years by his own reckoning. All this . . ." Tak indicated the refurbished street, "it wouldn't exist without him. He made it possible. In return the Myghtern grants him favours."

"Favours?"

Tak nodded. "He has some land, east of here."

Thorn slowed as they came to the steps and looked at Tak. "He must be a great man, this Jackson."

"Oh, he is," Tak said, the certainty in his voice making Thorn wonder what Tak's relationship to him was. Then, unexpectedly, Tak stopped and turned to him, holding his arm. "I've misread you, Thorn. I thought . . . Well, let me be frank with you. Jackson warned me that there were intruders in the Clay. Operatives, he calls them. When I had news of you I thought you were one of them. Yesterday, however, I took a prisoner. A big man, built like one of the Above. But he wasn't . . . well, he wasn't *real*. I didn't understand it at first, but Jackson explained it to me. My men thought he was a wizard, but he wasn't, he was just artificial. His hand . . . well, he detached his hand and used it to escape. And then, when I pursued him, his Above masters came for him in one of their half-tracks and rescued him."

Thorn nodded, stunned by Tak's outpouring. "I see."

Tak squeezed his arm. "It's all right. No harm was done. All he saw was the inside of a cell. But you . . . well, I must apologise to you, Thorn."

"There's no need," he said.

"Oh, there is. But come now, let's go inside. Jackson's waiting for us."

Jackson was standing with his back to Thorn when he entered, talking to the Myghtern. Tak touched Thorn's arm, indicating he should stay, then went across. For a moment Tak exchanged words with both men, then, with a pleasant laugh, Jackson turned to face Thorn.

Thorn stared at that face and felt the shock of it judder through him. DeVore . . . he was looking at DeVore!

Letting nothing betray the fact of his recognition, he stepped forward to greet the man, bowing, then looking to Tak as if for a lead.

"So you're the trader, huh?" Jackson said, his behaviour so pleasant, so at odds with what Thorn knew of the man, that his head swam at the great gulf that lay between the two. Why, this man was responsible for thousands, no . . . *millions* of deaths.

"My name is Thorn," he said, lowering his head, relieved to note that there was no sign of suspicion in DeVore's eyes.

"Well, Thorn, I understand you've done a good job for my friend the Myghtern. He's been in need of a good translator for some while. I do what I can, and Tak here struggles manfully, but from what I've heard you have a talent for it. Stick with it, Thorn, and you'll be well rewarded. Things are changing down here. Civilisation's coming to the Clay!"

Thorn nodded and smiled, as if pleased by what DeVore had said, but another part of his mind was furiously considering what this meant. If DeVore was here . . .

He had to let someone know, and the sooner the better. Everything else he'd seen and heard down here was as nothing beside that single, solitary fact. DeVore . . . DeVore was behind it all!

Good, he thought. *But how am I to get away?*

He could not just walk away. At least, not yet. Not until after the feast.

"Are you coming to the feast, this evening, *Shih* Jackson?"

DeVore smiled back at him. "I am afraid I can't. There are things I have to do. But if you'd be my guest this afternoon, *Shih* Thorn? My friends from the Above want to see what their money has paid for."

"I'd like that," Thorn said, surprised by the invitation.

"Good." DeVore reached out and held his shoulder. "Then meet me at the High Cross two hours from now. And wear some stout walking boots, *Shih* Thorn. You'll have need of them."

* * *

More troops had been arriving all morning, landed from huge assault carriers on the new strip the Security engineers had laid in the upper meadow. They had pitched their tents in the lower fields, their glossy black half-tracks – new machines used normally for the defence of the Plantations – lined up along the upper edge of the strip.

Ben stood with Haavikko in the lower garden, watching the activity in the fields surrounding the cottage. Everywhere you looked there were signs of hurried preparations. Equipment was being unpacked, weaponry stripped down and cleaned. Soldiers drilled, or washed, or simply took the opportunity to rest before the attack that evening. At the upper end of the field to the left of the cottage a huge mess tent had been set up. Soldiers in their shirt-sleeves queued to go inside, joking among themselves in the sunlight.

Ben sighed and looked to Haavikko. "It's a wonderful sight, don't you think, Major?"

Haavikko nodded, but he was uncomfortable in Ben's presence. The intensity of the young man was hard to get used to. And when he *looked* at you.

Ben smiled thoughtfully, the tiny remote that always hovered about him drifting slowly to one side. "Sometimes I wonder how it must have been in the old days, before the City. To see an army of a million men on the battlefield. Now *that* must have been a sight!"

Haavikko looked down. "I've seen half a million lined up ready for battle. In

West Africa. In the campaign against Wang Sau-leyan. And I've seen corpses stacked ten deep, six wide for half a *li*. The stench!" He grimaced.

"You don't like war, do you, Major Haavikko?"

Haavikko looked up, meeting Ben's eyes directly. "No. I've no love of it, if that's what you mean. I've had too many friends killed or badly wounded to be fond of so-called glory. But it's a necessity of our world, and I'll not shirk my duty."

"And yet you seemed keen earlier when I agreed to countermand the General's orders . . ."

"That's different."

"Why?"

Haavikko drew himself up straight. Ben might be his nominal superior, but he did not like this line of questioning.

"War . . . I mean war like we saw it in Africa, may not be a pleasant thing, but at least there's some element of honour in it. All this *skulking* in the darkness . . . that's a weasel's game!"

Ben laughed. "So you mean to cleanse the Clay?"

"Yes."

"Why?"

Why? Because the Enclave was their last hope. If it fell, then the darkness would be everywhere, and that could not be tolerated. To root out every last trace of opposition was his task, almost his obsession now.

"Because I must," he answered, damned if he'd justify himself any further than that. But Ben seemed to accept his answer, or perhaps sense his reluctance.

"Even so, Rheinhardt will be angry, don't you think?"

Rheinhardt . . . He sighed and looked down, disturbed. *Rheinhardt did not understand. He lacked the proper sense of urgency. Like all of the older generation, he was complacent: he did not see just how fragile their existence as a society was.*

He feared for the years ahead; feared for them in more than a personal sense. For himself he cared little; had cared nothing, in fact, since the death of his sister, Vesa. No, his was a generalised fear: a fear for humankind itself. Life here on earth was tenuous at best. Destroy the North European Enclave and there was the distinct possibility of radical ecological destabilization.

RED. It was the doomsday scenario, the one all his colleagues in the service talked of constantly; the final kicking away of the props of terrestrial existence.

"What will your soldiers use?" Ben asked.

"Pardon?"

"To cleanse the Clay?"

"I thought we'd use flame-throwers. We've some of the new high-powered models."

"Won't that be dangerous? There's not much air in there as it is, and those things devour oxygen."

"True. But my men will be wearing breathing masks and carrying their own air-supplies. Whether we burn them out or simply suffocate the bastards, it's all the same to me, as long as the job gets done. Minimal casualties, that's my prime directive."

"Maybe so, but I'd prefer it if you didn't use flame-throwers in there."

Haavikko frowned. He was happy to take generalised instructions from Ben, but if he was going to interfere in operational matters, then he might as well report back to Rheinhardt. "Why?"

Ben's eyes met his and held them. "Because I want something."

He swallowed. "What?"

"I want their king, the Myghtern. Alive if at all possible, but if not, well, I'd like his body at the very least, not some charred remnant."

Haavikko nodded, trying to keep the distaste he felt from showing in his face. "Are you sure?"

Ben straightened up, mock military for a moment, affecting Rheinhardt's voice with a frightening accuracy. "That is an *order*, Major Haavikko."

Haavikko bowed his head. "Then I shall ensure it receives priority, *sir!*"

Ben walked past him, then stopped, looking up the slope of the lawn towards the cottage.

Haavikko studied him a moment, trying to figure him out. "Forgive me for asking, but *why* do you want him?"

Ben half turned towards him. "Do you believe in vividness, Major?"

"*Vividness?*"

"Yes, vividness. It's the force that lies behind things. What the poet Dylan Thomas once called 'the force that through the green fuse drives the flower'. We can't see it, not normally, but sometimes – just sometimes, mind – it shows itself, in an event, or occasionally – very rarely – in a person. The Myghtern . . . *he* has vividness. I saw it at a glance. and I want him, even if it's only the shell of him. The rest . . . well, the rest I'll fill if I have to. It'll be my greatest art. To *re-create* him. To make him real for others."

Haavikko stared at him, astonished, wondering for a moment if it were true what they said and Ben Shepherd really was mad, then he turned and looked back at his men, busy in the fields near by.

What do you make of this? he wondered, his eyes travelling among the familiar faces. *To be here in this valley, on this afternoon.*

It was strange. Stranger than anything he'd ever known.

He let out a long breath, calming himself, forcing himself to bite the bullet, then turned, facing Ben again. "If it makes you any happier, I'll order the men to use their flame-throwers only as a last resort."

"Good. And the Myghtern?"

"I'll send a special squad to try and capture him."

"Good. I'm delighted you've seen reason."

Haavikko hesitated. "If that's all, I think I'll go now. Please, thank your sister for the tea. It was most . . . most pleasant." He bowed, feeling suddenly awkward, as if he'd outstayed his welcome.

Ben stared at him, an unexpected hardness in his face.

Again Haavikko felt himself at a disadvantage. Sometimes it was as if Shepherd were on a whole different level from himself. As if there were things he'd misread entirely.

"We go in at dusk," he said. "I think the men should rest until then."

Ben smiled, all charm again. "Of course. And come again some time, Major Haavikko. Please, call on us again."

* * *

They gathered in the High Cross, beside the cathedral; Tak, Thorn, the five from the Above, DeVore and two of his henchmen.

Hastings and the others were suited up – sleek, elegantly silvered suits, gusseted at the neck to take a helmet. They carried simple guns, holstered at the waist: primitive weapons, not lasers. Old models that worked on explosive principles. Thorn smiled on seeing them, realising that it was all of a pattern, deliberately old-fashioned, like the valve, the electric bulbs – all of it an elaborate charade to fool the Myghtern.

They went east, out past the sewage dump at Malpas – a vast reservoir of waste, contained within the old Fal's course. Twenty *li* south it stretched, and each year its level grew higher: a rich soup of effluence pumped down from the City. Life swarmed on the shores of this great lake of shit. A twisted, stunted form of life, admittedly, yet life.

Map orth caugh, Thorn thought, remembering what the old man had said when he'd first come into the Clay. *Pile of shit!* It was a truth down here, not an insult.

They crossed the clogged tributary at Tresillian, DeVore leading the way. From there the road headed north-east between stone walls, rising and then falling sharply, the roof of the Above sometimes close, sometimes far above, but always there, enclosing everything like the lid on a giant grave. That and the utter darkness.

The road was newly surfaced. Thorn bent down and examined it, trying to pick at it, then realised what it was. Ice! They were walking on ice, the multi-purpose polymer used throughout the Above!

After Grampound the road went down again and Thorn could see a glowing trail stretching away into the distance – dim but definite. Then, as they came to it, he saw the wire fencing either side, the warning signs. Electrified cables ran the whole length of the mesh and there were guards at the gate – heavily armed Security types, blunt-faced and anonymous-looking.

The gates hissed back and they went inside.

"Right now our main problem is distribution," DeVore said, turning to face them all. "Eventually, however, we'll cut an entrance overhead and ship the stuff direct into the City."

Thorn listened, not sure what "the stuff" precisely was, but realising that, whatever it was, it wasn't legal.

Past the fence the road ran straight, newly laid, like an ancient railway track. In places it cut straight through the hillside, in others it was built up, soaring over valleys on earth embankments. All of it spoke of years of planning and execution. Two years, Tak had said. Thorn nodded to himself and walked on, hurrying now to catch the others.

At the crest of the hill they had stopped, looking down into the wide and ancient valley of Treviscoe. Coming alongside them, Thorn gave a tiny laugh, unable to believe what he was seeing.

The building filled the centre of the valley. It seemed alive, glowing a muted gold against the velvet blackness, ten levels high, each hexagonal slice smaller than the one beneath, so that it had the appearance of an ancient zigurrat.

Thorn turned, meeting Tak's eyes, then walked on, following the others out on to the great bridge of ice that linked the hill to the topmost level of the building.

* * *

The bird sat on a perch of silvered wire. In places it had shed its feathers and the sore-pocked flesh showed through its ragged plumage. It was a songbird, but it sat there quietly, its eye dull, its beak scaled with a flaky whiteness. Wires ran from the back of its skull to a unit set into the wall behind the cage.

Its cage was one of many in the room, stacked in tiers from floor to ceiling. One came down into the room from above, let down on a platform through the ceiling.

It was a silent room, filled with the sour scent of chemicals. There was something horribly unnatural in that stillness. Thorn stood beside the cage, staring in at the wasted creature.

"What's wrong with it?"

DeVore turned then came across. "Ah, that one." He smiled, the light of pride in his eyes. "One of our more interesting experiments. He dreams, you know."

Thorn looked at the pitiful thing and frowned. "Dreams of what?"

DeVore consulted the computer clipboard in his hand, then answered. "That one dreams of being an eagle. A hunting bird. Of swooping on its victims and carrying them away in its talons."

From time to time the bird twitched, but that was its only movement. Its eyes were empty, its shredded wings were furled.

"It's an extension of the HeadStim principle. We feed the new information into the brain, ousting the old." DeVore smiled then put his fingers through the bars to groom the bird. It seemed entirely unconscious of his touch. "We wanted to see how effective it was. How far into a dream state these creatures could be induced to go."

Thorn stared at him, puzzled. "How can you tell?"

DeVore smiled tightly. "Watch."

He reached beneath the cage and moved his hand across. At once the wires retracted from the bird's head and snaked back into the wall unit. The bird stumbled then collected itself on its perch. Its eyes, previously dull, were now alert. Its head came up sharply, turning to stare at them. But that first, sharp, instinctive motion gave way to confusion. It went to open out its massive wings and found only the ragged, malformed wings of a songbird. It opened its beak to screech its hunting cry but uttered only the shrill notes of its kind.

The bird twitched, its eyes blinking rapidly. And slowly it began to tremble, its whole body shaking violently. In less than a minute it was dead.

DeVore turned, facing him. "We've found that it takes less than a week to create a situation in which the bird has lapsed totally into its new reality and cannot tolerate the old. That reaction is typical. The creatures would rather die than return to what they were. It's as if they switch themselves off."

"I see. And you plan to use this on humans one day?"

DeVore smiled, his eyes sharp. "Nothing so crude, *Shih* Thorn. But yes . . . some day."

In his mind Thorn was adding piece to piece, evaluating all he'd seen that afternoon: bacteria that could evolve and eat away the brain stem; chemicals that could be laced into the human bloodstream and activated by the presence of excess sugar in the blood, forming a potent explosive mixture; aggression drugs; acids that reacted only with calcium; and now this – this tinkering with reality in the brain itself.

He could make only one thing of it all. Terrorism. A subtle, insidious form of terrorism. What they had built here in the Clay was a complex of research laboratories designed to promote the ultimate downfall of Li Yuan and the North European Enclave.

Revolution, that was what it was. A direct assault on the Families and all they stood for. Against containment and the last remnants of the City-State.

"Come. We're finished here," DeVore said, motioning that he should step back on to the platform. Thorn turned, looking about him one last time, then did as he was bid. In a moment they were back in the central room.

DeVore bowed to him politely, then left to rejoin the others. As he did Hastings came across.

"You're a strange one, Thorn, aren't you?"

Thorn shrugged. "I don't know what you mean?" But it seemed that Hastings wanted to explain something to him, for when he spoke again it was in a low, confidential tone, as if he didn't want the others to hear.

"If there was any other way, I'd take it, believe me, but Li Yuan leaves us no option. The City is enough for him. Social order, that's all he seems to want. But we need more than that, don't you see that, Thorn?"

"Hastings' eyes looked away, as if searching the distance. "I want what Mankind has always wanted. New worlds. Fresh islands of being. New ways of living. I want it like . . ." His hands clenched and there was a look of pure need in his eyes, in the set of his mouth. For a moment he seemed to teeter on the edge of something, then he drew back. He laughed softly and looked at Thorn again, a wistful smile on his lips. "It seems so little to ask."

Dreams, Thorn thought. *Must we always murder for our dreams?*

"So many years we've been trapped here, festering away in the levels of the City. For centuries now we've been dying on our feet, watching it all fall apart, piece by piece. For centuries we've shut out the stars and denied our rightful place out there. But we *need* to grow. We *need* to venture outwards. It's either that or we'll die. You can see that, Thorn, can't you?"

Thorn stared back impassively. It was a pretty speech, but such dreams were dangerous, for to make such dreams come true millions, maybe tens of millions would have to die.

"War," Thorn said. "That's what you're talking about. A War against Li Yuan."

Hastings looked back at him, his eyes pained, then nodded. "If that's what it takes."

* * *

"Well, *Shih* Thorn, what do you think?"

Thorn turned from contemplating the wall hanging and met DeVore's eyes. He realised they were alone. "The others?"

"They've gone to eat. I thought we ought to talk."

"I see." Thorn licked his lips. "I've been impressed by what I've seen."

"Impressed?" DeVore echoed the word flatly, his smile fixed momentarily. "You seemed . . . well, unsurprised."

"I've heard . . ." he began, then realised what he had been about to say.

"You've heard what?"

"Nothing. It's just . . ."

DeVore moved his head back slowly, as if to see him better; or like a snake, about to strike.

"You know me, don't you?"

Thorn weighed the alternatives a moment, then nodded. "First time I saw you. It's just that I wasn't sure. I'd heard you were dead. But the rumours . . . Some said you were on Mars. Others, well, others said you'd changed your form."

"And you? What did you think?"

He gambled on a lie. "I thought you'd be here. It's why I came."

DeVore's eyes held him a moment, then slipped aside. His face made a tiny shrugging motion. There was a mild amusement in his eyes now and in the corners of his mouth. "You were talking to Hastings just now. What did he say?"

Again those brown eyes met his then slid away.

"He seemed . . . *concerned*. He was trying to convince me of the *rightness* of all this."

"And you? What do you think?"

Deeper and deeper.

"I am a revolutionary. It's my trade. Up Above one cannot move for spies and secret service agents. But down here . . ." He let his eyes glow with a revolutionary fervour. "Down here a man can be free to determine his own destiny."

"Ah . . ." DeVore's eyes were half-lidded, almost saurian in their sleepy watchfulness. His smile was the smile of an alligator crouched in his pool, waiting for his prey to come to him.

Thorn saw that look and laughed disarmingly. "I bet you hear a lot of such claptrap! The truth is, I can see the advantage of change. Unlike Hastings, I consider myself a realist . . . an opportunist."

DeVore considered that then nodded, as if some test had been passed, some barrier cleared.

"Hastings is a good man," he said, placing his arm about Thorn's shoulders. "Unfortunately he has a conscience. And that's an uncomfortable thing to have, don't you think, a conscience?"

His eyes were very close to DeVore's this time. He could feel the force of personality behind them. But was this the real DeVore or yet another fake?

"I like you, Thorn," he said after a moment. "You're a player. And a good one, too. But tell me . . . how did you recognise me? I'd have thought you were too young? Hastings and the others . . . they've no idea who I am. Do you like that?" He roared with laughter, as if greatly amused, then grew serious again. "But *you*, Thorn. *You* recognised me?"

It was time to be inventive. He conjured a name from memory and used it.

"My father was a friend of yours. He died twelve years ago. I was only seventeen when it happened. His cruiser came down in the mountains, so they say, but they never found any trace of it and it was rumoured that Security blew it up. His name was John Douglas and he revered you, Howard DeVore. He left me a hologrammic portrait of you in his will."

"John Douglas, eh?" DeVore nodded solemnly. "He was a great man, your father. It was a tragedy when he died."

He squeezed Thorn's shoulder then took his arm away.

"As I said, I like you . . ."

"John."

DeVore nodded. "I like you, John. You're . . . *different*."

He walked to the centre of the room and stood there pondering one of the doors a moment, then he turned, looking back at Thorn. "Come, John. I've something to show you."

* * *

The room was dark except for a small cone of illumination in one corner. There, beneath a small, wall-mounted spot, two men in white scholar's gowns – shaven-headed giants twice Thorn's height – faced one another cross-legged across a *wei chi* board.

"What is it?" Thorn asked quietly. "A hologram?"

"Come," DeVore said, touching his arm.

As they came close, one of the giants looked up.

"It's all right, Todlich," DeVore said, reassuringly. "I've cleared him."

The giant's eyes – the pupils large as a serpent's eggs, dark as ebony – looked down at Thorn, surveying him with a cool, clear intelligence, then, dismissing him, returned to the game.

"Three boards?" Thorn asked, realising with a start that what he'd thought was a *ch'i*-thick block of wood was in fact three separate stacked boards.

DeVore smiled. "It adds a whole new element of complexity, don't you think?"

Thorn nodded, but he was unable to keep himself from staring at the giant's arms. They were like corded silk, the muscles huge, the skin tone magnificent. *GenSyn?* he wondered. *Or had these men been bred?*

"Neumann," DeVore said, as if he read Thorn's thoughts. "I call them Neumann. New men."

"Their mother . . . ?" he began, but DeVore shook his head.

"Can't you guess?"

"You *made* these?"

DeVore's smile broadened. Stepping round the board he stood between the two, dwarfed by them, yet still, it seemed, their Master. They looked to him, patient, obedient.

"Thirty years I've worked to perfect them. Can you imagine that? Thirty years. Time and again I've seen my plans disrupted, but I've never given up. I knew, you see. I'd *seen* them, like this – exactly like this – picked out in the spotlight, playing the game. And having seen it I knew I had only to keep faith with that vision, even when things looked their darkest, because I *knew*."

"What *are* they?" Thorn asked, fascinated.

"They're morphs. Enhanced genetic stock. Tank bred."

"Like GenSyn?"

"*GenSyn?*" DeVore snorted dismissively. "Why, GenSyn's old news! Their methods . . . well, let's be kind and call them primitive. My techniques, on the other hand, are radical, *revolutionary*! These . . . these *creations* of mine are at the cutting-edge of evolution. They're the coming thing. The breaking wave. The *Inheritors*!"

"I see." Thorn crouched, studying the boards. The game, it seemed, was finished, the boards filled. He studied them a while, then looked to DeVore.

"White," he said. "By two . . . maybe three stones?"

DeVore raised his eyebrows, impressed. "Very good. You understand it, then?"

"I've played since I was three," Thorn said, looking back at the patterns of the stones. "My father taught me. It's very pure, neh? What a man *is* reveals itself in the stones."

"And what do *you* see, John Douglas?"

Thorn shrugged. "I see minds beyond mine."

DeVore stared at him a moment then began to laugh, and Thorn, looking back at him, made himself laugh along with the man. Yet deeper down he felt a profound disquiet; that and a fear great enough to eat away the beating heart of his world.

* * *

He tried to fall back, to lag behind somehow, hoping they would overlook him and go on ahead, giving him the chance to slip away, but it was no good, Tak stayed with him no matter what.

"Are you okay?" Tak asked finally, concerned for him.

"I'm fine," he said, deciding to give up on the attempt. Even if he did make a break, they'd surely come after him, and they were armed, he wasn't.

Even so, the compulsion to escape – to fulfil his prime directive and report back with what he'd seen – remained strong in him. Each step back towards the Myghtern's capital seemed not merely a step in the wrong direction, but a betrayal of basic duty.

"He seemed to like you," Tak said.

Thorn nodded, increasing his pace slightly. "An interesting man, *Shih* Jackson. What was he in the Above?"

Tak hurried to keep up with him. "He says he was a soldier, but that's just a tale he spins for the likes of Tynan. He was really a geneticist. One of the best."

"A geneticist?"

Thorn stared into the darkness thoughtfully; surprised not only that DeVore should give that story to Tak, but that Tak should understand what a geneticist was. Or maybe he didn't. Maybe he just liked the word.

"Who did he work for?"

Tak shrugged. "I don't know. One of the big Companies, I guess."

Thorn smiled. "What do you know of the Above, Tak?"

"I've seen pictures . . . you know, moving pictures."

"And what did you think?"

Tak was silent a moment, then: "I couldn't live like that."

"But surely it's better than this?"

"No. You think it's better, but it's all the same. There are big men and small men. Those who rule and those who are ruled. Well, I'd rather be a big man down here than a . . . what do you call it? . . . a *zao chen*, in the Above."

"*Hsiao jen*," Thorn corrected him. "But things surely *are* better up there. The darkness . . . how can you stand the darkness?"

Tak laughed. "How can you stand the light?"

"But what of the changes here? The light is coming to the Clay. The town . . . that's just the beginning of it, surely?"

Tak was silent, but his silence was telling. He didn't believe these changes would last. Or maybe he knew something the others didn't. Maybe DeVore had said something to him on that score.

They walked on, the darkness surrounding them, returning to the Myghtern's capital.

* * *

It was late in the celebrations. The wine cask was empty, the stripped bones of fowls littered the floor. Raucous laughter sounded, interspersed by the sober tones of Thorn as he translated the Myghtern's words for the benefit of the five outsiders.

A number of the minor chiefs had keeled over and rested against the walls or where they had fallen in the middle of the floor. Their smell was rank, their snoring loud. Only Tak seemed alert, his back to the wall behind his Master, no wine glass in his hand.

The Myghtern had drunk more than most, yet he seemed more sharp, more lively than ever. His broad face shone, and his ruddy mouth showed wetly through his jet black beard. He was talking of his dream again. Of the woman who would be his Queen. *Myghternes.* Queen Under the City.

Even in his cups he maintained the broad accent of his land. Not for a moment had he slipped and let them know he knew their language. That, more than anything, had impressed Thorn. The Myghtern was a man of strength and cunning. A beast, but also – in spite of all – a king. As once kings had been. Kings who were gods by vividness. These others were but pale imitations – shadows to the substance.

"She must be big," Thorn translated. But they had seen the gesture that
accompanied the words. There was no need really for Thorn to say more.

"I'll die before he touches an Above woman," Franke muttered under his
breath. But not quietly enough, for the Myghtern caught the words and turned in
his seat, eyes flaring.

"*Pandra ober an gowek cows?*"

It was said to Thorn, but the big man's eyes were on Franke, his mouth curled in
disdain. Thorn hesitated, but the Myghtern only repeated his words, adding
"*Styra!*"

His voice was calm, too calm considering the fierceness in his face. Thorn saw
how his hands gripped the arms of the narrow chair, his strong, thick fingers
flexing and unflexing.

What did the liar say? Translate!

"You heard," Thorn said, suddenly tired of the pretence. Let them make what
they would of it.

Franke frowned then looked to Thorn. The fierce expression on the Myghtern's
face had clearly shaken him.

"What is it? What did he say?"

Thorn smiled. "You'd better ask him yourself. He heard what you said. He
knows what you're planning."

For a moment there was silence – a tense, heavy silence – then, abruptly, Tak
moved. From his sleeve he removed a thin white cloth and threw it over his
Master's head and shoulders. As if at a prearranged signal, Tynan and Nolen
leaped forward, struggling to keep the Myghtern in his chair. He threw them back,
but sank down into his chair again, his hands going up to grab at the cloth.

Things were happening fast. Franke and Deng Liang had drawn their guns and
were turning on the minor chiefs. The explosions were deafening, the smell of
cordite strong and bitter.

The Myghtern was on his feet now, his broadsword half drawn from its
scabbard, but Tak's blade had slid between his shoulder blades and the tip of it
now protruded from the front of the Myghtern's chest, the small man's thrust
piercing flesh and metal. The giant's face was distorted in a snarl of agony. He was
bellowing, half-formed words frothing from his lips. He staggered forward,
catching hold of Deng Liang, and picked him up blindly. The young man
screamed.

There was a moment's silence after the body fell, then Nolen placed his gun
against the side of the Myghtern's head and pulled the trigger.

For a moment nobody did anything. Then Franke went round the body and
drew the massive sword from the scabbard. He tested its weight, then swung it
high, decapitating the rising body.

It was over. Only five men stood in the room. The rest were dead.

Tynan took a deep breath, then looked about him. "Where's Thorn?"

But the trader was gone.

"Where *is* he?" screamed Tynan. "If he gets away . . ."

"He'll not escape." It was Tak who spoke now. "We'll track him without trouble. This is unfamiliar territory to him. And then there's the fence. That'll stop him."

Tynan relaxed, but his face still twitched. Hastings stood back from it all, the blood had drained from his face. He was staring down at the butchered king; at the headless corpse that had once been a proud, strong man – the equal of any of them. Then, without warning, he threw up.

Franke laughed; a sour little noise. He was wrapping the Myghtern's head in the once-white cloth. The cloth dripped blood.

"Well, my friend," he said, turning to look at Tak. "So now you're king. King of Hell." And again he laughed – that same sour laugh, more mockery than enjoyment.

The once-lieutenant was watching Hastings however. Hastings, crouched forward, looked up at him, then turned his head away, disgusted. "You planned this, didn't you?" he said, staring at Tynan. "All of you. Without consulting me." He sounded bitter, close to tears.

"We had to," said Nolen. "There was no other way."

Hastings glared at him. "And we called *him* an animal." He spat out the last of his bile, then straightened up.

Tak was still watching Hastings, knowing this was the one he would have to deal with. He noted the weakness, the compassion, and kept his own counsel. It was useful to know such things.

Nolen stood over the body of Deng Liang, trying for a pulse at his neck. After a moment he straightened up and shook his head.

"A shame," Tynan said. "He was a good boy." He turned to face Tak. "You've done well today, Tak. As promised, I give you your freedom. That and custody of this land." He smiled. "These men are witnesses to that."

Tak nodded, then, for the first time that day, he smiled. "I'll not forget this."

"Nor we," muttered Franke, staring at the carnage all about them. "We'll do what we can to help you. Give you whatever you need to placate the chiefs."

The once-king's man, now Myghtern in his place, raised his chin and laughed, his laughter echoing eerily in that place of death.

CHAPTER·16

DEATH GROUND

I n the silent darkness of his room, Ben sat watching the half-tracks rumble through the Clay, their searchlights sweeping across a scene of devastation.

It was an eery sight, especially the ruined villages, and when Meg came into the room to bring him a snack, she stopped to watch, kneeling beside his chair.

"I can't imagine how they lived," she said. "There's nothing there!"

"It's a desert, true, but even deserts have their own ecologies. You know, there are insects in there, Meg, the size of your thumb. Long, white things with hard chitinous cases. Blind things that hunt by smell alone."

"And Haavikko's going to clear it all out?"

"That's what he says. This part of it anyway. His engineers are sealing it off to the east of here even now."

She was silent, then. "It's horrible. I keep trying to imagine what it would be like, being a child down there. Never knowing safety or happiness. Never knowing what it's like to see the sunlight."

He looked to her. "The City's little better."

"No, Ben. The City's awful, but *that* . . ." She shuddered. "That's hell, surely?"

"*Pi Yu*, the Han call it. The earth prison. Long before the City existed they believed in it. It was their underworld, their version of our Hell. The City . . . that was to be a Confucian Utopia – a place where every man could find his proper level. What they didn't realise was that in trying to create their ideal of Heaven, they also brought into existence – into *literal* existence, mind – their ideal of Hell. So it is, I guess. So it always must be. The further we reach up, the further down we go."

She stared at him a moment, wondering if that were true, then looked back. Ben had switched the image and was watching one of the half-tracks from close-up.

"Is that Haavikko?"

"Yes."

She studied the screen, smiling. "I thought he was okay."

"For a military type."

"You didn't like him, then?"

"He was a decent enough fellow. No imagination, but honest. And that's a rarity among them!"

"I thought he was nice."

He raised an eyebrow. "Like that other fellow, Neville?"

She laughed. "What are you suggesting, Ben Shepherd? It's just that I've few opportunities to meet nice men."

He reached down and pulled her up on to his lap. "Then maybe I should arrange a few more military campaigns? You could play Florence Nightingale to the wounded, perhaps?"

She drew her head back slightly, as if hurt, but his hand was curled about her back and she was in his spell.

"You know it means nothing."

"I know," he answered, drawing her face down to his and kissing her, while behind him, on the screen, Major Axel Haavikko turned in the command turret of his half-track and urged his foot-soldiers on, moving west through the Clay.

* * *

Haavikko turned, urging his soldiers on. They had met little opposition as yet, but that was hardly surprising. He had the latest weaponry and ten thousand crack troops, while they were a rabble, armed with stones and rusty metal bars. He sighed, thinking back to what Ben had said about the Claymen. It was true. He hadn't really thought about it before now; hadn't conceived them as people like himself. It was too easy not to. Moreover he had a duty to the Enclave. If *he* didn't do this then sooner or later someone else would have to, and by then it might prove difficult. Even so, the situation had begun to nag at his conscience.

Let's get this over with, he thought wearily, staring into the darkness up ahead through the infra-red visor of his helmet. *Let's get it done and get out of here*.

Nor did it help that he'd been proved right about the operative. It might silence Rheinhardt's objections, but it didn't silence the tiny voice inside.

The distress signal had come in half an hour back. At once he'd sent an advance team out after it, but ten minutes later the signal had died abruptly.

Too late, he thought sadly. *We're always too fucking late*.

* * *

Tak faced the screen uneasily; DeVore's face – four times its normal size – stared back at him impatiently.

"What is it, Tak?"

Tak tried to keep the fear from his voice, but it was impossible. "They've come!"

"Who?"

"Soldiers. The Clay is crawling with them!"

DeVore's face blanched. "Where are they now?"

"In the east. Near Tavistock."

"Shit!" DeVore considered a moment. "Are there many of them?"

Tak swallowed, then nodded.

The news sobered DeVore. "Are they on foot?"

"Not all of them. They have their machines. Their half-tracks."

DeVore let out a breath. "You did well, Tak. But listen. You must save yourself.

Withdraw to the west and take refuge. This storm will pass, but until it does . . .''

Tak made to speak, but it was too late. DeVore had gone. He looked down, trembling. They had gambled and failed. DeVore was right. There was nothing to do now but take refuge.

* * *

Ben's remotes flew on ahead of the invasion force, following the old road through the ruins of Indian Queens and Summercourt towards the Myghtern's capital.

The Clay was in turmoil, like an ant's nest opened suddenly to the air. The roads were packed with people, hurrying west with what little they owned, their eyes filled with a blind panic.

Where have they all come from? Ben wondered, amazed by their numbers; staggered, above all, that such a wasteland could maintain so huge a population. *Like insects beneath a stone.*

The gates to the town were open and unguarded. Again the crowd streamed through, unheeding, it seemed, of the strangeness of the place. That, more than anything, confirmed it. There had been rumours on the road, but now he knew for certain. The Myghtern was dead.

He found the body almost at once, lying at the foot of the steps beneath the great chair, headless, the handle of a broadsword poking from his back. Watching from afar, Ben sighed, remembering what a magnificent sight the man had been. It must have taken great strength to kill him. Great strength or greater cunning.

And even as he watched, he saw the small man – the Myghtern's lieutenant; the one who'd taken them and tortured his Claymen – come into the hall and, standing above the Myghtern's headless corpse, shake his head.

"Who's that?" Meg asked.

Ben turned. He had forgotten Meg was there. "The Myghtern's lieutenant."

"And the dead man? The giant?"

But Ben wasn't listening. Ben had turned back and was keying in instructions frantically, sending his remotes out hunting once more.

"Something's been happening," he said. "Something big . . . something *really* big. And I missed it. I bloody well missed it!"

* * *

The two half-tracks raced across the bridge into the dark. Behind them, at the centre of the valley, the building was on fire, flames blackening the translucent polymer of its walls and making it slowly buckle. From the six great ventilation vents black smoke billowed out, rolling like twisting dragons' heads along the ceiling overhead.

DeVore glanced back, experiencing a moment's regret, a moment's exasperation at all the wasted effort, then he let it go. After all, nothing was permanent. And he had taken all that was really important. To get away, that was the only thing that mattered now.

He looked ahead, at the road stretching out in front of them, lit up by the powerful headlights of the half-track, then ducked inside, giving new instructions.

At once the half-track slowed and slewed to the left, trundling down the embankment. The second vehicle followed at once, picking its way out across the open fields.

The cruiser station was almost directly south, some eight *li* south-east of the Myghtern's capital, tucked away in one of the dried-up bays of the old river Fal. If what Tak had said were true, the invasion force was somewhere near Lostwithiel by now, twenty minutes off. It gave him plenty of time.

It was getting hot, the air thin and tainted. He reached down and took a breathing mask from the rack, then, after slipping it on, used the lip-mike to order his men to do the same. At his back the Clay was lit up brightly now as the chemical fires he'd set took hold. Ahead the darkness seemed to rush towards him, the ceiling coming down, reflecting back their lights as they bounced over the uneven incline, then falling away as they went down the steep hill on the other side. Six miles. It wasn't far now.

He could see the approach lights of the station as they came down the hill above the bay. He had radioed ahead to have them prepare one of the craft for immediate use. The others would be booby-trapped.

They followed the coast road down, the half-track bucking on the steep gradient as the driver tried to brake without losing all his momentum. DeVore barked orders into the mike. There was no time for sophisticated planning. Five minutes, that was all they had. Five minutes to transfer the load on to the cruiser and get out of here. Whatever – and whoever – wasn't ready would be left behind.

As they came out on to the level, the compound's gates swung back and they sped inside, screeching to a halt beside the open hold of the biggest of the three cruisers.

DeVore smiled, pleased to see that the craft had been fuelled and readied as he'd ordered. Pulling himself up over the hood of the half-track he jumped down on to the metal-grid surface. He was about to turn back, to begin supervising the unloading, when two figures came out of the darkness by the control hut and walked towards them.

He felt anger well up in himself. *What the fuck are they doing here?*

"*Ah* . . . Jackson. Now that you're back, maybe you can tell your man to get one of the other craft ready. The bastard seems to think . . ."

"Nolan? Franke?"

The two men came up to him, Nolan assuming an immediate air of command. "Look, Jackson, things are hotting up. The Myghtern's dead and from what Tak says Security have sent in troops. Now be a good man and do as I've asked."

DeVore stared at him, amazed. "*Be a good man* . . . ?" He laughed. "Who the fuck do you think you're talking to?"

Nolan's eyes widened. His mouth popped open in surprise. "I beg your pardon?"

DeVore glanced at the timer inset into his wrist. There was no time for this. He looked at them, then drew his gun.

"I'm sorry, gentlemen, but . . ."

Two explosions echoed back from the cliffs nearby. DeVore holstered his gun and turned back, impatient now.

"Come on now, *move!*"

* * *

The Clay was filling with smoke. Already Haavikko could see only those soldiers nearest him, their heads – encased in the bright-lit bubbles of their helmets – seeming to bob, disembodied above the swirling mist.

The order to wear breathing apparatus had gone out half an hour back, but it was only now that he understood the true nature of the problems facing them.

The darkness . . . I could cope with the darkness, but this mist . . . It's like being dead. One feels like a phantom here.

If his instruments were right they were less than a *li* from the Myghtern's town, down a steep incline that began just a few *ch'i* up ahead, but their pace had slowed to a crawl and more and more time was being spent checking along the line to make sure no one had gone missing.

It's like a nightmare, he thought, swallowing drily. Their filters had not been designed for these conditions. If they did not find shelter soon . . .

A shout came down the line from his right, echoed from voice to voice. Someone was down. Haavikko called a halt, speaking into the open channel, then waited as slowly, much too slowly, two figures emerged from the mist, carrying a third.

There was another shout, a third. *It's too much for them*, he thought, feeling a sudden upwelling of despair. It wasn't just the darkness, nor was it the smoke – though those were bad enough – it was the sense of being trapped; the fear that they had stumbled through a door in reality and into the earth-prison itself.

"Gather round!" he ordered, knowing he must do something at once. "We'll take the wounded into the half-tracks."

Terming them "wounded" was technically inaccurate, he knew, but psychologically it would do them good. To be wounded was at least an honourable thing, whereas to fail because of the nature of the terrain – well, it was not "soldierly".

He pulled himself up on to the hood of the half-track and stood there, showing himself, watching as they grouped around the vehicle, all eyes looking up to him for their lead.

"Okay," he said, seeing how much easier they were now that they could see him. "We'll go down in formation. Lines of six, weapons to chest. Captain Freas, you bring up the rear. I'll lead us in."

He jumped down, to muted cheers and smiling faces. It was suddenly not so bad. The mist seemed suddenly less threatening, the dark less solid.

Below was the Myghtern's town. He would put it to the torch and then get out. The smoke would do the rest.

He moved between his men, smiling reassurance, touching an arm here, a shoulder there, then turned, watching them form up: soldiers again, with the indoctrinated pride of soldiers. He grinned, feeling his own fear melt away, then, turning to face the darkness, began to march, on and down, into the Myghtern's town.

* * *

Tak watched them, fascinated by the sight of their brilliantly-lit helmets bobbing in a regular rhythm – row after row of them – as they came through the gate and out on to the bridge.

All the rest had fled, or had choked and died where they fell. Only he remained now. He should have gone, should have taken Jackson's advice, but when it came to it he found he could not leave.

The breathing mask was tight about his nose and mouth, the tank almost empty, but they had served their purpose. He had stood and not run and now he, the Myghtern, would defend the Myghtern's town.

Tak drew his dagger, then took the old-fashioned gun he'd bought from Tynan from his belt. It felt strange and heavy in his hand. As the Above soldiers turned right into St Mary's Street, he began to walk towards them.

He could see them clearly now. There were a hundred, maybe more of them, and at their front a single man – an officer? their General, maybe? – marched alone.

You, Tak thought, stopping, then raised his gun to take aim. *I shall kill you. And then it will be over. Then both of us can rest.*

He sighted along the line of the gun, the way Tynan had shown him, and pulled back the safety. The gun was cocked.

The soldiers came on, like some strange non-human mechanism, the sound of their marching feet echoing now through the misted streets of the deserted capital.

He counted down. *Ten, nine, eight, seven, six . . .*

They did not stop, did not falter. It was as if he were invisible; as if they would simply march right through him, like an army of ghosts.

Five, four, three . . .

Something buzzed about him gnat-like, then clinked against the gun, putting him off balance. He turned, trying to shoo it off, and as he did the gun went off, the explosion deafening, a shower of hot, splintered metal hitting him full in the face and chest.

* * *

The column halted. Slowly, hesitantly, Haavikko walked towards the fallen man. He was dead. Haavikko could see that at a glance. No one could have survived an explosion like that.

"*Aiya!*" he said softly, stooping over the bloodied mess.

"He's the Myghtern's man." The voice came from close by and he recognised it as Ben's.

He looked up. Two of Ben's remotes were hovering close by. One of them seemed damaged; fire-blackened.

"Ah . . ." Haavikko nodded. But what was it doing with that ridiculously antiquated gun? It was a museum piece! No wonder the fucking thing blew up!

"The Myghtern is close by."

Haavikko looked up again. The undamaged remote was hovering much closer now. "What?"

"The Myghtern. You promised me you'd bring his body back, remember?"
Haavikko stood up, wiping his hands.

"Messy," Ben said, the remote moving in close over the corpse. "He would have killed you, you know."

"I know," Haavikko said, remembering those final few moments as he'd stared down the barrel of the gun.

The remote lifted, floated in the air beside Haavikko's face. "Didn't you mind?"

He shook his head. *And that's something you just can't understand, can you, Shepherd? But then, you haven't lost someone you loved. You haven't faced the emptiness the way I've faced it. After that . . .*

After that you had to live. Had to turn your face from darkness into the light again. And that was the hardest thing of all; to make that turn.

He shuddered, then brushed past the remote, facing his men again.

"Erikson, Byrne, Haller . . . come with me. The rest of you set charges on all the major buildings. I want us out of here within the hour!"

* * *

"Sir?"

The young man turned from the screen and looked across at his supervisor, the wire that linked him to the console stretching with the movement.

The old Han looked up and set his book aside. "What is it, Roesberg?"

"I think it's a hostile, sir."

Old Shao sighed then got up and came across, leaning over the young man to study the screen. There was a blip there where there oughtn't to have been – coming out of the south-western tip of the Western Isle – and it was heading directly into their air-space.

"Have we got anything on that sector? Are there any operations going on down there that we ought to know about?"

The young man punched codes, then went very still, listening to the data-stream. After a moment he gave a little shudder, then turned to the supervisor again, his eyes clearing slowly.

"There is something, sir, but that isn't part of it. There's a dozen Security cruisers in that sector and all of them are accounted for. Whatever it is, it isn't one of ours!"

"Then compute an intercept and scramble a crew. I want that identified or I want it down."

"Sir!"

Old Shao moved back, nodding to himself. Whatever happened now, he had done his bit: the cameras would show as much. Yet even as he watched it, he knew no intercept would touch it. It was moving too fast – much, much too fast.

You're right it's not one of ours! he thought, experiencing a glimmer of professional admiration. *Whoever you are, you've got one hell of a ship. Why, if those readings are correct, you must be travelling at something over two thousand six. Yes, and still accelerating!*

"Intercept on its way," the young man said, turning to him.

"Good. We'll have him, neh, Roesberg? Whoever it is."

But it was already out of reach, sweeping out over the Atlantic to the west of Brittany, accelerating all the way, heading for Africa.

* * *

The darkness was softer here, less intense. The gate lay just ahead. Outside, beyond the enclosing walls of the City, it was day.

Thorn stood at the cliff's edge, looking down into the echoing darkness of the water far below. The waves slopped gently against the rocks. Perhaps he should try to go down – get under the wall. For a moment he stood there, undecided, knowing how close he was, then moved on. The gate. He would try the gate.

The cave-like depression was just as he remembered it. The rock jutted up to meet the wall's smooth edge, but beneath it was a space, a way out. He went under, then stood there in the daylight, listening.

The wind played over his naked skin, tugged at the small pieces of burnt cloth that still clung to his body.

Thorn smiled to himself, thinking of the hole he'd made in their fence and wondering what they would make of that – whether they would be able to piece it together.

He crouched and went up the slope slowly, silently. The two guards were on the grass, in the sunshine, their backs against the bare rock, looking up at the settlement. A rough clay jug rested on the grass between them, liquid winking at its lip.

Thorn stood up and strode out in front of them. Startled, they clambered up hastily, clutching at their makeshift spears, but Thorn had no thought of fighting them; he held up his hands in surrender.

On the ground the jug lay on its side. One of the men reached down, cursing, and straightened it, the other poked timidly at Thorn with his spear, a sheepish look on his face.

He was outside. He had made it. Nothing could stop him now.

One of the men ran ahead. By the time Thorn came to the palisade a crowd had already gathered, their heads poking up over the crudely-built wall to stare.

Thorn turned, looking back at the vast, two *li* high ramparts of the City. What he knew could save that massive edifice. All that was needed was for him to report back what he'd seen.

He turned back, looking among the gathering for the figure of the chief. There was a sudden movement at the back of the crowd, a pushing aside of the mob.

The chief had changed greatly since Thorn had last seen him. He seemed smaller than before, and he hobbled, one shoulder resting on a crutch of flotsam. The right side of his face was badly burned and his right ear was missing. Seeing Thorn he glared at him then spat contemptuously.

"You!"

"Yes, *me*." Thorn looked beyond him, up the slope of the settlement. "I've returned."

The chief came forward until he stood in front of Thorn, looking down at him.

His breath was foul, his ragged sheepskin bore signs of the fire that had scarred his face. The necklet of animal skulls was gone, victim perhaps to the same accident.

He opened his mouth to say something, his yellowed, feral teeth showing, but Thorn's hand whipped out and gripped his throat, lifting him easily. He closed his fingers slowly, crushing the chief's windpipe, then let the body fall.

A low moan came from the crowd beyond the palisade. Behind Thorn the guard jabbed with his spear.

The blow jolted him. He turned, facing the man, and smiled. The thrust had torn his flesh but had glanced off the hard shell of his body. He could feel the wet, loose flap of skin against his buttocks, but it didn't matter. His arm flashed out, connecting with the guard's nose, thrusting it upward into the skull, killing him instantly.

He turned, seeing how they backed away. There was the high sound of keening from the middle of the retreating pack. Quickly the sound multiplied, moving from throat to throat – a dark, almost inhuman sound.

Afraid. They are afraid of me.

He went through, ignoring them, striding purposefully up the hill, then stopped.

It was gone! There, where the chief's hut had stood, was a patch of darkness. The site of a fire. of an explosion, possibly. There was a slight depression in the ground, a pit of ashes.

He understood at once. The valve – they had booby-trapped the valve! No wonder Tak had been so ready to trade.

So close, he thought. *I came so close.*

He crouched, looking out across the bay at the pearled walls of the City less than a *li* away. From the settlement below him the sounds of keening were diminishing as the tribe fled back into the Clay. Soon he would be alone.

He had seen in his head how simple it would be. The transmitter in his side had been damaged irreparably coming through the fence, its signal stilled, but there had still been the radio. One message and they would have come for him. But now?

He went to the edge of the cliff and stared down the steep flank of rock at the sea far below. After a moment he frowned and shook his head. There was no way down. He would have to go back inside. Back in to get out. Across the Clay once more.

But this time the Clay would be armed against him.

He turned, then began to make his way down towards the gate. As he came through the gap in the palisade he stopped. There, on the rocks beside the gate, stood a single tall figure – one of the five he'd encountered in the Myghtern's town.

Tynan was smiling – staring up the slope at Thorn and smiling. After a moment his smile turned into laughter.

So close. So bloody close.

* * *

Thorn descended the slope, knowing this was the end.

"You're hurt," Tynan said, waving his gun vaguely.

Thorn glanced round at the loose flap of skin, then reached back to tear it away.

"It's only flesh," he said, throwing it down at Tynan's feet. "There are more important things."

Tynan raised an eyebrow. "You're no trader, are you?"

Thorn stood there silently.

"I can always find out who you are," Tynan said. "Drugs. Torture. There are ways." But he was looking down at the thick flap of flesh. It lay there, glistening in the sunlight, the blood still wet on its surface.

"Nothing could make me say."

Tynan looked up, mouth open, realisation coming slowly to him. He stared at the singed threads of clothing that hung from Thorn and thought of the huge hole in the electric mesh he had seen.

Overhead seabirds wheeled and cried.

Thorn looked away, thinking of all he'd seen: of the Myghtern's town, shining in the darkness; of the small dark bird with golden eyes; of the great laboratory complex in Treviscoe Valley; and of the Myghtern himself, so strong, so vividly alive. He sighed, feeling the wind on his artificial skin, and sucked the sweet, cool air into his genetically-designed lungs, knowing it would not be long now before he would feel nothing.

"Well then," he said. "What now?"

Tynan raised the weapon. It was a sophisticated laser, not the crude weapon he had been armed with earlier. Aiming it at Thorn's chest, he depressed the trigger. At once, a beam of brilliant light flowed from the tip of the barrel, seeming to connect Thorn to the gun. Thorn's flesh began to peel back, blackening, boiling away into a mist. All about Thorn's torso thick bands of vivid light played, encircling him. The air was filled with the reek of charring flesh.

Thorn staggered, his eyes flickering as if in a fit, then he lurched forwards and grabbed the weapon from Tynan's hand, crushing it.

He turned, beginning to climb the slope once more, smoke spiralling up from the dark patch on his chest. Faint traces of static flickered from the exposed metal plate on his back.

Tynan drew a second laser and fired. The beam went wide, setting fire to the grass at Thorn's feet, then found its target, searing the flesh from Thorn's right shoulder.

Thorn stumbled and went down, then, pulling himself up again, headed for the narrow wooden bridge that led to the settlement. But he was in severe difficulty now; his movements were growing more erratic and with every step he grunted as if short of breath.

Tynan caught up with him and fired the laser from less than an arm's length away, holding the beam steadily on Thorn's side. The flesh boiled and bubbled, but still the trader didn't cry out. He swayed and half turned, looking back sightlessly at Tynan, then began to climb again.

Tynan threw the gun down then stood, watching him. Thorn was on the narrow bridge now, looking down at the water far below, as if fascinated by the way it crashed against the black, slaty rocks. Then, very slowly, he turned, facing Tynan. His mouth opened, as if to speak, but there was only the hum of static. He tried to smile, to raise his hand in farewell, but nothing functioned properly now.

Tynan was staring at Thorn in astonishment, realising at last exactly what he was. Thorn, looking back, would have laughed, but he had lost too much. He swayed and reached out for the frail wooden support. For a moment it held, then – with a resounding *crack!* – it gave.

The animating signal stuttered and then failed. A wave swelled and splintered on the steep, black slope of rock, dragging the machine under. There was a momentary glint of metal and then nothing, only the rise and fall of the sea, the crash of the big waves against the rocks, and the sound of seabirds calling in the sunlight.

PART 3 – SPRING 2222

TOWARDS EVENING

Towards evening there was Thunder and Lightning. Why was the lady
sad? The high lord did not reveal his majesty. What was he seeking?

Tien Wen (Heavenly Questions)
by Ch'u Yuan, from the *Ch'u Tz'u*
(Songs of the South), 2nd century BC

CHAPTER · 17

BETWEEN CITIES

I t was dawn, yet inside the Rift it was still dark.
  To the north the vast cliff-like face of the North European Enclave was studded with gun turrets and observation blisters. An irregular tangle of huge buttressed gantries loomed over the gap, camouflage nets of fine mesh ice draped between them like giant, glittering webs. Buzzing cycloids patrolled the upper air, giant black-shelled scarabs, their searchlights probing the air, while in the depths below deadly mechanopods, sprint-fast and armed with warmtrace homers, sought out their targets tirelessly.

To the south, exactly two *li* away, lay the White Tang's City, its face the mirror image of the Enclave's, a Great Wall of weaponry that ran three thousand *li* from Le Havre in the west, through Nurnberg and Dresden, then north-east to Stettin on the Baltic coast. Between, in a wasteland known to both sides as the Rift, a war was being fought – a war that had gone on for almost six years now. Two thousand one hundred and four days, to be precise. Fifty thousand, five hundred and eleven hours. Three million and thirty thousand six hundred and ninety-four minutes. And not a minute had passed without blood having been shed, lives lost. More than twenty million at the last count.

The Rift crawled with machines. Robotic mines, programmed to move in random patterns, scuttled about, like crabs at the bottom of the ocean, while ticking android bugs flittered and sprang, or hovered on see-through polymer wings, looking for prey. Only one thing was certain: nothing was what it seemed. Larger machines lumbered about slowly on tracks or jointed legs, heavily-armoured against their smaller brethren. Some were semi-sentient, some genetic sports. Among them were spies and mimics – infiltrators trying to win some brief advantage. But no advantage was possible here. The only reality was death.

And among it all went the men – the *jou chi ch'i*, or "meat machines", as the more cynical of the old Rift hands called themselves. Men who, in this deadly, mechanical cauldron, had been honed to machines themselves: the nerveless and psychotic, the brain-dead and the idiot-savants. The only common factor among them was the presence of some deep-rooted character abnormality in their psych-profiles. Normal humans didn't survive here.

War here wasn't a game or some temporary aberration, but the very condition of existence. War shaped the Rift. It also shaped all those who dared to enter it.

Karr's craft moved slowly, a shadow among shadows, remotes hovering at random distances from it sending out false radar images to the ever-vigilant eyes of the enemy. Karr himself lay on his back in the webbing couch, twin display screens above him showing both real and enhanced visuals of what was outside. Beside him lay his pilot, a middle-aged Han named Jeng Lo, his deeply-lined face hidden beneath a Wrap. Right now the old Rift veteran was twitching like an epileptic and mumbling incoherently into his lip-mike as the images danced across the insides of his eyes.

Karr watched, fascinated, as things swam towards them on the screen, were captured visually, identified, or – if unknown – destroyed with a short laser burst from one of the wall-mounted guns which were acting in close co-ordination with their craft. They themselves were unarmed.

Routine, Karr thought, trying to relax; to let his pulse rate return to normal. But he had not been out before, he had only read reports.

They drifted on. Beside him Jeng Lo twitched and mumbled, his right hand trembling jerkily, the fingers depressing touch-pads in a seemingly random fashion, moving with an eye-defying quickness across the control panel built into the couch's arm.

I wonder what he gets paid for this, Karr wondered, determined to look it up when he got back. *Not enough, I bet. Then again, who in their right mind would do this job solely for the money?*

Something swam towards them on the screen – something squat and tripartite, like a stunted ant, its outline a neutral black. The cameras seized the image instantly, enhanced it. Somewhere in the heart of the Enclave a computer calculated the mathematics of the machine's surface and deduced by that whether it was friendly or hostile. The shape changed colour. Now it glowed a cool, relaxing blue.

Friendly. Karr let out his breath, then laughed uneasily. How quickly his fighter's instincts had taken hold again. That old familiar buzz.

He watched the screen, waiting tensely now. *I have been fighting much too long*, he thought. *All of my life, it seems*.

Yes, but recently it had got much worse. Since he'd been made General he had come to conceive the world solely in terms of threat. It was true what the old Marshal said. There was no safety any more.

They drifted on, like a shark basking in the depths. Things sniffed them from a distance then moved on. Then, suddenly, one latched on to them. It came in fast from half a *li* up, spiralling towards them at first as if it were damaged and falling. The cameras saw it, enhanced it. For a fraction of a second its image was clear on the screen, outlined in black.

"*Fu lan te* . . ." Jeng Lo mumbled. *Rotten* . . .

The colour changed. The screen glowed red.

Hostile! Shit! Karr looked for something to press. His whole body ached to hit out at the oncoming hostile – to punch it or shoot it – but there was nothing he could do. It was up to Jeng Lo now.

"Hit the fucker! Hit it!"

The image seemed to expand, the red glow intensify. He felt a tiny shudder, felt the craft pushed to one side as if by a giant hand as the missile hit. On the screen the image shattered in slow motion, replaced by the Mandarin symbol *K'uei*, meaning to cut open and clean a fish, or to kill a sacrifice.

"*Wu Shi!*" Jeng Lo crowed triumphantly as the craft steadied. *Fifty!*

Fifty what? Karr wondered. Was that his strike rate for the week? The number of kills he'd made? He shivered. It had been so fast. A matter of two, maybe three seconds at most.

Not only that, but he felt absurdly grateful to Jeng Lo. The speed of his response had saved them. His instinct had been good. Even before the computer had confirmed it, he had known. *Fu lan te.* Too right the bastard had been *fu lan te!*

They sank lower, almost on the floor of the Rift now, searching, looking for rogues and runaways or anything unusual. Mines clustered thickly down below. They tickled them with radar as they passed above, soothing them with friendly codestream, searching . . .

"What's that?"

Jeng Lo grunted. For a second or two he was absolutely still, then he began to twitch twice as energetically as usual, both hands dancing across the control pads.

Karr's mouth had gone dry. *It couldn't be . . . It couldn't . . .*

The familiar shape glowed red.

"No!" Karr shouted, half lifting himself from the couch, the restraint harness pulling him back. "*No!*"

Jeng Lo's hand hesitated, then withdrew. On the screen the image pulsed a warning red.

A man – a running man – out here? Karr shook his head at the impossibility of it.

"What's he running from?"

Jeng Lo punched up a sector map, then enhanced it to show their locality. Their craft was at the centre of the screen, the running man a speck of red to their left. To their right, drifting in slowly, were a pair of blips, their parallel paths leaving Karr in no doubt as to what they were after.

"Deal with them, then let's pick him up."

Jeng Lo nodded, but even as he made to turn the cruiser something struck them with the force of a giant hammer.

"*K'uei!*" Karr yelled, his senses screaming as the ship disintegrated about him in a searing flash of flame. He died . . .

* * *

And woke, gasping, his chest on fire, his nerve ends singing, his skin feeling as if it had been burned in a thousand places.

"Sir? . . . Are you all right, sir?"

Karr lay there, letting his heartbeat slow, the trembling pass from him, then gave the smallest nod.

It had been so real.

315

Another voice, older, deeper in register than the first, spoke to him from close by, to his left. "General Karr? Are you all right?"

He turned his head and opened his eyes. A face swam into view. It was that of the AAD Project Director, Harrison.

"I died," he said.

Harrison nodded. "You had us all worried. That wasn't meant to be part of the show."

Karr tried to laugh, but it came out as a groan. His chest hurt.

"Lie still," Harrison said, laying a hand on his brow. The feel of it was cool and reassuring. "Your nervous system had quite a shock just now. It'll need a while to settle."

You bet, Karr thought, remembering the moment the missile had struck. Though he'd been safe – though his body had been here all the while, secure in this couch inside the unit – his mind hadn't known that. His mind had been out there in the Rift, in the robot cruiser.

"It's powerful," he said. "Too powerful. We should consider some kind of safety system. Maybe concoct some kind of drug-cocktail to be injected into the men as soon as something like this happens. Why, the shock of it could kill them."

There was an embarrassed silence, an exchange of looks between Harrison and the duty officer. Harrison looked back at Karr.

"I'm afraid Jeng Lo didn't make it. The strain on his heart . . ."

Karr felt a shock of disbelief pass through him. He turned, seeing at once the pale still figure on the couch beside him. "But it wasn't *real* . . ."

"It was too much for him," Harrison continued. "Fifty missions . . . it takes a toll. Most don't make it past thirty."

"Fifty . . ." Karr let his head fall back on to the couch, understanding. Thirty missions. Was that all they got out of their pilots? Just thirty missions? It was a good reason for trying something like this. But would this new system make it any better?

"And the running man? Was *he* real?"

Harrison looked to the duty officer, who shrugged. "I . . . I'll find out, sir. A man you say?"

"In the Rift. We saw him, just before the missile struck. He was being pursued."

The officer laughed. "Impossible, sir. He'd not have survived more than a few seconds."

Karr looked directly at the young man. "We saw him, Lieutenant. Before the hostile got us. Now go and check it, unless you want to be flying missions yourself!"

The young officer blanched. "Sir!" he said straightening to attention. With a curt bow, he turned and left the room.

Karr looked to Harrison. "I understand the reasoning behind this. That drug-induced belief that every situation is a life-or-death one gives our men an edge out there. But if they're going to have to go through this every time they get it wrong we'll lose just as many as we were by sending them in."

Harrison nodded thoughtfully. He turned, looking across at his two assistants who were standing nearby, then looked back at Karr. "We can do tests, of course.

See if we can come up with something that acts . . . well, like a parachute, I guess. Something to damp down the shock. But drugs take a while to take effect. It's those first few instants that do the damage, and I can't see what we can do about that."

"Work on it," Karr said, undoing the harness and sitting up. He took a deep breath, letting his head steady, then swung his legs round so that he was sitting facing Harrison. He was naked, a web of wires taped all about his body. At a signal from Harrison, two assistants came across and started to remove the wires.

The AAD system had been developed from Shepherd's "Shell" – a modified version geared to "At-A-Distance" experience. Harrison and his team had been working on it for two years now and had promised it would be ready for use a month back, but when they'd delayed yet again Li Yuan, impatient to see the project up and running, had ordered Karr to go and check it out first hand.

I could have died, he thought, angry suddenly, but not sure whether his anger should be directed at Harrison for not getting it right, or Li Yuan for forcing him to go through with it.

"How do you feel now?" Harrison asked, as his assistants stepped away.

Karr reached for the one-piece Harrison was holding out to him. "Sad. Jeng Lo was a good pilot."

"One of many. We lose two or three a day, you know, just in this one sector. But if this works . . . if we can iron out the snags . . . then maybe we can bring the death rate down. Think of the savings, and not just in terms of life. Think of the money the T'ang spends training up new pilots, not to mention the tonnage of equipment the rookies manage to lose in there. Now . . . if we were to have a whole team of AAD pilots, most of them with a thousand, maybe even fifteen hundred missions a-piece, *that* would give us an edge in there, wouldn't you say?"

Karr zipped up the one-piece, then met Harrison's eyes. "You think they're not working on this, too? Maybe those two ships that shot us down in there were AADs? Maybe that's how *they* got the edge on *us*? You thought of that?"

"I've thought of it."

Karr nodded, then looked across. The duty officer was standing in the doorway. "Well, Lieutenant?"

The young officer beamed. "We got him, sir! A snatch team took him only moments after you were hit."

Karr felt his spirits lift. "Excellent! So where's he being kept?"

"In Decon, sir. The lower cells."

"Okay." Karr clapped his hands together, pleased to have something real to do for once. He turned to Harrison and nodded, glanced briefly at Jeng Lo, then turned back to the young officer.

"Lead on, Lieutenant. I want to see this with my own eyes."

* * *

Decontamination was a whole deck – ten levels – at the bottom of the City, in what had once been called the Net. Emerging from the air-lock, Karr was greeted by Captain Lasker, in charge of the unit and three of his junior officers. It was not often they were visited by the T'ang's General, and they seemed prepared to make a ritual of it, but Karr waved aside all ceremony.

"Where is he?" he asked, moving past them purposefully. "Take me there now."

Lasker looked to his men, then hurried to catch up with the giant. "He's down here, sir. Surgeon Hu is looking at him right now."

They went through transparent flap doors and out into a large area lit by arc lamps. At one of a dozen huge work-benches, a surgical team was at work, crouched over a naked body.

As Karr drew close, he felt all of the optimism wash out of him. They were working on a corpse. The top of his skull had been removed and his chest was pinned open.

Karr moved two of the assistants aside brusquely and stood beside the Surgeon.

"What's the story?" Karr asked, as Hu looked up, about to scold him for interrupting the autopsy.

"General Karr . . ." Hu said, surprised. "I . . ."

"Have you found anything unusual?"

Hu shook his head. "Not yet. But we're still looking."

"Do you think they might have hidden something in him?"

"If they did, it's not something that's shown up on any of the scans. But we're checking the body physically. There's nothing up the anal channel, and nothing in the stomach."

Karr looked past Hu at Lasker. "Who captured him?"

Lasker turned, indicating one of his officers. "It was Daubler here."

Daubler, a fresh-faced young man in his early twenties, stepped forward, giving a curt bow of his closely-shaven head. "He was dead when we took him, sir. The craft that hit yours got him also. But it didn't get away. We got one, a mine got the other. Big things they were. Proper battle cruisers."

Karr stared at the young man a moment, then nodded thoughtfully. Now why would Lehmann have sent two battle cruisers after a single man? Why risk so much expensive hardware, unless there was a reason?

He looked at Surgeon Hu again. The man was cutting into the dead man's lungs now. Karr watched, undisturbed.

"Is there *nothing* unusual about him?"

Hu looked up, smiling. "About him, nothing. But you might look at his coat. It's over there, on the bench by the door. There's a team coming down from Bremen to look at it."

Karr went across and picked up the coat. It was a pure black, quilted thing, full length and padded like a flak jacket. He held it up, squinting into the overhead light to try to make out the pattern on the cloth. Tiny circles and spirals and what looked like exploding stars.

"They're tiny circuits," Lasker said, standing to attention just behind him.

"How do you know?"

"Try it on."

Karr laughed. "It's a bit small for me, don't you think, Captain?" He looked to Daubler. "Lieutenant Daubler. Try it on for me."

Daubler took the jacket and pulled it on.

Karr looked to Lasker. "Well?"

"Go over to the scanner," Lasker ordered his man.

They went across, Hu joining them there. As Daubler went behind the full-body screen, Hu activated the machine.

"Looks like it's broken," Karr said.

"No." Hu signalled for one of the other lieutenants to go behind the screen in Daubler's place. At once the screen showed the outline of the man and – at Hu's expert touch focused in on the major organs.

Karr nodded, understanding. "So that's why . . ."

"Exactly," Hu said, switching the machine off. "As soon as it became clear that there was nothing unusual about the body, I knew there had to be some other reason why an unprotected human being could run two *li* through the Rift and not end up as food for the bugs."

"So how does it work?"

Hu shrugged. "I haven't a clue, General. But it's a regular Magic Coat for you. A cloak of radar invisibility. Your ship only saw it because it came within visual range and you recognised it as being human in shape. To all the other machines out there it probably registers as a mirage . . . a shadow, like the 'shadows' your cruiser puts out all the time."

"I see." Karr turned, looking across at the body on the dissecting table. "So maybe they were after the coat, not the person in it."

"Could be."

It was one possible explanation. But Karr wasn't happy with it.

"The man . . . what checks have you done on him?"

"Checks?" Hu laughed. "I thought that was your department, General Karr?"

Karr looked to Lasker, who shook his head. "You mean, we don't even know who this is?"

"No, sir. We assumed it was one of Lehmann's men. You want me to check the files?"

"At once, Captain!"

As Lasker went across and sat at the terminal in the corner of the room, Karr followed Hu back to the bench.

"You think he stole the coat, perhaps, to sell to us?"

Hu laughed. "It's the kind of thing an enterprising man would do, neh?"

"Or a foolish one."

Hu stared at the face of the dead man and shrugged. "He doesn't look a fool. Educated, I'd say. And wealthy. Look at the layers of fat on the legs and chest. This one ate well. I'd say he was . . ."

"Sir?"

Lasker's call sounded urgent. Karr swung around. "What is it, Captain?"

"The dead man. He's one of ours. He lives inside the Enclave."

"Inside . . ." Karr went across, then stood behind Lasker, reading the details on the screen – details which were overlaid on a face which was, without doubt, that of the dead man. "But that's . . ."

He leaned across Lasker and punched in the man's ID code which was showing at the top of the screen, then REALTIME TRACE. For a moment the screen went blank, then a fresh image filled the screen. It showed a man at a desk, interviewing a young woman. A time-pulse at the top right corner showed that what they were seeing was happening right now.

"But that's impossible," Lasker said quietly. "He's dead."

"No," Karr said, a cold certainty gripping his insides. "But he would have been, had that thing on the bench got through."

* * *

Li Yuan could not relax; not even here, among those he trusted most. But then, the news his Chancellor had brought him was not of the kind that gave a man great peace of mind.

Nan Ho, watching his master from across the great council table, sighed, then signalled to Hu Ch'ang to hand out the sealed copies of the report.

There were six of them about the table; Li Yuan, Nan Ho, the old General Rheinhardt, Li Yuan's wife Pei K'ung, Ben Shepherd, and the Minister for Transportation, Heng Yu.

The reports having been distributed, Nan Ho gestured for Hu Ch'ang to leave. Only then, when the doors had been locked and they were alone, did he begin.

"*Ch'un tzu*," he began, "we meet here today in the light of a most serious development. If you would slit open the reports in front of you and read the summation on the first page, we can then proceed to discuss the matter."

There were raised eyebrows from Rheinhardt and Heng, a wry smile from young Shepherd. Pei K'ung, it seemed, already knew, for she, like her husband, slit open the report with a weary sense of inevitability.

It was a sad day for the Enclave. And a momentous one.

He looked about the table, watching them read; heard Rheinhardt's grunt of surprise, Heng Yu's sharp indrawn breath.

Ben, however, laughed. "What did I tell you, Yuan? Never trust a man with no vices."

Nan Ho could see how flat the joke fell on Rheinhardt's ears, but Li Yuan smiled tolerantly. "Joking aside, I wish now I had taken your advice."

"But is this true?" Rheinhardt asked, horrified. "I mean, have we *proof* of the man's infamy?"

Infamy . . . Nan Ho almost laughed at the word. It had a stark, old-fashioned ring about it. And yet, for once, it was almost the perfect word, for this *was* infamy, without a doubt: a betrayal so gross, so breathtaking as to make all other crimes against the State seem trivial by comparison.

"There is no doubt at all," Nan Ho answered, looking to his Lord before he spoke. "The evidence is detailed on pages 35 to 168. It is quite some catalogue. But the tenor of it is this, that Minister Chang is in the pay of our arch-rival, Stefan Lehmann, and has been these past two years. That much is true, *ch'un tzu*. What is less clear is how we are to deal with the man."

"Execute him!" Rheinhardt said without hesitation.

"Hear, hear!" said Ben, his face taking on the rock-like qualities of the old General, his voice the same stentorian bluster.

But Li Yuan raised his hand. *"Ch'un tzu* . . . it is not so simple. If it were, I would have acted already. Chang Hong would be dead and another appointed in his place. But Minister Chang is an important man. His influence and connections cannot be discounted. Even with the evidence ranged against him, to simply execute the man would be to welcome the wind of fresh dissent, and things are bad enough as it is."

"Then assassinate him."

All faces turned to Pei K'ung, who had spoken. She sat there, very still, her face composed like a mask.

Li Yuan narrowed his eyes, trying to make her out. "Are you serious, Pei K'ung? Assassinate him?"

But Ben picked up the idea. "That's good. I mean, why not? And you could blame it on Lehmann. Come up with some story about Chang being a bastion against the White T'ang . . . your right-hand man in the fight against him. The media would lap it up. And his family . . . well, you could give Minister Chang a full State funeral, with the honours one might bestow on the Head of one of the Minor Families. You could stand with the family and make offerings at his tablet."

"Are you serious?" Li Yuan looked horrified. "Honour a traitor?"

"Why not?" said Pei K'ung, nodding gratefully to Ben. "It's either that or face the prospect of further divisions within your own ranks. This way you could perhaps promote someone more suitable from the Chang family ranks. Someone more reliable."

Li Yuan nodded, liking the sound of that, then turned to Heng Yu. "Minister Heng . . . what do you say?"

Heng Yu looked down, uncomfortable in such company. When he had been invited he had not known all these people would be here. He had thought his T'ang wished to speak with him alone. To have to discuss the fate of a fellow Minister – one as much above him in status as Chang – had taken him aback.

"Forgive me, *Chieh Hsia*, but my view . . ."

"Is awaited, Heng Yu. Speak."

Nan Ho watched him, seeing how Heng weighed things before he spoke, and looked down, smiling.

"It is very difficult, *Chieh Hsia*," Heng began. "To act openly for once seems a course fraught with all manner of dangers. With respect to the Marshal, simply to execute Chang Hong, while it would be the most satisfactory of actions *personally*, could well prove the most expensive *politically*. In normal circumstances to even consider the use of assassination would be out of the question. But these are not normal circumstances, and the gains far outweigh the possible losses. As for the morality of it . . ."

"Let that hang," Ben said, interrupting him. "Do it, Yuan. And do it tonight. I'm sure that giant of yours, Karr, has a man or two who'd be good for the job. The levels could do with some entertainment – and what better than a full State funeral, neh?"

Again his voice had taken on the edge of mimicry, this time of Li Yuan himself, but only Nan Ho seemed to notice.

Li Yuan considered, then looked about the table. "Well?"

Ben nodded. Beside him Pei K'ung did the same. Nan Ho bowed his head in agreement. Rheinhardt grunted gruffly, signifying he had no objections. Which left Heng.

"Well, Minister Heng?" Li Yuan asked. "Should I have Minister Chang assassinated tonight, as *Shih* Shepherd here suggests? Or should I consider the moral implications further?"

Heng Yu looked up, meeting his Master's eyes, and nodded.

"Then so be it," Li Yuan said, closing the file, then pushed it away from him. "I shall have Karr assign a man this very evening."

* * *

Nan Ho sat back in his chair, greeting the face on the screen.

"Gregor! At last! I've been trying to contact you this past half hour!"

Karr bowed his head. "Forgive me, Master Nan, but an urgent matter has come up. I need to speak to you at once."

"And I you," he answered, conscious of the strange tightness in Karr's face. "How long will it take you to get here?"

Karr stood back a little, giving Nan Ho a glimpse of the view behind him. "As you see, I am at the East Gate guard post. I can be with you in two minutes."

Urgent indeed, Nan Ho thought, *and secret too, if I judge things correctly*. He nodded to Karr. "Come up at once. I'll cancel all other engagements."

"Master!" Karr bowed and cut the connection.

Nan Ho waved his secretaries away, then stood, feeling a charge of nervous energy run through him. What was it now? Another plot? Another batch of traitors? Were there no more honest men in Chung Kuo?

He crossed the great study and stood by the wall-to-ceiling window, looking out across the sunlit gardens. Guards patrolled the inner courtyards and the overlooking walls. In the old days guards would not have been allowed in the inner palaces, but times had changed. Now the threat was everywhere.

There was a sharp rapping on the door. He turned, facing it.

"Enter!"

The door eased open and Karr came in, closing it softly behind him. As ever, Nan Ho found himself surprised by Karr's stature. How many times had he met him now – four hundred? five? – and still he felt the same strange frisson of fear in the presence of the man. If *this* one should run amuck, then the gods help them all!

"Gregor," he said, stepping across and smiling. "How can I be of help?"

Karr came to the point directly. There was a strange sourness in his face as he spoke. "There are copies in the Enclave."

"*Copies*? You mean . . . ?"

Karr nodded. "Like the ones DeVore sent in from Mars that time. But these are much better. These are almost indistinguishable. Not even a surgeon could tell the difference."

"*Aiya* . . . And are there many of these . . . *copies?*"

Karr shifted uncomfortably. "Who knows? We were fortunate to stumble on the one we found. But if there's one then you can be certain there'll be more."

"And the one you found . . . who was it a copy of?"

Karr frowned. "That's the strangest thing. The man was a nobody. An Accounts Manager from the Mids. No connections, no importance. A cog, that's all."

"I see . . ." Nan Ho went to his desk and sat, then gestured for Karr to sit across from him. He was silent a while, thinking, then he looked up at Karr again. "Okay. What action have you taken so far?"

"The copy body is isolated. We're testing it right now to determine whether there's any way – however small – to distinguish it from the original. In that vein I'm also having the original brought in for a medical. That may help speed up the process."

"Good."

"I've also taken the step of placing all those who've had any contact with this matter placed under house arrest until further notice. I feel it's of crucial importance we keep this under wraps. If this gets out . . ."

"They would panic." Nan Ho nodded vigorously. "I agree. And what else?"

"I've got two teams working separately on the original's files – to try to work out just why he was targeted, and whether there might be any connections with other copies."

Nan Ho sat forward slightly. "But I thought you said this was the only one you had?"

"It is. But we're looking for more. I've got another two teams looking at the camera records for the stacks bordering the Rift. They're looking back a month to begin with. Anyone who hasn't a good reason for being there gets pulled in. If we can find a pattern . . ."

Nan Ho smiled tensely. "You seem to have covered all the angles, Gregor. Even so, we have little to go on. We are like blind men fishing in the dark, neh?"

Karr shrugged. "It's all we can do. That and pray we have another stroke of good fortune. One good thing has come of this, however."

Nan Ho raised an eyebrow.

"We have a coat," Karr said, smiling. "A magic coat, you might call it. It makes its wearer radar invisible. It's what the copy was wearing in the Rift."

"A magic coat! That's good!" Nan Ho shook his head in astonishment, then sat back, weary suddenly. "There is another matter, however. One that is almost as urgent as this matter of the copy. Li Yuan has a job for you, Gregor. He wants you to arrange something for him."

Karr sat forward. "Name it."

"He wants Minister Chang Hong assassinated. And he wants it done tonight."

* * *.

Karr was climbing aboard his cruiser when one of the guards from the palace ran up and hailed him.

"What is it, sergeant?"

The sergeant knelt, his shaven head bowed low and held out a folded print-out. Karr took it and read, then let the breath hiss from between his teeth.

The Plantations. Lehmann was attacking the Plantations!

"Get up," he said. Then, handing the man the paper back, urged him back towards the palace. "Hand this to the Chancellor. Tell him I'm going there right now. And tell him this. Tell him I'll deal with the other matter when I can."

* * *

Karr's cruiser was flying north-west at top speed, heading for the garrison at Kiev. Things were bad. Reports had come in of incursions by Lehmann's ground forces right along the line, with major invasions at Katowice, Ternopol and Kishinev. If this was true, then it was serious indeed. He had already committed all of his available cruisers – more than eighteen thousand in all – to fight off the threat in the air, and to fight three separate major land engagements without air support could prove extremely costly.

He leaned forward, chewing at a nail. Far below plantation workers had formed a straggling line from one of the large irrigation canals to the edge of a burning field, passing buckets from hand to hand, urged on by their supervisors, but the fire was burning fiercely and black smoke rolled out across the sky. From the blackened look of it, much of the huge, ten thousand *mou* field had already been consumed. Moreover it was one of many such fires he could see as he scanned the fields from horizon to horizon. Lehmann's craft must have penetrated their defences deeply to inflict such damage – either that or his agents had infiltrated the plantations themselves.

Karr sighed, pained by what he saw, knowing it would be worse further south towards the border with Lehmann's lands. So much destruction would take a long time to repair, and that would put a severe strain on the Enclave, but to lose it all would be catastrophic, for they could not survive on what the orbitals produced. This was a battle they had to win.

His stomach tightened with anxiety. It was six months since Lehmann had last made a concerted effort to destroy the Plantations; six months in which he had had time to build his strength. Over the same period, Karr's own forces had diminished.

The balance is swinging away from us again, he thought, watching as a hostile swept by below, pursued by two of his own ships, the curved wing shape of Lehmann's new craft unmistakable. *Yes, and he's winning the technological race too.*

"Sir?"

He turned, looking to his Communications officer. "Yes, Radow?"

"There's been an attack on the Ansbach Sector, sir. It looks like we've been overwhelmed there. Major Fiedler is leading a counter-attack, and reinforcements are being sent down from Bremen, but things look bad."

"Patch me in," Karr said, a cold certainty gripping him. Ansbach was where he'd been only that morning. Where the copy had been found.

The copy, he thought. *He knows we've got the copy and he wants it back. Maybe that's what all of this is about!*

But even as he thought it, he realised that it couldn't be true. The copy may have precipitated things, but this had the look of a long-prepared campaign. Lehmann could not possibly have organised all this in a matter of hours.

"Fiedler?" he said, as the Major's voice sounded in his head. "What's the situation there?"

"Bad, sir, but better than it was. Looks like Lehmann's put in an élite battalion. The way they're fighting you'd think our friend the White T'ang wanted something desperately."

He does, Karr thought, deciding not to commit his thoughts to the airwaves, just in case Lehmann was listening in, and glad at the same time that he'd ordered the copy removed to Bremen.

"Who knows?" he said, noncommittally. "For now contain him. Evacuate the surrounding stacks and fall back if he attacks again. Reinforcements will be there soon enough. If it's a bridgehead he's after, we'll know soon enough, but I suspect it isn't."

"Sir."

"And keep me advised of developments, Walter."

"How are things there?"

Karr looked out, noting the smoking wreck of a cruiser – one of his – in the field below. "Bad." He said. "But it's early yet. I'm going to make the fucker pay for this, believe me."

"Good. And good luck."

"And you."

He cut contact and sat back, closing his eyes a moment, thinking things through. If this was the Big Push, then they could expect a major campaign of disruption within the Enclave itself. Lehmann would be looking to destabilise things on every front, to try – almost literally – to kick the props away from under Li Yuan. So far, however, there was no news of any trouble within the Enclave itself. So maybe this was part of a longer term strategy. Maybe Lehmann had decided that he couldn't topple the Enclave at a single go.

And maybe he's right. After all, we've survived his worst for six years now.

Karr opened his eyes and leaned forward again, nodding slowly to himself. If Lehmann *had* committed himself prematurely, then maybe it was time to be audacious. Maybe it was time to hit him back. To take the War on to his territory for the first time.

His supply lines, they were Lehmann's weakness. He had a good staff, by all accounts, but he didn't have a genius like Heng Yu organising things behind the scenes.

He expects me to defend, as I've always defended. But if I go behind his lines and hit him where it hurts . . .

Karr laughed, then turned, calling to his Communications Officer. "Radow! Get me the Chancellor, right away! Tell him it's urgent. And if there's a problem, tell him the T'ang's General wants to fight a war."

* * *

Minister Chang was dressing for his afternoon appointment with his Junior Ministers when the news started breaking. Pushing his Steward aside, he stood before the big wall-screen, watching as the attack on the Plantations unfolded.

Too early, he thought, wondering why he'd heard nothing from Lehmann. *He's gone in too early. Nothing's ready yet.*

Unless something had happened.

Chang Hong turned, yelling at his servants to clear the room; then, the door locked securely behind him, he went to the corner and sat at his desk, punching out the contact code Lehmann had given him for emergencies.

He waited, tapping the desktop nervously, knowing the signal had to be re-routed several times. "Come on," he said, after a moment, anxious that it was taking so long. Then a face appeared; young, female, Han, in her twenties.

"Can I help you, Master?"

He shook his head, not understanding. "But the number I punched . . ."

"Is unavailable, Minister," she answered, bowing her head.

He stared at the screen a moment, then cut contact. *Minister . . . she'd called him Minister. Which meant . . .*

"*Aiya . . .*" he moaned softly. *They knew. The bastards knew!*

Out. He had to get out. Before they came for him.

Throwing the chair aside, he ran to the door and unlocked it, then went out into the corridor, calling for his Steward, knowing that time was against him.

* * *

Nan Ho hurried from his Master's study, almost running as he headed back to his own rooms. Things were happening fast. They had turned Lehmann's forces at Ternipol and fought off the worst of his air-strikes, but Karr was right – they had to do more than simply stand their ground. It was crucial – for morale, if nothing else – that they hit back, and swiftly.

As the doors to his rooms opened before him, he swept through, Li Yuan's signed order in his hand. It had taken a great deal to persuade the T'ang, but this would free Karr's hands to take decisive action.

And not before time, he thought, settling behind his desk and summoning his Secretary.

"Get Karr," he said brusquely. "Then tell me what the latest situation is with Minister Chang. Is our man still following him?"

"Karr is already on, Master," Hu Ch'ang said, bowing low. "As far as Minister Chang is concerned, we have taken his brothers to Bremen. As a precaution. They will remain there until Chang himself is apprehended."

Nan Ho nodded. While the situation was bad, there had been this one single benefit – that while a State of Emergency existed he could arrest Chang Hong openly, without fear of repercussions. Right now any allies Chang might have had were keeping their heads low.

"Okay. Let's take Chang Hong. Alive, if possible. I want to question the man. Find out what he knows!"

"Master!"

The Secretary backed away, head low as the big screen came down to Nan Ho's left. Nan Ho turned to meet Karr's eyes on the screen.

"Well, Master Nan?" Karr asked. "What does our Master say?"

Nan Ho held up the order. "He has given you permission, Gregor. A free hand to do what you must."

Relief flooded Karr's face. "Thank the gods!"

"One thing, however."

"Yes, Master Nan?"

"The copies. I want you to relinquish control of that to someone else."

"But . . ."

Nan Ho raised a hand. "Hear me out, Gregor. You have enough on your hands as it is, and I, for one, would be much happier if I knew your full attention was on the business of defeating Lehmann in the field. But for your own peace of mind, let me explain. I have asked the T'ang if I can bring in Ward on this matter."

"Ward? You mean the Clayborn?"

Nan Ho nodded. "I reason it thus. Ward has more experience than any of us on constructing morphs. More, perhaps, even than GenSyn – and certainly more than any single GenSyn employee. Who better to bring in on this? He has the mind for it, certainly."

Karr laughed. "There's no doubting that!" He considered a moment, then nodded. "Okay. But I'd like to liaise with him. All of this is tied in somehow, and I want to know how. It might be important."

"I'll make sure he does."

"Good. Then I'd best set to."

Nan Ho smiled, his face taut, strangely emotional. "And good luck, Gregor Karr. All our fortunes rest with you."

Karr bowed his head. "Take good care, Master Nan. And keep an eye out for my girls, neh?"

"I shall."

Nan Ho leaned forward and cut the connection, then sat back. It was eight minutes past three. "Get me Ward," he said, the heaviness he had been feeling earlier descending on him again. "Tell him his friend the T'ang requires his help."

CHAPTER · 18

THE DREAMS
OF MORPHEUS

T he naked boy crouched on the flat, wet stone at the cliff's edge, his wiry, five-year-old body hunched forward, watching the wave rush in – a pale green swell above the grey – and smash against the rocks below.

As it surged back he tensed, waiting, then threw himself in, his arms flicking out above his head, his body arching in a perfect dive. He struck the surface crisply, almost without a trace, his pale form powering beneath the incoming wave, his dark head surfacing in the green beyond as the water splintered against the steep face of the bay.

He took a breath then kicked backward, letting the outward flow carry then lift him up into the approaching swell.

This was the dangerous part. Judge this wrong and he was in trouble. He kicked hard, forcing his body back, climbing the wave that threatened to pick him up and smash him against the rocks. Kick, then kick again and it was gone, sliding beneath him like a whale's back heading for the shore.

He laughed and turned on to his front, his quick strokes pulling him through the water like a young otter, then ducked beneath the next wave and up. He was out of the bay now. The beach lay to his right, beyond the headland. He propelled himself across, letting the swirling current tug at him momentarily, enjoying the play of forces on his skin, then kicked shore, riding the waves until he beached, then letting the inward wash over him, lifting him gently as he lay on the shingle, relaxing.

Easy, he thought. *So easy.*

"Sampsa!"

He twisted sharply in the water, his head turning towards the sound. It was his father's voice, calling from the cliff path.

"Sampsa! Sampsa, are you there?"

He looked about him, then got up and ran quickly to the shore, disappearing among the rocks. There he hid, watching his father pass above him, calling.

"Sampsa! Where are you, boy?"

As his father's figure vanished among the trees at the top of the path, he scrambled up, climbing the path quickly, his feet finding the stones blindly. His clothes were where he'd left them, in a neat pile among the ferns. He reached in and pulled them out, then, shaking each item before he pulled it on, got dressed.

"Sampsa!"

The call was distant now, up near the house. His father would be getting worried.

"Here!" he called, beginning to run along the path, one hand combing the wetness from his hair. "I'm here!"

He didn't see him until it was too late. As he came out into the clearing at the top of the path, his father stepped out and picked him up, twirling him round above his head.

"You're wet!"

Sampsa stared down at his father, his eyes – one blue, one brown – wide with surprise. How had he done that? It was as if he'd come from nowhere.

"You've been swimming. Diving off the rocks again."

Sampsa made to shake his head, then smiled apologetically.

"Your mother would kill you, you know that? She worries enough as it is. You'll put grey hairs on her, Sampsa!"

"No," he said, pained by the thought. "You mustn't tell her."

"Then you'd best run to the house and dry yourself. I've got to go."

"Go?" Sampsa's eyes grew even wider, this time with curiosity.

"Into the City. I'm wanted. Li Yuan has asked for me."

Sampsa felt himself being lowered. His father stood back, smiling. "It won't be for long, but I want you to look after your mother. And no more diving. Not until I'm back, anyway. Then maybe I'll come in with you."

Sampsa's eyes were like saucers now. "You can *dive*?"

Kim laughed. "Of course. Where do you think you got it from?"

* * *

Jelka stood at the bedroom window, watching as the cruiser slowly settled on the lawn outside. Behind her Kim was packing an overnight case.

"Can't you do it here?" she asked, watching as the rotors slowed and the ramp slowly hissed down.

He turned to look at her. "The corpse is there, at Bremen. And all the information. They're loath to let it out of their sight. Understandably. Besides, they're hoping to get further copies. They can't bring them all here."

"Why not?" she asked, unusually petulant; the Marshal's daughter briefly. "If I had my way, I'd order them to."

He laughed, then grew serious. "I thought of asking to have it all shipped in here – after all, I've the laboratories. But then I thought, what if Lehmann has spies in Bremen? And what if they find out where the copies are being shipped to? And what if they try and attack this place?"

She shivered, then turned to him. It was the nightmare she'd always feared: that this, her safe place – her place at the eye of the storm – should be invaded.

"No," she said. "You were right. You must go there. It won't be long. It's just . . ."

He went to her and held her. He knew what it was without her saying. For six years now they had not been separated. For six long years they had spent every night together. And now, as the City slid once more into chaos, they were to be separated once more.

"Your father . . ." he said, drawing back from her. "Should I go to see him?"

She stared at him a moment, saddened, thoughtful, then shrugged. "What if he won't see you? He's always refused before now. Why should this time be any different?"

"Because I've heard he's ill."

He saw the movement in her face; the concern. She had ceased to be his daughter years ago. He had disowned her the day she'd married him. But still she loved the old man; still she worried about him.

"If he wants *me* to come . . ."

"We'll see, huh? But I must go." He smiled encouragingly. "The quicker I go, the quicker I'm back."

He turned and picked up his bag.

"Kim?"

He half turned. "Yes?"

"Where was Sampsa? I heard you calling him."

"Sampsa?" He laughed, then turned back, making his way out of the door. Jelka followed. "He was down in the cave. You know . . . in our special place. That's why he didn't hear me."

"Ah . . ."

He smiled then reached up, on tiptoe, to kiss her.

"I'll miss you," she said.

"And I you."

"Take care."

"I will."

"And Kim . . ."

"Yes?"

"If you do see him, give him this."

She placed a tiny, smooth-edged cassette into his hand. He knew what it was without asking. It was the holo she had taken of Sampsa last summer. The one where he'd recited "The Robbery of the Sun and the Moon" from the *Kalevala* – the old man's favourite piece.

He nodded. "I'll give it him, if I can. But I must go. I love you."

"And I you."

He turned and ran to the cruiser. The two guards jumped up after him and pulled the hatch closed.

Jelka stood there a while, watching the craft rise into the early evening sky, then turn and speed off south.

Gone, she thought, noticing Sampsa for the first time, sitting on the wall by the gate, watching the cruiser diminish to a speck.

You've been diving off the rocks again, she thought, noting how slick his hair was, how his clothes clung to him. *Good job your father doesn't know what you do, he'd go mad with worry.*

* * *

It was quiet in the barn. Shafts of light from knotholes in the weathered slats threaded the deep shadow. Among them crept the boy, like a cat stalking his prey. In a stall at the far end the Myghtern slept. You could hear his ragged breathing in the silence.

For a moment the boy rested, his back to the wooden barrier, his eyes taking in everything. Browns and golds dominated the barn; a hundred different shades of each, each one distinct, *nameable*. And the scents . . .

He closed his eyes and breathed in deeply, then, shivering, slowly turned and poked his head up, peering over the barrier.

The Myghtern lay on his back, mouth open, arms at his sides. His hands lay open, palm upward in drunken abandonment. The boy smiled and ducked down.

It would be easy.

He slipped the tinder from inside his cotton shirt and cupped it in his hands, staring at it a moment. That was the secret – the reason the magic worked – you had to *look* at it. Unless you looked, unless you took it all in, it meant nothing. The *meaning* was a result of focus. Without focus there was nothing.

He struck the tinder; saw the flame leap between the flint and the rasp; felt the warmth, smelled the burning in the air.

For a moment he saw himself from outside. Saw his ash-blonde, unruly hair illuminated by the flame, his oval, dark-eyed face gleaming in the tinder's flicker. Shadow surrounded him. Enclosed him.

He picked up a handful of straw and lit it, then, letting the tinder die, stood, letting the flames catch and crackle before he threw them out in a scatter of sparks into the darkened stall.

Impulse told him to run, but he beat it down and stood there, watching the flames catch and spread. Four separate tiny fires, spreading, merging to become a single, crackling blaze. The stall was bright now, the shadows beaten back into the corners. Up above the rafters were filling with thick, choking smoke.

He laughed, seeing the Myghtern stir then start to cough, one hand beating at the air. Turning, the boy made to run, but a hand grabbed him and lifted him high, twirling him about and, with a clout to the back of his head, threw him out of the barn door on to the sunlit grass.

He lay there, stunned, staring up at the roof of the barn. Smoke was billowing out between the broken tiles. The crackle had become a steady roar. As he turned, trying to focus, a tiny figure burst from the door, weighted down by its giant load, then collapsed, coughing, on to the grass nearby. It was Scaf. Beside him, untouched, was the Myghtern.

"You . . ." He coughed, a deep, wheezing cough from the pit of his stomach, then spoke again, forcing out the words between coughing fits. "You crazy . . . little boy. You . . . could have . . . killed him."

He met Scaf's eyes defiantly. "It's not alive. How could I kill something that isn't alive?"

Scaf scowled at him, then crawled across to the Myghtern, rolling him on to his back and listening to his heart. The big man coughed, then, moving onto his side, began to vomit.

The boy watched, his eyes like tiny saucers.

"Tom? Tom! What's going on?"

It was his mother. He turned, looking up the path towards the cottage, then scuttled off, up over the stone wall and away, down through the long grass of the upper field towards the bay.

*   *   *

Meg stood in the opening at the end of the garden wall, staring at the scene in disbelief. Then, wiping her hands on her apron, she walked hurriedly down the path toward them.

"Where's Tom?" she asked anxiously, looking past Scaf at the burning barn. "He's not in there, is he?"

Scaf shook his head, then pointed towards the bay.

She let out her breath, relieved, then looked down at the Myghtern. He had stopped heaving now, and was sitting up. He glanced up at her, his dark eyes miserable in his smoke-blackened face.

"What happened?" she asked, as if she were speaking to two children. "What was it this time?"

The Myghtern looked away, embarrassed. "I got drunk," he said. "I found some cider in the store rooms and I drunk it all. I . . . I must have kicked a lamp over or something. Scaf got me out."

She looked to Scaf, who shrugged.

"What will Ben say?" she said, shaking her head. "His barn. Look at it!"

The Myghtern glanced at it, then looked away again. Scaf stared stubbornly at the floor.

"It's a good job Scaf was there to get you out of trouble," she said, her anger at his stupidity tempered by her realisation that it could have been far worse. An old barn . . . Ben wouldn't mind losing it. His only regret would be that he hadn't been here to see it burn.

She turned, thinking of her child again, then walked across to the wall and, leaning on it, looked out across the field.

"Tom!" she called. "Tom! Where are you?"

But there was no sign of him. He was probably by the Seal. That was where she usually found him: down there where she had used to play with Ben; where they had found the diseased rabbit that time.

She turned back, surprised by the strength of the memory, then shook her head again. "Never mind. At least you're safe. Let's get you indoors and clean you up."

"But the barn?" Scaf said.

"Will burn itself out. But come now, Scaf. Give me a hand getting him up. The Master will be back in a while."

"And young Tom?"

"Tom will be in when it suits him," she said, as if giving the subject no more thought. *As he always is.*

* * *

She met Ben at the gate to the lower garden. Beyond him, the cruiser which had brought him back lifted and turned south, heading for the mouth of the estuary. He held her to him briefly, then turned and sniffed the air, looking to his right where the ruins of the barn stood out against the evening light.

"What happened to the barn?"

She laughed, making light of it. "Our friend the Myghtern got drunk and kicked a lamp over. Scaf got him out. They're both okay."

He nodded, then, putting his arm about her shoulder, walked on. "And Tom? How's he?"

"Our little shadow?" She met his eyes and smiled. "He's somewhere. Exploring probably."

He smiled then let his lips brush against hers.

"How was Li Yuan?"

"His usual anxious self."

She glanced at him anxiously. "And the launch?"

"It was okay," he said, with an unusual vagueness; then, sniffing the air again, he gave a grunt of approval. "Now *that* smells nice. Rabbit stew, unless I'm mistaken."

"With dumplings, carrots and potatoes," she said, squeezing his side. "I thought you deserved something special."

"It reminds me . . ."

"Of mother," she finished.

He stopped and turned, looking at her in the light from the open kitchen window. "And you . . . you remind me of her too."

It was some time since he had been inside the Enclave and she could see from his eyes the price he'd paid for his visit.

"Was it bad in there?"

He laughed, then assumed an actor's manner. "I had not thought death had undone so many."

She smiled, then joined in the game. "You who have sat by Thebes below the wall and walked among the lowest of the dead."

"You wonder what old TS would have made of it, eh?" He stroked her neck, then walked on, lacing his fingers between hers. "SimFic were pleased, anyway. It seems they've sold a record number of advance units. As for me, well, I smiled like the King of Villains himself for the cameras, and the critics lapped it all up. I'm *made*, they say."

"Made?" she laughed at the wealth of distaste he'd managed to pack into that single word.

"Constructed, manufactured, *fashioned*, like the lowest of the Clay!" He smiled wickedly. "I am *their* creature now. They own me."

"Or think they do."

"Which is the same thing, in *their* eyes."

She turned, making him stop and face her. "So why did you do it if you felt that way?"

His eyes gave her the answer. *For the experience.* She sighed, then, tugging at his hand, made to walk on.

"It's war, you know," he said. "Coming back the air was thick with troopships heading east."

"I know. There was talk on the news of a State of Emergency."

He nodded. "I may have to go back. Li Yuan has formed a special council. He's asked me if I want to be a part of it."

"And do you?"

His eyes sparkled. "It might be fun. To shape men's dreams and make them real."

"I thought that's what you did already?"

He smiled, then walked on, chuckling softly to himself.

* * *

Lehmann stood among his generals, watching through field glasses as his troops began a fresh attack on the Odessa garrison. In the last hour it had begun to rain, the black clouds billowing across the estuary from the sea to the south-east. Under its cover his assault cruisers swept in, firing salvo after salvo into the burning fortress.

Despite the rain, the smell of burning polymers was strong in the air and an acrid smoke mingled with the cloud, sending down a residue of flaky ash.

Lehmann pulled down his mask and looked about him. To his right the Overseer's House was on fire, its three tiers blazing like a giant tree. Beyond it his men were busy mining the bridges and setting booby-traps in the bunkhouses. To his left a mobile command unit had been set up and a bank of monitors showed scenes from the struggle for Odessa. Supported by two phalanxes of armoured vehicles, a body of five thousand men were trying to take the gatehouse, using flame-throwers and mobile rocket-launchers to prise their way in through the front door of the great fortress.

It had gone well. His feint to the north, at Kishinev, had drawn more than two-thirds of the garrison's strength, while the massive air battle further west had deprived Odessa of the critical air cover it needed to survive. He had only now to persevere and it was his – Li Yuan's "Pearl of the Black Sea", his prestige garrison.

Overhead the air was full of his cruisers, ferrying the wounded back to the base hospital in Galati. More than eighty thousand – killed in the first few hours of the assault – would never make that journey. They would be left where they'd fallen on the battlefield, for in this over-populated world nothing was so cheaply spent as soldiers' lives.

He smiled, pleased with how things had gone. His forces had penetrated deep into the T'ang's territory, destroying more than a hundred and twenty separate plantations in the process – almost a third of the Eastern European growing area. And though news had come in the last half hour of Karr's counter-attack, that barely mattered now, for they had served their purpose. He could lose all three armies and it would mean nothing, for what his enemies had taken to be a major attempt to take the Plantations had, in essence, been purely diversionary – a mighty, destructive cast of the dice, and all to win one single prize, Odessa.

Even so, he had been surprised by the resistance the T'ang's armies had put up. *That's Karr's doing*, he thought, feeling a great respect for the man. Unlike that vapid apologist Rheinhardt, Karr was a born fighter. He knew that it was never enough to contain one's enemy, one had to hurt him too. And so he had, today, no matter that it would not change the long-term progress of the war. Since Karr had been General things had changed a lot. Six months ago he might have swept the T'ang's forces back into the Baltic, but today his armies had been stalled and turned.

Unobserved, Lehmann smiled. *I shall send him the painting he admired. Schiele's painting of the fighter.*

"Fuhrer!"

Lehmann turned. His Communications Officer stood close by, his head bowed.

"Yes, lieutenant?"

"It's Soucek, Fuhrer. He says he's got it back."

"Ah . . ." *The copy! Soucek has got the copy!* He thought a moment. "Tell him to take it to Milan. I'll meet him there. Oh, and lieutenant?"

"Yes, Fuhrer?"

He looked past the lieutenant at his watching generals, seeing how they huddled together miserably in the falling rain, and knew which ones would live, which die before the night was out.

"Give the order to send in the reserves. I want Odessa taken within the hour."

* * *

Karr stared at Surgeon Hu a moment, then roared with laughter.

"They *what*?" Then, more soberly. "Poor bastard. I hope he doesn't suffer too much when they find out."

"Oh, they'll find out. How, I don't know. But if they made that thing, they'll know the difference."

Karr nodded. So Lehmann thought he'd got his copy back. Well, maybe he'd find out the truth and maybe he wouldn't. Maybe there *was* no difference – maybe these new copies were that good. Or, as Hu had suggested, maybe they were clones of some kind, grown from genetic material somehow obtained from the originals. One thing *was* sure, though, and that was that Lehmann's forces were retreating. For the past hour they had been withdrawing from most of the territory they had taken. Only a small pocket of land surrounding the Odessa garrison now remained in Lehmann's hands.

What does he want? Karr asked himself. *Why set such a host in motion and then withdraw with so little achieved? Was it just to test our strength? To weaken us?*

If so, then it was certainly successful. Lehmann could throw three armies at them – lose almost a hundred thousand men – and it was nothing to him; against which the destruction of a third of the plantations would have serious repercussions over the coming months. If Lehmann were to attack again in that time, then the position could easily deteriorate to the point of untenability.

Karr sat, offering Hu a seat across from him, then drew the investigation file toward him.

"You've heard what's happening?"

"He's here."

"Ward?" Karr looked up. "Why wasn't I told?"

"I believe he's gone to see the old Marshal."

"Ah . . ." Karr pursed his lips, then opened the file. "You'll co-operate fully with him, Hu. Understand me?"

Hu smiled. "It doesn't worry me."

Karr looked at him questioningly.

"That he's Clayborn," Hu clarified. "I know a lot of people find that difficult, but I can't see what the problem is. I've read his papers. There's no one knows the field better."

"Good." Karr smiled tightly. "Then you won't mind if I sit in on your first session."

"Not at all," Hu said urbanely. "If you've the time."

* * *

Kim leaned over the corpse and pointed to the exposed cranium, speaking through the surgical mask he wore.

"It's as I thought, the whole limbic system is generally far less developed than in a real human. It's *like* a human brain – much more than I imagined it would be – but it has the appearance of being damaged, *dysfunctional*."

He stood back slightly, looking to Hu, whose three assistants stood behind him, scrubbed up and masked as if for surgery.

"If I'm right, the pituitary gland will be undeveloped. Whoever built these wouldn't have cared whether they reproduced or not, so maybe they won't be able to produce those hormones that create sperm or eggs. Nor, I suspect, would they have bothered with creating a fully-developed emotional system. The amygdala might be very rudimentary – maybe even absent altogether. From Lehmann's point of view it would be useful if these things felt no fear. Against which, I'd guess there might be increased dopamine activity. We might look for pin-tight pupils in the living copies. They'll have eyes like dope addicts."

Hu gave a thoughtful nod. "I'll get started, then."

"Good." Kim bowed to him, then came away.

Karr, who had been watching through the window, greeted Kim as he stepped into the ante-room.

"*Shih* Ward," he said, bowing his head and extending a hand.

Kim looked up at the giant. "General Karr . . . Why, you could put me in your pocket!"

Karr laughed. "Ah, but would you stay there?"

Kim smiled, then took Karr's hand, his own enveloped by it. "If that thing in there is a copy, then it's the best I've ever seen. I didn't think Lehmann was even interested in copies. I thought that was more your old friend DeVore's line."

Karr released his hand, indicated that Kim should take a seat, then sat across from him. He leaned in, speaking confidentially.

"From what we can ascertain, when Lehmann captured the southern City, he took great care not to damage or destroy any of GenSyn's installations there. Our spies report that he's got the main factory at Milan working at twice its former capacity, and a great many of GenSyn's former employees are now working for him there. Even so, this latest development surprised us. There's not been a sniff of anything like this."

Kim nodded. "I see. It would have helped to have had some idea of Lehmann's thinking, but I suppose we can make a few assumptions, neh? My own guess is that Lehmann has targeted a group of very normal-seeming, stable men and women. Unemotional types."

"Why's that?"

"Because it makes things simpler. A mind is the most complex of things to create. Anything that streamlines the process has to be a plus. Bearing that in mind, we can make two fairly safe assumptions: one, that he's not planning to breed a new race, and two, that, whatever his scheme is, it's short-term rather than long."

Karr sat back slightly. "Why?"

"Because the longer you run a system the more invariables creep in and the more unstable and unpredictable it becomes. In this case, the more copies there are and the longer they remain in place, the greater grows the risk of discovery. As has been proved."

"So what do you mean by short-term?"

"A year. Eighteen months at most."

"So what we need to know is how long this has been going on."

"Which we won't know until we discover further copies, if then."

"So what do we do?"

Kim laughed. "Keep looking. It's all we *can* do. Is there any news on the camera sweep?"

Karr shook his head. "Not yet. But we should know something by tonight."

"I see." Kim looked down, silent a moment, then, more quietly. "Just how bad *are* things?"

"Bad," Karr confessed. "If he'd wanted, he could have carved us apart. Kicked the legs out from under us and watched us fall. As it is, it looks like we've lost Odessa, and that's a major blow. That whole sector has been destabilised."

Kim nodded. "So why did he stop?"

"I don't know. Maybe he thinks we're stronger than we are. But I doubt that. His spy network has to be as good as ours."

"And yet *something* stopped him."

Karr met his eyes. His own were troubled.

"I didn't realise," Kim said after a moment. "I've been away too long. Things have changed."

There was an awkward silence between them. Just then Surgeon Hu came into the room, a broad smile on his unmasked face.

"It's just as you said!" he announced triumphantly, looking to Kim. "The pituitary's a fifth the size it ought to be and the amygdala is missing completely. And there are other differences too. Enough, perhaps, for us to identify one of these things with a simple brain scan."

"Excellent!" Karr said, grinning at Kim. "Then I'll leave you to it. Good day, *Shih* Ward. I hope we can talk again."

"General Karr?"

Karr, who had been turning away, turned back. "Yes, *Shih* Ward?"

"Surgeon Hu seems to be in control of things here, so I wondered . . . well, I wondered whether I might leave matters in his capable hands and come with you. I'd like to see how things are. You know, get a feel of the broader picture. It might help, especially as all of this seems to be linked."

Karr hesitated a moment, as if embarrassed by the request, then nodded. "All right. But there's one thing I must do first. If you'll wait here for half an hour, I'll send my equerry for you. Maybe we'll have dinner, neh?"

Kim smiled and lowered his head respectfully. "I'd like that, General Karr. I'd like that very much."

*   *   *

Meg shouldered the door open, then turned and made her way down the steps, carrying the tray across the half-lit living-room.

"What's happening?" she asked as she set it down beside her brother.

Ben was sprawled out full-length on the sofa, watching the wall screen.

"They're announcing a great victory – our enemies trounced and peace restored – which probably means we've scraped through by the skin of our teeth and the grace of Almighty God."

She took one of the earthenware bowls from the tray and offered it to him. He sat up, his eyes never leaving the screen.

"The truth is," he continued, taking the bowl, "we're fortunate there's such a delicate balance of power. Lehmann is more powerful than any of the States surrounding him. Left alone, he could bring Li Yuan to his knees in a week. But his enemies – the African Mountain Lords and the West Asian Warlords – wouldn't let him. If they saw him go for Li Yuan's throat, they'd go for his. They're like jackals sitting beneath a tree, waiting for their prey to fall."

"And will we fall?"

Ben looked to her. "One day."

He sniffed at the soup, then, taking the spoon from the bowl, began to eat. It was a broth she'd made up from the remainders of the rabbit stew they'd had earlier. He grunted his satisfaction, then sat back, watching the screen again.

"The media can't tell the half of it. If they did there'd be panic in the levels. The Enclave would self-destruct. That's why they need what I do. Distractions." He laughed. "You know, that pompous puffball Tung Chung-shu was right for once. Distractions, that's precisely what I make. Artful distractions." He took a spoonful of the soup, then gave a thoughtful grunt. "Makers . . . It's all made, don't you think?"

"Made?" She narrowed her eyes and stared at him.

"Mankind. Intelligence. The Universe. It all has the stamp of something made. I can't believe that Chance threw it all together, however long it had to do the job. Chance could take three eternities and not create a piece of coal, let alone a thinking being. But what made the thing that made it? And what made that?"

"Maybe Chance and a piece of coal were enough."

He laughed. "It's not even that I want a god behind it all. Not someone like Great Father Amos, anyway. I want . . ." He sighed. "Well, to be honest with you, Meg, I don't know quite what I want, but I don't want a man with a white beard and a benign expression, nor even a woman with a white beard, come to that. I just want some kind of principle that explains it all. That makes sense of it without reducing it all back down to Chance."

"And a piece of coal."

He looked at her and smiled, mouthed another spoonful of soup, then carried on, the screen forgotten.

"That's why the darkness is so important. You know, some days I have the feeling that if I could just step through, *into* the darkness – if I could just tear that veil and penetrate it – then I might see and understand exactly how things are. As it is, it excludes me. It keeps itself from me."

She stared at him. Sometimes he frightened her with his talk of the dark. Darkness . . . for him it was not merely the absence of light, but a quality in its own right – not a negative but a positive, a different state of being. And sometimes – just sometimes – she was convinced that what he described by the term "dark" was that same thing that others called "death", the ultimate darkness.

She looked past him at the half-open window. Outside it was dark, the valley echoing still. Night birds called beneath the moon. She shivered.

"Will you sleep with me tonight?"

He looked at her and smiled, then looked beyond her. She turned, her eyes searching the shadows. It was Tom. He was crouched on the turn of the stairs, silent, his dark eyes taking in everything. Briefly she wondered what he thought, what exactly he saw with those eyes of his.

One day he would speak and tell her.

"Do you want some soup, Tom?"

He did not move. His eyes looked past her, watching Ben, his father-uncle.

"I was going to work," Ben said. "But if you want . . ."

She turned back. Ben was watching his son, an amused curiosity in his face. She heard a scuffling behind her, padded footsteps and the creak of the door as it opened and then closed. A moment later the outer door slammed.

"He'll be okay," Ben said, putting down his bowl, then coming round to her. "He always is."

She nodded, letting him put his arms about her and kiss her, feeling that same, strange thrill she always felt when he touched her. "Yes," she said. "But draw the curtains, Ben. Please . . ."

* * *

339

The boy ran down the sloping path beneath the moon, his bare feet making no sound on the tight-packed earth. The ground felt warm beneath him, the valley alive with mysterious secrets. The darkness was intense beneath the trees on the far side of the bay and if he closed his eyes he could forget the City crowding in on every side – that pale luminescence that towered above the valley's pleasant slopes. If he closed his eyes . . .

He stopped, opening his eyes again, staring out across the water's surface. He was standing on the edge. One step further and he would have fallen. He smiled. The moonlight was dancing on the water like a thread of silver. His eyes went up, finding the full moon in the sky. It was like a hole in the darkness. A portal into otherness.

He reached upwards, stretching, on tiptoe as he tried to touch it, then relaxed, a wistful little sigh rippling through him.

North, a voice said in his head. *Look north.*

He looked, no longer conscious of where he stood, drawn out of himself, that voice – familiar and yet strange – calling to him again across the miles, distant and yet close.

Yes, he said silently, shaping the word with his lips. *Yes* . . .

And felt the echo ripple back to him from the darkness. *Yes*, it said. *I'm here.*

* * *

Sampsa stood in the cliff garden of Kalevala, gazing south. Behind him, his mother sat on the low bench, looking out across the moonlit sea, her hair like spun silver against the black of her dress.

"He's there," he said, lifting his face as if to sniff the air.

She looked to him. "Who? Kim?"

"No. The other one. The one who never speaks."

She laughed uncomfortably, then stood and went across, kneeling and putting her hands on his shoulders.

"You imagine it."

He turned his face, looking at her. "No. I can sense him there. He's outside." He turned back. "North," he said softly, as if speaking to someone. "Look north."

She looked past him, frowning, then felt him shiver.

"Yes," he said. "I'm here."

"Sampsa?" But it was as if he was suddenly not there. His eyes were shining with an inner light, his lips smiling.

"You imagine it," she said again, squeezing his shoulders gently, feeling suddenly cold. "Let's go inside."

"Sampsa," he said. "Sam-psa . . . Yes."

She shuddered, then stood. "*Sampsa!*" she said, an edge in her voice.

He turned and looked up at her, his eyes still bright, still shining, then nodded. "He's gone now," he said, matter-of-factly. "I felt him go. He was standing beside the water, like we are, but much closer. And the moon . . . the moon was so bright where he stood. It was like an eye, staring down."

"Sampsa. Enough now."

He stared at her, then bowed his head. "Father's coming."

For a moment she thought it was more of his nonsense, then she too heard the sound of the cruiser. She laughed, the business with the "other one" forgotten, her joy at Kim's return making her pick Sampsa up and whirl him about. Then, setting him down, she hurried across to the open doors at the back of the house.

As the cruiser swept across the island, its powerful searchlights flickering across the blackness of the treetops, Jelka came out into the front garden and, shielding her eyes against the glare, watched the ship touch down.

As Kim stepped down, she rushed across and embraced him, moving back with him as the cruiser lifted and, turning in the air, accelerated into the night.

"I didn't think . . ." she began, but his kiss stopped her saying any more. When they broke, she moved her face back a little, studying his face in the moonlight.

"Did you see Father?"

He shook his head and sighed. "I went there, but he wouldn't see me. I left the holo for him."

"Ah . . ." She tried not to show her disappointment.

"Where's Sampsa?" he asked, turning and walking with her towards the house.

"I don't know. He was with me in the garden. He must have slipped away." She looked at him again. "So how did it go?"

There was a small movement in his face. "It's bad," he said. "I didn't realise how bad. We've been isolated here much too long."

She frowned, surprised by his words. "But I thought you liked it here."

"Here might not survive much longer. Not unless we do something. The Enclave is in trouble. The attack today weakened it badly. How badly we'll know in a matter of days. But things are in a critical state. I felt . . ." He shrugged, then looked away, embarrassed. "I felt as if I'd let them all down."

She reached out, turning his face gently with her hand until he was looking at her again. "Why do you feel that way? You've given them so much. Your inventions . . ."

"Are toys. What have I given them that's real? Have I given them the means to fight off their enemies? Have I given them the means to feed their population?"

"But those are not your problems . . ."

"No? Then why was I given my talent? Why, if not to make things better for everyone?"

"But that's perverse. You're not responsible for them."

"No? Then to whom do I owe my living, my existence? Without the City – without Li Yuan – I would have nothing. I would be dust. Without them I would not have you."

She felt the power of his love, of his conviction, wash over her, and gave a tiny nod. "If that's how you feel, then you must do something. But what can you do?"

He stared back at her and smiled, glad that she was with him. "I don't know, my love. Not yet. But I shall. Something will suggest itself."

* * *

Sampsa made his way down through the darkness with the stealth of a young fox. Where the path twisted and the ground levelled out was the clearing. Coming out into it he looked up and saw the moon, bright and full in the cloudless sky, and smiled.

Seven tall pines had once stood here, forming the shape of a staggered H beneath the stars. Fire from the heavens had burned them to ashen stumps. Now, where seven had once stood, only one now sprouted – a sapling of sixteen years, growing at the very centre of the clearing.

Sampsa made his way across, jumping from stump to stump until he stood beneath the sapling. It was a windless night and the young tree stood there, still and proud in the moonlight, a young giant, growing even as the great earth turned, slowly reaching for the stars.

For a moment Sampsa rested, his back to it, staring up at the house, at the lighted windows of the tower, then he slipped away, moving back into the blackness between the trees, heading down to where the land fell sheer to the sea.

There he stood, nodding to himself, understanding.

"Sampsa?"

He turned, surprised, staring at his father. "How do you do that?"

Kim laughed. "My mother taught me."

"You *had* a mother?"

Kim moved past his son and stood at the very edge of the cliff. His feet were bare, Sampsa noted. For a moment Kim stared out at the sea, listening, it seemed, to its faint sussuration, then he looked back at his son.

"I'll show you a hologram of her some time. As for the art of travelling silently, it's a trick I picked up in the Clay. We all did. Sound echoes in the Clay. Things are dry and snap easily, and there are enemies everywhere. You have to learn where to put your feet – how to see with your feet in the dark. Once learned, you never forget."

Sampsa nodded thoughtfully, then squatted. He picked up a pine cone and turned it between his fingers. "What is it like in there?"

"In the Clay?"

"No. Where you've just been."

"The Enclave?" Kim sighed. "It's like a box. A huge box, filled with teeming life. You know, sometimes it makes me think of the story of Morpheus, the god of sleep. Sometimes I think he has cast a great spell over humankind these past two hundred years – that we live, somehow, in his dreams."

"But not us," Sampsa said, staring up at his father, his eyes round. "Not here."

"No . . ."

"Are there other places? . . . Outside, I mean."

Kim turned, then squatted across from him. "There's Li Yuan's palace at Astrakhan. And the Plantations, of course. And . . . well, there's Shepherd's place. The Domain."

"The Domain?" Sampsa stared at the pine cone in his hand. "Where's that?"

"Oh, south of here. Far south, in the Western Isle. I've not been there, but I'm told it's idyllic. Not so cold as our island, nor so rugged. It's a valley. Shepherd lives there with his sister."

Sampsa looked up at him. "Just them?"

中
國

"I don't know. I assume there are guards. Like we have guards. Apart from that . . ." he shrugged. "Why?"

"Nothing." Sampsa looked away across the sea, then, standing, threw the cone out into the air.

"Shall we get back?" he said, turning, looking back at his father, his eyes – one blue, one brown – strangely troubled.

"If you like," Kim answered, getting up and brushing himself down. He reached out and touched his son's shoulder. "I have to go back. Tomorrow. I might be spending a lot more time there from now on."

Sampsa nodded.

"You don't mind then?"

The boy looked up at him. "I don't mind. As long as you keep your promise to come diving."

Kim grinned. "Tomorrow morning. First light. We'll go down before the cruiser comes for me, okay?"

Sampsa smiled, then, ducking beneath a low branch, slipped into the darkness, heading back towards the house. Kim listened a moment, hearing the faint sounds of his son's passage through the trees, then followed, melting like a shadow into the dark, the image of his mother burning like a candle in his head.

* * *

Neville let himself into the room of the SimFic stay-over, then, setting his case on a chair, sat down heavily on the bed and began to pull off his boots. It had been a long, hard day and he felt exhausted, but his mind was still racing, filled with the excitement of the launch.

It could not have gone better – not in his wildest dreams. First day sales figures were phenomenal, and the reviews . . .

He laughed. You could not have bought the kind of reviews Ben Shepherd was getting!

"Here, let me do that . . ."

There was the soft touch of a female hand on his shoulder, the faintest waft of scent. He turned, looking up at the girl. She was a young Han with a pretty face: one of SimFic's hospitality girls, chosen to fit his preference profile. Relaxing, he let her tend to him while he recalled the day's events.

He had met Shepherd only once before, when the deal had been signed, and had found him strangely cold, almost hostile, but today had been a revelation – today Ben Shepherd had been mesmeric. Why, he could have charmed the gods from the heavens!

There was a double beep, then the big screen in the corner of the room came on. He looked up at it.

"Jack?"

It was his boss, Reiss. A broadly grinning Reiss.

"Horst? What is it?"

"I just wanted to congratulate you on a superb job. I've just spoken to the board and they're delighted. In fact I've got them to grant you a bonus of fifty thousand, payable immediately!"

Neville leaned towards the screen, his grin unforced. "That's great, I . . . Well, shit, Horst, we had a *winner* today. I *told* you . . ."

"I know. And you were right, Jack. One hundred per cent right. But it was no accident. You put a lot of work into this one and I'm grateful. Hugely grateful. Between you and me, there's even talk of appointing you to the executive council. But we'll discuss that tomorrow, neh? Everything okay there? Our people looking after you?"

Neville moved back a little, revealing the smiling hospitality girl. "I'm fine, Horst. There's one favour you might do me, though."

"Name it."

"The media reviews. I'd like to run through them again – work out some angles for our campaign over the coming weeks. Can you plug me through say six or eight of the major networks? I'd like to sleep on them."

Reiss laughed. "If that's what you want, you got it. And again, great job, Jack. You've put us on the map again in a big way and the Company's grateful. Very grateful." Reiss grinned and gave a bow of his head. "Tomorrow, huh?"

"Right."

The screen went blank. Neville sat back, letting out a long whistling breath, then let the girl begin to kneed the tiredness from his shoulders. A place on the executive council, huh? He nodded to himself, imagining it. And maybe, in a year or two, Reiss might groom him for his successor. If things kept going right for him.

"You big man, huh?" the girl asked, poking her head over his shoulder, her smile innocent, disarming.

He smiled. "Seems like it."

She nodded, impressed, then returned to her task with a new vigour. Neville closed his eyes, enjoying her touch. "That's great. You're very good at what you do."

"You too, it seems."

He laughed. "Yeah. Seems the Company likes me."

"Seems so."

The screen beeped. Neville opened his eyes and looked. The MedFac logo had appeared on the screen, replaced a moment later by the image of a refined old Han with a long grey beard, flowing white silks and the contemplative eyes of an ancient sage. It was Tung Chung-shu, MedFac's most senior arts reviewer. He was walking in the familiar setting of his garden – a small but tasteful affair – speaking slowly to the camera in Mandarin, one hand pulling at his beard thoughtfully. A voice-over gave the English equivalent.

". . . and until now I would have said there was no future for the medium, but *Shih* Shepherd's work has convinced me that a work of art – of real and genuine artistic significance – can be created within this previously trivial form."

Tung stopped, one arm resting lightly on the wooden balustrade of a tiny plank bridge, and looked out over a small pond filled with lilies. The camera angle changed, looking across at him, the old-fashioned house framed behind him.

"More impressive, perhaps, is Shepherd's manipulation of the recipient – the audience – for his art. As you know, I have always scorned the term inter-active when applied to art. Most so called inter-active artforms are little more than games – distractions. True art requires a deeper, more inward quality. And that – miraculously, one might almost say – is the true genius of this new work. At all times I was the passive recipient of the experience. Physically I went nowhere – and yet, while I was *inside* Shepherd's work it felt as if I were in control of my environment, as if everything I did I had *chosen* to do. In that single respect – that of apparent volition – this experience was different, different *in kind*, from anything I have ever encountered in SimFic's product range, or anyone else's come to that. There is no doubt about it, Ben Shepherd's *The Familiar* is a conceptual break-through, a new generation Stim – the product of new thinking and, so I gather from Jack Neville at SimFic, of brand-new technologies."

Neville leaned back, nodding slowly, thoughtfully, as the screen blanked and a new logo – that of IntSat – appeared. *Little do you know of the troubles we had with it*, he thought, recalling the months they'd spent trying to perfect Shepherd's techno-gimmickry. But it had worked. And even the crusty old conservative Tung had had his silk socks knocked off by it!

"You want take this off?"

He nodded vaguely, then eased forward, letting the girl lift his silk one-piece and pull it over his head.

"That better, neh?"

But he was watching the screen, only half aware of the gentle movement of her hands on the skin of his back. The image had changed to show a studio set with four earnest young men – *Hung Mao* every one – leaning in towards each other. Behind them, forming a huge backdrop, was the cover of Ben's *The Familiar*, with its view of the idyllic German valley in which it was set.

That was a stroke of genius, he thought, *preparing two versions – one from the Han perspective and one from the* Hung Mao. *Only Shepherd would have thought of telling the same story from two entirely different viewpoints.*

Yes, and it had guaranteed an across-the-board sale. For the first time in living memory a single work had penetrated both markets. Indeed if reports were to be believed a lot of people were buying *both* versions.

There were a few introductory exchanges and then the presenter of the show, Jake Kingsley, a dark-haired, soft-featured man in his mid-twenties, began to speak.

". . . the soundtrack is simply filled with the sound of bird call and the hum of insects – strange sounds which, at the moment of one's immersion in the medium, seem natural and familiar things – as if it were always so – and yet afterwards, in the quiet of recollection, I found the hairs on my neck rise; found myself disturbed profoundly by the memory of that strange, insistent sound."

"That's true," another of them said, joining in. "What also struck me was the amazing openness of things – you know, the big open skies above the town and the constant feeling of sun and wind on your flesh. It was so . . . well so *real*. I mean, we're used to seeing these things on trivee dramas, but that's . . . well, it's like looking at a painting – it doesn't strike home. While I was there, inside the Stim, I was . . . *outside*. There's no other way of putting it. Shepherd's work . . ." He shook his head, awed. "Well, it's just masterful . . . the most brilliant thing I've yet encountered."

It went on: more, and yet more in the same vein, eulogising, professing amazement, astonishment, simple *awe*. And no dissenting voices. Not a single one. That in itself was amazing, for his experience was that when half the critics loved something, the rest would hate it with a loathing that was little short of spitting fury. This once, however, they had been caught off guard, overwhelmed by the shock of something totally, unexpectedly new. Ben's work had simply seduced them.

Neville smiled, then, turning from the now-blank screen, stretched out on his front, letting the girl straddle him, her hands massaging the small of his back.

He had been right to embargo the thing – to keep it secure in SimFic's warehouses until the day of release – letting the media and the public know only that SimFic had the greatest piece of product they would ever see, and risking the possibility that the hype would fall flat and no one like the thing. It had been a big risk – a huge fucking risk, now that he thought about it – but he'd been convinced about it, from the very first time he'd put on the HeadStim and experienced Ben's *Familiar* for himself.

Yes, and today's attack on the Plantations hadn't harmed things any, either. In his experience, the greater people felt threatened, the more they were in need of distractions – and Ben's "Shell" – even in its neutered Stim form – was the ultimate distraction.

"Is that nice?"

He grunted softly. Tired he might be, but not so tired that her tender ministrations weren't getting to him. He rolled over and faced her, enjoying the warm weight of her, the way she smiled.

"Today was a big day," he said, breathing deeply as she smoothed her hands across his chest then slowly eased them all the way down his groin. "Today I took a huge great gamble . . . and I *won*."

She grinned. "Fifty thousand. That big bonus. Fifty thousand keep me happy, oh . . ." she laughed, "many years!"

He smiled, liking her, enjoying the moment. Would there ever be a better moment – a moment when he felt more satisfied? Who could say? But even if there wasn't, even if this was all there was, it was enough. He chuckled, feeling generous suddenly, wanting to share his good luck with her.

"What's your name?"

She looked away, then looked back at him, her smile different somehow. "I called Jia Shu. You Jack, right?"

He nodded. "Okay, Jia Shu, how about this? How about you come and work for me alone? Be my maid. Look after me. I'll pay you well, make sure you're looked after, okay?"

Her hands had stopped, now they began again. She gave a tiny nod, her face suddenly tight as if keeping something in, but her eyes, when they met his again, were bright with gratitude, and her body, when it moved against his, was somehow more caring, more intimate than it had been only moments before.

CHAPTER · 19

FACES

The woman peeked through the screen, then quickly withdrew her head, tending to the stove once more. Uncle Pan had settled in the corner chair and lit his pipe. It looked like he was going to stay a while.

Without being told, she poured hot water into the *chung* to brew some fresh *ch'a*, listening as the old man began his regular tirade.

"They're weak, that's what they are! They let that bastard get away with murder! If I were T'ang I'd kick his arse, good and proper! I'd break him over my knee like a rotten twig!"

In her mind's eye she could see Lin look up from his work and smile his lop-sided smile, ever tolerant of his uncle's bluster.

"I'd crush him," the old man went on. "And no more silk glove treatment. I'd send a million troops against him and take back what's rightfully mine!"

She heard Lin stand and go to the door, listening a moment, then heard him speak softly to his uncle.

"Be careful what you say, Uncle. For myself, I do not mind, but if anyone should hear . . ."

"Let them hear!" the old man said belligerently. "That bastard should know the truth!"

She smiled and stood, lifting the steaming *chung* between her hands and carrying it through. The old man stared at her rudely as she emerged and made a scornful face, but Lin simply smiled at her and nodded.

"You took your time," the old man began, but a look from Lin silenced him. He would put up with most things from his uncle – out of respect and duty – but any criticism of her he stamped on instantly.

"Thank you," Lin said, taking over from her, encouraging her with his eyes to go back behind the screen while his uncle was there.

She went back through and squatted by the *kang*, busying herself with some mending, only half-listening to the old man's idle chatter, her mind dwelling instead upon his nephew, her protector, Lin.

In her mind she could see Lin's pale hands working as, smiling tolerantly, he listened to his uncle. Clever hands he had; hands that always knew the best way to fix a thing.

347

If something was broken, Lin could fix it, from the smallest, most delicate ivory to the biggest, most complex machine. People from stacks around brought things to him to be mended, and each year his reputation grew, each day more things would be brought for his clever hands to see to.

She smiled, looking at her own hands as they worked, neatly stitching the edge of the cloth so that it wouldn't fray again. That much she had learned from him: never to throw anything away. Everything – *everyone* – had a use. With patience and care, there was nothing that could not be mended.

She looked up, sighing, remembering how he had nursed her through the long months of her sickness; how patiently he had attended to her, clearing up after her when she was sick, and sitting with her in the night when she was feverish. *Mending* her. And though that was some years ago now, still the lesson of it returned to her whenever he smiled at her. In all the time she'd known him, never an unkind word had passed his lips, nor had he ever asked a thing of her. What she did, she did from gratitude and because – as he showed by his example – a life of idleness was a life of waste.

"His father . . . now, there was a man!" the old man said, his voice booming loud suddenly. "He was a *real* emperor. A lion of a man!"

She set the square of cloth down and, leaning across, checked the pots on the *kang*. There was little enough for two, but for three . . .

She decided she would go without. Lin needed his strength, and even to consider not feeding Uncle Pan . . . well, it was not done. Besides, she could eat later have some crackers, or finish off the er-prawn paste in the cold box.

Sitting back, she looked about the room. Like the other half that lay behind the screen, its walls were covered with shelves on which were packed a thousand things waiting to be mended. Their belongings, such as they were, were stashed in a small cupboard to her right, beside the *kang,* which at nights doubled as a bed for her, Lin sleeping on a bedroll in the other room.

People talked. She knew they did. She had heard them when she'd walked to the washrooms at the corner of the stack to empty the night-soil pot. But she didn't care. They said he used her at nights – abused her badly – but both she and Lin knew the truth of that. What did it matter what idle tongues said? Besides, there were many who spoke up for them. Many who knew Lin's worth and weren't afraid to state it.

She looked through the screen toward where he sat, working. "Everyone has a use, even those who seem most idle." That was what he always said, forgiving them. Yes, and he found work for people if he could; helped them in tiny but important ways – even those that spoke badly of him, so that when she thought of him she could not help but think of a great wheel, with Lin at the centre, the hub about which so many lives, her own included, revolved, every one of them dependent in some way or other on him.

He didn't look much, she knew. He was a pale, sickly-looking man, and his face . . .

She stood and went across to where, among a pile of chapter books he'd bought a week ago, she kept the mirror. It was a broken thing, the layer of reflecting ice bubbled on the right-hand side. Like his face, she thought, thinking of the way, when he smiled, the whole of the right-hand side was pulled into a grimace.

It was the kindest, loveliest smile she'd ever seen . . .

She held the mirror up and looked, holding it slightly away from her and moving her face to one side so she could see it whole. It was a strong-boned, healthy face. The face of a *Hung Mao* woman in her thirties, dark-haired and hazel-eyed. A handsome face, some said, describing it almost in boyish terms.

"Who are you?" she asked, her mouth forming the words silently. But the answer never came. Like much else, it was hidden from her, behind a screen much darker and thicker than the one that separated her right now from Lin. And Lin? If Lin knew, he wouldn't say. Or didn't know.

"I'd kick his arse!" Uncle Pan was saying, the tirade turning in on itself, like a snake swallowing its tail. "I'd break him over my knee like a rotten twig!"

She set the mirror back, then, with a tiny shudder, went across and began to prepare the meal.

* * *

Faces . . . what could one tell from a face?

As Karr scrolled through the file of faces, studying each of the seventeen suspects as they appeared, he wondered just what they had in common, and what could be read of them with the eye.

Was it true what was written in the *T'ung Shu*, that a man's fate could be read in his face? Did the shape of the chin determine one's strength, or the length of the brow one's intelligence? Or was Sun Tzu right when he wrote that a man's exterior – however fine – had little bearing on his character or destiny? For himself he believed the latter. Hans Ebert had had a fine face, and look how he had fared. And DeVore . . . Some said DeVore was handsome. But handsome was as handsome did, and the worldly face DeVore had put on had masked a nature so evil and so corrupt as to warrant a face as black and pestilent as a pit of swarming insects.

Karr froze the image and sat back, rubbing his eyes. He had been at it all night, trying to find connections between these men, but there were no connections. Not one of them knew or had dealings with any of the others, nor was there any point of common interest, as far as he could tell. The only thing they had in common was that they – or copies sent in to replace them – had been seen in the border stacks in the last four weeks, and had been there when they'd no business to be there.

It was time to call them in and question them. Time to take this a stage further. If Kim was right and the tests Surgeon Hu had devised worked, then maybe they'd find an answer to this mystery.

Karr sighed, exasperated. *I should have gone home*, he told himself. *I should have let one of my staff officers do this!*

That was true, but that was not his style. Tolonen's lesson was deeply ingrained in him. If you wanted something done properly you had to do it yourself. You trusted your own eyes – you didn't trust what others told you. But sometimes you had to let go. Sometimes you simply had to depend on others.

Kao Chen . . . what I could do with Chen at my side right now.

He smiled. It had been some while since he'd thought of his old friend Chen; some while since his face had crossed the screen of his memory. Now *there* was a case in point! Face like a thug. Ugly as sin. And yet an angel of a man. Loyal, trustworthy, the very best of friends. A man you could depend on in a tight corner. But Chen had long ago quit the service. It was nine years now since he had settled on the Plantations with his wife and family.

He chose well, settling so far north, Karr thought, recalling the devastation and loss of life he had witnessed yesterday. *If he had settled in a warmer clime he would be dead now. He and all his darlings.*

He ought to go and see him, once things were easier. It had been too long. Why, word was that Chen was a grandfather now. A grandfather! He laughed softly, then leaned forward, blanking the screen. It was hard to imagine. No doubt he had a few grey hairs . . .

"Sir?"

Karr looked round. His equerry was standing in the doorway.

"Yes, Pietr?"

"*Shih* Ward is here, sir. He'd like a word with you."

"Tell him I'll be with him in a moment. Take him through to my office and look after him, okay? I just want to finish here."

"Sir!"

He sat, resting a moment. To tell the truth, he'd done all he could, but he wanted a moment before he saw Ward again. Something was nagging at him. Something obvious he'd overlooked.

How often that happened. How often, when you focused on a problem, nothing would come, and then, just as soon as you'd relaxed and were thinking of something else – BANG! – there it was, the answer, as if from nowhere.

He laughed and stood. *Yes, but now I'm thinking about it again . . .*

Chen. Yes, he'd visit Chen. As soon as time permitted.

* * *

"*Shih* Ward . . . how are you?"

"Well, thank you," Kim said, standing and greeting Karr. "I understand the camera trawl threw up seventeen suspects."

"That's right," Karr said, going round his desk. "I'm having them brought in right now. We should know before lunch-time whether we've got more copies on our hands."

"But no connections, right?"

Karr stared at him, then nodded. "How did you know?"

Kim smiled. "Just a hunch. I was thinking about it earlier, when I was swimming with my son."

"And?"

"And I was thinking that if *I* was going to try to infiltrate the City I would ensure that there were as few connections as possible between those people I was going to replace. In fact, I'd make the whole thing as inconspicuous as possible."

Karr shrugged. "Fine. But to what purpose?"

"To whatever purpose I wanted. To assassinate targeted officials, maybe. Or to cause maximum disruption, perhaps by acting as human bombs. Or . . . and this only occurred to me travelling across . . . simply to sow despair."

"You're not serious, surely?"

"Why not?" Kim leaned forward, placing his hands on Karr's desk. "What weapon could be more effective? What could damage us more as a society than a whole group of individuals going about spreading the gospel of negativity?"

"But the expense! To make these things must have cost billions!"

"To develop them, yes. But to build them . . ." Kim shook his head. "My guess is that the hard work – the R and D – was already done. My guess is that once we start looking we'll find hundreds of these things!"

Karr stared back at him a moment then shuddered. "You're sure you're not one yourself, *Shih* Ward? To hear you speak . . ."

"Forgive me," Kim said, sitting back. "My words weren't meant to frighten you. Once we locate these things we can deal with them. But I think we ought to widen the scope of our investigation and look back through the camera records not just a month or two but over a much longer period. Several years, perhaps."

"But you said . . ."

"I've changed my mind. I think that whoever devised this is playing a long game. Placing sleepers among us. At some point, when he's enough of them in place, they'll be activated."

Karr whistled. "I see. I . . ."

His desk communicator buzzed.

"What is it?" he asked, touching the pad.

"I'm sorry, sir, but there's an urgent message for *Shih* Ward."

Karr looked to Kim. "Would you like to take it privately?"

"No. Patch it through."

The two men turned to face the screen as it came down. An aged Han faced them, his thinly-covered head bowed.

"*Shih* Ward?"

"Who calls me urgently?"

The old man raised his head. "Forgive me for disturbing you, Master. I am Steward Cui. We met yesterday . . ."

"Of course," Kim said, lowering his head slightly. "You have a message for me from your Master, Steward Cui?"

"He . . ." The old Han made a movement with his mouth as if finding it difficult to say what he was about to say. "He says he begs you to forgive him his rudeness yesterday. He says . . . if you would graciously visit him this afternoon?"

Karr looked at Kim. Something strange was happening in the young man's face. He saw the flickering emotions there, quickly controlled.

Kim raised his head proudly. "Tell your Master that I shall be most honoured to visit him. What time would be most convenient?"

Cui gave a grateful little bob of his head. "If you would care to be here at two, I shall prepare a light meal for you."

"That is most kind, Steward Cui. Until two, then . . ."

The screen went blank. Slowly it slid back into its ceiling slot.

"The Marshal?" Karr asked, then frowned, surprised by how unguarded Ward's expression was. For a brief moment his face revealed an unexpected vulnerability, then he composed himself again.

Kim nodded. "Yes. Now where were we . . . ?"

* * *

Lehmann walked swiftly through the massive entrance hall, the click of his booted footsteps carried back to him from the high, vaulted ceiling. The Shen Chang Fang at Milan was the oldest and most magnificent of GenSyn's installations, taking up seven whole stacks at the very centre of Milan *Hsien*, directly above the old city. The sheer grandeur of the place spoke of a different age – an age of fluted pillars and massive, echoing halls. It was said the ghost of Klaus Ebert walked their marble halls, but now the staff bowed their heads to another Master, kneeling hurriedly in the broad corridors as the White T'ang approached, his entourage hastening to keep up with him.

Steiger, the installation's Director, hurried to greet Lehmann as he bore down on the entrance to the new wing, bowing elaborately, but Lehmann swept past him as if he wasn't there, making his way through to the laboratory where the copy had been taken.

Soucek was inside, standing over the part-dissected corpse, watching the four-man team of technicians at work. As Lehmann entered, he stepped back, allowing his Master to take his place beside the operating table.

Lehmann studied the body a moment, then looked to Soucek, indicating that they should go into the next room.

Inside, the door closed, Lehmann went to the observation window. "So what do we know?"

"Nothing," Soucek said. "If I didn't know better I'd say that thing out there was real. A human being, born to a regular human mother."

"Then maybe he was."

Soucek looked surprised. "You think they know?"

Lehmann stared at the corpse thoughtfully, then turned to face his lieutenant. "More than us, perhaps. I'm beginning to wonder if these really are Li Yuan's creatures."

"They have to be. We know Ward was working on these long before the war began. He's had a long time to perfect them."

"Maybe. But word is he hasn't been working for Li Yuan for some while. And what happened yesterday makes no sense."

"Unless the thing just panicked."

Lehmann considered that, then shook his head. "I don't believe that. Its actions were too controlled. Too . . . *planned*. The coat it was wearing . . . the thing that made it trace-invisible . . . what *was* that?"

Soucek shrugged. "We don't know."

"We didn't recover it, then?"

"No. I took that place apart but there was no sign of it. They must have taken it to Bremen."

There was the slightest twitch of irritation on Lehmann's otherwise emotionless features.

"You want us to try to get it?"

Lehmann nodded. "Just so long as it doesn't affect any of our other schemes. Can we spare an operative?"

"I'll have two men on it at once."

"Good. Now about this body. If it's not one of Ward's – if that's not where they're coming from – then where *are* they from? What do we know about its movements before we chanced on it?"

"Not a lot. We've traced it to the south – to Almeria, in fact – but we can't be certain that's where it came in."

"Then let's find out for sure. Make that a priority, Jiri. If these are coming in from Africa, then it's more serious than I thought. If the Mountain Lords have copies . . ."

Soucek laughed. The idea was absurd. "But Fu Chiang buys technology off *us*! Why, if he'd developed *these* . . ."

He stopped. Lehmann was not listening. The albino had turned and was staring at the copy, his mouth fallen open.

"What is it?"

But Lehmann was shaking his head. "No," he said quietly. "It couldn't be . . ."

"Couldn't be what?"

"DeVore . . ."

"DeVore?" Soucek shrugged. *Who the fuck was DeVore?*

"It wasn't Ward," Lehmann said, meeting Soucek's eyes, his pale face burning with certainty. "We've been looking in the wrong direction. It's DeVore. Howard DeVore. He's back. The bastard's back!"

* * *

Uncle Pan had gone. Lin came back into the apartment and looked at her, letting a sigh of relief escape him. He was late now, she knew – had lost a precious hour of trading – but there was no sign of impatience, only a smile that seemed to say, "Ah, well . . ."

"Can I help you?" she asked softly, looking to his cart.

His eyes followed hers, then looked back at her. "Would you like to come with me this time?"

She stared at him, surprised. He had never asked before. Always, before now, he had gone to the market on his own, bringing her back some small gift at the end of the day, just to let her know he'd been thinking of her.

"Can I?" she said, her face lit up by the thought of it.

He nodded, his broad, answering smile distorting the right-hand side of his face.

"Clear the dinner things. I'll pack the cart."

* * *

Steward Cui let Kim into the darkened Mansion, placing a finger to his lips, then took Kim's jacket.

"He's resting right now," he said in a whisper, "But come through. I'll see if he's awake."

Kim looked about him at the shadowed hallway, remembering the last time he had been here. Then it had seemed a bright and bustling place – filled with Jelka's presence – but now the air was musty and the rooms had the feel of death about them. Even the boy, Pauli Ebert, had been taken from him – given into the care of a younger, healthier man. So Tolonen was alone now. Kim shivered. How long had he been living like this?

"*Shih* Ward . . . If you would come . . ."

He followed Cui down a long, dark corridor and out across a second hallway. Stairs went up into the darkness. Everywhere he looked doors were closed, as if the old house had been locked up.

Cui stopped before an imposing doorway and turned to Kim. "If you would wait just a moment, *Shih* Ward."

"Of course."

While Cui slipped inside the room, closing the door behind him, Kim turned, looking down the corridor. Military paintings filled the walls – portraits of famous generals and scenes from famous battles.

All lies, he thought, studying one that showed the victory of the Han armies at Kazatin, the Emperor Domitian – Kan Ying – bowing before the conquering general, Pan Chao. It was a familiar image and hung in schoolrooms throughout the levels, but it was a lie, for the battle had never been fought. In fact no Han army had ever marched upon the *Ta Ts'in* – the Roman Empire – let alone defeated it. Not in *this* reality. The truth was that Pan Chao and his handful of followers had reached the Caspian in 92 BC and withdrawn, leaving Europe to shape its own destiny. In this reality it had been fully two millennia before the Han returned as conquerors.

Lies. It was all built on lies. What he had said to Sampsa the other evening was the truth: the City was nothing but a box of dreams – the dreams of an evil god.

And now he must defend those dreams, lest they come crashing down. For in waking they might all die.

"*Shih* Ward. If you would step inside, the Marshal will see you now."

He went into the darkened room, his heart beating fast in his chest. How often he'd imagined this moment; how often he'd rehearsed which words to say, but his first glimpse of the old man robbed him of speech.

Aiya, he thought, pained by the sight.

Tolonen was propped up on his pillows. His mottled, shrunken head was completely bald and only his left arm – its golden surface polished brightly – showed above the dark-blue silken covers. The whole of his right side was paralysed and had atrophied – the result of the stroke he had suffered six years before. As for his face . . . Kim bit his lip, moaning softly at the sight. The old man's face was thin and drawn – a grotesque caricature of what it once had been. About his neck hung what looked like a thick black brace. Kim recognised it at once. It was a speech-enhancer; one of the inventions he had worked on while he was a commodity slave for SimFic.

Beside Tolonen, on the bedside table, was the black case of the holo Kim had left the day before.

"*Shih* Ward . . . ?"

The voice was thin, almost metallic: a perfect representation of the man.

Is that really you? Kim asked silently, appalled by how much the old man had changed. *Or is this some hideous, ill-shaped copy sent to haunt me?*

"Marshal . . ." he said, subdued.

The golden hand lifted wearily and beckoned him. "Come closer, boy. I cannot see you in the shadows."

He moved toward the bed, feeling a heavy reluctance. The covers had been perfumed, the room sprayed with strong disguising scents, but still he could smell the old man. A stale, unhealthy smell.

And in his mind – like some dreadful mockery – he saw Tolonen as he best remembered him, stripped to the waist and exercising, muscled like a god. Where had that gone? Where in the gods' names had that gone?

Kim stopped, an arm's length from the bed, looking down at Tolonen. A pair of watery-grey eyes stared back at him, one focused, one drifting in its orbit, let down by the muscles surrounding it.

"How is she?"

Kim smiled sadly. "She's well," he said. "And the boy. He's a healthy lad. He has his mother's nature."

"I miss her," the old man said, the enhancer making the words sound flat, unemotional. "It's been unbearable without her."

Kim nodded, understanding. "She misses you."

The old man swallowed painfully. His good eye blinked. "I . . . I was wrong."

"No," Kim said. There was a speech here he'd rehearsed; an angry, bitter speech about the wasted years and the stupidity of pride, but it meant nothing now. All that mattered was to heal the wound. To end this senseless feud.

"She loves you," he said.

The old man's mouth quivered, twisted strangely.

"What's done is done," Kim said. "Let it go. Come and live with us. It's what she wants. What we *all* want."

He waited, seeing how the old man struggled with himself. Even to agree to see him, he knew, had cost the old man greatly. His pride, his stupid, senseless pride – yet if he threw that away, what would remain of him?

"I . . .." He saw the last shred of defiance vanish like a wisp of smoke. The old man nodded stiffly, more a spasm of the neck than a nod, then closed his eyes. Slowly a tear rolled down his cheek.

Kim knelt and took the old man's golden hand between his own.

"It's over," he said, smiling, all the bitterness and anger purged from him. "You're going home, Knut. Home to Kalevala."

* * *

Sampsa lay on his back in the sunlight, the smooth surface of the rock warm beneath him as he listened to the gentle slush of the waves lapping on the shingle further down the beach.

Beside him a crab scuttled in the shallow rock pool, the pattern on its back like the Han symbol *erh*, the complex pictogram night-black against the meat-red shell. He watched it through half-lidded eyes, then looked up, studying the shapes of clouds.

Significance. Suddenly the world seemed to have significance.

He felt the tickling again, a dim presence at the back of his mind. The boy was searching for him, trying to find him with his mind.

For a moment he resisted, a faint reverberation in his head like an insect brushing against the glass of a fastened window, then, as if he'd unlocked it and thrown up the sash, the words rushed in.

Did you see the pearl?

He frowned, then answered. *Yes.*

Sampsa shifted slightly on the gently-sloping rock, then stretched lazily, spreading his toes. The dream. The boy was talking of the dream he'd had last night. For a second or two the silence in his head seemed vast, like the inside of some huge, sepulchral building, and then it came again.

That cloud . . . it's like a tiger . . .

He watched the air-show pass, the sun riding the great beast's back, feeling himself a channel, a window for the other's eyes.

Sampsa? Where are you?

He sat up and looked about him, letting the other see. "I'm on the island," he said, as if the other were blind and were sat beside him on the rock. "That house : . ." He looked up at the tower built into the rock face to his right. "That house is Kalevala. My home."

He stared at it a while, tracing its ancient shape, letting his mind fill with his memories of the place, then looked down into the pool. The crab was resting now, its huge front pincers slowly opening and closing.

Erh . . .

"The double". Sampsa leaned forward and, lightning quick, breached the surface of the water with his finger and touched the marking on the shell. As the crab scuttled away beneath a ledge of rock, he could hear laughter in his head.

He turned, looking south. "Why can't I see where you are?"

You can, the other answered. *Just close your eyes and look.*

He closed his eyes and looked. The blood-red of veins on the back of his lids faded to darkness and then . . .

The cottage seemed embedded in the hillside, the white of its walls vivid against the green. Beyond it similar cottages climbed the hill. And beyond that . . .

"What is that?"

That's the City. Its walls surround the valley.

"Ah . . ."

He felt the boy turn; saw fields and trees and then . . .

The bay. Slowly he moved towards it, past the charred remnants of an outhouse and down through fields until he stood beside it, looking out across the grey-green water.

"Where are the waves?"

Again there was laughter. Then, beyond what he saw, he sensed the memory of waves coming in across a pale white rock that jutted from a beach of yellow sand.

"What is that?" he asked, confused, but he could hear someone calling now, and as he turned to look the vision flickered and was gone.

Tom. The other's name was Tom.

Sampsa opened his eyes and shivered. From its place beneath the rock ledge, the crab eyed him warily, the message on his shell hidden from sight.

For the briefest moment he had glimpsed her, dark as his own mother was light, voluptuous where she was austere. And about her neck, the pearl; the same black pearl he had seen in the dream.

At once he saw himself in the water, forcing himself down, down into the sunless depths, his legs kicking strongly, his arms pulling him down through the hostile dark. For a moment he had glimpsed it, there on the shining, open shell – a perfect night-dark pearl, as large as the tip of his little finger – and had stretched to take it, but even as his fingers reached for it, he had felt himself drawn upwards and, lungs bursting, had kicked hard for the surface high above.

He had woken suddenly, gasping, his head ringing, his chest tight with imagined pain. The pearl. He had opened his hand and stared at his empty palm, the sense of loss powerful, unaccountable.

And then, that morning, diving with his father from the rocks, he had found himself searching the rocky bed of the bay, looking for it, expecting it almost, even though he knew no oysters grew in that frigid northern sea. And once again, his sense of disappointment had been sharp. But now he knew.

Did you see the pearl?

This time he smiled. *Yes. I saw it.*

"Sam-psa! Sam-psa!"

He turned and looked up at the house. His mother was leaning from the kitchen window.

"I'm coming," he yelled, beginning to make his way across the rocks towards the steps. Yet even as he did, he had the faintest sensation of grass brushing against his bare legs, the vaguest impression of an overpowering whiteness at the back of everything.

Doubled. Suddenly the world was doubled.

"Later on I'll show you the cave and the place where the trees were burned."

Yes, Tom answered. *And maybe we can row across the bay to where the ground is fused glass-black. There was a house there once . . .*

Sampsa smiled, then began to climb the steps, deciding he would say nothing to his mother.

At the top of the steps he turned, letting Tom look out through him a moment, sharing with him the rugged beauty of the view.

No. This would be their secret. Just he and Tom would know.

Later, Tom said. *Okay?*

"Later," he acknowledged, feeling Tom slip from his head. Then, alone once more, he turned and, pushing through the gate, made his way across the garden, heading for the house.

* * *

Tom sat in the corner of the room, spooning down his soup, while, on the far side of the room, his mother stood before the wall-screen.

On the screen itself, half life-size, three men – young men in their twenties – sat about a table, as if in a restaurant, talking and drinking wine. Tom glanced at it, uninterested, then concentrated on his soup again, aware only that his mother had gone suddenly from the room.

A moment later Meg was back, Ben in tow.

"There," she said. "That's him, isn't it?"

Tom looked up. His father was staring at the screen and frowning deeply as he listened. After a moment, he laughed coldly, then, speaking to the house computer, said, "Play this item from the beginning."

Tom finished his soup then pushed the bowl away. The programme began again.

He had not really been listening, yet his ears had taken in every word. As the discussion began, he found he knew what each was going to say. Not that that was odd: it was a skill – a talent – he had inherited from his father. Perfect recall. Sometimes it came in handy. Most times it was a nuisance – a barrier to simple being.

He slipped off the chair and – unnoticed by his parents – crossed the room, seating himself halfway up the stairs, on the turn where the rope was.

His father had crouched before the screen and was watching it attentively. The man in the middle was someone called Sergey Novacek, a sculptor, supposedly, though how a man with a shattered hand could be a sculptor was beyond Tom. To his left sat a man who called himself an art critic – one Ucef Agrafes, which sounded like a made-up name. To the right of the screen was someone Tom *had* heard of, the famous painter Ernst Heydemeier, creator of the so-called *Futur-Kunst* movement.

And their subject? Tom smiled, noting the tension in his father's body. The subject was Ben Shepherd's *The Familiar*.

Just then the comset in the corner began to bleep. His mother went across and picked up the handset. She was silent a moment, then turned, looking to Ben.

"He's watching it right now," she said, the words distinct enough to make Ben glance at her before looking back at the screen.

"Okay," she added, after a moment. "I'm sure he will."

She set it down then went back and stood beside Ben, her hand resting gently on his shoulder.

"For me it's not the concept," Heydemeier was saying. "I think the concept is quite a brilliant one. But then the concept isn't what's new here. The concept of shell technologies is actually more than two centuries old and Shepherd can no more take the credit for inventing it than any of us sitting about this table. No, what's new here is the degree of realism he's striven for, and I'm afraid that's just what's so deathly about the whole thing. It's just *too* real, *too* lifelike. Why, it's like someone has simply gone out with a new kind of camera and photographed the inside of someone's head. It's . . . well, I just feel it lacks all of those qualities that we recognise as being *artistic*. Art has to make some kind of statement about the world. It needs to reinterpret it for us, otherwise it simply isn't art. And Shepherd's *Familiar*, I'm afraid to say, simply isn't art."

Tom heard the tiny grunt his father gave, and noted how he had pressed his hands together on his knees, as if to still them.

Novacek, who was chairing the panel, now leaned forward and, lifting a bottle, began to fill his glass again as he spoke.

"I take what you say, Ernst, but you seem to imply that, even if it isn't art, there is, none the less, some kind of technical excellence at work here. Indeed that seems to be the single factor that swayed most of the critics who've thus far reviewed it – the surface glitter of the thing. For me, however, that so-called excellence seems more like sleight of hand; a kind of slick cheating. For me that smacks of the artist – and I define that term very loosely, I hasten to say – as magician. The whole thing is a cheap illusion, manufactured not by an *artist*, but by the worst kind of *con* artist."

"I quite agree," Agrafes chipped in. "In fact I'd go further and say that some of the scenes with the woman are no better than the cheapest Porno-Stims – the very lowest kind of titillation – and say more for the moral bankruptcy of my fellow critics than for the excellence of the work. For let us be quite clear, we are not talking about genuine excellence here. Ben Shepherd's *The Familiar* is – and let us not pontificate or try to obscure the point – the start of a new and quite disturbing trend which, unless something is done to try to prevent its proliferation, is almost certain to lead us down the path towards total moral degradation. To my mind it's filth of the lowest level – filth masquerading as high art!"

Ben stood, putting up a hand. At once the image froze.

"Well?" Meg asked quietly. "It *is* him, isn't it."

Ben nodded. His silence was the silence of anger.

"Do you know he married her?"

The look that came to his face was rare indeed; a look of shock. "You didn't say," he answered, his voice almost a whisper.

She shook her head, her eyes apologetic.

He looked back at the screen and shuddered. "He must have waited years for this chance to get back at me. Cheap illusions . . ." He made a snort of disgust. "As if that manufacturer of funerary items could even tell!"

"Distractions," she said. "That's what you said they are."

He glared at her, and then relented. "Achh . . . this is exactly what I wanted to avoid."

"Then ignore it. Don't lower yourself to their level."

"But the lies . . ."

"Are only lies. Or an opinion. You never know, he may even be sincere."

"Who, *Novacek?* No. He's a cunt! A shameless piece of shit! I should have snapped more than his hand!"

"Ben!"

The anguish in his mother's voice surprised Tom. He stared at her, not quite understanding what had happened. The past. This was a chapter of the past he hadn't read.

"What did Neville want?" Ben asked, after a moment.

"He . . ." She sighed. "Look, Ben, just forget this. It will do far more harm to answer them than ignore them."

"Maybe. But what did Neville say?"

She looked down. "He says he's booked a slot on three of the major channels for ten this evening. That's if you want to answer the criticisms. I said you'd let him know."

Tom watched, fascinated, not knowing what would come. For once this was a situation he could not recall.

"Tell him I'll pass," Ben said, and Tom, watching, saw how his mother let out a huge sigh of relief at that. But as his father turned away, he saw a strange glint in his eye and knew the matter wasn't over.

* * *

The day had gone well. According to Lin, they had taken more than twice what he usually did, and he was kind enough to put it down to her presence there behind the stall.

"We should do this regularly," he said in a quiet moment. "The customers seem to like you."

She smiled and looked down, abashed and yet also pleased by his praise. But more than that, she had enjoyed the day – enjoyed it more than she cared to think. For so long, it seemed, she had been caged. Not that she had ever looked at it that way before. And to even suggest it to him – well, it was unthinkable.

"If that's what you'd like . . ."

His lop-sided smile said that it was. Pleased, she attended to the stall, rearranging what was left so that it looked its best. Customers came and went, and for the next hour she barely had time to think. At the end of it, she looked to Lin.

"Well?" she asked, seeing how strangely he was looking at her.

"I should have known," he said with a little sigh.

"Known what?"

"That it was wrong. Wrong to keep you shut away. You needed this. Or something like this. I've never seen you so alive."

She looked away again, disturbed. "It wasn't wrong," she said. "You took care of me." She looked back at him, then reached out, holding his arm. "Nothing you could ever do would be wrong."

His eyes sought hers, then looked away, as if ashamed.

"What is it?" she asked.

"*Nu shi* . . ."

She turned, facing the customer who had interrupted her. "Just a moment . . ." But the look of surprise on the man's face at seeing her made her stop and frown. "Can I help you?"

"No . . . no, I . . . Forgive me, I made a mistake."

He turned and vanished in the crowd, leaving her staring after him.

"What is it?" Lin asked, seeing the look on her face.

"That man," she said.

"You knew him?"

"No . . . I mean, I don't think I did."

"Then what?" Unexpectedly he reached out and took her arms, turning her to face him. His face was more earnest than she'd ever seen it, his eyes searching hers. "Did you know him, or didn't you?"

"No," she said, certain about it now that she'd searched her memory. "But *he* knew me."

Lin swallowed. His face had gone pale. "Pack up," he said, pointing to the cart. "We're going from here right now."

"But . . ."

He shook her. "Do what I say. Now! Understand me?"

"Lin . . . ?"

"*Now!*"

* * *

Mach pushed his way through the crowd until he came out by the Market Inspector's Cabin. There was a queue by the window, but he ignored it. He went straight to the door and knocked loudly. Two men, who'd been standing near by, started to make their way across, but he turned and held up his pass. They stared a moment, then, satisfied, backed away.

As the door opened, he stepped through, pushing past the surprised Inspector who was getting up from the table.

"I want information," he said, showing the man his pass as he stared about the littered cabin. The man had been eating, and a half-empty bottle of Jung Shen wine rested on the table.

"Of course, Master . . . Harris," he finished, reading what was written on the fake pass. "What do you need to know?"

"Stall Five Three Seven," he said. "Who is the woman who owns it?"

The Inspector laughed. "Forgive me, Master, but you must be mistaken. Stall Five Three Seven is owned by Lin the Mender. There is no woman . . ."

He stopped, silenced by Mach's look.

"Today there *is* a woman there. So who is she? And where does this Lin live?"

"I . . ." The man wiped his mouth then went across and, searching among his records, returned with the card for Stall Five Three Seven. Mach studied it a moment, then pocketed it.

"But, Master . . ."

"I'll return it," Mach said brusquely. Then, without another word, he turned and left, slamming the door behind him.

* * *

"In here!" Lin said, thrusting the cart into a side room, then turned to grab her by the arm. "Quick now! Before he comes!"

Who is he? she wanted to ask. *And what's going on?* But the blind panic in his face, the very roughness of the way he pushed her into the room and slammed the door behind him, convinced her it was not the time to ask. Besides, his hand was clamped over her mouth. Outside she heard shouting, a curt demand – "Where are they? You . . . did you see someone come down here?" – then booted feet running past the door.

Lin waited almost a minute, staring open-mouthed at the door, barely daring to breath. Then, slowly, he released the pressure on her mouth.

"Forgive me," he said, realising suddenly what he'd been doing. "I . . ." He took a long, shuddering breath, then leaned towards her, whispering. "We are in great danger. That man . . ." He swallowed, the damaged side of his face twitching now. "I think he's trying to kill you."

Kill me? The shock of it rippled through her. She felt her legs go weak. "Why?" she asked, her voice tiny.

"I . . ." He stared at her, pained, remembering something – something he could not describe to her – then shook his head. "Believe me," he said. "I would never lie to you."

Who am I? she wanted to ask. *Who in the gods' names am I?* But she knew she had less chance of getting an answer from him than from the mirror.

"I have to go," he said. "There's a friend close by. He'll hide us until we can find somewhere else. We . . ."

"What's happening, Lin Shang?"

He tried to answer her – she could see how hard he tried to free the words – but the habit of the secret had become so strong it was impossible. Again he shook his head.

"Stay here," he said, placing a hand on her own. "I'll be back as soon as I can."
And don't open the door unless you hear my knock . . .

"And don't open the door unless you hear my knock . . ."

She smiled, the familiar phrase reassuringly welcome. "I won't," she said. "Take care." And then he was gone and she was alone, wondering if she would ever see him again.

For a moment she leaned against the door, recovering her strength, then reached up to throw the catch. It was a small thing, barely enough to stop a child if they were determined enough, but she felt strangely better for it.

She turned, then, moving the cart aside, looked about her. It was a store room, and beyond . . .

She crossed the room and opened the door, stepping into what seemed like a family room. There was a bed and a low table, two mats and, on the wall beside an inset screen, a picture of a family – a man, a woman and two children. Han. She wondered where they were, what they were doing. Then, because she could not stop herself, she wondered why someone should want to kill her. Someone she didn't know.

The accident . . . it had to do with the accident.

She stepped across and pressed the pad below the screen, some strange compulsion shaping the decision. For years now she had lived without it – could not remember a time, in fact, when there had been an active screen in a room she was in. Of all the things Lin had mended over the years, he had never touched a screen.

She watched as the image formed. There was a hall, a massive hall with pillars and balconies, and a host of men in white flowing robes trimmed with red, their heads shaven. On a platform high above it all was another man – a "priest" she realised, wondering where that word had come from. As the crowd below fell silent he raised his hands and began to speak. And as he began to speak the camera moved in close upon his shining face.

"Pasek," she said, shuddering. "Karel Pasek." And with the words the walls holding back her memory cracked and fell.

"*Aiya . . .*" she moaned, staggering back, then fell to her knees, gulping for air, while above her, Pasek's face slowly grew until it filled the whole of the screen, his eyes staring out, cold and soulless from the godless depths in which he lived.

And in her frightened mind she saw his lips smile, then move to form her name, his voice uttering the words the mirror had refused to offer up.

"Emily . . . Emily Ascher . . . So there you are."

* * *

As the acolytes queued patiently to climb the golden steps and kiss the Sacred Master's foot, Lehmann, seated in a balcony overlooking the scene, gestured to Soucek that he should come across.

"How much longer?" he said quietly to his lieutenant's ear, as the latest of the Blessed Thousand lingered above the sacred foot with a look of drug-induced bliss.

"Oh, there are hundreds of the bastards yet!" Soucek said, his tone almost as acidic as his Master's. "I've heard of paying lip-service, but this is ridiculous!"

"He takes too much upon himself," Lehmann answered coldly, speaking from the side of his mouth. "The man has ambitions above his station. One day he'll go too far."

"And then?"

Lehmann looked at his lieutenant; a look Soucek understood without needing to be told.

Right now Pasek was useful. He was a focus for the disaffection in their City. Religion – now that was something the Han had never understood. But harness it, as the great Hung Hsiu-ch'uan had once harnessed it in the time of the Taiping, and one could destroy Empires. Or build them. But religion was a two-edged sword, and its leaders invariably came to see themselves as gods.

But Lehmann had little time for gods, only for men he could use.

Soucek smiled, then stiffened, seeing movement in the shadows behind his Master. Drawing his knife, he stepped between Lehmann and the door, prepared to strike.

"Jiri . . ."

Soucek let his breath hiss from him, then sheathed his knife. It was Mach. He turned, noting how Lehmann was watching them, his own pearl-handled knife resting in his lap.

"What is it?" Lehmann asked softly, conscious of the ceremony continuing behind him.

In answer, Mach stepped past Soucek and handed Lehmann a slip of paper: a copy of a poster that had been circulating the levels in its thousands recently. On it was a photo of a dark-haired woman and a figure – a reward of half a million *yuan*.

"So?" Lehmann asked, meeting Mach's eyes again.

"So I've found her," Mach answered, smiling. "I've found Emily Ascher."

"Found her? Then where is she?"

"Nearby. I . . . I've tracked her to one of the local stacks."

"And you want my help to flush her out?"

Mach nodded.

"And when you get her?" Lehmann's eyes studied his old ally closely. "You fancy that reward?"

Mach laughed. "No, Stefan. I thought you'd like her. These posters . . . her old husband, Michael Lever is behind them. And Lever's a powerful man these days in Li Yuan's Enclave. I thought . . ."

Lehmann nodded. "You did well to come to me, Jan. A lesser man might have thought of the money. But you . . . you always were ambitious, weren't you?"

Mach shrugged, but all three of them knew the truth. Since Pasek had been taken up by Lehmann, Mach's own organisations had been under pressure. Pasek's Black Hand had all but destroyed the *Yu*. But if Lehmann gave his support, Mach could again be powerful.

"You could be useful, Jan," Lehmann said, turning to watch Pasek once more. "Our friend the Priest is getting rather high and mighty, wouldn't you say?"

He turned, letting his eyes say what he meant.

"Power's a delicate thing," Mach answered. "To rule, one needs to use checks and balances."

Lehmann nodded. "You understand, then?"

"And the woman, Ascher?"

"Take Jiri here. He'll help you flush her out. Oh, and Jan . . ."

"Yes, Stefan?"

"You've no . . . *beliefs*, have you?"

"Who me?" Mach laughed, then shook his head, scowling. "Why, if I met God himself I'd spit in his eye before I'd bow my head to him!"

CHAPTER·20

PUPPET DANCE

L i Yuan came down the dragon steps and stood over Karr, one hand gripping his imperial yellow silks, the other pointed accusingly at his kneeling General. Nearby his full Court had been drawn up for the audience, and his wife, his Chancellor and several other senior Ministers and Advisers stood watching as, his face dark with anger, he bawled Karr out.

"Odessa! How could you lose Odessa? Don't you understand how *vital* Odessa fortress was? And now it's his. *His!* Why, he has only to strike north to Kharkov and we are undone. I shall be trapped between his forces and the West Asian warlords. And what then?"

Then we must strengthen Kharkov, Karr thought. But he said nothing. He kept his head bowed, his face an expressionless mask, accepting his Master's blame, letting the young T'ang's anger wash over him like the tide.

"And Chang! Where is Minister Chang? You *promised* me him, General Karr! But he's slipped the net. You were watching him, neh?"

"I was, *Chieh Hsia.*"

"So what happened?"

"I do not know, *Chieh Hsia*. Much else was happening. The copies . . ."

Li Yuan waved the excuse away. "I gave that job to Ward. You, General, should have been concentrating on more important matters! I mean, what in the gods' names were you doing, losing Odessa! Surely you could see his purpose?"

Not until too late, Karr answered in his head, *and I defy any other man to say different.* But he kept the thought to himself once more, merely dipping his head a fraction lower, as if accepting the criticism at face value.

Rheinhardt, he thought. *Rheinhardt is behind this. He never forgave me for taking his job. And now he's whispering his poison in the T'ang's ear, setting him against me.*

He swallowed, gripped by a sudden bitterness at the thanklessness of his task. *After all I've done . . . to be treated thus.*

Li Yuan was still shouting at him, blaming him, returning time and again to his stupidity at losing Odessa.

It was a brilliant move, he thought, feeling a strange respect for his adversary. Like a cutting move in a game of *wei ch'i*, it had changed the shapes on the board at

365

a stroke. Li Yuan had always been on the defensive against a stronger player, but now things had entered a new and critical phase. Now the endgame was about to begin.

As Li Yuan went back up the steps, returning to his throne, Karr realised he had been dismissed. For the last minute or so he had been detached from it all, the T'ang's harsh words troubling him no more than a baby's babble. But now he had to stand and make his way from there, and that proved hard. As he stood he kept his head lowered, properly reverential, then, bowed at the waist, he began to back away, feeling a warmth at his neck that was as rare as it was unexpected. Never, before now, had he felt ashamed. Never, even when he'd lived beneath the Net, had he let another man do *this* to him.

Between the watching ranks of Courtiers and Ministers he went, head bowed, back beneath the great arch of the entrance, watching the great doors close slowly upon the scowling T'ang, perched atop his Presence Throne.

As the doors slammed shut Karr let a breath escape him, then turned, straightening up, making a tiny movement as if shaking off some dark and evil spell. He looked about him, noting how his men could no longer look at him; how their eyes slid away, embarrassed to see their General so belittled.

"Come!" he said curtly, gesturing for them to follow, then began to march at a pace towards the Eastern gate and the hangars beyond.

He was climbing aboard his cruiser when a shout made him turn. It was the Chancellor, Nan Ho. He was running across the grass towards the hangars, lifting his silks with one hand as he ran, while his other arm hailed the General.

"What is it, Master Nan?" he asked, over-politely, as the old man stopped, wheezing, at the foot of the ramp.

"Send . . . send your men . . . away, General . . . Karr." Nan Ho took a long breath, then spoke again. "We need to straighten a few things out. I could not see you leave like this."

Karr turned, waving his men out of the hangar. When they were gone, he faced Nan Ho once more.

"So?"

Nan Ho came up the ramp until he stood close, dwarfed by Karr. "You must be patient with him, Gregor. The events of the past few days have been a shock to him. He had thought to make a brand-new start, but now his plans are in ruin, there are intruders in his City and one of his key fortresses – perhaps *the* key – is in his enemy's hands. Would you not feel angry? Would you not – in some strange way – feel betrayed? And if not by fate, then by whom? In his mind he searches for a scapegoat, and for now he has found you."

Karr's anger – his frustration – suddenly boiled over. "And that should make me feel *better*?"

Nan Ho shook his head, a genuine distress at Karr's predicament in his eyes. "No. It must have been hard just now. Hard to say nothing when so much was being said, neh?"

Karr merely sniffed.

"Look, I understand. But before you do anything rash, let me tell you how things stand, Gregor. Minister Chang has fled to the southern City. I have word that his paymaster, the White T'ang, was none too pleased to see him. And no wonder. Here he was an asset, there he's merely another mouth to feed."

"And Rheinhardt? What's *his* role in all this? Is he counselling Li Yuan against me?"

Nan Ho looked away, suddenly uncomfortable. "You . . . you must trust me, Gregor. I shall do what I can. Just now the T'ang is set against you, but his mood will change. Ride out this temporary storm. Do nothing rash."

"Rash?" Karr laughed. "Do you not know me, Master Nan?"

"I think I do. And find no better a servant to the T'ang . . . bar myself, of course."

"And yet Li Yuan does not trust me? Our Master, it seems, prefers the prattlings of a bitter man."

Nan Ho sighed. "This is . . . *difficult*. Rheinhardt is here, at the T'ang's elbow, while you . . . well, you are about your business. You must be patient, Gregor. There are many here at the palace who wish you well. I would not have come to you were it otherwise."

Karr looked at him, then gave a small nod.

"Then trust me." Nan Ho put out a hand, holding Karr's forearm a moment. "To serve an ungrateful Master . . . that is true service, neh?" -

* * *

Nan Ho returned inside, troubled by what had happened. Then, hearing that his Master had retired to his rooms to rest, he went directly to Pei K'ung's apartments.

"Master Nan," she said, greeting him. "What can I do for you?"

He closed the doors and went across.

"That was a bad business just now," he said, deciding to come straight to the point.

"It depends on whose viewpoint you look at it," she answered, taking a seat on the high-backed sofa by the window and indicating that he should sit in one of the officials' chairs close by.

"Karr is a good man. An excellent servant."

"But a political liability," she said, looking past him and snapping her fingers. At once an aide slipped from the shadows and brought across a file.

"You've seen this, I assume."

He nodded. "The business with the young girl and the pamphlets . . . but that was years ago. Over a decade ago, so I understand."

"Maybe so, but Rheinhardt has been busy unearthing such things. It seems he's out to get our man Karr."

Nan Ho shook his head. "I don't understand it. Karr has done nothing to him."

"He took his job. No matter that he didn't angle for it, Rheinhardt sees it otherwise. Now he's out to destroy Karr, and the loss of Odessa handed him the ideal opportunity."

"But surely Yuan knows this?"

Pei K'ung sat back slightly. "My husband is beyond reason just now. I was there when he read that file. He feels . . . *betrayed*. And rightly so, perhaps."

"But Karr's behaviour since . . ."

"Has been exemplary, I agree. But that file creates a doubt, and where there's a doubt."

Nan Ho raised a hand. "I take your point. But what are we to do?"

"We?" Pei K'ung laughed, then, unfolding her fan, began to flutter it before her face. "What would you have me do? Speak to my husband? Why, he would tell me to mind my own business! Speak to Rheinhardt? Why, the man would simply say that he was acting in the best interests of his Master."

"Then we are to do nothing, I suppose, and let a good man go to waste!"

The fan stopped fluttering. Pei K'ung looked at him directly and raised an eyebrow. "Now, did I say that, Master Nan?" She smiled. "No. But there are other means."

"Other means?"

Pei K'ung stood abruptly, setting the file down next to her, then held out her hand for him to kiss the ring. He bowed and kissed it, then stepped back, unsure for once of her meaning. But he could see that she was not about to elucidate.

"You will forgive me, Master Nan, but I must rest now. I slept badly last night and . . ."

"I understand."

"Until tonight."

He bowed low. "Mistress . . ."

* * *

"Gregor? Is that you?"

Karr set down his knapsack and turned, smiling as Marie came out from the kitchen. They embraced, their four-year-old daughter, Hannah, watching from the doorway shyly.

"So what's this?" she said, breaking from a kiss and beaming at him. "Unexpected leave?"

He shook his head, the look in his face making her smile fade.

"What is it?" she asked quietly.

"I've come from Astrakhan," he answered, wondering how much he could tell her. "I . . . I had a personal audience with Li Yuan."

"So?"

"So he blames me for losing Odessa."

She closed her eyes briefly, pained by his pain, then looked at him again. "So you're demoted. Is that it?"

"No. But the whole Court was there. He . . ." Karr swallowed, finding it hard to say. "He *humiliated* me before them."

"Ah . . ." The tension in her face – around her mouth – told him she understood. Of course she did. No one understood him better. She was his other half – his other self. If she did not understand, no one could. He let her hold him a moment, then moved back slightly.

"So what are you going to do?" she asked, studying his face.

He looked past her, then smiled. "First I'm going to cuddle my little beauty."

Crouching, he put out his arms. Hannah ran across to him, letting him pick her up and hold her tight. He laughed, kissing her neck and cheek.

"And then?"

"Then I'm going to spend a little time considering my future."

She put a hand out, smoothing his shoulder. "Was it that bad?"

He nodded, then, kissing Hannah again, put her down.

"Master Nan says I must be patient. He says Li Yuan will come round, but . . . achh! I wonder if I can put up with it any more. I try my best, yet my best is never good enough."

She bristled at that, indignant on his behalf. "Your best is as good as any man's, Gregor Karr, and you know it! Why, it's certainly a lot better than that buffoon, Rheinhardt!"

The look in his eyes told her she had hit the gold. "Ah, so that's it! This is Rheinhardt's work."

He nodded.

"And you'll let him beat you?"

"No, but I'll not let him force me into making wrong decisions, either." He sighed. "Why is it never easy? Why does whatever I do feel wrong? It wasn't always like this, was it?"

She smiled sadly then reached out to hold him again, Hannah pressed between them, holding them both. "You can answer that yourself, Gregor. It's always been the same. You feel you owe a duty. It was the way you were raised. But sometimes duty isn't enough. Sometimes you have to believe in what you're doing, and for a long time now you haven't, have you?"

He stared back at her, reluctant to answer, then nodded.

"So what are you going to do?"

He laughed. "I'm going to think about it. As I said."

"And when you've thought?"

"Then I'll make my decision."

She kissed his ear, then spoke quietly to it. "Would you like me to get a sitter for young Hannah, Gregor?"

He turned his head and, seeing that look in her eyes, smiled. "I think that might be a good idea, my love. A very good idea."

* * *

A hammering at the door disturbed them.

"It'll be for me," Karr said, getting up.

Marie lay there, watching him dress, conscious of how magnificent a man he was. Nor was it just his form that was impressive. If a man was to be judged by the tenor of his actions, then her husband was a giant in more than one regard. She shivered, thinking of how gently he had touched her, of how his eyes had burned, adoring her, as he made love to her. That, in itself, was heaven. And whatever he decided – wherever lay their future path – she would go with him. For that was her fate now – to be with this man until her death. Or his.

He turned, blowing her a kiss, then went out. A moment later she heard him unbolt the door and throw it open. There were voices, the door slammed shut, and then he returned, carrying a large, flat, rectangular parcel.

"A delivery!" he said, laughing. "You weren't expecting anything, were you?"

She sat up, pulling her hair back from her eyes, then reached out.

He gave her the parcel. Reading the label, she frowned. "No, Gregor, this is for you. Look!"

He took it back, shrugging as he began to open it. As the wrapping fell away, she gave a tiny gasp of surprise.

"Why that's . . ."

"Lehmann's," he said, turning the painting to study it properly. He sat on the edge of the bed, letting her rest against him to look at it.

"This was *his*?"

Karr nodded. "It used to hang in his office."

"And that word, Kampfer. Is that the artist's name?"

Karr laughed. "I said something very similar first time I saw it. But no, Kampfer is an old dialect word for 'fighter'."

They both stared at the painting for a while. There was something clean and muscular about the line of it – something you never found in Han art.

He turned the canvas over. On the back, in a tiny, spiderish hand, something was written. Karr held it closer and read.

"To a worthy enemy. A fighter's fighter. Best regards. Li Min."

He turned it back. Again they studied it.

"It's beautiful," she said. "But you can't keep it. You know that, don't you?"

"I know. I also know that it's helped me to a decision." He met her eyes. "I'm going to resign. When one's enemy gives one gifts and one's Master only blame . . ."

"It isn't that simple."

"No?" The look in his eyes – of anger and bitterness and a deep-rooted frustration – was like nothing she had ever seen there before. Seeing it, she knew that this was a decision not lightly reached, however much this "gift" had triggered it.

"So what will we do?"

He took a long breath, stretching his jaw in the characteristic way he had, then smiled at her. "First, we'll visit Kao Chen and Wang Ti."

She laughed, delighted, and wrapped her arms about him. "And afterwards?"

He set the painting aside, then pushed her down on to her back, pinning her arms above her head and leaning over her. "Afterwards we'll do what we always do. We'll practise making more copies of ourselves."

* * *

Kim took the infodisc from the slot in his neck and slipped it back into its protective sheath, then sat back, thinking.

The old man was due to arrive within the hour, and once he was here he would get little else done, so it was imperative to make a decision now. There was a team of men at Bremen awaiting instructions, and if he did not provide them they would spend another day idle.

Of the seventeen "possibles" Karr had identified, only one had been human. The others had been proved by Surgeon Hu to be very good fakes. Human enough to fool the eye.

Puppets, Kim thought, wondering how, in a City of eight and a half billion people, he was going to discover just how many of these things existed.

There was, of course, only one answer. To be sure he would have to test everyone. All eight and a half billion. But would Li Yuan agree to *that*? The expense of it alone would be phenomenal, not to think of the logistical problems of ensuring everyone *was* tested.

Maybe they could hold a census. After all, it was over a decade now since the last.

He sighed. No. It was no good. After the devastating setbacks of the last few days Li Yuan would never agree to blanket testing. Which left them fishing with a net full of holes.

So clever, he thought. *So clever to make the things so ordinary.*

And when the puppets danced? What would happen then?

He sighed, then, leaning forward, tapped out Karr's private contact code. There was a delay then UNAVAILABLE came up on the screen.

"Odd . . ." He tapped in Hu's code. A moment later the Surgeon's face was on the screen.

"*Shih* Ward. What can I do for you?"

"I was trying to get hold of the General. He isn't there with you, is he? His private line registers unavailable."

"Haven't you heard?" Hu stared at him in surprise. "Karr is no longer General. The news came through an hour back."

"No!" Kim laughed with disbelief. "Has he been relieved of his command?"

"No. He resigned. This place is humming with the news. There's a lot of speculation as to who will replace him."

Resigned? Kim could hardly believe it. Karr had given no indication of it yesterday. So what had happened?

"Listen," he said, dragging himself back to the purpose of his call. "We need to start moving on the copies. The best thing would be blanket testing, but Li Yuan won't go for that. So what we need is to find a way of random testing. It would have to be done secretly, so my suggestion is that we rig up some kind of apparatus in the transits. Something that can scan at a distance for the differences we're looking for."

"No problem," Hu said. "The transits have camera surveillance, anyway, so we could rig something up at the back of that. You're talking of random testing in the Mids, I assume?"

"That's where we've found the majority of the copies, isn't it?"

"Thirteen out of seventeen."

"Then let's do that. If it proves successful, we can spread the net. I'll get a budget from Nan Ho. Meanwhile you get to work on the scanner. If there are any problems, contact me. Otherwise, I'll be in touch later this evening. Any questions?"

Hu smiled. "Only one. What are these things for?"

"If we knew that . . ."

Kim cut contact and sat back, looking about him at his study. This had once been Jelka's father's room, and the walls were lined with books – real leather books, the smell of them filling the air.

And now the old man was returning.

As if the thought were father to the act, there was the noise of a cruiser's engine, the distinctive whine of its decelerating turbos growing louder by the moment.

He went out into the hallway.

"Where's Sampsa?" he shouted, seeing Jelka in the kitchen, wiping her hands hurriedly on a towel. "He mustn't miss this."

"I'm here!" Sampsa answered, coming down the stairs just behind him. He was dressed in the clothes his mother had left out for him, his dark hair neatly combed back. For once he looked less like a wood imp, more like a young boy.

"Quick now!" Kim said, beckoning him across. "The cruiser's setting down. I want you to be there when they carry him down the ramp."

Sampsa nodded, then reached out, taking his father's hand. Together they went out, Jelka hurrying after, as the craft set down.

They waited, huddled together just beyond the stubby wing tip as the door hissed open and the ramp unfolded. Kim turned, looking up at Jelka, seeing the anxiety in her face. He had warned her what to expect, but the reality would be something else.

For the briefest moment he was beset by doubts. Maybe he should have left the old man there. This . . . this could only upset the hard-won balance of their lives. Yet to leave him there, to waste away in that darkened room, had been impossible. He would not have counted himself a decent man had he allowed that to happen. Besides, this was Tolonen's place. If he was to die anywhere, it should be here, with his daughter, in the place he had been born.

Kim looked back, at the house and the surrounding island, and wondered how Tolonen could have borne to leave it, even for a moment, let alone relinquish it to serve. But serve he had, for almost sixty years. Now his days of service were past and other actors – younger, stronger men – had stepped on to the stage he'd once frequented.

"There," Sampsa said, seeing movement inside before either of them. And sure enough, a moment later, two bearers began to edge out backwards from the craft, guiding a hover-unit down the ramp.

"Go," Kim said, urging Jelka forward, then pushing Sampsa after her. "Go and greet your grandfather, boy."

He watched, as Jelka crouched over the unit; saw the brief shock there in her face, the brave smile that quickly replaced it; saw the old man's golden hand lift from within the litter and grip hers weakly, the fingers visibly trembling with the effort.

The gods help us, Kim thought, disturbed and moved by what he saw. Such joy and pain as were in her face at that moment made his stomach clench in sympathy. At such moments he could not love her more. And the boy . . .

He heard himself laugh as Sampsa leaned into the litter and placed a kiss on his grandfather's brow. So unexpected a gesture . . . And then the old man laughed – a laugh like a startled cough.

You should have seen him, Sampsa, he thought, recalling what a rock Tolonen had seemed when first he'd met him. But now . . .

As the unit floated across he saw him for the first time in daylight and caught his breath in shock.

Out in the light Tolonen looked a corpse, the flesh melted from the bone, his skin so transparent one seemed to stare right through him into the earth in which he'd shortly lie.

Aiya, he thought, reaching out to take the old man's outstretched, trembling hand; seeing the gratitude in his watery eyes.

"Home," Tolonen murmured, the words as thin and pale as the flesh he so loosely wore. "I'm home."

Kim smiled and gently squeezed the hand, then looked to Jelka. She was sobbing now, the tears slowly coursing down her cheeks. He shuddered and looked back.

"We've prepared a room downstairs for you," he said, speaking slowly, loudly, so that the old man could hear. "It has a view of the sea and the cliff garden."

Again the old man smiled, like a pale sun glimpsed through thick cloud. "Thank you," he mouthed. Then, unexpectedly. "You're a good son, Kim Ward. A good son."

* * *

Lin Shang knelt on the littered floor, his hands bound tightly behind his back, his hair dishevelled. Soucek, standing over him, scratched his chin then, leaning closer, smiled.

"You're lucky, little Lin. We've found her. If we hadn't, I'd have had to kill you."

Lin winced but did not meet his tormentor's eyes. With the age-old stoicism of his kind – the five-thousand-year-old patience of the Han – he kept his head down and his mouth shut.

"I'm told you mend things," Soucek said, straightening up and looking about him at the shelves. "I'm told you have clever hands."

He drew his knife, then, reaching behind the kneeling man, grasped the rope and, slipping the knife between Lin's wrists, slit it. Sheathing his knife, he pulled Lin's right hand into view, holding it between his own to study it, his left hand on the wrist, the right curled about the four fingers.

"Yes," he said, nodding. "Clever hands . . ." Then, with a quick, hard movement – a technique he had learned from watching Lehmann – he tugged at the fingers, feeling the bones jump from the knuckles with a sharp resounding crack.

Lin's scream was the first sound he had made since Soucek had come into the room. Then he fell forward, unconscious.

Soucek stepped back, then looked to his two henchmen.

"Smash it all!" he said. Then, putting all his weight on his left foot, he stepped on to Lin's undamaged left hand, crushing it.

* * *

Lehmann looked up from his desk as Soucek came into the room, the writing stylus hesitating in the air. The woman was already there, seated in the corner, bound and gagged. Mach was due any moment.

"It's dealt with," Soucek said simply, standing to the side across from the woman.

He saw she was watching him; trying to gauge what his role in this was. He saw the contempt there, too, and wanted to tell her what he'd done to her boyfriend, but Lehmann would not have approved.

"Okay," Lehmann said, signing the document he had been reading and setting it aside. He stood and came round the desk, stopping beside Soucek to consider the woman.

"Mach's been delayed."

"Delayed?" Soucek looked to his master, but the albino's face was expressionless.

"Take the gag off. I want to talk to her."

This wasn't how they'd planned it, but Soucek did as he was told, standing back as she worked her jaw to ease the muscles.

"You're quite a celebrity, aren't you, Mary?" Lehmann said. "Or should I call you Rachel?"

"It's Emily," she said, meeting his eyes defiantly. "Emily Ascher."

"Ah . . ." There was sudden understanding in Lehmann's eyes. "So *that's* the connection. Mach was your friend. You were in the *Ping Tiao* together, weren't you?"

"Mach's a traitor!"

Unexpectedly, Lehmann laughed. "Mach's a useful man. He helped me find you."

She shrugged.

Lehmann turned and took the handbill from where it lay on his desk then held it out in front of her.

Soucek watched, seeing how her eyes widened, but also how quickly she controlled her emotions. It was impressive.

"I know you," she said, looking up past the paper at Lehmann. "You're DeVore's shadow. He grew you from a polyp on his arse!"

Soucek stepped past his master and swung his arm, slapping her so hard she fell from the chair. For a moment she lay there, stunned, then, turning her head, she laughed.

"The God of Hell's faecal puppet . . ."

Lehmann stepped forward, staying Soucek's hand. "It's okay, Jiri," he said softly. "Let her speak. Her words can't harm me. Nor will they help her."

He crouched over her, breathing into her bloodied face. "We've made a deal."

She swallowed painfully then made a small gesture of negation. "Michael would never deal with you."

"No?" He crumpled Michael Lever's poster in his hand, then pushed it brutally into her mouth, making her gag.

She spat the paper out and took a breath. Her eyes were angry now. "You don't frighten me, Lehmann. I've seen too much."

Lehmann studied her a moment, his face impassive, then he shrugged, as if it meant nothing to him.

"Your husband's a man of high principles, I understand. He must want you very much to have agreed to my terms."

Soucek saw how the words took the fire out of her. She closed her eyes, suddenly subdued, suddenly, unexpectedly defeated.

"Take her away," Lehmann said, straightening up. "And clean up her face. We don't want Lever saying we mistreated her."

* * *

After they'd gone Lehmann sat there staring at the door, seeing nothing, thinking nothing, then, returning to himself, he looked down at the message Michael Lever had sent back to him earlier.

"No deals," it read.

No deals, eh? he thought, screwing the piece of paper up and throwing it across the room. *Well, we'll see about that. Maybe when you start getting bits of her through the mail you'll change your mind!*

Deals . . . Everyone made deals. Kings more than most.

"Get me Fu Chiang," he said to the air, waiting as the screen came down. And as he waited, he thought, *I need a fortress. Somewhere more secure than this. Maybe at Odessa . . .*

"Master?"

The face on the screen was that of his ambassador to Fu Chiang's court, Cheng Lu.

"What's happening, Lu?"

"They're summoning Fu Chiang right now, Master. But I thought I should have a word with you about the situation here before you did. Things have been happening. Fu Chiang . . ."

"Is here," Fu interrupted, his image abruptly replacing Cheng Lu's. "Now, to what do I owe this unexpected call, Cousin Stefan?"

Lehmann raised an eyebrow. "We are still cousins, then?"

"Kissing cousins. The kind that kiss and die."

"Yet if we were to come to an arrangement?"

Fu Chiang's laughter was acerbic. He stared back at Lehmann scornfully. "You must really think me a fool . . ."

"But a meeting . . ."

"Would resolve nothing between us. We are enemies, Stefan Lehmann. Implacably so. You played the friendship card once already, or do you forget?"

"That was a misunderstanding . . ."

"On my part, certainly, to take your word of honour as having *any* value."

The two glared at each other a moment. It was Lehmann who broke the silence.

"Enemies, perhaps. Even so, to talk is better than to fight, *neh?*"

The threat was quite explicit, yet Fu Chiang merely smiled and shrugged, and at that moment Lehmann understood. Fu Chiang had made a deal with the West Asian Warlords – an "alliance". That was what Cheng Lu had meant to warn him about.

He broke contact and sat back, not bothering with the courtesy of farewells. Such courtesies were for fools or charlatans and Fu Chiang was neither. He, for one, knew how things stood. But if he *had* entered an alliance with the West Asian Warlords, then it was important to discover on what terms. Was it a defensive alliance? An agreement by each to come to the other's aid if attacked? Or was it more sinister than that?

Whichever it was, he felt frustrated for another reason entirely. In speaking to Fu Chiang he had not even touched upon the one matter he had wanted to raise with him – which was whether Fu had any news of DeVore. He would now have to trust to word from his spies in Fu Chiang's camp, and word from them was notoriously suspect. Most of them these days played a double game simply to survive.

There was, however, one other possible answer: one way not merely to create new channels of information, but also to undermine his "cousin", Fu. But that way was fraught with danger.

There was a knock, then Soucek entered.

"She's quiet now," he said. "Sweet dreaming on a tide of narcotics."

"Good. But listen. I'm going to give Mach his head. However, I'm also going to let our old friend Pasek spread his net far wider. I thought we might finally allow him to send missions into Africa."

Soucek stared at him. "But I thought . . ." He stopped, considering what he was going to say, then began again, spelling things out carefully.

"Here we control things. His church functions because we allow it to function and because we tie it in closely to our political machine. His priests are our men – as much as they can be, anyway. It *works*. We have our hand on the brake and he can't even shit without us knowing about it. But Africa . . . well, if we let him into Africa we lose control. The operation would be his, one hundred per cent. And if it caught on . . . well, think of the power we'd be granting him."

Lehmann nodded. "That's my assessment. It's a risk – a high order risk – but one we have to take. Fu Chiang is in alliance with the West Asian Warlords, and if I'm right, DeVore is somewhere in his City – maybe with his knowledge. In those circumstances, Pasek's fanatics could do our cousin Fu a great deal of harm. They might achieve, perhaps, what we could not by force."

Soucek sighed. "Maybe, but I don't like it. To give that cunt Pasek *anything* . . ." He shook his head. "The bastard thinks he's God, you know that, don't you?"

"He can think what he likes. The truth is that a knife or a single bullet would soon put paid to that belief. And if his grasp gets too long . . ."

Soucek nodded, understanding. "And Mach?"

"You heard what Mach said. But mind him, Jiri. Some men are vain and some foolish, some are too ambitious, others not quite skilled enough. Mach's none of those. He's a clever man who has no illusions about himself, but like that Han face he falsely wears to disguise his true origins, he's never quite what he seems. Watch him carefully, for of all our tenuous allies, he is by far the most dangerous."

* * *

Pasek held out his arms, letting the two serving boys disrobe him. Nearby, on the far side of his private chapel, one of the Priests Militant – masked and wearing the Cloak of the Seven Avenging Angels, wielded a brutal-looking whip, laying it time and again across the back of a stripped supplicant as two other priests chanted from the Book.

"And the fifth angel blew his trumpet, and I saw a star fallen from heaven to earth, and he was given the key of the shaft of the bottomless pit; he opened the shaft of the bottomless pit, and from the shaft rose smoke like the smoke of a great furnace . . ."

Pasek interrupted them at this point, stepping forward, naked now except for his breech-cloth, his hands raised as if blessing all present, his voice booming.

"And the sun and the air were darkened with the smoke from the shaft. Then from the smoke came locusts on the earth, and they were given power like the power of the scorpions of the earth; they were told not to harm the grass of the earth or any green growth or any tree, but only those of mankind who have not the seal of God upon their foreheads."

The whip had ceased falling, the room was silent now. There was only the faintest sizzle of the iron in the brazier. As the supplicant looked up, his drug-induced gaze falling with adulation on his Master, Pasek took the handle of the iron and lifted it into the air.

For a moment the air seemed bright with the glow of the heated iron, the symbol of the cross inside the wheel drawing all eyes. Then, as the Priest Militant drew back the supplicant's head, Pasek placed it against the man's brow, the room filling instantly with the sickly-sweet scent of burning flesh.

The man's scream was a scream of devotion – of acceptance. Thus marked, he would now be among the saved.

"And I heard the number of the sealed," Pasek said fiercely, setting the iron back upon the coals, then turning back to examine his handiwork. "A hundred and forty four thousand sealed, out of every tribe of the sons of the Hand."

The chanters closed their books and set them back on the shelf behind them, the Priest Militant hung his whip up on the hook on the wall. All three then helped carry the half-conscious supplicant – the Seal-bearer, as he would now be known – from the room, leaving Pasek alone with his attendants.

As ever, the ritual had inflamed him, filling him with the dark power of the animals from which his kind had come. His penis ached now for release; a release he must achieve at once if he were not to be tainted by its darkness. To be pure he must purge himself of it.

As the door slammed, he turned, looking to the two acolytes. Already they were waiting for him, their eyes as they looked back over their shoulders at him, eager that they be the one he chose.

But this once it was not to be. Even as he tore his breech-cloth off, freeing his swollen penis, there came a hammering at the door.

"What beast is this comes now!" he cried, rage making him spit the words. "Dress me boys, dress me!" he shouted, his heart beating furiously in his chest. "I'll kill the man! God help me I will!"

The hammering came again.

"Pasek! Open up! It's me, Soucek!"

Pasek groaned, grinding his teeth with anger. He would tear the man apart! He would blind him with the iron!

"Master!" one of the boys called up to him, seeming to speak to him from across a vast, misted distance. "Master . . . you must come back to yourself. There will be time . . . afterwards."

Time? The boy did not understand! He lashed out at him, sending him sprawling across the room. But the boy's words had their effect. Pasek took a long, calming breath, coming down, returning to himself – back from the darkness where he'd been – back from the bottomless pit itself.

The hammering came again. "Pasek! Open up!"

He looked to the boy and gestured, speaking gently now. "The door, boy. Open the door before he breaks it down."

As the door eased back he stood there, robed and calm, emanating the pure white power of his calling.

"Soucek," he said coldly, his eyes filled with dislike of the man.

"Master Pasek," Soucek answered, equally coldly, but with something resembling amusement in his eyes. He sniffed the air, then let his eyes fall first on the brazier and then on the boys, standing now at the back of the room beside the dressing-rail. "I bring good news."

Pasek waited, imperious as an eagle.

"Our Master, Li Min, has today granted you a great favour," Soucek began, stepping across to examine the iron, picking it up and sniffing at its heated end before setting it down again. He looked back at Pasek. "He is allowing you to send missions to our friends in City Africa."

Pasek's surprise momentarily betrayed him. For a second or two his mouth lay open like a suckling babe's, then it closed with a loud plop.

"Tell your Master he is very generous," Pasek said, looking down, angry that Soucek had caught him unprepared for such news, yet excited by the news itself. "And tell him I shall keep him closely informed as matters develop."

"He would expect no less," Soucek answered, walking behind Pasek and, unseen by him, making a lewd gesture and grinning at the boys. "But I will leave you now, Master Pasek. I'm sure you have much to . . . *organise*."

The unpleasant emphasis on the final word made Pasek meet Soucek's eyes and frown. What was the bastard implying? He watched Soucek go, heard the door slam and turned, facing the boys again. But it was no good. The power had drained from him, leaving its mark – a stain that would have to be purged from him some other way now.

Throwing off his cloak he went across and knelt, where the supplicant had knelt a while before, exposing his back. And, knowing what must be done, the eldest of the boys crossed the room and took the whip down from its hook, testing its heavy length in the air with a resounding crack before he turned and gently, almost lovingly, drew it across his Master's back.

Africa! Pasek thought, exultant, as the first stroke cracked and burned across his flesh. *Africa!*

* * *

Nan Ho was coming from Li Yuan's office when a servant ran to him and, kneeling, bowed his head.

"Master Nan! You must come at once!"

"Come? Come where, Steward Wang?"

"It is General Rheinhardt, Master . . . he has been taken ill."

The news took him aback. In his hand he had the document appointing Rheinhardt temporary commander of the T'ang's forces.

"Quick, then," he said, gesturing for Wang to get to his feet. "Has a doctor been called?"

Wang stood. "The Empress's own surgeon is seeing to him even now, Master."

"Then let us hurry there. If the General is unfit . . ."

No. He did not want to think of the problems it would cause if Rheinhardt were unable to take up his duties. It was bad enough that Karr had quit: to have to promote another from the lower ranks right now would cause nothing but trouble.

They hurried through the corridors. At the door to the Guest Apartments a guard made to stop them, then, seeing who it was, waved them through, his face troubled.

What's going on? Nan Ho asked himself, checking his pace in the doorway to Rheinhardt's room, seeing the long-faced crowd about his bed, Pei K'ung amongst them.

"What is it?" he said, going across to her and bowing.

"I am afraid General Rheinhardt is dead," she answered him, stepping back slightly so that he could see the pallid corpse. "It seems he ate a heavy lunch, then came back here to rest, complaining of chest pains."

Nan Ho looked down at the paper in his hand. He had been gripping it too tightly and his hand was wet where he held it. He looked to Pei K'ung's Surgeon, Yueh Li and raised an eyebrow in query, not trusting himself to speak, lest he say what was on his mind.

"His heart," Yueh said quietly. "He died before we could get to him. His brain . . . there was no calling him back."

Nan Ho nodded. This felt wrong. Everything about it felt wrong, but without causing a stir, what could he prove – if Surgeon Yueh – Pei K'ung's Surgeon – said he had died of a heart attack . . .

Besides, while this death would cause him problems, it might well solve others. With Rheinhardt dead, perhaps Karr could be persuaded to return.

"Master Nan?"

He turned, bowing to Pei K'ung. "Yes, Mistress?"

"Surgeon Yueh has prepared the death certificate, but it needs two further witnesses. I myself have signed. If you would oblige . . .?"

He stared at the piece of paper her foot-servant held out to him, knowing, both from the look in her eyes and the indecent haste with which she had prepared the paper that Rheinhardt's death had been no natural one but a result of those "other means" the Empress had mentioned earlier.

Poison. She has had him poisoned! The thought of it astonished him.

He took the inked brush and signed. *There! It was done!*

"Thank you, Master Nan," she said, smiling urbanely, giving no sign that this disturbed her in the least.

She smiled and leaned towards him, speaking softly, for his ears alone. "We are our Master's hands, neh?"

He looked at his, knowing they were not clean, then looked back at her again and, with a nod, began to back away.

"And Master Nan?"

"Yes, Mistress?"

She took the paper from his hand and, glancing at it to make sure it was the correct one, tore it in half and let it fall. "We'll not need that now, neh? Oh, and I'm told that Karr's to be found at a place called Kosaya Gora. It's one of the plantations close to the garrison at Moscow. If you act quickly . . ."

He nodded, understanding, then, with the feeling that he had been most thoroughly manipulated, turned and left the room, heading back to his Master to let him know the news.

* * *

Fu Chiang sat back from the screen, smiling broadly. He had just received the latest reports from his spies in his enemies' camps and was pleased with what he'd heard. Karr had resigned and Rheinhardt was dead. Pasek was to be given a free hand and Mach was to reform the *Yu*. In a more general vein, Lehmann's strike against the East European plantations had resulted in a loss to Li Yuan of more than eight per cent of his food production. That alone would have serious repercussions in the months to come, and not merely to Li Yuan. Lehmann himself relied quite heavily on food smuggled in from the Enclave, and if supplies were tight there the squeeze would be put on Lehmann too. As for Odessa, that might prove a mixed blessing for Lehmann. Certainly it had tipped the West Asian Warlords into his embrace, and who knew what might come of *that* alliance?

He turned, looking across the room to where DeVore stood at the rail of the fighting pit, staring down into the darkness.

"Things are ripening, don't you think?" he said, standing and going across.

"Well enough," DeVore said, turning to him. "But perhaps a little too slowly, no?"

"Constant dripping wears away stone," Fu Chiang answered, quoting the ancient proverb at him. "If we are but patient . . ."

"And if I'm impatient?"

Fu Chiang frowned. This was a side of DeVore he had not seen before. Wanting to avoid a quarrel, he raised a hand and smiled. "Perhaps there are things we might do to put a little pressure on."

But DeVore shook his head. "The trouble is they know."

"Know?"

"About my copies. Both Li Yuan and my old friend Lehmann. They know now what to look for. The element of surprise is lost. Or could be, if we don't act at once."

Fu Chiang stared at him uncomprehendingly. He knew about DeVore's copies – indeed he had gone down to Olduvai himself to see the factories there – but he hadn't known until that moment that DeVore had seeded his enemies' Cities with the things.

"How many have you got out there?"

"Not as many as I planned, but enough."

"Enough for what?"

DeVore met his eyes and smiled. "Just enough, that's all you need to know, Cousin Fu. It's time. Time to make the puppets dance."

CHAPTER · 21

AT ONE STRIDE COMES THE DARK

K im stood at the window, looking out at the night. The sea was still, a three-quarter moon floating high above it in a clear, blue-black sky. To his right, beyond the high brick wall of the garden, the pine trees bordering the cliffs were dark and still with a different kind of stillness to the sea's, a brooding mystery he had never fathomed.

It was just after four. Downstairs Jelka was tending to her father. He had stood there earlier, watching them, seeing how the old man looked to her, as a young child looks to its mother, totally dependent, and once more had felt a wave of regret that he had not acted earlier to bring Tolonen home.

Home. Standing there in the silence of the old house, he realised that, for the first time since he'd come here, it actually felt like home. Bringing the old man back – reuniting Tolonen with his daughter – had been the final, necessary act. And though the old man was dying, to die here where he belonged was somehow right. If he had died back there in that darkened room . . .

Kim shuddered, imagining it. If that had happened, Jelka would never have forgiven herself. She would have blamed herself for her father's death, and maybe part of her would have been for ever denied to him. As it was, the circle had been joined, the breach healed, and though it worried him to see her try to make up for the lost years in such a frantic way, he could understand it.

Such peace and yet such sadness he was feeling. Peace that he had at last done the right thing; sadness that Tolonen must inevitably die.

And maybe I could have prevented even that, he thought, remembering how relentlessly Old Man Lever had pursued him to work on his Immortality Project. Yet, sad as it was, he knew this death was necessary. For the old must always go, to let the new life breathe – to give it room.

Yes, and he'd seen how the old man's eyes had sparkled with pleasure at the sight of his grandson. Why, Sampsa had been a revelation, sitting with the old man at his bedside, reading from the Kalevala and talking of the old times. And after, how the boy had sat there, watching as his grandfather slept, his tiny fingers holding the golden fingers of the old man's artificial hand.

He sighed, then yawned, realising just how long a day it had been. Only a few years back it had seemed he could do without sleep at all, but now.

It's the air here, he thought, and smiled, turning from the window and looking back into the darkened room. It was only then that he realised the summons pad on the corner comset was flashing. He had turned off the audio earlier, in case it disturbed the old man.

He went across and closed the door, then, putting on a lamp, sat at the tiny desk and pressed the pad. There was a delay and then the screen lit up. It was Karr.

"Gregor?" he said surprised. "I thought . . ."

"Kim! Thank the gods! It's chaos here. They're active!"

Active? Then he understood. "The copies?"

Karr nodded. "We've reports coming in all the time. The City's in a state of complete panic!"

"Hold on," Kim said. "Back up a bit and tell me what's been going on. When you say 'active', what do you mean?"

"Stabbings, shootings, bombings. Maximum chaos. Maximum nastiness. Imagine five hundred psychos going ape-shit at once and you've just about got it."

Kim swallowed. "Five hundred?"

"I use the figure lightly. We don't yet know the full extent of it, but at last count we had over five hundred and eighty separate cases reported. And we're not talking single murders. Some of these bastards are taking out forty, fifty people apiece!"

Aiya . . . Then he'd been wrong. Wrong about both the scale and purpose of this intrusion. He'd thought their role was to be a passive one. But this . . .

"I've had to announce a City-wide curfew," Karr continued. "Not that anyone wants to be out walking the corridors with this going on."

"No . . ." Kim thought a moment, then. "Do you need me there?"

Karr laughed bleakly. "No. Stay there. It's probably the only safe place in the Enclave right now. We've had beserkers even here, in Bremen. These things . . ." The big man shuddered. "The stories I've heard are awful. Fathers turning against their families, trusted neighbours going from apartment to apartment and slaughtering old friends in their beds. The youngest we've had reported so far was a girl of six. She diced her whole family while they slept. What's made it worse is that it happened at so early an hour. By the time the alarm went out it was too late to do anything effective. Most of the victims didn't even wake."

"But now?"

"Now the whole City's awake. And terrified. Watching their screens and wondering if they're next. It's like these things are being triggered in waves. The first wave was the biggest, but reports are coming in of new ones all the time. That's the worst of it, perhaps. The uncertainty. The not knowing when it's going to end, or who's going to turn out to be one of these psychos. Can you imagine it, Kim? All of those people at home, behind locked doors, watching their loved ones and wondering if they're *really* real and not one of these things!"

"DeVore," Kim said. "It has to be DeVore."

"Yes," Karr said, admitting it for the first time. "It's what I said to Li Yuan when he reappointed me. Lehmann's a bastard, sure enough, but his imagination doesn't run to this kind of thing. This has DeVore's mark on it."

"So the thing you killed all those years ago . . ."

"Was a copy. It was what Tolonen always suspected. By the way, how is he?"

"Better for being here, I think. But look, is there *anything* I can do?"

Karr sighed, then shook his head. "Just pray for us, Kim. Pray to all the gods you know that we'll still be here come daylight!"

* * *

The palace was slowly waking. In the kitchens, servants were preparing the morning's meals, while in the stables the grooms had long since cleaned out their charges' stalls and fed them.

In the broad corridor leading to Li Yuan's apartments a servant walked, a towel over his right arm, a bowl of heated water balanced between his hands. His step was measured, orderly, as it ever was, but this time as he approached the great doors, Nan Ho, the Chancellor, stepped from the shadows to block his way.

"Master," the man said, bowing his head.

"I'll take the water," Nan Ho said, putting out his hands to take the bowl.

The servant glanced up from beneath his brows. "But it is beneath you, Master. Besides . . ."

"Give me the bowl," Nan Ho insisted.

He saw the bowl begin to fall, the servant go for the knife which, until that moment, had been hidden in the folds of his shirt, and knew he had been wise to take precautions. As he fell back, two guards stepped forward and, with the minimum of fuss, disarmed the servant, forcing him to the ground.

"Should we scan him, Master?" one of the soldiers asked, looking up at Nan Ho from where he crouched, his knee firmly in the servant's back.

"No," Nan Ho answered, picking up the discarded knife. "Whether he is or isn't, what's certain is he meant our Master harm." He bent over the servant and, grabbing his top-knot, pulled back his head so that he could see his eyes. It was just as Karr had said; it was as if the man were mad. That smile.

Steeling himself, he took the knife and drew it across the creature's throat. Man or copy, he could not be allowed to survive. So they must deal with their enemies from henceforth, for to be weak . . .

Nan Ho threw the bloody knife down. The creature spasmed then lay still.

"I want a squad posted here right away," he said, looking to the most senior of the two – a sergeant – he had rousted from his bed. "No one is to enter the great T'ang's rooms without my permission."

The two men stood and bowed. "Master!"

"Okay. *You* . . . go now and bring reinforcements! *You* . . . You will stay here until your comrade returns!"

"And the body, Master?" the sergeant asked, looking to the still-bleeding corpse.

"Leave it," Nan Ho said, feeling the bile rise in his throat. "It will serve as a reminder and a warning, lest others think the path to our Master's door be such an easy one."

* * *

Catherine sat on the sofa, the art folder in her lap, drinking. Sergey had been out all night. Out with one of his women, no doubt. There was nothing new about that. It was just . . .

She looked at the muted wall screen, then, forcing the glass to her lips, drained the last of the liqueur. It wasn't her habit to drink, and not this awful stuff, but for once she'd needed something.

The news was awful. All of that death. All of that senseless violence. It made one think that the world was ending. And perhaps that was no bad thing, for perhaps it was easier to end than to endure.

She set the glass down and turned her head, listening, but the child slept on. That at least was a blessing. She turned back, opening the folder.

It had been years since she'd looked at these. Years since she'd felt the urge. But tonight she had taken them down from the top of the wardrobe where she'd put them shortly after her wedding.

The first thing that struck her were the colours. She had forgotten – forgotten how Ben had made her look at things; forgotten how he'd pointed out to her the force *behind* the shapes. These – these paintings at the top – were the last she had done before she'd given up. The last and the best. Impressions. Sketches of things from memory. Sketches of him.

She stopped and moved her head back slightly, squinting at the painting. It was of Ben's face, side on, the light from just behind.

Or half his face, she thought, realising she had not finished it. *The half I thought I knew.*

Sergey had never seen these. In all probability he didn't even know they existed. Besides, he was too preoccupied with his own work – with his own obsessive versions of this face.

Ben. Ben Shepherd. How strange that she should think of him now, after so many years. Or maybe not so strange. After all, Sergey's attack on him was fresh in mind. He had tried to keep it from her, but she had overheard things, seen the bitterness in her husband's face as he was talking of Ben's work.

All that hatred, she thought, amazed that it had lasted all these years. Should one admire such a purity of purpose that nursed a hatred over fifteen years, or should one pity it? Whichever, it was certain that her husband hated Ben. Hated him for breaking his hand. Hated him, too, for having made her love him.

And herself? Did *she* still hate him?

She lifted the canvas, revealing the next work. This was a sketch – a pen and ink drawing of two lovers, their naked bodies abandoned to sleep after lovemaking. She sighed, remembering the day she'd done this. It was the day she had decided to accept Sergey's offer of marriage.

Yes, and she knew why. She had drawn this to purge herself. To finally accept that *this* was what she'd seen – Ben and his sister, Meg, asleep in his bed . . .

But that was no answer. Did she hate him still?

There was a sudden thumping on the outer door, the sound of someone trying to force their way in. "Cath-rine! Cath-rine, open this fucking door!"

She jumped with shock, then closed the folder. It was Sergey. He was back at last, and raging drunk by the sound of it.

"Cath-rine? The gods fuck you woman! Get off your arse and open this fucking door!"

Quickly she hid the folder. Then, taking a long breath to calm herself, she went out into the hallway.

"Cath-rine!" There was another thump, then a murmured, "Shit! Where *is* that fucking woman!"

She went across and reached up, drawing the bolt. Then, fearing the worst, knowing how angry he got when he was drunk, she undid the catch and moved back sharply.

Nothing. She frowned. Had he fallen asleep? She moved closer, trying to peek round the door. Then, very slowly, it began to slide back.

"Sergey?" she began, then caught her breath.

"Catherine. It's been a long time. Can I come in?"

"Ben . . ."

It was as if she had conjured a ghost. She moved back, letting him enter.

She closed the door, bolted it again, then turned, looking at him.

"These are good. They're Sergey's, I assume."

He was holding one of Sergey's heads. Three of them rested on the table in the hallway. Carved from black marble, each depicted Ben's face in various degrees of torment.

"Why did you do that?" she asked. "Why did you mimic him?"

He put the head down, smiled at her. "Why did you let me in?"

She shrugged, then moved past him, returning to the living-room. He followed.

"I often wondered," he said, looking about him at the room. "I thought his father was rich."

She switched the screen off, then turned, facing him again. "He was, *once*. But he died penniless. Sergey makes his own way in the world."

"Ah . . ." He stared at her, taking in the changes time had wrought in her, then smiled. She had forgotten how green his eyes were; forgotten the darkness behind the green.

"Do you want a drink?"

He shook his head. "I want you."

"No."

It wasn't possible. Too much time had passed. Too much had happened to them both.

He stepped across, taking both her hands in his. Then, without a word, he picked her up and carried her out into the hallway.

"The child . . ." she said softly, but he wasn't listening. He took her through, into the darkness of the end room where she slept, and laid her on the bed.

"What if Sergey comes?" she whispered, as he pulled her blouse up over her head.

"Sergey's not coming," he said, pausing to kiss her neck, her cheek, her mouth, his hands smoothing her naked flanks. "Sergey's sleeping it off at his club. I saw him there. He won't be home for hours."

"Ben . . ." Gently she pushed his face back away from hers. "Ben, we can't do this. What happened then . . ."

He did not answer her. Instead, his hands went to her breasts and cupped them, his thumbs caressing her nipples. Again his mouth was on her throat.

"Ben . . . Ah, Ben . . ."

And this time as his mouth brushed hers, she pushed against him hungrily, unable to resist.

"You bastard," she murmured, tugging his shirt up over his head and throwing it aside, her need mixed with a burning anger. "Why did you go away? Why the fuck did you leave me here with him?"

* * *

Lehmann looked about him at the smoke-blackened ruins of the gutted school. Most of the children had died in their beds, but those who'd woken had found themselves locked in and the fatty remains of their corpses were heaped beside the blocked safety exits. He had seen sections of the camera records; had seen how the two copies had covered the school's entrance from overlooking balconies, picking off anyone who tried to help the screaming children, like machines functioning at prime efficiency. It had taken almost thirty of his men to subdue them, and eight had died in the process.

In all, over seven hundred had died here; elsewhere the news was just as bad. More than two thousand "berserker" outbreaks had been reported – more than twice the number in the Northern Enclave – and news of yet more was coming in by the moment.

It could no longer be denied. Things were falling apart. Local guard posts had been attacked throughout the levels and apart from a few key areas surrounding his major garrisons there had been an almost total breakdown in law and order. Even at the best of times his forces had enjoyed only minimal popular support, but now, it seemed, the mob was getting its own back on those minor officials who, before today, had held the power of life or death over them.

He turned to Soucek. "Is there any news from Pasek?" he asked, looking past him at the mobile communications centre parked just outside the entrance. Soucek crunched through the debris and lifted his mask.

"Nothing yet. But it's chaos out there. We're not even sure where Pasek is."

"So where are the two who are supposed to be looking after him??"

"Dead? Unless *they* got *him*."

Lehmann stared back at him, then shook his head. "I've a bad feeling about this. This is Pasek's chance. If he doesn't take it . . ."

"Master!"

Lehmann turned, facing his captain.

"What is it?"

"It's a broadcast, Master. I think you should see it."

He went through, his white boots smeared with ash. Soucek followed. Inside the mobile centre eight men were crowded round the screen. As Lehmann entered, they made room for him.

"Play it back," Lehmann said curtly, recognising Pasek's features. "Let's hear what the bastard has to say."

At once the image jumped. The screen went white. Music played. Music that was familiar only because Lehmann had heard it so often at Pasek's rallies for the faithful.

"Brothers," Pasek said, his face forming from the whiteness, his flesh glowing almost golden. "The day is here. The day of final judgement. Yes, it is time to prepare ourselves for the weighing of souls, for the great sifting of the worthy from the unworthy. And I, Earthly Son of the Most High Celestial Master of the Five Directions, am here to tell you what must be done to be among the worthy . . ."

Lehmann leaned forward, killing the image. He turned, meeting Soucek's eyes. "Kill him," he said simply. "Find out where he is and kill him for me, Jiri. I want that bastard's head on my desk before nightfall, understand me? I want that fucker nailed!"

* * *

Catherine sat on the sofa, draped in her emerald-green night silk, her flame-red hair tied back, her head tilted to one side as she fed the baby from her breast. Ben, stepping into the room, stopped, staring across at her.

In the softly-pearled lamplight her skin seemed almost transparent, like a sheen of ice over the bone. It had always been so, of course, but what had been pallid was now pellucid.

It was fifteen years since he'd last seen her. Then she had been little more than a girl. Nineteen and an arts student at Oxford. Now she was a woman of thirty-four and a mother.

Twice, he thought, remembering what she had said about the little girl she'd lost. *That too has made her brittle.*

She looked across at him and smiled, the child sucking healthily at her breast. "Do you remember that time you took me down below the City?"

He went across and sat, facing her. "I remember."

"Of course," she laughed, at peace with herself. "You *can't* forget, can you? You're incapable."

"Do you remember the bird?"

"In the Café Burgundy?" She nodded, suddenly more thoughtful. "I never dreamed . . ."

That you'd be caged? He looked about him at the opulence of the apartment. She was like a bird, a flame-haired hunting bird. But she'd let herself be trapped. Now why was that?

She looked back down at the child and smiled, like the Virgin Mother herself, yet there was a tightness in her features that had not been there back in her youth. Even so, he could still see what had moved him in her. There was still beauty in that face.

He closed his eyes and saw her as she'd been; saw her clear, as if she sat before him in that time, her skin unblemished, all lines of age removed. When he opened them again, she was watching him, her green eyes curious.

"I was remembering."

She looked away, a small movement in her face which for once he could not read.

"Why did you marry him?"

"Because he asked me," she said, not looking at him; then, as if she realised it sounded insufficient, "And because I wanted to."

"He's been good to you, then?"

Her quiet laughter told him all he needed to know. That and the hardness in her face.

"And the baby? Was that your idea?"

This time she turned her head, meeting his eyes. "I thought it might bring us closer."

"And did it?"

She looked back down at the child. She was sleeping now, sucking only fitfully in her sleep. "No. And yet it's something."

He looked away, his eyes returning to the folder he had noticed, there beneath the table. Standing, he went across and picked it up.

"Can I?" he asked, turning to her.

"If you want."

He sat, the folder in his lap, studying each painting intensely before he moved on. At the sketch of himself and Meg he stopped and looked at her.

"This is good. The best you ever did. It has life."

She was staring at him; her intensity for once almost matching his. "I wanted to kill you. Did you know that? I wanted to take a knife and stab you through the heart for what you did. I . . . ."

The baby stirred on the breast. She removed it gently from the nipple and covered herself.

He stared at her. "I'm sorry."

She stood, rocking the baby gently in her arms, making sure she was asleep, then carried her through into her room. A moment later she was back.

"Would you like a drink?"

"I . . ."

"We've done that," she said, almost sharply, as if angry with him.

He closed the folder. "What is it?"

"You. Just coming back like this. For fifteen years nothing, and then . . . What am I supposed to do?"

"Come with me? Back to the Domain?"

She stared at him, then shook her head. "It doesn't work like that, Ben. You can't just click your fingers and everyone comes running. That's how a child thinks."

"I'm serious. Come back with me."

"And the child?"

"Bring her with you."

Again she shook her head. He stood, setting the folder aside, then took her arms. "Look," he began, but he said no more. At that moment the wall screen behind him came alive. They both turned, surprised.

"Jesus . . ." he said softly.

"Who is it?" she asked, not recognising the urbane, middle-aged *Hung Mao* who stared down at them.

"It's DeVore!" Ben said, as the man began to speak. "It's Howard fucking DeVore!"

* * *

Karr stood at the back of the huge room, watching while a hundred different experts and technicians sat at their screens, scrolling the taped speech back and forth, analysing it in the minutest detail. Everywhere he looked he could see DeVore's face – or parts of it: his mouth, expanded to fill the screen, a single eye, the image of the pupil covered by a computer-generated grid.

"Well?" he asked after a moment, turning to Director Lung. "Have we any kind of consensus yet?"

The old Han turned to him and smiled apologetically. "It takes time, General Karr. Such precise analysis is a science. We are not *Wu* here."

"I understand," Karr said, keeping his impatience in check, "but time happens to be the one thing we don't have much of right now. That part in his speech about the sun and the stars . . . have we any trace on where that comes from?"

Lung turned and snapped his fingers. Behind him, one of his assistants sorted quickly through a file, then handed him a piece of paper. The old Han studied it a moment, then, smiling, answered Karr in a leisurely drawl.

"It appears that that part of DeVore's speech relates to proscribed writings. One of the banned poets."

"And?" The man's manner was infuriating to say the least. The very slowness of his speech lit a fuse in Karr's head.

The old man studied the paper again, then handed it to Karr.

Karr looked at it, then shrugged. "Coleridge . . . Ah yes, that was it . . . The sun's rim dips, the stars rush out; at one stride comes the dark."

He shivered, hearing again how DeVore had said that. *At one stride comes the dark . . .*

DeVore's ubiquitous appearance on every media channel had come as a real body-blow, just as they were beginning to get on top of things. It had been just the thing to set it all off again. Now there were riots throughout the levels. People were panicking – as if it were already over.

Which is, of course, DeVore's intention.

It was pure Sun Tzu. The great man had always argued that it was best never to fight a battle unless it was absolutely necessary. And what better way to prevent the necessity of conflict than to demoralise your enemy before a single blow had been struck? That was what DeVore was doing here. He was psyching them all out, trying to destroy their nerve. But he couldn't be allowed to win – not without a fight.

Karr turned to the Head of Department. "As soon as you have anything more, Master Lung, let me know."

Then, knowing time was against him, he hurried from the room, heading back for his office.

He had barely stepped through the door when his equerry rushed in and, bowing hurriedly, thrust a piece of paper into his hand. Karr glanced at it, then pointed to the screen on the far side of his office.

"Get him! *Now*!"

A moment later the screen lit up and the face of a young cadet officer appeared.

"What's this?" Karr said without preliminaries, waving the piece of paper at the screen. "What do you mean all of our near-space surveillance satellites are down? That's impossible!"

The young soldier swallowed. "No, sir. They're dead. Contact was lost eight minutes back. Right now we're blind."

"Are they destroyed?"

"We . . . we don't know, sir. Without physically checking . . ."

"Then *do* it! Send someone up to look!"

He cut contact and sat back, a cold certainty forming in him. This was it. This was the end. First the copies, then the face on their screens, and now this.

The sun's rim dips, the stars rush out; at one stride comes the dark.

He looked to his equerry. The young man stood there, staring at his General, his face openly afraid. Seeing it, Karr knew he had to do something, and fast.

"Okay, lad. Now listen. I want you to summon every officer of the rank of Colonel and above and I want them all here in my office within the next fifteen minutes, understand me? It's time we dealt with all this nonsense. Time we held a proper Council of War."

He saw how the boy straightened up; how his face lit with a sudden sense of purpose. Yet once he'd left the room, Karr felt his own spirits slump.

Marie . . . I ought to speak to Marie before it begins . . .

But there was no time. No time for anything now but war.

* * *

Sergey stumbled from the transit, then stood there in the empty corridor, swaying slightly, getting his bearings as the doors closed behind him and the lift began to descend.

Home, he thought, recognising the familiar wall-hangings, the tiny statue of the horseman that rested on the plinth beside the wall opposite. *I made it. I fucking made it . . .*

He shook himself and frowned. It was chaos out there in the levels. And if they got through the coming days he'd have that Steward's balls for turfing him out at such an ungodly hour. He had *never* been so insulted. *Never!*

He swallowed, feeling distinctly nauseous, then, turning to his right, began to stagger towards the apartment. He had got only halfway along the broad, dimly-lit corridor when the urge became insistent and, lurching to his right, he held on to the porcelain edge of the decorative plant trough and, doubled up, began to heave.

"There!" he said, laughing, then straightened, wiping his mouth on his sleeve. "Better out than in!"

For some reason that amused him and he began to giggle. But then he remembered. Remembered just *why* he'd got so drunk.

The thought sobered him. He spat bile, then turned and stumbled on, fumbling in his jacket pockets for his code-key.

"Shit!" he swore, coming to a halt. He must have dropped it back at the club, or on the way here. Still, Catherine would open up. He'd wake the bitch.

He looked up and frowned. The door was open. He could see into the apartment.

"Wha . . . ?" He stepped unsteadily across, then pushed the door open wide. The hallway was empty, but there was a light on in the living-room. He turned, closing the door quietly behind him, then, as quietly as he could, tiptoed exaggeratedly towards the living-room door.

He peeked inside, not certain what he'd find, but the room was empty. Then, as he stood there, holding on to the jamb, the baby began to cry.

"Fuck it!" he mumbled. "Where *is* the fucking woman?"

There was another noise beneath the baby's crying; something he couldn't quite make out. He turned, looking back into the darkened hallway, then went out, making his way along the wall towards her room.

He stood there, sniffing the air. The bitch! The fucking bitch! He knew that smell. She'd been having men in there while he was out! He staggered across and felt for the bed in the darkness, half stumbling over it. It was unmade, the sheets crumpled. He put out a hand, looking for confirmation of his fears . . . and found it in the dampness of the sheet.

He sat, nausea making him swallow hard.

"You bitch!" he muttered. "You fucking bitch!"

A sudden anger washed through him. So this was what she did while he was out. Well, fuck her – he'd make her pay for this!

He pulled himself up and staggered out, looking for her. As he came into the living-room again, she was standing across from him, framed by the kitchen doorway. The baby was still howling, but she seemed unaware of it. Her eyes were red, as if she'd been crying.

"You!" he said, pointing an accusing arm at her. Then, with a bellow, he launched himself at her.

She yelped and tried to get away but, drunk as he was, he was still too fast for her. Grabbing her hair he pulled her down savagely on to her knees, then leaned over her, putting his face almost into hers.

"Who was it? Who've you been screwing in my bed, you fucking bitch?"

She made to shake her head, but he tugged at it hard, making her cry out.

"It was Shepherd," she said, her eyes glaring at him venomously now.

He let her go, then staggered back. "Shepherd . . ." The name seemed to deflate him. He stood there, swaying, his eyes shocked. "Ben Shepherd?"

"That's right!" There was a pure hatred in her eyes now. "And he wasn't screwing me. We made love, Sergey . . ."

He swung his arm and felt his hand connect, hard.

"He's used you. Used you like the cheapest whore to get back at me!"

Her laughter stung him.

"*You*? You think he cares about *you*?" Holding her swollen jaw she glared up at him. "He came for *me*, Sergey. Not you. He came to take me back with him."

He swung again, knocking her down, then crouched over her, his hand raised. "I'll kill you! I'll see you dead before he touches you again!"

He drew his hand back and saw her flinch, then stood, backing off a pace, as if he'd finished with her. Then, with a savagery that surprised them both, he turned and kicked her in the stomach.

He stood over her, watching her gasp with pain, then leaned in, pointing at her, his fingertip directly under her nose. "You're dead, woman! You're fucking dead, hear me?"

Sergey moved back, trembling now, the thought of what had happened making the muscle beneath his eye twitch violently. He turned, looking back at the darkness of the doorway, and wiped his mouth, his eyes full of imagining. For a moment he was somewhere else, and Catherine, seeing that, reached up and, taking the heavy lamp from the table beside the sofa, pulled herself up.

"Wha . . . ?" he began to say, turning back towards her, but it was too late. As his face came round, the lamp caught him on the side of the head and shattered.

For a moment she stared at him where he lay, the blood bubbling from the deep gash in his skull, her hand out, her mouth open in shock. In a daze she went through into the baby's room and lifted her from the cot. Then, knowing there was nothing for her there, she began to walk, out of the room and down the darkened corridor, heading for the transit.

* * *

"What can you see?"

The pilot shifted in his seat then lifted his visor. "The satellite's there all right but . . . well, it's just dead. And from the infra-red readout it's cold as a piece of rock. It's as if it's been frozen."

He waited as his craft slowly drifted in an arc about the satellite, wondering what ground control would ask him to do next.

There was a click and then the disembodied voice sounded again. "Is there any obvious sign of tampering?"

He put his visor down again then readjusted the tracking cameras, trying to get as clear a view of the inert satellite as he could. *See for yourselves*, he'd have liked to have said, but audio was the only thing working right now. Someone was jamming all the other wavelengths.

"I can't see anything," he said, after a moment. *Then again, if whoever did this was any good at what they did – and there was no reason to assume they weren't – then there would be no sign. All it would take was a few bursts of accurate laser-fire and . . .*

"Oh, shit!"

"Pardon? Can you repeat that message?"

"I said . . ." He fell silent, watching as the ships peeled off – huge, saucer-shaped ships, as white as the autumn moon; hundreds of the fucking things, coming out of deep space like stones falling from a giant's hand.

"Oh shit! Oh fucking shit!"

* * *

DeVore stood on the edge of the sandstone outcrop, looking out across the rugged gorge of Olduvai as the great ships came down.

A gift of stones, he thought and laughed, remembering the time when he had sent Li Yuan a betrothal gift of three hundred and sixty-one white *wei ch'i* stones – stones carved from the bones of his victims, symbolising death.

Yes, and now for delivery on that promise.

Three hundred and sixty-one bone-white ships, sailing out of Charon, the ice-moon, Pluto's twin.

He laughed, watching them come down. Each ship a stone, and within each ship a hundred thousand copies of himself, cloned in the body factories of Charon – conjured from ice and chemicals and the structured dance of atoms: a vast army of the unborn.

He watched them march in lines of ten down the broad white ramps, forming up in the early morning heat, parading openly before the final battle; the cameras hovering overhead, letting the great world know just what had fallen on them from the darkness.

Olduvai . . . The significance of it had been lost, the truth of it buried beneath the Han's great Cities, but it was here, five million years ago, that Man had taken his first steps on his long journey towards the stars.

And towards her, he thought, turning to look at his companion.

In the glaring African light, Emily's pallor seemed an unnatural perfection. Towards this those ancient apes had striven. Towards this high peak of physical perfection.

He took her hand, examining it. Like Adam and his companion, he thought, grinning: only this had been grown not from Adam's rib, but from the severed finger of the original.

And where are you now, Emily Ascher? he wondered. *Are you still alive? Do you still burn with such a pure, fine flame?*

The only woman he had ever wanted.

He put the thought aside and looked toward his generals, gathered by his tent.

"Are you ready?" he asked, knowing the answer. Then, turning towards the great army that was gathered beneath him, he raised his arms and uttered the words he'd long prepared, knowing the young T'ang was watching him.

"Alas! alas! thou great city, thou Mighty City, Babylon! In one hour has thy judgement come."

CHAPTER 22

COPIES OF
SOME GREATER THING

Naked, the great T'ang stood before the mirror; last of the Seven, the One Man under Heaven, Son of the Celestial Emperor himself. He had washed and now he waited for his maids to dress him, perhaps for the final time, in the dragon robes of imperial yellow silk.

In his thirty-second year he had begun to fill out. Regular exercise had kept his muscles firm, his stomach trim, yet time had left its mark, even on him, in the lines about his eyes and mouth.

The cares of kingship, he thought and tried to smile, but it was impossible. Behind him his maids were sobbing as they went about their work, their faces wet with tears. Indeed the whole palace had a strange, funereal air about it. Servants and their families had been fleeing throughout the night, abandoning him.

Yes, and he had had to order his guards not to fire upon those who chose to run rather than face what Fate had ordered for them.

He nodded to his image, as if acknowledging a stranger. And maybe there was an element of truth in that. As a younger man he had often stood before the mirror, studying his own face, staring into his own eyes, asking himself questions. But lately?

He stepped up to the mirror and, placing the fingers of his left hand to the glass, met his own eyes, trying to look through into himself.

Do you still know who you are, Li Yuan? Are you still so sure about things? Or has the world eroded more than your trust in your fellow creatures?

He stared and stared, yet there was a wall, a barrier of consciousness he could not penetrate. He might look for ever and not see what he was searching for, for it was he himself who was hiding it, he who directed his eyes away from the dark corners where what he sought was hidden.

"*Chieh Hsia?*"

He drew his hand back, watching as the four moist circles where his fingertips had touched faded and disappeared, then looked to the maid who stood behind him.

"What is it, Sweet Fragrance?"

The young girl met his eyes in the glass, then quickly looked away, wiping her eyes with the back of her sleeve. "We are ready to dress you, *Chieh Hsia*. If you would come across?"

He sighed, then answered her softly, feeling a great compassion for her. "Of course."

Sweet Fragrance was only fifteen. She had not seen life, and now it was ending. By evening she could be dead.

He turned, then, on whim, drew her to him, holding her close and warm against him, and as he did his thoughts went out to his first wife, Fei Yen. He had tried to find her, or at least to get some news of her, but his efforts had come to naught. East Asia was in a state of constant turmoil as the Warlords fought for dominance, and there had been no word.

Where are you? he wondered, closing his eyes, pained that he would die without ever knowing what had befallen her. *Are you even still alive? You who caused me so much pain, yes, and yet gave me so much joy. And the boy? Is my son with you where you are? Are you some Warlord's concubine? Or did some peasant conscript rape you and gut you with his bayonet?*

Not that it mattered now. Not that anything mattered. He had seen those dreadful images from Olduvai. Forty million DeVores! He shuddered at the thought.

He released the girl, then went across and stood there, letting them dress him. And as each article of clothing was placed on him, he nodded inwardly, as if to say, "This is the last time this shall be done."

Finally two of them carried across the dragon robes, holding the silks out as he stepped into them. And as they buttoned them he felt the certainty of his situation harden in him.

This, then, was what my father dreamed, the night I was born. This is his vision – the City burning and his old friends dead, their children's bodies torn and bloody on the nursery floor. And darkness . . . darkness bubbling up into the brightly-lit levels.

He shuddered at the thought and gritted his teeth against the pain he felt remembering it, for that was the night he had killed his mother and robbed his father of all earthly joy.

It was not my fault.

Maybe not, but he did not *feel* that. He had never felt it. Impatient to come into this world, he had sent her from it. And all that had followed – *everything* – had stemmed from that.

"*Chieh Hsia?*"

He looked down. Sweet Fragrance was staring up at him. "Yes?"

"*Chieh Hsia* . . . why are you weeping?"

* * *

The last of them had gathered in the Great Hall, beneath the steps of the Throne. As Li Yuan stepped into the huge, high-ceilinged chamber, they knelt and bowed their heads, like a single creature, subservient to his will.

As he took his place above them on the dragon throne, he cast his eyes over those that had stayed. There were no more than four hundred in all – friends, courtiers and retainers. So few they seemed, huddled together between the great stone pillars, and yet he felt inordinately pleased to see so many familiar faces.

In the end this was all that remained. Friendship and loyalty. The rest meant nothing.

He lifted his chin proudly, recalling who he was – a Son of Heaven, last of the Seven who had once ruled the great empire of Chung Kuo – and saw how they responded to the gesture, pleased that he was their Lord.

"Kuei Jen," he called, looking to his son. "Come stand behind me."

The young man did as he was told, his father's shadow.

"Master Nan . . . the screen."

Down below, Nan Ho turned and instructed his assistant to lower the great screen. Slowly the lamps in the great hall faded, the glowing screen came down.

Olduvai. The images were from Olduvai.

He watched as the cameras panned across that mighty host, sensing the fear that rippled through the watching crowd below as they saw what had fallen out of the dark upon them. Only Pei K'ung seemed unafraid. She stood there at the foot of the steps, looking up at him, concerned, alone in all that crowd in not watching the screen.

He met her eyes briefly, then looked back at the screen, all hope, all spirit draining from him. "Look!" the images demanded, "Look and despair!"

He saw the great ships waiting on the far side of the plain, their hatches open, ready for embarkation, the fluttering pearl-white banners of the mighty army, and felt his stomach tighten.

"Are you afraid, Kuei Jen?"

The young man laughed softly. "I would be foolish to say no. That is some sight, neh, father? I know now how the enemies of Ch'in must have felt when the great Ch'in army took the field against them."

Li Yuan half turned and smiled at his son. This much, at least, had been a blessing: to have had so fine a son.

"That may be so, but we would do well to remember what happened at Ch'ang P'ing, neh, my son?"

Kuei Jen bowed his head, chastened. At Ch'ang P'ing, in 259 BC, the army of the kingdom of Chao had been starved into surrender by the King of Ch'in, the First Emperor's father. In a gesture of the most supreme barbarity, the King had ordered that the army of Chao be exterminated and a great mountain of heads had been piled up on the plain of the battle. Four hundred thousand men had been executed that day and Chao deprived of every able-bodied man it had.

And now history, it seemed, was to repeat itself. For one thing was certain. DeVore would spare not one of them. They must fight or die like curs.

There was a knocking at the far end of the Hall and then the great doors swung open. Li Yuan turned and looked. It was his Major, Haavikko. As the man straightened up from bowing, Li Yuan beckoned him across.

"What is it, Major?"

Haavikko knelt and touched his head to the stone flags, then looked up at his Master.

"There is news from Odessa, *Chieh Hsia*. Li Min's army has withdrawn."

There was a gasp, then a murmur of urgent, whispered voices from the crowd.

"Withdrawn?" Li Yuan leaned forward, unable to believe what he had heard.

"Yes, *Chieh Hsia*. It seems . . ."

"*Chieh Hsia!*"

Li Yuan got to his feet, staring past Haavikko at the newcomer. It was Karr. The big man stood there, getting his breath, a scroll held up in one hand.

"What is it?"

"It has come, *Chieh Hsia!* A message from Li Min. He sues for peace, and for an alliance against our common enemy, DeVore."

The silence that fell was profound. Li Yuan stood there a moment, astonished. He had assumed Lehmann was in league with DeVore. Why, the men had been allies! Trembling, he went down the steps and, bidding Haavikko rise, walked over to Karr and took the paper from him, reading it through. He turned, handing it to Nan Ho who had come across.

"It cannot be," Li Yuan said, shaking his head. "Peace, certainly. I'll agree to peace. But the rest . . ." He met his Chancellor's eyes. "How can I possibly ally myself with him? For ten years he has been my mortal enemy. To embrace him . . ." He shuddered. "The men I've lost, the loyal friends . . . It would be a betrayal."

"You have no choice," Pei K'ung said, stepping up and taking his arm, forcing him to turn and face her. "You must do this, husband. You *must* or there is no hope."

He met her eyes briefly, then looked away, troubled. "Perhaps . . . But I must have time to think."

"Then think. But don't take long." She pointed up at the screen. "See. He is loading his armies back on board their ships. Soon they will fly north to meet us. So think hard but think fast, Li Yuan, for you must decide. Before the god of Hell descends on us."

He stared at her, then, knowing she was right, nodded and turned to Karr. "General Karr . . . send a messenger. Tell Li Min . . . tell him I shall let him know within the hour."

* * *

Fu Chiang had fled, escaping the assassin's blade by hours, yet the people of his great City – a city he had wrested by cunning and the force of arms from his fellow Mountain Lords – had come out on to the sandstone cliffs to witness with their own eyes the host that had gathered on the plain near Olduvai. In awe they stared as phalanx after phalanx of massive soldiers – seven, maybe eight *ch'i* in height – marched aboard the ships, their uniformity of appearance as much as their massive size sending a ripple of chill apprehension through the watching crowd.

There was a strange and eery silence to the scene, a stillness such as might happen in a vast airless jar, and then a trumpet blew, deafeningly loud.

A great gasp of fear greeted the apparition in the sky above the ships. It was a horseman, a giant horsemen almost two *li* in height, dressed totally in white, its horse as pale as snow. In its hand it grasped a bow.

The trumpet blew again, making the watchers clasp their ears in pain.

A bright red horse appeared beside the first, its rider – his face cowled – dressed in vermilion silks, a broad sword in his hand.

Again the trumpet blew.

This time it was a black horse. It reared proudly, its black-cloaked rider holding a set of scales.

Once more the trumpet sounded.

And finally, a pale horse, mounted by a white-cloaked skeleton.

DeVore, watching from his vantage point, smiled. The crowd was running now, screaming, trampling each other down to get away, while above them the air rustled with the presence of the four gigantic figures.

He turned. Pasek, who had arrived no more than twenty minutes back, was on his knees, his mouth open, his eyes staring in wonder. Behind him, those of his acolytes who had made the journey with him did the same.

"You have done well," DeVore said quietly, putting out his right hand so that Pasek might kiss the black iron ring that rested on the knuckle of his index finger. "You have laid down a path of fire for me."

As Pasek grasped his hand and kissed the ring fervently, DeVore smiled inwardly. It was no lie. Pasek had sown the seed – had planted these startling images in the minds of friend and foe alike – and now he, Howard DeVore, would reap the harvest.

The battle is already won, he thought, retrieving his hand, then turning to watch as his fleet lifted slowly from the plain. *All the stones are mine, while my enemies . . .* He laughed, a cruel, unfeeling laughter that broke finally into a high cackle of triumph. *My enemies play with an empty pot!*

In the air above, the horsemen began to turn, rising into the pure blue of the sky, leading on the pure white circles of his ships as they began their journey north to the coast.

And at his back he could feel the dark wind blowing, cold and pure, coursing through him with a silent, steady pressure, streaming like an unseen tide of photons from the endless blackness at the core of him.

The game had begun.

* * *

"That face . . . that fucking face!"

The man swung the lamp, smashing the screen, then stood back as it popped and sputtered into blackness.

Lehmann, standing in the corridor outside the room, nodded and walked on quickly. He understood. Everywhere he went people were destroying the screens. He had destroyed more than a hundred himself. Even so, DeVore's face still followed him wherever he went – awaiting him in silent rooms and at intersections, there on every new screen he encountered.

The purest form of solipsism, he thought, his gun searching the intersection before he hurried on. *That need to fill the world with copies of himself. It was the ultimate in xenophobia: not just a hatred of other races but of otherness itself. Was that how God had started – filling the pristine world with copies of himself?*

He stopped momentarily, listening. Most of these levels had been abandoned, but there were still some of Pasek's men about. He took three slow paces backward and peeked inside. Another screen – DeVore's face speaking to the empty room.

DeVore was jamming all visual communications channels and beaming down his own programmes; replacing that great multiplicity of images that characterised the levels with the single image of his face.

Or so it had been this last hour. That face . . . murmuring that awful litany of Last Things, Pasek's "Book".

He hurried on. His ship had been brought down short of his destination – by one of his own gunners, no doubt – but that was the least of his problems right now. Sofia garrison lay up ahead. That at least should be safe. But he was growing anxious now, afraid in case he should get there and find it had all fallen apart while he'd been making his way across.

The last he'd heard his men had been deserting by the thousand, abandoning their posts. Pasek's declaration for DeVore had been more damaging than he'd possibly imagined. For once Soucek had been right. He had underestimated the power of the religious impulse. He had thought it simply another addiction, like drugs and sex. But he'd been wrong.

And if Li Yuan says no?

Then it was over. Alone he could do nothing. Alone he could not stand against DeVore. Even so, he would fight him to the end. For there was no other choice. He knew DeVore. If he fled, DeVore would track him down. Only his death – the death of them all, perhaps; every last autonomous being on the planet – would satisfy that madman.

He slowed, the gate in sight now, the final intersection just ahead.

It did not matter that he'd been careful all these years. All of his patient work meant nothing now. In less than two days DeVore had destroyed it all. Yet strangely it wasn't bitterness he felt, or disappointment, but a curious excitement. The kind a gambler feels.

It was only now he realised how far he had strayed from his intended path. Only now – with DeVore's reminder – did he begin to understand. He had let himself become a king; acting as a king, *thinking* as a king. He had forgotten his original intention – had let that pure flame of hatred for the system gutter and die in him. But DeVore . . .

He stopped, looking across at an unbroken screen, seeing his old Mentor's face staring back at him, and smiled. DeVore, at least, was pure. DeVore had not forgotten.

There was no doubting it. He admired the man. Admired his style, his ability not merely to plan but to carry out such long-term, sweeping plans; his skill for the long game. But he could not let admiration cloud his judgement. He had no illusions. DeVore was no friend of his. It was either/or now – him or DeVore. For there was no room on this world for them both.

One more corridor, he thought, beginning to run, his spirits strangely lifted by the challenge that lay ahead. Whatever the odds against him, he would fight on, and not merely because there was no other choice, but because he would bow his head to no man.

No, nor to the copy of a man.

* * *

The guard stopped at the bottom of the road, beside a low, white-walled cottage with shuttered windows, and pointed to the white-painted gate at the side.

Catherine stared at him, her eyes questions.

"Go on," he said, bowing politely but anxious to get back, then waved a hand at her, gesturing that she should go through. "The Mistress knows you're coming. Go round. There's a door at the side."

She made to say something more, but he had turned away and was making his way hurriedly up the curve of hill, disappearing after a moment between the white-washed cottages. She sighed then looked down at the sleeping child in her arms. Now that she was here she felt like turning back. It had been a mistake. She should never have come.

Turning, she looked at the gate. Like everything here it was strange, dreamlike. The smells, the sounds, the way the air moved on the skin. It was like being brushed by hungry ghosts.

She shivered then reached out, trying to open the gate, feeling the wooden frame judder beneath her hand, resisting her attempts. She peered over it, then, finding the catch, lifted it.

There, she thought, surprised by how fast her heart was beating. *As easy as that.*

She looked up, smiling, pleased with herself, then saw her. Meg. It had to be Meg. Despite the years she recognised her.

"You came," Meg said. "I wondered if you would. He said you wouldn't. He said you'd stay inside."

Catherine swallowed, feeling awkward. "And you?"

"I thought you'd come. He usually gets what he wants. But come through. You look like you could do with a drink."

"Do I?"

Meg smiled, her eyes sympathetic. "Is it bad in there?"

She nodded. It was terrible. Worse than she could ever have imagined. If she hadn't had help . . .

Meg came across and, unexpectedly, took her arm, looking down at the sleeping child. "Hey . . . it's all right now. You're safe here. Both of you. All that . . ." She looked up past her at the massive wall of whiteness that began beyond the hill's crest. "All that's *inside*."

Meg put her arm about her shoulder then, turning, led her down the stone-paved path and up two steps, into a kitchen that was filled with sunlight and smelled of beeswax and flowers.

"This is all so . . . *strange*," she said, letting Meg seat her on a wheel-backed wooden chair, then watched as the other woman filled a copper kettle from the tap at the sink. "I didn't know."

"No." The look of sympathy was back. "Your face . . . you want me to see to that?"

Catherine reached up and touched her cheek, then winced. It was very tender. She looked at Meg and nodded. Meg smiled, then went over to one of the cupboards and, reaching up, got down a wooden box marked with a red-painted cross. Setting it down on the table, she opened the lid and began to search through the jumble of things within.

"He didn't forget you, you know."

"Forget me?" Catherine stared at her, a clear memory of the first time she'd met Meg coming back to her. Then she'd seen her with jealous eyes, thinking her Ben's lover; unaware she was his sister. She had been wrong, and at the same time right.

She looked down, wondering if Ben had mentioned what had happened between them. Whether now as then, he told his sister everything. But something stopped her asking.

Meg looked up, setting a tube of ointment and some gauze to one side, then smiled at her again. "The picture you painted . . . you know, the one of Ben. The one you left in his apartment. It's upstairs, on the wall."

Catherine stared at her, surprised. *He'd kept that?* She shivered, not from cold, but from a sense of displacement. Sitting there, it was like she couldn't wake. It was like . . . well, like the "shell" Ben had made her experience that time, so real and yet unreal. Totally unreal.

"Your daughter's very pretty," Meg said, smiling at her.

"Her name is Sasha, I . . . ." She smiled. All of the anxiety she had been feeling had gone, she realised. "You aren't angry with me, are you? I mean . . . about Ben."

"Angry?" She laughed. "God, no. It'll be nice to have some decent company around. Now . . . turn your head slightly towards the light, so I can see what I'm doing."

* * *

She opened the door quietly and stepped inside. There was a long casement window to her right. Beneath it a broad wooden table was crowded with all manner of things – a part-sculpted clay head, an oddly-shaped piano keyboard, some sketches, pots of paints, brushes, scalpels and rags, and, in a chaotically-disordered pile, a stack of old folders labelled in Ben's precise hand. Ben himself had his back to her, working on a canvas. For a moment she stared out of the window, still surprised by how beautiful the valley was, how strange it felt to be outside the City. It was all so different, so frighteningly, confusingly different. No wonder Ben had seemed strange when she'd first met him; no wonder he'd seemed out of place back there in the levels.

She looked back at him, then took two silent steps, moving to the left so that she could see the canvas better. It was a huge thing and took up most of the wall on that side of the room.

It was a picture of the valley – of the Domain – but changed, horribly transformed. In the top half of the canvas all seemed normal. Sunlight bathed the valley, creating a sense of great repose. Birds nested in the branches of the ash trees, and a swan glided on the golden, sunlit water. She could see the cottage to the right of the canvas, the tree – the same young oak she could glimpse from the window – just beneath it on the slope. Yet there, beneath it all, was a second world, so different from the first as to make its normality appear sinister, a mask to what was really real.

There, in the centre of the picture, the earth had cracked and the water fell through a thin crust of darkness into what seemed like a vast flame-lit cavern. And as it fell, the water changed. Its vivid blue became a deep yellow. Its smooth liquid flow suddenly, violently fragmented – as if its very atomic properties had changed – tiny splinters of bright yellow glass scattering in a shower of exploding crystal on to the rocks below. The effect was startling.

She took a step towards it, feeling a ripple of fear run down her spine. It was the dance of death. To the far left of the cavern, a tall, emaciated figure led the dance, its skin as pale as glass, its bare arms lithely muscled, the long legs stretched taut like a runner's. Its body was facing to the left – to the west and the darkness beyond – but its horse-like, shaven head was turned unnaturally on its long neck, staring back dispassionately at the naked host that followed, hand in hand, down the path through the trees.

In its long, thin hands Death held a flute, the reed placed to its lipless mouth. From the tapered mouth of the flute spilled a flock of tiny blackbirds, the cruel rounded eyes like tiny beads of milky white as they fell on to the host below, pecking at eye and limb.

In the very centre of the cavern, beneath the great gash in the earth, the settling crystal had formed a sluggish flow – like the flow of glittering lava. She recognised the allusion. These were the Yellow Springs, beneath which, the Han claimed, the dead had *their* domain, *ti yu*, the "Earth prison".

So bleak it was. So hopeless those forlorn and forward-staring figures. A scene of utter torment, and no release – no sign of simple human compassion.

She shivered, watching him lean towards the canvas to make the tiniest of changes to one of the figures.

"It's called 'The Feast of the Dead'", he said quietly.

"It's extraordinary," she said. *Yes, and horrible, and frightening and . . . and beautiful, all at the same time.* "Was it a dream?"

"Yes," he said. "But not one of mine. I saw this once. Or a version of it. Do you remember? I told you about it."

She shrugged. If he had, she didn't recall it.

"The Oven Man," he said, as if that were the key that would unlock the memory. "He painted this with ash."

It meant nothing to her.

"Well, he'll be busy tonight, neh?" He turned, then frowned at her. "Where's the child?"

"Meg's looking after her."

"Ah . . ."

She watched him, surprised by how calm he was, how untouched by events. "It's ending," she said. "The world is ending, Ben."

His eyes were cool, unmoved by her words. "You don't think I know? We Shepherds have been awaiting this for centuries!" He turned slightly, looking back at the canvas, then laughed quietly. "When things break down, we artists forge new links. We make sense of it all. That's our purpose."

He turned back, staring at her, the full intensity of his gaze bearing down on her, then, beckoning her closer, he offered her the brush. "Come . . . add your own figure to the dance."

* * *

Sampsa crept slowly down the hallway, then, kneeling beside the open doorway, looked into the room.

His grandfather lay there, propped up on the cushions, completely still, his hairless, skull-like head turned towards the window and the sea.

One quarter of his genetic make-up had come from the old man. One quarter of all he was. Slowly, like a fox creeping through the grass towards a chicken pen, he crawled into the room, making his way to the foot of the bed.

He could hear the old man's breathing, smell that strange, musty smell that seemed to cling to him. Carefully he raised his head, looking over the carved wooden foot of the huge bed.

The old man's head looked like something that had been carved in jest. Those features which, in the portrait in the hall, created a sense of rock-like strength, now seemed merely ludicrous, the chin too wide, the nose too long for the collapsed bone-structure of the face.

The skin itself seemed stretched over the bone, like animal hides over a nomad's tent, its surface blotched and yellowed, blighted here and there by tufts of coarse ice-grey hair.

Slowly he moved round, creeping towards where his grandfather's hand lay on top of the sheet, its gleaming gold extending to the leather pad at the shoulder. Sampsa stared at it a moment. It was easy to imagine that the old man's body was slowly being turned from flesh to gold; that he would come back in the evening and the whole of the old man's chest and head would be made of the same bright, gleaming metal.

"Sampsa?"

Tolonen's head turned the slightest amount, those watery-grey eyes still fixed upon the distant sea.

"Yes, grandpa?"

"Ah . . ." The old man's mouth formed the suggestion of a smile. For a time he was silent, then he gave a little cough. The fingers of his hand flexed, like a machine coming to life. "Come closer, boy."

He stood, stepping to his grandfather's side, careful not to block his view. From this close the smell of the old man was much stronger. It was like the smell of old cupboards, of drawers that had been kept locked for years, their contents slowly rotting in the darkness.

"What do you see, grandpa?"

"See?" The voice was like the wind whispering through the treetops. The old man made a sound that might have been either laughter or discomfort; he couldn't tell which. "I see old friends. Li Shai Tung. Klaus Ebert. Young Vittorio Nocenzi. They're out there, waiting for me."

Sampsa turned and looked, but there was nothing; only an old man's imaginings. Turning back, he reached down and laid his hand against the old man's palm. The metal was soft and warm – not metal at all, he realised, but something that resembled it.

Looking back at the old man's face he saw Tolonen was watching him.

"Something's happening," the old man said, his voice a sigh. "I can feel it." Something of the old strength flickered briefly in those eyes, then vanished, like a fish slipping back into the depths. "What is it, boy? What's happening?"

It's the old world, grandpa, he wanted to say. *It's dying. Just as you are dying. And the new is being born. That's what you feel. The death-pangs of the old and the birth-pangs of the new.*

"It's nothing, grandpa," he said, feeling the old man's attention slip from him, his eyes returning to the sea.

But it was true. New blood was coming into the world.

Sampsa drew his hand back, then, careful not to make a sound, he backed slowly from the room.

And in his head, he heard the other singing.

* * *

Tom sat on the wall overlooking the cottage, singing softly to himself. He had seen the woman come down the road with the soldier; had seen her go inside with his mother and, a while later, climb the stairs and go to the end room where his father worked. That had been an hour ago. Now he saw them come out from the shadow on the other side of the cottage and walk down the path towards the bay.

Clouds were forming high overhead and there was a sense of heaviness in the air. A storm was coming. He could feel it on his skin.

He watched the walking couple for a moment, then jumped down, running towards the cottage. Inside he stopped, listening but hearing nothing. Only the regular tick of the grandfather clock in the hallway.

He went on, past mute screens that showed the same unfamiliar face – the face of a middle-aged man with near black hair and cool green eyes – then made his way up the stairs. There he paused, staring at the painting of his father. Instinctively he made the connection. The woman who had come . . . *she* had painted this.

He hurried on, padding along the polished wooden boards, his bare feet making no sound. The door to the end room was open. He could see the painting there. But that was not where he was headed. Halfway along he stopped, trying the door to his right. It was locked, but that was no problem. He took the skeleton key from the pocket of his shorts and slipped it into the lock. A moment later he was inside. It was dark, the curtains drawn. The screen on the desk – like all the screens – contained the face.

Tom glanced at it, then climbed into his father's chair, pulling himself in closer to the desk. Then, closing his eyes, he placed his hands upon the keyboard.

Sampsa? Can you hear me? What's happening? What are we waiting for?

At once he felt himself on the island, far to the north, staring out through Sampsa's eyes. The sea . . . he was high up and looking out across the sea again.

Something's happening, Sampsa answered. *That face. His name's DeVore. He's brought a great army here to Chung Kuo from the edge of the System. Copies, they are. My father . . .*

He stopped abruptly. Someone was calling from the house behind him. Sampsa turned, looking. It was his father. He had thrown the window to his study open and was leaning out.

"Sampsa! Sampsa! Come quickly!"

Tom's eyes flicked open. *The screen*, he said silently, talking to Sampsa across the miles. *The image on the screen has changed.*

The face was gone. In its place was a black screen. Or almost black. At the top right a circle of white flickered fitfully, like a full moon obscured behind thick, fast-moving cloud. As he watched a tiny figure formed at the right-hand side of the screen – a white stick-man no bigger than his little finger. Above the hollow circle of its head three tiny, glowing spheres orbited like atoms.

Slowly, almost indiscernibly, the figure began to walk. Tom closed his eyes. At once the image of a second screen filled his head – the one Sampsa was staring at in his father's study.

What does it mean? Sampsa asked. But before Tom could even frame a thought, a voice sounded in the room where Sampsa stood: a deep, rich-sounding voice of great intelligence.

"Kim . . ." it boomed. "It's been a long time since we talked. Sit down. It's time I told you what's been happening."

* * *

"It is no good, *Chieh Hsia*," Nan Ho said, looking up from the inert keyboard. "I can get nothing but this . . ."

DeVore's face stared back at them from the screen, supremely confident, as if he'd already won.

Li Yuan sighed. He had hoped to bring Kim and Ben together – to use his two best minds to find an answer – but it was no use. DeVore was jamming everything. Everything except the short-wave radio bands.

He turned, looking to Karr. "All right, Gregor. Send someone to Lehmann. Tell him the answer is yes."

Karr bowed. "Perhaps I ought to go, *Chieh Hsia*. He knows me."

"You know where he is?"

"The last we heard he was heading towards his garrison in Sofia. If he's there we could arrange a meeting somewhere between."

"Odessa?"

Karr smiled, aware of the irony in his Master's voice.

"Odessa, then," he answered, coming smartly to attention. "I shall go to him myself."

* * *

Li Yuan stood on the wall, watching Karr's cruiser disappear into the haze of the south, then turned, looking at his son.

Kuei Jen had really blossomed this past year. The lanky youth of twelve months back had become a young man, broad of shoulder and thick of arm. But it was not merely in his outward form that he had changed. In the last year he had matured immensely, throwing off the last vestiges of childishness. Lo Wen, his tutor, acknowledging this, now bowed his head respectfully to the Young Master, as he called him. The transformation was complete: the boy had become a prince.

Yes, Li Yuan thought sadly, *but will he ever take my place?*

It was strange. When he looked back over the years that had passed since his own father's death, it was with the feeling of a man who had begun to run downhill only to find the slope too steep, his footing uncertain. Now he was tumbling helplessly towards a sheer drop.

"Father?"

He smiled at his son. "It is all right, Kuei Jen, I . . ."

His hand, searching absently in the pocket of his silks, had fastened upon the tiny cloth bag Nan Ho had given him earlier.

"Here," he said, taking the bag out and handing it to Kuei Jen. "I want you to have these."

Kuei Jen took the bag and, untying the string at its neck, shook the contents out into his open palm. He looked back at his father, frowning. "What are they?"

Li Yuan took one of the eight tiny black figures and held it up, studying it in the daylight. "They were a gift from the Marshal's daughter. She gave them to me on the day of my betrothal to Fei Yen, my first wife. My father tried to keep the matter from me, but I found out. There were two gifts that day. The first was from DeVore – a *wei chi* set."

"But I thought he was your enemy, father."

"He was, even then. It was the stones, you understand. There were no black stones, only white. And the stones themselves . . . they were all carved from human bone."

"Ah . . ." Kuei Jen looked down at the figures in his palm. "And these?"

Li Yuan returned the eighth figure to his son's palm. "These are the eight heroes with blackened faces." He smiled thoughtfully. "White for death, black for honour. My father, your grandfather, was delighted with the gift. He felt that the bad luck of DeVore's gift was balanced – *nullified* – by the good luck of these. But now . . ." The smile faded. "Now DeVore is back. And once again he brings his gift of stones."

Kuei Jen nodded, then looked down at the eight delicately carved figures. "Which one is Pao Kung?"

Pao Kung was the Chinese Solomon, the epitome of wisdom. Li Yuan searched among them a moment, then picked out the one he'd taken earlier. "This one. See. His baldness is meant to denote his wisdom."

"Ah, so *that* is why . . ."

Kuei Jen gestured towards his father's full head of hair and laughed. "Maybe it's time to shave our heads and call on the spirit of Pao Kung for aid?"

"Perhaps," Li Yuan answered, saying nothing of his vain attempts to contact Kim and Ben. And yet he smiled, his spirits raised. It had been a long time since he'd looked at Jelka's gift; a long time since he'd held one of these tiny figures in his hand. When Nan Ho had given them to him this morning he had not understood, but now he did. Somehow the balance would be made, DeVore's advantage cancelled out.

"*Chieh Hsia!*"

He turned at the urgency of the summons. Nan Ho stood at the top of the steps that led up to the wall, his hair dishevelled, his eyes alarmed. Seeing him thus, Li Yuan felt all hope burn away, like a mist touched by the first rays of the winter sun.

"What is it?" he said soberly.

"You must come, *Chieh Hsia*. The screen . . ."

He hurried down, letting Nan Ho lead him through to the room where they had set up their headquarters. A group of men were clustered about the screen. As he entered, they fell back, letting him approach.

Li Yuan stepped closer then stopped and gave a tiny moan.

It was himself. Or, rather, it was his copy – his *ching* – taken from the place where it had been kept, awaiting his death. The *ching* stood before the camera, indistinguishable from himself, its silks torn, its hands bound with coarse rope, its eyes downcast, defeated as it spoke to the watching billions.

"It is over," it said, unable, it seemed, to meet the camera's eye; feigning shame at its fate. "You must submit to your new Lord and put down your arms. The Mandate of Heaven is broken."

He shuddered as the image froze and then replayed from the beginning.

"*Aiya*," he said softly, feeling the last tiny flicker of hope die in him; seeing how even those most loyal to him now looked at him with eyes of pity and regret. Yes, even Nan Ho. This . . . this *pretence*, had been the final blow. Nothing now remained.

"Is Karr still in range?" he asked, looking to his Chancellor.

"I think so, *Chieh Hsia*."

"Then call him back. There is no point in meeting Lehmann now. It is over. This . . . there is nothing after this."

"*Chieh Hsia* . . ." Nan Ho made to obey, but a voice from the doorway made him halt and turn.

"Hold a moment, Master Nan! We are not beaten yet."

Pei K'ung strode into the room and faced her husband. "What is this, Yuan? Are you to let this showman beat you? Are you to meekly bow before this Prince of Lies and Illusions?" She shook her head. "No. You must act at once to counter this. You must send out messengers to all your garrisons to let them know what has happened. Master Nan . . ." She turned to the Chancellor again. "Bring paper, ink and brushes. My husband must write to his commanders. And Yuan . . . remember who you are."

He stared at her a moment, then bowed his head, honouring her. Looking about him at his men, he drew himself up to his full height. "You heard. Let's get to work at once. The Mandate is not broken. Nan Ho, do as my wife requests. Bring paper, ink and brushes. And Haavikko . . ."

The Major came to attention. "Yes, *Chieh Hsia*?"

"Prepare the imperial cruiser. We leave for Odessa within the hour."

* * *

Odessa was a gutted shell. Its outer walls concealed a scene of utter devastation. More than a hundred thousand had died defending the great Black Sea fortress and pieces of their charred bones littered the landing platform, cracking underfoot as Karr paced back and forth, awaiting his Master's ship. Across from him, Lehmann waited patiently beneath his banner, his lieutenant, Soucek, at his side.

"You're certain he's coming?" Lehmann asked tonelessly.

"He'll be here," Karr answered, glaring at his one-time enemy. "My Master is a man of his word."

If there was any implied criticism in that, Lehmann chose to ignore it. He walked across.

"You received my gift?"

Karr nodded. "You knew I couldn't keep it."

"That was your choice. It was not a bribe. You're not a man to bribe . . . or flatter, come to that."

Karr stared back at him, conceding nothing.

"I would have beaten you," Lehmann continued, "in time."

"I know."

"And yet you remained loyal to Li Yuan. Why?"

Karr looked past him at Soucek. "Why does *your* man stay loyal? Why does any man?"

"Foolishness?"

Karr was silent. Lehmann studied him a moment, then turned away.

"We'll not beat DeVore," he said, so casually that it was almost as if he didn't care.

"Maybe not," Karr answered, looking out to the north-east, his eyes searching the cloudless sky.

"And yet we have to fight, neh?" Lehmann laughed; a cold, strange sound. "We have to fight because if we don't he'll annihilate us. Oh, he'll annihilate us anyway, but a man must have the satisfaction at least to know he was a man and not an insect."

Karr turned back. Both Soucek and Lehmann were watching him. "I shouldn't be here," he said quietly. "I should be with my family."

"Then why aren't you?"

Lehmann came back to him, stopping very close, looking up into his face. "Just why *are* you doing this, Gregor Karr? After all you've witnessed. After all your Master's done. The Wiring Project. The torturing of good men and women – people who shared your ideals. Ah yes, and the deals. The pandering to greedy, selfish men. Your friend, Kao Chen . . . *he* saw the shape of things. That's why he got out, isn't it? But you . . . you stayed inside. You *served*. Why was that?"

Karr shrugged. *A sense of duty? Of loyalty? . . . Simple habit? Or was it because he'd still too much pride in himself as a fighter to get out – to become a man of peace and till the earth like Chen?*

Pride . . . or stupidity.

He looked up. There had been movement in the two gun turrets that still worked. They had swivelled, tracing an incoming. He strode to the edge of the platform and stopped, shielding his eyes, unconscious, it seemed, of the two *li* drop only a step from where he stood.

"He's here," he said, seconds before the gun commander confirmed it. "I said he'd come."

"As you said, your Master is a man of his word."

Karr turned, frowning, trying to make out what Lehmann meant by that; but the White T'ang's face was blank, unreadable. *Inscrutable*, he thought, thinking for the first time how much that face, despite its superficial differences, resembled his Master's. Then he turned back, awaiting his Master's arrival.

* * *

They had shared a cup of wine; now the two great men embraced, sealing the compact between them. The paper lay on the campaign table to one side, the ink still drying, the T'ang's great seal lying beside Lehmann's on the cushion.

It was done. The Cities were reunited. At least, until he came. Until DeVore's great fleet swept them into the cold northern sea.

Karr looked down, a bitter taste in his mouth. He had never thought to see the day.

Chih yao yu heng hsin t'ieh ch'u mo ch'eng chen, he thought, recalling the banners that had hung before Lehmann's gate that time he'd gone to meet with him.

If only there is persistence, even an iron pillar will be ground into a needle.

Well, so it was. Lehmann's persistence had certainly ground them down. Unfortunately for him, that same persistence which had made his enemy, Li Yuan, so weak had likewise weakened his own forces. Both now were vulnerable.

How DeVore must be laughing now, Karr thought sourly. *Laughing as a jackal laughs, watching his prey fall from exhaustion.*

He sighed. They had learned the lesson far too late – that even persistence can mean nothing in the face of Fate.

"General Karr . . ."

He glanced up, meeting Lehmann's eyes, then looked to his Master. But Li Yuan merely nodded, his eyes instructing Karr to listen.

Lehmann stood before him, handing him a scrolled paper. "As from this moment you are in command of our joint forces. We shall draw up a plan of action which you shall carry out on our behalf."

Again he looked to Li Yuan.

"It is what we have agreed," Li Yuan said quietly. "We feel there is no better man to lead our forces."

"But *Chieh Hsia* . . ."

"Please, Gregor. Do what we say. Little time remains and we must make the most of it. First we must devise some means of communicating between our garrisons, then . . ."

The blare of a siren drowned out his words. All turned, staring to the south. A ship was coming in fast.

Karr ran across, climbed the steps of the turret and leaned inside.

"Who is it?" he yelled over the siren's wail.

In answer the gun commander pointed to the screen. It was blank, the gun-controls dead. Karr climbed inside and, pushing the two men aside, tried to reactivate the control panel, but it was no use. He hammered it with his fists, then scrambled out again. He could see the thing clearly now. It was less than half a *li* away, screaming in low over the plain to the south-west.

"Down!" he yelled, knowing it would do no good. "The bastard's jammed the guns!"

Li Yuan looked to Lehmann, expecting a trick, but Lehmann seemed just as surprised. He turned back, frowning, then strode across to Karr and stood beside him, facing the incoming ship.

"Let it come!" he shouted.

They waited, expecting the flash of a missile, the sudden explosive warmth of detonation. Instead the craft flashed over them, the sharp crack of it breaking the sound barrier making everyone duck – even Lehmann.

"What the . . . ?"

The sirens fell silent. Slowly the craft turned in the air, slowing in a great arc that brought it round to the front of the fortress once again.

"Is that him, do you think?" Li Yuan asked, looking to Lehmann who had come to stand beside him.

Lehmann shrugged, then patted the gun at his belt. "If it is, I'll shoot the bastard where he stands, copy or no copy. I'll have *that* satisfaction."

Li Yuan smiled. "You're sure he'll send a copy, then?"

"Oh, he'd not come himself. Not DeVore. He's the Puppet Master himself, that one."

They stepped back, under their banners as, slowly, the craft came down, settling between their own.

As the engines whined down towards silence, Karr stepped out, facing the hatch, and drew his gun. Now that the moment had come, he understood why he was here. This was not for Li Yuan. No, nor for that callous bastard Lehmann. This was for Marie and his girls. For them.

I killed you once, he thought, *and I shall kill you again. However many times it takes. However many copies you send against me.*

The hatch bolts fired, the door hissed slowly open.

Karr raised his gun.

"Gregor Karr . . . is that you?"

The man who stepped out into the light was not DeVore. He wore black, as DeVore might have worn, and his hair was shaven close to his skull in a distinctly military style that DeVore might easily have affected, but it was not DeVore. Karr frowned, staring at the man.

Where his eyes should have been the sockets were hollow and empty. *Burned out*, Karr realised with a shiver of revulsion. Over the blind man's head three tiny bug-like remotes hovered, slowly orbiting.

Karr stared a moment longer then gave a surprised laugh. *No . . . it couldn't be!*

"*Ebert?*" Li Yuan stepped past Karr and stood there, looking up the ramp. "Hans Ebert?"

Slowly the blind man came down. Then, unexpectedly, he dropped to his knees, touching his head to the floor before Li Yuan.

"*Chieh Hsia*," he said, drawing the dagger from his belt and offering it to Li Yuan. The T'ang took it and stared, recognising it. It was the dagger he had given Ebert the day he had appointed him his General. With a shudder he dropped it and stepped back.

"*Aiya!* Now he sends ghosts against me!"

"No, *Chieh Hsia*," Ebert said, making no move to retrieve the dagger. "I come to serve you. That is, if you'll forgive me."

"Serve me?" Li Yuan laughed bitterly. "As you served me before, no doubt, by betraying me to my enemies!"

"If you think that, *Chieh Hsia*, kill me now. Pick up the dagger of my shamed office and carry out the sentence you and your fellow T'ang passed in my absence. But I am not the man I was."

Li Yuan stared at the knife, then looked back at the kneeling man. "No. Get up, Hans Ebert."

As Ebert got to his feet Karr stepped forward. "Shall I kill him, *Chieh Hsia?*"

Ebert turned towards him. "Is that you, Gregor Karr? Ah yes, I see it now. I did you wrong, not once but many times. I see you're General now. Well, no better man deserved it."

Karr made to answer but Lehmann laid a hand on his arm, then stepped past him, confronting Ebert.

"How did you do that? How did you jam the guns?"

Ebert smiled. "Stefan Lehmann . . . I didn't expect to find you in this company. But as for your query, look . . ." He pointed unerringly at the bank of screens beside Li Yuan's craft. As he did the face of DeVore vanished from all twenty screens, to be replaced by the tiny walking matchstick figure.

"What does this mean?" Li Yuan asked, looking about him as if expecting some sign of trickery to be revealed.

"It means I am here to help my Lord again. Not as servant, but as guide."

"Guide?" Li Yuan was totally bemused.

Ebert bowed his head again. "Am I forgiven?"

"Forgiven?" Li Yuan turned, looking to where Kuei Jen stood with Pei K'ung and Nan Ho. Urged by his stepmother, Kuei Jen stepped forward and gave a nod. Li Yuan stared at him a moment then turned back. "I . . . I forgive you, Hans Ebert, and lift the sentence of death that hangs over you."

"*Chieh Hsia*," Ebert answered, bowing his head smartly. Then, turning towards the darkness of the open hatch, he extended an arm. "Look!"

Karr glanced at the hatch, then looked at his Master, seeing the sudden astonishment there in Li Yuan's face. Surprised he looked back. Eight men now stood in the open hatchway: big men dressed in strangely old-fashioned space-suits. *Black* men.

"The heroes . . ." Li Yuan whispered, real awe in his voice. "You brought the eight black-faced heroes!"

Ebert beckoned for the men to come down the ramp, then faced Li Yuan again. "You remember, then?"

"The gift of stones."

"Yes." As they formed up behind him, he straightened, for the first time seeming something like the old Hans Ebert – a prince in disguise, returning to his kingdom. "If we win you must promise to tear it all down."

"Tear it down?"

"The City. The evil of the levels. You must tear it down and start again. This way . . . it's wrong."

Li Yuan turned once more, looking first to Nan Ho, then to Pei K'ung and finally to Kuei Jen. Each nodded. He turned back.

"All right. But how? He has forty million . . ."

"And we have eight." Ebert's smile was unexpected. "As I said to you, old friend, I am not the man I was."

He turned and, going to the edge of the platform raised an arm. At once the sky was lit suddenly with the searchlights of a hundred cruisers, the machines forming a great circle about the gutted fortress.

"*Aiya!*" Karr said, noting how not one of the cockpits held a pilot. "What dark wizardry is this?"

But Ebert merely laughed and pointed to the screens. "No wizardry at all, friend Gregor. Look!"

They all turned, looking to the bank of screens. And as they looked the twenty screens, which, for long hours past, had shown a single duplicated image, now broke into a cacophony of images and sound as the commanders of all their garrisons appeared suddenly, clamouring for orders.

"The eyes," Ebert said, coming back to them and standing in their midst, reached out, touching first one and then another of them in turn, smiling at them blindly. "The eyes are open now. Let us use them to see our way out of the darkness."

CHAPTER·23

A SPRING DAY AT THE EDGE OF THE WORLD

F ar off across the bay the sea was boiling. The great space-mounted lasers fired down – broad, dazzlingly-bright beams that ripped like pillars of fire through the clouds. And where they touched, the surface turned to steam. Great thunderheads were rolling across the sky. The air was heavy. Again and again the lasers struck, burning the elements, stripping away layer after layer, down to the rock.

From her vantage point on the City's roof, Emily watched in awe. The air itself was burning and the roar of the boiling sea hurt her ears. She hobbled across, joining the small group who had climbed up out of the levels and had gathered there to see the end of things. Silent, they waited at the edge of the world, watching.

Last things . . . She stared out at the boiling, bubbling sea, her eyes filled with last things.

It was over. All that she'd ever known was being broken down and refashioned. It was the universe's way. Even so, she felt regret. Regret that she would never see them again: never see Michael, Mach, or – and this she regretted most – Lin Shang, with his clever hands and crippled face. For the world was finally ending. The seas were burning and the air was filled with the roar of dissolution.

And when the seas had finally boiled away and the air could not be breathed, what then? What could little men like Lin do to mend that?

She gritted her teeth, pained by the thought that he would suffer. Pained that she could not be with him when it ended. That, at least, would have been something, but to die alone . . .

She shuddered, thinking back, remembering all that had happened to her. Remembering her family's fall from grace, her father's death, her mother's long-suffering stoicism. And afterwards, all those years spent with Bent Gessel building the *Ping Tiao*. Before DeVore had come. Before the great Prince of Inauthenticity had come and destroyed it all.

And yet DeVore had saved her, sent her away. She glanced down at her severed finger and frowned. To America she'd gone. To America and Michael Lever. Her fate. To become the Eldest daughter, before that City fell in flames and she came scuttling back to Europe.

Oh, I've seen much, she thought, remembering it all. And yet nothing suddenly mattered one half as much as what she had felt these past few days, knowing what Lin Shang had done for her. Little Lin, who had had no power and no beauty, yet who had risked himself for her.

Risked himself, and asked nothing back from me.

And now he would die, as they'd all die, unrewarded, just as others went unpunished. And no sense to it all, no justice, no apparent order. Only the chaos of fate and time and dissolution.

Yes, dissolution, at the back of it all. Death's maggot, wriggling in the bone.

It was getting hard to breath now. Her eyes stung and her throat was getting sore. And her skin . . . her skin seemed to burn.

Inside, she urged herself, hearing the crack of rock, the demonic hiss of the burning sea. *Inside* . . .

She turned, making her way back to the shaft. But it was almost over now, and, looking back, she saw first one and then another of the group step out into the nothingness beyond the edge.

* * *

They had built a temporary encampment on the plain below the ruined fortress. Beneath a flapping banner that displayed the *Ywe Lung*, the great Wheel of Dragons, Li Yuan paced up and down. Behind him Kuei Jen stood looking on.

"Just what in the gods' names is he doing?" Li Yuan asked, pointing to the bank of screens – at the cluster of images sent back from their remotes, high above the burning sea.

"He's draining it," Karr said, pointing to a display at the side which showed the whole of the Mediterranean basin. "He's dammed it at Gibraltar, and at the Bosphorus and again down here where the old canal was. Now he's burning it off. When he's finished he'll probably march his army straight across."

Li Yuan's eyes were aghast. "But *why?*"

"Because he can," Nan Ho answered quietly. "It's how he is. He wants us to see just how powerful he is before he destroys us. Because it all means nothing to him. The game . . . Only the game has meaning for him."

Li Yuan stared at the display in disbelief. *The Mediterranean . . . the madman was draining the Mediterranean!*

This was why his father had so feared the idea of Dispersion – *this* was why he had fought it so vigorously – for out there there were no limits, no controls. Out there Man could do exactly as he wished. He could take the very elements and reforge them; could reshape himself in a thousand different ways and then return – with unlimited energy, unlimited destructive power. Dispersion: it was merely another word for dissolution; for the destruction of all that was decent, all that was truly human.

The wind was coming up now, gusting steadily through the encampment. Li Yuan pulled his cloak tight then turned to look at Ebert, seated by the far wall of the enclosure, his men surrounding him.

"DeVore brings a mighty force against us. What will you eight do against that?"

"Do?" Ebert turned towards the watching faces of his dark companions and murmured something in their tongue. There was laughter, a rich, warm laughter, and then Ebert looked back at him.

"Wait and see," he answered, his face tilted up as if to the sun. "Just wait and see."

* * *

Ben gripped Catherine's arm, hurrying her up the slope towards the lights of the cottage. Overhead the sky was black with cloud and the wind was howling down the valley, tearing branches from the trees and whipping the surface of the bay into a frenzy. As they struggled on, the wind tore at them, threatening to claw them back into the water.

Catherine turned towards him, trying to speak, but the wind whipped away her words. Up ahead the shutters of the cottage were banging violently and there was the sudden tinkle of breaking glass.

"Come on!" he yelled, tugging at her, knowing they'd not be safe until they were inside, but she had frozen suddenly, her eyes tight and fixed like the eyes of a trapped and frightened animal. He pulled at her again, but it was no good; she was too heavy, the wind too strong. Unless she helped him . . .

There was a sudden shout – a bellow close by that sounded over the roar of the wind. He half turned then lost his footing and went down. Yet even as he did, even as he felt Catherine's hand slip from his grasp, he felt someone – someone huge and muscular – pick him up and head towards the cottage.

"The woman!" he yelled at the Myghtern, his voice making little impression on that vast, unending roar. "Get the woman!"

As the giant turned, a sudden gust hit them full on and the Myghtern went down, on to his knees, knocking the breath from Ben as he fell. When Ben came to he was inside, the howl of the wind more sinister, more threatening somehow now they were out of it. The very air was alive, it seemed, making the hairs on his arms and neck bristle.

"Catherine . . ." he began, starting up, then saw her, sitting in the chair beside the door, his sister, Meg, attending to a cut on her forehead. Behind her Scaf and the Myghtern looked on concerned. And Tom? He turned then smiled. Tom was in his usual place on the turn of the stairs, silent, staring.

The cottage juddered and groaned, the shutters banged. The howl intensified.

"It's getting worse!" Meg said, turning to him, her eyes worried. "What is it, Ben? What's happening?"

"I don't know," he said. "I . . ."

He shrugged, but it was like something he'd read in Amos's journals, about the wind that followed a nuclear explosion: the great inrush of air to fill the vacuum. *DeVore*, he thought. *DeVore's the vacuum at the heart of this.*

But this wind had some physical cause too. Something must have happened. Something catastrophic. He glanced at the screen, but it was blank. Communications must be out. Yes, of course they were out. The storm . . .

He got to his feet then shook his head to clear it, but still the constant roar of the wind sounded deep within.

"Come on," he said, going across and helping Catherine to her feet. "Let's go down into the cellars. This is one storm we'd better ride out below."

* * *

Nwibe looked to the sky and laughed.

"Hear how old Mother Thunder rebukes her son."

Along the line the others stopped fastening their harnesses and looked up at the thick layer of cloud overhead and smiled inside their helmets.

Dogo, the biggest of them, Ezeulu's son, answered Nwibe, his voice sounding in every earpiece. "When her son is angry, there is always trouble in the village, no?"

"There will be trouble enough without those two adding to it!" Aluko Echewa answered, clipping himself into the harness and adjusting the straps about his shoulders.

On every side the floor of the great sea steamed, shrouding the strange, uneroded shapes of the freshly-exposed rocks with swirls of mist. *Perhaps Mars was like this once*, Aluko thought, *millions of years ago*. He turned, looking to his left, then to the right, making sure everyone was ready. Then, pulling down the rigid armatures of the flying-suit and slipping his hands into the gloves, he checked along the line.

"Ugoye?"

"Ready."

"Chike?"

"Done."

"Nwibe?"

"One moment, Elder. . . . Okay, I'm ready."

"Odile?"

"Ready."

"Elechi?"

"Done."

"Dogo?"

"Itching to go, Elder."

"Nza?"

"Ready."

He closed his eyes. At once an image filled his head; sent back from one of the remotes that were tracking their progress. It showed the eight of them spread out in a line along the dry bed of the ancient sea, the special harnesses they were wearing making them appear twice their normal size.

"Okay," he said, placing his fingers over the control pads. "Let's lift. Slowly now."

His thumb closed with a gentle pressure on the pad. At once he felt himself lifted; felt and saw . . . for at the same time the eight figures in his head lifted and began to drift forward.

Even as they climbed, emerging from the deep rift in which they'd been hidden, the storm broke overhead.

"See how the young ram loses his temper!" Dogo said in his earpiece, laughing his rich, deep laugh, as a bolt of lightning struck the brittle rock less than a *li* to the left of them with a sharp crack of destructive power. And then the thunder spoke, exploding all about them, shaking the air with an unexpected violence.

"The night is our mother," Aluko began, speaking into the heads of his brothers, repeating the words of the litany for those who, unlike Dogo, had the sense to be afraid. "She comforts us. She tells us who we are. We live, we die beneath her. She sees all. Even the darkness deep within us."

* * *

"How? *How?*"

DeVore glared at man on the screen, his face hard, his anger kept tightly in check.

"We're not sure, Master," the Technician said warily, conscious that his very uncertainty was guaranteed to upset DeVore. "He's gone behind things. *Tweaked* them, somehow."

"Tweaked them?" DeVore let out a snort of disgust then shook his head. "How? *Exactly* how?"

"We . . ."

"Find out! Understand me? And when you know, tell me. Until then, your life is forfeit, man. You're dead."

He turned from the screen, his anger matched only by his curiosity. It was meant to be foolproof, tamper-proof. But somehow Li Yuan had managed to get round the back of things and override his systems.

Ward! he thought with a sudden certainty. *This is Ward's work!*

Okay. But how did he use that knowledge? How could he regain the advantage he had temporarily lost?

I should have hit the island, he thought. *Yes, and the Shepherd place too, while I was at it.* The only reason he hadn't was because he'd thought he could take them as prizes once the rest was his. To have them work for him.

You were too greedy, he told himself, calmer now, beginning to think again. *But never mind, it's still all yours if you play this right. The advantage is still yours. After all, you still have all the stones.*

"Master?"

There was a new face on the screen. His own face, but a copy. Overlaying it was the printed number 154. It was the Commander of that craft.

"Yes, 154, what is it?"

"There's something coming at us from the north."

"Something? Be more specific."

"Eight men, Master. Eight men in rocket-suits."

DeVore gave a laugh of disbelief. "Is this a joke, Commander?"

"I . . . I thought you should see what our remotes are sending back."

"Okay. Patch it through."

He stood back, relaxed, chuckling to himself. Eight men in rocket-suits! Whatever next?

His laughter died. The image on the screen was none too clear; even so, he recognised those suits and knew what colour the faces were behind the dark reflecting surfaces of their visors.

"*Osu* . . . What in the gods' names . . ." And then he saw it. Then, with a strange little laugh, he understood.

"Eight stones," he said softly. "Is that all you can muster, Li Yuan? And what of your father's boast that time, that he would place the last stone on my grave? Vanity . . . an old man's vanity, that's all that was. Vanity and boastfulness. And now you'll pay the price."

He laughed, then spoke to his Commander.

"You will engage, 154. You will attack those eight and destroy them, understand me?"

"Master!"

And then he would deal with Ward. Yes, and with Shepherd too.

He cleared the screen, then looked about him at the silent room, smiling. It was time to clear the board.

* * *

At the still and silent centre of it all, Hans Ebert sat, facing Tuan Ti Fo across a rock, a *wei chi* board set up between them.

All about them the drained sea shimmered in the late afternoon heat, its sculpted surface like the vision of a demented child.

Ebert stared blindly at the board, the remote overhead sending him back an image of the game. Leaning in, he slapped a white stone down in *shang*, the south, then sat back, frowning.

"I feel uncomfortable, playing white. It seems wrong somehow."

Tuan Ti Fo chuckled. "It is several years since I played black, but there is a purpose to this, Hans."

"A purpose?" Ebert laughed. "Let's pray to Mother Sky there is a purpose behind your thinking, Master Tuan, for the King of Hell himself is upon us."

"Relax," Tuan Ti Fo said, playing a black stone at the edge of the board, in *ch'u*, the west, safeguarding a line.

Ebert studied the board a moment, then looked across at the old man. "I still don't understand it. If the Machine can do this much, why doesn't it finish the job outright? Why all these half measures?"

"The Machine acts as it must," Tuan Ti Fo answered, pulling gently at his beard. "There must be a balance in all things. When that balance is lost . . . well, that is not healthy, neh? Our friend DeVore . . . his thinking is the thinking of a child – an unhealthy child."

Tuan Ti Fo leaned forward, moving his hand over the board. At once all the stones became white. Tuan gestured at the board. "So our friend would have it. But where is the skill in such a game? Where the beauty?"

He swept his hand over the board once more, returning the stones to their original colours, then smiled at Ebert.

"You must understand. It is not our purpose to win the game for you, merely to

419

allow it to be played. Our friend DeVore . . . he plays the game well, but he does not understand its purpose. He thinks that winning is the all of it, but the game is not meant to teach Man ruthlessness. No . . . it's object is to teach us balance, to school us in the dance of opposing forces. As for the greater game . . . this game he chooses to play out with men's lives, well, we cannot possibly contest the matter. Forty million against eight." Tuan laughed. "Those are poor odds, neh?"

Ebert stared at him. "You speak as if we can't defeat him."

"And you speak as if you are surprised." Tuan Ti Fo gestured towards the board. "Play your stone."

Ebert slapped down a second stone in *shang*, then drew his silks about him irritably. "You play with me, Master Tuan."

"Of course . . . But that's not what you really mean, is it? Nor do you understand me. We cannot defeat DeVore. Have no illusions about that, Hans. However, we *can* let the man defeat himself."

"Defeat himself? How?"

Tuan Ti Fo leaned across and placed a stone in the very centre of the board. "By keeping him here. By forcing him to look into the nothingness at the centre of it all."

"You speak in riddles," Ebert answered, slapping down a stone beside the Master's last.

"Not at all," the old man answered, pointing to the stone Ebert had just laid. "Just as you were forced to shadow my play, so we might force our friend DeVore to shadow ours."

Tuan Ti Fo placed another stone to the right of his last, extending the line towards his group in *ch'u*.

"Time," he said, meeting Ebert's sightless stare with his own. "We must buy time. For time, not force of arms, will win *this* contest."

* * *

"There!" Dogo shouted, pointing down to his right. "I see them, by that loaf-shaped rock!"

Master Tuan turned as the eight descended toward him, then stood, greeting them. Behind him, Ebert also stood.

"You took your time," Ebert called, grinning at them, turning his face to the clear sky overhead. "Can't you get the hang of those things?"

Aluko, setting down, looked back at him and laughed. "Dead seas I'm used to, but these . . . Whose idea was this?"

"We merely play his game," Tuan Ti Fo said, turning and throwing a cloth over the board. "DeVore likes symbols. Well, we shall give him symbols, neh?"

Aluko frowned at him. He had grown used to the old man's vagueness over the years, but sometimes – as now – it worried him.

"What can symbols do against such a mighty host?" he asked. "What if they simply shoot us down?"

"Oh, they will," Tuan said, folding his silks about him.

"Great!" Dogo said, coming alongside Aluko. "So now we're suicides!"

"That troubles you?" The old man asked, smiling faintly.

Dogo looked to Ebert, then shook his head firmly. "Whatever Efulefu asks, we shall do. It is our debt to him."

"And DeVore?" Ebert asked, looking to Aluko. "Do you still owe DeVore a debt?"

Aluko laughed coldly. "We repaid that monster years ago, as you know, my friend. Nothing would give me greater pleasure than to destroy him. But Dogo has a point. Are we to be merely symbols?"

"Merely?" Tuan Ti Fo chuckled. "You think men are mere machines – even DeVore's kind of men? No. Men have fears and deep-rooted instincts. Like you, my brothers, they have beliefs – even when they profess to believe nothing. Why, even the most pitiful rogue will believe in ghosts and demons. So . . ."

"So?" Nza came and stood with his fellows. A moment later the others joined them. The eight stood there, facing Master Tuan, dwarfing him in their harnesses.

"So it is time," Tuan answered, turning and lifting a hand towards the sky.

They looked. As they did the sky seemed to shimmer and take shape. There, where a moment before there had been nothing, was a massive dragon with seven heads and ten horns and seven diadems upon his heads. The sight was awesome, fear-inducing.

Tuan Ti Fo spoke into the sudden silence. "See. He sends his dragon against us."

There was a low moan of fear from the eight, but Ebert only laughed.

"I who have no eyes can see what you cannot. You asked about symbols, Aluko. Well, what you see is but a symbol. A mere air-show. Yet it has a purpose, neh? It is there to drain the courage from those who might dare to stand and fight." He stepped forward, looking from one face to another, his blind eyes seeming to take each of them in before he nodded and looked to another.

"Aluko . . . Nza . . . Dogo . . . Chike . . . Elechi . . . Odile . . . Nwibe . . . Ugoye . . . Your names will live for ever. And your deeds today . . ." Ebert smiled, then, as if he'd heard something in his head, turned and looked to the south. "But wait . . . one of their ships is coming."

Aluko stared at Ebert, then looked to Tuan Ti Fo. "But what shall we do? I thought there would be weapons here."

"Weapons?" Again Old Tuan laughed. "Weapons will not help you against DeVore. No. You must defeat him by other means. Here . . ." He bent down and, removing the cloth, revealed a pile of circular shields.

Aluko stepped across and picked one up. It was perfectly normal on its back, but its front . . .

"But it's a mirror!" Aluko said, staring at Tuan Ti Fo in astonishment. "You mean, we are to fight DeVore's great fleet armed only with mirrors?"

"How quick are you?"

"How quick?"

Tuan stooped and, without warning, picked up a rock and aimed it at Aluko. Instinctively Aluko raised the shield and fended off the rock. He frowned at the old Han, then turned the shield, dusting it off, examining it for cracks.

"Unmarked," he said, looking back at Tuan.

"Good," Ebert said. "That's all you have to do. Defend yourself. Now . . . who will be first?"

Nza stepped forward, staring at Ebert fiercely. "Let me go, Efulefu."

"You, little bird? You want to fly up and pluck the stone from the air?"

Nza nodded.

"Then fly, Nza. But fly quickly now, for our enemy is almost upon us."

* * *

The target was just ahead. There was nothing now for him to do but wait. The ship's computer had locked on to the distant figure and, as it grew on the screen, the Commander felt the certainty of a kill ripple through him. He could do it now – he could destroy that drifting figure in a blaze of laser-light, but he wanted to get closer – wanted a good visual display to send back to his Master.

"Slowly now," he said, conscious of the presence of his senior staff behind him, watching his every move. Lesser copies, they might be, but they would share the glory of this first encounter. The glory, and the rewards.

He could make out details of the figure now. It was a man. One of the eight the remotes had pictured earlier. At first he seemed empty-handed, but then, as it came clearer, he saw that the man was carrying some kind of shield.

"It's a mirror, Commander," the technician at the desk nearby stated flatly, the wire at his neck linking him to his console enhancing the image he saw.

"Direct the cannon to avoid that area," the Commander said. The last thing they wanted was their own fire coming back at them.

"Kill speed," he said quietly.

Let him come to me. Let him fall upon my spear.

He waited, counting in his head. *Ten, nine, eight, seven . . .*

He stopped. Something was wrong.

"How big is he?"

"Twelve, fourteen feet . . . No, sixteen. No . . . Oh shit!"

The technician's words merely confirmed what was obvious to the eye. The figure was growing. Growing perceptibly and by the moment. Slowly, very slowly it expanded, the mirror it held growing with it, until it was like a tiny moon, reflecting back their own image.

"Disarm the lasers," he said, a tiny ripple of fear running down his back. "We'll hit him with missiles. Prime and fire. Don't wait for my order."

The figure was so big now that it filled the screen. The image was recalibrated, so that again the figure could fit into it, but still it grew. It had to be half a *li* tall now.

It's some kind of trick, he thought, trying to reassure himself, but that wasn't what the instruments were telling him. "What he saw was what was happening. All of the readings confirmed it. As the figure grew, so its mass grew, in direct and correct proportion to its size.

"It's impossible," he whispered, awed now that he'd had time to consider just what was happening out there. And even as he said it, he felt the slight judder of the ship as the first of the missiles were launched, then another as a second pair streaked out towards it.

The giant raised his shield. The Commander watched in astonishment as the missiles vanished into it, then gasped as a beam of pure white light bounced back at him from the mirror's surface.

"Take avoiding action! Now!" he yelled, but even as he gave the order he knew it was too late.

* * *

DeVore stared at the screen in disbelief.

"188. You're in that area. What happened?"

There was a moment's hesitation, then a sobered voice answered him. "It blew up, Master. It simply blew up."

"But the giant . . ."

"Giant, Master? What giant?"

What was happening? What in the gods' names was going on out there?

"188. Go in there now. Hit that target. And pay no attention to anything you might see on your screen. Just kill it. Understand?"

"Going in now, Master."

He let out a breath, then shook his head. *An illusion. It had to be an illusion. But how? And when had an illusion ever registered with such solidity?*

He shivered. He didn't know. He simply didn't know.

"260," he said. "Follow 188 in. I want to make sure we've nailed that target. If anything happens to 188, you take over the mission."

"Understood, Master!"

And if they all blow up?

He looked up at the screen again. "All ships in Shang Command go in there at once. I want that sector scoured and cleaned out, and I want it done now!"

* * *

Coming to the top of the slope Ebert stopped, then laughed, surprised by the sight that met his eyes.

Tuan Ti Fo was sitting on a low rock, DeVore's fleet to his back, studying the *wei chi* board that was set up before him.

Ebert went across and looked down at the board. It was the same game they had been playing earlier. As he watched, Tuan Ti Fo laid another stone, extending his line.

"Isn't it rather late?" he asked.

"Play a stone," Old Tuan answered him.

"Where?"

Tuan looked up at him and smiled. "Deep into his territory. Turn him. Play behind his lines."

"Behind?"

Tuan nodded. "You must distract him a moment longer. The storm . . . the storm will decide it all."

Ebert frowned, then looked up at the darkening sky. And as he did the first drops of rain fell on to his face, trickling down his brow and pooling in the hollows of his eyes.

* * *

The storm drains were full, the sluices overflowing, but still the rain fell, heavier by the moment. Chen looked up at the sky, drawing his fingers through his soaked hair, then looked back towards the village, urging the last few stragglers on towards the safety of the bunker. His son Jyan was last of them, coming down the street between the big farmhouses, carrying Old Mother Ling, a waterproof sheet wrapped about her. Seeing how he was struggling, Chen began to wade towards him, his feet sticking in the mud that was everywhere now – that pulled and sucked and threatened to send one sprawling at any moment.

"Come on!" he yelled, taking the old woman from his son, then turning to half walk, half limp towards the steps.

Handing her inside, Chen turned back. "Is that everyone?" he yelled, making himself heard against the wind, the thunder that now rumbled incessantly.

"I've checked the houses," Jyan answered him. "You want me to check the barns?"

Chen shook his head. "We'll do a head count down below. If there's anyone missing . . ."

Jyan nodded and then laughed. "What's happening, father? It's like the Great Flood out here! I've never seen so much rain!"

"No . . ." Chen looked at the sky thoughtfully. "Still, let's get inside, neh? You know how your mother worries."

"I know," Jyan said, laughing, letting his father hand him down the steps.

He watched his son vanish inside, then turned back, shielding his eyes against the beating rain as he looked up at the sky once more. The clouds were dark and menacing, and even as he watched, lightning flickered between them with a crack of thunder.

Where are you now, Gregor Karr? he wondered, concerned for his old friend's safety, but glad that Marie and the girls at least were safe here in his charge. *I'll look after them*, he vowed, as the rain redoubled its efforts, stinging his exposed flesh and throwing up spray off the muddy steps.

He stepped back, into the shelter of the bunker, then reached up and pulled down the storm shutter.

It would be a long time until daylight.

* * *

DeVore stared aghast at the screen, watching one after another of his craft fall slowly to the ground. It was like they were being switched off, one at a time. He watched another wobble in the air, then begin to topple to the dry sea bed, and shook his head.

It made no sense. There were no beams, no rays, nothing whatsoever to explain it, yet ship after ship was losing power. Soon there would be nothing in the sky. And the storm . . . the storm was fast approaching.

Too long, he thought. *I've spent too long here on this single play.* Yes, and now he would pay the price for his hesitation.

It was time for more drastic measures.

"Destroy the Cities," he said, leaning over the communicator. "Let the missiles fall."

The image on the screen changed. It was now a view from space. A dozen huge launchers lazed like alligators in a pool, awaiting their moment. As he watched tiny twinkles of light appeared along the sides of each, like matches being struck. A closer view showed a single rocket haring from its launch hatch, silently falling towards the dark mass beneath it.

There was no satisfaction in this, yet if he could not take the board he would at least destroy it.

More missiles launched, and then a final salvo. Seventy-two in all. Enough to leave the continent a bed of smouldering cinders.

He watch them fall, streaking into the upper atmosphere. In two minutes it would be over. He turned, calling one of his men to him, and as he did the screen was lit with brilliant light.

Shielding his eyes, he looked back, trying to see what had happened, but the light was too fierce. Slowly it intensified. Then, with a strange little fizzle, the image on the screen dissolved into a fuzz of static. DeVore lowered his hand and looked about him. Every single screen in the cabin was the same.

"No . . ." he said, unable to take in what had happened. "No . . ."

* * *

Those who had survived the fall of their ships had clambered out into that nightmare landscape, dazed and uncertain of their bearings. The rain was falling steadily now, lightning flashes briefly illuminating the darkness, casting rocks and hollows into deep shadow. Then, with a startling suddenness, the whole sky lit up. For ten, maybe fifteen seconds the light was painfully intense and those that glanced up found themselves staggering about blindly, their flesh tingling, their retinas burned away.

Among them Ebert walked, truly blind now, his remotes destroyed in that same moment when he had reached out and – feeling his way behind the fine lines of the missile's wiring – had tweaked the signal and detonated the leading rocket.

As the darkness fell once more, the rain intensified. Rain like a solid wall falling endlessly from the night-black heavens. Rain so hard it beat the blinded stragglers down, sucking at their feet, filling their mouths, its noise like the sound of a million drummers drumming.

For a moment, the universe was rain. And then, with a rumble that shook the rocks beneath them, the tide came in again.

* * *

The Machine watched all. It saw the great sea burned away; it watched the ships lose power and fall, the missiles detonate high above the troubled earth. And as the great wave swept across the dry sea bed, it spoke to the eight who were in the air, directing them, urging them on, until the one it had chosen was safe.

It watched, knowing how close it had come to doing nothing, not certain even now that it had done the right thing in interfering in the affairs of men. Millions had died. Hundreds of millions. And many more would die in the months to come – of starvation and plague and simple misery.

It watched, seeing how the eight flew high above the Flood, Ebert held safe between the central pair. Let DeVore make what he would of that. Let him slowly figure out just what had happened here today.

Maybe that's why, Tuan Ti Fo said, speaking from the space at the centre of it – from that point of emptiness it could not see into. *Maybe you simply couldn't let him win.*

Maybe . . . But such a thing was incalculable. It was not even something it could rationalise. On Mars it had acted to preserve itself. But here . . . Here it had acted out of instinct.

Instinct? Tuan Ti Fo asked and laughed; a gently ironic laugh. *Since when did a Machine possess instinct?*

Since . . .

But it did not know. Just as it did not know how it had come to be self-aware, so this too was a mystery to it.

Another step, Tuan Ti Fo said. *Another tiny step.*

And then laughter; a gentle, ironic laughter, slowly fading.

* * *

Li Yuan sat in the great tent, alone at his desk, the rain drumming on the canvas overhead. Nan Ho had left him for a moment, gone to greet the latest arrivals on the far side of the encampment, but there was much to do, and while he waited for him to return Li Yuan busied himself with matters of State, trying not to think of what was happening in the greater world, keeping his thoughts within the tiny circle of lamplight in which he sat.

How many millions had died already? And how many more would end their lives before this day was done?

That was the worst of it, the reason he could not dwell on it too long: it was the impotence he felt; the inability to change a single thing that had happened or was to come. Slowly, degree by degree, they had lost control. Seven had become One – himself. And now that One no longer held the reins. The world ran foaming-mad towards the brink and he could do nothing.

He sighed and looked up, rubbing his eyes, then tensed. There had been a movement in the shadows across from him; the faintest noise.

"Who's there?"

He waited, his heart pounding, squinting into the dark. Had he been mistaken? Yes. It was only the wind, moving the canvas on the far side of the tent. He sat back, frowning, angry with himself for letting his imagination run away with him. There were guards outside, after all. It was just not possible . . .

He felt a shiver at the back of his neck and looked up. Lehmann was standing there, not three paces from him, watching him, those cold pink eyes staring.

"No speeches," Lehmann said, drawing his knife. "You know why."

Li Yuan threw the desk up between them, then tugged the knife from his belt. But he had no intention of fighting Lehmann. Scrambling back, he slashed at the tent's soft wall then threw himself out through the gap his knife had made, Lehmann close behind.

"*Help!*" He yelled, his feet slipping on the wet grass. "Hel . . .!"

A hand caught him, picked him up and threw him aside unceremoniously. He rolled awkwardly then slammed into the palisade, the breath knocked from him. Groaning he turned his head, looking back.

Lehmann was standing beside the rip in the tent's wall, crouched like a fighter in the flickering torchlight, his knife in his left hand. Facing him, holding the gusting torch, was a huge figure of a man, head and shoulders taller than the albino. As he slipped from consciousness the man's name flickered like a guttering lamp. Karr . . .

* * *

Lehmann looked past Karr at the crowd that was gathering and straightened, making himself less threatening.

"I have no fight with you, Gregor Karr. You served your Master well. But enough's enough. One must respect one's Master, surely? One must be in awe of him, neh?" He gestured towards the fallen bundle by the palisade. "But how can you be in awe of *that?*"

Karr looked to Li Yuan then back at Lehmann. It was in his power to choose. For this one brief moment, as the rain fell and the storm gathered strength, he had been granted the freedom to determine how he lived.

And the choice? The choice was simple. It was whether he chose to carry on, confused, struggling to make sense of things, to bring some form of good from the chaos of his life, or to submit to the certainties – the rigid order – of this other way.

Li Yuan groaned again and opened his eyes.

"Is the promise good?" he asked, looking to him.

Li Yuan coughed, then struggled to his knees. "Promise?"

"What you said to Ebert."

"Ah . . ." Li Yuan looked to Lehmann, then back at Karr. "I swore."

"You'll tear it down?"

The rain beat down. The torch gusted in the wind. Across from him Lehmann waited, crouched now, the knife slowly turning in his hand.

"I'll tear it down."

Lehmann sprang. His knife arced towards Karr's throat, his foot towards his guts.

Karr shifted back a fraction, the torch spinning from his grip. His left forearm turned the knife thrust, his knee met Lehmann's foot. His right hand punched.

Lehmann was dead before he fell.

Fate. In a second he had decided what would be. As the thunder growled, he stepped back, letting a shuddering breath escape him. It was done with. *Finished.*

Someone picked up the torch and held it up. In its light he saw the dead man shudder then lie still. Turning, he saw that Li Yuan was watching him, his dark eyes staring, trying to understand just what had happened.

"*Chieh Hsia*," he said, kneeling. Yet somehow the balance had changed. In a single moment he had made sense of his life. One single action – one single, physical action – had changed the shape of things. Had he died – had Lehmann triumphed over him – the future would have been different, the balance altered.

He shivered, then stood and stepped away. The rain was falling hard now. They would need to find better shelter than a tent afforded them.

He looked to Li Yuan again. The T'ang's silks were sticking to him, his dark hair plastered to his head. Karr frowned, understanding it at last. There were no levels, only those Man invented for himself. And Li Yuan . . . Li Yuan was just another man.

"Come," he said, holding out his hand, offering it to the man. "We'd best get out of this."

Li Yuan took the offered hand, letting himself be helped up, then smiled.

"Round everyone up," Karr said, looking about him. "We'll go to the island. To Kalevala. It's no good here. This weather . . ."

Thunder cracked and rumbled over the plain. The rain intensified, drumming madly on the canvas close by. The torch hissed and suddenly went out. As it did, lightning played on the rim of the ruined fortress to the east.

Li Yuan looked up at Karr and nodded. "We'd better wake them. Warn them we're coming."

"Wake them?" Karr laughed. *Yes, wake them*, he thought. A new age beckoned. A new way. He felt a thrill flash through him, then, laughing, wiped the rain from his face.

So it began. So the Wheel turned and the world changed. He looked down at the corpse of the albino and nodded to himself.

So it began.

* * *

DeVore sat in the pilot's seat of the tiny one-man craft, hovering above the boiling sea, the rain hammering at the craft's wings as he looked out through the rain-streaked window.

The sea was awash with corpses, his own face, dead, forty million times dead, staring up at him blindly, endlessly.

As he watched the last of his ships slip beneath the darkness he nodded to himself. The game was lost. It was time to cut and run, back to the no-space. Back to the cold dark space from which he'd come.

STARLIGHT AND NON-BEING

Starlight asked Non-Being: "Master, are you? Or are you not?"

Since he received no answer whatever, Starlight set himself to watch for Non-Being. He waited to see if Non-Being would put in an appearance.

He kept his gaze fixed on the deep Void, hoping to catch a glimpse of Non-Being.

All day long he looked, and he saw nothing. He listened, but heard nothing. He reached out to grasp, and grasped nothing.

Then Starlight exclaimed at last: "This is IT!"

"This is the furthest yet! Who can reach it? I can comprehend the absence of Being. But who can comprehend the absence of Nothing? If now, on top of all this, Non-Being IS, Who can comprehend it?"

(Chuang Tzu, 6th century BC. *Writings*, xxii, VIII)

STARLIGHT
AND NON-BEING

S he had walked for four days, through abandoned levels and empty rooms, past broken barricades and scenes of desolation, returning to him. Through the nightmare vistas of a ruined City, through scenes of misery and torment and the utmost degradation she passed like a shadow, unseen, untroubled by the gangs of thugs and madmen who roamed like pack-dogs in those half-lit regions.

Eventually she stood there in the room she had shared with him, looking about her at the wreckage, and felt the last faint glimmer of hope die in her. She had been so sure – so certain he'd be here.

She sat, weary now, letting her head fall. If she died it would not matter. Let the sky fall and the earth crack open, it would make no difference now.

For a long time she slept, beaten, finally defeated by the world. Then, pulling herself to her feet, she turned and went from the room, not knowing where she'd go.

Main seemed echoing and empty. Glass littered the floor from broken screens, but one still functioned at the far end by the clock tower. Beneath it a small crowd had gathered, standing idly or sitting on their bundles, as if waiting to see this last transmission before they too moved on.

She walked across and stood there at the back, looking up at the screen, her eyes registering nothing. Dead. This world was dead now, and she with it. She looked down, meaning to walk on, then saw him, there at the front, leaning against the barrier.

"Lin?" She went towards him, not sure at first that it *was* him. Then, as the certainty of it gripped her, she called to him, louder this time.

"Lin! Lin Shang!"

He turned sharply, fearful, his lop-sided face grimacing fiercely, then saw her. The grimace became a smile. He took a step towards her then stopped, looking down, the smile vanishing. Both his hands were bandaged. In one he loosely held a scrap of paper.

"Lin!" she said breathlessly, coming up to him and gripping his upper arms. "Lin! What happened to your hands?"

He shook his head, refusing to look at her.

"Lin! What is it?"

Slowly he held out the paper. She took it and unfolded it. On it was a picture of her face. She recognised it at once. It was one of the handbills Michael had been distributing throughout the levels before the War. She stared at it a moment, then, looking back at him, held it out.

"Lin Shang . . . look at me."

Slowly, fearfully, he raised his eyes.

She tore the paper, then tore it once again and let it fall. Then, reaching down, she picked up his pack and, placing her arm about his shoulders, began to lead him away.

"Come Lin," she said gently. "There's mending to be done."

* * *

Beneath the camera's solemn gaze, the funeral cortège crossed the bridge then climbed the great steps, pausing beneath the gate of Bremen fortress for those senior officers who had survived to remove their caps and bow respectfully before the Marshal's body.

Tolonen was dead. Now he lay in the great coffin, his face made up to resemble life, his corpse padded out to fill his Marshal's uniform. Ten stout cadets carried the great casket, while behind it the Marshal's daughter, Jelka, walked slowly, dressed from head to toe in white, her son one side of her, her diminutive husband the other. Beyond her, bare-headed and dressed in sack-cloth, honouring his father's General, walked Li Yuan, and behind him his court.

Karr was next, his old lieutenant Chen beside him.

Last came Ebert and the Osu, their eight black faces exposed to the watching eyes of those millions who had survived to witness this final act.

Li Yuan, looking up at the casket, sighed. Ice, flood and fire, they had survived it all. And now, it seemed, they were to place the old world in the earth: for Tolonen had been the keystone of the arch, and, as his father had so often said, without the keystone, the arch must surely fall.

He had had a plot cleared at the centre of the fortress, at ground level. There he would bury the old man, and around his grave he would begin the task of rebuilding his world, of fulfilling his promise to Ebert and the Osu. The promise he'd renewed to Karr.

They had been given a chance – a breathing space in which to bring about a change. Change such as his father would never have dreamed of.

You must not fail, he told himself, stepping beneath the arch into the sepulchral darkness of the great atrium.

That morning, against habit, he had called his wife's *Wu* and had the old man cast the oracle.

Wei chi, it had been . . . Before completion.

He smiled, recalling the old man's words.

"Before completion. Success.
But if the little fox, after nearly completing the crossing,
Gets his tail in the water,
There is nothing that would further."

He understood. Ahead of him lay his greatest task, that of leading his world from disorder into order; of shaping it into a newer, healthier form; of giving the world he had inherited true balance. But in so doing he must be like an old fox walking over ice. He must be the unifying force behind it all, stopping often to listen for the cracking of the ice where it was thinnest.

Yes, and he must keep his tail out of the icy water!

* * *

After the ceremony, Li Yuan went across to Ebert, who was standing with the Osu between the huge pillars of the Hall.

As the Osu stepped back, Ebert turned his blind eyes on the young T'ang and bowed low. "Li Yuan."

"There is some final business between us," Yuan said, turning to take the two documents from Nan Ho. "Promises I made you."

Ebert smiled. "You gave your word. That is enough for me."

"Perhaps . . . but maybe I have less faith in myself than you, Hans Ebert. These . . ." He handed them across. "These are as a sign to all men. The one returns your name to you and absolves you of all blame for your father's death, the other is a statement of my government's policy from henceforth."

"Then you will tear it down?"

"I shall. Beginning here, at Bremen."

"And in its place?"

Li Yuan shrugged. "Who knows? The oracle bids me be like an old fox on the ice. It will doubtless be many years before the crossing's made."

"But beginning is something, neh?"

Li Yuan smiled and nodded. "And you, Hans Ebert? Will you stay and see those changes come about?"

Ebert bowed his head slightly. "Forgive me, Li Yuan, but I have other plans. I have a son I do not know, and a people who must find a proper home. Now that DeVore has gone, they have an itch to return from whence they came so long ago."

"I see."

"Make sure you do," Ebert said, laughing softly. Then, with a bow, he turned and went to join the Osu.

* * *

It was silent where he sat between the worlds. Silent and dark. Outside the stars shimmered redly, elongated towards him as his craft sped out towards the System's edge.

He had begun a new game; had placed the first stone on the board. Now he stared at it fixedly, conscious that he must learn it all again.

"What do you want, old man?" he asked, looking up at the shadowy figure seated across from him.

"To travel with you," the other answered, leaning closer as he placed an answering stone. "And to enlighten you."

DeVore laughed. "Enlighten me?"

The old man stared back at him, his dark eyes narrowed. "You think yourself *beyond* enlightenment?"

"No. No . . . it's just . . ." Again he laughed, amused by the whole thing.

"You lost," the old man said, sitting back.

"You cheated," DeVore answered, placing a second stone. "I don't know how, but that's the only way you could have beaten me."

"The *only* way?" It was the old man's turn to laugh. "You stare into the dark and think the dark is all."

In the beginning there was nothing. And in the end . . ." DeVore shrugged. "Nothing."

"And yet we live in-between, neh?" The old man slapped down another stone – carelessly, it seemed.

DeVore stared at it, then shook his head. "It's all such a mess, don't you think? All so . . . *confused.*"

"That is one way of looking at things. But there are others, surely? As Chuang Tzu said, the human form has ten thousand changes that never come to an end. In consequence one's joys, as one's sorrows, must be uncountable. Life . . . life cannot be reduced. It cannot be tidied up, the way you wish to. It simply is."

DeVore snorted. "Nonsense! Life's there to be shaped, to be changed into other, *better* forms. Why give us knowledge if we are not to act upon it? Why give us power if we cannot *use* that power?"

"To teach restraint?" The old man waved a hand across the board. "It is like the game. It must not be mistaken for life."

DeVore stared at him, then picked up the board and threw it at him. It passed through the old man, landing on the floor, the stones scattering.

The old man was gone.

"Light and air," he said contemptuously. "That's all you ever were, old man. Starlight and nothingness!" He stood, stretching, looking about himself at the tiny cabin.

The room was dark. He was alone now. He had always been alone. Outside the stars shimmered redly.

Restraint, he thought and laughed. *Just wait. I'll teach you cunts restraint!*

NOTE
White Moon, Red Dragon concludes the second phase of the great "War of the Two Directions", but the history of Chung Kuo – of the struggle for balance – enters a new and final phase in Book Seven, *Days Of Bitter Strength*, as Li Yuan begins to build his new world order.

AUTHOR'S NOTE

The transcription of standard Mandarin into European alphabetical form was first achieved in the seventeenth century by the Italian Matteo Ricci, who founded and ran the first Jesuit Mission in China from 1583 until his death in 1610. Since then several dozen attempts have been made to reduce the original Chinese sounds, represented by some tens of thousands of separate pictograms, into readily understandable phonetics for Western use. For a long time, however, three systems dominated – those used by the three major Western powers vying for influence in the corrupt and crumbling Chinese Empire of the nineteenth century: Great Britain, France, and Germany. These systems were the Wade-Giles (Great Britain and America – sometimes known as the Wade system), the École Française de L'Extrême Orient (France) and the Lessing (Germany).

Since 1958, however, the Chinese themselves have sought to create one single phonetic form, based on the German system, which they termed the *hanyu pinyin fang'an* (Scheme for a Chinese Phonetic Alphabet), known more commonly as *pinyin*, and in all foreign language books published in China since January 1st, 1979 *pinyin* has been used, as well as now being taught in schools along with the standard Chinese characters. For this work, however, I have chosen to use the older and to my mind far more elegant transcription system, the Wade-Giles (in modified form). For those now used to the harder forms of *pinyin*, the following (courtesy of Edgar Snow, *The Other Side of the River*, Gollancz, 1961) may serve as a rough guide to pronunciation.

Chi is pronounced as "Gee", but *Ch'i* sounds like "Chee". *Ch'in* is exactly our "chin".
Chu is roughly like "Jew", as in *Chu Teh* (Jew Duhr), but *Ch'u* equals "chew".
Tsung is "dzung"; *ts'ung* with the "ts" as in "Patsy".
Tai is our word sound "die"; *T'ai* – "tie".
Pai is "buy" and *P'ai* is "pie".
Kung is like "Gung" (a Din); *K'ung* with the "k" as in "kind".
J is the equivalent of r but slur it as rrrun.
H before an s, as in *hsi*, is the equivalent of an aspirate but is often dropped, as in Sian for Hsian.

Vowels in Chinese are generally short or medium, not long and flat. Thus *Tang* sounds like "dong", never like our "tang". *T'ang* is "tong".

a as in father
e – r*u*n
eh – hen
i – see
ih – h*e*r
o – l*oo*k
ou – g*o*
u – s*oo*n

The effect of using the Wade-Giles system is, I hope, to render the softer, more poetic side of the original Mandarin, ill-served, I feel, by modern *pinyin*.

This usage, incidentally, accords with many of the major reference sources available in the West: the (planned) sixteen volumes of Denis Twitchett and Michael Loewe's *The Cambridge History of China*; Joseph Needham's mammoth multi-volumed *Science and Civilisation in China*; John Fairbank and Edwin Reischauer's *China, Tradition and Transformation*; Charles Hucker's *China's Imperial Past*; Jacques Gernet's *A History of Chinese Civilisation*; C. P. Fitzgerald's *China: A Short Cultural History*; Laurence Sickman and Alexander Soper's *The Art and Architecture of China*; William Hinton's classic social studies, *Fanshen and Shenfan*; and Derk Bodde's *Essays on Chinese Civilisation*.

The version of the *I Ching* or *Book of Changes* quoted from throughout, is the Richard Wilhelm translation, rendered into English by Cary F. Baynes and published by Routledge & Kegan Paul, London, 1951, and all quotations from that text are with their permission.

The Chinese sage, Chuang Tzu, is quoted and referred to several times in the text, and a collection of his "Basic Writings" (title *Chuang Tzu: Basic Writings*) can be obtained from the Columbia University Press, translated by Burton Watson [1964]. I strongly recommend this to anyone with more than a passing interest in Taoism, for its delightful wit and charm. The quotations are used here with the kind permission of the publishers.

The quotations from *Kalevala: The Land of the Heroes* is from the edition translated by W. F. Kirby and first published by J. M. Dent in 1907.

The quotations from *The Magic Flute* are from Act Two, from Sarastro's "Air", and translate as follows:

> Within these sacred halls,
> vengeance is unknown;
> if a man should fall,
> loves leads him back to duty.
> He is guided by a friendly hand,
> happy and contented,
> to the better land.

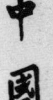

and, for the final two lines:

> He whom such teaching does not delight
> is not worthy to be a man.

The lines Ben and Meg quote of T. S. Eliot are from "The Wasteland" and are used by kind permission of the publishers, Faber & Faber.

The translation of Ch'u Yuan's "The Greater Master of Fate" is by David Hawkes from *The Songs of the South: An Anthology of Ancient Chinese Poems*, Penguin Books, London, 1985, and used with their kind permission.

The translation of Li Ho's "Song of the Bronze Statue" is by Yang Xiangyi and Gladys Yang and is taken from *Poetry and Prose of the Tang and Song*, published by Panda Books, Beijing, 1984.

The game of *wei chi* mentioned throughout this volume is, incidentally, more commonly known by its Japanese name of *Go*, and is not merely the world's oldest game but its most elegant.

David Wingrove, March 1994

ACKNOWLEDGMENTS

M ajor thanks this time to Brian Griffin who, as ever, put in long hours trying to work out – for my benefit – just what I was up to in the text. Thanks too to my editors, Carolyn, Jeanne and Alyssa, and to good friends Robert Carter, Andy Muir, Mike Cobley, John Hindes, Andy Sawyer, Vikki and Steve, Robert Allen, Brian King, my brother Ian; and to Edinburgh-based band Tranceport, whose Chung Kuo music has kept me going through many a long night – to Stewart, Robert and Alan – a huge thanks.

And, of course, to my girls, Susan, Jessica, Amy and Georgia, without whom none of this would be worth doing.

GLOSSARY OF
MANDARIN TERMS

aiya! – common exclamation of surprise or dismay.

ch'a – tea.

Ch'eng Hsiang – "Chancellor", a post first established in the Ch'in court more than two thousand years ago.

ch'i – a Chinese foot; approximately 14.4 inches.

chiao tzu – a traditional North Chinese meal of meat-filled dumplings, eaten with a hot spicy sauce.

Chieh Hsia – term meaning "Your Majesty" derived from the expression "Below the Steps". It was the formal way of addressing the Emperor, through his Ministers, who stood "below the steps".

ching – literally "mirror"; here used also to denote a perfect GenSyn copy of a man. Under the Edict of Technological Control, these are limited to copies of the ruling T'ang. However, mirrors were also popularly believed to have certain strange properties, one of which is to make spirits visible. Buddhist priests used special "magic mirrors" to show believers the form into which they would be reborn. Moreover, if a man looks into one of these mirrors and fails to recognise his own face, it is a sign that his death is not far off.

chung – a porcelain *ch'a* bowl, usually with a lid.

ch'un tzu – an ancient Chinese term from the Warring States period, describing a certain class of noblemen, controlled by a code of chivalry and morality known as the *li* or rites. Here the term is roughly, and sometimes ironically, translated as "gentlemen". The *ch'un tzu* is as much an ideal state of behaviour – as specified by Confucius in his *Analects* – as an actual class in Chung Kuo, though a degree of financial independence and a high standard of education are assumed a prerequisite.

Hei – literally "black"; the Chinese pictogram for this represents a man wearing warpaint and tattoos. Here it refers to the genetically manufactured (GenSyn) half-men used as riot police to quell uprisings in the lower levels.

441

hsiao jen – "little man/men". In the *Analects*, Book XIV, Confucius writes: "The gentleman gets through to what is up above; the small man gets through to what is down below." This distinction between "gentleman" (*ch'un tzu*) and "little men" (*hsiao jen*), false even in Confucius's time, is no less a matter of social perspective in Chung Kuo.

Hsien – historically an administrative district of variable size. Here the term is used to denote a very specific administrative area: one of ten stacks – each stack composed of thirty decks. Each deck is a hexagonal living unit of ten levels, two *li*, or approximately one kilometre in diameter. A stack can be imagined as one honeycomb in the great hive of the City.

hun – the "higher soul" or spirit soul which, the Han believe, ascends to Heaven at death, joins Shang Ti, the Supreme Ancestor, and lives in his court for ever more. The *hun* is believed to come into being at the moment of conception (see also *p'o*).

Hung Mao – literally "redheads", the name the Chinese gave to the Dutch (and later English) seafarers who attempted to trade with China in the seventeenth century. Because of the piratical nature of their endeavours (which often meant plundering Chinese shipping and ports) the name has connotations of piracy.

kang – the Chinese hearth, serving also as oven and in the cold of winter as a sleeping platform.

Kan pei! – "good health" or "cheers"; a drinking toast.

Ko Ming – "revolutionary". The *T'ien Ming* is the Mandate of Heaven, supposedly handed down from Shang Ti, the Supreme Ancestor, to his earthly counterpart, the Emperor (Huang Ti). This Mandate could be enjoyed only so long as the Emperor was worthy of it, and rebellion against a tyrant – who broke the Mandate through his lack of justice, benevolence and sincerity – was deemed not criminal but a rightful expression of Heaven's anger.

Kuan Yin – the Goddess of Mercy; originally the Buddhist male bodhisattva, Avalokitsevara (translated into Han as "He who listens to the sounds of the world", or *Kuan Yin*). The Chinese mistook the well-developed breasts of the saint for a woman's, and since the ninth century have worshipped Kuan Yin as such. Effigies of Kuan Yin will show her usually as the Eastern Madonna, cradling a child in her arms. She is also sometimes seen as the wife of Kuan Kung, the Chinese God of War.

lao jen – "old man"; normally a term of respect.

li – a Chinese "mile", approximating half a kilometre or one-third of a mile. Until 1949, when metric measures were adopted in China, the *li* could vary from place to place.

Nu Shi – an unmarried woman; a term equating to "Miss".

Pa shi yi – literally "Eighty One", here referring specifically to the Central Council of the New Confucian officialdom.

pai nan jen – literally, "pale man".

pau – a simple long garment worn by men.

Pien hua – literally "Change".

Ping Tiao – "levelling". To bring down or make flat. Here used also as the name of a terrorist (*Ko Ming*) organisation dedicated to bringing down (levelling) the City.

p'o – the "animal soul" which, at death, remains in the tomb with the corpse and takes its nourishment from the grave offerings. The *p'o* decays with the corpse, sinking into the underworld (beneath the Yellow Springs) where – as a shadow – it continues an existence of a kind. The *p'o* is believed to come into existence at the moment of birth (see also *hun*).

san k'ou – abbreviation of the *san kuei chiu k'ou*, the sixth stage of respect, according to the "Book of Ceremonies" it involves striking the forehead three times against the ground before rising from one's knees (in *k'ou t'ou* one strikes the forehead but once).

Shen Ts'e – special élite force, named after the "palace armies" of the late T'ang dynasty.

Shih – "Master". Here used as a term of respect somewhat equivalent to our use of "Mister". The term was originally used for the lowest level of civil servants to distinguish them socially from the run-of-the-mill "misters" (*hsiang sheng*) below them and the gentlemen (*ch'un tzu*) above.

t'ai chi – the Original, or One, from which the duality of all things (*yin* and *yang*) developed, according to Chinese cosmology. We generally associate the *t'ai chi* with the Taoist symbol, that swirling circle of dark and light, supposedly representing an egg (perhaps the Hun Tun), the yolk and white differentiated.

ti yu – the "earth prison" or underworld of Chinese legend. There are ten main Chinese Hells, the first being the court-room in which the sinner is sentenced and the last being that place where they are reborn as human beings. In between are a vast number of sub-hells, each with its own Judge and staff of cruel warders. In Hell it is always dark, with no differentiation between night and day.

T'ieh Lo-han – "Iron Goddess of Mercy", a *ch'a*.

Wei chi – "the surrounding game", known more commonly in the West by its Japanese name of "Go". It is said that the game was invented by the legendary Chinese Emperor Yao in the year 2350 BC to train the mind of his son, Tan Chu, and teach him to think like an Emperor.

Wu – a diviner; traditionally these were "mediums" who claimed to have special psychic powers. *Wu* could be either male or female.

Wu Ching – the "Five Classics" studied by all Confucian scholars, comprising the *Shu Ching* (Book of History), the *Shih Ching* (Book of Songs), the *I Ching* (Book of Changes), the *Li Ching* (Book of Rites, actually three books in all) and the *Ch'un Ch'iu* (The Spring and Autumn Annals of the State of Lu).

Wushu – the Chinese word for martial arts, refers to any of several hundred schools. *Kung Fu* is a school within this, meaning "skill that transcends mere surface beauty".

wuwei – non-action; an old Taoist concept. It means keeping harmony with the flow of things – doing nothing to break the flow. As Lao Tzu said, "The Tao does nothing, and yet nothing is left undone."

yang – the "male principle" of Chinese cosmology, which, with its complementary opposite, the female *yin*, forms the *t'ai chi*, derived from the Primeval One. From the union of *yin* and *yang* arise the "five elements" (water, fire, earth, metal, wood) from which the "ten thousand things" (the *wan wu*) are generated. *Yang* signifies

Heaven and the South, the Sun and Warmth, Light, Vigour, Maleness, Penetration, odd numbers and the Dragon. Mountains are *yang*.

yin – the "female principle" of Chinese cosmology (see *yang*). *Yin* signifies Earth and the North, the Moon and Cold, Darkness, Quiescence, Femaleness, Absorption, even numbers and the Tiger. The *yin* lies in the shadow of the mountain.

yuan – the basic currency of Chung Kuo (and modern-day China). Colloquially (though not here) it can also be termed *kwai* – "piece" or "lump". A hundred *fen* make up one *yuan*.

Ywe Lung – literally the "Moon Dragon", the great wheel of seven dragons that is the symbol of the ruling Seven throughout *Chung Kuo*. "At its centre the snouts of the regal beasts met, forming a roselike hub, huge rubies burning fiercely in each eye. Their lithe, powerful bodies curved outward like the spokes of a giant wheel while at their edge their tails were intertwined to form the rim" (from "The Moon Dragon", Chapter 4 of *The Middle Kingdom*).